The Castle of Heavenly Bliss

Gerard Charles Wilson

Gerard Charles Wilson Publisher

The Castle of Heavenly Bliss

Sixties Series Book 7

Copyright © 2019 Revised 2025 Gerard Charles Wilson

Gerard Charles Wilson Publisher

Mount Martha VIC

Australia

Email: gerard.wilson1@bigpond.com

ISBN 978 1 876262 28 0 paperback

ISBN 978 1 876262 08 2 ebook

Cover illustration Moon PIR04D

Dedication

To those dedicated nuns, brothers, and priests who gave me an excellent education and a love of reading

Contents

Chapter 1

The mission

THE SUMMER SUN was dipping down over the dry countryside of north-western Victoria. The hot hours of the day had driven the folk of the sleepy town of Binawarra into their homes, leaving the streets parched and deserted. Some ten miles out of town, travelling in the subsiding heat, a car made its way along the narrow, patched road. The car's occupants squinted and shaded their eyes against the flickering glare as the sun danced in and out of the gum trees with the curve of the road. The driver hummed a ragged tune and tapped the steering wheel while the woman, with a cigarette stuck between her fingers, had her eyes fixed on the papers she shuffled on her lap. The scene of rolling and peaking hills covered with eucalypts and expanses of dry brown grass was not appealing enough to break her concentration. Now and again, she stopped the shuffling and stared at the jottings on a piece of paper held loosely in her left hand. Eventually, she flicked at the sheets and frowned at her notes. The driver glanced at her and then at the paper. Casting a quick look along the road, he leaned closer. She was alerted to his movement and saw the bored expression fade.

'What?' She drew on her cigarette and blew a puff of smoke out of the side of her mouth.

'Your notes are in Dutch. Not usual,' he said, in heavily accented English.

'Well?' She folded over the sheet of paper in her left hand, making no attempt to hide her irritation.

He smirked.

Gerda Vrouwendijk had contempt for the man she had to put up with when circumstances warranted his unique skills. He was a mere caricature in her mind—a savage brute brandishing pistols and swearing blood oaths. As brutish as he was, though, he served his purpose well. Methodical and unfeeling in his tasks, he backed up these useful qualities with great natural strength and physical conditioning. More than anything else, his lazy indifference to her plans provided her with the compliance indispensable to her work. He revolted her as no other man could. She called him Boris, almost always with a sneer. She did not know his real name and did not care to know it. Boris remained unperturbed.

He assumed the name during their travels, having a false passport and business cards produced for the purpose. The full significance of the nickname, oddly enough, seemed to escape him. So she thought. Despite the show of indifference, she had to reassure herself occasionally when he shook his head and cast a menacing look from under those dark brows or when he perpetrated some unspeakable violence on command and absently sucked the blood from his split knuckles. But he dared not touch her. Apart from any other consideration, his objectives in their association, whatever they were, depended on her.

She unfolded the sheet and contemplated it. What was it to him that her notes were in Dutch? He recognised the different European languages and even spoke some Eastern European and Arabic languages, but she was unsure how good his Dutch was. These sorts of things, he was cunning enough to hide.

'I do not pay you to concern yourself with such matters,' she felt compelled to emphasise. 'In any case, the reason would not advance your font of knowledge.' Then, knowing how much she would need him in the coming months and how effectively she could exploit the energies of his dark hatreds, she forced out, 'These notes are of the briefing reports you gave me. Right? I was tired at the time—unconsciously reverted to my first language. It's the easiest way of organising your thoughts. You should know.'

Boris frowned, stared at her, and returned his distrustful eyes to the broken road in front of him. Gerda prided herself on remaining elusive, but she must not antagonise him. She needed him. Reinforcing Boris's chronic distrust would be an unnecessary risk. He was right about the jottings in Dutch. She had been lax. Through tiredness? The preparation and travel had been demanding. Through common human frailty? Who knows, she thought, not wanting to dwell too much on such irrelevance. It was essential to keep in character. She would be more alert.

'But thanks for pointing it out,' she added, feigning a conciliatory tone.

Calmly stubbing out her cigarette, she pretended to return to her paperwork. She hoped her casual, accommodating remarks would wipe the distrust off the face of the frightful man she would have to spend the following months with. Boris resumed his humming and tapping. She was relieved. That savage Balkan could be a nuisance when he had a mind to it. A glance from Boris showed he was playing the same sly game and keeping an eye on his companion.

During this time, the car wound its way upwards between two peaks. Close on their right, the land rose steeply out of the undulating fields in a stream of rocks, dirt, dry grass, and stunted and spiky eucalypts until it reached a sharp peak towering over them. Near the top of the peak, a strange, grey, rocky outcrop jutted. Like a platform put there for some purpose. Underneath the platform was a sheer drop along a scaly cliff face for about sixty feet. From there, a short levelling incline to the roadway. Further on, on their left and not as close to the road, a massive mound rose to reach a height above the sharp peak. Its huge, hunched, squatting form was treed all around its rugged slopes. Though burnt brown in the Australian summer, the grass was long and thick, hiding any sign of the reddish-brown earth that appeared on the opposite peak. Its top was inviting and negotiable by a fit and eager bushwalker.

Gerda and Boris drove on past the rocky outcrop, ignoring the hunched, squatting form on their left. The road reached its highest point, then descended, bursting from the hills and trees onto a broad view of farmland, with Binawarra nestled cosily below. In the distance, the farmland rose again to form a chain of low-lying hills. On their slowing descent, the township's pattern of roads, its settler-period public buildings, and the clusters of pioneer houses with their verandahs opened to them. As dull as their observations of the countryside on their approach to Binawarra were, this enchanting rural scene intruded on their purpose. They silently stared as they emerged from the trees between the peaks. The uneasiness was soon gone. For as they drove on, two figures walking hand-in-hand towards the town drew their attention.

'That's her,' said Boris, indicating with a raised index finger.

'Keep calm,' said Gerda. Boris remained unmoved. 'Don't give any sign that we have seen them. Drive on, but slowly, so I can get a clear view. Easy ... I said easy!'

Boris took his foot from the accelerator. The two people, a very tall man and a tall, well-formed young woman, both of darkish complexion, gave no sign they were aware of the approaching car. As the car coasted level, Gerda turned and looked around Boris's head. 'Don't move!' she hissed. She had an unimpeded look, satisfied that the two walkers paid no attention to the car, let alone show any interest in its occupants.

'Well,' said Gerda, more to herself than to Boris, 'reports about her have not been exaggerated. She is exquisite ... quite exquisite ... unusual ...' She turned to Boris: 'You stay away from her. Don't forget it.'

Boris laughed loudly. Gerda did not respond to this mocking reaction. She knew, as he did, that they were playing out a little theatre and that a general warning had been repeated. Binawarra was worlds away from his style of pleasure, and, more importantly, he would stick to his task. They drove on in silence. Stunning. Absolutely different. Not only the physical appearance: tall, sturdy, and well-formed, but with a manner, an allure, like nothing Gerda had seen before. This was indeed a prize. Gerda was not one to rush to judgment. She had been sceptical and hesitant when the idea arose, and the possibilities suggested. The results, on a long shot, almost far-fetched, did not promise to reward the time and effort. But now. Defying her own rules, she rushed to judgment. This would be worth the risk. If this girl could capture her, Gerda Vrouwendijk, so directly, surely she would have the same effect on others. The car, slowing almost to a stop, broke in on her musings.

'What are you doing?' she said, glancing back over her shoulder.

'Well, where do you want me to go?' Boris tapped the steering wheel and looked in front of him.

'Keep driving.'

They had crossed the bridge over a fast-flowing creek and headed towards the town centre. Gerda stroked her cheek and then her chin, staring but not seeing in front of her. Boris glanced at her with smirking interest.

'Show me where the publisher of *The Binawarra and District Mail* lives,' she said, waving her hand without bestowing even a sideways glance. 'Go on and mind your business.'

She put on her sunglasses, took a broad-brimmed sunhat from the back seat, and positioned it on her head. She lit up another cigarette and exhaled, deep in thought. Waving the smoke away, Boris made a turn at the end of the large, lush park in the middle of the town's shopping centre, took a turn to the left, and drove several blocks to a fashionable part of the town. He stopped outside a smart, restored colonial-style cottage. Despite the presence of a few people on Binawarra's cooling streets, Gerda took on the attitude of an interested visitor to the picturesque town and surveyed the living quarters of the publisher of the principal organ of communication in the district.

'Our publisher is a discerning man with a taste for the finer things of life,' she murmured. 'A most tastefully restored property. Your report has not been amiss as yet, it pleases me to say.'

Boris nodded in acknowledgment.

Dropping ash from her cigarette, she flicked through the papers on her lap and, with a wave of the hand, directed Boris to drive on. She isolated one of the sheets, looked around, and then motioned him to stop. She read for a minute. 'How reliable is this? Is there really something between our publisher and the wife of the Returned Soldiers League President?'

'It's a reasonable suspicion. They come into contact quite often. Collins fancies himself... the sophisticated type ... targets the rich and upper-class in the town ...'

Gerda rubbed her chin again. 'Keep an eye on them—for whatever may be going on. It might be useful.' She returned to the sheet of paper. 'This debt and his ambition to set up a chain of country newspapers. Too vague. I want a clear picture of his financial circumstances. The urge to build a media empire can be a virulent one.' Not expecting a reply to this gratuitous opinion, she waved him to drive on. 'Take me on a tourist drive around the town.'

Following his companion's promptings, Boris made his way at a tourist pace around Binawarra while Gerda took in as much as she could. When they returned to the square, she said: 'Now the high school.' Boris drove around the square, at the end of which he turned into Melbourne Road, the main road out of the town. He drove several blocks and then turned right into Goldminers Road. The town's high school was at the top of a slow incline, from which there was an arresting view of the town centre. The administrative block looked out over the fields to the range of hills, where the great hunched mound and the sharp peak were prominent. The sports fields, set into the treed slopes, were lower down on the hill. They stopped there, contemplating the view.

'Now show me where *he* lives,' said Gerda.

Boris drove back down the hill and turned right into Eureka Street. They proceeded about half a mile to the outskirts of the residential area. The house with a view of the hills was the last on a large block. All around was an abundance of plants in well-cared-for gardens. Behind the house, the farmland stretched out. Eureka Street continued, taking a curving swing to the left, and met Melbourne Road before the bridge over the creek. As Gerda and Boris drew abreast of the house, the man himself appeared on the verandah. Gerda motioned Boris to drive on. Boris did not blink. He drove on through the curve until he was out of sight and turned back. The man ignored the car as it approached a second time. He stood with a rapturous expression, running a proud eye over his flower gardens, and breathing in the fresh country air. When the car was abreast of him, he looked up and gave a friendly wave. Boris lazily returned the gesture.

'You fat old fool,' said Gerda, happy that this first sighting had reinforced the picture she had formed of Bill Huckerby. 'You are going to be rocked out of your complacency.' A woman appeared on the verandah and put an arm around the man's ample waist. She gave him a kiss and snuggled up to him. Gerda turned her head away. 'Quick, get going,' she ordered. Boris jerked the car forward and drove off.

'Now, the girl,' said Gerda, ridding her mind of the detestable sight.

Boris turned right at Goldminers Road, headed across Melbourne Road, and took the third turn to the right into Old Melbourne Road. As with Eureka Street, Old Melbourne Road was an alternative way south out of the town and joined the main road around fifty yards before the creek. The last house on a large parcel of ground and hemmed in by two long dry-stone walls stood snugly among a welcoming array of flowers, bushes, trees, and vegetable gardens. Boris nodded at this house. 'Where the girl lives.' He slowed the car while Gerda fixed her eyes on the house, mingling with the early evening light. The girl emerged from the yellow glow. She stood motionless, facing the hills at one end of the verandah. At the risk of being seen, Gerda looked around as they passed.

'Stunning,' she said and added, 'Drive on a little further, turn around and come back. I think she is too preoccupied to pay attention to us.'

The girl seemed to recollect as the car returned for a second pass. She turned and walked to the other end of the verandah, where she sat on a swing seat and gazed at the hills. Gerda could not help but lean around and have a last lingering look. When Boris turned into Goldminers Road, she told him to pull up somewhere unobtrusive. There seemed nowhere more unobtrusive than where they were, and he brought the car to a halt. From there, they had a clear view up Goldminers Road to the high school at the top of the hill. Gerda was lost in thought.

'Is she always like that?'

'Like what?'

'Serene, detached, aloof. Like she was gazing on the world from a different place, you know.'

'Yes,' he said, contemplating the question in his lazy way. 'People her own age say she's as cold as a dead fish. The boys call her the "Ice Maiden." She has most of them in awe of her.'

'Good. What about other people in the town, the older people?'

'I've heard that some of the men, prominent men, have thought it necessary to protect her.'

'Against what?'

'They've warned the town's youth—'

'Hypocrites.'

'That's what I've heard. There is only so much questioning I can do. My accent is already a signal that I do not belong. You know the way country people are.'

'I certainly do.' She consulted her papers again. There was silence for a while. 'You say there is frequent contact between the girl's family and that fat fool and his wife. It's a long walk from one house to the other.'

Boris shrugged his shoulders. 'It may be, but I have often tracked her on her way there or coming back again. She is a keen walker. She is known for her lone walks in the bush and farmland. The farmers keep an eye on her. It's easy to see she is fit and strong. A year or so ago, people thought she would be a champion athlete.'

'That's not in your reports.'

'Well ... the story was too vague. People say she lost interest. She takes part in the school sports but does not try.'

'Extraordinary,' said Gerda to herself. 'To look like that and have the potential to be—'

Silence followed, and then: 'A close connection with the Catholic priest, that's expected. But this relationship with that woman. You don't say much about her.'

'There's not much to say. Miss Barker, as she insists on being called, is a shrivelled spinster in her fifties. She keeps to herself. Or when she does speak, it is often to abuse someone. Most people stay out of her way. She works part-time as the school's nurse and lives cheaply. They say she had a bad experience with the Japanese during the war. Not much is known about her. She is not important—just a sad, lonely figure. You don't have to worry about her.'

Gerda happened to glance at the house they were parked outside of. One slat of the Venetian blinds on the lounge room window was raised at an angle.

'You had better move on. Otherwise, someone might see us parked here doing nothing. Drive into the shopping centre again, and then to where the Vatican stooge lives.'

Without reacting to the melodramatic request, Boris drove to the shops, took a turn around the square, and came to a stop outside the little blue-stone church with its charming steeple. 'St Philomena's Church.'

'This is it, is it? Not very impressive.'

While Gerda was looking at the church with unfeigned disgust, the priest appeared at the entrance's stone archway. He walked stooped with much difficulty, supporting himself on a walking stick. He had to stop and turn himself round so he could shut the cumbrous set of wooden doors before locking them. His face was weather-beaten, and his emaciated figure was covered loosely by a cassock that was patched, discoloured, and frayed at the edges. Gerda watched in silence, contempt showing on her face. Taking notice of Gerda's uncovered expression, Boris drove to the opposite side of the park, where the trees and shrubbery hid the car. They watched as the stooped figure checked the front area and sides of the church. He was in some pain, for he grimaced now and then.

'There you have him,' said Boris, smiling for the first time that day, 'a compatriot of yours.'

'Yes, but from the south-east of Holland, the Province of Limburg,' Gerda hastened to say, unguardedly. 'I'm from the south-west, the Province of Zeeland. Very different.'

'Are there not Catholics in the south-west of Holland?' said Boris, the mocking smile lingering on his lips.

Gerda ignored the question. 'Besides, your notes say he has spent much of his life out of Holland, in New Guinea.'

'Yes, his disabilities date from that time. I don't know what happened to him. Nobody knows except his doctor, and he will not talk about it.'

'That may be useful.'

'They say he's been put out to pasture.'

'Out to pasture?'

'There are few Catholics in Binawarra, the girl's family among them, so the order of priests responsible for this small parish has never had a priest stationed here—that is, until they exiled Fr. van Engelen to this God-forsaken place. It seems that he is a sort of recalcitrant.'

'About what?'

'He cannot adjust to the Second Vatican Council, they say. So they put him where he could not cause trouble, which did not please some of the townsfolk, at least in the beginning. I don't know how much of this is true, but it is plain he is not popular with his superiors. Otherwise, he would not be here in such poverty. He is very close to the girl and her parents. He gives the girl special instruction, which, they say, she laps up.'

'This priest will be my biggest obstacle. Focus on him. I want to know all about him. Find anyone antagonistic to him and his Church. Now drive me once more around the town. Show me where some of the minor figures live.'

Gerda Vrouwendijk leaned back and settled into assessing what she had seen. A self-satisfied expression appeared on her face as she listened without comment to Boris's bored commentary while he spent another half-hour touring the town. At length, Gerda gave the signal, and he headed out along Melbourne Road. They drove up the fast-rising incline into the hills, passed the dark, squatting mound on their right and the rocky platform on their left. The hills, peaks, and trees disappeared into the growing darkness behind them while they remained occupied with their thoughts. The tall, striking figure of the girl with the darkish complexion stayed in Gerda Vrouwendijk's mind. Boris resumed a vacant expression.

An hour and a half later, they were in their rooms in different motels in the provincial city of Bendigo. Gerda booked two international calls. Drawing heavily on her cigarette, she walked up and down her room in a distracted manner. Boris threw himself onto his bed and flicked through the motel's flyers. At about one o'clock in the morning, two young women knocked on Boris's door. Gerda Vrouwendijk, who stood opposite under a tree, smoking, watched as the door opened, flooding the area with yellow light, then shut, plunging the area into darkness. She looked at the dull, lifeless, overcast sky. She must ensure she slept through the night. All her energy and alertness were needed for what lay ahead.

Chapter 2

Estella

IT WAS TUESDAY morning, the 4th of February 1975. The rays of the early morning sun streamed through the large pane glass windows of Charles Winterbine's workshop. He and his assistant were finishing several wooden window frames, part of a commission from the Binawarra town council. Charles would not be satisfied until the style was right and the workmanship flawless. He stood back and surveyed all the delicate joins. He motioned Ken to stand back, too. They ran their eyes over each section.

'We have it right, Boss,' Ken said. 'There were a few difficult points, but they are now exactly the same as the plans.'

Charles walked to the charts pinned to the wall. 'Okay. You're right. We cannot do any better than this.'

'Better! What we have done is better than the original!'

Charles gave his young assistant a smile of approval. 'Right, let's have a break. Get yourself a cup of tea. I'll be back in a minute.' Charles stopped before the crucifix hanging in the workshop, bowed his head for a few moments, and then continued his way.

Ken went to the workshop bench, where Mrs Winterbine had prepared his morning tea, as she did each day. He was used to the routine of the Winterbine household and knew the Boss was off to say goodbye to his daughter, who would be setting out for school shortly. Ken took his tea and biscuits to the front garden, where there was a bench. He said it was a comfortable place to sit and relax. Nobody was fooled; he wanted to get an eyeful of the girl without equal in his town—or anywhere else. She always gave him a friendly wave and sometimes spoke to him.

At that moment, the object of Ken's aesthetic appraisal was finishing her preparations for school. Estella Winterbine stood in front of the full-length mirror in her bedroom and looked at her reflection. Her rich, dark brown hair was drawn back to form a ponytail that dangled in a bunch of naturally streaky curls between her shoulder blades. She smoothed the hair on her temples with both hands to ensure it was gathered with no loose strands. She examined her blue school uniform. She frowned again at the hem. It was too short. But she was reluctant to lower it further. Her classmates wore their dresses much shorter, and she would stand out too much if the hem were any longer. The last thing she wanted was more attention. She had to be satisfied that her school clothes were neat and spotless. She brushed her hands down both sides of her dress as if to keep it at an optimal level of modesty. Then she bent down to fold and align the gleaming white socks set off against her glowing light-brown skin and the polished black shoes. She considered herself for the last time; she had to be happy with what she saw.

The books lying on her bed were gathered up and returned to the shelves. A duster gave the books a quick brush. The top shelf housed her books on Scripture, doctrine, devotions, and the saints. The next shelf had her favourite novels, mostly nineteenth-century English classics. The exceptions were *The Lord of the Rings* and *The Hobbit*. On the shelf below were her gardening books. They filled that shelf and part of the bottom shelf. The rest of the bottom shelf was taken up with a miscellany of books on history, languages, and the arts. They were her favourite school subjects. She dusted all this, bending down frequently to ensure she had removed every speck of dust.

Satisfied that all was neat and in order, she turned to the adjacent wall where she had set up a shrine to the Virgin Mary. On a polished wooden shelf, which her father had fixed to the wall at her request, she had placed a statue of Our Lady of Fatima. On each side of the statue were candles and two little flower vases. She stood before her shrine, closed her eyes, bowed her head, and made the sign of the cross. She repeated prayers of thanksgiving and intercession. Finally, she checked the flowers in the vases. They had to be replaced. That was a job for after school. Taking up her school satchel, she slung it over her shoulder and headed for the front verandah.

She opened the front flywire door to find her mother and father holding hands and waiting for her. She took her mother into her arms. Aine Winterbine was not short. She was rather on the tall side, but her daughter seemed to dwarf her. Estella was a couple of inches taller, but the contrast was in the fullness of her figure. Estella had inherited her father's physical features. Her height, her darkish complexion, the sturdiness of her body and the evident strength in her limbs were from her father. And standing next to her mother made her mother appear even more delicate than she was. However, a subtle blending of her father's robust physique with delicate, unblemished features and an expression radiating a sweet manner was all from Aine. Only in her dreamy hazel eyes did she differ from her mother. It was this combination of features and manner that drew everyone's attention. People could not help giving Estella Winterbine a second look. Some of the Binawarra folk wanted to see augury in the presence of someone so different and so striking.

'The first day of your final year at school, my darling,' said Aine, with her arms still around her.

'I'm all right,' said Estella. 'Really.' She let her go and flung her arms around her father, resting her head for a moment on his shoulder. Then she stepped up on her toes and kissed him loudly.

'Okay! Okay!' Charles said, pretending to resist as he did each time he was subjected to his daughter's unrestrained affection. 'Enjoy your day.'

He traced the sign of the cross on her forehead with his thumb and then kissed her.

'Are you going to come home for lunch?' said Aine.

'Yes, of course.' She took Aine's hand and kissed it. She turned to leave. 'I'll see you then, okay?'

'Is everything all right?'

Estella stopped at the top of the short flight of verandah stairs. 'Yes, of course.' She looked at her father. 'Everything's all right.' She descended the steps and turned. 'I'll see you at lunchtime.' She was about to head off when her father called to her.

'I forgot,' he said, coming to the front gate. 'Please give this to Roley Seddon.' He took an envelope from his overalls pocket. 'It's his account. Say hello from me to Roley, and Terry, too, if you see him.'

'I'm all right,' she repeated. She walked up the road, turning twice to wave. Once out of view, she pondered. Why were they worried? She had not said anything. She could cope with her problems. She knew the answer. It was her mother. It was as if her mother had a separate sense of how she felt. For the way her father felt, too. They could not hide the slightest worry. It was a problem.

Estella often thought in recent years that her mother's periods of incapacity were due to some undefined feeling for her family and not to any physical cause. It was something above the physical. The doctors had found nothing wrong with her. They said she was physically healthy. She looked very healthy, and Estella knew she was admired for her youthful beauty. On one occasion, Dr Enright had taken her father aside and said that her mother should learn to relax and not take things so to heart.

Charles had repeated this to her in exasperation. She rarely saw her father like that, but she could understand his upset. The doctor made her mother seem childish or immature, and that was just not true. When she saw how well she organised the household and cared for her father and herself, the last thing she could accept was that her mother was mentally or emotionally weak. Her intense feeling was akin to a mystical insight into how she and her father felt. So often had her mother anticipated a worry or a threat of something about to bother her. It put a strain on her. But what was it she saw now? What was causing these warning signs?

By this time, Estella had reached Goldminers Road. She looked to see if Miss Barker was in her front garden. That forbidding woman was often there at this time to wave at her. And yes, there she was again. Estella waited to catch Miss Barker's attention. She did not have to wait long. Miss Barker was in the habit of surveying her surroundings. She beckoned.

'So, Miss, how do you feel now that you are starting your last year at school?' she said when Estella came up to her.

'Oh, I don't really feel anything. It's just another year.' She knew she did not sound convincing. She was also aware of what was on Miss Barker's mind. There had been hints enough during the last few months.

'Just another year? Have you thought yet about what you will do after school?'

'I have, but it's a question I don't have an answer for at the moment.'

'Well, my girl, you'll have to put your thinking cap on.'

'Yes, of course, you're right.' She tried to smile.

'It may not be an easy time for you,' said Miss Barker, softening her manner. 'You can always talk to me about things. You know I'm not that fearsome, don't you?'

'Of course, I do,' said Estella. She had long seen past Miss Barker's stern manner. At times, this notorious spinster deliberately reinforced her reputation. Why she did so was not clear. Miss Barker was otherwise a capable, well-organised woman who showed concern and affection for those she held dear.

'Come here,' Miss Barker said. She took Estella into her arms. 'I want to wish you all the best for this determining year. I hope ... no, I know you'll come through it.' She let Estella go. 'And I know you're not cold and aloof.'

Then, putting her hand on Estella's breast: 'In here is the warm heart of an affectionate little girl.'

Estella was so surprised by Miss Barker's unanticipated words and uncharacteristic behaviour that she was initially lost for words. 'Thank you,' she said vaguely. 'I'm sure things will be all right.'

'Be watchful. Now, be off with you. People will get the wrong idea if they catch me going on like this. Perhaps I will see you at the school's assembly.'

Estella crossed over Goldminers Road, gave Miss Barker a final wave, and then walked towards Seddon's Timber Yard. Miss Barker's words stayed with her. Fr. van Engelen had said similar things. They were both concerned about her future. She was, too. It wasn't her future, however, that bothered her mother. It was something else. What exactly? On reaching Seddon's open yard, she peered around to see if Terry Seddon was there. She liked Terry. He was one of the few boys in Binawarra whose manner with her was friendly and unaffected. Perhaps Terry was different because he was in love with her dearest friend, Jenny Brougham. She turned to go to the front office.

'Hey, Estella, wait!' Terry called as he emerged from one of the sheds. 'How's Jenny?' he said as he came running over.

She expected the inquiry about Jenny, but could not tell him much. For the first time in their lives, she and Jenny had seen little of each other during the Christmas break.

'I'm not really sure. I haven't seen much of her recently.'

'Oh,' said Terry, shrugging. 'I've tried to call her, but she won't come to the phone. What's going on? Six months ago, there was no separating us. Now it looks like she can't stand the sight of me.'

'Jenny has other interests and other friends now. Perhaps it's better to forget her for the time being.' She put her hand briefly on his arm.

'I can't.' He sighed and shrugged again. 'Put in a good word for me if you can.'

'Of course.' She handed him the envelope.

'Thanks,' said Terry, fiddling with the envelope. 'Call in here if you've got any news. Okay?'

She left him standing in the middle of the yard. Checking her watch, she saw she still had time for a visit. She hurried to St Philomena's. As she knelt in the back pew, Fr. van Engelen came hobbling from the sacristy. His face lit up when he caught sight of her.

'Do you have time for a few words?' he whispered after hobbling down the aisle. He nodded towards the front doors. 'It won't take long.'

'It's such a beautiful morning,' he said when Estella joined him outside. 'Let's sit in the park. We can enjoy the fresh morning air together. I want you to console this broken-down old priest. Here, give me a shoulder.' He put his hand on Estella's shoulder while they walked across the road.

'The first day of your last year of school, isn't it?' he said when they were seated on the nearest park bench. Estella nodded. He looked at the ground in front of him as if he were considering his words. Estella cast a glance around the square. Mr Foley, the President of Binawarra Returned Soldiers League, was at the far end of the plantation. He spotted them and started towards them.

'Good morning,' he called. 'Just the place to be on such a beautiful morning. How are you, Father?' A brief exchange of greetings followed before the RSL President continued. 'Father, we are well down the track with organising Anzac Day. The committee has authorised me to ask you to do the blessing at the dawn service. Actually, it's on Bill's insistence. Are you okay with that? Only need a commitment now. I'll discuss the details later with you.'

'Certainly, I would be honoured. But do you really want an old priest like me to appear on such a formal occasion,' he said with a smile. 'And me with my accent! Don't you want a local voice?'

'Don't be silly, Father. There'll be plenty of local voices,' said Ray Foley. 'Far too many before the old diggers close their eyes that night. And forget about your accent. You're an honoured member of our community.'

Fr. van Engelen offered no more resistance and again said he would consider it an honour.

'Last year of school for you, Miss,' said Ray Foley. 'It's amazing how time flies. It seems like yesterday that your dad arrived in Binawarra with Aine, eight months pregnant. What excitement that was for everyone! Let's see. That was around eighteen years ago, wasn't it?' Estella nodded. 'Blow me down. And look at you now! And how's that twin pal of yours?'

'Okay, I think.'

'Father, did you know Estella and Jenny Brougham were born on the same day, in the same hospital?' Yes, Father did know that. He had heard it once or twice before. He glanced at Estella, who shifted.

'Yes, it's quite true,' said Ray Foley, wagging a finger. 'People forget these things. Two such striking girls, never seen anything like it. And they've been like sisters ever since. Inseparable.' Then, looking at his watch: 'Goodness, I must fly. There are many things for me to follow up on. Have a good day, Father, and you too, Estella.' He turned to head off but exclaimed, 'Look, speak of the devil, there she is now!' With another wave, he was on his way.

Estella looked across the square at Jenny walking along the shops with some friends, her long, wavy blond locks streaming behind her. She twirled and giggled and looked around at the boys following on her heels. They were the friends Jenny had acquired during the last year. Estella watched as she danced out ahead of the group, throwing comments behind her. She watched as Len Dawson threw some back in the sly, smirking manner she was so familiar with.

'What is it?' asked Fr van Engelen. Estella hesitated, glancing at his lined face. He passed on. 'We all have our pitiful anxieties. I do, too, you know.' Estella smiled faintly. 'Last night I was reading some reports about Holland.' These last words, as he murmured them, brought on a sadness that bent his emaciated shoulders. 'If I close my eyes and let my mind wander,' he went on, after a long pause, 'it goes straight back to the town of my childhood. The images, though jumbled, are clear. I can feel and smell and see the changes in the seasons, the mists tumbling over the freshly ploughed fields. I can hear the birds in the trees early on a summer's morning. I see the bare trees of winter beside the frozen canals. I see the distinctive gables of the houses lining the canals and the narrow streets—' He hesitated and looked at Estella.

Estella was content to listen to the crippled priest for whom she had much affection, especially now as he told her of his sadness. She was relieved, too, that he was moving away from the subject of her future. She smiled.

'That's why my heart breaks over my country,' he continued. 'Everything that seemed to be wholesome in Holland, everything that seemed to make Holland what it was, is being turned over. A hardness of heart is washing over its people. Along some of the main thoroughfares of my hometown, Middelburg, are shops that are proud to sell all the dirt and degradation of the human mind. That same hardness of heart is like a tidal wave flowing over the world and submerging all that's innocent and pure.' He took Estella's hand. 'That wave has not yet reached this beautiful little town, but there are signs of its approach. You are on the brink of adulthood. You have much to learn about people and the world. Your mother and father, the best of people, have protected you from the rough edges of life so far. In the future, you will be on your own. You know that, don't you?' Estella nodded.

'You need God's graces to help you along. You need to understand that God has given a good spirit to help you, your guardian angel. Don't worry about the world laughing at the idea of angels. God's good spirits exist. Pray for their help when things are difficult. You will be protected against the evil spirits always there to urge you to do the wrong thing. They will help you to protect the goodness that is inside Estella Winterbine, to keep that innocence shining that everybody sees in you.' He let go of her hand

and reached into the pocket of his habit, struggling until he found what he was looking for. He held up a little shiny medal.

'Do you know what this is?'

'Yes, it's the Miraculous Medal. My mother has one attached to the bracelet she wears.'

'But do you know of its significance?'

'Only that it is to remind us of the tender spotless heart of Jesus's mother.'

'That's right. Do you have one?' She shook her head. 'Then I give you this one. This represents a devotion for our times when the degradation of the human spirit is celebrated, when much pleasure is taken in befouling and destroying the innocent soul. Wear it on a chain or on a bracelet. It has no magical qualities, of course. It merely signifies a devotion to the purity and holiness of the Blessed Virgin Mary.' He paused. 'We all are prey to temptation, and you will be too, even though at this point you might not understand how. Let this medal be your symbol of resistance and protection.'

'I will put it on a cherished silver chain and wear it.'

Fr. van Engelen took Estella's hand again and held it. At that moment, a woman appeared from the milk bar a little distance down the square. She carried the local newspaper in one hand and packets of cigarettes in the other. She was flicking the paper open in a clumsy manner as she tried to read the front page. Looking around her, her eyes alighted on the priest holding Estella's hand.

'*Goede hemel!*' he exclaimed. '*Het is niet waar!* It can't be true!'

Estella turned to see what had caused the exclamation. She recognised the face. The woman composed herself and got into her car.

Father van Engelen said nothing as Gerda Vrouwendijk drove by. 'She was staring at us,' he murmured, and then in a normal voice, 'Do you know her?'

'No,' said Estella, not understanding the priest's reaction. 'But I saw her yesterday driving into town. I mean, she was a passenger in a car that passed Daddy and me on the road. I'd never seen her before then. She also drove by our house twice.'

'Did she? Twice?'

'Who is she?' said Estella, intrigued by the priest's sudden change. It was not like him to become excited over something so ordinary.

'Eh..., I mean, I don't know, at least I'm not sure. She looks like somebody I was acquainted with a long time ago in Holland. Well, not her directly, people close to her.' He frowned, deep in thought. 'In any case, that's not of interest now. And it's time for you to go to school. You must not be late on the first day. Now, come on. Give your tired old priest help in getting across the road.'

Estella left the priest at the church entrance and hurried to school. Fr. van Engelen slipped into one of the back pews and bowed his head. But the sight of Gerda van den Donker, if it was she, intruded on his prayers. No, there was no mistake. He threw off the inclination to deny what he had seen. It had been fifteen years since he had seen Gerda van den Donker, but the intervening years had not changed her much. It was she. But what was she doing in Binawarra? What had brought her to the sleepy, picturesque country town of Binawarra? The shadows of that dirty room arose, and the fresh, innocent face of Truus van den Donker emerged from the darkness. The thought of her being subject to Cees van den Donker filled him with sadness and revulsion. He struggled to drive it all from his mind.

BEHIND a clump of bushes at the side of the lower school oval, some boys were lolling about smoking. There had been a pause in the conversation. With a mocking grin, Len Dawson waited. Nobody seemed inclined to comment or even to be thinking about it. Len let out a half-laugh and took a long draw on his cigarette. 'None of you losers can do better than that.' He blew the smoke into the air. He still got no answer.

'Nobody can do better than Jenny Brougham,' Len teased. 'It has been the best summer of my life.' He dragged on his cigarette and blew the smoke at his friends.

'Somebody could, you know,' said Larry Burgess, who had walked away from the cover of the bushes.

The boys swung towards him.

'What are you on about?' said Len. 'Who's better than Jenny Brougham?'

'The Ice Maiden.'

'The Binawarra Virgin doesn't count.' He waved his hand. 'There's a fortress around her.'

'But she is better.'

'She doesn't count.'

'But she is better,' John Sayer insisted, nodding at Larry.

'Not really,' said Len unconvincingly.

'Come off it. Jenny Brougham is stunning. But the Ice Maiden ... and we all know she thinks Len Dawson stinks.' Dennis Lorimer pointed at Len as if that were an adequate answer to his boasting.

'Here she comes,' said Larry.

The boys moved forward. From there, they could see Estella, eyes on the ground, walking up the pathway around the oval's embankment. Lost in her thoughts, she appeared aloof and detached as usual. The five boys looked at her in silence.

'That's something that'll remain untouchable, even for Len Dawson,' said John Sayer. The other boys murmured their agreement.

'No girl is untouchable,' said Len, retrieving his offhand, confident manner. 'There's always a vulnerable point. You just have to find it.'

'Well, it won't be Len Dawson to find it. She thinks you stink.' He held his nose. The others laughed.

Len held out his hand. Don McGlashan, who was closest, grabbed it.

'Three months,' said Len.

'Right,' said Don. 'You've got no hope.'

'You bunch of girlie pikers!' Len dropped his cigarette in front of him and ground it in the soft earth with his heel. Estella was now level with the trees, obscuring the boys.

'Hey, Estella!' he called. Estella stopped and turned towards the voice. Len stepped into full view. The familiar cold stare greeted him. Len looked a little unsure for a moment, but then walked over to her, his mates looking on.

'How are your parents? Is your mother well?'

'They are all right, thank you,' said Estella, in a soft but steady voice. Her expression remained unchanged.

'I heard your mother suffered a relapse at the beginning of the holidays. She's okay now?'

'She is quite all right. There was nothing wrong with my mother.'

'Oh, I heard there was. That must be a worry for you and your father.'

'She's quite all right.'

Estella gave a sign that she had nothing more to say.

'Look, Jenny hasn't seen much of you—spends most of her time with me. I'm sorry. I know she's your best friend. Why don't you join us—share the fun?'

Estella looked him in the face and frowned. Len took a step back. As she walked on, she saw the others. She frowned again, her gaze lingering on Larry Burgess. The boys' eyes followed her in silence. The tall, well-formed figure, the healthy sheen of the skin against the spotless blue uniform and the gleaming white socks, the slim, firm calves and ankles, the gliding upright posture, the gorgeous flowing brown hair, it was all too much for them. Too much even for Len to make one of his waggish comments.

'Well, I hope you can do better than that,' scoffed Don, breaking the silence when Estella was out of sight.

'What?' said Len, roused from his thoughts and glancing around at them. 'That's the trouble with you dunces,' he said, lighting another cigarette with a shake of the hand. 'You're just ignorant of the way the female mind works. You just want to barge in. This is the start of a campaign for a great trophy. And that was the first move.' His lips curled in a grin. 'I'm the lion. She's the gazelle. I must draw her slowly and expertly into the open plain where I can swoop. By the time I've finished, that shrine in her room will be to Len Dawson.'

'Nobody's fuller of it than you,' said Dennis Lorimer, putting his finger in his mouth.

Len seemed not to hear. 'Why did she look at you like that?' he said to Larry.

Larry blushed. 'How would I know? She didn't, anyhow.'

BUT SHE did, and Larry did know, but he wouldn't admit it. He dropped behind his friends as they made their way to the assembly hall. He had to avoid giving Len any reason to pursue his last question. Seeing most students crowding the side entrances, he turned towards the back. As he broke free of the milling students, he found himself walking beside Estella. There was a moment of surprise.

'How are your parents, Larry?' said Estella.

'Um, quite well,' he stammered. She usually walked right past him. He wondered whether he should stop and let her go on alone.

'I haven't seen them for a while. Didn't you go away on holidays this Christmas?'

'Yes.'

'Where to?'

'New York.'

'Oh, so far away? What was it like?'

'A whole lot of tall buildings. My father had to attend a conference there, an agricultural conference.'

'Oh.'

They were now at the back entrance.

'We used to have fun together,' said Estella, stopping. 'You remember, when Daddy was working on your house.'

'Yes, um, I remember,' he stuttered. He could not recall the last time Estella had spoken to him in such a friendly way.

'It seems a long time ago now, doesn't it?' She hesitated. 'You have such lovely parents. Your mum was always so friendly ...' Mr Seaver, the Deputy Principal, appeared at the back door to save Larry from further discomfort.

'Come on, you two, Estella, Larry. Mr Huckerby is almost ready.' The hall was noisy with the students' chatter. 'You can sit over there.' He indicated two seats in one of the back rows. 'No, Larry,' he added, seeing Larry looking around, 'you go and sit there where I told you. There's no time.'

Many eyes followed them. Larry knew everyone would be wondering what he was doing with Estella. As they sat down, it occurred to him that Len would try to make the most of such a situation and carry on a double conversation. This was one of Len's envied skills. He could talk on one level to the person he was addressing and on another for the people listening. He had tried it on Estella with his false concern for her mother, but Larry was pretty sure he had not fooled her. That was why she had let her gaze rest upon him.

'I have such good memories of playing with you and Jenny,' said Estella, taking up the conversation again.

'Do you?' said Larry, not knowing what else to say. He tried desperately to think of something. What could he say to such a girl? Then he felt the attention of his friends around them. He glanced at Estella. She seemed oblivious to it. A comment from Len rose above the chatter. He glanced in the direction of Len's voice and then saw the coolness returning to Estella's face. He felt such a fool.

Estella had been seeking an opportunity to reconnect with Larry. He was not like Len and the others. She could only do so while he was not in Len's company. It would be useless now that Len had his attention. She caught sight of Jenny's blond head bobbing around as she chatted. It hurt her to think she could sit there ignoring her. If Jenny had abruptly cut contact with Terry, it had been almost the same with her, the break coming after some painful cooling. It was around the time that she began mixing with Len and his friends. The thought that she would prefer the company of a person like Len Dawson was heartbreaking. Feeling tears welling in her eyes, she turned to the rostrum and was surprised to see the woman who had caused such a strange reaction in Fr. van Engelen. Uncle Bill spoke to her in his usual welcoming manner, while she listened, her head cocked. To the side of the rostrum, Miss Barker was observing her. Then the principal motioned her and the others to take their seats. Miss Barker moved to the side of the hall, keeping her eyes fixed on the woman.

'Hello, hello, right, we are ready to start,' said the principal, tapping the microphone. 'All right, everyone, can I please have your attention!' He waited until the chatter had died away. 'I want to warmly welcome you all on the first day of another school year. As usual, we will carry out the flag ceremony at the end of the assembly. I want to remind you that it is just on thirty years since the end of the Second World War. The town is making a special effort to commemorate Anzac Day this year. I want to encourage you, students, to contribute. Remember that many of our diggers who lost their lives were no older than many of you.' He paused, and the hall fell silent.

'You know, it is one of the unique qualities of this great land that our nation was born amid failure. It was born in the blood sacrifice of those young men landing on a deserted beach at the other end of the world. Many of our youth make a pilgrimage to what we often call the old country. That is a great experience. There you will recognise the origin of so much of our social and political heritage. For me, however, the first destination of a pilgrimage for young people these days should be to that deserted beach, Gallipoli, on that barren peninsula of modern Turkey, to meditate on the spot where those young men willingly shed their blood. They shed their blood willingly because they believed that our society, our Christian civilisation, was worth saving, worth fighting for.

'I invite you to walk around our town centre and reflect on what you see. There are not just shops, businesses, municipal and government buildings, churches, and other private premises. There is more to them than just the material structure. Embodied in them are all the beliefs, values, traditions, customs, and political ideas that they presuppose. It's worth thinking about. Those places, our town, did not materialise on their own. They are built on all those beliefs and values, and so on. We are a Christian civilisation, and that is the foundation of our free society. You young men and young women should think about these things. That's what our young soldiers fought to keep. Now, I don't want to be too serious on this first day, so I will stop there. Let me get onto other matters. First, there's the class timetable and your teachers for the year.'

Estella's mind drifted as the principal went through the timetable. She could not help looking over at Jenny, whispering in Tricia Barry's ear. Tricia, with her hand over her mouth, returned the whisper. They both giggled. Jenny smiled teasingly at Len, who wore the same smug, self-satis-fied expression. Jenny's every action continued to draw her attention: the wavy blond hair flicked this way and that; the playful teasing look in her sparkling blue eyes; the movement of her shoulders; and the pout of her lips. Estella forced herself to turn away.

'Lastly, I want to introduce you to the teacher who has joined the staff this year,' the principal was saying. And then, turning to the woman

Estella had seen that morning: 'Miss Bicknell, I welcome you on behalf of myself, the staff, and the student body to Binawarra High School.' Then, addressing his audience: 'Miss Edith Bicknell comes to us with some very impressive qualifications and experience. She will be taking up a new position in the school.'

'In addition to teaching English and history, she will be the senior year coordinator. She will be looking after your welfare, not only regarding your coursework but also your general welfare. Let me assure you that Miss Bicknell is well qualified for this. I must say it is a privilege to have her on staff. I do not doubt that the senior students will benefit from Miss Bicknell's expertise.' He turned and gave a little bow in Miss Bicknell's direction. Miss Bicknell gave a perfunctory nod. 'Miss Bicknell will say a few words.' He stepped away from the microphone.

Miss Edith Bicknell rose and approached with confident steps. 'Thank you, Mr Huckerby, for the welcome on behalf of the teachers and students. It is much appreciated. I won't keep you. You have already heard too much. Such assemblies can be a little tedious, can't they?' A flicker of a smile passed across her lips. 'I want to take a moment to introduce myself and say that I am looking forward to working with the teachers and students and providing whatever help I can. I will be indeed rewarded if my experience and qualifications are of benefit to you.' She looked around the hall.

'You have heard that our freedoms can come under assault from the heavy-handed tyrant riding at the front of a military machine. Unfortunately, that is all too true. But the restrictions on personal freedom come not only from an enemy carrying a gun. The deprivation of freedom can come in a much more insidious form. That is when you don't realise that you are being oppressed, when you have been so long in chains you don't recognise it anymore. Like the woman trapped in a marriage with a violent husband, or worse still, the woman prevented from fulfilling herself by a demanding, thoughtless husband, or even worse still, a woman trapped in the grip of traditions that keep her silent. A great philosopher wrote these words in one of his famous works:

Men and women are born free; and everywhere they are in chains. One thinks himself the master of others, and still remains a greater slave than they. How did this change come about?

'An important part of my task is to help the final year's students fulfil themselves, to reach their full potential. And that means throwing off the restrictions that society has placed upon you. I want to help you all focus on the answer to the question of how and why people are not free. I am sure you have noticed the awakening of women in the last few years. Their issues are just as important as the subjects you will study in class. One thing before I finish. Forms of address are just one small part of the problem. It is now accepted that the form of address for all adult women is "Ms." Please address me as Ms Bicknell. Thank you.'

Ms Bicknell returned to her seat with the same confident steps. The students looked on in silence and expectation, while bemusement and indecision seemed to have overtaken the rostrum. Bill Huckerby struggled to his feet and shuffled to the microphone.

'Well, thank you, Miss Bicknell, for that inspiring speech. I'm sure we have all been encouraged to reflect on issues that seem to take a back seat on such occasions as this.' He paused, his eyes on the floor in front of him. 'Yes, I think the young men here can profit by contemplating how they relate to the young women in their class. I don't want to sound like I am reprimanding you in the first assembly of the year, but it is well worth encouraging you all to consider how you treat the fairer sex. Girls are not the same as boys. You need to treat them with care and respect. Some day they will be mothers of children just like you. Some of them may be the mothers of your children, as you must be aware.'

'I won't say any more now, but I think the boys here know what I am talking about. The same roughhouse behaviour and language are not for people emotionally and physically more sensitive than you boys. There has been a sad deterioration in the attitude of boys towards girls over recent years. Some very bad influences are abroad. You boys should reflect on why this is so. But now, let me finish on this subject. There are other matters to get on to before we start the ceremony of the flag.'

Miss Bicknell's face darkened as the principal extemporised while Miss Barker continued to observe her. Eventually, the principal announced the flag ceremony. Four final-year boys marched solemnly two abreast down the middle aisle to the rostrum. Bill Huckerby held the folded flag aloft and then handed it to the boys. Each boy took one corner and mounted the rostrum. They turned the folded side showing the Union Jack.

'This side of the flag shows the flag of Great Britain,' Bill Huckerby announced. 'But at a deeper historical level, this unique design represents the common origins of Great Britain and our great nation. The superimposed flags of England, Scotland, and Ireland (those of St George, St Andrew, and St Patrick) that make up the Union Jack represent our shared Christian heritage. They represent our system of morality and the system of law and political organisation that has grown out of it. They represent a system of law and political organisation that has evolved over hundreds of years. We honour and cherish that system and commemorate and honour the people who bequeathed that system to us, their descendants, to all their descendants in spirit and hope who now make up the great land of the southern seas.'

With the principal's nod, the boys turned the flag around and held up the side depicting the Southern Cross.

'The Southern Cross of the night sky: mysterious, hopeful, and unifying. While the superimposed flags of the old countries bid us to look back to acknowledge and honour our origins, the Southern Cross represents the new, the future, and our aspirations. It is symbolic of a unity that binds together those who were here and those who have come, a unity that will take us forward under God in building this great nation.'

The boys unfolded the flag and, carrying it aloft, set off down the aisle with Bill Huckerby close behind, followed by the teachers and students. They processed to the flagpole in the recreational area, where they attached the flag to the flagpole ropes. Then, with the students and staff gathered around, the boys raised the flag until it fluttered in the warm blue sky above Binawarra.

Chapter 3

Revolutionary disturbance

AMID THE NOISY bustle of students leaving the flagpole, a voice whispered over Edith Bicknell's shoulder, 'I bet you've not often witnessed anything as ridiculously reactionary as that.'

The voice belonged to a slim, attractive woman with fashionable slacks and a matching top clinging to her trim figure. A pair of elegant wire-frame glasses perched a little forward on her nose. Her sleek, youthful complexion and bright blue eyes were an arresting contrast with the rather studious-looking spectacles. The senior boys eyed her as they passed.

'Jane Cox,' she went on, putting a hand on her arm and bending towards her. 'History and social studies, senior years.'

'Ah, yes,' said Ms Bicknell, 'I'll be working closely with you.' They turned to walk towards the final year students standing around the entrance to the classroom block. 'Like what?'

'You know, all that stupid stuff about Christian heritage and that embarrassing flag ceremony. Enough to make you throw up endlessly! Who could believe it? When was the last time you saw anything like that?'

'It's very unusual to make such an elaborate ceremony around a mere flag.'

'Huckerby is such an absurd clown. It's a travesty in this day and age that someone like that is still the principal of a state high school. Preaching at us! How out of touch can you get? You would think the political revolution of the last decade, the betterment of society, was unheard of here. He barely mentioned the Aboriginals.' Ms Bicknell feigned an uncommitted response. 'I know just what you meant about freedom and oppression,' Jane Cox continued, 'I've been dying to say something for ages, but never had the support. The man provokes me like ... I don't know what. You probably heard you did not get through that thick skull of his. You know, you're going to find out that a gang of men just like Huckerby run this town. Thick as bricks, they are.'

They were now standing in front of the students.

'Can't talk now,' said Ms Bicknell, glancing at the restless students. 'Let's meet later. Does anyone else feel the same way?'

'They certainly do.'

'Really? How many?'

'At least five who feel strongly and a few others too lazy to act.'

'Are you prepared to act?'

'Yes!' she hissed.

'Okay, all right, I understand,' said Ms Bicknell, putting a finger to her lips. 'Let's get the students organised first. Then we can talk about getting together. I would like to hear more.'

'You just wait! You don't know what you're getting yourself into.'

When the students broke away after the flag ceremony, Estella approached Larry.

'Larry, you do remember when we used to play together, don't you?'

'Yes,' said Larry, a little more at ease.

'We had fun, didn't we?'

'Yes ... yes, we did.'

'And you just thought of me as a good friend to play with?'

Larry hesitated. 'You came with your father. And my mother liked having you around.'

'Your mother is a good person, so kind and considerate. Your father is kind, too. Do you think they're happy with you mixing with Len Dawson?'

'What do you mean?'

'You know what I mean, Larry.'

'No, I don't,' he said, blushing from the blatant lie.

During this time, they walked to the classroom block and stopped with the others while awaiting further direction. Larry shifted and fidgeted, noticing Len not far away.

'Larry, I'm no different from that little girl you used to play with. I'm still the same person. There's no reason we can't be friends. There's no need to change just because we are older. Think of me as the sister you don't have.'

'What ...? Okay,' he said, seeing Len approaching.

'Hey, lover boy!' Len cried as he came up to Larry with the others in tow. Estella backed away and walked to the other side of the group.

'She still thinks you stink,' Don laughed as they watched her retreat. 'You're not getting very far.'

'What is it suddenly with you and the Binawarra Virgin?' said Len, ignoring the dig.

'Nothing.'

'Come off it!'

'She just asked about my mother and father. We saw a lot of Estella and her dad when he was working on our house.'

'I saw a lot of her, too, when her old man was working on my father's properties, but that has not turned into the Binawarra Virgin sucking up to me.'

'Estella wouldn't suck up to anybody. I know her too well.'

It was a fatal mistake.

'Ohhhh, lover boy!' the boys chorused.

'Lover boy here knows the Ice Maiden too well,' John sneered, 'but is obviously no threat to the wall of ice.'

The students close by laughed. From the other side of the group, Estella watched. They were mocking Larry because of her. It was sad. Larry's self-respect could not overcome the prestige of belonging to Len's in-group.

MISS BARKER positioned herself so she could observe Miss Bicknell. A faint look of disgust grew as the flag ceremony progressed. That was very careless of her. In her short speech, Miss Bicknell made it evident, except perhaps to the naïve and unobservant, that she had an agenda. If that agenda went against the powerful interests in the school and town, it would be incautious to play one's hand openly, even a little. Miss Bicknell thought she was safe.

When the flag ceremony ended, Bill Huckerby returned to his office with his staff. Miss Barker was about to follow when Jane Cox approached Miss Bicknell. She hesitated. Usually, she would now go to the school's sick-room, where she, as the school's nurse, would be on duty until lunchtime. The students had almost dispersed, leaving her vulnerable, standing alone, clothed in white. She glanced once more at Miss Bicknell and Jane Cox deep in conversation, and then made her way to the sickroom. After en-suring everything was prepared, she walked to the principal's office.

'Is the principal available?' she said to Mrs Joyce Charing, the principal's secretary, 'I want to take his blood pressure. Tell him it is essential we get this over with now.'

Mrs Charing regarded Miss Barker stonily and put her pen firmly on her desk. She went to his door. 'The school nurse says you must have your blood pressure measured,' she said, shooting an indignant glance at Miss Barker. 'Do you want me to show her in?'

'Blood pressure! Why does that old witch want to take my blood pres-sure now? Okay, show her in,' he said, laughing. 'Thank you, Mrs Charing, please shut the door as you go.' The secretary closed the door, looking down her nose at the nurse.

'I wonder if that woman is suited to her position.'

'You leave the administration to me,' Bill Huckerby shot back, pretending to be affronted. 'She's all right.'

'I wonder.'

'Don't wonder. It's not good for you. Come on, let's get on with it.' He rolled up his shirtsleeve.

'That can wait for the moment,' she said, sitting in the armchair in front of his desk. 'There's something I want to talk to you about first.'

Bill Huckerby raised his eyebrows and gave an uncomprehending gesture with two open hands.

'What did you think of that little speech the new teacher, Miss Bicknell, gave?'

'I thought it was good, a sort of pep talk. What about it?'

'Didn't you think there was something discordant in it, something that clashed with your own ideas?'

'Not really. Or perhaps a little. So what? Miss Bicknell is a young teacher. Like a lot of young people, she has those sorts of matters foremost on her mind, you know, personal freedom, women's issues, and so on. That's okay. That's just something I have to work with.' He stopped. 'What's this all about, Flo? I can see now you didn't come here expressly to take my blood pressure. Come on, cough it up.'

'What about the student radicalism that has gripped the university campuses for some years now?' she said to prod him.

'What about it? You're not suggesting it's being exported to our town in the form of Miss Bicknell, are you?' he said with a grin. Miss Barker remained unmoved. 'In any case, it's the same thing. Those students have got to have something to get excited about. That's part of being young. You were young once, weren't you? Kicked over the traces? Entertained weird, idealistic ideas?'

'No, I didn't. At least not in that way.'

'Oh, come on, Flo! I know it's a serious business on campus. That's all city stuff. I don't think we have to worry about it here in sleepy, isolated Binawarra. This is a bad place to export your student revolution to. Your ordinary student radical will soon run out of puff when the responsibility of being a teacher in a country high school comes to bear on him. Miss Bicknell was producing the rhetoric of undergraduate student politics. In a way, it's inspiring for the young minds here. It will help them reflect on the rights and responsibilities of adult life. In the bigger picture, old fogies like you and me, fixed in the rhythms of the bush, are here to keep things in perspective, aren't we? We should be happy we have such an earnest and enthusiastic teacher. No, the ramparts aren't about to be stormed yet in Binawarra.'

'On the subject of revolution, do you know where Miss Bicknell's quotation came from?'

'What quotation?'

'The one in her speech, the lines she quoted to emphasise the need to undertake a struggle for freedom.'

'What are you talking about?'

'Oh, I see. The principal of Binawarra High School wasn't listening, was he? Too busy thinking about other matters, no doubt.' And before the principal could answer, 'Miss Bicknell quoted some lines from the opening page of *The Social Contract* by none other than Jean-Jacques Rousseau. Rousseau is generally considered to be the architect of the French Revolution, the revolution that was to be the paradigm for most revolutions over the next two hundred years.'

Bill Huckerby frowned and looked hard at Miss Barker.

'Oh, Flo, Flo ... look, I'm not a political philosopher, and the French Revolution is not part of my stock of usable knowledge. I'm just a simple-Simon economist by training. It's not that I have no interest in such high-flown academic matters. I don't have the time. I have a school to administer. Have a look around at the filing cabinets here. All chock-a-block.' He waved his arms around the room. 'On the moral and political side, I'm ruled by what is already established in this great land of ours. I don't need any academic texts. The rights and responsibilities of the citizen are in everything we see. That's why I told the students to reflect on what we have in this town of ours. The lessons are there as clear as can be.' He paused and then wagged his finger at her. 'You know what? You've been spending too much time in that library of yours. You're becoming too bookish! Loosen up. This is the real world.'

Miss Barker could not hold back the trace of a smile.

'Hey!' cried the principal, 'get me a camera!'

'You're more of a political philosopher than you think,' she commented, but then, realising there was no point in pursuing the subject, said, 'Tell me, Bill. Why did Miss Bicknell arrive in Binawarra this morning? That's unusual, isn't it? Generally, new teachers arrive well in advance to settle into their new accommodation.'

'She had to stay with an aunt of hers who's not well. She's an invalid, and there's no one else to take care of her. Miss Bicknell rang me in good time to discuss it. It was all right with me as long as she was prepared for the first day of school, and she was.'

'Really? An aunt, eh? And where is she staying now that Miss Bicknell is in Binawarra?'

'I don't know. I didn't ask. Why are you so suspicious about this particular teacher? What's going on? This is not like you to be imagining things.'

'Am I imagining things?'

'Yes! You are!' he said, his face reddening. 'I spoke several times with Miss Bicknell on the phone. All her paperwork is in order. She has very good qualifications and references. Her qualification in psychology is particularly useful in helping the final years, I think. So that's what I am going to work on.' He paused. 'Flo, get out of that dark library of yours. There are too many heavy volumes there, and they're weighing on your brain!'

'All right, I give up,' said Miss Barker, pursing her lips. 'I'm just alerting you to things. If you disagree with me, at least keep what I have said in mind. There's not a good smell about this Miss Bicknell.' She rose. 'I suppose we should be relieved she did not quote from Marx.'

'Marx! Dear oh me, Flo.'

She took up her blood pressure apparatus. 'Okay, give me that arm of yours.' The principal held up his arm. 'It's not satisfactory. Far too high. You must do something about it, or you will have trouble. You should go and see the doctor.'

'I know, I know. Joanne is on to me, too, about it. I'll do something about it after the busy period has passed. Now, what about coming around this evening for a cup of tea? Joanne will be pleased to have you over. You can tell her all about your suspicions. She'll be amused, too. You know, Flo, as a spy, you would make a good nurse!' He laughed loudly, leaning over the desk and wagging his finger at her.

Miss Barker packed her apparatus up and gave him a stern look. 'See you tonight.' She opened the door to find herself staring into Mrs Charing's face.

'Oh!' said Mrs Charing, 'I was about to knock.'

'That's all right, Mrs Charing,' said the principal. 'Come on in. See you tonight, Flo.'

Miss Barker let the startled and embarrassed secretary walk by her and, with a grave nod to the principal, walked to the sickroom. She sat at her desk and gazed through the window. Her friend, Bill, was not susceptible to her misgivings. Would it have made any difference if she had mentioned she had seen Ms Bicknell the day before, driving around the town with a man who had recently begun visiting the town, ostensibly for business? On the other hand, what if he were right? That Miss Bicknell was just another idealistic left-wing teacher who talked more about changing the world than did anything about it.

No, too much about her actions gave the impression that she was following a plan. Her speech during the assembly might have resulted from an unexpected provocation, but what she said was well prepared, just waiting for the right moment to come out. She must be patient. If Miss Bicknell was up to something particular and not just general left-wing agitation, it should become clear in time. Meanwhile, she would keep an eye on her and on the salesman with what sounded like a Balkans accent. On that point, she was not sure. He had an accent that sounded Balkans, but there was something else mixed in there. What it was, she could not say.

WHEN ESTELLA left for school that morning and Charles took himself off to his workshop, Aine Winterbine busied herself with the housework. For some time, she walked around distractedly, dusting and cleaning. At length, she stopped and bowed her head, her fair shoulder-length hair falling around her face. She brushed the hair out of her eyes and sat in the nearby lounge chair. The insistent vision of Estella walking to school alone, standing alone in the schoolyard, and being isolated in class came to mind.

Over the last two years, Estella's small group of friends broke off one by one. There was no conflict evident in the dissolution of her friendships. A divergence of interests was the cause. While some of the girls had boyfriends early and others couldn't stop chatting about them, Estella had shown no interest. She had always been friendly with a few, Larry Burgess, for example, but she was not interested in them as boyfriends. And those few boys now seemed unable to be just friends.

Another cause was the girls' obsession with the latest fashions and music, some of which was vulgar and in poor taste. That meant the conversation often was, if not about boys, about clothes, make-up, and pop stars. Estella had little interest in following the latest youth fashions, even less in the music they liked, preferring folk and classical music. Besides her extensive reading, she developed a fervent interest in gardening. None of the girls had the slightest interest in messing with plants and dirt. They laughed at the idea. Her favourite pastime of long walks in the surrounding fields and bush turned them off even more. They could not understand how a beautiful girl like Estella could indulge in such boring pursuits.

Estella was not too deterred by the desertion of most of her friends. The comfort of her mother and father, together with the Huckerbys and Miss Barker, who made up her small surrogate family, was enough for her. Fr. van Engelen also showed the same constant care and concern. They were all she needed for family love and consolation. But it was different with Jenny Brougham. She and Estella had been as close as sisters.

Jenny's temperament was as bright as her blue eyes and golden, wavy hair. Nobody could have as much fun with so little as Jenny Brougham. In contrast, Estella was quiet and subdued, matching her complexion and dreamy hazel eyes. Tall and perfectly proportioned, she appeared to glide rather than walk, while Jenny, a little shorter and slimmer, was always bouncy and exuberant. The boys in their age group were besotted with both girls. The difference was that Jenny exploited their interest while Estella backed away from the attention.

Without knowing the incident that caused the final break—there evidently was one—Aine was convinced it related to their religious beliefs. From one day to the next, Jenny refused to go to Estella's room. From one day to the next, Jenny noticed, as she never did before, the crucifixes and devotional objects around the Winterbine house. She was uncomfortable with things she had seen for years. Worse still, they repelled her. The estrangement broke Estella's heart.

She rose and went to her bedroom. There she knelt before pictures of the Sacred Heart and Our Lady of Perpetual Succour, which formed a modest shrine in the corner of the room. She bowed her head and repeated several prayers of intercession. At length, she returned to the lounge room to resume her work. The gradual onset of the darkness, which had started earlier that morning, could not be resisted. With a sinking heart, she dropped her dusting cloth on the floor and fumbled her way to the front of the house, holding one hand over her eyes. She emerged into the bright light of day and felt along the wall to the end of the verandah.

'Charles!' she called. She waited, but he did not appear. The whirr of the electric saw filled the air, smothering the bird and insect buzz of summer. She reached for the rope of a bell Charles had attached to the wall and pulled on it. He appeared on the gravel driveway within seconds, looking up at her. He mounted the verandah stairs, took her in his arms, and clasped her close. Aine let her head rest on his chest as she had done for the first time nineteen years earlier. He held her for a few minutes, then led her to the swing seat. He caressed her cheek and neck and then kissed her on her smooth, pale forehead. At length, recovering from her swoon, she opened her eyes, and he kissed her lightly on the lips.

'Do you remember that night at Bill and Joanne Huckerby's,' he said, 'before I left to return home to the South Coast?'

She nodded.

'Remember? We were sitting on the verandah alone while your parents, Bill, and Joanne were inside, just like we're doing now. We were looking up into the clear night sky, peering at the stars. I pointed out the Southern Cross and said it was strange that the great symbol of the Southern World was shaped like a cross. Do you remember?'

'Of course.'

'Remember, I said we had been brought together under that symbol, and there it was in the night sky. When I left, I said that you were to look up in the sky each night while we were apart, find the Southern Cross and know that I was looking at it, too, that evening, looking at you in the love of Jesus. I was so happy.'

'Me, too,' she whispered.

'I drove into a crystal-clear night back to the South Coast. The stars sparkled like diamonds against the dark, icy sky. I suppose I should have stopped. But I wasn't sleepy. I didn't want to sleep. I had driven away from Fr Bertollo and my aunts, not knowing where I was going. Now I was returning, knowing where my life would go. It would go with you no matter what. No matter what, do you understand?'

'You have been too good. I will never forget the pain I caused you when I—'

'No, don't say it.' He put a finger on her lips. 'You couldn't help ... there were other things at play ... you came through it. I'm so grateful to God for bringing us together in the strangest way and for His continuing protection. Sweetest Aine, you have been good to Estella and me. It has never been a burden if I have been good to you.' He kissed her again.

They sat for a while, without speaking. Aine raised her head. 'Let me go and lie down for a while. I will be all right if I do that.'

Charles walked with her to their bedroom. He made sure she was comfortable and then made a cup of tea. He continued to talk about that week when they first met, the climb to the top of his mountain, his trip home, and telling Fr Bertollo and his aunts all about it, how their joy scarcely exceeded their astonishment. When he was satisfied she was calm and resting, he returned to the workshop.

Aine slid down, so her head was resting on the pillow. She closed her eyes and pondered Charles's efforts yet again to comfort her. He knew talking about the circumstances of their first meeting always acted as a restorative. It reassured her when that terrible darkness came upon her and filled her with doubts about herself. She could not help it. Charles always had to reassure her, and he did. But why, oh why, did it happen? she kept asking herself. Her thoughts drifted back all those years to the convent, Virginia, Jannie, the promising career as a model, the near disaster with Harry the photographer ... She became aware of someone caressing her arm. She opened her eyes to see Estella sitting beside the bed.

'What's the time?' she said, sitting upright.

'Half past twelve.'

'Oh, I am late.'

'No, don't worry, Mamma. Lunch is ready. I have already called Daddy.'

THE EFFECTIVE break occurred when Jenny began teasing one of the teachers. Estella did not think it was fun. Worse, it was cruel and unfair. Up to that point, the teacher, in his mid-thirties, was relaxed, outgoing, and popular with the students. As Jenny led him on with a sauciness that only he seemed unaware of, he became infatuated with her. When it changed him from outgoing to depressive, Estella made her disapproval known. She could not help it. Jenny should know how reprehensible her behaviour was. Jenny sorely resented her disapproval. It wasn't her fault, she said, waving both arms. He should keep his eyes to himself. A man of that age should not be looking at her like that. Like what? Don't be so naïve. Paul Egan got Estella involved by bringing it up himself while helping her with an essay. They spent some time in discussion when he broke off and, embarrassed, asked her if she minded talking about something personal.

Though suspecting what it was about, she did not object. Mr Egan said he was reluctant to bring up what was on his mind, and he would never have said it to just anybody. He was sure she would keep his confidence and not misjudge his intentions. He knew Jenny and their friends were talking about him. His manner with her was not right, but he could not help it. It is difficult to have problems in your personal life. It is even more difficult when you come across someone you think suits you. But it is worse than difficult when your feelings are pointless, besides being improper.

He was sorry to be so explicit and regretted making her uncomfortable, but he wanted Jenny to know his feelings were blameless. He was a complete fool, and even more so for admitting his affection. That Jenny was teasing him was plain, but he was sure there was no malice behind it. Her state of mind was a factor in his feelings and in his decision to bring it up. Jenny was infatuated with a fellow student whom Estella did not regard well. He would do anything to get her out of reach of the unprincipled person who had no genuine interest in her. But his hands were tied. Besides, he would look like a hypocrite. He hoped Estella could do something.

He would not say who it was. She would see in the end if she did not already know. He finished by saying that the situation had become irresolvable, and he had to remove himself from the school for everyone's benefit. The principal had his application for transfer on urgent personal grounds. Mr Huckerby was very understanding and guaranteed a smooth transfer to a school in Melbourne. He would be gone before long, and the matter closed for good.

Mr Egan's honesty embarrassed Estella, but the tragedy of his circumstances moved her. She was sure he would never do anything to harm Jenny. Full of compassion and doubting her power to do anything, she saw him alone in his sorrow and prayed he would receive the grace to rise above his trials. The next day, she tried to warn Jenny about Len Dawson. But Jenny would not hear about it. Not a word. She slapped the bench they were sitting on and rose.

'You're too strict, unbending, and ready to preach like a nun. And I'm sick of it.'

Her heart aching, Estella could only watch as Jenny left to join her new friends.

Chapter 4

Planning the revolution

FR VAN ENGELEN completed the blessing of the ashes and turned to the congregation. 'Today, Ash Wednesday, is the first day of the holy season of Lent. The forty days of Lent are in memory of Christ's forty days of fasting and penance in the desert. It is a time when we unite ourselves with the suffering of Christ as he went to meet His death, the death that would become our redemption. The sprinkling of the ashes is a sign of our bodily destiny and the repentance we should feel. "Remember, man, thou art dust, and that unto dust thou shalt return."'

He turned towards the tabernacle, genuflected, and moved to the right to say the first prayer before the sprinkling of the ashes. The small choir sang the Antiphon psalm:

> Listen to us, Lord, of Thy gracious mercy; look down upon us in the abundance of Thy pity, Lord. O God, save me, see how the waters close about me, threatening my life.

THAT EVENING, Gerda Vrouwendijk hurried around her lounge room, trying to bring order to her mess. Books and papers lay everywhere, wrappings of fast-food dinners spread over every available space, and ashtrays were full to the brim with twisted, discarded butts. A stale food and tobacco smell pervaded the house. She stacked the books on the floor next to the chairs or wherever they were out of the way. She scraped whatever rubbish came to hand into a bin. She checked her watch. It was not yet eight o'clock. She grabbed the telephone receiver.

'Get around here now,' she ordered. 'Walk. Go to the back laneway entrance as I showed you.' She slapped down the receiver, making it rattle in the cradle. Twenty minutes later, Boris strolled through the kitchen doorway into the lounge room.

'I wouldn't leave the back door unlocked if I were you,' he said, with a lazy nod over his shoulder.

'We are not where you come from. It would arouse suspicion here if people found the new teacher locking all her doors in the evening. Besides, it's none of your business.'

'As you wish,' replied Boris. He sat down in a lounge chair and stroked his thick, dark moustache with his index finger. He looked up at Gerda from under his bushy eyebrows.

'Well?'

'Well!' she snapped, coming and standing before him. 'Come on. I don't have much time. I'm expecting people.'

'It's only been a week since I saw you. I cannot come to Binawarra more than once a week. I don't want to arouse suspicion. People have to be comfortable with me.'

'You've got to get onto it.' She clicked her fingers. 'Come more often if it's necessary.' She walked to the mantelpiece and snatched at a packet of cigarettes.

Boris blinked long and deliberately. 'Don't try to force things more than is possible,' he said, taking his cigarettes from his shirt pocket. He lit up and lazily blew the smoke at Gerda. 'You could get yourself into a compromising position.'

'I don't need you to tell me such things.'

'I have told you as much as I know about this place,' he said, relenting. 'I am cultivating some contacts. They are on the point of bearing fruit. I don't want to push them. They must think they are confiding the information I want.'

Gerda sat and composed herself. She agreed on that last point. Nevertheless, she must keep up the pressure on Boris. She wanted nothing to distract him. 'All right, have you got anything at all?'

'Perhaps more on the two points you asked about. You must keep in mind that the Dutch priest is well-liked. The people are sympathetic towards him because of his disabilities. He often sits in the park across from his church, greeting people as they pass by. Even the young people shout hello to him. People say he is not the sort of preaching figure they have imagined Catholic clergy to be. He's been chosen to say prayers, or whatever it is, at the dawn ceremony on Anzac Day this year, the day commemorating the soldiers who fought in wars, if you did not know. I would be careful how you deal with him. People like him for the person he is.'

'He must have a weakness somewhere,' Gerda muttered. 'He clearly exerts more influence over the girl and her family than I assumed.' She got up and walked up and down. Boris waited. 'What about this injury of his? That causes so much pain. What do people know about it? How genuine is it?'

'Nobody knows anything about it, as far as I can gather, except his doctor, who is not local. He sees a Catholic doctor in the city from the Dutch community.'

'Okay, find out what it is and why he needs a special doctor.' Boris gestured his assent. Gerda, fidgeting and blowing smoke out of the side of her mouth, continued, 'Right. Now, what about the other matter?'

'What about the Dutch community?' said Boris. 'Haven't you got better contacts than me?'

'I give the directions, not you. And don't refer to my national background. How many times do I have to tell you? What else?'

Boris fixed his dark eyes on Gerda and then flicked ash into the ashtray. 'About Alan Collins's debts, people in Binawarra have a lot to say. Much of it is the rumour of envy. Mr Collins has airs, they say. He settled in Binawarra about five years ago. In that time, he has built up a nice little newspaper business. People whisper that he has debts. The size of the debt is exaggerated, though. His bank manager hinted that the debts were nothing to worry about. But there is this: Collins is a bankrupt runaway.

'Apparently, he ran a tourist business on the Gold Coast, and clocked up big debts, causing it to collapse. The creditors got almost nothing in the wind-up. Collins cleared out as soon as he could, leaving everything, including his wife and kids, in Brisbane. You can guess what rumours followed him, can't you? He had a nice little stake to start up a business in semi-retirement in country Victoria. None of this is generally known in Binawarra. It is in the interest of those who do know to keep it to themselves. Their business and advertising tariffs depend on it. Finally, to show just how fortunate our newspaper editor is, Collins's plan for semi-retirement flew out the window because of the paper's success. But there were no tears. He sees a promising future in media and has thrown himself into his newspaper's development. He is not without ambition.'

'Well, this is something we can work on,' said Gerda, taking a seat in the armchair opposite him. 'What about women?'

'I can't find a connection with any woman in Binawarra. I have checked out Rita Foley, the wife of the President of the Returned Soldiers League. It's likely there's nothing in it. She's just a busy beaver. We'll see.'

'Other women?'

'Nothing is known. No names are connected with him. He frequently travels to Ballarat and Bendigo, and often to Melbourne. I cannot imagine that he remains celibate, especially someone so sophisticated and obviously concerned with his comfort. It's not credible that if he has a woman in this forsaken place, nobody would know.'

'You're right. I want you to find out what female connections he has. There's got to be something there I can exploit.' There was a brief pause as they looked at each other. 'Is that it?'

'There's nothing more,' said Boris. 'Tomorrow, I will return to Melbourne. I'll be back next week.'

'I'll look forward to it,' she said, unable to suppress her sarcasm. 'Some of my teaching colleagues are coming around this evening. Situate yourself behind the ferns and shrubs on the front verandah. Just in case.'

'Just in case?'

'Just in case. Understood?'

Boris sat back in a deck chair behind the shrubs and ferns, prepared to observe those inside. He gave no more than a glance at the street. Nobody was there then. Anyhow, who would be interested in a get-together of high school teachers? But across the road, standing in the dark, hard up against one of the towering eucalypts lining the street, a tall, slim figure had been observing for some time. She now watched Boris installing himself out of sight on the verandah.

Jane Cox, dressed in tight, gleaming white slacks and a pink tank top showing off her shapely, suntanned shoulders and perky breasts, hurried through the front door. Her fashionable wire-frame glasses still sat a little forward on her delicate nose. Her shampooed hair was swept back over her head. On her feet, she wore expensive white leather sandals.

'Edith, I've been looking forward to this!' she gushed, looking around her. 'About time someone did something.'

'It's merely a get-together, a meeting of like minds,' said Ms Bicknell. 'We will see if it's worth doing anything.'

'Yes, yes, it will be,' She enthused. I've got a good feeling about this. This town desperately needs change, and we can start with that fat ass Huckerby.'

Stephen Calder, a history and social studies teacher, strolled in with one hand in his pocket and the other carrying a can of beer. Trim and muscular with short, cropped hair, he wore soiled, faded blue jeans and a white T-shirt.

'Welcome, Stephen,' said Ms Bicknell. Stephen nodded, mumbled a greeting, and flopped down on the lounge settee. He looked at the two women and brought the can to his lips. 'I hope we're not wasting our time again,' he said as he withdrew the can and wiped his mouth.

'No, no, we're not,' cried Jane. 'Be positive! This is a real chance to organise.' She sat next to him, tapped his thigh and grabbed the cigarette pack that he had thrown on the coffee table.

'We'll see,' he said, balancing the can on his knee.

Faye Crofts and Lesley Conos entered, one behind the other. They looked around, said their hellos, and took their place in the nearest chairs. They caught sight of the beer can balancing on Stephen Calder's knee and frowned at each other.

'This is an opportunity,' whispered Jane, coming and kneeling beside them. 'This is a chance to plan for change.'

'We hope you're right,' said Faye Crofts.

'We're behind any attempt to replace that fat fool,' said Lesley Conos.

'I like that anger,' said Jane, patronisingly patting Lesley on the shoulder. 'Keep it up.'

'Who are we still waiting for?' said Ms Bicknell, coming through the blue haze.

'There's Rick Juddery and Pat Dillon,' said Jane. 'There's also Suzie McNamara. I don't know if she'll be any use. She's bright and full of resentment but needs the right direction. She insists on bringing that stupid American Bob McKinnon with her. It's a mystery why. He's not with us on everything. He should scurry back to San Francisco. He and his ... whatever you want to call them, are more at home there.' She shivered. 'I hope he doesn't mess things up.'

That seemed the cue for that named couple to breeze in, dragging the sultry summer air in with them. Bob McKinnon stopped and looked around at the gathering in an ostentatious manner.

'The usual suspects, I see,' he commented in a light American accent. He held up one hand in an elegant gesture. 'I sincerely hope this will come to something at last.'

The others watched in silence as he sat in the nearest armchair while Suzie, a petite girl dressed scantily for the summer weather, pushed a chair next to him. He took a black and gold pack of cigarettes from his shirt pocket, opened it, and offered it to his companion. She took one, and he lit up for both of them. He drew on his cigarette, exhaled, and vaguely looked around him, paying no attention to the others. Plumpish, he was dressed in a bohemian manner: sloppy oversized pants, white shirt hanging out, a little goatee beard, and curly hair just falling over his forehead and ears. He was in his late thirties, while the others were mid-twenties to early thirties. Suzie McNamara was the youngest. At that point, Pat Dillon entered, followed by Rick Juddery.

'Good, I think we can start,' said Ms Bicknell, taking a seat.

'Another baby boomer meeting, I see,' Bob McKinnon threw out with a slight sneer before Ms Bicknell could continue. 'Well, come on. Let's get on with it. Let's see if it's *extractus digitus* finally. I hope we don't have that collectivist nonsense you usually go on with and—Oh Lord, spare us—the sisterhood speeches.'

'That's all we need right now—your stupid comments,' said Jane Cox. 'Typical of you, you selfish pig!'

'Oink, oink,' Bob replied without looking at her. 'Give me a wholesome drink. I don't care for the swill here.' He daintily put his cigarette to his rounded lips, still without looking at Ms Cox.

'We'll have something later,' said Ms Bicknell, taken unawares by the sudden flaring of emotions but mistaking Bob's meaning.

'You know, Comrade Sister Cox,' Bob McKinnon continued, 'I once read somewhere that one of the sisterhood had written that men were such brainless depraved animals they would swim through torrents of vomit, floods of snot, and other such disgusting fluids, to relieve their sexual urges. I don't remember the precise wording. I must say that if you were the reward on the opposite bank of that raging river in your pretty pink top, I might be tempted. Maybe.' He smiled and looked down his nose at her. 'You don't make Stephen work nearly hard enough.'

Stephen Calder glanced at the ceiling and shook his head while Jane Cox grabbed the nearest object, which happened to be a book on the pile next to the lounge, and threw it in Bob McKinnon's direction. 'You sexist pig!' accompanied the flight of the book across the room.

'Quite the contrary,' said Bob McKinnon, unmoved and turning to give the book lying on the floor a curious glance. 'I don't discriminate. I think we're all equal. I'm the genuine liberal. Men and women are the same. You and your pal Stephen can do whatever you want, wherever you want, as you do like hyperactive rabbits. I have no moral judgment. No, none at all. Indeed, if it were Steve here in a fetching pink top at the other side of that torrent of deliciously disgusting fluids, I would be tempted to dive in—against my better judgment, of course. But, no, it's you who thinks we're different. It's everything about you that denotes the discriminating mentality.' Then turning to Edith Bicknell: 'I say, Lady Chairperson, I'm already weary of the usual, uncontrolled childishness of Sister Cox. Would you please bring this meeting to order before Comrade Sister becomes incontinent and spoils her dazzling white slacks? A pity to ruin such an expensive garment.'

Ms Bicknell said nothing, frowning, looking from one to the other. Suzie looked on expectantly. The other women clamoured their disapproval, soon arriving at a resolution that Bob McKinnon's words were highly offensive and that he should apologise or leave immediately.

'Get lost if you can't help being an offensive pig!' Jane Cox shouted as the group's conclusion.

Bob McKinnon stood and bowed with dignity. 'Brother and sisters, comrades,' he said, holding out his arms in a gesture of appeasement. 'I fervently apologise.' He tapped his breast. 'It was a moment of weakness when those unrestrained thoughts bubbled up from my subconscious and escaped through my fat, lazy lips.' He sat down and winked at Suzie. Suzie smothered a smile.

'There's a lot of unresolved tension here,' Ms Bicknell began.

'Oh, bravo!'

'That's something you should work on to resolve,' Ms Bicknell went on, ignoring Bob, 'but not here tonight. There are other matters to discuss, so let's get onto them. Some of you approached me after the first assembly to comment on the few words I was permitted to say—'

'May I respectfully interrupt at this point, Madam Chairperson?' said Bob, raising his hand. 'That was a very fine quotation you inserted into your few spontaneous words. Unmistakably from Rousseau's *Social Contract*. Very theatrical and very effective. And it should be. It worked well for Robespierre and his mates in the Terror. And indeed, parts of the *Social Contract* would have appealed to the Nazis, and no doubt they did.'

Ms Bicknell stiffened. 'Would you explain yourself, sir?' she said, with a trace of contempt at the corners of her lips.

'Very willingly, my dear lady,' he said, smirking. 'Rousseau's concept of the General Will of the people can be exploited by any fanatical group that claims to have its authentic interpretation.'

'That's a perversion of Rousseau's meaning.'

'You think so?'

'I do.'

'I think otherwise. But Madam Chairperson is undoubtedly sure of her facts. Please go on. My interruptions are objectionable and disruptive.' Despite his played-out cooperation, he could not suppress the impression of a backdown.

'They are out of place at this meeting. But we can discuss the matter whenever you want.' She paused for a reply, but Bob waved his arms in mock surrender. 'Okay, as I said, some of you remarked on the message of my little speech. It's obvious you think things are not what they should be in the high school. That's the reason I suggested we have this informal meeting. I want to learn from you. I propose that each of you give your version of the problems. Who wants the floor first?'

'I do,' said Jane Cox, jumping to her feet. 'There are so many problems in this corrupt town that I hardly know where to start.'

'Everybody happy to hear Jane out first?' said Ms Bicknell. There was no objection. 'Okay, Jane, you have the floor. Keep it brief and to the point.'

'We are waiting with bated breath on those pure drops of sisterhood wisdom,' said Bob, as Jane was about to speak. Jane glared at him and was about to respond, but was stopped by Suzie McNamara, who could not suppress a snigger. Jane reacted first with surprise, then with disdain.

'So that's it, you little slut!'

'Oh, well done, Suzie, my dear,' said Bob, with a little clap and feigning surprise. 'To earn the title of a slut at this juncture is truly an honour. If our efforts to rid us of that real straitjacket on our freedom, debilitating Christian morality, earn the title of slut for you, then we can consider that a shiny medal in reward for our feverish revolutionary efforts.' Then, looking around the assembly, 'If Suzie here earns that title by applying her feminine charms in all her youthful vigour to seducing a fat old fool like me, making me groan with pleasure, then I say, well done, Suzie. That's hitting out at what really wraps this school and town up in its invisible prison.' He paused. 'I hope we can concentrate on the real obstacles to freedom and equality.'

The women ignored Bob's congratulatory speech and gazed at Suzie in dismay. Stephen Calder, for the first time, looked animated and smiled.

'What are you about, you immature little bit of nothing?' said Pat Dillon.

'You disgusting little pervert,' said Faye Crofts.

'How could you?' said Lesley Conos.

'Easy,' replied Suzie, deploying all her girlish charms. 'I agree with Bob. Our personal freedoms are everything. The ability for me to act as I am inclined from moment to moment is essential. Surely that's true freedom: the ability for spontaneous and random acts of pleasure?'

'Well said, my soiled sweetness,' said Bob, reaching out and patting her shoulder.

'This town is paralysed from the top down,' Suzie continued, encouraged by the revulsion she had excited, 'by a hierarchy of people who police a code of morality that keeps the individual in check. Discrediting the Christian religion with its power-wielding clerics will destroy that code. It's not only the high school principal who props up that offensive system. It's a clique of men supported by their dimwitted wives. Bob and me support any action to disempower those props. There's nothing else.'

'Brilliantly explained,' Bob followed, clapping in support. 'We are not interested in replacing one repressive system with another equally repressive. *Nota Bene*, Sister Cox. Do you follow?'

'The world would be a much better place if the Christian religion had never existed,' Ms McNamara announced with finality.

'Where did you get all that stuff from, you silly little bimbo?' said Jane. 'As if we had to guess.'

'Please, everybody,' Ms Bicknell appealed, 'we must speak in order. We will not get anywhere unless we listen to what others have to say. Let's not become emotional about it.' The suspicion of being emotional about a rational enterprise was enough to subdue the heated feelings for the moment. 'Now that Bob and Suzie have stated their position,' she went on, 'it is only fair to give someone else a turn.' Bob McKinnon gave a generous, encompassing flourish of his arms to signify his resignation. 'Good. Go on, Jane.'

'Of course, we want to rid the world of debilitating Christian morality,' she began, glancing at Bob and Suzie. 'We agree with that. That's not an issue. The legitimate expression of individual sexuality is just one issue.' There was no discernible reaction from Bob, so she proceeded with more confidence. 'What has escaped Bob McKinnon is that the Christian religion is not only a code of morality. It's an institution. It's a powerful, wealthy institution with a parallel system of government. It parallels the institutions and governments of our democratic society. And no matter that some of the churches have officially broken from the Catholic Church, its powerful apparatus acts to coordinate all the traditional Christian groups.

'What's worse is that the Vatican is really the predominant apparatus, with the so-called secular government beholden to it. People think it's the other way around. But clearly, the capitalist system arises from the Catholic view of private property, family, and racial and sexual distinction and orientation. There has never been a real separation of church and state. And there never will be while the Vatican exists with its massive ability to propagate on a world scale. Without its destruction, the capitalist system will prevail.'

'You talk about democratic society? Come on!' cried Bob, taking advantage of a pause in Jane's speech. 'No, look, I'm sorry. With respect, I must interrupt.'

'You had your chance!' Jane cried. 'Now give me mine!'

Bob looked at her and smiled: 'You look so cute when your face is flushed. I could almost be aroused. But not quite.'

Suzie's lips curled while she gripped the sides of the chair and looked at the floor. A few moments of silence seemed to hold the air in suspension. Jane jumped to her feet, but Calder grabbed her arm and forced her back into her seat. Unable to resist, she burst into tears.

'Will you stop reacting! He's just trying to wind you up.'

'I know,' said Jane, between tears and sniffles.

Calder placed the beer can on the floor, got up, and walked over to Bob.

'The knight in shining armour, no doubt,' said Bob, drawing back as he looked up at him.

Calder bent over and, with a quick movement, inserted his index finger into one of Bob's nostrils and gave it a violent flick, jerking Bob's face up and to the side. 'Lay off! Otherwise, we'll get nowhere.' Leaving Bob clasping his nose, he returned to the settee. He reached down, picked up the beer can, and with his eyes on Bob emptied its contents into his mouth. 'And stop crying,' he said, glancing at Jane. He rolled the empty can onto the floor.

'It's so frustrating,' she said, wiping her face with a tissue handed to her.

'We won't get anywhere unless we can bring order to this meeting,' said Ms Bicknell, barely able to hide her exasperation. 'Bob, you had your say. It's fair to give someone else theirs.'

'Madam Sister Chairperson, I only wanted to save time,' said Bob, red-faced and wiping a trickle of blood from his nose. 'We have heard Sister Cox's views *ad nauseam*. What she has just imposed upon us, yet again, is a prepared speech she reels out at the slightest opportunity. It's like a stuck record.'

'You should talk, you revolting fairy!' Jane shouted.

'Oh dear, we are losing it, aren't we? Remember all that stuff about sexual freedom and the sexual revolution, comrade hypocrite?' Bob said with an unrestrained sneer. Then, turning to Ms Bicknell: 'The point I was going to make is that she never ever addresses the objections I raise to her waffle. It's always as if I had never uttered a word.'

'As if you don't do exactly the same thing.'

'I can tell you what's coming next,' he said, ignoring her. 'She's going to give us all that bull about the capitalist system, class struggle, organising, getting up committees, subcommittees, sending delegates, and so on. But good friend Stephen here has just illustrated the failure of that allegedly peaceful democratic system: if the delegates—we know what that means—don't get their way, then force is brought to bear. Sister Cox is all persuasive power when Stephen's muscles are backing her.'

'He should have put more than his finger in your nose,' said Jane.

'I wish,' said Bob, laughing. Suzie continued to look at the floor with tightened lips.

Edith Bicknell, giving up all hope that the meeting would drift onto the desired course, decided to risk an intervention.

'Bob, perhaps you have a point,' she said while signalling to Jane to relax. Bob nodded his acknowledgment, and Jane was now too wrung out to speak. 'You have both expressed your general ideas. But let's stick to the school. What are the specific manifestations of the problems you perceive?' She paused. 'If anything is to be done, we must know exactly what the problems are.'

'That fat misogynist fool, Huckerby, is the manifestation,' Faye Crofts said, taking the cue.

'Absolutely agree,' said Lesley Conos, leaning forward.

'Okay, explain ... and, Bob, give them a chance.' Bob gave an indulgent wave. 'You have the floor, Faye, and Lesley, but keep to the point.'

Disregarding the injunction to be brief, Faye Crofts and Lesley Conos opened in a furious relay. When they arrived in Binawarra, they expected a position commensurate with their academic qualifications. Instead, Bill Huckerby lectured them on the need to gain classroom experience. It would be best to start with the junior classes as freshly graduated teachers. Students in those years needed the kind of care and attention that reaches beyond the lessons of the university lecture hall. There he had them, called to attention like schoolgirls in front of his desk. When they tried to explain that they were qualified for more responsible work, he gave them a long lecture on the value of practical experience.

'Father knows best,' said Faye, signalling a break in the relay.

'The great patriarch telling the women to keep in their place,' echoed Lesley. 'Special care and attention, my fat foot! He just wanted us to look after the children, wipe their noses, and take them to the toilet. That's a woman's job, isn't it?'

'Have you ever noticed how he orders his secretary around, fetch this and fetch that?' Pat Dillon offered. 'How does she put up with it?'

'Isn't that her job?' said Bob.

'Funny how a woman always does that sort of work.'

Bob shrugged, twisting his rounded lips this way and that.

'How does Mrs Charing feel about that?' asked Ms Bicknell.

'She hates it. Oh, how she hates it! You haven't been here long enough to notice the sour looks and bad moods. But you will.'

'Why didn't you invite her to this meeting?'

There was silence as if the thought had never occurred to them.

'Perhaps because she is not at your exalted level?' said Bob.

'Please, Bob,' said Ms Bicknell, holding out her hand to suppress any reaction. 'I suppose it has just been an oversight. Mrs Charing might have something valuable to say in a meeting like this. She is closest to the principal. If there is any misconduct or incompetence, Mrs Charing will be an important source of evidence.'

'Misconduct and incompetence,' repeated Jane Cox, now recovered from her emotional episode, 'that describes it to a tee.'

There was a long pause. It seemed as if the full seriousness of the principal's attitude and behaviour had just penetrated their minds. Ms Bicknell looked around the group with satisfaction.

'Then let's make sure we invite Mrs Charing to our next meeting. I will tell her we're all in solidarity with her.' Ms Bicknell turned to the aggrieved women. 'You have been at the school for three or four years, haven't you? Nothing seems to have changed.'

The sympathy in Ms Bicknell's voice was like pouring ointment over a burn, and the two junior teachers again went at it in tandem. Yes, they were still in the same positions. They had spoken regularly to Huckerby, but it had all fallen on deaf ears. Of course, all important positions were to go to the principal's mates—exclusively male.

'How do you account for the positions of Ms Bicknell and our fair Jane here?' asked Bob, through rounded lips.

'Ms. Bicknell's appointment has come from outside. He had no influence there,' said Faye. 'Jane's the token woman. Just ask her whether she gets equal treatment from that fat pig.'

'God forbid I should ever put Sister Cox's competence in question. Has it occurred to you that Sister Jane, for all her endearing imperfections, may be considered a good teacher and that you, in the eyes of the principal, are not yet at that level of competence?'

'No, it has not!'

'Jane ...?'

For the first time that evening, Jane Cox looked as if she did not have a ready answer. Bob smiled at Suzie, and Suzie, no longer able to keep a straight face, bent forward.

'You horrible, jealous little slut!' Faye sneered. 'Two minutes in the school and you think you know everything. I hope this middle-aged slob works you over real good and then spits you out like the piece of filth you are.'

'Oh dear!' said Bob, putting his hands over his ears.

Suzie smiled and said nothing, which infuriated the women even more.

'You're a disgrace to the feminine.'

'The sacred corrupts within you.'

'What kind of nonsense is—?' Bob began, sitting up.

'Bob,' said Ms Bicknell, interrupting and casting a sharp inquiring glance at Faye and Lesley, 'please refrain from teasing. You, too, Suzie. Faye and Lesley have justified grievances. It should not be a source of fun for anyone.' She continued to glance at the two women with interest.

'Madam Sister Chairperson, we take the point,' said Bob. 'We apologise to Faye and Lesley if we have offended them. We are indeed on the same side, more or less.' He held an admonishing finger in front of Suzie. Suzie nodded but looked like she barely contained her amusement.

Jane Cox rushed to confirm everything Faye and Lesley had said. The discrimination of the fat, complacent principal was rooted in his corrupt social ideas. The school was only part of the problem. Huckerby was the principal of a school in a town structured along patriarchal lines. It was a small band of reactionary males that held the authority. Huckerby himself had formed a committee of men to parallel the elected officials in council. The council did not dare do anything that departed from the edicts of this powerful, unelected committee. Injustice was institutionalised in Binawarra.

And so, Jane Cox held forth in this manner, welcoming many supportive interventions from the other women, while Rick Juddery nodded his agreement and Stephen Calder continued to look bored. At one point, Calder ambled out of the room to return shortly after with another can of beer. There was no interruption now from Bob McKinnon, who now and then put his hand over his mouth to suppress a yawn but gestured an apology the next moment. Suzie leaned against his armchair and stroked his arm now and then, drawing an indulgent smile from Bob.

Eventually, Ms Bicknell brought Jane's tirade to a gentle close. 'Very good. Now I am beginning to understand your grievances. I am surprised nobody has done anything about it. Why don't they? Do you think it's due to the influence of the priests and ministers here? Is it a religious influence? Or is it something else?'

Yes, the lack of action was due to the constricting influence of religion. The ministers of religion in Binawarra were very, very powerful. The most dramatic influence of all was, of course, the Catholic priest, even though the Catholics in the town were relatively few. But the hold over them was extraordinary.

'What do you mean? On whom in particular?' said Ms Bicknell.

'Well, for example, you must have noticed that striking girl among the final year's students,' said Jane, happy to take the lead.

'Yes, of course,' said Ms Bicknell. 'Estella Winterbine.' She paused. 'I've noticed something odd about her. It's as if something constrains her. She is very subdued. That's very unusual these days with a girl like that.'

'Exactly!' exclaimed Jane, almost leaping from her seat. 'When you see her mother and father, you'll understand where she gets her looks from. The father is one of the most handsome men you will ever see. She looks a lot like her father. Her mother's beauty is quite different, an unblemished medieval paleness and as fair as you could imagine, like a garden fairy. She must be in her late thirties, but looks like she's in her twenties.' The others nodded their agreement. 'Instead of their appearance giving them confidence, let alone conceit, it seems to have the opposite effect. They are timid and subdued, as you say. They don't understand the significant social advantage of their appearance. Worse, they don't like how they look or the attention it attracts. No guesses where that comes from—from the Catholic Church in the form of that puritanical, manipulating priest.'

Faye, Lesley, and Pat called their enthusiastic support for Jane. They, too, expressed their incredulity about the timid and retiring Winterbines, especially Mrs Winterbine, who not often appeared in public and never alone. Estella could have every boy in the town daily on their knees before her. But, incredibly, she did all she could to discourage their attention.

'Estella, without a doubt, is still a virgin,' Jane said, now on her feet. 'No, there can be absolutely no doubt. The boys call her the Binawarra Virgin. The first boy to have Estella Winterbine will at once broadcast it to the whole world. He'd be a hero. No, no, there's no doubt it hasn't happened yet. It won't occur in Binawarra, either.'

'Let me just add here,' said Bob McKinnon, with a slight smirk, 'that the males who supervise the running of the town have let it be known to the town's youth that Estella Winterbine is under their protection. Quite clearly, those middle-aged men think such a beauty is wasted on the grubby youth here. Of course, they're right, too.'

'To show how damaged the Winterbines are,' Jane continued, 'a couple of years ago, Estella looked like developing into a champion athlete. Then, she suddenly refused to enter the races. Well, nobody could work it out at first. Then the story came via the principal that she found the athletic shorts and singlet immodest. Immodest! Can you believe it? Huckerby did not want anyone to talk about it. People should have respect for the family's ideas on these matters. It left those who had to know speechless. You see, she didn't like baring that stunning body to the public gaze. Incredible, isn't it? Jenny Brougham tried reasoning with her. But Estella wouldn't listen.'

Ms Bicknell nodded slowly with raised eyebrows.

'Jane's right,' said Faye, taking the baton. 'That priest has the three of them psychologically tied up so tight they can hardly move. The spirit is chained within them. The mother is the worst of the three held in that prison. She never ventures from the house by herself. She has these episodes which apparently leave her prostrate.'

'Prostrate? What type of episodes?' said Ms Bicknell, again eyeing the two women with interest.

'Well, few of us know exactly,' Lesley said, 'because nobody except the doctor, that Barker woman, and the Huckerbys ever see her at these times. Oh, of course, the priest, too. He's always there. None of them will speak about it.'

'Really? But why the Barker woman and the Huckerbys? What's the relationship there?'

'I'm not sure, but they are very close. Everybody knows that.'

'This is something I know more about,' said Bob, holding up his hand. 'I've been here long enough to be acquainted with the story. Bill Huckerby met Charles Winterbine and invited him to come to Binawarra to work on the Returned Soldiers Club. The Huckerbys had taken a shine to Charles and Aine and urged them to settle in Binawarra. Bill and Joanne Huckerby were responsible for introducing Charles to Aine.'

'What about Ms Barker?'

'That's a strange one,' Bob continued in the same vein. 'To start, be careful of Miss Barker, as she insists on being called. A more cantankerous, sharp-tongued witch you'll never meet. Not afraid of the devil, she isn't. Don't get on the wrong side of her, or you will feel the lash of her tongue.'

'Really?' said Gerda Vrouwendijk, and for the first time, let her guard drop. 'You're not serious, are you?'

'Deadly serious.'

'I will be careful, then,' said Ms Bicknell, composing herself. 'Why the connection with the Winterbines?'

'It's through the Huckerbys,' Bob continued. 'That's the strangest thing. For some mysterious reason, Miss Barker gets on well with Bill and Joanne Huckerby. It's got to be Joanne Huckerby because Bill and Florence Barker are completely different personalities. I don't understand how she puts up with him. He even jokes with her, something nobody else would dare do in their right mind. It's a mystery. Through the Huckerbys, Miss Barker is friendly with the Winterbines. She does seem to care for them, especially the daughter, who, again, incredibly, does not object to Miss Barker. Others of her age treat Florence Barker as if she were the wicked witch of the west, or the east, whatever it is.'

'What about those episodes? Do you know anything about them?'

'Only that she is incapacitated for a while but gets over it without being the worse for it. The cause? Entirely psychological in my view, induced by her wretched religion and reinforced by the priest.'

'Reinforced? How?'

'It's not directly apparent. It may just be his influence, although I suspect it's more deliberate and ritually specific.'

'Ritually specific?'

'If you saw the inside of their home, you would get an idea of the psychological maladjustment,' Jane broke in before Bob could explain. 'There are grotesque religious objects everywhere. Estella has a shrine in her room. Can you believe that of a typical girl of these times?'

'A shrine?'

'A shrine to the Virgin, as they call her. It's time the state stepped in. It's really an abuse of parental authority. It's child abuse.'

'How do you know about the shrine?'

'Jenny Brougham. All that religious nonsense has put her right off. It's sad to see religion breaking up such a close friendship. There's nothing like religion to cause conflict and misery. Jenny says she gets the horrors now when she goes to the Winterbines. Well, she doesn't go anymore.'

'That's serious,' said Ms Bicknell. 'I mean the shrine. That's a bad sign. I can see what you mean about psychological maladjustment. It sounds like a neurotic disorder. There are well-known cases in the professional literature on religious obsession. Such cases sometimes lead to violence; others result from violence or abuse.'

There was another pause as her audience considered a point that had never occurred to them.

'You mean violence and abuse from someone close to her?' said Jane.

Ms Bicknell nodded.

'Do you mean sexual abuse?'

Ms Bicknell nodded again. She glanced at Bob. He had nothing to add.

'But who? Not the father, surely? I've heard people speak of his unimpeachable character when it comes to his work.'

'It may be different in the home,' suggested Ms Bicknell. 'It's often the case.'

'No, I can't believe it,' Jane said. 'He seems such a gentle person. He doesn't involve himself in any of the antics of the ruling group. His manner is not at all threatening. I know because I have had several conversations with him and Mrs Winterbine. I found it hard to keep my eyes off him.'

'I'm not saying he is responsible,' said Ms Bicknell. 'I'm indicating the possibilities. Others could have abused the girl. The priest. He obviously has tremendous power over the family. The confessional box is often the occasion for Catholic clergy to abuse those in their power.'

'Oh, I can believe it of the priest,' said Lesley.

'What about the principal?' suggested Ms Bicknell. Once more, everybody considered this unexamined possibility. 'Didn't you say the Huckerbys have been in close contact with the Winterbines since they came to Binawarra? And wouldn't he have had close contact when the mother had those episodes? I'm assuming she has had those episodes from the beginning.'

The women were startled by these possibilities. Boris, peering from the darkness of the verandah, shook his head.

'You know,' said Ms Bicknell, deciding to bring the subject to a close, 'the professional literature indicates that such sexual abuse is most often a question of power or the desire to dominate the victim. The potential is present in any man. The abuse occurs when the impulse to dominate gets out of control. There are manifestations of the problem well beforehand.' She glanced again at Bob, but he kept silent.

'And I thought Huckerby couldn't be any worse than he was,' said Jane Cox. 'What a disgusting man!'

'Be careful,' said Ms Bicknell. 'I have only suggested possibilities. Don't forget the priest.'

'Old Huckerby can hide behind the law, but that's enough for me,' said Faye.

'For me, too,' added Lesley, putting her hand on Faye's arm.

'Just one more thing before we close,' said Ms Bicknell, rising from her chair. 'That name "Winterbine," it's obviously a made-up name, given sometime after settlement. Is anyone aware of its history?' Nobody was. 'It's a terrible injustice to inflict a name stinking of the English countryside and symbolic of the burden brought to this land on someone so foreign to that world.' Her listeners appeared taken aback by the feeling in Ms Bicknell's voice but said nothing. 'I want to know about that name. But we have said enough. It's time for a drink.'

Within a few minutes, the drinks were served, chips and peanuts put in bowls around the room, and cigarettes lit. Ms Bicknell drew on her cigarette and looked with satisfaction at the gathering. 'I am glad you came. I have learned a lot about the problems in the school and town. And they are not small. The next step is to plan the action. We will not get anywhere unless we organise ourselves and decide on a strategy.'

'At last!' said Calder, coming alive. 'We've gone over all this before, but nobody has had the guts to do anything. This meeting, like the others, will be useless unless we take action. Real action, I mean, not pansy stuff.'

'Ah,' said Bob, 'we can have no doubt what that means. Stephen is eager to break heads. All that pub rock experience must not count for nothing.'

'You shut your face, or I'll start with breaking your fat head. It would probably squash like an overripe marrow,' he replied, without bothering to look at him. But then he got up and walked over to Bob. 'Are you going to let me say something without me having to stomp on you to keep you quiet? I advise you to stick to arranging tents and leave the action to those with balls.'

The women looked on with interest as fear passed over Bob's face.

'It doesn't suit your image to make stupid jokes,' Bob said, trying to sound blasé. 'As for your threat, you and your Trotskyist friends have fortunately not managed to usurp the public authorities in this country.' There was a waver in his voice. 'As deficient as it may be, the system of government still has in place a local police force, ready to grab you and your mates and put them away. As I've told you before, in the face of such threats, the moment you lay a finger on me, that is the moment I will be off to the police. The force and rush of criminal and civil charges will follow so quickly that you'll be breathless. I'll have your bank account squeezed dry, and you drummed out of every school in the land. I know more about you than you think.'

'You would too, you litigious American weasel,' Calder sneered. 'Personally gutless and politically gutless. You're all like that—prancing San Francisco boys.' He resumed his seat beside Jane Cox. 'Be careful. I can hurt you without leaving a mark.'

'And you, you violent unconscionable bigot, would be delighted, no doubt, to do so,' said Bob, rising from his chair and putting his glass of wine on the coffee table. Suzie rose, too, and placed her glass beside his. 'Don't forget, comrade. I know more about you than anyone else—including the principal.' He waved his finger at Calder. Calder stared at him, his eyes narrowing. 'Madam Sister Chairperson,' Bob went on, 'it has been an entertaining evening, but the time has come for us to part. You have your discussions before you on how to tackle the perceived problems. As long as this Marxist thug has anything to do with the planning, I will not be a part of it.' Suzie nodded in solidarity, and Bob, noticing, took her hand. 'We will not be part of it.' He bestowed a smile on her. 'I needn't point out that Suzie and I share many of the group's concerns. We are in solidarity on those points. And how to tackle the problems? Not by sudden violent action that aims to bring on a resolution of the class conflict.

'No, we aim to be far more subversive. Without doing away with the great gains of our liberal society, we will undermine the foundation of the current problems at every opportunity. I am a science teacher, and this bright young woman is a science and mathematics teacher. Note well, my dear Faye and Lesley,' he said, nodding at them. 'Not being science teachers, at least, not real science teachers in the case of Stephen, you would never understand how subversive a science or math class can be.

'We, on the other hand, ignoring such pseudo-scientific ideas as the materialist dialectic but relying on the unrelenting logic of mathematics and the empirical truths of science, make religion a laughingstock. We, standing before the blackboard, bring the students to laughter without effort about the truths of revealed religion. The Virgin birth? The Real Presence? Original sin and the act of redemption? Do we have to say that it's all nonsense? No, that conclusion arises from the texts and course material prescribed by the state's educational authorities. We only have to present it properly.

'You see, my dear comrades and sisters, direct criticism and a direct attack on these matters will only excite the parents, who are a lost cause. Next thing, you'll be explaining yourself before the principal, the town hierarchy, and possibly the central authority, who don't give a damn about your attack on Christianity but are only concerned with avoiding controversy. No, we want the field of the battle, the classroom, to remain solely our preserve where the laziest and sloppiest of us will book victory after victory.'

'Aren't you finished yet, you great bag of wind,' Calder broke in, pointing his beer can at Bob. 'You've had your say. Now get lost before you get thrown into the street.'

'I'm almost finished, my dear Stephen. Your way will never get anywhere in the Western democracies. It is my way that will prevail. In twenty years, nobody will worry if you and I, dear Stephen, kiss passionately in the city centre. Even more exciting, if, when that time comes, we stand up naked on a float in the main street of any capital city and kiss in the most frightful manner, it is almost assured that our action will be met with cheering rather than disgust. Mark my words. It will come to pass.

'And the crowning achievement in those days will be the automatic disqualification of those espousing any religious belief, particularly Christian belief, from serious intellectual debate. That won't happen through legislation. The community will automatically understand that those people adhere to a kind of nescience and are not to be trusted or relied upon. Their isolation will be self-imposed.'

He bowed to his bemused audience with a final flourish of his arms. 'Come, Suzie, my dear, shall we go?' With an impudent smile on her face and her hand still in Bob's, Suzie skipped after him as he walked with much ostentation between the people and out through the front door. Suzie's sniggering drifted back to the mute group.

'Now that bag of wind with his boring speeches is gone,' said Calder, breaking the silence, 'we can get down to some real planning. That is, if you want to make the hard decisions.'

'Are you all ready to make the hard decisions?' said Ms Bicknell.

They were. What those hard decisions would be, they decided to think about before another meeting. They broke up, agreeing with Ms Bicknell's suggestion that Anzac Day, with the principal's involvement, would present the most favourable occasion to strike at the pernicious structures of the town. As they were preparing to leave, Gerda whispered to Faye and Lesley to stay on a minute. Across the street, still standing motionless, hard up against the gum tree, Miss Barker watched the teachers depart. Shortly after, Boris emerged and disappeared into the lounge room.

Jane Cox and Stephen Calder drove in Stephen's utility to one of their favourite parking spots, a bushy picnic area under the squatting sentinel. There was no containing Jane's chatter.

'You see, it did work out. Edith is an impartial observer; she shares our views and will act to resolve our differences and bring us together.'

Stephen mumbled and leaned over to kiss her on the neck. She talked on while his lips moved along her neck and onto her bare shoulder. He ran his hand up under her top, slipping it over her head.

'No, Stephen,' she said, trying to wriggle away. But Calder held her tight. Unable to resist his vice-like grip and his hurrying actions, she succumbed.

An hour later, she was undressing in her bedroom. She was tired. She was weary. But it was physical tiredness. Her spirits were elevated. She was excited about the prospect of doing something effective to address the injustices she had endured at the school and in the town. Leaving her clothes lying on the floor where she had wriggled out of them, she turned out the light and dropped exhausted onto her bed. She looked sideways at the slacks and top, her eyes fixed by the pink and the white gleaming in the little moonlight that came in through the bedroom window. There was no point in hanging them up; they had to go in the wash. She closed her eyes and was soon breathing in a deep, satisfying sleep.

Chapter 5

Bill Huckerby's worries

BILL HUCKERBY pushed open the neatly painted green flywire door and stepped onto the front verandah, a frown marking his usually cheerful face. An early evening dinner was behind him, and Joanne was busy clearing the table and preparing to do the washing up. The faint clinking and clacking of crockery and cutlery echoed up the hall. He put his hands on the railing and shook his head.

He should have felt at peace with the world, like most Sunday evenings. After all, he was happy with what he had and what he had achieved. He was grateful his nature was hopeful and cheery, even when things seemed to be going badly. It was known, even celebrated, that he always had a smile and a joke, no matter what happened. Most people appreciated that. He saw his temperament as a gift of Providence and was thankful for it. But for once, Bill Huckerby stood on the verandah wrestling with a strange mixture of powerlessness and foreboding. His beautifully tended gardens and the manicured lawn in front of him counted for little this Sunday. The inspiring view of the hills away to the south counted for little. The fresh late-summer air, blowing the fragrant smell of leaf and earth from the brooding hills, counted for little. What was bothering him? He tried to analyse the feeling, but as a feeling it was not to be analysed. He did not like that. No, not at all. He slapped the railing.

He prided himself on his ability to march straight up to a problem and deal with it on the spot. Problems were practical issues, and there was always a practical solution. Several weeks into the school term, there were no problems beyond the usual ones with students, staff, or the school's general administration. He had learned to take such things in his stride. But there was something new, something indistinct, imposing itself on the school activity. Could he call it a problem? No, it was more like something hanging over him. Why should he feel that way? What was there to cause this almost irrational fear? Yes, it was a sort of fear. Of what? He felt Joanne's arms slide around him.

'What's wrong? Why does William look so worried?'

'Do I look worried?'

'To me, you do. I've known you long enough, Bill Huckerby, to know the meaning of every wrinkle, twitch, and spot on your face. Come on, what is it? We always sort these things out together.'

'I'm not sure,' he said after a long meditative silence. 'I have this uneasy feeling about the school. There's no unsolvable problem anywhere. No, it's something in the atmosphere, in the manner and mood of many people. Sounds silly, doesn't it?'

'No, not necessarily. Can you be more precise?'

'No, I can't,' but then reconsidering, 'For example, Mrs Charing, she's always been anxious and moody about her work. I've been able to manage her moods by reassuring her. But that tenseness seems to have changed into resentment. And I can't guess why. I've asked if she has any worries and whether there's anything I can discuss with her. She says no but continues to look resentful.'

'Are you sure you're right about it? Joyce Charing has always been difficult. We've had no end of trouble with her moods at the Country Women's Association.' She patted him on the shoulder. 'Anyhow, we must go now, or we will be behind. We can discuss it on the way.'

'Let's leave the subject for the moment. I don't want to spoil our Sunday evening.'

A few minutes later, they were in the car, driving towards the town centre. Neither spoke. Joanne leaned around twice to check the parcels and boxes on the rear seat. She glanced at Bill. She put her hand on his arm and drew a reluctant smile. Soon they pulled up outside St Philomena's presbytery. They peered through the passenger side window. There was a dim light in the front parlour.

'He's there,' said Bill, 'Let's go.'

He took a cardboard carton and a plastic bag from the rear seat, and they walked to the front door. A pause followed their knock, and then they heard uneven hobbling steps and the shuffling of a walking stick. The porch light went on, and the door opened to reveal Fr. van Engelen's inquiring face.

'Bill, Joanne, so nice to see you,' he said, his face brightening. He grimaced and fell back against the hall wall as he opened the door. 'Come in, come in. I'm just about to make a cup of tea. How about a cup? Or what about some coffee? I've just received some delicious Dutch coffee from the family in Holland. I'm really pleased to see you.'

'Love a cup of tea, Father,' said Bill, as he followed Joanne into the dark hall. 'We'll leave that strong Dutch coffee for you.'

'Let me fix it, Father,' said Joanne. She set off down the hall to the kitchen.

'Thank you, Joanne. Please, Bill, come into the parlour and make yourself comfortable.'

They entered a small, dimly lit room, austerely arranged. Old-style lounge chairs and a lounge settee with broad armrests were in front of a fireplace covered for the summer. A large woollen rug hid the stained floorboards that bore the years of trampling feet. An oak cabinet stood against the far wall, an oak writing desk near the front windows, and a traymobile to the side of the lounge settee. In the corners were medium-sized statues of

St Michael the Archangel and St Anthony of the Desert on carved wooden pedestals. A large crucifix hung above the fireplace.

'You have a kind wife, Bill,' said Fr. van Engelen. 'You are very fortunate.'

'She's the best, Father. I'm all too aware of that.'

'Well, you are both very good to me.'

Bill was going to protest, but Joanne entered the parlour.

'Father, I put some vegetables and fruit away in the kitchen. Make sure you keep up your vegies, won't you,' she said, sitting next to Bill. 'You have to follow the doctor's orders.'

'Yes, Joanne, of course. I appreciate your concern. I will not waste your garden's produce.'

'Now, Father, there's something else for you here,' said Joanne, bending down. 'I wanted Charles, Aine, and Estella to bring this to you. But they refused. They said it was Bill's idea, and it was, and so he should be the one to bring it along.'

Fr. van Engelen stared, lips parted as Joanne drew a neat, clean cassock from the cardboard carton.

'Yes, Father, Bill has been saying it was terrible you couldn't afford new clothes. So he rallied around the townsfolk and collected enough money in no time. The order went to Melbourne, and now, presto, here you are, new clothes for you. There are others still in the carton. Some odds and ends I imagine you will need.' She held a finger up. 'No, no objections, it's all done, no sending them back. Don't forget you're presiding over the blessing on Anzac Day. You must look your best for the old soldiers. It's your duty to look your best.'

Fr. van Engelen helplessly held his hands up. 'You are all very kind. I don't deserve such kindness.'

'Bill's doing, Father,' said Joanne. 'The rest of us just cooperated.'

'You are a good man, Bill Huckerby,' was all the crippled priest could say.

'Now, now, none of that. You're part of this town. We care for our own.'

'You are proof of the workings of charity,' said the priest. 'You exemplify Our Lord's teaching—and the teaching of the Church.' And then, to break the seriousness of the moment: 'Are you sure you don't want to join us, Bill?'

'Oh no, none of that either now,' said Bill, catching on. 'You know what we Anglicans say about Catholics!'

'No, I don't. Tell me.'

Bill laughed heartily. 'I don't know anymore. I've forgotten!'

'Ssssh, Bill, not so loud,' said Joanne, getting up. 'I'll go and pour the tea. Bill, about charity, why don't you tell Father what's worrying you?' She was gone before he could object.

Bill looked away, his mouth twisting in indecision. 'I don't want to be a wet blanket,' he said. 'We came here for some cheerful conversation, not to burden you with my worries.'

'If anything is bothering you, and I can help, please let me know.'

'It's a school matter,' said Bill after long considering the bare floorboards in front of him. 'It's not really your field.'

'It's up to you, Bill. I'm happy to listen.'

'It's Sunday evening, and we've come for some cheerful conversation,' he repeated, 'not to discuss dreary school matters, the sort of things you're unfamiliar with. I don't want to be a wet blanket.'

'You, a wet blanket!' said Joanne, walking into the room carrying a tray loaded with all the things necessary for the tea. 'I don't think so.' She put the tray on the traymobile and began serving the men.

'Come on, Bill, a pair of neutral ears might help.'

'Well, okay, Father,' said Bill. 'It's just that I have perceived a change of mood in the school. Our school, like most, is not trouble-free. There are the usual things, you know, but this mood is different. There is something new about it. And I don't understand what it is exactly. I don't even understand why I have noticed it. I'm usually unresponsive to that sort of thing.'

'What sort of mood?'

'People seem anxious, dispirited. There's less patience and less willingness to cooperate. I've noticed disagreements over trivial things, like where people sit in the staff room, where they have their desks, who teaches what, and so on. And it's not as if the disagreements pass either. No, they go on even after a resolution. There must always be a compromise in settling disputes. You would know that. Sensible people seek compromise. But now, people claim their rights have been denied. For heaven's sake! Human rights over seating arrangements! Incredible! I can't afford the time to adjudicate on such trivial things. It's just not like this town. It's a mystery why so many have suddenly taken it into their heads to make an issue out of a triviality. Or is it me? Am I changing as I get older? Am I less flexible, less able to cope?'

'Well, I can vouch for you there,' said Joanne.

'If it's a staff matter, perhaps you should turn your attention to changes there,' said Fr. van Engelen. 'Do you have new staff? If so, have they made a difference?'

'Not really,' said Bill. 'One new member of staff has joined us. She comes to us highly recommended and with excellent qualifications. She does her work efficiently and appears to have the respect of the other teachers. But, so far, I haven't had much cause to talk to her. Everything looks well under control. Besides, one individual would not make such a difference.'

'Why don't you tell Father what Flo said about her?' said Joanne.

'Oh, Joanne, dear,' said Bill. 'Flo should stick to her nursing and not meddle in such things.'

'What did Miss Barker say?' prompted the priest.

'I'm not sure if we should repeat it. It sounds too much like idle gossip, malicious gossip, too.'

'Bill!'

'Oh, I don't mean Flo is malicious. I just mean her suspicions will sound malicious. You know how most people regard her. It wouldn't do her reputation any good for people to hear about it.'

'Miss Barker strikes me as a no-nonsense woman,' said the priest. 'What are those suspicions, if you don't mind telling me?'

'If I repeat it, you must treat it as under the seal of confession, Father.'

'It will be in the strictest confidence,' said the priest, with the trace of a smile.

'The seal of confession!'

'Absolute confidentiality, I promise.'

'Come on, Bill,' said Joanne, sighing. 'Don't be silly. You're not in confession here. You're not even Catholic, I don't have to remind you!'

'Well, okay,' he said, waving his hand. 'You know who we're talking about, don't you?'

'Yes, I think I do. I have seen her about the town, on occasions, visiting the office of the *Binawarra and District Mail*. She seems to have a lot to say to the editor of the district newspaper.'

'Have you? Okay. You know who Miss Bicknell is,' said Bill, seeing nothing in the priest's observation. 'It's simple, really. Flo's of the opinion that Miss Bicknell is here with a political agenda. She won't say what that agenda is or give convincing reasons for thinking it. It's ridiculous. Absolutely ridiculous! I'm surprised at Flo.'

'What evidence does she give?'

'The slimmest of evidence! She bases everything on a quotation Miss Bicknell included in her speech during the school's first assembly.'

'It's more than that,' said Joanne. 'And I don't like the look of her. She looks like someone with something to hide. It's a contrast with the people of Binawarra.'

'The look of her! Yes, that's it precisely, and the rest is suspicion!'

'What was the quotation?' said the priest.

'I don't remember,' said Bill. 'I wasn't listening at that point. I have so much to attend to. I can't possibly concentrate on every little thing uttered in an assembly. Flo said it was from Rousseau, the architect of the French Revolution. She called him that, the architect of the French Revolution, I mean.' He shrugged.

'Was it, by chance, about people being born free but ending up in chains due to the corrupt nature of their society?'

'That's it,' said Joanne. 'Flo told me later that evening.'

'It's a very famous quotation,' said the priest. 'Just about every undergraduate student anywhere in the world will come across it at some time or another. It's on the first page of *The Social Contract*. Do you want me to read it to you?'

'Well, I never read it as an undergraduate student. I was too busy preparing myself for a life of work,' said Bill. 'And don't bother, Father, it's not relevant. I told Flo that all young graduates are going to entertain radical ideas. That's part of being young. But, when it comes to the practical world, they'll find it tough to apply them.'

'I wouldn't call Miss Bicknell a young graduate, dear,' said Joanne.

'There is a second part to the quotation you've alluded to,' said the priest. 'If people born free are in chains, Rousseau said, they have a right to take back their freedom in the way it was taken from them. Many have considered the full quotation justice for violent revolution. Indeed, the French Revolution was an enactment of those thoughts.'

'Still doesn't change anything,' said Bill. 'I need more than a quote from a dusty old book to take serious notice of Flo's suspicions.'

'Perhaps you should be at least aware of those ideas.'

'Yes, that's wise,' said Joanne.

'That's what Flo said. And I'll do just that if it pops up to distract me. Flo's fantasising about the new teacher's political inclinations is no help to me.'

Fr. van Engelen regarded Bill with concern. If his good friend failed to make a connection between the quotation from *The Social Contract* and the school's mood, he did not. Miss Barker's reaction was enlightening. It was unlike Miss Barker to play the role of the paranoid conspiracy theorist and to suspect a person's motives without any solid foundation. He had had little to do with Miss Barker, but as he observed her over time, he had developed respect for her. There was far more to her than the stiff, short-tempered person of reputation. Seeing Bill redden and fidget, he decided to leave it. Sometime later, there was a knock at the front door.

'I'll get it, Father,' said Joanne. She opened the door to reveal the Winterbines smiling shyly in the porch light.

'Come in,' she said. 'Father, it's Charles, Aine, and Estella.'

Charles stood aside for Aine and then followed with Estella, clutching his arm. 'Please don't get up,' said Charles, offering his hand to the priest as he entered the parlour. 'We've just come to bring your washing and a few things from the garden. We won't stay.'

'No, no,' said Bill, now back to his cheerful self. 'You stay. We're just going before Father makes another attempt to rush me from Canterbury over to Rome! We won't be crossing the Tiber just yet. You can keep him company for a while. Keep him in order!'

'I won't give up on you,' said the priest, going along with Bill's permanent joke after Joanne had given him a helpless look. 'And, yes, Charles, please stay for a moment.'

'They are such good people,' said the priest when the Huckerbys had gone. 'Bill jokes about my trying to convert him, but I have to say he sets an example in charity that would put many of us Catholics to shame.'

'We know all too well, Father,' said Aine.

'You're familiar, of course, with where it says in the Gospels that those entering heaven are the ones who tend to the sick, the naked, the hungry, and the destitute, for Christ is present in the downtrodden. All those lonely and poor people in the Binawarra district who Bill and Joanne visit will testify when he and Joanne at last stand before the Lord.' He paused. 'But I fear Bill will be tested over the coming months.'

'What do you mean?' said Aine, putting her hand on Charles's arm.

The priest hesitated. 'Perhaps I shouldn't say such things. Perhaps it's not the time— ' He glanced at their querying faces. 'There have been, as we have discussed, many changes going on in the world. Those changes appear not to have reached our sleepy little town. Now I fear there are signs the enemy is not far from the gates.'

'What signs?' said Charles.

'I would rather not say at this moment.' He shook his head. 'Bill Huckerby is such an open, honest fellow. I fear that his honesty, good nature, and trust in his fellow citizens will blind him to what may happen under his nose.' He noticed the anxious look on Aine's face. 'But come,' he said, 'let's not be down in the dumps on this Sunday evening. I am so glad to have had both my families here this evening.' He smiled warmly. 'Now, what about a cup of tea?'

'Let me prepare it, Father,' said Estella.

'Thank you, my dear.' Estella took up the tray and disappeared down the hall. 'Now Charles, Aine, what's the news with you? How is your work for the renovation of the courthouse going?'

'Well, Father,' Charles said. 'It's meticulous and painstaking work but very satisfying.' He was in the middle of a detailed description of his work when he broke off and glanced at Aine, who had somehow got his attention. He nodded. 'Father, we were not going to stay long,' he resumed, 'and we didn't intend to get into a serious discussion, but now that you have mentioned worrying changes, we would like to tell you something.'

At the priest's encouragement, Charles related how the new senior teacher, Miss Bicknell, had called Estella to her office during the week for a vocational discussion. Miss Bicknell began by holding her pen up and asking Estella how she knew she had a pen in her hand. At that point, Estella returned. She glanced at her father as she put the tray down.

'Perhaps you could tell me in your own words what was said,' said the priest. 'About the pen, I mean. Try to remember the exact words.'

'Well,' Estella said as she poured the tea, 'Miss Bicknell, as Daddy said, held up her pen in front of me and asked me how I knew she was holding her pen.' She handed the priest his tea. 'I found it a strange question. I wasn't sure what to say. In the end, I said the obvious, that I knew she was holding the pen because I could see it. It seemed I gave the right answer because she said, "exactly!" She then said the truth is sometimes so simple that we miss it or just pass over it without realising what we have before us. And not realising what we have before us, we sometimes make our lives more complicated than necessary.'

'Go on.'

She poured her parents' tea and handed them their cups.

'She asked next how I knew the pen was smooth, and I said because I could feel its smoothness. Then she asked how I knew she was talking to me, and, realising that her questions had to do with the senses, I said, because I could hear her. Then she asked how I would know that I was drinking orange juice, and I said because I could taste it.' She sat down with her cup and waited for the priest's response.

'She then asked how you knew heaven was real, or something like that?' said the priest.

'Why, yes.'

Aine and Charles looked from Estella to the priest. 'What was the point of all that?' said Charles.

'Let Estella finish first.'

'She asked me if I believed angels were real, and I said, yes, of course. Then she asked how I knew angels were real. Had I seen one?'

'And what did you say?'

'I didn't know what to say at first. I've never seen an angel, so I could not say I had seen one like I saw the pen. After thinking for a bit, I said I knew angels were real because I had been told they were real. She asked me who told me and how they knew angels were real. I said my mother and father had told me, and you, too. I realised what her next question would be.'

'No, I've never seen an angel, either,' he said. 'How did you answer that question?'

'I didn't answer it. Instead, I asked what the point of all those questions was. It seemed so strange and unconnected with talk about vocations.'

'Good girl.'

'She said she would let me think about it to see if I could come up with an answer. She would talk to me about it again. It was crucial that I understood the answer.'

'And then what?'

'I said, okay. After that, she asked me what I planned to do after leaving school. I said I hadn't decided. She said that was something I should also direct my mind to, because I needed to have some idea of what I would do with my life. I would not want to waste my great talents, she said. I could be influential if I wanted to be.'

'Did she mention what your great talents were and how you could be influential?'

'No, the rest of the time was spent going over the subjects I was studying. She spoke to me in a kind and sympathetic way. She seemed to have my interests at heart.'

'What do the other students say about her?'

'I don't know. I haven't heard anyone talking about her yet. They usually do if there is something noticeable about a new teacher.' She shifted a little.

The priest contemplated Estella and then turned to Charles and Aine: 'What do you make of all that?'

'We don't know what to think,' said Charles.

'She seemed to be questioning Estella's religious beliefs or making Estella question her beliefs,' said Aine, 'although I'm not sure how.'

'You are right, Aine. She was getting Estella to question her beliefs. Now, how she was doing it may be new to you, but I can assure you it is not new. It was the first time Estella's beliefs were assaulted in this way, but it certainly will not be the last.'

'I've never heard anything like that before,' said Aine. 'It does not sound like a temptation.'

'No, it doesn't,' said Charles. 'What a strange business.'

'I probably have the explanation for that,' said the priest. 'And, indeed, it's not a temptation. At least, not at first. First, the social environment was different when you met all those years ago at Bill and Joanne's. Even though the divide between the Catholic Church and the Protestant churches was sharp and sometimes antagonistic, basic Christian beliefs, shared by Catholics and Protestants alike, prevailed. There was a natural guard in everyday life against attempts to subvert Christianity. No school would have tolerated an open attempt to undermine a student's religious belief, which is what Miss Bicknell was doing. Religious belief was a matter for the family. I mean the authority of the family.

'What you must understand is that outside the conflict of Catholic and Protestant belief, there were people who maintained that the claims of Christianity were not true, regardless of the Christian group one belonged to. They claimed that no part of its body of belief could be demonstrated by reason or by empirical evidence. The arguments they brought for centuries against Christianity remained for a long time restricted to small feverish groups of intellectuals. Their efforts to subvert Christian belief, however, were unrelenting. This is a long and complicated story, too long to tell now. But it is not wholly off the mark to say that the breakthrough in their propaganda came through the insistence of their right to free speech, as they understood that right, I should add. Under that banner, they succeeded in having their views propagated without restriction. Institutional and general safeguards fell one by one. It has amazed me how quickly all those safeguards fell once there was a breach in the wall.

'It was the same in my country, in the Lowlands. My countrymen, both Catholic and Protestant, seemed to flip over in a short space of time. Then, with the success of the free speech propaganda, the tables were gradually turned, and Christian teaching ended up banned from public life. The agitation for free speech was, in essence, a very successful political tactic. It was a pretext for the gradual introduction of an ideology that allows only speech consistent with it. You see how things are now. People are likely to get into trouble if they try to present arguments for Christian belief within any public institutional setting. If ordinary Christian teaching happens by odd chance to come up for discussion, it is never presented truthfully, faithfully, or fairly. That ideology is yet to reach its end.'

'You, Charles and Aine, were even more protected from these developments. Aine, at the time that young people of your background would have been exposed to the arguments against Christian belief, you were either working in your father's business or testing a vocation in a convent. Then you met Charles. It is a very rare thing that you two have experienced. Charles was just as preoccupied with testing his desire to join the religious life. Providence brought you both together at the point when you had to face the fact that you were not being called. You were protected at a vulnerable time and have since protected each other. You are very fortunate. Of course, others are likely to say you are unfortunate because nobody has ever given you the chance to break free of the indoctrination of the Church.'

'The indoctrination of the Church?' said Charles.

'Father means Miss Bicknell thinks we have been tricked into believing because we haven't been given a chance to hear a different view,' said Estella. Charles and Aine greeted their daughter's explanation with surprise.

'Very clearly put, my dear,' said the priest. 'That's about it. The different view, of course, is the truth for these people. They believe that Christians are programmed to think unreflectively about their beliefs. Only mentally affected people would believe things that have the quality of fairytales. The Gospels are fairytales manipulated by the powerful to keep gullible people under their thumb. I'm afraid some people consider me a political criminal.

I experienced such animosity the moment I stepped into public dressed as a religious.'

'Is this all really true?' said Charles. 'I know people don't believe as we do. I'm aware that non-Catholics disagree with us, but I haven't met the animosity you are speaking of. Not in my hometown or here in Binawarra.'

'No,' said Aine. 'Nobody here has ever said anything against us or our religious beliefs. And everyone knows how important it is to us and—' She glanced at her daughter.

Estella looked away.

'Has there been a problem?' said the priest. 'Have any of your friends said something? Is it something you want to talk about?'

Estella shook her head while Aine gave the priest a sign.

'I'm all right,' said Estella. 'May I talk to you about it another time?'

'Of course, any time you wish.'

Fr. van Engelen bowed his head. The Winterbines, unembarrassed, waited for him to speak. At length, he looked around the room. His eyes came to rest on the tray on the traymobile.

'Would you mind bringing the cups closer so I can reach them?' he said to Estella. She did as he wished.

'What is this?' he said, picking up a cup.

'A cup.'

'And this?' he said, picking up a second cup.

'A cup.'

He held up two more cups with the same question.

'And how do you know that they are cups?' he said when Estella had repeated her answer.

'Because I can see them.'

'That's not actually answering the question. You see something, of course, but how do you know that what your eyes are seeing is, in each case, a cup?' The Winterbines had no answer. 'You see, there is something more than just sense perception here. The mind or the intellect is in operation independently of the sense perceptions. It seems to be seeing something beyond the material or recognising something non-material, that is, something in the mental sphere. So, is there "seeing" in terms of understanding, in addition to 'seeing' as sense perception?' He paused. 'Miss Bicknell is telling a tiny part of a big story that has been raging through our civilisation for centuries. That story is about knowledge and reality. What can we know and how can we be sure we do know it? What is the real? Philosophers through the centuries have come up with many answers, some of which are so complicated and abstract that the ordinary person cannot follow the language used, let alone understand the theory.

'The position that Miss Bicknell and those like her adopt goes under the general heading of materialism. Now, there is a variety of theories in this area, some in sharp conflict, but the primary claim is that the senses are our source of knowledge, that our senses determine what is "the real." The real is the material world and nothing else. What cannot be verified by way of empirical measurement cannot be called genuine knowledge or a real object. You can see how that position can be a weapon to attack Christian belief and teaching.

'Nobody sees angels, God, heaven, hell, and so on. The conclusion: those things do not exist. Even more radical: it is meaningless to talk about things that cannot be verified empirically. The conclusion appears so watertight to those adhering to the position that they cannot accept that others cannot see what they see. They go on to conclude that people rejecting what to them is so patently true must be ignorant, backward, deluded, and above all else, deceived. And the deceivers are people like me. The pressing task then is to rescue the deceived from the deceivers. Ironically, most people who think this way seem unaware—and unbothered—that their views rest on an unprovable proposition. There is no argument or material evidence that justifies the claim that all knowledge comes through the senses and that only the material exists. That is the fallacy of scientism.'

'But what is Miss Bicknell's object in saying all this to Estella if that's what she was doing?' said Charles.

'Yes,' said Aine, 'what's the purpose? Why should she concern herself with what we believe? Why should she concern herself with our daughter?'

'Charles, I can assure you that Miss Bicknell's aim was to get Estella to question her religious beliefs. I have not the slightest doubt about that. I am very familiar with the approach and, indeed, was often subjected to those arguments in my younger days as a priest. And what Miss Bicknell's ultimate purpose is, Aine, I can't imagine. As I say, it might just be that she feels obliged to convince everyone that religious belief is not true. Such people go about society in a proselytising spirit. They feel the need to disabuse all their fellow citizens of their ignorant opinions. They see those ignorant opinions as functioning as a prison for them. It may also be that Miss Bicknell has targeted Estella. Why? As I say, I could not guess at this point. But it did seem significant that she exhorted Estella not to fail to develop her considerable talents.'

'But what possible object can she have in targeting our daughter?' repeated Aine.

The priest shrugged. 'Perhaps I should not speak before I have clear evidence that Miss Bicknell has a distinct purpose regarding Estella. Remember, too, that Estella has said that she is kind to her. Perhaps it is just her good intentions, however misguided.' But he could not believe that. Too many strange things were happening around the new teacher. And then there was what he knew that nobody else knew.

'Yes, Father,' said Charles, 'that must be it. Surely, there can't be any other explanation. It is some misguided attempt by someone who does not share our faith to convince us of their way of thinking. If that's the case, it's our job to explain to Miss Bicknell what we believe. Perhaps she will stop to consider the truth as we know it.'

It was a naïve suggestion, but the priest would not try to dissuade him. Miss Bicknell should be aware of what she was up against. It would also give him time to search for a purpose in what could be seen as sinister be-haviour. Not least sinister was Juffrouw van den Donker's masquerading as a teacher with counselling expertise. It was known she was a gifted lin-guist. She had written learned pieces about the origins of human language and was an expert in the dialects of their region. But he had never heard that she had studied psychology, and he had never heard that she was teaching in schools.

'By all means, go and explain your beliefs to Miss Bicknell, Charles,' he said. 'But I would prepare for an unsympathetic ear and stubborn resistance. People like her do not hold their beliefs casually. Indeed, they are just like the devoted faithful. We hold our beliefs tenaciously, do we not? Miss Bicknell and those like her hold to their theories about people and society with a religious fervour. Tell me, though, has she made any difference with her little demonstration?'

'Not in the slightest,' said Charles. Aine and Estella nodded. 'We could never think about Our Lord's love and teaching in the way Miss Bicknell reasoned with Estella. For us, the Gospels' teaching of love for one's fellow man and the misery caused by sin is self-justifying. Our Lord's teaching makes sense of the world and its purpose.' He paused to consult his wife and daughter. 'There is something in the Gospels that is inexpressible and unfathomable, and at the same time coercing in a liberating manner. No, Miss Bicknell's demonstration, whatever it was about, makes no differ-ence.'

'No, none at all,' said Aine. 'It's rather a cause for worry because we don't really understand her reasoning.'

'Yes, I can understand that,' the priest said. 'The arguments for the empiricist view Miss Bicknell holds are quite abstract. By that, I mean that they seem little related to the reasoning that the ordinary person uses in his everyday life. Ordinarily speaking, the mind has to be prepared to accept such arguments. The irony is that the people who embrace them most unreflectively are usually those who have had a good education. By "good education", I mean the style of theoretical education that school and university students undergo these days.

'It is not worth my trouble taking you through the theoretical background to the principles of empiricism and the objections that can be raised. The Church has long wrestled with the intellectual debate she is continually drawn into and has always come up with the answers, right from St Paul through some of the greatest minds of European civilisation, including the great St Thomas Aquinas.

'No, the ordinary faithful Christian does not need lessons in philosophy to maintain his belief in God and His Church. We have the enduring witness of the Church received from the apostles. In any case, nobody was ever converted solely by a theoretical exposition. That is the delusory hope of the blind atheist. In the end, faith is a gift of grace. God is mysterious in his ways, but we know that the gift of grace is ours if we turn with a sincere heart to Him.'

The priest said these words simply and without fuss. He wanted to explain the background to Miss Bicknell's strange questions, but also to reassure them, stressing that their faith did not depend on learning or obscure theories. There was, however, no need for Fr. van Engelen to worry. Charles and Aine stressed that they were happy with the explanation of Miss Bicknell's questions and did not consider them a threat to their own beliefs, only a puzzle. When it came down to it, there must surely be some misguided and benign purpose behind it. Estella, though, appeared unsure. 'Thank you for explaining all that to us,' said Charles. 'You have reassured us. I think it now best that we go and see Miss Bicknell.' Aine nodded. 'We can explain our beliefs to her. At least that way she'll understand better and understand that we do have our daughter's interests very much at heart.'

'Well, that's up to you,' said Fr. van Engelen. 'I warn you that she may not be so receptive.' The priest was torn between protecting Charles and Aine's endearing naivety and exposing Miss Bicknell. Few in Binawarra would be more knowledgeable about the Bible than the daughter of strict Reformed parents. 'But let's put aside all that now,' he went on. 'Before I forget, I want to thank you most sincerely for the new clothes. I must look a sorry sight to raise such concern about my cassock, particularly to people who are not Catholic!'

'It was all Uncle Bill's idea,' said Aine. 'We just got behind him.'

'Yes,' said Charles, 'we're rather embarrassed that we didn't think to do anything about it ourselves.'

'Oh no, Charles, you are not to think that. I'm a worn-out old priest. It was appropriate that I wore old, worn-out clothes. It served to remind me who I was. You understand.'

Charles and Aine did understand. 'We have spent long enough with you tonight,' Charles said, offering his hand to Aine. 'Thank you for your hospitality, Father. And explanation.'

'Drop in whenever you want,' said the priest, letting Charles help him to his feet. 'There is not much for me to do in the town. I love your company, too. Estella, please come and talk to me anytime you want. You know where to find me.'

After seeing the Winterbines off, Fr. van Engelen limped back to the parlour. Steadying himself as best he could, he got to his knees in front of the crucifix that hung above the mantelpiece. He bowed his head and remained motionless. At length, he struggled to his feet and went to his writing desk. He took paper and pen from the drawer.

'Dear Frans,' he wrote, 'This is a short letter. It is for your eyes only. Please keep my confidence. I want to ask about a particular person who is well known to us. It's Juffrouw Gerda van den Donker. Would you please tell me what you know about her and where people think she is at this present time? I cannot tell you my reasons for asking now. I hope you will bear with me. I need the information urgently. It is very urgent. I don't want to sound alarmist, but it could be that a person's well-being depends on it. Please make enquiries, as discreetly as you can, avoid looking like you are on a search, and tell me whatever you can find out, no matter how trivial it might be. I warn you that there may be more to Juffrouw van den Donker than any of us has suspected. I suppose knowing her occultist father the way we do, we should not be surprised. I think of his poor wife every now and then. And, also, could you bring me up to date on Meneer van den Donker's activities? I remember you telling me about his business success. Has anything changed there? Is there any connection with his daughter? Tell me whatever you can find out, as long as you do it discreetly. This all sounds very mysterious, I know. Just bear with me for a while. Your affectionate brother, Jos.'

He folded the page, drew an airmail envelope from the drawer and inserted the folded note into it. He sealed and addressed it thus:

De Heer Frans van Engelen
p/a Pater Matthijs
Sint Augustinus Kapel
De Middel Delft
Middelburg, The Netherlands

Chapter 6

Meetings and visits

THE SATURDAY following the evening visit to Fr. van Engelen, Aine was sitting on the verandah swing seat. With eyes closed and head tilted back, she gently pushed the seat to and fro with her sandaled foot. She clasped a book of the Psalms in the ample folds of her long summer dress. The vague whirring and singing of Charles's electric saw drifted from the workshop through the sparkling summer air, rousing the familiar picture of her husband bending over the saw, feeding through the wood, slat after slat. The shuddering thud of a closing car door interrupted that comforting image. She opened her eyes to see Paul Egan coming to the front gate. He stopped and stared self-consciously at her. With a friendly wave, she went to greet him.

'I'm sorry to disturb you, Mrs Winterbine,' he said. Do you remember me? Paul Egan. I was Estella's class teacher last year.'

'Yes, Mr Egan, of course,' said Aine. 'I remember you well. Would you like to come in?'

'Yes, yes—' he stammered. 'It was a while ago, and I wasn't sure—' He made no move to pass through the gate. 'I wanted to have a few words with Estella to see how she is going. Well, you see, she was such a good student, a girl of such high principles—' He looked away, unable to meet Aine's gaze.

'Thank you, Mr Egan. Estella thought well of you and was sorry to see you leave the school.'

'Was she? I was rather afraid she had lost respect for me.' He blushed at this admission. His expression of unease changed to one of resignation. 'Do you know why I left—why I had to leave?' When Aine did not reply, he went on, 'I see. You do. I'm sorry.'

'Mr Egan, please don't stand there. Come in. Estella would be disappointed if she missed you. She's in town, but we expect her back anytime now. You can stay for a cup of tea? You have nowhere to go in a hurry, do you?'

'No, I was on my way back to Melbourne when I ... eh, decided to see how Estella was going.'

'Good, then, you can stay for a while. My husband will finish his work shortly, and we can have a cup of tea together.'

Paul Egan followed Aine onto the verandah. He looked around at the arrangement of furniture. 'This is like the verandah at the Huckerby's.'

'Yes, you're right. Charles and I met at Bill and Joanne's. I was standing on the verandah there when I saw Charles for the first time. We like to have these small things as a reminder.'

'You are fortunate.' Aine regarded him with sympathy but said nothing. 'If you know why I left the school, you must know that my wife has some problems.' Aine nodded. He put his hands together and rubbed them as if in pain. 'Dealing with something like that is not easy. One has only so much endurance. Makes you vulnerable to all sorts of feelings and inclinations ...' He stopped and wiped his brow with his handkerchief. 'You do stupid things ... there's not much you can keep secret in a small town, I have found out. That's one of the reasons I wanted to speak to Estella.'

ESTELLA HAD left the music shop at the busy end of the shopping circuit. In one hand, she carried a bright brand bag, and in the other, her carry bag and a broad-brimmed straw hat. Ignoring the many stares that accompanied her, she put on her hat and walked across the road, through the busy Saturday morning traffic, and between the sunlit gardens to a park bench. She sat down, put her bag beside her, and took the record from the brand bag. She and her mother loved this Vivaldi piece. She stared at the album cover and pictured her mother's happy expression as she gave it to her. She imagined the warm look of approval on her father's face when he saw what she had done. A smile crept across her face as she pondered their reaction. She loved to please her undemanding mother.

'Still the same old Stell, lost in her dreamworld,' said a laughing voice that broke in on her thoughts. A surge of joy passed through her. Jenny was at the other end of the park bench. She wore tight-fitting white shorts and a bright pink top revealing her suntanned shoulders. On her slim, elegant feet were old sandals, and her painted, manicured toenails made an attractive contrast.

'Here you are, lost in your thoughts while every male in the town has walked by and had a good gawk at you. Totally oblivious! How is it possible?' She giggled and sat down next to her. Then, with the tip of her little finger, she scooped up the tear that had appeared at the corner of Estella's eye. She smiled and, in her naughty way, put her little finger in her mouth.

Estella put the record back into the bag, embarrassed that she had made her feelings so obvious. It was the same old Jenny, the same bright, naughty face, and expectant expression. But as Estella continued to look, a hint of strain appeared in those eyes. She took Jenny's hand and raised it to her lips.

'You silly girl!' said Jenny, pulling her hand away. 'It's not me you should be kissing. Look around. Take your pick! And take off that silly hat and let everybody feed on your beautiful face.' In one swift movement, the hat came off and landed on Estella's lap. 'And that head of hair!' With another quick movement, she untied the red ribbon that bound Estella's hair into a ponytail. She ruffled her hair. 'That's better! Not so proper.'

Estella did not resist. She was pleased with the attention. On Jenny's insistence, she cast a disinterested look around the square. Many passing eyes stole a glance at them. Loud, shrill whistles came from somewhere. Jenny did not react. She rubbed her suntanned legs and flicked her long, wavy blond hair, wriggling a little each time.

'They haven't seen us together for a while, have they?' She smiled. 'It'll drive them mad. The contemptuous Jenny and the ice-cold Estella! They deserve to suffer.'

She said this without seeming to move her eyes from Estella. Estella, pained by the hardness in her voice, turned again towards the shops. People were still looking at them. Then, at the sound of shouting, she looked further up the shopping precinct. Outside one of the hotels, a group of young men shouted and waved.

'Don't look at them like,' Jenny whispered. 'Keep them in panting expectation. They're here to play cricket and to pick up what they can. We will not make it easy for them. Most of them are slobs, anyhow. How dare they even consider us!' She glanced slyly at them and then turned to Estella. Again, there were shouts and hoots. 'There, they imagine they have a chance now. But it'll be like waving a lump of raw flesh in the face of a starving lion and whipping it away at the last moment.'

Estella gazed at her. That vengeful tone was not like her. It disfigured the sunny face with the pretty lips and cute nose.

'What?' Jenny demanded. Estella looked away. 'What's wrong? Icing up again?'

'No,' said Estella, taken aback by the sudden change. 'You know I'm not like that.' She was long aware of her nickname. That did not bother her because she knew the reason and had not the slightest inclination to thaw in the manner expected of her.

'I'm sorry,' said Jenny, taking her hand. 'That was not fair.' She caressed her hand. 'I just don't understand why you aren't prepared to use the assets you have. Yours are huge. They're our weapons. They're our defence. We must know how to use them.' Her manner was now rather sulky, again unusual for Jenny. 'And I don't understand how you can have no interest in any of the boys in the town.' She discarded Estella's hand and turned so that she was sitting straight and looking ahead of her.

'It's not that I have no interest. I'm just not interested in the way you and they expect. I would like to be friendly with everyone, even the boys, but it's not that sort of friendship they want.'

'Listen to yourself! You can't be serious. You can't seriously expect normal boys of our age to sit down with you as if you were at a tea party. Have you looked in the mirror recently?' She snorted in disgust. 'You have to play the game with them. This is where we both have an advantage over the other girls. We should use it. You can have the boys wrapped around your little finger if you're smart about it.'

'I don't want to play that game,' said Estella. 'I want an ordinary friendship like we always had. If that should lead to something else, something I cannot imagine, it will be on that basis.'

'You're unbelievable.' Then, after some moments of silence: 'Isn't there anyone you find attractive?' She glanced at Estella.

'No. None at all,' said Estella, not seeing any meaning in the glance. 'Anyhow, I don't regard them in that way. It's the way they are and behave that I take notice of.'

'And how are most of them?' replied Jenny, shaking her head.

Estella hesitated. 'Do you want me to be honest?'

'You will be.'

'Aimless, crude, and full of silly talk and bad language.'

'All of them are like that?'

'That's what I see.'

'Well!' There was a blink of relief.

'Perhaps Larry Burgess is different,' Estella said, after some reflection, 'but he doesn't seem to have the courage to resist the influence of the others. He was different when we were young.'

'Larry Burgess! It gets stranger by the minute!'

'Larry is a sweet boy deep down. It's sad that he's under the influence of the others.'

'Of Len, I suppose you mean.'

Estella did not answer.

'So, there is someone you like? I don't think anybody suspects it, least of all Larry.'

'He does know. I told him.'

'You mean stuck-up Miss Winterbine told him she liked him, and he didn't rush around telling everyone?'

'I would like him as a friend, like we used to be, nothing more.' She paused. 'And I'm not stuck-up. I just don't want to do the things you and the others do.'

Jenny opened her mouth but retreated into her thoughts while Estella observed her. 'You know, you are so judgmental,' she said at last. 'I'm sure nobody realises how much contempt you have for us.'

'It's not contempt. It saddens me that you all seem so content to lead an aimless, degraded sort of life. The boys seem to regard me as an object to have. I find it revolting. I've heard some girls talk about their experiences and what the boys do to them. It makes me sick. How can they let them do such things?'

'You're such a prude! Don't you realise that the girls like it? That's natural.'

'That's the way I feel about it.' She shook her head, which action riled Jenny.

'What's wrong with thinking somebody is attractive and wanting to have pleasure with them? Have a look at yourself. You're like a bitch on heat, dripping signals everywhere you go. You're fighting nature.' She stopped as if she didn't know what else to say. 'It's wasted on you. You've got hang-ups!'

Two of the young men who had been outside the hotel minutes before suddenly appeared before them with silly grins. Estella frowned and looked away.

'Get lost!' Jenny snarled. 'We're not interested.'

The two young men refused to get lost. With arms flopped around each other's shoulders, they began an uninterrupted stream of silly talk as if to demonstrate on cue what Estella had just said.

'I said get lost!' Jenny shouted, drawing the attention of those nearby.

The boys jumped back together with their arms held up in mock fear. They grinned at each other, one gesturing towards the bench. His friend plopped himself between Estella and Jenny and smirked at them. Estella got up and retreated a few steps.

'Oh, chilly!' He tried to put his arm around Jenny. Jenny shoved him away and stood up. The boy continued to grin stupidly.

'Okay, fellas, that's enough,' said a voice from across the road. Bill Huckerby came lumbering over to them. 'Come on, leave the girls alone.' He pointed at his watch. 'You want to play cricket today, don't you? I wouldn't push my luck if I were you.' In a friendly manner, he pulled the boy to his feet. 'Come on, get on up to the oval, now. And stay off the beer until the match is finished.' He waited until they walked off. 'Fat chance,' he said before turning back to the girls.

'Thank you, Uncle Bill,' said Estella.

'Thank you, Mr Huckerby,' Jenny added.

'That's all right. They don't mean any harm. A little exuberance helped along by some early beer. Yes, much too early. I'll have a word with their coach. We can't have that sort of thing happening. It's not cricket.' He winked. 'Paul Egan has been with me this morning,' he said, directing his attention to Estella. 'He asked after you. He has a high opinion of you, you know.' He did not divert his eyes. She glanced at Jenny. 'I told him you were doing well and that you would be glad to hear he inquired after you.

He seemed pleased with that. He's a good man. It's a pity he had to leave the school.' Still, he did not divert his eyes.

'Thank you,' said Estella.

'Okay, girls, have a good day. I must be off now.' He gave them a little bow and walked across the road to join a young man and a young woman with whom he had been before the beery young cricketers provoked his intervention.

'That creep Egan is in Binawarra!' said Jenny. 'I thought I'd seen the end of him.'

Estella did not respond. The young man and young woman had caught her attention. The young woman was in her mid-twenties, dressed conservatively but smartly for the summer weather. Short and plumpish but attractive and carrying herself confidently, she fixed an examining stare on Estella. Estella made nothing of her undisguised interest; it was the young man who held her attention.

He was in his late twenties, tallish, solidly built, and dressed in the typical manner of the farmer: fawn slacks, dark tan riding boots, short-sleeved blue check shirt. His short fair hair was thinning at a rate usually unacceptable for his age. He fiddled with a battered Akubra hat as he looked across at her. It was his expression that stopped her gaze from passing on to avoid the usual staring eyes. In the few seconds before Bill Huckerby led him and his companion away, Estella caught a shy, respectful expression that reflected a spirit at ease with itself. For those few moments, she was being looked at in a way she was unused to, a manner neither intrusive nor offensive but rather amounting to an old-fashioned country greeting. Before she realised it, she returned the greeting with a modest smile.

'What are you looking at?' said Jenny, glancing at Estella and then in the direction of her eyes. 'It's just another farmer and his proper little wife. Huckerby is probably quizzing them about their cows, or their sheep, or their wheat, or whatever else they grow. Boring.'

'I'm sorry,' said Estella, embarrassed to be caught staring and even more embarrassed that she had smiled at the unknown man. 'What did you say?'

'That creep Egan is in Binawarra again. I thought I'd seen the end of him.'

The young couple passed from Estella's mind as the inconsistency of Jenny's attitudes struck her.

'What?' said Jenny, and then, understanding, 'He is a creep. He's twenty years older than me! He shouldn't leer at me. It's no excuse that he has a dotty wife.'

All the meanness and unfairness of Jenny's attitude toward Paul Egan appeared again, but Estella did not want to return to what had caused the first heartbreaking rift between them.

'You still think I'm wrong, don't you?' said Jenny, flicking her hair back.

Estella looked at the ground in front of her. 'You know, some of the tender love stories in literature have been about a young woman and a much older man. Think of Marianne Dashwood and Colonel Brandon in Jane Austen's *Sense and Sensibility*. Colonel Brandon was nearly twenty years older. In the beginning, Marianne considered the colonel too old for anything, let alone love, but she fell in love with him. She got to see him as he really was.'

'What...? But they're just stories.'

'One of history's most famous liaisons was a young woman of twenty-two and a man of fifty-three.'

'Who?'

'Cleopatra and Julius Caesar.'

'How do you know all that? Since when have you been interested?'

'I read about those things,' said Estella. 'I've always read a lot. I've always had my interests. They're just not the same as yours anymore.' She paused. 'Marriages between men and women with a big age difference were not uncommon in the past. It often happened in England in the eighteenth and nineteenth centuries. It was common in the early days of Australia.'

'I don't care. Egan's a creep.'

'I'm not saying you should respond to his affection. He's married. But you should not think of it as something dirty. I'm sure he would not do anything to hurt you.' She hesitated. 'And you should not abuse or exploit his feelings, either.'

Jenny sat up and turned on Estella. 'I don't understand you. You speak of the rest of us as if we're a bunch of dirty children, and you defend a man old enough to be my father who does nothing but leer at me!'

'He doesn't leer. I've seen the way he regards you.'

Jenny's eyes flashed. They were on the brink of furthering the rift. But before she could give full vent to her anger and frustration, Terry Seddon walked up to them. He fixed his eyes on Jenny. She looked up at him and turned away.

'How could you?'

'How could I what?'

'You know.'

'Know what?' she barked.

'I didn't think anyone could willingly soil themselves with such a stinking grub.'

'What I do has got nothing to do with you. So go to hell!'

'It has something to do with anybody who has a sense of shame.'

Jenny jumped to her feet. She raised her hand, ready to slap him, but all she did was open her mouth. Terry did not move. He appeared prepared to be screamed at and have his face slapped. Long seconds passed, and then Jenny burst into tears. Next thing, she was running up the centre of the plantation between the trees, shrubs, and gardens, her blond hair flowing behind her. In consternation at the sudden turn of events, Estella rose to follow, but realised it would be a fruitless pursuit. She turned to Terry. He sat on the bench and sighed.

'I must appear pretty hard-hearted to abuse Jenny like that. And she's right. It's none of my business. But that creep, Dawson ...!'

Estella sat beside him.

'I got the full story last night. You're also involved.'

'In what ... what story?'

'In Dawson's plans.'

She stiffened.

'I was in the pub last night when Dawson came in with some of his friends. You know, the grovelling grubs he hangs around with. Seeing me, one of his mates loudly asked him how Jenny was.' He stopped and kicked at the ground. 'That rotten creep! To the laughter and filthy comments of his grub mates, he answered in detail. I wanted to punch the hell out of him. But I wouldn't do that. Nothing would please him more than to be the object of jealous rage. And he knows he could count on the sympathy of all his girlfriends. How could Jenny fall for him? He's a creep. He's a sneak. He's deceitful. He's weak. Why do so many girls fall for him?'

It upset Estella to have her suspicions confirmed. And she could not answer his question. It was a mystery. 'I have no idea why,' she said, at last.

'Do you think he's good-looking? I think he's a weed. Even if he had the guts, which he doesn't, he couldn't fight his way out of a wet paper bag on a rainy day.'

'No, I don't think he's attractive.'

'Do you find him appealing in any way?'

'No, not at all. He, least of anyone.'

'I'm relieved to hear that.'

He fell silent and looked around. Estella watched his mouth working. 'There's more, you know,' he said eventually, 'and it concerns you.'

'What is it?'

'You had better prepare yourself because I'm sure you don't suspect anything.' Estella blinked and shifted. 'Len and his mates count Jenny as a great conquest. She had long been the object of his grubby tricks. After going through the charade about Len's success with Jenny, for my benefit, one of his mates shouted, "Now what about the "Ice Maiden"?

You know they call you that?' Estella nodded. 'They looked at me and laughed themselves silly. They all thought it such a tremendous joke.'

'What do you mean?'

'I mean, you're now the object of Len's nasty plans.'

'You can't be serious.'

'That's what I heard.'

'They must be joking.'

'I wouldn't say so. In fact, I know they're not.'

'But Len Dawson must know how I feel about him. Ever since we first met, I have shown nothing but disdain.'

'I doubt that Estella Winterbine's polite efforts to show disdain would make an impact on Len Dawson. The fellow is a snake, an unprincipled grub who wouldn't hesitate to do the dirty on his own mother.'

'No, no, I can't believe it,' said Estella, shaking her head. 'How could he think I would respond to his advances? He's the last one in the town I would have anything to do with! No, it's not true. They're playing a joke on you.'

Terry shook his head.

'No, no.'

'I'll tell you why it's not a joke.' He contemplated her for a moment. 'There's a bet on with a fair bit of money at stake.'

'A bet?'

'Yes, the bet started among his school friends and then extended to his pub friends. The pub bookie grabbed the opportunity and has taken the bets. They're trying to keep it quiet. They don't want the police sergeant, the mayor, and especially Huckerby breathing down their necks, but it hasn't stopped a whole bunch of the usual lowlife from having a go. The money wagered for and against him amounts to several thousand dollars. Len has backed himself, I heard later. The odds against him are high. There's a big payout if he succeeds.'

Estella stared ahead of her, trying to comprehend the full meaning of what she was hearing.

'You mean ... you say they're betting on whether Len Dawson can seduce me?'

'Yes, that's a fancy way of putting it. Now, put crudely, you know what that means, don't you?'

'Yes ... what?'

'It means having him ... you know ...'

Estella shuddered. There had been a build-up in her mind. Her body felt now under assault, and her flesh began to crawl. She put her hand to her forehead and leaned forward.

'Are you okay?' said Terry, grabbing her shoulder.

'I don't feel well,' she whispered. A cold, clammy sweat broke out around her ears and neck.

'Can I do anything?' said Terry, alarmed at Estella's rare loss of composure.

'No thanks,' she said, with her eyes closed. Her head drooped further forward. 'Yes, you can stay with me for the moment.'

Some passers-by came hurrying over. From the coffee shop a little way up the square, Boris sat looking on as he drank his black coffee and calmly smoked his Middle-Eastern cigarette. For a long minute, Estella said nothing.

'I'm all right, thank you,' she said. 'I just felt a little sick.'

The people around her looked at each other and drifted away. She gathered up her things. 'Thank you for your comfort, Terry. I appreciate it.' She put on her sunhat and smoothed her hair back over her shoulders. She looked around for the red ribbon as she picked up her bags. It was nowhere in sight.

'I'm sorry, Estella. I didn't want to upset you, but I thought you should know. I didn't expect you would take it so badly.'

'No, it's all right. I'm fine now. Thanks for telling me. I need to know that sort of thing.'

'Do you want me to go home with you?'

'No, thank you, I will be all right by myself. Please don't tell anybody you told me. I will deal with it myself.'

'Okay. But are you sure? Don't underestimate Len Dawson. You should be prepared.'

The idea that anybody could believe she would succumb to Len Dawson filled her with indignation. But it was not directed at Terry. She understood he was concerned for her.

'Anybody who has bet on Len Dawson will lose their money. I would rather die ... I would rather die like Saint Maria Goretti.'

'Who is Maria Gor ...?'

'She was an eleven-year-old Italian girl stabbed to death for resisting the advances of a neighbour.'

'Really? I ... er ... never heard of ...'

Seeing Terry reduced to bemused silence, she thanked him again and set off, reflecting. How could someone think and behave like Len Dawson? There seemed to be no idea of right and wrong, of honour and respect for others. It was like there was a deep, dark abyss in his soul. She shuddered. She was determined to shake off all thought of him. She turned her mind to Jenny and her flight through the trees. Why did Jenny appear after months of silence and looking away every time she came near her? Was it a coincidence that she came across her sitting on a park bench in the middle of the town? Or was she there for some purpose? She could not help the feeling that Jenny had sought her out. She would not have carried on as if nothing had changed if she had not had some purpose. Surely?

That surge of joy passed through her again as she recalled hearing her happy voice. It was enough to erase all the hurt of the previous months. Then her heart sank when it had not taken long for the conversation to go the same way. She could not bear the thought that the meeting would end in further estrangement. She arrived at the end of the park and was about to pass the last picnic shelter when she caught sight of a familiar figure sitting in the shade. She came in under the roof, out of the glare of the midday sun.

'I had an idea you would come along this way,' Jenny said, exhibiting neither pleasure nor regret that she was right. Estella sat on the opposite side of the picnic table. 'I watched you walking up the park,' Jenny went on. 'I watched you dressed in that knee-length fawn skirt and white short-sleeved blouse that would make anybody else but you look daggy. Ordinary leather sandals on those gorgeous feet, an old straw hat shading the beautiful face and the gleaming brown hair ... I watched that perfect figure with the perfectly shaped breasts.' She stopped as if to contemplate that thought. 'You know, your breasts alone make us all ragingly envious.'

'Don't—'

'There you were walking along with that dreamy expression, driving everybody mad.'

'I was thinking of you.'

Jenny stared hard at Estella. Her face tightened. Her lips quivered. Estella shifted next to her. She put her arm around her, observing the struggle on her face. She drew her towards her and held her in an embrace, kissing her forehead and cheek.

'Stop,' said Jenny, pushing her away. 'You make me nervous doing that.' She moved along the bench.

'I'm sorry. I only meant to comfort you.'

'I know. I know. I'm just not in the mood for it.'

'What's wrong?'

Jenny responded to the question with a look of disbelief.

'What is it?' said Estella.

Jenny would not answer. A few more moments passed in silence, and then Jenny began scrutinising her. Her gaze rested on her face and then moved on. She focused on her hands. She grabbed her right hand and twisted it this way and that. She bent over and had a look at Estella's feet under the picnic table.

'Well, you have gone to the trouble of manicuring your finger and toe-nails. And look, you have taken care about it, too.' She grabbed Estella's left hand. 'That's a bit vain, isn't it?'

Estella pulled her hand away. 'I want to be neat and clean. No other reason.'

'Neat and clean!'

'Yes, it's important. Mamma taught me that as far back as I can remember. It's important to be neat and clean in everything you do. That's part of being a good person.'

Jenny threw her head back. 'Neat and clean and being a good person! Are you for real? And why do you call your mother "Mamma"? Why don't you say "Mum" like everyone else? You really want to be different, don't you?' She pouted. 'That's it, isn't it?'

'What's it? I don't understand.'

'Don't you?'

'No, I don't.'

Some moments passed as they looked at each other. Then Jenny said, 'All right. Come on, turn.' She pushed Estella around so that she had her back to her. The sunhat was thrown on the picnic table. She slipped her hand into her shorts pocket and pulled out the red ribbon. She grasped Estella's hair and gathered it in a sequence of fluid movements. Estella closed her eyes, enjoying the caressing of Jenny's slender hands.

'What's this?'

There was a pull on the chain around her neck. She felt Jenny turning the medal over in her fingers.

'Mary, conceived without sin, pray for us who have recourse to thee,' said Jenny, with increasing disgust.

'It's—'

'I know what it is,' said Jenny, poking the chain and medal back inside Estella's blouse. 'I don't understand why you believe all that stuff. It's sick.'

'Why is it sick to want to—?'

'Stop!' She held her hand over Estella's mouth. Then, satisfied that Estella would not speak, she resumed forming her hair into a ponytail. 'Sit still.' She pushed her head straight. 'Relax.' She bound the hair with the red ribbon and fixed it with a bow. 'I've done that many times, haven't I?' She rested her head against Estella and put her arms around her.

'Yes, but not for a long time.'

'Well, let's change that,' she said, patting Estella on the back and then sitting straight. Estella turned to face her, sorry that the attention had ended. 'That's what I came to see you for. That stupid Terry Seddon interrupted us. Well, we're having a party next week, and we'd love for you to come. We've decided you spend too much time alone. So you've got to join us.'

'A party?'

'Yes! Come on. There's nothing strange about it. You look like I've asked you to jump off Death Rock! Go on, go on, come,' she said, in a tone she resorted to when she wanted something from Estella.

'I wouldn't go anywhere near that cliff,' said Estella. 'I've always been surprised you and the others went there.'

'Well? Don't change the subject.' She put her arms around Estella again and squeezed her. 'Come on.'

It was too much for Estella. Jenny knew she could not refuse her.

'But it's Lent,' said Estella, remembering.

'Lent?'

'Yes. It's the time of penance and fasting and going without. You know that. We observe that each year in the approach to Easter.'

'Lent!' Jenny huffed impatiently. 'Well, it's not really a party. It's more of a friendly meeting. Only we girls will be there. You know, we'll just chat and play music.'

'I don't know. It still sounds like something I should leave until after Easter. Can't you arrange it then?'

Jenny coloured and shifted. 'Okay, we won't have any music, then. Come on, what will you be doing that evening anyhow? Just sitting at home? You might as well be among friends.' She took hold of Estella's arm. 'You should be friendly and charitable during Lent, shouldn't you? Isn't that part of being a Christian?'

'All right, then,' said Estella, amused at Jenny's attempt to use her religion against her. 'I'll come for a little while. But I don't understand why you can't leave it until after Easter.'

Jenny coloured again and turned away. 'I've got to go now,' she said, pushing Estella along the bench so she could get by. She got past Estella and stood in the bright sunlight. She brushed her shorts and her tanned legs, flicked her hair back, and then posed in the saucy way she was known for. Estella, smiling, sighed, picked up her sunhat, and came from under the shelter. She went to put her arms around her, but Jenny backed away, her mood changing yet again.

'Somebody's waiting for me. I've got to hurry.' She moved off a couple of steps. 'It's probably Wednesday evening for the party. Okay? It will be at Trish's place. I'll tell you more about it at school on Monday.' She came back, grabbed Estella, hugged her, let out a whimper, then turned and hurried towards the shops without looking back.

Estella walked to the curb of Explorers Road. Something was going on with Jenny, she was convinced, something behind her abrupt appearance and something behind this party.

LARRY BURGESS had been on his way home when he saw Estella and Jenny emerge from the picnic shelter. Ordinarily, he would have walked straight on, thinking they would not be interested in talking to him. Jenny confirmed that by passing him without so much as a glance. But Estella's last conversation with him was still fresh in his mind, and he slowed, at last stopping at the curb. Estella was only ten or so yards away. He coughed.

'Larry! I didn't see you,' she called, hurrying over to him. 'Have you been there long? I was just talking to Jenny.'

'Yes, I saw you, and I saw her, too. She didn't see me, though. No, I just got here. I've been into town to do messages for my mother.'

'Are you going home?' He nodded. 'I'll walk with you.' She looked at her watch. 'Oh, I'm late. Mamma would have been expecting me by now. Come on.'

They crossed over Explorers Road and then headed along Melbourne Road. Larry waited for Estella to speak.

'Larry, I meant what I said. I want to be friends like we used to be. Can't we do that?'

Larry looked into that beautiful face, so close as to set his face on fire. How could she be serious? How could she expect him to be just plain friends as if nothing had changed? Could she really believe looking like a goddess made no difference? And what about her religion? Everybody knew about the shrine she had in her room and her relationship with that old priest. And the trips to that convent in Melbourne? It was unbeliev-able. It was impossible for anyone her age, let alone the boys, to think in conventional terms about Estella Winterbine.

'Things are not like they used to be.'

'Why not?'

He did not say anything. They walked on. Estella stopped and took him by the arm. He looked at Estella's hand holding his arm, and he gazed at the face now even closer. It was unbearable.

'Larry, I'm still the same person I was when you and Jenny used to come to my place to play. I may look different, but inside I'm still the same. Please think of me like that.'

Larry struggled to say something, but nothing sensible would come out.

'Larry, I like you. I like you as a friend. I like your mum ...' She stopped and let go of his arm. 'I have no interest in any boy. No one. I have no feeling for that sort of thing. That part of my life is a complete blank. Do you understand? It's pointless to talk about it.'

'Yes, I do ... I do understand. I'm sorry, but I have nothing to do with it.' He coloured as he remembered that he was the one to provoke Len.

Estella appeared not to understand, but then: 'I appreciate that, Larry. I really do. Can I now rely on your friendship?'

'Yes ... yes, of course,' he said, surprised she wanted his support. Then, as she stood before him pleading for his friendship, he caught a glimpse of the real person. Len Dawson's plans were sick.

They arrived at the intersection with Goldminers Road. Estella looked towards Miss Barker's house. That was another oddity, the relationship with that battle-axe who was in the front garden, tending her flowers. It was not long before Miss Barker caught sight of them and beckoned.

'Do you mind if we stop and talk to her for a moment?'

Larry looked at the forbidding spinster. 'I'd better go on home. She just wants to speak to you.'

'Okay, but please wait for me. I won't be long. Just a minute?'

Larry nodded, still finding it difficult to reconcile Estella's behaviour towards him. That she should be pleading with him to wait for her! It occurred to him, as he waited and looked on, that Estella, the person, had become isolated because of her religion and appearance. Len Dawson's bet was worse than sick.

'MISS WINTERBINE is with a boy, alone, too,' said Miss Barker. 'I don't think I have seen that before.'

'Larry's a friend,' said Estella. 'At least, I want him to be a friend like he used to be.'

'Hmmm,' said Miss Barker, looking at Larry. 'He's led by the nose, that boy. I hope you can do him some good. Be careful. Don't rely on him too much.' Larry turned away when he saw Miss Barker looking at him. 'Anyhow, that's neither here nor there.' She clapped her hands and rubbed them. 'I want you to come for dinner one evening. We will have a pleasant evening together, just the two of us, two girls together.'

'Of course, Miss Barker, I would love to,' said Estella, surprised at the unexpected invitation. 'I'll discuss a time with Mamma and give you a call. Is that all right?'

'Yes, fine,' said Miss Barker, distractedly, as she looked towards the intersection. 'Has that man been following you?'

A man was on the corner opposite Larry, looking at them. He turned away as soon as he had attracted their attention. He casually crossed the road, said something to Larry, and then walked on out of sight.

'I don't know. I haven't noticed. Why would he be following me?'

'Oh, you silly girl! You've got to be more careful, have your wits about you. Do you know him?'

'No. I once saw him with Miss Bicknell in a car that drove past Daddy and me. Oh, and then they passed by our house later the same day.'

'Are you sure they were in the same car? You're not mistaken?'

'No, not at all. I remember very clearly. I thought they were on a drive around the town, sightseeing like many people do. Why do you ask?'

Miss Barker frowned, then, as if shaking off some unpleasant thought, said, 'Tell me if you notice him hanging around you, will you? Now be off with you. I will expect a call—soon.'

WHEN ESTELLA joined Larry, she asked what the man had said.

'He made a stupid joke about men always having to wait for their girl-friends.'

'What did you say?'

'Oh, I said you weren't my girlfriend, and I was just walking home with you.'

'Did he say anything after that?'

'He said it was a good day for a walk in the hills and kept on walking.'

They turned together. Boris was indeed strolling towards the hills.

'Why are you asking about him?' said Larry. 'He comes to town on business, my father said. He stays at the Country/City Motel, which he has just walked by.'

'No particular reason. Just curious. Come on. Let's go. My mother will wonder where I am.'

They set off at a brisk pace to Diggers Road, where Larry lived. Estella reminded Larry that they used to play in the bush behind his house. Yes, it was a time of innocence, he said, now responding to the girl he remembered. Soon, they had forgotten about Boris.

Chapter 7

Ruby and Geoff

CHARLES CONSULTED his watch. 'Something must have held her up, though I can't think what.' Paul Egan stood up. 'It's now lunchtime. You must stay for lunch,' Charles insisted. 'It's a long way back to Melbourne. You need to have something.'

'Yes,' said Aine, 'please be at ease.'

'No, no, I have stayed too long already. I will—'

At that moment, Estella and Larry appeared among the trees and brush on the land opposite. Estella waved excitedly, but, noticing a visitor, calmed herself. She and Larry crossed the crumbling bitumen road.

'What's he doing there?' Larry whispered.

'I have no idea.'

'I'm going now.'

'Hello, Larry,' said Aine, who had come to greet them. 'It's nice to see you here. It's been so long.'

'Hello, Mrs Winterbine,' said Larry, his feelings of awe returning. The youthful, reclusive Mrs Winterbine was no less striking than her daughter. It was almost overwhelming to have them both confronting him. 'I ran into Estella on the way back from the shops, and she walked home with me. Mum asked me to accompany her home if she insisted on walking through the bush.'

'That's very kind of you, Larry. Would you like to stop for lunch? You're very welcome.'

'No, thank you, Mrs Winterbine.' There was no way he would undergo the excruciating experience of trying to eat a sandwich while Mrs Winterbine and her daughter were looking on. He glanced again at Paul Egan. He didn't want to talk to him, either.

'All right, Larry, please say hello to your mother for me. Call anytime.' She left Estella to say her goodbyes.

'Thank you, Larry, for accompanying me home,' said Estella. 'You know, Mr Egan is a nice man. His manner towards Jenny was misunderstood. Please try to think better of him.'

With a nervous wave, Larry walked across the road and onto the vacant land. As he took the path through the trees towards his house, he pondered his meeting with Estella, trying to put everything in its place. Yes, they were great friends when they were young, and, he must admit, Estella was the same girl on the inside. She still behaved in the same quiet, earnest manner. She was gorgeous in those days, too. But then, it didn't bother him, even when his mother and father exclaimed over her pretty looks and manner. It occurred to him that he had kept company with the most stunning girls in Binawarra and that while everyone thought Len Dawson a grubby, deceitful weed of a boy. How things had changed! Now it was different, entirely different. The onslaught of puberty had reorganised their relations. He could not regard somebody who looked like a goddess as just another friend. The appearance must have something to do with it, surely. Estella must see that.

He was entertaining these thoughts while grabbing at the bushes, crumpling and throwing away the twigs and leaves. As he neared the back fence of his house, he looked up and came to a sudden halt. He felt a rush of fear as he caught sight of a silhouette between the trees. He walked on and recognised the man who had passed him on Melbourne Road. The man was standing still, gazing up at a tall eucalypt. He turned when he heard Larry's steps crushing the leaves and twigs on the bush track.

'It's you again?' Boris said. 'Are you following me?' He gave a little laugh. 'What happened to your girlfriend? Did you lose her in the bush?' He wagged his finger.

'She's not my girlfriend,' said Larry, indignant at the implication. 'She's nobody's girlfriend,' he added, becoming suspicious of the stranger's interest. 'And she's not likely to be.'

'I'm sorry, young fellow,' said Boris, 'I meant no offence. Just trying to make a friendly joke, nothing more.' He looked up at the tree again. 'Tell me, is that a White Cheeked Eastern Rosella or not?' He put a heavy hand on Larry's shoulder.

Larry stiffened and peered up into the tree. He could make out a few Rosellas on the top branches, but they were silhouetted against the glare of the summer sun.

'I don't know. They are Rosellas, but which ones I can't see.'

'Ah, well, they are beautiful birds all the same.' He looked at his watch. 'I must be getting back now. Have a good day, young fellow.' He took his heavy hand off Larry's shoulder and strolled off along the bush track towards Melbourne Road.

'HELLO, MR. Egan,' Estella said as she joined the group on the verandah. 'Uncle Bill told me you were in Binawarra.'

'Did he? I had not intended to come by.'

'Please sit down, Mr Egan,' said Charles. 'You must stay for lunch now.'

'Yes, do sit down,' said Aine. 'Estella, darling, will you entertain Mr Egan while we prepare lunch?'

Neither said anything when left alone. Paul Egan shifted on his chair.

'How have you been?' he said at last. 'I've thought about you and Jenny Brougham ...' He blushed. 'It was such a sudden departure last year. It's not always easy to make a sudden break like that.'

'I understand.'

There was more silence.

'There's a reason I dropped by,' he said eventually. 'I did plan to leave Binawarra as soon as possible. There is too much pain here ... I want to tell you something before your parents return. You can tell them later if you like. I heard something about Jenny and ...' He looked at her as if he were trying to discern her thoughts. 'You're aware of ...?'

Estella nodded.

'So you know that unconscionable Len Dawson has ... has taken advantage of Jenny. That poor girl. To have someone like that exploit and abuse you in that manner.' He shook his head. 'She gives the impression she's full of confidence, but you would know, as her best friend, that she is sensitive and easily hurt. She's all bravado a lot of the time, but when it comes to it, she has a soft heart. It's not fair that she should fall prey to the likes of that fellow. It could leave her traumatised... and hating all men in the long run.'

Paul Egan's simple, unaffected sympathy wounded Estella. Of course, she knew Jenny was a warm and happy girl. Nobody had given her more hugs and kisses. Scenes of Jenny jumping around her, laughing, grabbing, and hugging her came back.

'It has upset me, too. I know how you feel,' he said.

To her disgrace, he was not aware of her feelings. Preoccupied with her own hurt, she had not sensed the suffering Jenny might have endured and now blamed herself for her insensitivity. The contrast between Mr Egan's admirable sympathy and Terry Seddon's childish bout of jealousy occurred to her.

'Now he has had Jenny, he is turning his attention to you. You do know, do you? That's what I wanted to tell you.'

'Yes, I heard it this morning by chance. It upset me at first, but I'm all right now.'

'Are you sure? Len Dawson is the sort of boy not to be underestimated.'

'Mr Egan, I would rather die.'

He looked at the verandah floor in front of him. 'Estella, males like Len Dawson make a study of how to flatter and fool the female sex. You girls can see through the tricks of most of us silly males, but some men work on that ability to get under your guard. Len Dawson might not be as obvious as you expect.'

'Whatever he does, it won't work. It's not just Len Dawson. I'm not interested. I can't imagine it.'

'Please be on your guard, nevertheless.'

'Yes, I will. I'm thankful for your concern.'

Moments of silence followed. They could hear the muffled sounds of Aine and Charles's preparations for lunch floating up the echoing hallway. The phone rang. Estella listened to her father's footsteps coming up the hall.

'Hello Bill,' they heard Charles say. 'No, that's okay. We're about to have lunch. Mr Egan dropped by ... yes, we know ... Who? This afternoon? What time? Righto, we'll be there, cheerio.' Footsteps followed back down the hall.

'Was that all you wanted to tell me?' said Estella.

'Yes, but that's bad enough, isn't it?'

'I don't understand how someone can plan something like that,' she said, not wanting to say it could be, and was, worse.

He looked thoughtful. 'How is Jenny?' And then, 'There's one thing about you, Estella. Your honest nature will not hide anything.' He reached into his shirt pocket and drew out a business card. 'If Jenny is ever in any need, I mean real, urgent need, will you contact me? It doesn't matter when.'

'Yes,' said Estella, taking the offered card.

They could hear Aine and Charles walking up the hall. Estella got up to open the fly screen door.

'Thanks, darling,' Charles said, as they passed through and then addressing Paul Egan, 'Bill Huckerby called. He has invited us over to meet some people later this afternoon. One's an old soldier. Bill has invited him to Binawarra for the Anzac Day celebration. The other is from the university. He said you would know her. Ruby someone.'

'Yes, Ruby Waiting. She's the school's contact at the university.'

'The invitation is for you, too. Apparently, the soldier is interesting.'

'No doubt he's interesting for Bill. What soldier isn't? Please thank Bill for me. I must be on my way after lunch. I imagine, too, that Bill has a purpose in inviting you to meet Ruby. Ruby is a competent, well-organised young woman. You can be sure she will act in your best interests.'

'Act in our best interests?' said Charles. 'What do you mean?'

'No, I should leave that to Bill. I can't imagine what part the old soldier has in this, though.

AT AROUND three o'clock that afternoon, the Winterbine family arrived at the Huckerby house to find Joanne and Bill chatting on the verandah with their visitors.

'Hey, where's Paul?' said Bill, coming to meet them and grabbing Charles's hand. 'Welcome, welcome all of you. He probably had to go back to Melbourne, did he? Quick, come on, I've got some people to introduce you to,' he said, puffing as he ascended the stairs.

'Please take a seat,' said Joanne. 'Estella, darling, it's best for you to sit next to Ruby.'

She moved aside to reveal the young woman and man Estella had seen with Bill earlier that morning. Neither seemed surprised to see her as they rose.

'This is Ruby Waiting,' said Bill. 'She's an executive officer with Sandhurst University. And this upstanding young man is Geoff Shawcross, formerly of the Royal Australian Army. A captain, no less. But what he did was hush, hush!' He added this last comment in a loud whisper with his hand half over his mouth. 'Ruby, Geoff, these are our very dear friends, Charles and Aine Winterbine and their daughter, Estella.'

Geoff Shawcross gave a self-conscious smile and a little bow, but his companion came forward, offering her hand.

'Yes, it's true. Waiting is my surname, as odd as it sounds. But mind you, I'm the one who makes the most jokes about it. I'm always waiting,' she said with a quick, self-deprecating laugh. She gave the former soldier a meaningful nod, who reacted with surprise. Ruby looked Estella up and down. 'Well, Bill's right. I'm glad he told me about you. Usually, girls like you are scatty and self-absorbed and need a bit of prodding. But Bill tells me you are quite different, and I see that already.'

'You'll have to get used to Ruby,' said Joanne. 'She's blunt. Very blunt!'

'Am I blunt?' said Ruby, looking around with feigned innocence. 'Come on, Miss, sit next to me. We've got things to talk about.'

Estella felt herself being led to the chair and pushed onto it. Ruby tapped her arm with a satisfied expression and looked around at the company. On one side of Estella were Ruby and Geoff, with Geoff sitting a little forward and facing along the verandah so that whenever Estella turned to speak or listen to Ruby, she found herself looking at him. Her mother and father sat next to her on the other side, and Bill and Joanne sat forward with their chairs facing Geoff. Together they formed a cosy semi-circle.

'No doubt, you're wondering why I have asked you over to meet Ruby and Geoff,' said Bill, beaming. 'Ruby is the school's contact at the university. We started a program a few years ago to give the senior students the opportunity to chat to an official about prospective courses. Ruby has been instrumental in expanding that program so students can spend time on campus to see how they like university life, you know, touring the different departments, attending lectures, using the library, that sort of thing. Getting a close look at campus life in their final school year is very helpful to some of them. Miss Bicknell has suggested that Estella would be well-suited to a career in public relations. She thinks Estella, with a little more confidence, would be excellent for that type of work. She is yet to convince me. But that's something you have to decide on.'

'Public relations?' said Charles. 'This is sudden.'

'Just routine vocational discussion, Charles. Taking advantage of Ruby's presence.'

'What is involved in that work?' said Aine.

Bill gave a brief explanation and referred Charles and Aine to Ruby.

'Let me first explain how the plan works,' said Ruby, 'and then I'll outline the course that will qualify someone for public relations work.'

When Estella turned to Ruby, she found herself looking at Geoff, who was looking at her. Before Geoff averted his gaze, she noticed the same friendly, respectful look in his eyes. It was strange. No man had ever looked at her like that. She turned to Ruby to follow her explanation, but found her eyes drifting back to Geoff. Now those eyes were focused on Ruby. She saw warm admiration and wondered what their relationship was. Perhaps they were engaged. No, there was no ring on Ruby's left hand.

'Now, what do you think?' said Ruby, turning to Estella. 'You haven't said anything yet.'

Estella started. At that point, she had her eyes on Geoff. Geoff directed his gaze to her. She flushed at being caught staring, but he didn't seem to notice her interest or embarrassment. 'I don't know.' She shifted in her chair.

'Is there something you don't understand?' said Ruby, tilting her head.

'No, no, it seems clear,' she said, trying to gather her thoughts. 'I'm just not sure about the sort of work. I've never thought about it. This is a surprise.'

'That's all right. Give it some thought. What about spending a few days at the university?'

'I don't know,' said Estella, realising she had missed part of the conversation. 'I'll have to think about it.'

'Of course, she has,' Bill said. 'It's all new to her and her parents. Don't put her under pressure.'

'Pressure! Get away with you. She doesn't know what pressure is. Geoff can tell you what pressure is, can't you, Geoff?'

Geoff smiled, shifted, and shook his head. He looked around at the company. Estella again saw the warmth in his eyes.

'I bet he can. But you know what I mean, Ruby,' Bill said, wagging his finger at her. 'Estella needs time to weigh up the pros and cons. Charles and Aine, too.'

'Right!' said Ruby, after a few moments considering Estella. 'I'll tell you what. I have a unit in Bendigo. You can come down for the weekend, and we can go out and visit the university while there is little activity on campus. If you are interested, we can arrange for you to come at another time to find out what the course is like. What do you say to that?'

'What an excellent suggestion!' exclaimed Bill. 'She couldn't be in better hands.'

'That's a very generous offer,' said Charles. 'We'll have to discuss it. It is all so sudden. This is the first mention ... we need the time. But we thank you.'

'There's no rush,' said Ruby. 'You can decide at your leisure. I'm here by coincidence, not to interview you and Estella.'

'Well, we've finished with the business part, haven't we?' said Joanne, rising. 'Now for afternoon tea.'

Bill began talking about the Vietnam War with Geoff as soon as Joanne and Aine left for the kitchen. Ruby rearranged the seating, so Geoff was sitting next to Bill.

'That's better,' she said in a half-whisper to Estella. 'I've heard it before, and I'm sure you're not interested. But, anyhow, you don't know why I'm here with Geoff, do you?'

Estella shook her head, resisting the inclination to look at Geoff.

'Well, it's a coincidence, as I said.' She glanced at Bill in animated conversation with Geoff. 'Do you know him very long? It's strange that he has never mentioned you before this.' Estella explained the relationship between the two families. 'Well, you surprise me. You're close, almost family. I wonder why he has never said anything about you.'

'Why would he?'

Ruby burst out laughing, attracting the men's attention, before dropping her voice. 'You silly naïve girl!' She grabbed her by the arm. 'I really like you. You're the genuine article.'

Estella did not understand but could not help smiling at Ruby's forthrightness.

'That's a pretty name: Estella. It suits you.'

'Mamma and Daddy let Uncle Bill choose the name because of all the help he gave when they moved here. They had some trouble then, and Mamma was pregnant with me.'

'Did Bill really choose your name?'

'Yes, he called me Estella after a character in *Great Expectations*. You know, the book by Charles Dickens.'

'I don't think Bill has read *Great Expectations*,' said Ruby, leaning back and laughing, now quietly.

'No, he saw the film long ago,' said Estella, happy that Ruby understood the incongruity. 'Auntie Joanne teases him about it, and all Uncle Bill can say is that it was the lovely name of a lovely girl, and he didn't realise she was so cold.'

'Just like Bill! Had no idea of what the film was about, I bet. Probably slept through it.'

They giggled together, and Estella realised it was the first time in a long time that she had a good giggle. She couldn't stop her eyes from filling. Ruby was too sharp to miss the sudden change.

'What is it?' she whispered, caressing her arm.

Estella shook her head and looked at the two men. They noticed nothing. She was relieved and composed herself. 'It's nothing.'

'Not half. But we can discuss it when you come and stay with me. Girls together.'

Estella nodded, surprised that she had made such a commitment. But then, she liked Ruby's matter-of-factness, cheeriness, and confidence. She was a bit like Jenny.

'You will make me look twice as dumpy. But I don't care.' She squeezed Estella's arm. 'I began to tell you why I am here with Geoff, but sidetracked myself. Well, Geoff is sort of my boyfriend. We've known each other for a few months, but I suppose we can say that by now. I'll be honest with you. I'm fond of Geoff, and he's fond of me. I'm not sure when I'll be ready to settle down, though. There's so much I want to do. My work is important to me. Then again, I'm twenty-four, and I suppose I should be thinking about getting married. Geoff is such a good bloke, too. He's more of a good, solid farmer than a soldier in my view.'

Joanne and Aine arrived, and their conversation was cut short—much to Estella's regret. She learned over afternoon tea that Bill had invited Geoff to lead a small group of Vietnam veterans at the Anzac Day march. It was the first time he had managed to have a group of 'Vietnam Vets' in the ceremonies. Having a former Special Air Services captain to lead the march thrilled him. It was the only time the warmth faded in Geoff's eyes and the only time he spoke up. He told Bill he preferred that he not make too much of his rank or his SAS background.

'Of course, of course, Geoff, my boy,' said Bill. 'I understand some things are still classified,' and he gave him a wink. Geoff frowned. The reaction was brief, and the conversation resumed its easy, light-hearted course, and the warmth returned to his eyes.

Eventually, Ruby rose, saying they must be off. Estella watched them to the car, keeping her eyes on Geoff's every move, on every gesture he made to Ruby. She watched the car turn and Geoff give a wave through the open window. She watched the car drive up the street. She tried to see if Ruby shifted closer to Geoff. She did not. At least, she could not see if she did. On the way home, while her mother and father were busy talking about the university and the plan for her to stay with Ruby, Estella wondered what Geoff thought of her. She wondered if he saw her looking at him. It would be embarrassing if he had. Well, she was embarrassed that she had looked at him. Why did she do it?

AT EIGHT o'clock that evening, Boris was strolling along Melbourne Road towards the shopping centre on Anzac Square. The tall eucalypts running along that side of the road blocked out the light from the street-lamps so that he walked enveloped in grey-flecked darkness. Ahead of him was the glow of the lights coming from the two pubs and two coffee lounges on the square.

As he neared the square, a light-colored utility passed him by and pulled up a short distance away. He sheltered behind the nearest gum tree while the car remained stationary, with its heavy engine humming smoothly. A girl emerged from around the nearby corner and hurried to the car. The door opened as she reached it. 'Quick, hop in.' The light caught the gleaming hair, the white top, and the bare shoulders. The door slammed behind her. With a squeal of the tyres, the car did a U-turn and headed out along Melbourne Road. Boris checked his watch. Ten minutes later, he wandered through the back door of Gerda Vrouwendijk's house.

'Glad to see you on time,' she said, lighting up a cigarette.

Boris lounged in an armchair, drew a packet of his Middle-Eastern cigarettes from his pocket, and lit up. 'Have you got my coffee?' he asked, blowing the smoke into the air in front of him.

'I'll get it in a moment.'

'I want it now.'

Gerda looked at him, expressionless. 'You have something important to tell me?'

'While I have my coffee.'

She went to the kitchen and returned five minutes later with a small cup and a glass of water.

'Well, what have you got?'

'I just saw Calder pick up a girl and head out of town.'

Gerda frowned and held her cigarette in front of her for a moment. 'Are you sure it was Stephen Calder?'

'His car is unmistakable. There's no other utility like that in the town. You can't miss it.'

'Are you sure he wasn't picking up Jane Cox?'

'Absolutely. Jane Cox would never agree to be picked up like that. No, it was one of the girls from the school. I know who it is. I am just not sure of the name. Barry, I think.'

Gerda described Tricia Barry, and Boris confirmed it was her.

'That's playing with fire,' said Gerda, getting up and proceeding to pace the floor. 'Stephen Calder should know better. He's making himself vulnerable.'

'That works in your favour, of course.'

Gerda remained silent while she considered this new information. Boris smoked his cigarette, sipped his coffee, and looked bored.

'What else is there? You have something else, I assume?'

'Your treasure will need more supervision. That will mean more outlay.'

'Why?' She sat down again.

Boris related the bet that Len Dawson was running with his friends in the pub. Gerda, alarmed, jumped to her feet.

'Are you sure of this?'

'I'm sure I heard the details of the bet. I was in the pub while it was being made. Len Dawson has bet he can seduce the Winterbine girl within three months. There's a lot of money being bet against him, most thinking she is too protected. The odds are against him. He has bet a lot on himself. He will get a healthy payout if he succeeds.'

'What chance does he have?'

Boris shrugged. 'Who knows? Apparently, Len Dawson is known for his success with the girls. All women are vulnerable. You have to find the right spot. He must have a knack for finding that spot. He's a creep otherwise. I would enjoy squeezing the life out of such an example of corrupt Western life.' Gerda subjected him to a look of contempt. 'Okay, not all women, but I would say the Winterbine girl is as vulnerable as the next.'

'She must remain untouched!' said Gerda, slapping the chair she was standing behind. 'As pure as fresh-fallen snow.' She slapped the chair again. 'You must do whatever is necessary to protect her. I mean whatever is necessary.'

'Then my input will be greater than what we have agreed. I will have to spend more time and run far more risks. We must renegotiate the agreement.'

'You mean you want more money?'

'Not only money. I am not on my own.'

She rubbed her ear and drew on her cigarette. 'I want you to use violence as a last resort. Right? Let me handle Len Dawson for the moment. But don't forget, the protection of the girl goes before all else. I am committed. There is now a lot at stake for you and me.'

'Understood.'

Gerda Vrouwendijk fetched a pen and a pad. 'I will need to consult about renegotiations.'

'Whatever.'

Her pen was poised. 'I want you to proceed as if it is confirmed. Agreed?'

Boris kept his eye on the poised pen. 'Agreed.'

THREE HOURS later, Boris stood behind a gum tree near where Stephen Calder had picked up Tricia Barry. At around twelve-thirty, Calder's utility hummed to a stop at the same corner. There was no movement for a minute or so, just the pulsating hum of the finely tuned engine. Tricia Barry hopped out, shut the door, and walked out of sight around the corner. Calder drove towards the town square, where the lights from the two pubs and coffee lounge lit up the grass and gardens of the plantation.

From the sheltered porch of his presbytery on the square, Fr. van Engelen saw the girl descend from Calder's car. He watched as the car made its way around Anzac Square to park outside one of the pubs. He stood for some minutes, steadying himself on his walking stick and looking around the square, slumbering in the clear night air. As he was about to turn to go inside, a dark figure emerged from behind one of the gum trees near the end of Melbourne Road, crossed the road and made its way down between the trees and gardens of the park. The figure took shelter behind the bushes opposite the pub. Fr. van Engelen remained where he was, despite the discomfort of having to stay standing.

Half an hour later, the man belonging to the white utility emerged from the pub with two men. They got into their cars and headed out of the square. The dark figure came from behind the bushes and hurried along the park in the direction he had come. At the end of the square, he broke into a jog and disappeared into the darkness along Melbourne Road.

THE NEXT morning, after Mass, Fr. van Engelen knelt in front of the statue of the Blessed Virgin on the side altar. A few pews behind, Aine, Charles, and Estella knelt with their heads bowed. Aine was immersed in her post-communion prayers when fast-appearing images penetrated her consciousness: Estella and Miss Bicknell; Estella and Jenny; Estella and Larry; Estella and Ruby Waiting; and between those images curled a dark aura. Soon, she was struggling with a chaos of clashing images. The aura grew out over the chaos. She let out a faint moan and began to sink in the pew. Always alert, Charles and Estella took her arms. Fr. van Engelen turned and made the sign of the cross. Aine was sliding into a swoon when the darkness dissolved and the feeling of despair with it.

'I'm all right,' she whispered, running her hand over her forehead.

Charles and Estella let go of her arms. Aine continued her thanksgiving, but she could not concentrate. Some threatening palpable form was emerging from that darkness. When they came from the Church into the cool early morning air around the old stone building, they found Fr. van Engelen waiting.

'You are all right now?'

'Yes, Father,' said Aine. 'It was just for a moment this time. I think I'll be right.'

'Be careful,' he said, shaking his head.

'Yes, Father,' said Charles, 'we will be careful.'

'Good morning!' a cheery voice called from the street.

They turned to see Ruby Waiting and Geoff Shawcross on the path outside the church's front gates.

'You're surprised to see us, I bet,' said Ruby. 'Can we come in?'

'Yes, of course,' Fr. van Engelen said. 'Everybody's welcome here.'

Geoff decisively opened the gate and stood back to let Ruby pass.

'After we had left you yesterday, we drove around Binawarra,' said Ruby. 'It's such a beautiful old gold mining town, and there's so much to see. We decided to have dinner at the Commercial Hotel when it became late. Then it got so late, and we were so tired—well, at least I was tired—that we decided to spend the night here.' She put her hand half over her mouth and, in a quiet, emphatic voice, said to Aine, 'In different rooms, of course, Mrs Winterbine,' and then continuing, 'And here we are walking around, taking a last look. A marvellous old music rotunda there,' she said, pointing down the square.

'Yes, we're very proud of the town,' said Charles. 'We have a committee that looks after the planning and restoration. Bill has a lot to do with that committee.'

'I bet he does,' said Ruby.

When Charles made the introductions, Geoff gave Fr. Jos a second inquiring look at the mention of his name, but the moment passed after Charles invited Ruby and Geoff to morning tea.

'That's very kind of you,' said Geoff. 'But we must get back to St Arnaud. My mother's expecting us, and I must be back on the farm this afternoon.'

'Yes, we have to go, unfortunately, but we would like to come here again,' said Ruby, 'and if the offer is still open—'

'Of course, you're always welcome,' said Aine.

'Do you like bushwalking?' said Charles to Geoff. 'There are many bush tracks around here. Estella knows them better than anyone. I'm sure she would act as your guide.'

'I'm not a great bushwalker, but Geoff is,' Ruby answered. 'It was part of his soldiering—running around the bush looking for the enemy, I mean, and he can't forget it, can you?'

Geoff smiled at Ruby and nodded. 'Yes, I like bushwalking. It's very relaxing.'

'Then you must take advantage of the tracks here.'

'That's up to Ruby,' said Geoff, 'but I would like to.'

'We'll see next time we are here,' said Ruby. 'Now, just a short turn around the square, and we'll be off.' She put her arm through Geoff's.

'Would you like Estella to accompany you?' said Charles. 'She knows a lot about the buildings here.'

'We would love her to,' said Ruby, showing surprise, 'that is, if Estella does not mind.'

Estella was no less surprised than Ruby at her father's invitation, as she was at his volunteering her to lead them on a bush walk. It was not like him or her mother to let her go off with people they did not know well.

'No, I don't mind,' said Estella, searching their faces to see if they were being merely polite. Ruby's eagerness was enough. As for Geoff, he looked at her with the same friendliness he had shown from the first moment she had seen him.

'Good, come on, you can give us a guided tour,' Ruby said, letting go of Geoff's arm and taking Estella's hand. 'We will drop her off at home on our way, Mr and Mrs Winterbine. We look forward to seeing you again. Goodbye, Father, nice to have met you.'

Ruby walked off with Estella, who was nearly a head taller. Geoff stood for a few moments and then gave them a slight self-conscious bow. 'Nice to have met you, Mr and Mrs Winterbine, and Fr. van Engelen.' He hurried after Ruby and Estella, who had already passed through the gates.

'Come on, stop dawdling,' they heard Ruby call.

Chapter 8

Bob McKinnon's threat

ESTELLA ENTERED the school by the gate below the sports fields. She had gone a few yards along the bushy dirt track when she heard her name called. The voice was not directly recognisable. She looked around and saw Len Dawson emerge from behind a clump of bushes. Half-stopping and then stumbling a little to the side, she scolded herself for forgetting that everybody knew she came that way to school. She made a move to hurry on.

'Estella, wait, I know what's on your mind,' he said, running up to her. 'Please, stop. I want to explain.' He came up beside her. 'You've been told about the bet, haven't you?' He held his school bag in one hand and gestured with the other. His frank admission and the absence of the swagger brought her to a stop. 'I don't blame you for being upset. It was all a stupid joke that got out of hand. It's not true. The bet, I mean. Some of my friends were having a go at Terry Seddon and went too far—way too far. I'm sorry. Terry Seddon can't stand me. Because of Jenny. We were just giving him the business.' For once, he looked sincere.

'It's true. Jenny's my girl, and Seddon can't cop it. And I know you think I've taken her away from you. I'm sorry, but I really like her. She really likes me, too.' She hesitated. 'Seddon's jealous, and he can't take it. Jenny's not his property.' She agreed. Terry had no right to attack Jenny. 'If Jenny chose him, I wouldn't like it, but I would accept it. That's the way things go. You can't control your heart.'

That was also right. Len Dawson had for once said something profoundly true. She was softened, but her long aversion to him was not nearly overcome. She did not trust him. Whatever the case, she was relieved to hear him claim the bet was a prank.

'Good morning, young people,' they heard from the fence.

They turned, Estella recognising the man in the car with Miss Bicknell. 'Where does that track go to?'

'It goes up to the school,' said Estella.

'Oh, does it?' The man came through the gate and took off his hat. 'I was looking for walking tracks that I heard were around here.'

He gave Estella a little bow and stood beside Len, ignoring him. He was tall and solid like Geoff Shawcross. Dressed in a spotless blue shirt and fawn slacks and wearing heavy walking boots, he stroked his trimmed moustache as he spoke. Len looked frail and boyish beside him.

'There are walking tracks over there,' she said, pointing. 'You have to follow Huckerby Way right around the border of the school. You'll see some signs.'

'Huckerby Way?' said Boris. 'Named after the school principal?'

'Yes,' said Estella, wondering why Len said nothing.

The man glanced at Len, raising an eyebrow.

'Look, I'll leave you to it,' Len said, looking from one to the other. 'Jenny's waiting for me.' He hurried up the track.

'You say there are signs there?'

'Yes, not far along. Uncle ... Mr Huckerby has organised signs all around the town for the walking tracks.'

'Yes, I have noticed. They are very handy for those who like bushwalking. This is a well-organised town. Do you like bushwalking?'

'Yes, I do,' said Estella, finding this man with the accent polite and respectful.

'Would you mind showing me where the signs are?' Estella looked at her watch. 'If you are running late for school, it doesn't matter. I thought if you had the time.'

'I am running a bit late,' she said, not wanting to be unfriendly. 'You can't miss the signs. They're a little way along the curve in the road.'

'Thank you. I will find them.' He looked up the track. 'That goes up to the school, does it? Do you mind if I walk with you? I would like to see the school grounds.'

'No, of course not.'

He gestured for her to go ahead, which she did, acknowledging his attention. He came up beside her as she walked on, only dropping back when the track narrowed. He was careful to keep a respectful distance. It was uncommon behaviour, very polite, and Estella felt quite at ease as she walked with him. He asked her about the surroundings, the birds they saw in the trees, and the animals found in the district. Estella was happy to answer.

'I see you like the bush around your town. You seem to know a lot about it,' he said as they came from the trees and onto the grassy area where the sports fields began. 'This is so beautifully arranged and kept,' he continued, without waiting for an answer. 'The school principal knows what he is doing.'

'He does a lot for the town,' she said with pride. 'My father says the town would be a lot less attractive without him.'

'I think your father is right, young lady. Now I must let you go. I thank you very much for letting me walk with you. I'm glad to see the school grounds with such an excellent guide.' He reached into his shirt pocket. 'Here's my business card, so you know who I am. I don't want your parents to think you have been talking to strange men.'

'Thank you,' she said, taking the card.

'And now I must let you go on to school. Have a nice day, Miss.' He gave her a polite bow and walked off, relaxed, along the way they had come.

Estella watched him as he strolled along, looking around at the trees. She held up the business card.

Boris Rostowski
Importer of Middle Eastern Wares
Snead St
Upfield VIC

It was strange that Miss Barker appeared suspicious of him. There was nothing in his behaviour to cause suspicion, surely. On the contrary, his manner was reassuring. She glanced towards the school as she resumed her way and saw Len Dawson standing alone on the upper level of the first oval and looking down at her. He turned away when she returned his gaze and walked out of sight. At recess, Jenny came up to her as she was about to leave the classroom block to go to her usual place under the trees.

'Hey, Stell, where do you think you're going? Wait!' She took Estella's arm. 'I'm coming with you today.' They walked to the bench under the trees, Jenny babbling on as she used to do. 'Now, about our get-together,' she said when they sat down. 'We've decided to wait until after Easter. That's only fair to you. That'll be better because we can also ask the boys to come.'

Estella was grateful for the change. She had not been happy about going out during Lent, especially as Holy Week was approaching. But now it looked like a party. She would not enjoy it if it were their usual sort of party. She had been to such a party once and could not tolerate more than half an hour. It was one of those episodes that got their backs up, and earned her the nickname Ice Maiden.

'I'm not so sure,' she said, reluctant to cause trouble now that their relationship seemed on the mend.

'Come on, Stell, it will be different now,' Jenny pleaded. 'Things have changed. We're not as excitable anymore. It was all new for us. Perhaps we were out of control for a year or two. But we've settled down now.' She paused. 'I don't understand how you resisted it and still don't.'

Estella did not want to resume that conversation again. How could she explain if Jenny did not understand?

'Okay, don't try to explain,' said Jenny, seeing Estella's reluctance. 'I just want you to give us a chance. You know, some of us do love our boyfriends. Maybe the way we express it is not your way.'

Estella strained to keep quiet. Submitting to the things the boys did to them, how could anyone call that love? She shuddered. Love was something else. Her mother and father loved each other. The way they treated each other—that was real love.

'You'll think differently when it happens to you,' said Jenny, when there was no response from Estella, 'when you experience this sort of love.'

Estella shrugged. In a way, Jenny had a point. She hadn't experienced the kind of relationship the others had when they said they were in love. 'I may think otherwise,' she admitted, 'but it won't change what I know to be right. Anyhow, there's no point in talking about it. There's nobody in Binawarra that I could imagine myself in love with.'

'Be careful, Stell. Few people choose the person they fall in love with. The heart will not be controlled. It's a rebellious creature.' She laughed nervously.

Len had made the same comment that morning. Was it just a coincidence? Or were they so like-minded on this?

'What?' said Jenny.

'Nothing, but I agree with you. There've been many examples in literature of people falling in love unexpectedly or against their will. In some cases, it became a terrible fixation. Bradley Headstone in Dickens's *Our Mutual Friend*, for example.'

'You and your stories!' said Jenny. 'I had no idea you've been reading all that stuff.'

'We've been doing different things the last two years. I've read a lot ... I read a lot. You know that.'

Jenny looked uncomfortable for a moment. 'You must experience it yourself—not read about it. Love, I mean, not obsession.'

They became aware of Len walking toward them.

'Hi,' he said as he came up.

Again, Estella noticed his different demeanour. A relaxed, attentive friendliness had replaced the nonchalant sneer and the swaggering brava-do. She was not happy, though, that he should interrupt her time with Jenny. She nodded. Jenny took Len's hand and pulled him onto the bench. He gave Estella a friendly glance.

'I've told Stell that we will wait until after Easter,' Jenny said. 'That has made her happy. She has no objection now.'

'That's good,' said Len, frowning.

GERDA VROUWENDIJK sat at her office desk and studied the sheet of paper in front of her. It was decision time. Of the group at her house, only Bob McKinnon was unacceptable. Susie McNamara was young and impressionable and may be brought around in time. The others were en-thusiastic. Jane Cox was almost jumping out of her skin in her eagerness to act against Huckerby and the 'pernicious influences' in the town. Getting rid of Huckerby was necessary for Binawarra, but her immediate task was to neutralise his influence over the girl. She tapped her pencil on the desk and looked out the window at the students emerging from the classrooms. At length, she put the pencil down and, checking the teaching roster, left the room.

BOB MCKINNON walked towards the trees where Estella, Jenny, and Len were sitting. He could not help but be drawn by their youthful beauty and let out a soft whistle as he approached them. What a rarity. Not even on a crowded beach in full summer would you expect to see such specimens. Len and Jenny were outstanding enough, but the Winterbine girl—she was spectacular, like a rare rose that preserved all its pristine beauty. The one and only fleeting possession of that untouched prize would be a life's ecstasy. That child-woman, he mused as he got near, didn't realise what the spotless school uniform did to her as she sat with her legs together and the dress hem drawn over her knees.

'Bob!' he heard from the side.

'Oh, how irritating.'

'Can I have your attention for a moment, Bob?'

'For a moment, Edith?'

'Okay, for more than a moment. There are things to discuss.'

'This is not about teaching, is it?'

'No, it isn't, but it's just as important. You know that.'

'Do I?'

'That was your commitment.'

'My commitment? How boring.'

'Let's go over there,' she said, pointing to a bench under the trees not far from the three young people.

He followed her, dragging his feet. 'You're such a party pooper, Ms Bicknell.'

She raised her eyebrows, but then noticed Estella, Jenny, and Len sitting nearby. 'You'll have time enough for your pleasures later,' she said as she sat down. 'It's time to get down to business. The others agree that Anzac Day will provide the best opportunity for making a move against Huckerby and his cronies.'

'Really? You mean Jane Cox thinks that's the best way forward? You should be careful about following that mad, hysterical woman. She may perform satisfactorily in the classroom, but as a political agitator, she deserves to be locked up. Permanent PMT. I hope you don't regret getting into bed with her.' He smirked and added, 'Oh, that's just a figure of speech, my dear lady. She's not your type at all.'

'Will you stop your juvenile talk for once. I don't have time for it.'

'Ah, the unflappable Ms Bicknell is not so unflappable. It's good to see there's some emotion in that cold Germanic breast.'

'What do you mean by that?' she demanded, with a slight twitch at the corner of her mouth.

'Nothing.' He waved his hands, looked around, and shrugged.

'Nothing?'

'Yes. What's wrong? Don't like being described as Germanic?'

'What do you think?'

'Then you should try not to appear so cool and organised in your manner and terse and peremptory in your speech. You're like an overbearing German commander a lot of the time. Loosen up!'

'And you should learn to control your irritating tongue.'

Bob smiled, winked, and ran his index finger and thumb along his pursed lips.

'The others, including Stephen Calder, agree that Anzac Day provides the best opportunity,' she resumed, shifting.

'Ah, Stephen. Let me guess,' he said, putting his hand to his chin and stroking his trimmed beard. 'Our dear Trotskyist wants to show dramatically how Huckerby and his henchmen are representative of the capitalist class in that they glorify war, and that the glorification of war is a tactic to keep the working class in check by imbuing them with the bourgeois virtues of honour, bravery, selflessness and so on and so on.' He waved his hand in a broad flourish in front of her. 'The trouble, my dear woman, is succeeding in getting that message across to people less than susceptible. Do you think the burgers of Binawarra are so oppressed by the capitalist class that they are thirsting for such liberating messages?'

'Don't be so negative. There's a message that needs to be conveyed,' she answered. 'The glorification of war does support the present political and social regimes. Besides, you want to see the oppressive regime of Christian virtue collapse, you said.'

'It is collapsing. You see, we don't need to smash everything up in the style of our dear friend Stephen. The infrastructure of our liberal society delivers more materially than any other society. We want that intact. By all means, prepare for a counter ceremony on Anzac Day that subtly raises the right message about the oppression of the Church and its morality. I'm with you on that. But mark my words, if you go ahead with Calder involved, there will be violence. That'll just put everyone off. Changes are on their way. Inexorably. People like Calder, who in reality has his own personal agenda, will only delay the victory.'

'Why are you against him? What violence has he been guilty of in Binawarra? And what's this personal agenda?'

'Ah, Ms Bicknell, I know more about that young man than anyone else, far more than he suspects. You are warned. Be careful.' He wagged his finger, a mocking grin spreading across his face.

'Well, tell me ... so I don't have to suffer your childish games.'

Bob McKinnon laughed heartily. 'Did you know that Binawarra High School is the third school he has been assigned to since he graduated?'

'No, but does that matter?'

'He's been a teacher for six years. Three schools during that time. Doesn't that raise a question in your mind?'

'Not directly.'

'You surprise me, Edith,' he said, becoming serious. 'A person who seems so calculating and well organised as you. It just does not fit. Perhaps you have your own preoccupations?'

She searched his face. 'You just can't keep on the point, can you?'

'Can't I?'

'Get on with it.'

'Keep calm, dear lady,' he said, holding his hand up. 'There's never any need for impatience.' He raised his eyebrows in an admonishing manner. 'Well, if it doesn't raise a question in your mind, it did in mine. I made inquiries, discreetly, you see. I know who to ask. And I found out two things about our Stephen Calder. The first should be no surprise to anyone who knows him. He belongs to a radical Trotskyist group that is enamoured of the materialist dialectic and aims to bring the opposing elements in our society into conflict. Violence and general social disturbance are the tools for bringing on the cleansing revolution, which will lead to the new society. You know, all that stuff, blah, blah, blah ...' He flicked his hand up and down and sighed. 'Calder has been involved in a string of violent incidents, including pub brawls, rock concert melees, and just bashing people he perceives as inimical to the revolution. This last focuses on people his age. He knows they're reluctant to go to the police.'

'Go on.'

'You have no comment?'

'Not at the moment.'

'Okay. He was warned not to get involved in actions that might link him to his school, you know, to discredit the school. As one would expect, he gave the one-finger salute to that. He's such an indiscreet lad. It's embarrassing to see how careless he is with our dear Jane. By the way, can you explain why that hysterical promoter of women's rights endures the slave treatment he subjects her to?'

'You must ask her. Get on with the rest of the explanation.'

'I have asked her, and incredibly, she doesn't seem to understand the question. It's amazing. Calder clearly uses her for bodily relief while she slaps the face of another male who dares to open the door for her. Do you have an explanation for this mystery?'

'No. Will you get on with your story?'

'Tut, tut,' he said, pouting. 'Is the question too hard for the women's movement?'

'We don't have much time. Will you get on with it!' The bell sounded the end of recess. 'Come on,' she said, pointing. 'We must ensure the students move to their classrooms. After that, we can resume our conversation in my office. And keep to the point—if you have a point. There's a lot to organise.'

'My, Ms Bicknell, the organization. It's like the military. Are you sure you're not from German extraction?'

'Can you, for once, stop being offensive and consider that there are duties to attend to?' she said, the twitch returning. 'It makes sense to be efficient. That makes it easier for everyone, including you.'

'Of course, you're right, dear lady,' he said, getting up.

He watched her walk to the threesome, now heading towards the classroom block. She stopped to speak to them. Len and Jenny nodded and kept walking, while Estella stayed with her. Estella listened for a while, then nodded and resumed walking to the classroom block.

He gave a snort of dissatisfaction and lazily followed the students, most of whom had already disappeared through the doors. Checking his watch, he weighed up whether it was worth going to Ms Bicknell's office. Because it did not concern school business, he could ignore her invitation. Then again, he was intrigued by Ms Bicknell's interest in the Winterbine girl, an interest very different from his. He had no qualms about admitting his desire to possess an object of flawless beauty. All that was lost on the dour regimented Ms Bicknell. There was not even the dullest flicker of lust in her eyes as she looked at the woman-child. She was motivated by something else, something no less keen than lust. He was intrigued enough to relieve his boredom by going to Ms Bicknell's office.

Smiling gaily, he poked his head inside when he arrived at the door. She was busy poring over papers on her desk, which she shifted around as she read. She was so preoccupied that she did not hear him enter. He stood there regarding her with an interested smirk. He leaned a little forward, trying to see what held her attention. He moved a few steps forward. Ms

Bicknell looked up and, seeing him looking wide-eyed and smirking at the papers, shuffled them together.

'What do you mean by sneaking in like that?' she demanded. 'Don't you think of knocking? Where I come from, people knock when they enter someone's office.'

'Ah, yes, where is it that you come from? I wonder about that?'

They looked at each other.

'Bob, I'm not interested in rising to your bait,' she said, drawing her hand across her chin. 'I want you to sit down and continue your account of Stephen Calder. We have limited time. I'm assuming it's relevant to the plans.' She pointed to the chair in front of her desk.

Bob flopped down and looked around him. 'What a mess! You should be ashamed of yourself. How can a person who seems so well organised keep their office in such a state? And the food you eat! How can you eat all that junk food? No wonder you don't look exactly a picture of health.'

She leaned on her elbows and stared at him without saying anything. She blinked a few times. 'I'm waiting.'

'Okay. Where was I? Oh yes, Stephen, our dear Stephen,' he said, maintaining his good humour. 'Well, that's the first thing about Calder. He likes to break heads and uses our good friend Marx as a convenient cover for his psychopathic tendencies.' He stopped and made as if he had an illuminating thought. 'You know, that was probably Marx's real heritage: providing an excellent moral justification for people who get a thrill out of beating people to death.' He smirked and raised an eyebrow.

'Get to the point.'

'To the point? Yes, well. The second thing about Calder and what everybody in this school is ignorant of, except me, that is, is that Stephen not only has a taste for young flesh—that's not wrong in itself—but in his inimitable way, he does not care how he indulges that taste. The real reason he has been moved on from the two schools is that he was caught taking the pleasures of fourteen and fifteen-year-old students. Girls, that is. He has no taste for boys, it seems.' He stopped content for the moment to observe her reaction.

'Are you sure of this?' she said at last.

'Positive.'

'Were there any problems?'

'The incidents were covered up. The underage girls were just the worst of it. He had several relationships with older girls who would not speak against him.' He paused, scrutinising her expression. 'Bill Huckerby has no idea of Calder's background and why he is now among us in Binawarra. He would be furious if he knew. He would be furious if he discovered that a teacher's illegal actions had been covered up, and he had been sent on to him.'

'Really?' she sneered.

Bob considered Ms Bicknell's expression. 'I have no idea why you're fabricating that image in your mind of Bill Huckerby, but you need to understand that he would not tolerate Calder's presence in the school if he knew of his activities. You've been told what happened to Paul Egan, haven't you? He was merely infatuated with the Brougham girl. He didn't do anything, and I rather doubt he would have. Like Huckerby, he's - afflicted with a Christian bourgeois conscience. But it was enough for Bill Huckerby to get him moved on before he would have been obliged to ac t officially.'

'How many underage girls were involved?'

'It's not clear. At least one in the first school and two in the second. They were the known cases, mind you.'

'Are you sure of your information?'

'For the second time: positive.'

'And nobody else knows about this?'

'No. I haven't thought it necessary to mention it until now. I mention it now because of your proposed plans for Anzac Day. The whole thing may backfire on you if he draws attention to himself through his indiscretions.

Mark my words: his indiscretions will come out in the end. It may be the ruin of Bill Huckerby unless he finds out beforehand.'

'I'm glad you told me,' she said. 'It does make a difference. I need to reconsider the action.'

'Don't mistake me, dear lady. I am not against any action. On the contrary, I'm only concerned with the type of action and those involved. You are running a risk by following those two lunatics, Cox and Calder.'

'I'll think about it,' she said. She leaned back in her chair and picked up a pencil. She tapped the desk a few times. 'Do you really think the principal would be so keen to make an issue out of sex with an underage girl? Perhaps Stephen is safe.'

'You're persisting with that, are you?' he said, dropping his playful tone. 'Dear Edith, you're not talking to Jane Cox or those other two dills. If you seriously entertain Bill Huckerby's interfering with the Winterbine girl, you are deceiving yourself. I know for sure that Bill and Joanne Huckerby have always been helpful to Aine and Charles Winterbine, especially with Mrs Winterbine's health problems, and that they're deeply grateful for it.'

'I have given my opinion about the possible causes of the psychological problems the girl suffers from. She shows the classic effects of sexual abuse.'

'And those are?'

'Timidity, fearfulness, lack of confidence, withdrawal. Her withdrawal into obsessive religious ritual and myth is symptomatic.'

'Your expert opinion is that she suffers from these things, is it?'

'That's my professional opinion.'

'Is it not possible you're mistaking character traits for these afflictions? Is it not possible that religious indoctrination has suppressed her natural feelings and desires?'

'What character traits?'

'The girl is quiet, studious, a little innocent, and naïve. Indeed, her naivety is a pleasing quality in her.'

She looked at him for a few moments. 'You're not trying to make excuses for yourself, are you?'

'What do you mean?' he said, with a waver in his voice.

'I mean that the idea of children having sex does not seem to perturb you. It did not escape me that you went quiet when the group discussed the girl's psychological problems.'

He got up and closed the door quietly. 'How many children play doctors and nurses?' he said, resuming his seat.

'You tell me,' said Gerda, a hint of a smile at the edges of her mouth.

'Every child does. I'm sure you were at times all dressed up in your little nurse's uniform and administering to the local boys in the back room or garden shed. Or perhaps it was the local girls?'

'What does that prove?'

'It proves that children experience sexual pleasure.'

'Go on, give me the whole story.'

'The whole story?' he said, leaning back. 'You're not here for a seminar on sexual politics and the liberation of desire, so I will be brief. I am a scientist, first and foremost. All genuine knowledge is scientifically verifiable. Anything else is myth, custom, dreams, or delusion. Religious belief, morality, and fixed social structures fall into this category. There is nothing fixed, nothing objectively right or wrong. Thus, we organise ourselves socially and politically by consensus and organise our private lives according to our desires.

'These are only limited by the effect they may have on others. Therefore, our first law, the greatest commandment, is that, in maximising our pleasure, we may not interfere with the pleasure of others, or the converse, we may not cause pain to others, as others must not cause pain to us. In a way, we mimic the Christian rule: do unto others as you would have them do unto you, but we fulfil the truth of the rule, which is essentially about pleasure. I think we can agree on this, can't we?'

'More or less.'

'We can be pleased that desire to some extent has been liberated from the straitjacket of Christian morality, the most gratuitous, oppressive scheme of morality ever imposed upon civil society. But there is a long way to go. The sexual revolution, which it is our duty to push forward, is not complete. The increasing acceptance of homosexuality is just a breach in the wall. Apart from the sub-categories of this general term, other forms of sexual desire have been brought to the centre of the public stage as "deviancies", which in turn are to be normalised. Among these so-called deviancies are cross-generational desire and adult/child relationships. As we have convincingly demonstrated and irresistibly demanded the rights of same-sex relationships, we must do the same for the rights of children to express their sexuality, exercise their power, and bestow their consent. The same rules, the same arguments, and the same acceptance must prevail for this form of desire and those relationships issuing from it. To deny this is to be cowardly and inconsistent.'

'Then why are you criticising Stephen Calder?'

'That's perfectly clear, my dear Edith,' he said, with another flourish of his hand. 'I have no objection to any sexual relationship Stephen or anyone else has, as long as consent is present on the part of all parties. If those fourteen-year-old girls fully consented, then I have nothing to say about their sexual activity—well, apart from their bad taste. What I do object to is the complete lack of regard for the practical, concrete situation, and thus the political disadvantage.

'It is simply the fact that certain moral rules prevail in our present society. It is imprudent for anyone to engage in sexual relations with someone they work with; it is madness for a teacher to become sexually involved with a student; and pure insanity with an underage student. It is action that will cause great harm to the political campaign if found out. Such behaviour, when it is uncovered, affects everyone who wants to see the full liberation of desire.'

'So you would not get involved with a student in the school here?'

'No, never. I may look and appreciate, but touch, never. My record in Binawarra is clean. And it will stay that way. This fat, indulged old fool can stick to his plans, too, when it's important enough. Like you, I don't lose sight of my objectives. Besides, there are enough avenues to indulge oneself. You must be aware of the dialogue on university campuses. There's a cautious but insistent academic defence of cross-generational relationships. This will grow. At the same time, there's an opportunity to pursue one's particular desires. I can testify to this. Calder should attend these occasions instead of focusing on some pea-brain girl who may spill the beans if found out. Incidentally, that was the way he was found out. The girls were either too talkative or too indiscreet and, when confronted, pointed the bone at him, fool that he is.'

'Are you sure you will never succumb here?'

'What are you alluding to?'

'I saw the way you were gazing at the Winterbine girl. You didn't look like you were trying to suppress your temptation.'

'Temptation! Oh, such a biblical notion. I hope you're not giving yourself away.' He laughed.

Gerda Vrouwendijk did not reply. She tilted her head a little as if she was prepared to ignore his mockery until he answered.

'Everybody looks at her,' he went on. 'She is such a rare combination of blinding beauty and disarming childish naivety. There wouldn't be a man in Binawarra who has not turned lustful eyes on the girl. It wouldn't be human to do otherwise. No, dear lady, I may look and dream, but I know she is out of bounds. There is too much riding on her. The area around her is fraught with danger. Female beauty of that degree possesses enormous power. She doesn't yet know how to use it, but I have no doubts others are contemplating its use.'

Gerda Vrouwendijk drew breath and made a nervous movement of the hand. With a slight quiver of her head, she picked up the papers on her desk, drawing Bob's attention away from her face. 'You are being a little melodramatic, aren't you?'

'Am I?'

'I think so. The girl has psychological problems that point to the cause I have outlined.'

'I advise you not to pursue that idea.'

'Why?'

'First of all, you're wrong. The girl dotes on Uncle Bill, as does her mother. If you knew anything about the Winterbine family, their affection for Joanne and Bill wouldn't happen if Bill had interfered with the girl. You're deluding yourself if you think otherwise. Second, you shouldn't be so cavalier in assessing Bill Huckerby. Don't pay any attention to Jane Cox and those two incompetent twittish teachers. Bill Huckerby is a sad example of the Christian mentality. He can't help himself. He's merely a product of his upbringing in a particular society. He is not a bad man; he doesn't intend the enormous harm his society brings on us all.

'On the contrary, Bill Huckerby, in his way, is a good man, kind and considerate to many people in the town less fortunate than him. He is also an outstanding administrator despite his clownish manner. I won't bore you with the material benefits his stewardship has brought to the school. The assembly hall is entirely his doing. If you and your friends succeed in destroying Bill Huckerby, you will destroy so much else that is materially beneficial to the town and the school. There is a more efficient way to reduce and eliminate the social and political effects of Bill's Christian mentality. It's already happening. Bill will drift out of public influence in a short time, but he'll leave behind the benefits of his administration. My way will prevail. Mark my words. Thus, and this is my last word, the political action during the Anzac celebrations in thanks for the courage and sacrifice of the returned soldiers should be subtle. It should be aimed at an incremental step forward in the campaign to liberate the human spirit.'

'That's a nice speech.'

'Then you had better pay attention to it.'

'Is that a warning?'

'It's my advice. It would be a pity if you went to a whole lot of trouble only to make a fool of yourselves and end up being unpopular among the townspeople. Have a look at the Returned Soldiers monument on Anzac Square. You'll see many names of youngsters from the district who died in the two World Wars. People here attach a lot to the sacrifice and bravery of those young lads.'

'Perhaps it's time to show that the reality is otherwise?'

'Don't delude yourself. I'm against war for similar reasons, but I'm not so stupid as to believe the little old ladies who live in the town will change their minds about the sons they lost sixty years ago.'

'It's a hard message that should be conveyed.'

'It won't be a bad thing for Faye Crofts and Lesley Conos to totally discredit themselves in front of all the town's notables. It will justify Bill Huckerby's correct decision not to give them any responsibility. They're complete idiots and should be drummed out of teaching. My fervent hope is that they succeed where Bill's hints have failed.'

'You are making your position abundantly clear.'

'I am,' he said, tapping her desk. 'I'm willing to participate in a demonstration, but it has to be understated. I will take no part in something that causes violence or aims to bring the principal and his friends down. It won't succeed.'

'I will keep you informed,' she said, indicating the interview was at an end.

Bob McKinnon remained seated, regarding her thoughtfully.

'What are you about, Ms Bicknell?' he said at last.

'What do you mean?' She stood.

'Your driven way of organising things and the interest you seem to have in the Winterbine girl suggest you have some sort of agenda. I repeat: what are you about?'

'Under that detached, sarcastic manner, there is some paranoia, I see.'

'No, dear lady, that won't do. You'll have to do better than that. As I said, I have my contacts. I have a network. You should have realised that. I have made inquiries. In some quarters where you should be known, nobody has heard of you. In other quarters, there's confidentiality to be maintained. It all sounds rather sinister.'

'Bob,' she said, making a show of her weariness, 'I'm not interested in being your straight man. You can use others who are more susceptible to your taunts.' She went to the door and opened it.

Remaining seated, he turned. 'Jane and her twittish friends are known where they ought to be known.'

'Why are you so far away from San Francisco? There's likely a story in that.'

'There is, but it won't help you.' He smirked. 'You'll have to do better.'

'I have work to do, Mr McKinnon,' she said, looking out the door and tapping her foot.

Bob got up. 'Don't worry, my dear Edith. I'm not interested enough to pursue the matter. I would get bored. You are not interesting enough. I'll probably forget about it within five minutes. I'm like that, you know.' He tapped her on the shoulder as he passed through the doorway. But then he stopped.

'If you go to San Francisco, you, Edith, will take more than a flower to put in your hair, I bet.' He sniggered as he continued his way.

Waiting until he was out of earshot, Gerda Vrouwendijk returned to her desk, picked up the phone, and dialled. After a brief conversation in a lowered voice, she stood at the desk, knocking lightly with her knuckles. She shuffled her papers into her briefcase. Checking her watch and the timetable, she locked her office door and hurried down the corridor, paying no attention to the classrooms as she passed.

Chapter 9

Frans and Anneke investigate

FRANS VAN ENGELEN stood by the lounge room window, contemplating the grey mist swirling in wraiths over the canal that ran along the Seissingel, the road on the outer side of the last canal ring circling the old medieval town of Middelburg. Through the mist and a half-hearted drizzle, he could make out the grassy slopes of the *Bolwerk* on the opposite side of the canal. On the same side, further on, the upright sail of the windmill, the *Seismolen*, was faintly visible above the mist that hung at its thickest not far above the glassy green surface of the water.

In the winter months, when the morning light was little more than a greyish pall over the town before ten o'clock, Frans was accustomed to having his morning coffee with Marijke before going to his office in Middelburg's centre. He checked his watch and walked to the small, elegant oak desk that stood against the wall on one side of the broad window. He could relax. There was not much happening. Besides, he had a successful notary practice, and at his age, he could afford to take it easy. On the wall above his desk hung a small, framed photo of him and his brother. It was taken in 1960 during his brother's visit to Holland. He fixed his eyes on the photo. The phone on his desk rang.

'Good morning, Van Engelen speaking,' he said, as he stared at his emaciated brother disguised in a beret, civilian clothes and wearing unfashionable sunglasses.

'Good morning, Frans, it's Fr Matthijs here. I have something for you.'

'Oh, yes, good morning, Father,' said Frans, sitting up straight. 'This is unexpected.'

'That's all right, lad,' said the old priest. 'I'm sorry to disturb you. Just drop in when you can.'

'Yes, Father. What is it?'

'Whenever you have time, Frans, I'm here the whole day.'

'Certainly, Father.'

He put the receiver back in its cradle as Marijke walked into the room with coffee and biscuits on a tray. He wondered whether he should say anything. No, Fr. Matthijs's mysterious manner told him he should wait. A short time later, all rugged up, he was cycling along the Seissingel. He crossed the bridge over the canal and a minute later emerged from Vlasmarkt. He rode over Marktplein and headed down Lange Delft. Not long after, he arrived at an ancient brick archway in Middel Delft under which was the unobtrusive entrance to Sint-Augustinus chapel and presbytery. He pulled on the small length of rope at the side of the door and heard a bell sound in the distance. A minute later, Fr. Matthijs opened the heavy wooden door, which looked like it had not been opened in centuries. He led Frans down a dark hallway and ushered him into a dully lit parlour where logs were flaming and crackling in an open fire.

'Sit down, my boy,' said the old priest. 'There.'

He pointed to an armchair close to the fire, beside which stood a small table. On the table lay a letter. Fr Matthijs chatted to him about his family for a while. When it seemed they had exhausted the priest's inquiries, the priest pointed to the letter.

'That's for you.'

Frans picked up the letter. 'Why is Jos writing via you, Father?' Frans could not help but ask.

'I have no idea, my dear boy.'

Frans looked at the envelope and put it into the inside pocket of his coat. He rose. 'Thank you, Father. I, too, have no idea.'

'Think nothing more of it, Frans,' said the priest, not showing any curiosity. 'Fr. van Engelen knows he can always rely on us. You won't stop for a coffee?'

Frans declined. The old priest gestured to Frans to kneel. Closing his eyes, he said a short prayer for the welfare and safety of his family, after which he blessed him.

'May the spirit of Jesus and His Blessed Mother accompany you always,' he said, finishing.

A few minutes later, Frans was riding over Damplein on the other side of the Abbey complex. Behind him, the *Lange Jan*, the church tower, rose to dominate the surrounding buildings, and on his right as he rode along, he glanced at the house that had served as the German commandant's headquarters during the war.

Once in his office, he checked the morning's correspondence with his chief clerk, Juffrouw van der Wal, planned the day's schedule, and then climbed the stairs to his room. From his desk, he had a clear view over Middelburg. He fixed his eyes on the *Lange Jan*, wondering about the unopened letter that had mysteriously arrived by way of perhaps the most secretive place in the ancient town. He turned on his swivel chair, taking in the panorama until his eyes rested on the dome of the Oostkerk, which poked above the buildings not far away in Singelstraat. At length, he sliced open the envelope, unfolded the letter and read it. He read it again, more slowly. After staring through the window for some time, he returned to Juffrouw van der Wal.

'Juffrouw, what do you know about Meneer van den Donker's business activities?'

Nothing more than the connections he had had with the business that came through their office, she said, expressionless. Did he want her to get out the information? Yes, that was a good idea. His chief clerk had her finger on all the practice's files. And another thing, when she had a minute later in the day, would she check the relevant public registers about his property holdings on Walcheren? He left her to carry out those tasks, but came back to her a half-hour later.

'I suppose you're acquainted with Gerda van den Donker?'

'Not really. She's my age but mixed in a different group. I had no interest in those issues that occupied her and her friends. When she went to university in Amsterdam, I lost track of her. I hear she did well there, studied languages, something like that. But, really, she didn't interest me. I know more about her father because of his business activities and his connections with our clients. She has turned up a few times in recent years, but I only caught glimpses of her. I once saw her with her mother on market day. Her mother always attends market day, you know. You could ask her about Gerda if it's important.'

'Yes, I know. I see her now and then.' He hesitated. 'Have you ever seen her with her husband on market day?'

'No, I haven't, come to think of it.'

Frans tapped the desk while Juffrouw van der Wal waited. 'What was she like as a person? I mean Gerda van den Donker,' he said at length. 'They say she was hard to deal with when she was young,' he added, seeing some reluctance. 'She was expelled from the Girl Guides. There was an episode with my daughter...'

'Yes, of course, I remember Anneke had more to do with her. She was not afraid to speak her mind about Gerda. Actually, she did more than that,' said Juffrouw van der Wal, a slight smile disturbing her composure for a moment.

'Have you heard anything about her since she finished her studies?' Frans said, side-stepping Anneke's well-known clash with Gerda when they were teenagers.

No, Juffrouw van der Wal had heard nothing, not even from friends who had seen more of her. 'Gerda van den Donker had no close friends here on Walcheren,' she added. 'There were the political associates— There was also talk— No, her political interests and the way she went about them put everybody off, especially with those environmental actions. She was too fanatical. That masculine way of dressing put us off, too.' She stopped. 'Is there any particular reason you're asking about her, Meneer van Engelen?'

'Oh, not really,' said Frans, aware his questions were not related to their usual business. 'Talking about her father reminded me of something that happened at the end of the War.' He paused and then: 'Have you seen any indication that the daughter has any part in her father's business?'

'No, surely that's the last thing Gerda would get involved in. I'd have thought she was opposed to her father's business interests. Capitalism and all that, horrifying for a socialist.'

'Hmm, you're probably right.' And then on reflection: 'Was she a socialist, I mean, was she aligned—?'

'I assumed so.'

Later in the day, Juffrouw van der Wal brought a summary of Cees van den Donker's business processed through their office. He ran his eye down the list. He noticed that most property transfers and business acquisitions were before 1965. After that, there were a few small transactions, insignificant compared to some of the acquisitions of the previous years. That was curious. From casual conversations with some of his clients, he had learnt that Cees van den Donker was highly active. Either the business was going elsewhere, or Cees van den Donker's name had retreated into the companies he had formed or acquired. It struck him that he had invested widely in hotels and restaurants. Several exclusive hotels in the vicinity of

Domburg had fallen into his portfolio. This was a sector that Cees van den Donker specialised in.

That also raised the thought that he could have been investing outside Holland. It was more than probable. In that case, it would be difficult to track down the extent of his activities. Cees van den Donker had a reputation as a dour, irascible man hard to get on with and ruthless in business. Hiding his activities was consistent with his character. The more he thought about him and his daughter, the more intrigued he became with his brother's inquiries. What was Jos tied up in? What was the danger?

That evening, after dinner, Frans sat with Marijke and Anneke in the lounge room. Frans glanced at his daughter, who was reading a fashion magazine. He was trying to decide whether he would broach the subject of Gerda van den Donker with her there and then. Leaving questioning to more private circumstances might raise some unwanted curiosity. Anneke became aware that her father was looking at her.

'Pappa?'

'Has there been any news of Gerda van den Donker lately?' he tried to say casually. 'Are you aware of what she is doing now?'

Jolted, Anneke looked blankly at her father.

'Whatever has made you ask about her after all this time?' said Marijke, distracted from the television.

Frans hesitated, a little frustrated. 'I can't say. It's connected with a confidential inquiry about Meneer van den Donker.'

'I'm curious about who would want to inquire about that frightful, bad-tempered man and his equally frightful daughter?' said Anneke, composing herself.

'Anneke,' said her mother. 'I thought you had—'

'I can't say. It's business. But has anything been said?'

'No, I haven't heard anything about her since university days,' said Anneke evasively, a reaction Frans noticed and wondered. 'She studied language and linguistics in Amsterdam and did extremely well. She had a lot to do with student politics, you know, left-wing stuff. You know what she was like. She went to London to continue her studies at Thames University. By that time, she could speak English as well as any Londoner. Mamma heard that when we came across her in London in 1965. Friends have said she's been here a few times recently, but I've not seen her. Fortunately, there's not much for her to do on Walcheren, and nobody's interested, except for her weird contacts here.'

'There's nothing else?' said Frans. 'You've not heard whether she is still in London or what she's doing?'

'No, but what's this all about?' said Anneke, shifting.

Frans noticed her unease and again wondered

'Yes, what's going on?' said Marijke, glancing at Anneke.

'I can't say,' said Frans, irritated that his questions had excited more than their curiosity. 'And please don't mention to anybody that I have asked about her.'

'You're just feeding our curiosity,' said Anneke.

'It's confidential.'

He drifted off into his thoughts while Marijke returned to the television, and Anneke thoughtfully picked up her fashion magazine. He had asked only his secretary, his wife, and his daughter about Gerda van den Donker; yet it was strange that they knew little about her after her departure to Amsterdam. It was strange because Middelburg was not a big town, and people usually were aware of the comings and goings of their fellow citizens, especially of people like Cees and Gerda van den Donker.

Cees van den Donker's story was well known to everyone. He had metamorphosed from a country boy into a successful businessman, enhancing his reputation not just for his sullen, irascible manner, but also for the wealth he had cleverly acquired. He and his wife had one child and had spared no cost in maintaining her in their social class. Gerda gave a good return on the investment by excelling at school. She could have attended whatever university she wished, but chose De Witt University in Amsterdam. There, however, Gerda's trail ended for him.

He could not help comparing her with Anneke as he continued to glance at his daughter. As a teenager, Gerda had paid little attention to her manners and her clothing, despite the ample financial support she received. She had been slovenly in her dress and disrespectful and tactless in her speech, all of which only emphasised her unfortunate appearance. As a young adult, she dressed in a bohemian style, which was hardly an improvement. As for boyfriends or marriage prospects, he thought her chances nil. Her poor mother, he thought, having a husband and daughter like those two. And that was so odd. Truus van den Donker was so different.

Anneke, on the other hand, was always well-groomed, largely due to the regular work she did as a photographic model. She was a confident, feminine young woman who, despite being candid, understood when to be polite and respectful of others. After graduation, she had no trouble securing a teaching position in one of the high schools on Walcheren and was a valued member of staff. She had a circle of friends, most of whom were now married. There had been a couple of relationships a few years ago, but nothing came of them. So, at twenty-seven, she was still unattached with no candidates in view, which seemed not to bother her. Indeed, living with her parents seemed a strategy to discourage candidates.

'You're looking at me again,' said Anneke, rousing Frans from his meandering thoughts.

'I'm sorry. I couldn't help comparing you with Gerda van den Donker.'

Anneke put her magazine down and came to him. She was not a big girl, being slight, of average height and with fine, delicate features in keeping with her size. She plopped herself down on his lap and put her arms around his neck. 'I've told you: you're never going to get rid of me if you continue to spoil me.' She kissed him on the cheek and then retreated to her room.

The following day, Wednesday, Frans spent almost the entire time trying to track down information about Gerda van den Donker. He got Juffrouw van der Wal to continue her search into the father's business holdings. At the end of the day, however, they had got no further. There was nothing more they could discover about his business dealings, and the daughter's trail to London still ended there. Nobody knew anything about her after that, although some people knew she had visited Middelburg several times in recent years. The surprising feature of those visits, they said, was that they seemed to be no more than visits. All the political agitation of earlier years was absent. She stayed with her parents, which was a relief for most aware of her presence.

It was strange, thought Frans. He had to be discreet in his questions, and he thought he was, but surely somebody would know whether she was still in London. Whatever the case, there seemed nowhere else for him to go, except to approach her parents. The father was out. He would not dare ask him about his daughter. Their confrontation of 1945, thirty years ago, was still vivid in his mind. He saw him around town, but they regarded each other with suspicion. He had spoken to him during their mutual business transactions, but it had never been more than strictly necessary. There seemed to be no choice but to talk to Truus van den Donker, who still lived at their farm outside Middelburg while her husband lived in their house on Seissingel. Although their separation made it easier, he was still reluctant to go that far. That would appear to be meddling. That evening, he turned the question over in his mind. In the end, he decided there was nothing for it but to approach her. The only opportunity would be on market day, which was the next day. Mevrouw van den Donker rarely missed market d ay.

The following morning, he waited at the end of Nieuwe Burg and surveyed the rows of stalls. The sun was peeking through the clouds, warming the chilly air, and already many people were wandering along the stalls. He took a seat at an outside table at a restaurant on the square. Two cups of coffee were emptied before he caught sight of Mevrouw van den Donker. He paid his bill and hastened to the fishmongers. It would take another

ten minutes for her to get that far, so he walked to the end of the row and
waited. His calculations were not far off. Truus van den Donker appeared
from the other end and eventually arrived at the display of the fish lying
on ice in their baskets. Frans strolled to the stall, stopped beside her and
pretended to examine the fish. She did not notice him.

'Hey, Meneer,' he called to one of the men behind the table, 'what sort
of fish is this?'

'You don't have to ask, Meneer van Engelen, surely?' the man said scorn-
fully. 'That's cod, of course. You know very well.'

'Just checking,' he said, with a foolish grin. He saw out of the corner of
his eye that she turned towards him. She did not say anything. He bent a
little forward to look at the fish in front of her.

'Pardon, Mevrouw, I'm in your way,' he said. 'Oh, Mevrouw van den
Donker, it's you. I'm sorry. I wasn't paying attention?'

'No bother, Meneer van Engelen,' she said awkwardly. 'How are you?
It's been a long time since we spoke.'

Frans noticed her healthy complexion and her still smooth, rounded
cheeks. What a difference with her daughter. He stepped back from the
display, and she followed him.

'The family's well—'

'How's your brother?' she asked before he could go on.

'As well as can be expected,' said Frans, eager to ask about Gerda.

'He's still in the same place?'

'Yes, in Australia, in the country. And your family?'

'Has his health improved?' she said anxiously.

'Yes, he seems well,' said Frans, frustrated that he could not turn the
exchange to Gerda.

'I'm glad to hear it. Wish him well from me.'

'I will. What about your family, Mevrouw? I heard Gerda was in London.'

'Gerda is—

'Aren't you finished yet?' came from a rough voice behind them.

Fear passed over her face as she turned to her husband. He had somehow approached unnoticed. She became flustered and seemed unable to answer.

'It's you, is it?' said Cees, not showing any surprise that he should see Frans there talking to his wife.

'I was just asking after your wife, Meneer,' said Frans, recovering from Cees's sudden appearance. 'Nothing more.'

'Have you finished here?' her husband said to her.

'No, I've just a few purchases.'

'Then hurry up, and we'll be on our way.'

She walked back to the counter and gave her order. Cees eyed Frans with a slight shake of the head. He walked a few paces up the row away from his wife and beckoned him with a flick of his head.

'What are you up to?'

'What could you mean, Meneer?'

'Don't give me any of that slimy Catholic stuff. I'm aware you've been asking about me. What are you up to?'

'I ask questions about a lot of people in my business, Meneer,' said Frans, standing up to him. He would be polite and discreet, but would not move a pace backwards if he got it into his head to push him around.

'I ask you a third time, what are you up to?'

'And I will answer a second time that I ask a lot of questions on behalf of my clients about matters that remain confidential.'

Mevrouw van den Donker came and stood on the other side of Cees.

'Finally finished, are you?' he said, noticing her.

'Yes.'

'Then go on to the Trefcenter, as we arranged. I'll meet you there in half an hour.'

Without saying anything or acknowledging Frans, she turned and set off with her head bowed.

'I'm not going until you tell me what you are up to,' said Cees, inching towards Frans.

'Then you will be left staring at the fish until they stink.'

'I warn you, I'm not the sort of person to get on the wrong side of.'

'You can warn as much as you like,' said Frans, not backing away and holding his angry stare. 'If you're playing your usual badgering game, then I should tell you it hasn't the slightest effect. I act calmly and without prejudice on behalf of my clients, whatever the tricks of the people who come my way. But if your warning is more sinister, I will remind you that the law of the land still operates and that the courts and the police are still established in our ancient city.'

'The law of the land,' he scoffed. 'The law of the land supports people like you, doesn't it?'

'People like me?'

'Yes, you know, the ones that built the Abbey and led an opulent lifestyle while the peasants here starved.'

'Still reconstructing history to suit yourself? Have you forgotten the clandestine churches the simple Catholic peasant had to hide in after the Calvinists usurped power in the province?'

'I bought one of the country retreats of the papist prelate that once inhabited the Abbey,' said Cees, pushing his face into Frans's. 'I turned it into a restaurant and reception centre. The chapel functions nicely as my office. I have installed a personal toilet where the altar stood.'

Frans regarded the animated, hate-filled face with scorn. Cees van den Donker, appearing to become conscious of his belligerent appearance, drew back and moderated his expression.

'No peasant starved during the time the Norbertine Abbey presided over the welfare of the people of this island,' said Frans. 'You should get your history right.' He stopped himself from saying more, remembering his brother's admonitions when he had his dander up. It occurred to him that he was not familiar with the reception centre Cees spoke of. 'Which reception centre?'

A mocking smile spread across Cees's face. 'Hah! You don't know, do you? Haven't been able to find that out?' He nodded and smirked. 'That's for me to know, and for you to find out. Good luck.'

'Is it such a secret?'

Cees responded with another mocking smile. 'What were you doing with my wife?'

'Doing with your wife? We were at the same market stall. You're living up to your reputation for offensiveness.'

'Oh, you find me offensive, do you? Then it's about time you took your own medicine.' He looked around him. 'I've nothing more to say other than this, Meneer van Engelen. I'm not happy with your inquiries. I will keep an eye on you. I'm not where I am because I'm stupid.'

'That's the last thing I would accuse you of, Meneer. Cunning and abusive, yes; stupid, no.'

Cees gave Frans one last look of contempt and hurried off. Frans was not surprised by their clash. Making inquiries about him always ran the risk of his finding out. He was sorely frustrated that he had got nowhere. He had hardly the chance to mention Gerda to her mother. As he made his way back to his office, he again felt sorry for Mevrouw van den Donker. How terrible it would be to fear one's husband. It would be difficult, if not impossible, to approach her again. How would he find out where the daughter was? There was something strange going on. That he could not trace Gerda's whereabouts and that the father had got so excited about inoffensive inquiries into his business activities were just the start.

ANNEKE VAN Engelen stood in front of the rows of flower-filled buckets outside the Trefcenter, Middelburg's leading supermarket. She rubbed her cheeks while she surveyed the bright display. She happened to glance in the direction of the nearby bridge over the canal. At that moment, Truus van den Donker turned from the bridge to go to the supermarket. Their eyes met, and Truus gave her a smile of recognition. Anneke returned a warm smile.

'Goedemorgen, Mevrouw,' Anneke said when Truus had reached her. 'I see you remember me.'

'Of course, Juffrouw, I know you from your time in the Girl Guides. You haven't changed much.'

Like her father, Anneke could not help admiring how well Mevrouw van den Donker looked for her age.

'I also know your father and your uncle,' Mevrouw added. 'At least I have had occasion to speak to them. I just saw your father at the market—'

'I hope it wasn't at the croquette and frites stall,' said Anneke. 'He'll be in trouble if he's caught eating between meals. Please call me Anneke.'

Truus smiled, and Anneke saw how pretty she was.

'No, it was at the fishmonger's.'

'How's Gerda going? I haven't seen her for a while.'

'She's well, I think. I don't hear much from her these days. She seems too busy. Her father talks to her more than I do, from his office or from the house in Middelburg.' She paused. 'You know, of course, that my husband lives in the house on Seissingel, not that far from you, and I returned to the house on the farm just outside Vrouwekerke. I find it peaceful there. My husband's business takes over the house in town.'

'I did know,' said Anneke, now seeing the low spirits behind her polite expression. 'It's nice to live out in the country,' continued Anneke to encourage her.

'It's nice enough. The fresh air is good for me. When Gerda visits, she stays in the house in Middelburg.' She glanced at her watch. 'She's no longer used to the silence of the countryside, she says. But I like it. I need it.'

'Where does she live now, then?'

'London. Didn't you know that?'

'Well, I knew she studied in London, but I didn't know she settled there.'

'Oh. Yes, she's the head of an organisation there. I thought it was common knowledge.'

'I don't believe it is.'

'Oh. My husband seems so well known, and I leave everything up to him ... I just assumed ...'

'I didn't know.'

'Yes, she's the head of an organisation attached to a university.'

'What sort of an organisation?'

'Something to do with her field, languages, that kind of thing.'

'Does she enjoy her work?'

Truus van den Donker glanced again at her watch. 'I think she does. She seems busy. I can't always reach her. I ring now when I must. Otherwise, I wait until she calls.' She looked at her watch. Anneke decided not to detain her. She didn't want to make her life harder than it was. But Truus made no move to end the conversation. 'You have such a lovely family,' she said. 'You are blessed. You and your brothers, such nice-looking children, and now confident, handsome adults. I suppose they're either working or studying?'

'Yes, Joop and Pieter have graduated and now work in Rotterdam. Lodewijk is still studying. There's just me living at home.'

'Do you know how I know your father and uncle?'

'No. I assumed it had something to do with my father's business.'

'Actually, it was your uncle I first met. You know nothing about that?'

'No, is there something to know?'

She looked at her watch and then at Anneke. 'I'll tell you something in confidence, Anneke. Please promise not to tell anyone else.' She glanced back at the bridge. 'Your father knows and your mother, probably.'

'What is it?' said Anneke, uneasy and curious at the same time.

'Your uncle, Fr van Engelen, saved Gerda and me from certain death at the end of the war. Nobody knows about it except my husband and me, and your father and uncle. Not even Gerda. My husband doesn't want her to know.'

'Why? Why are you telling me this?'

'I don't know. You're such a sweet, sympathetic girl. Somehow, I feel I have to tell you. But I can't stay any longer.'

'But Mevrouw, I don't understand.'

'Ask your father. I must go.' She glanced over her shoulder at the bridge, moved away a couple of paces and then stopped. 'Your uncle was hurt badly in New Guinea and is now in Australia. Do you hear much from him?'

'Yes, very badly. He's now a cripple. No, I don't hear much, only when my parents talk about him.'

'Thank you, Anneke.'

Mevrouw van den Donker turned and disappeared into the Trefcenter. Anneke stood where she was, perplexed. Mevrouw's story and questions about Fr. Jos must relate to her father's sudden inquiries about Gerda. It was too much to be coincidental. She saw Meneer van den Donker walking over the bridge and turned back to examining the flowers. She walked along the buckets, picked up a bunch and handed it to the florist. She cast a glance towards the entrance of the Trefcenter. Meneer van den Donker looked over his shoulder. He stopped. Anneke turned to the florist and handed him a ten-guilder note.

'Aren't you Meneer van Engelen's daughter?' he said, arriving beside her.

'Yes, Meneer van den Donker,' she said, with an inquiring look as she turned to him.

'You know my name?'

'It's not a big town, Meneer. You are a well-known businessman, and I am a schoolteacher.' She added a slight aloofness to her usual confident manner. 'Is there something I can do for you?'

'I had a few words with your father.'

'Did you? That's nice.' She took her change and looked him in the face.

'Has he spoken to you?' he said awkwardly, glancing back at the supermarket.

'I beg your pardon? Goedemorgen, Meneer.' She paid him no further attention as she cycled off.

She made straight for the school library. She took the London phone directory and checked all the possible names of a language institute affiliated with a London university, but found nothing that seemed to qualify. She concentrated. Perhaps it was connected to a department of Thames University? She checked the list of departments. Nothing. It may be an organisation or institute that was not listed. She scribbled down the university's phone number. When she arrived home for lunch, she gave her mother the bunch of flowers with a kiss, received her thanks, and then called London.

'Good afternoon, Thames University,' she heard.

'Yes, good afternoon, madam, can you tell me whether you have a language or linguistics institute attached to your university?'

'Do you have the name of the institute, madam?'

'No, but it should have a name like the "language and linguistics centre," something like that.'

'There's nothing here,' said the voice.

Anneke concentrated.

'Are you there, madam?' the voice said wearily.

'Yes, yes, I am here,' said Anneke. 'Sorry to keep you. Please put me through to the Department of Linguistics.'

There was a long pause. 'Department of Linguistics,' a curt female voice said.

'Yes, good afternoon, do you have a centre or institute for languages and linguistics attached to your department?'

'Not that I know of.'

'There must be,' said Anneke.

'Must be?'

'Yes, check with one of the senior people there.'

There was another long pause during which Frans arrived home. She held up a hand when he came into the lounge room.

'Yes, madam, you're partly right,' said the voice, returning to the phone. 'There is an institute that has a loose association with our department, I am told. It's not officially attached to the university.'

'What's it called?' Anneke grabbed some notepaper and a pen.

'It's called The Institute for the Rights of Regional Dialects and Language Custom.'

Anneke repeated the name as she wrote it down. She glanced at her father, who regarded her with interest. She raised her hand. 'Do you know who's in charge?'

'No, but I can give you their number.'

Anneke wrote down the number and thanked the voice. 'Just a little more patience, Pappa,' she said, dialling the number. 'Could I speak to Ms van den Donker, please?' she said to the male voice that answered.

'There's no Ms van den Donker here.'

Anneke noticed tension in the reply. 'Are you sure?'

'Who am I speaking with? Are you from Holland?'

'Yes, I'm an acquaintance of Ms van den Donker's. I was told she was a member of your institute, and I could contact her there.' It was a stab in the dark.

'Just a minute,' said the voice. Another long pause. 'The head of this institute is Ms Gerda Vrouwendijk,' said the same male voice at last. 'She knows where Ms van den Donker is. Please give me your name and contact number, and I will pass it on to her.'

'Isn't she there?'

'No.'

'Where is she?'

'On assignment. Please give me your details.'

'When will she be back?'

'Not for a while. Please, your details.'

'She must be on an important assignment.'

'Madam, I will not be answering any more of your questions,' said the voice.

'Don't worry, then,' said Anneke. 'It's not important. I'll call again. Just tell her that an old acquaintance from Middelburg rang. She'll know who it is.' It was another stab in the dark.

'Okay, I understand, I'll pass on that an old Middelburg friend called,' said the voice, but then, realising what he had given away, 'if that's where Ms Vrouwendijk hails from.'

It was too late. Anneke had what she wanted. She adjusted her notes and then handed them to her father. 'I think we can safely conclude that Gerda van den Donker is the head of The Institute for the Rights of Regional Dialects and Language Custom and is going under the name of Gerda Vrouwendijk.'

Frans sat in his armchair and studied the notes. 'You are a smart girl, aren't you? You've got the information I've been trying to get for the last two days. How did you do it?'

It took Anneke five minutes to run through the meeting with Truus and Cees van den Donker outside the Trefcenter.

'Clever girl. But why has she changed her name?'

'Doesn't the name mean anything to you?'

'No. It looks like another odd Dutch name.'

'I suspect it's a play on words that Gerda wears as a sort of badge.'

'What do you mean?'

'Pappa, I didn't realise you were so innocent.'

After lunch, Frans and Anneke left together, cycling along Seissingel. When they reached the bridge over the canal, Anneke stopped. 'I would like to see you this afternoon, at four o'clock in your office. Will you be there?'

'Yes, but why?'

'There are questions about this business with Gerda van den Donker.'

'I don't know how much I can tell you. I'm following up on a confidential request.'

'Has it something to do with Fr Jos?'

'How...?' her father stammered before he could compose himself.

'Something Mevrouw van den Donker said.'

'Of course, she asked about him, didn't she? Okay, come to my office at four o'clock. See you then.' He leant over, and they kissed each other on both cheeks.

At four o'clock, Juffrouw van der Wal ushered Anneke into Frans's office. He bade her sit in a chair in front of his desk. Before her, he placed an envelope.

'Okay, *dochterje lief*, you're sometimes too smart for your own good,' he said, with a reluctant smile. 'Now I don't know what you're getting yourself into. I'll be honest. I don't know for myself.' He held his hand up when he saw that Anneke was about to speak. 'No, wait until I have finished. I've thought about it, and I have decided to tell all I know. It's not much, and you would probably get it all out of me in the end, anyhow. First, Fr. Jos. You have something to ask about him.'

'Mevrouw van den Donker said Fr Jos saved her and Gerda in the war. What happened?'

'He saved her and her daughter from being crushed in a stampede caused by the Germans firing into a crowd. I know no more than that. I first learned about it during a conversation your uncle and I had with Meneer van den Donker. Well, it was more of a clash with me than a conversation. It appeared that Meneer van den Donker didn't like the idea of a papist priest, as he called him, saving his daughter and wife. As you can imagine, I was furious. I don't know how much you know about our illustrious businessman, but one thing is sure: he is the most frightful anti-Catholic bigot.'

'Of course, I know. Anti-Catholicism is a feature of his social group.'

'Certainly not in the aggressive manner of our friend. Besides, the community he belonged to expelled him many years ago. He's a sort of free-thinker now, but there's nothing liberal about it. Anyhow, I asked brother Jos what happened, but he wouldn't tell me the details. He said it was better to keep quiet about it if Meneer wasn't happy.' He held up his finger to Anneke. 'I don't know any more about it before you start quizzing me further.'

Anneke thought for a few moments. 'What's the connection between Fr. Jos and Mevrouw van den Donker?'

'Connection?' he said, shifting. 'There's no connection. Fr. Jos is in Australia, and Mevrouw van den Donker is here.'

'Mevrouw van den Donker seemed concerned about Fr. Jos. She seemed upset that he had been injured.'

'That's normal, isn't it? After all, he saved her and her daughter. She feels enormous gratitude. Do you remember when your uncle was staying with us in 1960?' he said to evade further questions about a relationship. 'We went for a bike ride one Saturday afternoon and ended up on Marktplein. She came and spoke to him while we had a croquette. Do you remember?'

Anneke hesitated. 'Oh yes, I remember now. Gerda scowled at us because we were looking at her and Ilse Rijswijk. Her mother turned up and took Fr. Jos aside to speak to him.'

'Yes, Mevrouw van den Donker wanted to express her gratitude to Uncle Jos once again. Understandably, she's very grateful and embarrassed, I suppose, that her husband doesn't want anyone to know about it. He has forbidden her to talk about it. Outrageous, isn't it? That's the only connection between them.'

'But she seemed so upset.'

'It's understandable, as I say.' Because Anneke made no further comment, he picked up the envelope and handed it to her. 'This is the letter that prompted my inquiries about Gerda van den Donker. It must remain confidential.'

Anneke scanned the envelope's contents twice. 'This would have sounded baffling before, but now it sounds mysterious, not baffling. Something is going on, for sure. Just what, and Fr. Jos's connection with it, is not obvious. What are you going to do now?'

'Nothing for the moment. I'll relay what information I have to Jos and wait for further reaction.'

'I see here that Uncle Jos thinks of Mevrouw van den Donker now and again.'

'Of course. He feels sorry for her. You should have heard the offensive way that man spoke about Catholic priests. I'm sure Jos thought, no, knew, that living with him would not have been easy.'

'Yes, you're right.' She gave the letter back. 'I suppose we can only wait for Uncle Jos to respond now.'

'We?'

'Well, yes, I know this much. You'll keep me involved, I hope. Besides, I'll keep alert to any news about Gerda—discreetly, of course. I'm in a better position to learn something about her, you know.'

'All right. You'll have it your way eventually, anyhow,' he sighed. 'You'll have to be careful, though.'

'I'll be a model of discretion.' She got up, came around the desk and kissed him on the forehead. '*Dag lieverd,*' she said, as she disappeared through the door.

Frans swivelled to face the window with a view of the Abbey tower and pondered the conversation he had had with his daughter. She had sniffed something in Jos's remark about Truus. He had tried to allay her suspicion that there was something more than sympathy in the remark. The trouble was that there was indeed something. Truus and Jos were thousands of miles apart, and they did not correspond, but what they felt for each other, as displayed that evening in Middelburg six years ago, was love—pure, undefiled, love. If Jos's mysterious request for information about Gerda and Cees proved to be ongoing, Anneke was sure to find out the truth. Cees and Truus had already become involved.

ANNEKE'S cheerful, playful expression, which her father so liked, disappeared when she left his office to cycle home. The memory of those traumatic events seven years ago, of which Gerda was the cruel architect, seized her mind. Despite the devastation, she had worked with her best friend Nienke to contain the damage, both moral and reputational, and to isolate herself. She cut ties immediately with the men—refused all contact—and carried on with her modelling and study as if nothing had happened. Cousins James and Danny were in Australia and could do nothing except write letters, which she didn't even open. Wolter, with Katja's help, was mor e difficult, but he eventually gave up.

Gerda appeared happy with the results of her savage action and left her alone. To reveal what she had done would have damaged her reputation and whatever academic research she was engaged in. When she finished her studies and found a teaching position in Zeeland, she moved back home for further isolation and reputational protection. Nienke insisted she keep up her modelling to ensure an additional layer of protection. Liesje and Fiene were more than happy to feed her with work. She should not waste what gifts nature had given her. Anneke could not be blind to the irony. After all, it was what nature had given her that had led to her ruin. Now, after all those years of successful isolation and Gerda's disappearance from the scene, Gerda should suddenly appear in her uncle's correspondence from Australia. In this case, at least, it had nothing to do with her. Whatever it turned out to be, she would stay firmly in the background.

Chapter 10

The real Florence Barker

JANE COX parked down the road from the Commercial Hotel on Anzac Square. She adjusted the rear vision mirror and checked her lips and cheeks, twisting her face this way and that. She applied her lipstick, rubbed her lips together, and then lingered to assess the results. How fortunate to have a pretty face with well-shaped lips, a cheeky nose, and fresh, smooth skin that had some colour, whether it was summer or not. Why did Edith Bicknell insist on making the worst of some very plain features, making their heaviness worse by wearing poorly fitting clothing, little make-up, and having her greying hair cropped into the form of a Prussian helmet? It was perplexing.

She checked her appearance in the reflection of the shop windows as she passed, admiring her shapely legs shown to their best advantage by her short summer dress. She recalled, with barely suppressed amusement, a few of the senior boys' comments about her unfortunate colleague. She laughed to herself, flattered no end by the attention of the leading bucks. Handsome Len Dawson, the darling of the class, openly flirted with her to the frowning displeasure of the girls. The enjoyment of Jane's self-admiration was interrupted by the sight of Ms. Bicknell walking from the offices of the *Binawarra and District Mail* on the other side of the square. Ms Bicknell caught sight of her and started across the park.

'Jane, I wanted to talk to you today after classes, but missed you.'

'Oh, I wanted to talk to you, too, Edith,' Jane enthused, pushing the wire-frame glasses up her nose.

'Do you have time now?'

'I'm meeting Stephen at the pub, but he probably won't turn up for a while. You know what he's like ... has no idea of time. A drink?'

'Love to,' Ms Bicknell hastened to say, to moderate her stiff manner.

They entered the saloon bar, with Jane looking around. There was nobody yet of note, just a few dusty farmers who looked at her. She let her disapproving gaze rest upon them. 'They just come here to leer at the women. They should stay in the public bar,' she whispered as they settled themselves at a table. 'They're the types that support Huckerby and his mates on the Council. Just look at them.' She gestured in their direction.

'They're like most men,' Ms Bicknell said, hardly glancing at the men standing at the bar, talking among themselves. 'I wanted to speak with you about the Anzac Day demonstration. It is critical that we get the procedures right. It's five weeks away, but that'll rush by. I want you to take charge of the demonstration.'

'Yes, of course.'

'How many women can you get to join in?'

'I can count on ten teachers from the primary and high schools. There should be more from the town itself, some of the younger women. We can forget about the older women from the Country Women's Association. They'll be slavishly supporting the men. Huckerby and his criminal mates will see to that.'

'What if you keep the surprise element to the core three or four of the group? Will that make a difference? Will you get more?'

'Yes ... probably. Can we keep it a secret, though?'

'Tell the others everything except the key part. Its impact will depend on surprise. I suggest we keep it between the two of us for the moment and inform the core group when the time is right. As for the rest, keep telling them it will be a demonstration against the glorification of war and the rape of women in wartime. This concerns all women, whatever their views. Tell them that. Agreed?'

'Yes,' said Jane, 'you're right. We must keep it from the others. Keep it to just the two of us. Wow, it will really rock this town!' She wriggled as she brushed her hair over her head yet again.

'What can I get you ladies?' said the barman as he walked by, collecting the empty glasses.

'Ladies!' said Jane. She looked to Ms Bicknell for support.

'What are you, then?'

'Persons,' said Jane.

'Then, what do you persons want?'

Jane consulted her companion and then, frowning, ordered two gin tonics. The barman returned a few minutes later.

'There is no table service here,' he said, putting the glasses down. He took their money and returned some change. 'I took your order as I was passing the table. You must come to the bar to order from now on. It'll get busy shortly.' He walked off without waiting for a comment.

'What a rude pig of a man!'

'I've been talking with Bob McKinnon,' said Ms Bicknell. 'He's not with us, I'm afraid.'

'I told you so,' said Jane, taking a few sips of her gin tonic. 'He's the most irritating, divisive man. He's always a problem.'

'I want to leave him out of things, but I don't want any trouble. Any confrontation may cause a leak in the plans. I want to string him along for the moment under the illusion he's abreast of our plans.' She paused. 'You know, the problem is that he's too sympathetic towards the principal. He may tell him what's going on. We can forget about the demonstration if that happens.'

'Sympathetic towards the principal? Are you sure? He's never finished ridiculing Huckerby's Christian mentality.'

'He's in sympathy with him on the pernicious economic structures of the town. I've heard it from his very mouth.'

'I knew it,' said Jane, almost throwing her glass on the table.

'The only thing he condemns the principal for is his Christian morality. You will see I'm right if you pay attention to what he says. It all has to do with the liberation of desire. The issues for him revolve around sexuality and sexual politics, nothing else. You know what his tastes are like, I imagine.'

'Yes, I do. That disgusting little Suzie McNamara—'

'It's more than that. Did you notice he went strangely quiet when we were discussing the possibility of the principal interfering with the Winterbine girl?'

'No, I didn't. Did he?' said Jane, wide-eyed.

'Yes, and I now know why.'

'Why?'

'He supports the current tentative movement on university campuses to liberate cross-generational relationships. So, you see, he would not consider the principal's abuse of the Winterbine girl wrong as long as the girl did not object.'

Jane Cox looked long at Ms Bicknell as if she was unsure of her response.

'Really?' she said at last.

'Yes, it's quite unbearable. We're in full support of liberating desire, but we are not about giving men even more power to control and oppress females. The movement to normalise cross-generational relationships is, in reality, the movement to give men more opportunities to control and abuse women. If women are to maintain control of themselves from birth, we must defeat this movement. It's vital that Huckerby and McKinnon are exposed. Young females are exclusively the concern of women.'

'Yes, you're right,' said Jane, in a desperate whisper and leaning forward. She slapped the table. 'Those monsters! I was convinced there was something fundamentally wrong with McKinnon.'

'Well, we know his attitudes, but there's no concrete proof. With Huckerby, it's otherwise. We must work on it so that he is fully exposed. I've already made a few moves in that direction.'

'What?'

'I would rather keep it to myself now, but I will tell you when I'm sure it will be a step forward. About Bob McKinnon, we must wait for our chance, keep an eye on what he does and who he speaks with. He's very cunning, you know. He has been able to hide his activities from the people in Binawarra.'

'Not anymore,' said Jane. 'I won't rest.

IT WAS six o'clock when Estella, a bunch of flowers in one hand, knocked at Miss Barker's door and then turned to admire her roses.

'Good girl!' said Miss Barker, opening without delay. 'You're right on time. That's what I like, someone I can depend on. Come in.' She took the flowers that Estella handed to her. 'Thank you,' she said, bringing them briefly to her nose.

Taking Estella's hand, she led her into the lounge room to the left, off the small vestibule. Miss Barker's house was late colonial style, with the hall curving off the front vestibule and giving access to the other rooms as it wound its way to the kitchen at the back of the house. The lounge room was not large, but it was comfortably furnished with armchairs and a couch upholstered in dark brown fabric. The armrests were thick, square, and broad. The floor was carpeted in brown, and on the cream walls, right around the room, there were a variety of framed pictures, reproductions of well-known artworks, and black-and-white photos of people.

'Dinner is almost ready. So I won't offer you anything beforehand except a glass of orange juice. Take a seat.'

She disappeared through the doorway into the dining room. Estella remained standing and looked around the room, which she had rarely been in and never by herself. On the sideboard to her left was a framed photo of a young woman in her late teens, a photo she had never seen. There was something familiar about that face. She peered at it without picking it up. The smiling young woman had a handsome oval face and long hair that flowed elegantly over her shoulders. Miss Barker walked into the room carrying a tray on which she had a vase with Estella's flowers, a tumbler of squeezed orange juice, and a glass of sherry.

'Yes, that's me,' she said with a smile and placed the vase close to the photo. 'I know what you're thinking. Come on, sit down, and drink your juice. I will show you more photos and more surprises later.'

'I've never seen that photo before,' Estella said, sitting in the armchair indicated by Miss Barker.

'That's because it's not there normally.'

Dismissing the photo with a wave of her hand, she sat opposite Estella and chatted about family matters while sipping her sherry. Just when Estella thought the conversation was focusing on her mother for a purpose yet to be revealed, Miss Barker asked if she had seen that strange man again.

'Do you mean Mr Rostowski?'

'Oh, you know his name, do you?'

'Yes, he gave me his card. I've come across him several times, and he is always polite and friendly. He asks me about the town and where the best bush walks are. Nothing else. He doesn't seem at all like someone to be wary of.'

'Friendly, is he?'

'Yes, and polite, too. He's very well-mannered. He doesn't bother me at all.'

'Any special requests?'

'Only once. He asked if he could walk into the school grounds with me. That's when he gave me his card. He didn't want my parents to think I had been talking to strangers.'

'Oh, did he?'

'Yes. It was considerate.'

'As long as he remains polite and friendly ... but you should still keep your wits about you. You're a young woman who attracts a lot of attention.'

'Yes, Miss Barker.'

She invited Estella to sit at the dinner table, where she served grilled fish and a green salad, a concession to Friday and Lent.

'Now tell me how school is going,' she said. 'Tell me all about it.'

Estella did as requested, speaking randomly about her classes, teachers, and friends. When Miss Barker posed probing questions about her friends and fellow students, she could hear herself sounding evasive, which she covered rather clumsily. Curiously, Miss Barker seemed interested in the revival of her childhood friendship with Larry Burgess, about whom Estella felt less guarded.

'You could have a beneficial influence on that boy. Your efforts are commendable.'

That last comment about Larry ended her interest in her friends. Miss Barker moved on to Miss Bicknell. At first, her questions were general, but then Estella became aware of a keen, narrowing interest. And when she told of her vocational meeting with Miss Bicknell and the questions about the evidence of the senses, which Fr. van Engelen interpreted as an attempt to undermine her religious beliefs, alarm disturbed Miss Barker's usually composed face. She asked her to repeat the demonstration with the pen and Fr. van Engelen's counter-response. Estella had no trouble with Miss Bicknell's demonstration, but she struggled with the priest's counter-response.

'I understand Fr. van Engelen's point, but I'm not quite sure about the reasoning behind his explanation,' she said in conclusion.

Miss Barker regarded her without speaking. 'Yes, I understand,' she said eventually. 'The explanation is more complicated than Miss Bicknell's.'

'Miss Bicknell said that reasons for some things are so simple that we often pass over them, causing ourselves a lot of unnecessary trouble.'

'Oh, she did, did she?'

'I should reflect on what the evidence of the senses meant to me and judge whether the claims for such things as the existence of angels can be supported. That's how she put it.'

'Your parish priest is right. More than materialism is behind her thinking. It was a brazen attempt to undermine your religious beliefs. Have you thought about it?'

'Not very much. It makes no difference to my beliefs, anyhow. Daddy was right when he said there was more to our beliefs than the odd demonstration Miss Bicknell presented to me.'

Miss Barker fell silent again. Estella waited, observing the same keen interest Fr. van Engelen had shown in Miss Bicknell's demonstration. The coincidence was curious. She had an idea of what Miss Barker's next question would be.

'Did Fr. van Engelen perceive a purpose in Miss Bicknell's attempt—I mean, apart from undermining your religious beliefs?'

'He suspected there was a higher purpose but said he could not guess what it could be. It could just be an attempt to convince me of her views about religion.

'What do you think?'

'I have a feeling there's more to it. I had the impression that Fr. van Engelen thinks so, too. He seemed cautious about what he said. He might be worried about Mamma. Mamma and Daddy think it's just a sincere but misguided attempt to convince me of her religious views. They're going to see her, talk to her about our beliefs, present them to her.'

'I imagine Fr. van Engelen didn't think dialogue with Miss Bicknell would be fruitful.'

'That was my impression.'

'Time will tell.'

Estella expected the conversation to shift to Miss Bicknell's exhortation to develop her talents. She looked forward to this discussion because she was keen to hear what Miss Barker thought her talents were and whether it had ever occurred to her that she would be suitable for work in the public relations field. It had not entered anyone else's head except Miss Bicknell's. To her surprise, the end of dinner brought a stop to the subject of Miss Bicknell and her plans, whatever they could be. Miss Barker had Estella remain at the table while she cleared up. And then, coming from the kitchen carrying a tray, she said: 'Come on, young lady, we'll have coffee and cake in my study.' She led the way from the dining room across the hall to a room lit by a small desk lamp.

'You have never been here before, have you?'

'No, Miss Barker,' said Estella, looking around at the bookshelves that ran from ceiling to floor on two sides.

Miss Barker placed the tray on a coffee table. 'This is my library. This is where I escape to, to shut out the world.'

On the wall free of shelving, against which the desk stood, there were various framed photos. Estella peered at the pictures, trying to make out what they were in the soft light.

'You are the first person, other than me, to enter this room,' said Miss Barker after she had served the coffee and cake. 'Now, relax and listen to what I'm about to say.' She settled into her chair and looked around, first at the books and then at the framed photos, as if deciding on a starting point.

'See that photo there?' She pointed to a framed photo of a man in his thirties, with his arm around the shoulders of a young woman. As Estella focused on the picture in the soft light, she saw that the young woman was

Miss Barker with an expression she had never seen before. 'That's me with that man. I was twenty-two. He was thirty-three. He was a doctor.'

Miss Barker gazed at the picture. Her expression softened. The more she contemplated the photo, the more her face seemed to undergo a change. She loosened the knot of hair she always had tied at the back of her head, letting the long, greying hair flow around her shoulders. Estella couldn't see what it was, but the change in the hair, the softened expression, and the softly lit room made Miss Barker look different. She could now see traces of the handsome, elegant face in the photos.

'That was thirty-three years ago in Singapore. Have you read about the fall of Singapore in the Second World War?'

'I didn't know you were there.'

'That's because I have never told anybody in Binawarra.' She paused, assuring herself of Estella's close attention. 'Everything I say to you is to stay between the two of us. Not even your parents are to know. You do understand?'

'Yes, of course, Miss Barker.'

Miss Barker's gaze returned to the photo. 'That is Doctor Tom Buchanan, my husband.'

'Your husband!' exclaimed Estella. 'But—'

'He was my husband for the six happiest weeks of my life. It ended when the Japanese murdered him.'

Miss Barker embarked on a long wistful account of how she had met Tom Buchanan in a hospital in Singapore when the Japanese forces were moving down the Malay Peninsula, of how they fell in love, of how Tom with much urgency proposed and arranged their marriage, of how on the day the Japanese troops approached the hospital, he walked out in front of them as a distraction.

'He had left me behind a tree in the gardens with strict instructions not to move, no matter what happened. I watched him walk out in front of them, raising his hands and indicating that he was a doctor. They shot him on the spot and bayoneted him to ensure he was dead. The soldiers continued to the hospital. That night, many innocent people, patients, and medical staff died in an orgy of murder. I stood behind that tree for many hours with the crushing realisation that my husband had walked to his death to protect me.' She paused long, her eyes glistening. 'With the help of a local family, I retrieved his body and went into hiding.'

Estella shed a few tears as Miss Barker described how she had wept over, cleaned, and prepared his body for burial in a lonely spot out in the bush. At the end of her story, Miss Barker rose, unhitched the photo from the wall, and gave it to Estella. 'It was taken on our wedding day.'

'Miss Barker ...,' Estella murmured, brushing the tears from her cheeks.

'It's time for a fresh cup,' Miss Barker said, collecting the empty cups. 'All my talking and your patient listening have made us thirsty.'

Estella contemplated the photo while Miss Barker went to the kitchen. The happiness it reflected gave not the slightest hint of what would happen less than two months later, not the slightest sign that Miss Barker would bury her husband before two months were up. She would never view Miss Barker in the same way.

'Now, I can't tell you what happened to me after that,' said Miss Barker after she had returned. 'I have reasons for keeping that part of my life quiet for the moment. You will know eventually. All you need to know now is that I survived the occupation. When the Japanese surrendered, and Singapore came under Allied administration, I revealed myself. I made arrangements to return to Australia, then went about retrieving whatever property was left of mine and Tom's and settling with the bank and the solicitors. So much of what Tom said made sense after his murder. As I got my affairs in order, I became increasingly aware that he suspected what might happen. All our affairs, bank accounts, wills, property, and so on, had been arranged in such a way as to avoid problems for me in the event he should not survive. One of those eventualities was the loss of our marriage records in the Japanese destruction. Legally, I am still Miss Barker. I could hardly fathom the depth of his love. I still can't.

'Can't you take steps to have your marriage recognised? Surely, you would want to be Mrs Tom Buchanan?'

'It suits me to leave things the way they are,' said Miss Barker, with finality. 'Anyhow, everything was put in order, including Tom's exhumation and return to Australia. Tom came from a wealthy family. His parents settled much property on him before he travelled overseas. They were so shocked by his horrible death that they only survived him for several years. That meant his property and theirs, which they bequeathed to Tom, came to me. That tragedy has made me very wealthy. Before their deaths, they shipped Tom's belongings out to me. One of the most precious possessions sent is this library. He had mentioned the collection in his will but never spoke about it. So I was surprised to open all those boxes and find them full of books, some with notations in the margins.

'I understood as I unpacked the books and saw the titles that I now had Tom's mind with me. I certainly had his spirit in those books. Sometimes when I am reading a particular book, I hear his voice. That's why you see this separate room devoted to what remains of him—photos and books. In a way, it's a shrine to him. I spend time here every day reading or contemplating. It fills me with Tom's spirit—sometimes unbearably so.'

There was a moment of disturbing silence as if that spirit had fleetingly passed through the small room, brushing against Estella's feelings. Miss Barker turned on the ceiling light. 'You are on the threshold of adult life,' she continued as she resumed her seat. 'I wanted to tell you about my experiences, so you know me better—so that you find more than the grim woman who appears in public—'

'But we don't see you like that,' said Estella.

'Yes, I know, dear girl,' said Miss Barker. 'I count myself fortunate to receive the affection of your family. When I came to Binawarra, I never expected to meet people like you and your parents. But let me continue.

I wanted not just to reveal more of myself as a person. I want to explain what love has meant for me. I mean the love between a man and a woman. I have a point, perhaps a concern, in telling you this.

'Some people may think I have suffered a tragic experience,' Miss Barker continued, with a glance at the photos on the wall, 'but that I would get over it and go on to live a fruitful life and form new relationships, perhaps meet someone else and get married. Otherwise, I would condemn myself to unhappiness and a wretched, unfulfilled life. It hasn't been like that. I didn't plan it. It happened the way it did. I was going along without craving a man's love and companionship, and then Tom appeared. To use a worn image, it was like the sun rising. It brought a new life. There were feelings and yearnings I had never experienced before, and they were returned. Tom and I were one during those short weeks. We were of one spirit. I had never been so happy. And then he was gone.

'When I overcame my grief, I realised I had been wounded forever. It was a precious wound. Without him, I was ready to die, but then it forcefully occurred to me that I should go on. Tom would have wanted me to go on and live a fruitful life, with his love always with me. And that's what I have done. Those few weeks of happiness have stayed with me all these years and continue to sustain me. They sustain me in my activities. There's a depth to such constancy in love that many of your friends will never experience, and they will scoff at it. It is their loss.' She stopped and smiled. 'There now, I have finished. Thank you for your patience, my dear innocent girl.'

She rose, took the framed photo from Estella, and hung it in its usual place. 'When next time a woman like Miss Bicknell sermonises about the need for young women to break the chains of oppression,' she said, gazing at the photo, 'I would like you to think about what I have said and what feelings I have for the man who died to save me. Now, do you want to see the rest of the photos?'

Estella was glad about the invitation because, apart from nodding, she did not know how to respond. It was all so unexpected; it was all so stunning. Never would she have suspected—nobody in the town would suspect it. Not even Uncle Bill, who had more to do with her than anyone else, would suspect it. He had often said that Florence Barker was a closed book, and he would not be the one to try to open the pages. Oh no, not h e!

'Come on, my girl,' said Miss Barker. 'I know what you're thinking. How could anything like that happen to a person like Florence Barker? But that's one of the reasons I've told you. Appearances often don't tell the full story or even the right story. You're too used to yourself and your parents. The world is not as honest. So, beware!'

She took Estella by the hand and led her from photo to photo, describing where it was, what she was thinking, or what she was saying to Tom, or what Tom was saying to her. It was thrilling for Estella to hear it. She asked about her feelings when she had Tom's body beside her in the little room of bamboo walls. She struggled to understand the emotion. She could only compare it to the feelings she would have if she had to kneel beside her father's body. She shuddered. She could not bear the thought. She squeezed Miss Barker's hand.

'What was that for?' said Miss Barker, turning to her and smiling.

'I was imagining myself kneeling next to my father's body to try to feel what you must have felt.'

'It would break your heart to see your father like that, but it is not the same. With the husband you love, you become one. When he goes, part of you goes with him.'

They talked in this manner for some time. The privilege of the confidence Miss Barker had placed in Estella was sinking in.

'Now, young lady,' said Miss Barker abruptly. 'I'm taking you home.'

Estella had brought nothing with her besides the flowers, so she was ready to go. Miss Barker hesitated at the front door, holding Estella's hand, then quickly opened the door, pulled Estella with her, and hurried to the front gate. A bemused Estella noticed Miss Barker glance up and down the street. She did not see the tall, solid figure hurrying around the corner into Melbourne Road in the faint rays of the streetlights. Miss Barker lingered on the front footpath, commenting on her roses. Another furtive glance went up the street.

BORIS WAS relieved to see Miss Barker and the Winterbine girl walk off towards the girl's house. He thought that wretched woman might have seen him. But she gave no sign. He came from behind the fence and walked a little way along Goldminers Road, intending to follow them. But, no, there was no point. That sterile witch was taking the girl home. Keeping track of that predictable woman would be a waste of time.

Chapter 11

Geoff Ruby and Estella

GEOFF SHAWCROSS and Ruby Waiting were making their way along a narrow bitumen road, badly fraying at the edges. Ruby was lost in thought while Geoff remained alert to the bends where the trees hid the oncoming traffic and to potholes that became visible at the last moment. It was not a bothersome task, though. It was a fine sunny day, with a light breeze blowing across the fields of maturing grain. And he had pleasant company.

'Are you happy to go?' said Ruby.

'Of course.'

'Can you spare the time?'

'Yes, of course.'

'Are you sure?'

'Yes, of course, I'm sure. I've committed myself to Bill Huckerby, in any case. Why are you asking?'

'Well, you have the farm. Isn't it busy at this time of the year?'

'It's busy, but I can take time off. I want to take time off.' He glanced at her. 'I want to spend some time with you.'

Ruby looked at him but said nothing.

'What do you think of Estella Winterbine?' she said eventually.

'You've already asked me—several times.'

'I want to hear your answer again.'

'Why? Why does it matter?'

'It doesn't matter, really.' There was a long pause while she looked through her window. 'She's such an unusual girl. I'm intrigued. I'm intrigued because we seemed to hit it off.'

'What's there to be intrigued about?' said Geoff, wrestling to keep the wheels out of the dusty shoulder of the road. He looked in the rear-view mirror at the car speeding away in a cloud of dust.

'You really don't know?'

'No,' he said, frowning.

'Girls who look like Estella Winterbine are not usually friends with girls like Ruby Waiting. Gorgeous girls stick together. Have you ever seen a tall, trim, beautiful girl good friends with a dumpy creature like me?'

Geoff glanced at Ruby. Ruby was attractive. He was sure other men thought so, too. She was always well-groomed, with a regular face and a healthy complexion, all with an engaging personality. She was never lost for words, and her conversation was friendly and amusing. What a contrast with him! He was continually tongue-tied and often felt like a goose in company. She may be a little short and a little plump ... well, she was pleasantly rounded. As far as Estella went, in his wildest dreams, he, Geoffrey Shawcross, former SAS Captain, would never have thought such a girl would give him a second glance. All he saw at the Huckerby house was a girl who belonged to another realm. She disappeared from his thoughts the moment he drove off with Ruby.

'What's that silence mean?' said Ruby.

'You're too critical about yourself,' he said at last. 'You're attractive.' His fair complexion was no match for his blush.

'You're very sweet,' she said, giving him a light pat. 'But you can't compare me with that apparition in Binawarra, can you?'

'In what way?'

'Come on, Geoff, be serious!'

'About what?'

'Come on, tell the truth. What do you really think of her?'

With a sigh and a glance in the rear-view mirror, Geoff gathered his thoughts.

'She's a beautiful girl to look at. But there's more to a person than appearance. She's young, too.'

'Is that all you've got to say after taking so long to think about it?' Ruby laughed and gave him another pat. 'What's being young got to do with it, anyway?'

'Just that she's young. She's just a teenager, isn't she?'

'Well, she may be a teenager, but she has the body of a fully mature female. That's what we're talking about, the beauty of a physically mature young woman. She must be at least five foot nine. Surely, as a man, you don't stay unmoved by so much womanly beauty. It might be different if she were a slight little thing. Then I could imagine you seeing her as a young girl, but not with that body.'

Geoff looked ahead of him. His mind was distracted by the whoosh of the wind and the scattering and jerking rumble of the tyres as the car sped over bitumen, gravel, and shallow potholes, throwing up dust clouds along the way. What did he think about the Winterbine girl? Well, not much. She was beautiful, no doubt, but a female of that sort was out of his league. It did not bother him; that was the way it was. Besides, he looked for other qualities in a female companion. What those qualities were, he was not sure. He knew he liked Ruby, though.

She was cheery, open, and honest. She was also a hard worker. A farmer's wife had to be like that. Beauty in a female? It was not something that occupied him. Then, when he thought again about their meeting at the Huckerby house, Estella had a sort of sparkling factory-newness about her. Those unblemished, perfectly proportioned features. Like an inanimate object of beauty. It was when her full lips parted, once sticking in one corner, that she seemed a real person.

'You poor fellow,' said Ruby. 'I don't mean to put you under pressure. You know, you should learn to relax when you're called upon to give an opinion. If you relaxed, the words would come with more ease. Talking or expressing an opinion is like any skill: you must practice.'

Now that was what he liked about Ruby; she was considerate and forbearing. She was the first girl to understand the difficulty he sometimes had in expressing himself in company. 'I have thoughts. I sometimes find it difficult to get them into words when people are around.'

'Perhaps you try to say too much at once? You should try expressing one thought at a time. Try keeping a sequence in mind rather than holding the whole content in your head. It's not the same as your soldiering work. Then, you had a context that your mind had to grasp. It was very much a non-verbal activity, wasn't it? At least, that's the impression you have given me from the little you have said about your experiences in Vietnam.'

'You're right,' said Geoff, reflecting. 'I had never seen it like that, but you're right.'

'Okay, then, concentrate on the proposition: Estella Winterbine is beautiful.'

'I'm concentrating,' said Geoff reluctantly, fixing on the last image he had of her as they drove away from the Winterbine house.

'First of all, do you judge her beautiful? Consider now.'

'Yes, she's a very beautiful girl, physically, I mean.'

'That was my next question. So, for you, beauty is more than the physical appearance?'

'More than physical beauty attracts me.'

'But is attraction beauty?'

'I don't suppose it is,' he said, after some consideration.

'What is beauty, then? What do you mean when you say Estella Winterbine is beautiful?'

'Why are you asking all these questions?' said Geoff, feeling the strain of concentrating on the dusty, broken stretch they were now driving over and on the tight questioning.

'I'm intrigued. There is an increasing focus on female beauty these days. Just look at the advertising industry, films, and pop stars. I'm wondering what you, as a man, consider female beauty to be, what it means, and how you react to it. I want to compare your thoughts with mine.' She looked at him and saw he was concentrating on driving. 'The road is rough here, isn't it? Well, I will tell you what I think. You take every physical aspect of Estella—face, arms, hands, breasts, legs, ankles, height, hair, complexion, whatever you want to name—and those features are just about perfect, aren't they? Whichever way you look at her, you see perfection. Classical perfection. It seems almost impossible that someone could be like that. Do you see that?'

'Physically, she is stunning.'

'Now,' said Ruby, 'that's what I wanted to hear. So you think she is physically stunning?'

'Yes. I've already said that a couple of times,' said Geoff, baffled by the repetition.

'But there's more to it than the bare physical aspect, isn't there?'

'What do you mean?'

'Well, her manner of conducting herself. Those physical aspects are not stationary, so to speak. They are in motion. I'm talking about the elegant way she moves, stands erect, and sits modestly but elegantly, all those things. There is also her manner of regarding the world around her. You would think she is aloof at the first meeting, but you can see that it's not aloofness after a while. She has an ethereal manner of looking at everything around her. It's sometimes like the gaze from another world. Now, my question is this: is the motion of the physical entities a part of the beauty we attribute to her? Is that part of what we understand as female beauty?'

'That's all rather complicated, isn't it?'

'But do you agree or disagree? When you say Estella Winterbine is beautiful, do you mean she has unblemished skin, trim ankles, shapely arms and legs, and all those sorts of things? Or do you mean more than that, that a manner of moving is somehow a part of being physically beautiful?'

There was another long pause as Geoff tried to apply those contrasting standards to the picture of Estella he had in his head.

'You're right now that I consider it,' he said. 'The girl has a manner about her that's quite different. It does add to her appearance. I mean, it seems to be part of her beauty or a part of her being beautiful.'

'Which is it?'

'I'm not sure,' said Geoff, trying to fathom the distinction he had made.

'That's a good question: is beauty the same as being beautiful?'

'I don't know.'

The bitumen road ended, and they found themselves on an unsealed section. The dust flew everywhere as Geoff drove on, barely slowing the car. Ruby kept silent. After a period of noise, wind, and dust, the car seemed to lurch out of the dust cloud onto a wider, smooth, sealed road.

'Ah, that's better,' said Geoff. 'The road here is much better, and we don't have much distance to cover. We'll be there shortly.' He glanced at his watch.

'No need to hurry. Bill and Joanne are not expecting us before twelve. We'll stop in the town centre for a cup of tea before we see them.'

They drove on for a while without saying anything, but both had their minds on Estella.

'You know,' said Ruby, 'the fact that Estella's appearance has us talking about her means something, doesn't it?'

'You've been talking about her, but what?'

'It means something about her promotes such a discussion, to state the obvious. But obvious or not, it points to something about female beauty. Does anyone ever talk about male beauty in that way? And are we right to apply the word beautiful to the male appearance? I don't think so.'

'I certainly don't think about a handsome man like I would talk about a beautiful woman,' said Geoff, now able to concentrate. 'In any case, I don't notice if a man is handsome, or less so, at least, than I would think of a woman in that way.'

'But you have noticed that Estella Winterbine is beautiful?'

'Really, Ruby ...'

'You think she is stunning?'

'Ruby ...!'

'Okay, what does that mean for you?'

'Why are we covering the same thing all the time?'

'You notice she is beautiful. Well, does that fill you with desire?'

'No,' said Geoff, 'certainly not. I just observe that she's a beautiful woman.'

'You started off saying she was a girl.'

'She is, too.'

'Which is it?'

'She's a woman physically, but she's a girl to me. She is so much younger than me. It's wrong for a person of my age to be feeling desire for a girl at that stage of maturity ... all round development.'

'Well said, Geoff!' said Ruby. 'See, you can express yourself well when you're relaxed and have the time for reflection.'

'Thank you,' said Geoff, pleased with the compliment.

'But are you serious?'

'What? About desire?'

'Yes.'

'Yes, I'm serious. It's wrong to regard her in that way.'

'What if she were older, say, my age?'

Geoff blushed badly.

'I'm sorry, Geoff, that wasn't fair.'

'It's still wrong. It's not right to regard a woman as an object of desire,' said Geoff, eager to cover his embarrassment.

'You're a strange combination, Geoffrey Shawcross. Normally, people like you think about women as objects of desire.'

'People like me?'

'Yes, highly trained soldiers. I have had my experiences with soldiers, you know. With one, I mean, when I was in my final year at university. I went out with him just once. He spent the evening talking loudly about himself, and at the end, I almost had to fight him off with a stick.' She snorted in disgust, not noticing Geoff's change in expression.

'Not all soldiers are like that,' he said. 'Some SAS soldiers have families, you know. One of the most painful experiences I have had is telling a wife with young children that her husband was killed while on a mission, and she was not allowed to say anything.'

'That's sad. I'm sorry.'

'That's all right. I know some soldiers behave badly. They ignore the bad name they give the rest of us. One of the reasons a soldier is chosen for special service is his sense of honour and firm commitment. It's not a job for weak, indulged, undisciplined men. A loud-mouthed man who treated a woman as an object of desire wouldn't have the right strength of character for a genuine SAS soldier.'

There followed a silence. As they were about to enter the township of Binawarra, Ruby said, 'You know, I have learned more about you during this drive than all the weeks since we met. I say again: you're a strange combination, Geoff Shawcross. I mean that in a good way.'

Geoff could not have felt more pleased. He wanted Ruby to think well of him. They drove onto the circuit without further conversation while he looked for a parking spot. It wasn't until they were outside Fr. van Engelen's presbytery that they found a free spot. They noticed the priest sitting not far away in the mid-morning sun.

'Let's say hello before we have a cup of tea,' said Ruby.

Fr. van Engelen, who seemed preoccupied, looked up when they were within a few yards of him.

'Hello, Father. How are you this morning?'

'Oh, well, Miss ...'

'Waiting, Ruby Waiting, but call me Ruby. We met you last weekend, do you remember? This is Geoff Shawcross.'

'Yes, of course, I remember you both. Estella Winterbine showed you around the town centre ... please forgive me if I don't stand up.'

'No, Father, you remain seated. We just wanted to say hello.'

'You've come to see Estella?'

'Well, we've come to see Bill Huckerby, but we hope to catch up with Estella and her parents later today.'

They exchanged some more pleasantries. Ruby noticed the old priest was distracted. When she said they must be off, he came to. 'Oh, I meant to ask you. Are you Catholic?'

'No, Father,' Ruby laughed. 'Do we give that impression?'

'You do a bit,' he said, smiling. 'I'm sorry. I didn't mean to intrude.'

'That's quite all right, Father. We'll take it as a compliment, won't we, Geoff?' Geoff nodded. 'Have a nice morning, Father. We're off to have a cup of tea before we go to the Huckerby's.'

As they were about to enter the coffee lounge, Bob McKinnon blundered out, almost bumping into them.

'Oh, oh, it's the girl with the delightful but inappropriate name, Ruby,' he said, with the usual flourish of one arm. 'That name better suits me. And what brings you to our humble town? Oh, with a boyfriend, I see. Quite nice!' He looked Geoff up and down in his impudent way.

'Good morning, Mr McKinnon,' she said, shaking her head in a showy attempt to be patient. 'Can't you control your decadent inclinations?'

'Never! You know me. That's my object in life: decadence! Now, introduce me to this strapping young man, and,' he emphasised, wagging his finger, 'no need for such formality, Ruby dear.'

'Bob, this is Geoff, Geoff, this is Bob.'

'Is that all I am to know?' he said, pretending to be wounded.

'Geoff is a farmer and a good friend,' said Ruby. 'He was in the army before returning to the family farm.'

'A soldier, eh? You're not perchance here to visit Bill Huckerby about the Anzac Day celebrations?' he said, tapping his nose.

'How did you know?' said Ruby.

'Oh, just a guess, perhaps more than a guess, really. You don't often come to Binawarra to discuss the university's arrangements, and you never come on weekends.' He looked Geoff up and down again. 'A Vietnam veteran, no doubt. You're not afraid you and your fellow soldiers will cause a disturbance, are you?'

'What do you mean?' said Geoff.

'Oh, nothing,' said Bob, raising his eyebrows and looking away.

'Come on,' said Ruby, 'don't play your stupid games. Tell us if there's going to be trouble.'

'You know, Geoff, that's what I like about our little fascist friend here. No, steady on,' he said, seeing Geoff stiffen. 'I mean it in the nicest possible way. In contrast to some of my weak, dimwitted left-wing colleagues, our Ruby has some gumption. But that's it. I have said enough. I'll be hung by the ankles and have my treasure ritualistically cut away if I am caught betraying the comrades.'

'Don't take any notice, Geoff. He delights in teasing people.'

'Did you know, Geoff,' said Bob, nodding in mock seriousness, 'that our buxom little friend here was once a flower child?'

'Flower child?'

'Don't talk rubbish,' said Ruby, amused despite herself.

'Yes,' said Bob, spurred on by Geoff's bemused expression and Ruby's helpless smile, 'there she was in her gypsy floral skirt, psychedelic top, crocheted beret, sandals and—'

'Stop it, Bob!'

'And free love, and the rest,' he continued, in high amusement at Ruby's growing embarrassment. 'And who could have resisted the sweet teenage face, the long hair ... If you go to San Francisco, be sure to wear some flowers in your hair,' he sang.

'Don't mind him, Geoff,' said Ruby. 'I was in San Francisco in 1969—'

'And such a cute, sweet little teenager with the brightest flowers laced through her hair,' Bob interrupted again.

'I was dressed in the fashion ... I was only nineteen, but none of the rest ...'

'It is the dawning of the Age of Aquarius ... harmony and understanding ...' Bob continued to sing.

'Come on, Geoff,' said Ruby, 'we'll leave Bob to his fun.' She took his arm. 'Bob seems to forget about the Manson murders and what happened in Berkeley that year. That ended the peace and harmony.'

'And whose fault was that?'

'Spare me, Bob. I've heard it all before.'

'Okay. I'm a little bored with it these days, anyhow. But you were such a cute little thing—'

'Do you know Estella Winterbine?' said Ruby.

'Dear girl, what a question. Who doesn't in this town? She's a phenomenon that causes every male thigh in the district to quiver. And have you forgotten: I actually teach at the school she attends?'

'What do you think of her?'

'Think of her? You mean apart from her extraordinary beauty?'

'Yes.'

'What's prompted this question?'

'Nothing ... well, it has been proposed that she come to the university for an orientation visit. One of her teachers has suggested that work in public relations may suit her.'

'Public relations! Who has suggested that?' he said, dropping his simpering manner, but then reflecting, 'Oh, don't tell me. It's that Bicknell woman, isn't it?'

'I understand Miss Bicknell is in charge of career counselling. Do you disagree with her?'

'That girl's destiny is to be a goddess. She doesn't have to open her mouth. She just has to be there—' He stopped and went silent. He stared at the ground in front of him. Ruby and Geoff looked at each other. 'A goddess ... the Age of Aquarius ... so, that's it,' he murmured.

'What's it?' said Ruby.

'Perhaps Edith Bicknell is right,' he said, resuming his effusive manner. 'Come to think of it, the Winterbine girl would probably be suited to public relations work. But Ruby, my darling girl, I don't have time to stand around and gossip, as pleasurable as it always is to see you. Geoff, I salute you. I warn you, though, you'll have a handful with this converted Boudicca of the Right. Cheerio.' He left them as if on some urgent errand.

Curious, Ruby and Geoff watched him hurry to his car and drive off.

'That's an odd character,' said Geoff. 'Not my type.'

'You said it,' said Ruby. 'You couldn't have anybody further from the bloodstained battlefield. I wonder what got into him. But, come on, I'm dying for a cup of tea.' They were seated and waiting for their order a couple of minutes later. 'I wonder what got into him,' Ruby murmured. 'The idea of Estella Winterbine in public relations seemed to set him off.'

'I wouldn't have a clue,' said Geoff. 'His whole manner was odd. How could someone as strange as that hold down a job teaching in a high school?'

'That's a good question,' Ruby laughed. 'But it wouldn't occur to the powers that be. Bob is actually a good teacher. Bill vouches for him, though I see a side of him that Bill doesn't see or doesn't want to see. Bob and I are at opposite ends of the political spectrum. I see him occasionally at the university, where he has a network of like-minded friends. You know, he likes to have a dig at people like me and will not pass up an opportunity.' She shook her head. 'Morally and politically, he is totally unsuitable for teaching impressionable young people.'

The waitress arrived at the table with a pot of tea, cups, saucers, and a plate of pastries.

'He was friendly enough towards you,' said Geoff, after he poured the tea and offered Ruby the pastries.

'He doesn't dislike me. And I don't dislike him. He's different from many lazy left-wing bigots who inhabit the campus and feed on state money. He's kind in his way. He can like a person who differs from him on political and moral matters. You heard him. He doesn't hesitate to criticise people from his side or to say something complimentary about someone like me. I'm sure he means it.'

'Does he? Is he married?'

'Married!' said Ruby. 'Geoff, I wonder about you sometimes. How could anybody who has roamed the jungles of Vietnam ask such a question?'

'Oh,' said Geoff, after a moment.

'Yes, it's "oh",' said Ruby, laughing again.

'What was all that about San Francisco?'

'You know, flower power and all that. He was ribbing me. Don't take any notice,' said Ruby evasively.

'What flower power? I was in the army, remember.'

'Yes, you were, weren't you? You're right to remind me.' She turned to gaze through the window.

Another period of silence followed while they sipped their tea and gazed at the busy crowd walking up and down the pavement. Eventually, Charles Winterbine stopped and peered inside. He waved and headed for the entrance.

'Good morning, Ruby, Geoff. Fr. van Engelen told me you were in Binawarra to see Bill Huckerby and thought you might contact us afterwards. I wanted to say you're very welcome. Please come over to our house when you have finished with Bill. You don't have a fixed arrangement with Bill and Joanne?'

'No, Mr Winterbine,' said Ruby. 'We're here to discuss the Anzac Day march with Bill—at least Geoff is. We would like very much to visit you.'

'Good, I'll call Bill and arrange a time to suit. If you decide to stay the night, please, you are our guests. I've checked the forecast. Tomorrow will be fine and sunny, and not too hot. So Estella can take you on the promised bushwalk. And please call me, Charles.'

Thank you, Charles,' said Ruby, taken aback. 'We do intend to stay over. Are you sure it's all right? We can stay at the local hotel, you know.'

'Yes,' said Geoff. 'We don't want to inconvenience you and Mrs Winterbine.'

'No inconvenience. It's our pleasure. Estella likes you.'

'We're flattered,' said Ruby. 'I like her, too.'

'No need to be flattered,' said Charles, giving the impression he did not quite understand. 'She's a quiet girl. It's not always apparent when she likes somebody. That changes when she gets to know you. She may be a little reticent, too, because of the age difference.'

'Oh, there's no need to worry about that,' reassured Ruby. 'Friendship depends on other factors, doesn't it?'

'It certainly does,' said Charles.

'We would be delighted to accept your invitation,' said Ruby.

'Aine and I look forward to seeing you this afternoon. I'll tell Estella to think about where you can go tomorrow. We'll see you later.'

'We look forward to it,' said Ruby.

GEOFF'S thoughts returned to Estella on the way to the Huckerbys. In the discussions with Ruby, he had discovered more about her. It was not just about her appearance; it was as much about her as a person. He was stupid to think of her as a young woman with a beautiful face, devoid of thought or feeling. It was ridiculous to describe her appearance as 'factory newness.'

His mind passed to the meeting with Bill Huckerby, and he recalled that odd teacher's comment about Vietnam veterans in the Anzac Day march. Was there going to be a demonstration? He had already experienced the rage of anti-war people. Shortly after his arrival back in Australia, a group of university students and unionists had abused and spat on him and some soldier mates. His inclination was to avoid situations where his uniform could provoke the anti-war anger that still appeared. The last thing he wanted was to be part of a march that would rile some people. When he and Ruby sat down with Bill and Joanne, he asked whether there was any strong anti-war feeling in Binawarra.

Bill scoffed at the idea of anti-war demonstrations in Binawarra if that was what was on Geoff's mind. Some people in the town did not agree with the Allies' role in Vietnam, but they were not fanatical about it. People were conscious of the sacrifice of the soldiers who went to fight on behalf of Australia, and they wanted to acknowledge that on Anzac Day. Geoff could rest assured that he and his companions would be welcomed and celebrated. Forget about any demonstrations, he said, waving his hand dismissively.

Geoff mentioned Bob McKinnon's oblique warning. With a snort and another dismissive wave, Bill told him not to worry about Bob McKinnon. He was a good teacher, but he was not to be taken too seriously outside the classroom. Bob's outlandish behaviour was an act to shock and tease people. By coincidence, he had just had him on the phone, warning him that not everything is as it appears and that he should keep alert.

'There was a whole lot of vague stuff about—well, about the students. Do you see?' Bill said. 'I asked whether it was my turn to have my leg pulled. He knew I was a wake-up. So, don't worry about Bob. He's just having a go at you. There'll be no problems on Anzac Day.'

Despite the reassurance, Geoff could not get rid of his uneasiness. Anyhow, he had committed himself and four other Vietnam veterans to the march. He would not go back on his word. Besides, there was no withdrawing without looking weak and foolish. He would not do that to his mates. After he and Bill had completed the arrangements, he could not help greeting Bill's satisfied expression with a doubtful smile that passed Bill by. When he and Ruby were preparing to go to the Winterbine's after lunch, Joanne remarked that it was a tribute to them that they had been invited to stay. 'Charles and Aine are not at all proud, but they are particular about their friends, especially when it concerns Estella.'

'It's all got to do with Ruby,' said Geoff.

'Yes, I like her,' said Ruby. 'There is something direct about her that you don't meet so often. I like honest souls. I'm just so surprised an exquisite creature like that likes dumpy little me.'

'Oh, don't be so hard on yourself, you silly girl,' said Joanne. 'We all have to admit that Estella is something out of the ordinary. Besides, you're an attractive young woman. I don't have the impression you're without your admirers.'

'Well, that's while the youthfulness lasts,' she laughed. 'What if that passes me by and I have not landed a catch? What will happen when all my feminine charms desert me, and I'm a wrinkly old woman?'

Joanne and Bill laughed, telling her not to be so melodramatic. Geoff smiled weakly. Not long after, as he and Ruby approached the Winterbine house, Ruby began fidgeting.

'You see what someone's appearance can do?' she quipped when she saw Geoff's curious glance. 'Such girls can reduce you to hand-wringing awe. Come on, Ruby girl, control yourself.' She forced herself to laugh. 'Don't you feel a little unnerved by her? Not just a little?'

'No,' said Geoff, as he parked the car. 'I feel shy and uncomfortable in most company. I'm no more affected by Estella Winterbine than by others.'

'You're incredible, Geoffrey Shawcross!' exclaimed Ruby. 'I thought I had you worked out.'

Geoff did not reply. He had already explained. On reflection, though, Estella did arouse feelings of protection in him. Her appearance, or more exactly the way of her appearance, gave her a vulnerable aspect that made a claim on him. He would not express it that way publicly. He was observant enough to know how ridiculous such thoughts could sound. Ruby remained seated, staring at the front of the house. Then Aine Winterbine appeared from behind the plants and vines on the verandah and waved. Ruby responded, and all uneasiness disappeared. 'Look,' she whispered, 'she looks like a Northern European princess, dressed in that long summer dress and her hair loosely tied behind her.'

AFTER depositing their bags on the verandah, they followed Aine to the workshop, where Charles greeted them warmly. He had a few tasks still to complete, but would be with them in a while. Aine could show them around the gardens in the meantime. They're worth seeing. Estella was responsible for a great deal of it, he added. She had a mind for garden design. They left Charles to his work and made their way to the back of the house. Their eyes widened in surprise. The Winterbine house was on several acres of land that ran down a rolling incline towards the creek, not far beyond the border of their property. Along the border on all sides were trees of various sorts, both European and Australian. An acre or so of the land had been set aside as a garden. A dry-stone wall enclosed the garden on each side. Between the wall and the property borders, the untouched ground was grassy and uneven, with rocks and boulders of varying sizes scattered about. There was an orchard behind the garden. Dispersed throughout the whole were several imposing eucalypts. A weaving pattern of gardens, thick with a mixture of flowers, shrubs, and small trees, spread out in front of them.

Aine led them on through the maze, stopping here and there to point out flowers or shrubs that were not common. Estella had several books on old-fashioned colonial plants and had tried planting quite a number. She was mostly successful. They loved working in the garden, and although Charles did most of the heavy digging and landscaping, Estella chose the plants and shrubs and the pattern of the paths. They arrived on an open lawn. In its centre was a broad archway about ten feet long with a climbing rose bush lacing the metal framework. Under the archway lay gleaming white gravel, and on either side stood two white stone benches. The climbing rose grew so vigorously that its branches, green leaves, and blooms cosily enclosed the stone benches and the white gravel space between them.

'How romantic!' exclaimed Ruby as she walked under the archway and sat on one of the stone benches. She peered about her. 'It would never have entered my head ... and you, Geoff?'

Geoff sat on the bench next to her. 'I don't know ... It's well planned and well organised. My mother would love this.'

'Does your mother attend the garden at the farm?' Aine inquired.

'Not anymore,' said Geoff. 'My grandfather bought a house in St Arnaud a long time ago. It was for the family to stay overnight, enjoy social occasions, and avoid making the trip back to the farm. My father never got rid of it, even when the roads and transport became easy. After he died, my mother moved to town. She said she couldn't bear to live on the farm without my father. The farm is left to me; unfortunately, I don't have the same way with gardens and flowers. It's okay, just not as good as my mother used to keep it. There is a small garden at the house in town, but she cannot walk very well. A gardener looks after it.'

'I didn't know that,' said Ruby.

'I suppose the subject has never come up.'

'I'm sorry to hear your mother is not mobile,' said Aine. 'That would be a big loss if you liked gardening.'

'Yes, it is,' said Geoff. 'She really feels it sometimes. She was always active.'

Ruby walked from under the archway, plucking a pink rose bloom. Aine and Geoff followed her. They stood in the open green space, looking around at the gardens.

'It's beautiful,' said Ruby. 'I've not seen anything quite like it. You have definitely outdone the Huckerbys. You must spend hours on it.'

'We do spend a lot of time in the garden, the three of us,' said Aine, 'but Estella comes into the garden almost every day. She gets lost here.'

'I can imagine,' said Ruby, in awe of the surroundings. 'What do you think of it, Geoff?'

'I agree. It's impressive. A lot of hard work has gone into it.'

Ruby frowned but did not reply. Aine led them into the path through the gardens. Before long, they were enveloped in waves of cascading flowers and shrubs washing over the pathway here and there. The further they advanced, the thicker it became. Without warning, they emerged at a dry-stone wall with several gaps through which they passed, to be confronted by a line of chestnut trees that appeared to stand guard over the space beyond. They walked past the line of chestnut trees and came out onto an open area hemmed in by apple trees on either side.

The open space was a vegetable garden, its plots divided by two long paths that formed a cross. The four sections of the cross were separated by curving paths that, together, traced three concentric circles throughout the whole. The plots were full of lushly growing vegetables. At the end of the garden was a hedge. In the centre of the hedge was a white shelter. On the bench under the shelter sat Estella, holding a hoe and looking dreamily at the garden plot in front of her. On her head, casting a shadow around her eyes, was a wide-brimmed straw hat with a red band. She wore a red short-sleeve blouse and khaki trousers. On her feet were short gumboots.

Ruby and Geoff stood in silence, looking at her. Ruby turned to Geoff, fixing her gaze on him. Impressed as Geoff was with the vision of Estella framed within that gleaming white shelter, he was as much impressed with her work. It had never entered his head that a girl like Estella could not only be interested in gardening but also undertake the extensive work needed to complete all he had seen. Aine roused them from their trance-like state and, beckoning, led them up the middle path that formed the upright of the cross. Estella did not look up until they were close by. Her first reaction was surprise, and then, smiling shyly, she got to her feet.

'Estella, we had no idea you were such a fantastic gardener,' exclaimed Ruby. 'It's beautiful. How have you managed? I'm surprised Bill has said nothing about this. Have you considered doing this for a living?'

'Not really,' said Estella, hesitating, 'or perhaps a little.'

'Mrs Winterbine, have you thought about this sort of work for Estella?'

'Yes, Charles and I have talked about it, but for now, we are leaving it to Estella to ponder. We are following Uncle Bill's advice. It would not harm to investigate other choices. We are inclined to agree. But please call me Aine.'

'I suppose it's wise to consider all reasonable options,' said Ruby. 'But when I see this—' She waved her hand around her. 'Aine, if she's enjoying such work and is good at it, she should go for it. There are courses in gardening and landscaping. What do you think, Estella?'

'I don't know,' she said. 'I've always enjoyed gardening. I began helping Mamma and Daddy when I was very young. Everything developed from there. Mamma gave me a patch of ground to work on, and it got bigger and bigger. Then I started to read about gardening and landscaping.'

'That's right,' said Aine. 'That's the way it happened. It all developed naturally. We didn't encourage or discourage her.'

'Really? Forget about public relations, then,' Ruby said. 'Well, that's my opinion, anyhow,' she added hastily.

'We value your opinion, of course.'

'There are courses in horticulture and landscaping at the technical college linked to Sandhurst University,' Ruby continued. 'When you come to stay with me, we can have a look there, too. What do you think?'

'A course in horticulture is far more appealing than public relations, I have to admit,' said Estella. What did Geoff think as he stood there saying nothing? She glanced at him now and then but could not see whether he was committing himself one way or the other. She wanted to ask his opinion but did not dare.

Aine left her to show Ruby and Geoff around until afternoon tea and returned to the house. Estella took them on a tour of the vegetable garden and orchard, which, with its plum, orange, apple, and peach trees, ran to the lower border of the property where they could make out the creek. Ruby continued to pepper Estella with questions. All the while, Geoff remained silent. He seemed to be regarding everything with patience but without enough interest to say something. Estella wished he would say something. Only Ruby seemed to raise his interest.

WHILE Aine and Estella cleared up following afternoon tea, Charles showed Ruby and Geoff around the house. They admired the finish of the homestead-style house's woodwork with its matching furniture and décor, but showed restraint at so many religious objects. They returned to the verandah, where Geoff asked about the layout of their property. Charles was delighted to answer Geoff's questions, and very soon, the conversation was restricted to the two men. Aine excused herself and disappeared inside.

'Will you excuse me, too?' Estella whispered to Ruby, 'I would like to change.'

'Of course, girl, don't mind us. Just go about your business. I have to unpack my clothes, too. So I'll go with you.'

When the two young women rose, Charles and Geoff stopped talking while they moved towards the front door. Once in the hall, Ruby commented that she was not often treated with such politeness. It was a pleasant change. She could live with it. Estella said that good manners were important to her parents. Good manners were a part of being a good person. It was a constant demonstration of charity, the most important virtue.

'From anybody else, such comments would sound unbearably pompous,' said Ruby, smiling.

'Why? What do you mean?'

Ruby, without thinking, had followed Estella into her bedroom. She was about to answer Estella's question when she saw the shrine. Her mouth dropped open.

'It's my shrine to the Blessed Virgin,' said Estella.

'Is it?'

'I have a devotion to Our Lady.'

'Do you?' said Ruby, still staring.

Estella nodded, ready for more questions. Ruby took a closer look at the small statue on the varnished wooden shelf and the vases with their fresh flowers.

'I have never had much to do with religion,' she said. 'My parents were strict about their moral principles and good manners, but they never had any religious affiliation. And, I might add, they rarely criticised religion or the churches. Any criticism they had was aimed at the people responsible for wrongdoing. Individuals were independent moral agents. They didn't follow the present trend of blaming everything except human wrongdoing. That's what I was exposed to growing up, and I suppose it accounts for my moral and political views. I mean, my parents taught me lessons I agree with. What I am saying, Estella,' she pointed at the shrine, 'this is new to me. I know Catholic churches have this sort of thing, but I have never been so close to it.'

'Do you want me to explain?'

'No ... no, not now, let me think about it first,' Ruby said, looking around the room. 'May I look at the books?'

'Of course,' said Estella, sitting on the edge of her bed.

'All Jane Austen's novels, a good selection of Dickens, the Bronte sisters, and Thackeray. 'Oh, and here's *The Lord of the Rings*! What are your favourites?'

'*The Lord of the Rings* and Jane Austen's novels,' said Estella.

'Which of Jane Austen's books do you like best?'

'*Persuasion.*'

'Really? That's not the most popular. Usually, it's *Pride and Prejudice* followed by *Emma*.'

'I like them all, but *Persuasion* is my favourite, followed by *Pride and Prejudice*,' said Estella, pleased, at last, to be talking to someone familiar with the sort of books she liked.

'Why do you like *Persuasion*?'

'Because of the purity and selflessness of Anne Elliot's love for Captain Wentworth.'

'That kind of long-suffering devotion is not valued much these days.'

'Isn't it?'

'No.' Ruby looked around the neat, tidy, and well-organised room. 'You're a surprise packet,' she said, tapping Estella on the shoulder as she walked over to the half-opened window. She noticed the book lying on the bedside table beside her rosary. 'What's this?'

'It's a book about St Maria Goretti.'

'Who's that?'

'She was an eleven-year-old girl, stabbed to death for resisting the advances of a neighbour.'

'That's putting a high price on one's virtue,' said Ruby, turning the book around in her hands.

'The Church says that's behaving with heroic virtue. That's why she was made a saint.'

'Most people today would call that heroic madness. It's just physical, they would say. Unpleasant, but you get over it. Not worth dying for.'

'Would you let just anyone touch you?'

'No. Yuck! Never! I'm very particular. Even more so these—' She did not finish the thought.

'But why, if it is all just physical?'

'Yes, of course, you make the right point,' said Ruby, with her eyes on the book's cover. 'But is it worth resisting unto death?'

'It's the virtue and goodness in the integrity of the body that is being protected. We are made up of a body and a soul. Our body is the temple of the Holy Spirit. Fr. van Engelen explained it all during Mass one Sunday. We have an example in Our Lord—resistance to evil to the point of death.'

Ruby put the book down. 'You know, I'm inclined to agree with you,' she said. 'There is some link between the physical, the moral, and the a-ffections. I don't know what it is, and at this point, I can't grasp all that justification that comes from religion.' She stopped and fidgeted. 'I should let you have your shower. I'm sure we'll talk about it again.' She walked to the door. 'You've never had a boyfriend, have you?'

'No, I've never met anyone I could like that much.' She flushed at what was now probably a lie and looked away.

'Amazing. You may see things differently when you do,' said Ruby, not noticing Estella's sudden unease.

Estella watched the door shut and reflected on her growing friendship with Ruby. She had not known her for very long, but it seemed long. Ruby's unconscious way of patting her on the arm or shoulder as a big sister would do was endearing. It was comforting. It was a gesture of solidarity. Her familiar, generous, sympathetic way of listening was just as endearing and comforting. She was seven or eight years older and successful in her work, but she did not for one moment hold it over her. It was not just politeness, either. Estella was sure she liked her, and she wondered why. Perhaps she should not wonder too much, she told herself. She should be grateful that Ruby was compensating for her disappointment with Jenny. For the moment, anyhow. Perhaps it was temporary. She did not want to think about it. She gathered her clean clothes and headed to the bathroom. What motivated Geoff to become a soldier? Did she really like him?

GEOFF and Charles continued chatting on the verandah when Estella and Ruby went to attend to their different tasks.

'Do you mind if I have another look around your back garden?' said Geoff during a lull in the conversation. 'I'm so impressed.'

'Of course, Geoff, I'll come with you.'

As they wandered through the gardens, Charles explained how and why he had laid the garden's borders where they now were. It was not evident at that stage, though, that his daughter would play a vital role in developing the gardens. To his delight, she showed in time that she had a good feel for garden design. He pointed to the pattern of the paths through the garden plots. She gave them a purpose: this path had to wind here and there in a friendly way, with warm, friendly plants on either side; that path had to have a predominance of native plants, giving it an air of mystery; other parts had to reflect a fairytale atmosphere. After reading her novels, she wanted romantic scenes in which lovers could meet in secret to declare their undying love.

'She is such a soft romantic, my daughter,' Charles said, 'but in an innocent way. The archway over there with the pink climbing rose was designed from a picture she had in her mind of two young lovers sitting beside each other with hands held.' He turned to Geoff, smiling. 'It's true. I did all the heavy work in the early days. As she got older, she took over a lot of the digging. I still lift heavy objects like rocks, large pots, and so on. She does what she can. She comes to me if anything is too heavy. You know, Geoff, you might not think it, but she's quite strong for a young woman. And she's not afraid of hard work.'

'I see what you mean,' said Geoff, whose admiration for the garden and its layout increased as he followed Charles.

They came to the left-hand border, stopping at the dry-stone wall. The grassy open space was just visible, with the archway covered by the climbing rose in its middle. Geoff looked over the wall. The rough rolling grassy terrain contrasted sharply with the well-organised gardens behind him, and it seemed all the more untamed because of it. He then followed Charles to the vegetable garden, whose design was also Estella's doing, Charles wanted to point out. The cross was deliberate. It was a tribute in nature to God. The concentric circles expressed the infinity of God and His love, and His wisdom.

Geoff had never heard such things. His upbringing was, in many respects, like Ruby's. His parents had not been religious, but they had been insistent on the sort of moral principles the Winterbine's religion dictated. It was interesting, even fascinating, to hear how the grounding in religious belief expressed itself in the symbols of nature. At length, Charles excused himself. Geoff was happy to go on alone. He walked around the plots admiring the lushness of the plants. He passed around the hedge and walked the full length of the orchard before he retraced his steps. After passing the chestnut trees and the dry-stone wall, he headed to his left to follow the path he could make out between some native shrubs.

The pathway wound out from the stone wall between shrubs and ornamental trees whose slender leafy branches hung from either side, forming a light-flickering archway. Then it swung back, widening to end in a clearing. There, erected on the wall, was a little stone grotto. Geoff stopped. A small statue stood on a ledge in the upper part of the grotto. He examined it, deciding it was Estella's work. It bore her mark. Why, he did not know. He walked on, lost in his thoughts, until he came out onto the grassy space with its archway of climbing pink roses.

He walked under the archway, feeling the white gravel crunch under his feet, and sat on one of the white stone benches. Nothing about the work was haphazard or careless. Everything was done with much care. How did Estella have the time and energy to do all this? Even considering that her parents worked with her, it was pretty incredible. He had wanted to ask such questions when he was following Estella and Ruby, but every time he was on the point of saying something, his tongue would not work. He saw Estella glancing at him occasionally, but thought she was checking that he was following. He heard the slight scuffing of feet on the path leading from the house and turned to see Estella approaching. She was looking at him with neither a smile nor a frown.

He stood up as she came under the archway. She wore a long, cream, loose-fitting dress, the style her mother wore, and her hair fell loosely around her shoulders. She wore leather sandals on the slim, tanned feet that appeared from under her dress with each step. Ruby was right, he had to admit. There was something almost unearthly about the girl's appearance. She stood next to the stone bench opposite Geoff and focused her clear hazel eyes on him. He did not know what to say. The teenager's unexpected appearance left him tongue-tied.

'Daddy asked me to come and fetch you,' she said. 'Ruby is helping Mamma in the kitchen.'

'Oh,' was all Geoff could say.

'Do you like the garden?'

'Yes, very much,' he said. He must make an effort to say something sensible. 'You've done a lot of work here.'

'I enjoy it. It doesn't seem like work.'

'Nevertheless, I can see how much effort is needed to establish something like this. I have a farm ... I know what is involved.'

'Thank you,' said Estella, sitting down. 'Daddy and Mamma do a lot of the work, too.'

Geoff sat on the bench across from her and waited for her to continue.

'Would your mother like it?'

'My mother?'

'Yes, you said to Mamma that she liked gardening.'

'Yes, I did. Yes, she'd be in as much awe as I am.'

Estella smiled modestly and looked at the ground in front of her, giving Geoff the best indication so far of what she was thinking and feeling.

'You have an enormous variety of plants here. Where do you get them from? Is there a big nursery here in Binawarra?'

'There is a nursery, but it's not very big. I receive plants from different people. Uncle Bill and Auntie Joanne let me have anything I like in their garden. I have a lot of books about plants and plant cultivation. When I see something I like, and nobody has it to spare, and Daddy allows it, I ask them at the nursery to order it. They do that usually. Sometimes it takes a while for the seeds or plant to arrive, but I have the time. One must be patient about these things.'

'Yes, nature won't be hurried, will it?' he said and was rewarded with an unaffected smile.

'No, it won't. That's one of the things I like about gardening. One sees the orderly workings of nature.'

'Plants are more predictable than people, aren't they?' Geoff found himself saying.

Whether that comment or some other unrelated thought brought the change in Estella's expression, Geoff could not know. She rose.

'They will be waiting for us,' she said as she walked from under the archway with a slight nod towards the house.

Geoff followed as she walked on. He was not too perturbed about the sudden end to the conversation. There could have been any number of explanations. Her shyness was one. He should not forget how different they were: she a beautiful young girl with the world before her, and he a rather plain, unexciting returned soldier who was now a farmer. He should be happy she was friendly towards him.

Chapter 12

Miss Barker and Fr van Engelen

AT AROUND 11 o'clock on the previous Friday evening, when the streets of Middelburg's town centre were deserted, Anneke van Engelen set out from her friend's place on Kinderdijk to cycle home. Intent on getting home as soon as she could, she rode briskly along the canal ignoring the lights prettily reflected in the dark, glassy water, crossed over Spijker Bridge and continued along Dwarskaai to Damplein. She was on the point of passing the former German commandant's quarters when two darkly clad cyclists appeared on either side of her. They had woollen beanies pulled down to their eyes and folds of scarves covering their mouths. One brushed against her.

'Careful!' she cried, her bike wobbling. The other bumped her. 'Hey, what are you doing?' Her right foot scraped along the rough paving to prevent herself from falling. She came to a stop. 'I will call the police,' she said to scare them off, but knew it was an empty threat.

The two men stopped beside her. 'It's your fault, you little tart,' said a rasping male voice. 'That's what happens when you get in the way. Watch what you're doing, or you'll fall and scar your pretty face. That wouldn't do your modelling any good, would it?' He pushed his hand inside the opening of her coat and pinched her breast. She let out a muffled scream and grabbed at the man's hand. He brushed her off, laughing. The other figure wrenched the bag from her shoulder, rode a few yards further on and emptied its contents in the gutter while his companion sniggered. The empty bag and its contents were kicked around, and then both men rode across the square, disappearing into Molstraat.

Anneke, shaking, watched them go. She heard the faint sound of the bike tyres on the paved road and then silence. There followed the opening and shutting of car doors and the soft revving of a car engine. The whir of a highly tuned engine faded into the cold night air. She looked around. Was it possible that nobody had heard or seen what happened? There were lights on in the vicinity. No one had ever treated her like that, not even in Amsterdam. She felt sick and humiliated. She took out her handkerchief and dabbed her eyes, trying to compose herself. She picked up the contents of her bag, her tears falling on the road pavers. When she had stuffed everything back in her bag and checked to see nothing was lying in the gutter, she mounted her bike and rode off, taking the most open and protected streets through the town centre to her parents' house on Seissingel. There could be no doubt that the assault was connected to her father's inquiries and her efforts to contact Gerda at her London office. It was a warning, typical of Gerda.

THE FOLLOWING morning, while Ruby and Geoff were racing across country towards Binawarra, Father van Engelen was settling down in the front parlour to read his Divine Office. No sooner had he opened his breviary than the phone rang. He picked up the receiver to hear the operator announce a call from the Netherlands.

'Frans, is that you?' he said before the voice on the other end said anything.

'Yes, Jos, it's me. You'll have to tell me more about Gerda van den Donker and her delightful father. It's getting a bit rough here.'

'Rough?' Frans related the incident with Anneke. 'Good Lord! Is she all right?'

'Yes, there's no physical hurt, but she's still in shock, more from the humiliation than anything. She's sitting with Marijke and me in the lounge room. I'm sorry, Jos, you must fill me in. It looks like the incident has resulted from our inquiries, discreet as they were.'

'Give me the details.'

Frans had already posted a letter describing what had followed his inquiries about Cees van den Donker and his daughter. Jos should read the letter and then get back to him. In the meantime, the main points were that Cees became belligerent when he learned he had been asking about him; that Anneke found out that Gerda was parading as Gerda Vrouwendijk, head of an institute associated with Thames University called The Institute for the Rights of Regional Dialects and Language Custom; and that Anneke was assaulted the next night. It was too much of a coincidence.

'You're probably right. Anneke must be careful from now on.'

'I've told her. She knows the sort of person Meneer van den Donker is. She's a sensible girl.'

'Good,' said the priest. 'But that organisation, you said, The Institute for the Rights of Regional Dialects and Language Custom?'

'Yes, what sort of an organisation is that?'

'What sort of an organisation? Yes, that's a pertinent question,' Fr. van Engelen said. His mind was racing, trying to make connections with what he already knew. Was there a link with the quotation from Rousseau? What on earth was Gerda van den Donker doing in Binawarra in the guise of a teacher of English with counselling qualifications, and at the same time functioning as the head of a London language institute that promoted the rights of dialects? And what did it mean for Estella Winterbine, in whom she seemed to have more than a passing interest? It was bewildering.

'Jos, don't drift off on me now,' pleaded his brother. 'This silence is costing money.'

'I'm sorry, Frans,' said the priest, reflecting. 'Look, I don't want you or Anneke to do anything more about Cees van den Donker and his daughter. No more questions. I urge Anneke to report the assault to the Middelburg police, mentioning no connection with the father and daughter. We should assume the assault and Anneke's inquiries are connected. Making it known that you have reported the assault will put the Van den Donkers on their guard, make them more careful about using violence, and not mentioning them will take the attention away from you. I'll write a letter explaining everything, at least as much as I know. Please be careful. The more I find out about this business, the more sinister and stranger it becomes.'

'What business?'

'No, Frans, wait until you get the letter. Be patient.'

'Yes, big brother.'

'You said Anneke spoke to Truus van den Donker? Did she tell you how she was?'

'Anneke, Fr. Jos is asking how Mevrouw van den Donker was,' the priest heard his brother say.

'Yes, hello, Uncle Jos ... Father. Mevrouw van den Donker was very agitated and fearful of her husband. I could've got more information out of her about Gerda, but she was evidently afraid her husband would catch her talking to me.'

'That's sad. Are you all right?'

'Yes, I'm okay now. It was a bit of a shock, but I'll deal with it and be more careful. I won't let them scare me.'

'Be careful. I don't exactly know what all this is about. I'm sorry that you've become involved.'

'I'll be careful, Uncle Jos, I promise.'

'Good.'

'Mevrouw van den Donker looks well for her age, feminine and healthy looking, but her eyes and expression reveal a sad person. She asked after you.'

'What did you tell her?'

'That you had been severely injured and were left a cripple. She knew that already because Pappa had told her. He spoke to her at the market.'

'Your father spoke to her, too?'

'Yes. She told me what happened at the end of the war, that you saved the lives of her and Gerda and that Meneer van den Donker has forbidden her to talk about it. Gerda doesn't know.'

'She told you all about that?'

'Yes, and I told her you were in Australia.'

'Did you say where?'

'No, I didn't know.'

'That's good.'

'Why? And why is she asking after you?'

'I suppose because she sympathises with me,' he said, noting Anneke's curiosity. 'She knows about my injuries from New Guinea.'

'Yes, Pappa reminded me.'

'There is a story to tell, but it's confidential. One day, I will tell you. I don't want to speak about it now because of her husband. She is interested in our Catholic faith. Prayers are what she needs.'

'Yes, Father, I will say prayers for her.'

'Please do not tell her where I am in Australia. Her husband could cause a lot of trouble. It's not too much to say that he hates the Catholic Church. Ask your father to tell you about that part of the story, including the clash at the Abbey. You know so much now. You might as well know the rest of it. It is better if she makes her inquiries through a neutral source. Pray that the Holy Spirit will lead her in that direction.'

He hung up and began turning the events over in his mind. At length, he went to the phone and dialled. 'Good morning, Miss Barker, are you free?'

'This is a surprise, Father,' said Miss Barker. 'Yes, I am free.'

'Bill told me about your—'

'Excuse me, Father,' she interrupted, 'would you mind hanging on a moment. I'm sorry.'

'That's quite all right, Miss Barker.' He waited a minute or so.

'I'm sorry, Father, something has come up,' said Miss Barker, coming back on the line. 'Can I speak to you later? Give me an hour.'

'Of course, Miss Barker.'

The line went dead. Miss Barker was known for her abruptness. This was the first time he had experienced it. It was odd. He prepared to wait until she rang back. He picked up his breviary but could not concentrate. The one question kept on recurring: if Gerda van den Donker was in Binawarra pursuing a political agenda, then what had Estella Winterbine to do with it? Her connection with regional dialects was too tenuous to make any sense. It was most baffling. Sometime later, he decided to sit in the park. Perhaps the fresh air would precipitate some enlightenment.

He had been sitting on his bench, lost in his thoughts, when Ruby appeared with the Vietnam veteran. Her warm greeting and the respect she showed him, using his clerical title, were the qualities that had prompted him to ask whether she was Catholic. He was embarrassed when she laughed and said no. It was rather presumptuous of him to ask such a question. He watched them walk off, pleased that they were making friends with Estella. A few minutes later, Charles hailed him from the presbytery. He signalled he was leaving Father's washing at the front door. When he joined the priest and learned of Ruby and Geoff's plans to stay overnight in Binawarra, he was off to find them. Another minute had hardly passed when Miss Barker arrived from across the other side of the square, carrying shopping bags.

'Good morning, Father,' she said. 'I'm sorry to have ended your phone call so hurriedly. May I sit down?'

'Of course, Miss Barker.'

'Father, as I talk to you, I want to give the impression we are having a friendly conversation. That may sound a little mysterious, but let me explain. You were going to say you had spoken to Bill Huckerby about something.'

'That's right.'

'That was the first time you had ever called me. In fact, we've never exchanged more than a few polite greetings, have we?' The priest nodded. 'I figured that it was something important. My mind made a connection with Miss Bicknell because I had expressed rather strong opinions about her to Bill. I suspected you wanted to talk about this. Am I right?'

'You are right, Miss Barker. That is a reasonable deduction.'

'It's as much about being alert.'

'Few of us are that alert.'

'That may be so, but if I was right, I did not want to discuss it on the phone. There is always the possibility of someone listening.'

'Someone listening? Who would want to listen to this old priest? Who is in a position to listen?'

'You'd be surprised.'

'Perhaps I would. I'll leave it to your judgment, then.'

'Before we talk, I would like to ask you to keep our discussions confidential. If need be, we will meet here so that no one thinks we are having more than a casual conversation. Agreed?'

'It's a bit cloak-and-dagger, but yes, I agree.'

'Good. Now, what did you want to say?'

'Bill told me you had the impression that Miss Bicknell was here in Binawarra with an agenda. Do you have any idea what that agenda is?'

'No, or only in the most general terms. I'm basing that on her comments during the first school assembly when she quoted from the first page of

Rousseau's *Social Contract*. That might seem like little to go on. However, it wasn't just the quotation. There was an aggressive tone attached to it. That's not to mention her comments before and after it. It rang a bell with me. It seemed to presuppose an agenda.'

'Well, I can confirm that the right bell was ringing because I have information consistent with your impression. To begin with, Miss Bicknell is not this lady's real name, and her nationality is not Australian.'

'Should I be surprised?' said Miss Barker, pursing her lips. 'You're going to tell me she's Dutch, I suppose.'

'Yes. But remember, most of what I can tell you is known only to a few people.'

He began from the beginning, from his rescuing Truus and her daughter, right through to Frans's phone call that morning. He also mentioned Miss Bicknell's interview with Estella.

'You've given me a lot to think about, Father,' she said when he had finished. 'Edith Bicknell is in Binawarra for a purpose that is somehow connected with Estella Winterbine. The mildly sounding Institute for the Rights of Regional Dialects and Language Custom is likely something more radical beneath the surface. What that could be, is anyone's guess. It may have to do with language protection; it may not. That's all the more reason for us to keep this to ourselves. I want time to think about it. We've spent enough time together, anyhow. She glanced around at the growing number of people walking through the park and around the shops. I'll see you here whenever we need to make contact. All right?'

'Yes, of course, Miss Barker.'

'There's something else you're not aware of. A foreign man, Boris Rostowski, visits Binawarra on business. He represents an importer of Middle Eastern wares. Do you know who I mean?'

'Not really,'

'He's a large, solid man, dark hair with a well-cultivated moustache.'

'Oh, yes, I do now. I have seen him coming out of the office of *The Binawarra and District Mail*.'

'He is linked to Edith Bicknell or Gerda whatshername,' said Miss Barker. 'They are very careful to keep the link secret.'

'Van-den-Donker. But how do you know they are connected?'

'Observation. The man seems to be some sort of support. He is tracking Estella. Not in a threatening way. She has said he is friendly. He seems to be keeping an eye on her. The question is why?'

'I saw this same man shadowing three men on the square last Saturday night,' said Fr. van Engelen. 'One of the men was the Dawson boy. I could not see who the others were. One drove a white utility. He had dropped off a girl at the end of Melbourne Road before he met up with the other two.'

'Stephen Calder, no doubt,' said Miss Barker. 'There's someone who doesn't make much effort to hide his activities. But why is Rostowski shadowing Calder and Dawson?' She had gathered her bags and was standing.

'Just one last thing, Miss Barker,' said the priest. 'The name that Gerda van den Donker has assumed as head of her institute—Vrouwendijk—it means in English "women's dyke."'

'That's interesting, but not surprising. Good morning, Father.'

FR. VAN Engelen pondered over Miss Barker and her interest in Gerda van den Donker as he returned to the presbytery. What motivated her interest? What facts about her were presupposed by that interest? How and why did she see an agenda in Gerda's speech to the students? It was not the mere fact that Gerda had quoted a passage from Rousseau's *Social Contract*. There must be something more. He had long suspected there was more to Miss Barker than the picture of the cantankerous, demanding woman that she seemed at pains to project. And then, nobody knew much about her, not even Bill Huckerby, who astonished everyone by getting on with her and apparently keeping her in check. Or was that part of it: letting Bill think he was keeping her in check?

Everyone in Binawarra had a distinct idea about Miss Barker, and it was the same idea. Did that suit Miss Barker in a life that was not quite what everyone thought? And that preoccupation with security, did she have a good reason, or was it a part of the act? Whatever the case, he had confidence in her. He hoped that she would find out what Gerda van den Donker's purpose was and whether there was any threat to Estella and her family. Back in his front parlour, he eased himself into the lounge chair and took up his breviary. But Estella's safety remained in his head, distracting him. Some minutes elapsed before he struggled to his feet and reached for the phone.

'Miss Barker, has Bill Huckerby spoken to you about the veterans' celebrations for Anzac Day?' he said quickly to avoid the possibility of her putting the phone down without hearing what he had to say.

'Only briefly,' she said. 'I'm never involved in the plans. That's Bill's particular interest. Why do you ask?'

'You do know that he intends to have some Vietnam veterans for the march?'

'Yes, and a good thing, too. It's about time they received their due.'

'One of the Vietnam veterans and his girlfriend have struck up a friendship with Estella?'

'That must be a recent development.'

'Yes, very recent. The girlfriend, Ruby Waiting, is with Sandhurst University and has regular contact with Bill. Ruby and her boyfriend met the Winterbines at Bill's place. It seems Aine and Charles like the couple and are happy for the friendship to develop. The soldier is an impressive young man.'

'Well, Father, you have the jump on me this time. I will tick Aine and Charles off for not keeping me up to date with their goings-on.'

'Geoff Shawcross, the young man, was a commando in the army. It seems he was specially trained for the war in Vietnam.'

'That's interesting. It will be a remarkable coup for Bill if he can get an SAS soldier to take part in the march.'

'I suppose it would,' said the priest. 'Anyhow, you might be interested in the latest about a family we both have much affection for. One more thing: the young couple is staying with the Winterbines this weekend.'

'What are their names again?'

'Ruby Waiting and Geoff Shawcross.'

Miss Barker thanked the priest and, without more ado, rang off. The priest resumed his seat satisfied he had provided useful information. Five minutes later, the phone rang. No doubt Miss Barker with a follow-up question, he thought, picking up the phone.

'Goedemorgen, Father,' said a formal voice, 'Fr. de Jonge here. I want a final word with you about introducing the New Mass, the *Novus Ordo Missae*, into your parish. The time has come, and it will not be put off. Your priestly brothers have been patient long enough.'

This was the call that Fr. van Engelen had been expecting from the Oceania Provincial of the Wounded Heart of Jesus. He had been in a struggle with Fr. Hans de Jonge's ideas of liturgical reform long before he had risen to the position of District Provincial. Indeed, it was not only liturgical reform that they had clashed over. His resistance to the order's introduction of the New Mass was, however, the issue that brought the conflict to a head. Fr. van Engelen's objections were not against the legitimate decision of the Pope to introduce a new form of Mass in the vernacular. It was the order's free-wheeling ideas of liturgical reform to which he objected. The illicit inclusion of liturgical dance and mime in the New Mass was only the worst of it. He could not in conscience go along with it.

He had suffered a series of disciplinary measures, the last of which resulted in his banishment to the tiny parish of Binawarra. This last action backfired. When the news slowly spread around the district that Fr. van Engelen said the old Tridentine Mass, the Latin Mass, the church filled on Sundays. His superiors were not at all pleased. They reminded Fr. van Engelen that he was permitted to say the Old Mass in private and for those old people set in their ways. His continued stubbornness was outright disobedience. They threatened intervention. Fr. van Engelen's reply was to raise the stakes.

An Instruction issued by the Vatican, 5 September 1970 (*Third Instruction on the Correct Implementation of the Constitution on the Sacred Liturgy*) made it clear he was not the only one questioning the direction some parishes were taking with the new Mass. He sent a copy of the Instruction to Fr de Jonge, underlining the passage where the Pope warned those who 'acting on private initiative, arrived at hasty and sometimes unwise solutions, and made changes, additions or simplifications which at times went against the basic principles of the liturgy. This only troubled the faithful and impeded or made more difficult the progress of genuine renewal.'

The provincial's reply to this 'open act of rebellion' was swift, dismissive, and threatening. Fr. van Engelen was not only breaking his vow of obedience but also arrogating to himself authority that was not his. The implementation of the Council's decrees required specialist understanding and recognised competence. Father had neither, as he must know. The interpretation of the Council's documents was the task of those who did—those with privileged knowledge. Left in the hands of the unqualified and those beset by fear of change, the documents would not be given the chance to fulfil their prophetic task. Father's most recent communication led members of the order to think that his medical condition, resulting from the assault in New Guinea, affected his judgment. Perhaps it was time for Father to undergo a medical examination to see if anything could be done to help him overcome the problems that he created for himself and his priestly brothers. In the meantime, the provincial required a program for the introduction of the New Mass, as set out by the order's liturgical committee. It would be considered a healthy sign of a willingness to cooperate if Father, at the same time, provided a sketch of a series of sermons that were consistent with the liturgical committee's views on the New Liturgy.

Fr. van Engelen did not reply. Some painful months of reflection had passed before another communication arrived. It was a brief second request to submit a timetable for change. Enclosed with the formal letter was the latest bulletin from the order's liturgical committee detailing the most recent developments in liturgical practice. The bulletin confirmed Fr. van Engelen's decision on the basis of faith, not obedience. He ignored the second request. A third arrived a month later, in December the previous year. It was more of a demand than a request. Fr. van Engelen realised he could not keep ignoring the provincial, even if it were for the sake of good manners. He wrote, telling the provincial that his conscience forbade him to accede to the order's directives. The order had put itself outside the Church on the matter of the liturgy. He pleaded for exemption on the grounds of a sincere conscience.

The provincial's reply was terse. Each brother had a duty, and his duty as provincial was to implement the Spirit of the Second Vatican Council, whereas Father's duty was to obey, however much his uninformed conscience deviated from the directives legitimately issued by his superiors. Father should know that an appeal to conscience implies following a properly formed conscience. That was the Church's constant teaching on the nature of conscience. Father's priestly brothers were patiently waiting for him to properly form his conscience and join them in fraternal solidarity. Fr. van Engelen put the letter aside and waited for the intervention. Now the voice on the other end of the line signalled it had come.

'I have already explained my position, Father,' the priest replied in Dutch, his heart sinking.

'I am all too aware of that,' said Fr de Jonge. 'I am afraid it means unpleasant and necessary intervention by the order for the sake of your parishioners. We have a duty to bring the fruits of the Council to all the faithful. I respect your inability to see the truth of things—your medical problems are a factor—so I will postpone further disciplinary action. My brothers agree that we should continue to view your resistance with charity. I propose to come myself with my religious brothers and sisters to introduce the New Mass to your congregation.'

'Brothers and Sisters?'

He had not anticipated this action, and it came as a shock. Until then, he had been able to protect his parishioners from the liturgical anarchy promoted everywhere by priests, religious sisters, and self-appointed lay groups. That protection had become a duty and major motivation in the stand he had taken. He had kept his timid and bewildered flock together by taking the brunt of the pressure himself. Direct intervention now threatened to disperse them.

'You mean you are coming personally?' he said, knowing too well that it was the case. 'And with—?'

'Yes, I mean to come and personally take in hand a long overdue task.'

'But do you have the time?' Fr. van Engelen said stupidly.

'I always have time for such sacred tasks.'

'When?'

'I propose to conduct the liturgy for Easter Sunday. It will be the Day Mass of Easter Sunday. Please note that it will be the only Mass said on Easter Sunday. It will be at ten o'clock. There will be no midnight Mass. I want all your parishioners to be in attendance for this great occasion.'

'Easter Sunday! Would you please put it off until after Easter,' Fr. van Engelen pleaded. 'I have been conducting the full Easter Vigil ceremonies since I came to this parish. The parishioners look forward to it.'

'Is it the new liturgy for the Easter Vigil and the Mass of Easter Night? No? Then it will be as I say.'

'I beg of you ...'

'Please, Father, do not embarrass us both. We must do our duty. That is the end of it. I will be in contact with you to discuss the details. I must consult Sister Parker in Melbourne about the proper form of the dance.'

'Dance? But that is illicit. Nothing could be clearer ... according to the Vatican directives.'

'Father, we are about following the Spirit of the Second Vatican Council. That's what we're doing. Unfortunately, the written word often lags behind the dictates of the Spirit. And that Spirit is telling us to redress the injustice to women.'

'Redressing injustice to women in dance! What ... what real spirit are you being led by?'

'Father, don't be offensive. That is not going to get us anywhere,' the provincial admonished. 'Indeed, the real spirit is hidden from you in your stubborn resistance. Women have a prophetic role in the Church. I don't have time to discuss this now. That time will come. Your task is to prepare yourself for the occasion. Oh, and one final matter: two seminarians will accompany me. They will mime the Gospel of the Resurrection.'

'Mime?' was all that Fr. van Engelen could say.

'Yes, Father, that will be an integral part of the ceremony. And now I have other matters to deal with. I will be in contact. Goedemorgen.'

'Goedemorgen,' Fr. van Engelen whispered, as he put the phone down. He dropped to his knees in front of the crucifix. He remained there, praying and beseeching.

AT THREE o'clock that same day, Edith Bicknell welcomed Jane Cox and Mrs Joyce Charing, the principal's secretary, to her house.

'Come in, Mrs Charing. I'm very sorry we've not had time to talk before this,' she said, ushering the women into the lounge room. 'Would you like something to drink? Jane, you too? What about a glass of wine?'

'Please call me Joyce,' said Mrs Charing, nodding eagerly. 'Yes, I would like a glass of wine if that's what you're having.'

'Yes, of course, it's Saturday afternoon. What's better than a glass of Chardonnay? And please call me Edith. But please sit down. You do like Chardonnay, I hope?'

'I certainly do.'

'It's Green Valley Chardonnay. Is that to your liking?'

'That's a coincidence. That's my favourite wine. I don't have it too often because it's so expensive.'

'That's lucky,' said Edith, disappearing into the kitchen.

Jane smiled encouragingly as she took her seat. She had not had much to say to this older woman. Mrs Charing seemed in a permanent sulk. The students even joked about it and her ridiculous, snooty manner. A minute later, Edith reappeared with a bottle of wine, crackers, and three glasses.

'Joyce, I must apologise for not inviting you to our meeting,' she began. 'It was an oversight. That was my fault. When I organised the meeting, I asked Jane to invite teachers with similar views. It was foolish and thoughtless of me not to consider a person in such an important position for the school's running. I hope you will forgive me.'

'Oh, Edith, no apologies necessary, I assure you,' said Joyce, beaming. 'I'm just so pleased that someone understands the importance of my work. I appreciate the compliment. It's so often a thankless task with you-know-who ordering me around.'

'I understand your position, Edith. You have my sympathy. We're here to change things.'

'Yes, we're here to bring about dramatic change,' said Jane Cox. 'We want to establish a regime of justice. You're not the only one who has complaints about the discriminatory policies of the school principal.'

'Discriminatory policies—?'

'Yes. That's why we're getting together to discuss action. The principal and his mates on the council have had it their way for far too long.'

'The council, too, you think?'

'Let's leave that for the moment, Jane,' said Edith. 'I would like to hear about Joyce's experiences with the principal. We need to understand it clearly. If we are going to support Joyce in her efforts to receive proper recognition for her crucial role in the school, we must know exactly what she experiences. Joyce, we need you to keep a diary of what happens. Can you do that?' She raised her eyebrows as if she were asking something difficult.

'I already do!' said Joyce. 'It used to get me down so much that I felt I had to keep a record of it.'

'Splendid!'

'Have you actually been keeping a diary?' said Jane. 'For how long?'

'A couple of years now. I note down everything that happens in the office. It helps me deal with Mr Huckerby's attitude towards me.'

'What sort of things do you note?'

'The things he says to me, the manner he says them in, the organisation of the office—he's always contradicting me and having his own way—the phone calls he makes. That sort of thing.'

'What phone calls?' said Edith.

'Well, he makes many calls to people outside the school, people who have nothing to do with the school.'

'What people?'

'The mayor, for example. He's always calling the mayor. He calls people on the council. He has long conversations with them.'

'What about?'

'I don't know exactly. He always shuts the door after the call has been put through.'

'Are you the one to put the calls through?'

'No, not always. Mrs Corrigan usually answers the phone. I always ask who it is when the caller wants the principal. I keep track of who calls him that way.'

'Can you listen in on the calls if you want to?'

'Yes.'

'Have you done that?'

Joyce shifted and looked into her wine glass.

'That's all right, Joyce. This conversation is strictly confidential. What you say remains strictly between us.'

'Well, I have on occasions when I thought it was necessary. But, you know, he's not supposed to be conducting private business on the school property.'

'He's certainly not!' said Jane. 'What private business?'

'Property negotiations. He buys property. He's actually bought loads of property in Binawarra, and outside, too.'

'Why should we be surprised?' said Jane, looking at Edith.

'It's not only private business,' said Joyce, leaning forward after taking a few sips of wine from her fast-emptying glass. 'It's also questionable business.'

'What do you mean?' said Edith, topping up Joyce's glass.

'I'm glad you're concerned about the men on the council because there has been some funny business between them and Huckerby.'

'Funny business?' said Jane, also leaning forward.

'Yes, there were two adjacent buildings owned by the council in the town shopping centre. Do you know the two old buildings—they're renovated now—a few doors down from the office of the *Binawarra and District Mail*? Well, these passed from the council to the principal without so much as a boo. Nobody else knew about it. They weren't advertised.

Huckerby secretly bought them for an amount he and the council members agreed on.'

'That's corrupt!' exclaimed Jane. 'There you have it, the capitalist system in its full glory. How did he get away with it?'

'Are you sure about this?' said Edith.

'I have all the details. There were many phone calls between Huckerby, members of the town council, the economic committee, and the bank. It went on for weeks. It was obvious Huckerby was squeezing the council for the lowest price.'

'You have it on paper?'

'Yes, everything. I recorded everything I heard.'

'Can I have a copy?'

'Of course. I'll make one for you on Monday.'

'Does anybody else know about this? I mean, anybody except for those involved?'

'I told my husband, but he just told me to forget about it. He said I should not meddle in things I don't understand. That was typical of him. He treats me like a fool, my husband does.'

'All men are like that,' said Jane. 'Men from your generation treat women like dirt. I sympathise. You must have a lot to put up with.'

'I do. I truly do. I get it at school and at home. They treat me like a fool.' Her eyes filled, her cheeks tightened, and her lips twisted.

'When did you tell him, and has he said anything about it to anybody else?' Edith intervened.

'It all happened three or four years ago. Let me think,' she said, brushing her eyes. 'It was four years ago, 1971. No, he hasn't mentioned it since. He wouldn't. He's never treated me seriously. Anytime I say something to him, he just tells me to relax and have another wine, and that's it. He just goes on his way. I have no idea why I married him. My mother said I was good-looking enough to get a much better man than that. I was pretty in my twenties. Look at me now.' She took a short sip of wine and brushed her eyes while Edith and Jane regarded her sympathetically.

'The way he put me down just made me more determined to prove it was true,' she said between her teeth. 'I was careful to get all the information I could about the sale. I checked the transfer of ownership and so on. I have all the information. I'll show him. I'll make him look the fool he is.'

'Who?' said Jane.

'My husband, and Huckerby, too, of course. I'll get them both at the right time.'

'So nobody else knows about this?' said Edith.

'No, not that I'm aware. No, there's nobody else who knows. I've waited purposely to see if anything happened. It didn't. They covered it up. At least they thought they'd covered it up.'

'Excellent. You have done very well, Joyce,' said Edith. 'We'll support you one hundred per cent when you want to bring it into the open.'

Joyce's face began to tighten and twist again.

'Are there any more examples of his corrupt business dealings?' asked Jane eagerly.

That was the cue for Joyce Charing to launch into an account of the principal's property purchases made over the last ten years. From memory, she could name the dates, the address of the property, the property's attributes, the previous owner, and her own reasons for the sale and purchase of the property. She assembled the information from the official records and the many conversations that Huckerby had had on the school premises. She had it all on record. It took some doing, but she had the time and space while her husband ignored her. And that was just about every evening.

She continued for some time while Gerda and Jane took turns expressing their sympathy. A long account of her husband's miserable treatment and the principal's torment spilled from her mouth. It was all torment for her at work and at home. Edith ventured to ask her why she thought the principal wanted to acquire so much property. Joyce gave the indignant, burning reply that Huckerby wanted as much of the town as he could grab. His ambition was to set up a sort of kingdom where he could lord it over as many people as possible. He lorded it over her and others at the school. That was just the start. He wanted to lord it over all Binawarra. The man was power drunk and bent on tormenting everyone, especially the women. Jane Cox, holding her empty glass in front of her with her mouth slightly open, blinked at her. Edith emptied the last of the second bottle of Chardonnay into Joyce's glass and lit up.

'You don't have an easy life, do you, Joyce?'

'No,' said Joyce, taking the refilled glass and blubbering into its contents. 'I don't.' She took a sip. 'But I can't tell you how comforting it is to have people listening who understand my misery.'

'You can count on us,' said Edith, with a slight movement of one eyebrow at Jane.

'Yes, you can rely on us,' said Jane. 'We will support you in your struggle against the men of this town.'

'Thank you,' said Joyce, sniffling and again wiping her eyes.

'Now, how are we to tackle the problem from here?' said Edith, and without waiting for a reply, 'We must hit on an occasion where we can nail the principal and his friends. To bring you up to date, Joyce, we think the best occasion is Anzac Day.'

'Anzac Day? Why?'

'Because War Veterans' Day is the grand celebration of men over women,' said Jane.

'Is it?'

'Yes, it's the time when men celebrate their aggression and brutality. War is the great expression of male aggression and brutality. War is the time when men rape women. While Anzac Day is a time for men to celebrate war, it is a time of mourning for women. It's a time to mourn the victims of war: we women—'

'We are arranging a demonstration against the brutality of war to take place on Anzac Day,' said Edith, interrupting Jane's flow. 'Now, you have an important role in this.'

'Have I?' said Joyce, shifting her wide-eyed gaze from Jane to Edith.

'Yes, and I'll tell you why. We must know what the principal has planned for the day. You're in the best position to see that.'

'Yes, I am, definitely. I already know a lot about the plans. I've had to type the program.'

'Can you get us a copy?'

'Of course, but it's only preliminary. But don't worry, I'll provide an updated copy whenever there are changes.'

'Good. Well done. I'm glad we have you to rely on. But it's all to remain secret, just between us.'

'Of course, of course. I'll keep it secret. You can rely absolutely on me.'

'It's a mystery why the principal undervalues a person of your ability,' said Edith.

Struggling to control her tears, Joyce looked into her half-empty glass. 'It's a hard thing to take. He just orders me around as if I were a bit of dirt. Go there, come here, do this, do that, is all I hear. No appreciation at all. And then there's that horrible witch of a woman who just strolls in to see him whenever she wants. He's all smiles and jokes when she's around. She's horrible. She treats me like dirt, too, horrible woman.'

'You mean Florence Barker?' said Jane.

'Yes, that tall stick of offensiveness. They make a good pair, those two—Laurel and Hardy of meanness.'

'Why is the principal so friendly with Ms Barker?' said Edith.

'I have no idea. It's insulting. Whenever she turns up, I have to curtsey and announce her as a sort of majesty who has come to visit.'

'You don't have to put up with that, do you?'

'You do unless you want your head bitten off,' said Jane.

'Is this woman so frightening?' said Edith. 'I've only seen her at a distance. She looks so shrivelled and deprived. How could she be so frightening?'

'She is, believe me. She doesn't have much to do with the town. But don't get on the wrong side of her in those few things she has an interest in.'

IN THE meantime, the subject of Jane Cox's dire warning had approached the Winterbine house. She surveyed the front verandah as she reached the front gate. A female head poked above the vines that ran along the rails. She mounted the stairs and greeted a surprised Ruby.

'Good afternoon, young lady, you must be Miss Ruby Waiting.'

'Yes, madam,' said Ruby, getting to her feet.

'I am a friend of the family. Miss Barker is my name. Please call me Miss Barker, and I will call you Miss Waiting. I don't go with all that first-name nonsense. It's presumptuous.'

She sat in the nearest chair and waved to Ruby to resume her seat. She looked Ruby up and down in a way that left Ruby bemused and waiting until she was required to speak.

'Hmm, short, perky and cute, a steady look in the eyes, and polite,' said Miss Barker. 'I like that.'

'Thank you, Miss Barker.'

'You know you have been paid a great compliment, don't you?'

'I have?'

'Few people would have been welcomed into the Winterbine house the way you and Mr Shawcross have. Charles and Aine are not proud people, but they have certain standards. They obviously see something in you and your friend.'

'Let me assure you, Miss Barker,' said Ruby, 'I am flattered by their attention. I like them very much. I seem to have become friends with their unusual daughter. I'm not quite sure why it has happened. But I'm honoured.'

'Well, young lady, I'm beginning to see why. I think we'll get on.' She looked around. 'Where are the others?'

'Charles is helping Aine in the kitchen. Estella has gone to fetch Geoff, Mr Shawcross, from the back garden. And I'm here enjoying the fresh air of the late afternoon.'

'Well, we might still have a few minutes, Miss Waiting. Let me get straight to the point, and please don't subject me to a series of "whys" after I have said my piece.' She tapped the armrest of her chair. 'I have some concerns about Miss Winterbine. Dangers are lurking around her that Charles and Aine are not aware of. Your friendship with Estella is fortuitous. You and your friend could help in protecting her.'

'I don't understand. What dangers?'

'I don't want you to discuss this with anyone except Mr Shawcross. Indeed, you must discuss it with him. Understood?'

'Yes, but—'

'He is a former SAS soldier, I believe.'

'Yes. He left the army around two years ago. He now looks after the family farm.'

'What rank was he?'

'Captain.'

'A captain, was he? That's no small thing. But you are probably unaware of what he has done.'

'Yes,' said Ruby uneasily. 'He avoids talking about it, and I don't ask.'

'Excellent. Now, I don't know how long the danger will last, but your friend's protection might be critical. There is a man in Binawarra, an outsider, who is stalking Estella. Whatever his reasons are, nobody is aware of it except me—and the person who's directing him here.'

'Stalking Estella? Are you sure?'

'Miss Waiting, I'm not a fanciful person.'

'No, of course not. It's just that I've never experienced this sort of thing before. It sounds so … indeed, it sounds fanciful. How would Estella be in danger in this quiet place?'

'You must trust me for the moment, young lady. A lot is going on that I cannot reveal, things that reach outside this sleepy hollow. I'm telling you this on the strength of Charles and Aine's good opinion of you. I am relying on you not to let me down.'

'Miss Barker, it goes without saying. I'll keep your confidence and try to do what I can. But what can I do?'

They heard voices coming from the hall.

'It's more about what Captain Shawcross can do. Here is my card. Call me before you leave Binawarra. Don't forget.'

Ruby slipped the card into her blouse pocket just as Aine and Charles opened the flywire door. They exclaimed when they saw Miss Barker, greeting the rather still older woman warmly. It was so unlike her to visit without warning and at that time of the day. The next moment, Estella and Geoff appeared in the front garden. Estella hurried up the steps and hugged and kissed Miss Barker while she and Geoff looked on.

'Now, now, you'll spoil my reputation,' said Miss Barker. 'Introduce me to this young man I see before me.'

Geoff came forward before Estella could say anything and held out his hand.

'Geoff Shawcross, ma'am, glad to meet you.'

'I'm pleased to meet you, too, Mr Shawcross. You are a former Special Services Captain, I believe?'

'Yes, ma'am,' he said, looking at Ruby, who shrugged.

'I know a little bit about the army,' she said. 'I was caught in Singapore during the Japanese occupation. I saw a good bit of the army when the war finished. I know Brigadier Penathy. I believe he had much to do with special operations during the Vietnam War.'

These comments left Geoff frowning and shifting.

'Never mind, we can talk about that some other time. We don't want to bore the people here, do we?'

Miss Barker, to the Winterbine's surprise, was very talkative. She had a lot to say to Geoff, who was forthright in his answers, always addressing her as 'ma'am.' She asked him when he joined the army, how he came to join the SAS regiment, and whether he liked it. To these questions, he gave general answers. However, when it came to his time after the army, he was vague, only mentioning his farm. Miss Barker seemed happy with all that he said.

Unbeknownst to Estella, Miss Barker had observed the change in her expression whenever Geoff spoke. No one else seemed to notice her shy interest in the self-effacing but quietly confident former SAS officer, not even the sharp, confident Ruby.

'And now, Miss Waiting,' said Miss Barker, turning to Ruby, 'I have heard enough about Mr Shawcross. Let me hear from you.'

Ruby described her background, her job at the university, her contact with Bill Huckerby, and the reason she met Estella and her parents.

'What do you think, Miss Waiting, of the suggestion that Estella is suited to public relations work?'

'Well, it's something that Estella has to decide for herself—'

'But what do you think?'

'I believe it's the wrong field for her. I had only to walk around the garden here for five minutes before I understood the sort of work Estella would enjoy and could do as an occupation.'

'Good,' said Miss Barker, which seemed more of an invitation to continue than approval.

Ruby then explained the plan of having Estella come and stay the weekend with her in Bendigo, for which Miss Barker expressed her support.

From that moment, Miss Barker took a backseat in the conversation, content to let the Winterbines talk freely with their new friends. As she left the Winterbine's house at about eight o'clock, a murky shadow flitted between the trees in the bush opposite. Miss Barker took no notice. The meeting with Ruby and Geoff the next day was more important.

Chapter 13

Estella and Geoff

FR VAN ENGELEN stood in the sacristy with his head bowed. He had on the amice, alb and the girdle, which tied the stole across his chest. In front of him on the bench lay the maniple and the chasuble. Two altar boys in red robes and white surplices stood behind him. At length, taking his stick and gesturing to the boys to stay put, he entered the sanctuary and headed for the ornamented wooden pulpit.

'I have sad news to pass on to you,' he said, after a painful pause. 'For some time now, my superiors have been requiring me to introduce the liturgical reforms in compliance with the Second Vatican Council's Decree on the Sacred Liturgy. As some of you know, I have been resisting because of irregularities appearing in many parishes. I have continually asked for clarification of the present trends, trends which seem entirely out of step with the Council and certainly out of step with Holy Mother the Church. I have kept my negotiations from you because I did not want to cause anxiety unless it was necessary. I am afraid to say that it is now necessary. My superiors have taken the matter of the liturgy out of my hands and are intending to introduce the new liturgy, as they see it, into this parish on Easter Sunday.' Fr. van Engelen held up his hands to check a murmuring that was gathering.

'Some of you have come from a great distance to attend this Mass. I understand your disappointment and dismay at the news. Let's not despair.

Let's pray to Our Lord and His Blessed Mother that this plan is thwarted. I will keep you all abreast of whatever happens. Let's say before Mass begins an Our Father, a Hail Mary, and a Glory Be.' He bowed his head and led the congregation in the prayers. 'Remember today is Passion Sunday,' he resumed. 'It is the beginning of Passiontide. It's that period when we contemplate Our Lord's suffering and death on the cross to redeem us, to make us, as Saint John tells us in the Mass's last Gospel reading, sons and daughters of God, born not of the flesh, but of God.'

After Mass, the Winterbines went to the front gates to wait for the priest. They arrived there as Ruby and Geoff approached.

'Hi there,' said Ruby. 'We thought we would have a walk around the town while you were at Mass. We can't sit still, you see,' she laughed. 'We'll go home with you when you're ready.'

'Of course,' said Charles, 'but a quick word with Fr. van Engelen before we go.'

'Take your time,' she said. 'There's no hurry. We'll sit on the park bench opposite.' She took Geoff by the arm, and they walked across the road.

Estella kept her eyes on them all the way over to the park bench. She watched Ruby talking in her usual animated way while Geoff listened, all attention. Then Ruby caught sight of her. She waved and blew a kiss. Estella returned a clumsy, half-hearted wave. Geoff waved back. She flushed and looked first at the ground and then at her parents. Seconds later, she stole a look at them. They were now talking, their attention directed elsewhere. Just as well, she thought, again embarrassed and confused by her response to Geoff's simple, friendly gesture.

RUBY'S attention soon returned to the group in front of the church. 'There must be some trouble, judging from their body language,' she commented.

'Yes, they had looked anxious.'

'So you noticed, too, did you? Something's up. And what about Miss Barker's request? It's strange—and unnerving.'

'It sounds odd that somebody could be stalking Estella in this town. I mean for reasons other than ... you know. On the other hand, you wouldn't think Miss Barker would make baseless claims.'

'Is that the officer's experience speaking?'

'Perhaps. Miss Barker's manner—she said a few things that suggest there's more to her than appears. She may have the skills to assess such a situation.'

'What are you saying?'

'Nothing for sure. I had a hint that Miss Barker has knowledge or even experience with surveillance methods. How much is the question? I'll find out before too long, I suspect.'

'What will you say to her when we speak tomorrow?'

'I'm still thinking about it. It depends on what she says.' He shrugged.

Seeing Geoff retreat into his non-speaking mode, Ruby turned her attention to the Winterbines and Fr. van Engelen. Their demeanour still reflected worry. Then Charles turned and beckoned.

'Come on,' she said, taking Geoff's arm.

'Miss Waiting, forgive my question about your being Catholic,' said the priest, 'That must have sounded presumptuous. I was a bit distracted.'

'No need for an apology, Father. We took it as a compliment. Truly. We have no religious affiliations, if you're wondering. Our background is classical humanist.'

'I take it you have little sympathy with the prevailing social and political views.'

'That's pretty much it,' said Ruby, noticing that Charles, Aine, and Estella were looking on as if aware of what was on Fr. van Engelen's mind. 'Religious practice stopped in my family long ago—Anglican when it was there. The same for Geoff, too, I think.'

'And now you are staying in the most Catholic of homes.'

'We are staying in the homes of charming, friendly, hospitable people, aren't we, Geoff?'

'Yes, that's right,' said Geoff, with a nervous cough.

'You share a lot of values. Anyhow, I am pleased you have made friends with Estella. You will find her a good, loyal friend when you get to know her.'

'You certainly will,' said Charles.

'We already know that.'

'Miss Waiting,' the priest continued, 'you and Mr Shawcross could be like a big brother and sister to her.'

'If Estella looks on us as a sister and brother, I would be pleased,' she said, smiling at Estella. 'We would be delighted, wouldn't we, Geoff?'

Geoff shifted, nodded, and glanced at Estella, who blinked at him and then looked away.

'But I won't detain you anymore,' said Fr. van Engelen. 'I must get on with my duties. Have a pleasant day.'

As the group set off to walk home, Ruby put her arm through Geoff's and told Estella to take his other arm. If they were brother and sister, she said gaily, this was the way a brother escorted his sister home from church.

'No,' said Ruby, 'hold it properly, you silly thing. He won't bite you. Geoff, make her take your arm.'

Geoff drew Estella's arm into place. Estella looked ahead of her as they followed her parents, who, having regarded Ruby's rearranging with amusement, were now several paces ahead of them.

BY ELEVEN o'clock that morning, Estella, Ruby, and Geoff were behind the Winterbine's property, making their way through the gardens and the long grass to the creek. Estella was dressed in khaki slacks with a white short-sleeve blouse. A broad-brimmed sunhat was on her head, and sandshoes on her feet. Geoff wore the clothes and boots of a seasoned bushwalker. Ruby looked at them and laughed. Her light shirt and shorts, and sandals did not seem suitable for the purpose. She scolded herself for not even bringing her hat when she always insisted that Geoff had his hat on when in the sun. She had to make do with a spare cloth hat that Estella had given her. Estella was in her element, and Geoff was happy to be on the move. He asked Estella about the bush around Binawarra. In a short time, they were swapping comments and questions. Ruby said they were obviously peas in a pod when it came to the bush, but made no further allusion for a while.

Although the way was not hazardous, Ruby struggled. Geoff had to help her over rocks or tree trunks that had fallen across the path. Estella observed how attentive he was to Ruby's surprising clumsiness. When she led them down the bank and across the fast-flowing creek, jumping from boulder to boulder with the water splashing around them, she and Geoff had to help a fearful Ruby. 'I'm such a fat little dunce,' Ruby exclaimed several times. How did she get it into her head to go bushwalking with such big, fit people, a little girl like her? Geoff and Estella laughed together, and Ruby commented that it was not funny that her misfortune was the sign for them to lose their shyness towards each other.

Ruby found the going so tiring that Estella had to cut short the walk and head to the picnic ground where they had arranged to meet her parents. Aine, noticing Ruby's fatigue, was quick to comfort and reassure her. Her daughter and Charles were fit and demanding walkers. She said it would take someone like Geoff to keep up with them. That was why she did not often go with them and certainly not on their day walks.

'You mean they walk a whole day like that?' said Ruby, fanning her red face with the floppy cloth hat and sitting on the bench under the picnic shelter. 'It's not right that someone is so fit and beautiful at the same time. There should be a law against it.'

Estella turned away, but the next instant, threw a sly glance at Geoff. Geoff looked non-committal. Embarrassingly, she had trapped herself into doing what Jenny and her friends did. It annoyed her. For the first time, she was conscious of the utility of her appearance in attracting a man's attention, and that man belonged to somebody else. What could she be thinking? She went to help her mother, who was preparing the picnic table, but kept her ear attuned to the conversation between her father, Ruby and Geoff.

Lunch passed agreeably while the conversation turned mainly on Geoff's farm and his life as a farmer, which Ruby spiced up with her witticisms. Charles asked where the farm was exactly. It was no more than fifteen miles north-east of St Arnaud, said Geoff. Or perhaps it was more easterly than north-east. Looking around, Charles pondered the direction. Then the farm must be about the same distance northwest of Binawarra. He and Estella may have walked on Geoff's property at some time or another. They sometimes walked long distances during the day, always keeping to the outskirts or uncultivated areas of people's property. Estella put her hand to her mouth, then quickly took it down. Ruby exclaimed about the coincidence.

'Well, I—' said Geoff, glancing at Estella. But he appeared unable to finish the sentence.

'I'll have difficulty climbing all the way up there,' said Ruby, staring at the slopes of the squatting sentinel. 'In fact, there's no way I could do it.'

'Are you sure?' he said.

'Yes, but that won't stop you and Estella. You don't have to stay here with me. Aine, you're not going to climb up there, are you?'

'No, I'm staying here. It's too much for me.'

'Yes, Geoff,' said Charles. 'You and Estella can do the climb. We will keep Ruby company. We have lots to talk about.'

'Aren't you going, either?' Geoff said.

'Oh no, I'll keep Aine and Ruby company.'

'Go on,' said Ruby. 'You want to do the climb. You don't need my permission.'

'As long as Estella is happy to go with me.'

'Estella will be glad to go with you,' said Aine. 'It's one of her favourite walks.'

'Yes, I would like to go,' said Estella.

Ten minutes later, Estella and Geoff set off.

AT FIRST, they walked in silence, negotiating the trees, shrubs, and rocks at the foot of the slope. As they approached the climb's beginning, Geoff asked if she had a particular route in mind. They would take the way she and her father always took. It was the way he went when he and her mother had climbed the mountain. Her father always walked that way in memory of that time.

They climbed in silence across the side of the hill at a steep angle. Estella made her way steadily in front of Geoff. Several times, he was on the point of asking if she was all right and if it was not too tiring for her. But he saw she was taking it in her stride, slightly raising her breathing. He marvelled as he looked at her from below. The trim figure in loose-fitting clothing against the grassy, rocky hillside, the shapely ankles in the white sandshoes, the luxurious streaky brown hair with the ponytail dangling under the broad-brimmed hat—it was mesmerising. Every couple of minutes, she turned as if to check if he was managing. She check him! He gave her a signal each time that he was following without any trouble. At length,

Estella stopped and waited for him to come up beside her. She pointed out her parents and Ruby, whom they could see sitting under the gum tree below. She waved back when her mother waved. Geoff waved, too.

'We have a good view of the town from here,' he said.

'It's much better from the top. Let's go on a bit further, and then we can sit down and rest.'

Geoff followed as Estella set off, this time taking a steep angle across the other way. She climbed at the same steady pace, sometimes grabbing the grass in front of her when the slope became rough through erosion or when she had to negotiate a boulder embedded in the side of the mountain. After ten minutes, she stopped and waited for Geoff to come up beside her again.

'This is where Daddy and Mamma stopped when they came here for the first time,' she said, pointing to a small rock marked with a dash of white paint. She sat down.

'When was that?' said Geoff, sitting beside her.

'When they first met, about nineteen years ago,' she said, fiddling with the long grass beside her.

'Those occasions are very special for your parents, aren't they?'

'Yes. They celebrate all those things. Every time I come up here with Daddy, he talks about it. He never expected to meet and marry someone like Mamma.'

'I see they love each other very much.'

'Everyone notices. Everyone likes them, Mamma just as much as Daddy, even though she doesn't go out very often.'

'She's a beautiful woman,' said Geoff, surprised that he should make such a comment. 'I mean that many women like that are usually more likely to go out ... I mean ...' He felt so stupid as he tried to correct one clumsy comment with another.

'I know what you mean,' she said. 'Mamma puts no value on appearance. Many times she has pointed out to me the impermanence of physical beauty. Anyhow, I don't notice it in my mother. I see how beautiful she is on the inside.'

'You're very fortunate with your parents.'

'I know. I say a prayer of thanksgiving every day.'

'Do you really?'

'Yes,' she said, turning to him.

'I don't hear people talking about prayer very often.'

'Did you ever think about God when you were in Vietnam?'

Geoff's mind flashed back over a lot of violent situations. 'I'm not sure I did. There were times when the danger was so extreme that I could only survive by committing acts of brutality most people would not even dream about. I didn't have a chance to reflect. That's what war is about. It is a necessary but dirty business.' He paused. 'But ... I don't know. Perhaps there was sometimes this overwhelming feeling of fate ... I mean of fate guiding the events.' Becoming conscious of what he was saying, he said, 'I'm sorry. I didn't mean to go on like that. It's not the sort of thing I should be saying to a young person with no experience or idea of such things—of how cruel the world can be.'

'That's all right,' she said, 'I appreciate your confiding in me.' Her hand on the grass beside her moved compulsively towards him.

'Look,' he said, not noticing, 'we can see Ruby and your parents from here, too.'

'Yes, we can.'

'Come on.' He stood. 'We should make a move.'

He gave her his hand without thinking. She took it and let herself be pulled to her feet. She waited for him to let her hand go. He let it go and gave her a self-conscious smile while he waited for her to lead the way. Five minutes later, they reached the crest of the hill. She led him around the grassy open space, pointing out the landmarks and the major towns in the area. Geoff exclaimed at the view from all angles. They came to a point from which Geoff had a view below them of the sharp peak with its strange rocky outcrop. He looked at it and then at Estella, who was gazing at it.

'That's a strange peak there,' he said. 'That platform of rock looks almost as if it were man-made.' She seemed reluctant to speak. 'Is there something about it?'

'Daddy does not like it. He doesn't like the look of it.'

'Has he ever climbed it? It drops sharply on the roadside, but a ridge runs off the back with a much shallower incline leading around to where the road ascends to pass between this hill and that peak. Can you see that?' Estella nodded. 'Somebody could reach the top from there quite easily.'

'No, Daddy's never been there,' she said. 'And he told me to keep away from it. But friends of mine went up there once and said it was eerie. One of my friends calls it Death Rock.'

'Death Rock? I'm not surprised.'

'Shall we go on?'

'Yes, of course.'

She was not comfortable. It was strange, he thought, following her as she moved away. The daughter seemed to share the father's feeling about the land and its formation. They walked out of sight of Death Rock to where they had a view over the town and the farming land beyond.

'Can we sit here?' she said. 'Mamma and Daddy won't mind if we're a little longer.'

'If it's all right. I don't want to take advantage of your parents' hospitality.'

'No, they won't mind,' she said, sitting down after choosing a spot just below the crest of the hilltop. 'They know I like to sit and look at the view. Daddy and I can sit here for hours.'

'Can you? What do you see?'

'We see a lot,' she said, her eyes focused on the expanse before them. 'If you sit here for a while, you see the beauty of the hills around here and the broad flat farmland that reaches out, right up to those low-lying hills in the distance. But the longer you sit here, the more you see. Daddy pointed it out the first time I came up here when I was about ten.'

'What are they? What do you see?'

'If you keep looking—well, it's more than looking. It's more like contemplation. If you contemplate the scene, you begin to see different patterns, sort of life patterns. The land becomes alive. It points, it marches, it breathes, it warns, it guards— We humans are situated on top of the life of the land.' She stopped, and they sat in silence.

'I see what you mean,' said Geoff.

'Then, after a while,' she continued, 'you can name the parts of the land. Daddy calls where we are sitting, the sleepy wombat. He will awaken when there is danger. He has a story about it. He used to tell stories before I went to sleep.'

'When you were ten?'

'Yes,'

'Really?' said Geoff, looking around. 'Yes, I can see that.'

'Do you see how the creek runs past our property?' She pointed to their right. 'That's the sly black snake. We always have to be careful around the sly black snake. Then there's the echidna. That's where the high school buildings are, with the little forest of gums on the low side. The echidna is shy and trusting but mistaken in thinking its spikes will guard it against danger.'

'Amazing!'

'And do you see that string of low hills over there in the distance? Daddy calls it the Goanna. The Goanna is the knight of the bush: strong, powerful, and ready for action. The land is clear around it because of the awe and fear it creates in nature.'

Geoff looked around him. He glanced up at the position of the sun and then stood up. 'That must be due north there,' he said, pointing across the middle of the town. 'Then the Goanna must be northwest of here, almost exactly.' He sat again. 'You know, Estella, the Goanna is just behind my farm. That's where my farm is. I have looked at those hills all my life, and it has never occurred to me that somebody could see a goanna in them.' He shook his head. 'But I see it. I'll never look at those hills in the same way again.'

'You live under the Goanna?' she murmured, without looking at him.

Geoff's mind was too full of what Estella had told him to notice any feeling in her question. 'What does your father call the sharp peak on the other side there?'

'He doesn't call it anything. He says it's a dark spot in the world. We always turn away when we pass it.'

'Astounding!' There was silence for a while more. 'Did your father make all these things up? I mean, does it all come from his imagination, or is it part of a mythology?'

'No, they're his stories,' she said, gazing before her. 'They are stories whose origins are in the land, but also stories giving form to the virtue and vice in the world. They came to him as he contemplated what he saw in the actual space before him and how people behave in that space. They're also, in a way, like portents, like the stars. They exemplify not only vice and virtue linked to the physical world, but they are also pointers to things that can happen. Underlying it is God and the mystery of God's creation. Daddy says that after sitting here a long time, he can almost see God touching the world.'

'Do you see that, too?'

'Yes, I think I do. When we sit here in silence, we cannot conceive that someone could deny God and all His goodness exist. It's unthinkable.'

'You explain your father's thoughts very clearly.'

'They are mine, too.'

'Are they also your mother's?'

'The thoughts about God, and how they lead to God's coming into the world as Jesus, are the same. I don't know about the stories. I haven't heard him talking to Mamma much about them. It is something between the two of us.'

'Then I suppose I am privileged.'

She blinked a couple of times and then looked at the grass in front of her. She pulled out a long stem. 'It's the first time anyone other than my father has come with me to the top of the Wombat.'

'You mean none of your friends has been here?'

'Not that I'm aware. At least, they have not been with me.'

'That's sad. Such beautiful surroundings, and with the meaning you can see in them.'

'They're all too preoccupied with modern music, boys, and fashion. They have no interest.'

'Aren't you interested in those things?'

'No, not really.'

'I appreciate your confidence.'

'Thank you,' she said, pulling at the grass in front of her.

'Come on. We must be getting back.'

He held out both hands, and she let herself be pulled to her feet. She looked into his eyes. There was a glint of recognition. Unaware of its meaning, Geoff began descending along the same route they had come by. Following closely, she commented that he had a good memory for the way. He remembered such things, he said. Twice, he offered her his hand at an awkward spot. Estella, who had negotiated the route countless times by herself, took it.

'Geoff's farm is next to the Goanna, Daddy,' Estella said when they joined the others.

'Is it really?'

'Next to the goanna?' said Ruby.

'Charles and Estella have names for the different formations in the landscape,' said Aine, who was putting the last of the cups and plates in the picnic basket. 'The Goanna is the string of hills to the north of here. You can see them from the top of Charles's Mountain.'

'Oh, really?' said Ruby, 'That's interesting.'

'You can tell Ruby about it later if you want, Geoff,' said Estella.

'Did you tell Geoff about the stories?' said Charles.

'Yes,' she said, glancing at Ruby.

'Oh,' said Charles, looking curiously at Geoff.

'Fancy that, Geoff,' said Ruby. 'All these years, Charles and Estella have been staring at your farm from the top of that hill.'

'Yes, that was my reaction, too. I told Estella I had been looking at those hills for years, and the thought that they looked like a goanna never entered my head.'

Estella glanced from one to the other and turned to help her mother. It was as if a curtain came down over the sweet engagement of their conversation, and the aloofness reappeared—at least its appearance. What had happened? He did not have time to wonder much about it, for the preparations to leave were almost complete.

GEOFF opened the car door and was about to get out.

'Wait,' said Ruby, grabbing his arm.

'What for?'

'I have no idea what to say. And that woman is so overwhelming.'

'Let's just listen. I imagine you won't have to say anything. It's me she wants to talk to.' He put a foot outside the door. 'It's not like you to worry.'

'This is different. We've just spent the last couple of days with the Winterbines. There hasn't been a sign of one single spy or thug anywhere. It just doesn't make sense, suggesting that someone in this little town is stalking Estella or wants to harm her. Have you seen anyone?'

'No, not directly.'

'Not directly? Have you been looking?'

'Yes.'

'Really, do you mean it?'

'Old habits, old training, are hard to forget.'

Miss Barker had that odd habit, too, of looking furtively around her. He had seen how she kept her eye on Estella the previous evening. She had also turned her eyes on him when she thought he was not paying attention. 'Just listen to her calmly, without preconceptions.'

Once inside, Miss Barker lost no time. 'Miss Waiting, a down-to-earth person like you, will find this talk about threats and danger and stalkers a bit hard to take. But, again, I ask you to trust me.' Ruby gave a sign of resignation. 'Good. In Binawarra, I propose to keep a close eye on what's happening. If I judge that Miss Winterbine is in danger, I can raise the alarm. It's different outside the town. This is where you come in, Captain Shawcross. I assume Miss Waiting has filled you in?'

'She has.' For some reason, he did not object to Miss Barker's calling him 'Captain.'

'You're familiar with surveillance methods, I assume?' Geoff nodded. 'I would like you to accompany Miss Winterbine to Bendigo when she goes to stay with Miss Waiting.' She held up her hand. 'Yes, I realise it will take you away from your farm and constitute an expense. However, I'm willing to pay for all your expenses. And don't worry, I can afford it.'

'Miss Barker—'

'Hear me out first, Mr Shawcross. I want you to stay somewhere away from Miss Waiting's residence. I want you to keep Miss Waiting's residence under surveillance or be with them while she and Estella are home. When they go out, no matter where, I want you to go with them or shadow them in the usual way. You are to make notes of anything unusual. You know the routine. I'll send you a photo of the man who is stalking Estella. His name is Boris Rostowski. He comes to Binawarra as a sales representative for an importer of Middle Eastern giftware. The company is legitimate. I have checked. I will also send you a photo of the person he is working with. That person is Miss Bicknell.'

'Miss Bicknell?' Ruby exclaimed. 'What ...?'

Miss Barker gave a brief account of her shadowing of Boris and the time and manner of his meetings with Miss Bicknell.

'What's going on?' said Ruby.

'You would be surprised at the political manoeuvring and agitation that goes on in the most unexpected places,' said Miss Barker, 'sometimes right under the eyes of an authority that chooses or is rewarded for remaining blind.'

'Miss Barker, you don't have to pay any expenses,' said Geoff. 'If it's true that Estella's welfare is at stake, I'll gladly foot my own expenses. As for the farm, I can afford several days' absence. I still have my farm manager.'

'No, Mr Shawcross, I have my reasons for wanting to take all the expenses. It may not be obvious, but ensuring Miss Winterbine's safety may eventually require a lot of money. You should not risk yourself or a delay by suddenly finding yourself under a financial burden.'

'You think it so serious?'

'To be honest, Mr Shawcross, I don't know how serious it is. I can only say it has the marks of something sinister. Miss Winterbine seems to be at the centre of a plan of some sort. The kinds of people who author such plans are quite ruthless. The ideological plan goes before all else. I don't have to tell you, Mr Shawcross, how little lives are worth in political conflict.'

'You certainly don't.'

'What's that supposed to mean?' said Ruby, glancing from one to the other.

'The Vietnam War has been a political war,' said Geoff, knowing what Miss Barker had alluded to. 'Ideology has driven the conflict. It has excused the barbarity of a type I never imagined when I decided to become a soldier.'

'But that war's over.'

'It's almost over. The enemy is now poised to take Saigon. All that bloodshed for nothing, all those brave men who thought they were fighting for freedom. It was all lost outside the battlefield. It was a political and ideological betrayal of the selfless soldier.'

'You're right, Mr Shawcross,' said Miss Barker. 'We think alike on this subject, as I expected. The difference, Miss Waiting, is that Mr Shawcross experienced it.'

Ruby was silenced.

'All right, Miss Barker,' said Geoff. 'I'll go along with you. I'll undertake the surveillance of Estella. I would rather do it at my expense, but I understand you have your commitments. I'm assuming there's more to the affair than we know.'

'Yes, indeed.'

'Will we know more about it in due course?'

'Perhaps. Yes, more than likely, you will. You may become involved. Are you ready for that?'

'Of course.'

'Good, I appreciate it, Mr Shawcross.' She turned to Ruby. 'Miss Waiting, try to remain calm. You will not be involved beyond entertaining Miss Winterbine at your residence. I don't want you to do anything else. The surveillance's success depends on your going about your normal business. So leave everything to Mr Shawcross. And don't ask him any tedious questions. Is that clear?'

'Yes, Miss Barker.'

'Good, I know I can rely on your good sense. That's all I have to say on the matter. I will now get you a cup of tea.' She rose and pointed to a pad and pen on the coffee table. 'Please write all your contact numbers there:

home, work, everything. If the need is there, I don't want to scratch around trying to find you.'

Ruby and Geoff had listed their contacts by the time she returned.

'Good, that's in order,' she said, looking at the pad and placing the tray on the coffee table. 'Miss Waiting has my card. Here is one for you, Mr Shawcross. How do you find Miss Winterbine?'

'How do I find her?' he repeated, taking the card and putting it in his shirt pocket. 'She's a very nice girl. I'm glad she and Ruby get on so well.'

'A very nice girl? That sounds wishy-washy, sir. Surely you think more about her than that.'

'Geoff's not a great talker, Miss Barker,' said Ruby.

'Come on, Captain Shawcross, you can say more than "she's a very nice girl"?' insisted Miss Barker, silencing Ruby with a glance.

'Well, she's a little different from what we first thought,' he said while he withstood Miss Barker's demanding stare. 'She appeared at first a little aloof, perhaps passive, but we have since found her to be the opposite. She is shy and sensitive.'

'Is that all?'

'That about describes it.'

'You mean you have not noticed her appearance?'

'Yes, of course, but I didn't think your question was about her appearance. Everyone sees she's very beautiful. She is also young. Her appearance, in a way, hides the way she is inside.'

'Does it?' said Miss Barker, as if she was weighing up Geoff's words. 'Well, I'm glad to hear all that,' she added, in a tone that meant the examination was over.

Geoff gave a faint shrug and glanced at Ruby, who sat forward and upright in her chair, looking at Miss Barker. Miss Barker's manner softened, and she switched the conversation to mundane topics. It wasn't long before they finished their tea, said farewell to Miss Barker, and were in the car driving towards St Arnaud.

'That's a terrifying woman,' said Ruby when they were outside the town. 'People say I'm too confident, officious, and overbearing. I'm nothing to that woman. Phew!'

'She's less terrible than she seems.'

'Do you think so? I wouldn't mind betting you have come across Vietcong less terrible.'

'Some of it is an act. She's playing a part. You shouldn't take her so seriously.'

'It takes an ex-SAS soldier to say that. You can, but I'm not willing to take freedoms.'

They drove on in silence for a while.

'Why do you say it's an act?' said Ruby.

'Well, it's a cover. There's more to her than on the surface. The way she is organising the surveillance of Estella is telling. Not everybody goes about that sort of thing with such precision and confidence. She's definitely had experience. It's one of the reasons I have gone along with the plans.'

'And the other reasons? Or should I say the other reason?'

Geoff glanced at Ruby. 'The answer is obvious, isn't it?'

'Obvious, is it?'

Geoff smiled and cocked his hand on the steering wheel at Ruby. He did not want to be the butt of Ruby's playfulness on this.

'She likes you, you know?' she said with a mischievous smile.

'Does she?'

'Yes, she does. It's amazing. She looks at you with the respect a child has for an imposing adult. You really have made a good impression.' She gave him a poke in the arm: 'Such a beautiful specimen of femaleness being impressed by Geoffrey Shawcross, it's amazing! I'm impressed. You have every reason to be flattered.'

'I'm glad you have said it's a child's attitude to an adult. It would be nothing else, I assure you. If it's true, I'm flattered.'

'It is true, and you should be flattered, you duffer. She's not easily impressed with specimens of the male sort.'

Geoff did not reply, and Ruby seemed not to expect a reply. They drove on in silence for a while.

'Yesterday, we started talking about female beauty,' said Geoff at length. 'The question was whether beauty is just physical, or was female beauty also connected with movement and attitude. What do you think now about Estella, about her beauty, I mean?'

'Should I think differently?'

'We're better acquainted with her now. She's affectionate. Deep down, she's not at all aloof or impassive. Her appearance is like a cloak. It's the inner person who seems beautiful, as I said to Miss Barker.'

'What's your point?'

'I don't know whether I have a point, other than Estella is different from how she appears.' He struggled to think through his thoughts. 'Is there a link between the appearance and the person inside, where the real beauty lies?'

'You can't disregard appearances when discussing beauty,' said Ruby. 'Isn't the idea about beauty really about appearance? Surely, it's the appearance that moves. It is a power to move. And someone of extreme beauty has the power to move extremely. Estella's unique appearance possesses great power, even though the personality—what you're calling the inner beauty, not seen with the eyes—is soft and sweet and affectionate. We have experienced that power.'

'There is then a difference between physical beauty and inner beauty, the beauty of the person,' said Geoff, still trying to sort out his thoughts.

'That seems obvious.'

'Then the great power attached to outer beauty is rather brittle, isn't it?'

'Why?'

The car was now on the dusty, unsealed road, and Geoff had to pay closer attention to the way before him. He struggled to put the idea that had come to him into words.

'The beauty you see in the physical appearance is like the bright wrapping around a gift box. You don't know what's inside until you remove the bright wrapping. What you find on the inside depends on what has been put there. It may be an empty space. It could be an ugly ornament. It may also be a pure gold ingot. In the end, what's on the inside is the important part. You throw the wrapping away when it has served its purpose. Someone too attracted by the wrapping to open the box for the gift is foolish, don't you think?'

'Well, you're quite the philosopher.'

'I'm just working from what you have said about beauty.'

'But is the analogy a good one?' she said. 'The wrapping on a gift box bears, it is true, no real relation to what's inside the box, but is that true of a person? Couldn't the physical exterior of a person determine what's on the inside?'

'Would a beautiful exterior make a beautiful interior? A beautiful person may be ugly inside.'

'You're right,' she said. 'These days, it seems more likely that a beautiful exterior goes with an ugly interior. So often, you find beautiful girls empty-headed, conceited, and selfish.'

'So exterior beauty doesn't necessarily have anything to do with interior beauty, does it?' said Geoff. 'Interior beauty comes from the way the person is. What the person is could also determine what that person does with their exterior beauty.'

Ruby said nothing for a while. The car raced on over the dusty dirt road, eventually came on the deteriorating sealed road, and bumped and shuddered along as Geoff kept up the pace.

'Okay,' she said at last, 'I'll grant a meaningful distinction between exterior beauty and inner beauty, but I'm not wholly convinced that exterior beauty is as superficial as you seem to think. For example, is Estella's extraordinary appearance only on the surface and wholly unrelated to what we have seen as a soft, affectionate girl? And there's something else we have not yet mentioned: her high principles. Those principles are just not what one would call "Catholic principles." Her decency, her modesty, her politeness, the lack of vulgarity, all these things make up what we have referred to as her inner beauty. When you look at Estella, you see a person of extraordinary beauty. When you continue to look, you perceive a depth to that beauty. The decent, mature adult would see further into that beauty than the ignorant, vulgar types that harass young women in pubs. So there could be more of a connection than you think.' She paused. 'Perhaps, the beautiful girl with the ugly interior is guilty of warping a gift of nature ...?'

'Yes ... perhaps,' said Geoff, concentrating on the road.

'You know,' said Ruby, 'it's a form of desecration, isn't it? I mean, for a crude, ignorant yobbo to leer at and pester a person like Estella Winterbine. What was that biblical quotation again, you know, about casting pearl before the swine or something like that?'

THAT EVENING, Aine expressed her satisfaction with Ruby and Geoff's visit. She was pleased their first impressions had been correct. It was gratifying that Ruby and Estella had taken to each other. Charles agreed and remarked on Ruby's willingness to accommodate Estella while deciding what work she should do. Estella would go to Bendigo on Easter Monday and return the following evening. Estella was happy with the arrangements and looked forward to her visit.

Then, said Charles, it remained for him and Aine to discuss the matter with Miss Bicknell and Bill Huckerby. It would be an opportunity also to talk to Miss Bicknell about their faith. She should know why and how strongly they and their daughter were attached to their faith. It might impress her and bring her to consider the power of Christian belief rather than the other way around. A person's life must be empty and despairing without Christ's promises. But Aine was not so sure now that Miss Bicknell would be susceptible. Feelings were gathering in her about the new teacher. They were indistinct at that moment, so she did not utter them. She would wait before she caused Charles worry.

Estella left her parents to be with each other. She knew they liked time during the day to share their love in silence. The love between husband and wife? She now wondered what lay ahead for her. She had never imagined herself attached in that way to someone else. What would it be like to love a man the way her mother loved her father? What would it be like to be held in the arms of a man she loved as much as her mother loved her father? She walked around the side of the house, picking off dead buds from the overhanging plants. What lay ahead of her? Fr. van Engelen had asked her whether she felt a calling to the religious life. No, she did not feel a calling. She did not feel anything drawing her away from her parents, her house, her garden, and her town. She did not think it would make a difference to her prayer life and her devotion to Jesus if she were in Binawarra or anywhere els e.

She made her way along the winding paths to the grassy, open space where the archway, covered in the climbing rose, sprinkled its pink rose petals and leaves on the ground around it. She walked its length over the white marble gravel and emerged on the other side. She turned and came back. Thin, loose streamers of rose bush hung around her, and the fragrance of the plants and flowers of the surrounding gardens blew softly and whisperingly through the archway. The sun was going down, and the sparkling early evening air was yellow-tinged. She sat on the bench where she had sat the previous day, facing Geoff. She saw the face with the warm, friendly eyes.

She did not know what to think about him. It was all confusion whenever she tried to work out what she was feeling. He was a lot older than her, a lot more experienced, and a lot more mature, but she liked him in a way that she would like someone of her age. She was happy he was friendly towards her, that he seemed, in a way, protective. That was good. But it did not make her feel good. She saw the feeling he had for Ruby. It was tender and considerate. That was also good. But it did not make her feel good.

She sat for some time, feeling a mixture of pleasure and unease and looking at the spot where Geoff had been sitting. She stood, walked from under the archway, and took the path to the right. She could not be more pleased with her new friendship with Ruby. Ruby was like Jenny, but with more confidence, maturity, and understanding. She had taken on the role of a big sister, a big sister who was reliable and trustworthy. This was just where Jenny failed.

Ruby's reliability and trustworthiness brought Estella's attention back to Geoff. Thinking of him so much made her uneasy. She struggled to suppress a sob. Her feelings for Geoff were not the feelings of a normal friendship. It was her first time. She had to confess that she was responding to him as a man. She felt the force of the betrayal in those feelings. She arrived at the little grotto. She lifted her dress to kneel with her bare knees on the ground. In the fading light, the dress fell about her in a white circle as she bowed her head.

AT AROUND eight o'clock, Boris was walking under the eucalypts at the end of Melbourne Road. He stopped under some low-hanging branches and waited. Fifteen minutes later, Calder's white utility hummed to a stop at the same spot. Two girls who had pressed themselves up against the bushes at the front of the property on the corner raced to the car and jumped in. He watched the utility make the same manoeuvre and head out of town. A short time later, he was seated in Gerda's lounge room, smoking and drinking his specially prepared coffee. Gerda walked up and down, furiously blowing smoke into the air.

'Tricia Barry and a younger girl! How could that fellow be so stupid? He could risk everything. The younger girl is almost certainly Tricia's sister. She's fourteen.' She turned to Boris. 'Why are men so stupid?' She stubbed her cigarette out in the nearest ashtray. Boris shrugged and assumed a look of boredom. It was obvious he could not have cared less. She would have to handle it through him, if necessary. She must not be too hasty, though. Boris's mindless violence should be used sparingly. Perhaps she would leave Stephen to hang himself. That might be engineered. Moreover, the shock of a teacher's dealing carnally with a fourteen-year-old female student might distract people from seeking connections with other activities. Then it hit her. Jane Cox would prove her real worth at last. She sat on the couch opposite Boris.

'Got something going?' he said, breaking his boredom with a mocking smirk.

'What have you got for me?'

'I can say there's less chance of the Winterbine girl losing her treasure now.'

'Go on,' she replied, irritated by his lazy, mocking manner.

'That witch, Florence Barker, is paying more attention to her. I don't know what that's all about. From reports, she's always poked her nose into their affairs—the Winterbines, I mean.' He shrugged, not bothering to look at her. 'Something trivial, no doubt.'

'Go on.'

'The girl has struck up a friendship with a young couple. From the man's appearance, Dawson had better be careful. The man has a military background. His build, his manner of walking and standing, it can't be otherwise.'

'Who are they?'

'They're from out of town, here to visit the principal. I'd guess the man will be part of the veterans' celebrations.'

'What about his girlfriend?'

'I don't know at this stage. That's as much as I have learned.'

'Good,' said Gerda, and she fell to thinking. 'Do you have access to marijuana?'

'Yes. I have a special price for you.' He raised an eyebrow.

'Good. I don't care about the price. Now I've persuaded Huckerby to consider a career in public relations for the girl. I might have had difficulty arranging a vocational visit to the Media Studies Department at Sandhurst University, but he obligingly suggested it himself. You must keep an eye on her everywhere she goes in Bendigo. Without fail. I especially want you to keep an eye on my contact there. He has a taste for young female students. He knows what he has to do, but in the past, he has proven weak. Is that all clear?'

'When and what's the contact's name?'

'I will give you all the details in time.'

'What about the marijuana?'

'How soon can you get hold of it?'

'Whenever you wish.'

'This is what I want you to do, and you must do it discreetly. You bear the responsibility for any failure.'

Boris emptied his coffee cup and reached for another of his foul-smelling cigarettes.

Chapter 14

The darkness emerges

ON MONDAY afternoon, not long before the final bell, Bill Huckerby made his way to Edith Bicknell's office. Finding the door locked and no sign of her, he turned to retrace his steps. He had gone a few paces when, glancing through the corridor windows, he noticed her talking to Len Dawson at the end of the recreational area under the shelter of the trees. Len was bent forward with one ear directed at her. They came to attention upon his approach. Miss Bicknell said something to Len, who, acknowledging the principal with a quick nod, walked off towards the school ovals .

'Ah, Miss Bicknell, I'm glad you've finished. I wanted to inform you of the Winterbines' decision.'

Ms Bicknell, with her head a little tilted, did not answer but waited for the principal to speak, an attitude Bill Huckerby did not miss. He had noted it before, and it seemed increasingly like an expression of weary forbearance. But there was no time to dwell on that. Charles and Aine Winterbine had decided it was worth investigating the public relations proposal for Estella. The visit to Bendigo had been fixed for Easter Monday and Tuesday. Miss Bicknell welcomed this information, saying she would inform her contact in the Media Studies Department at the university and encourage him to give Estella every possible help. The only requirement remaining was for Charles and Aine Winterbine to discuss Estella's future with her. They settled on a meeting at eleven o'clock the following day.

'Good,' said the principal, as they walked back to the school wing, 'that's one task completed without a hitch. I'm glad, Miss Bicknell, that we've been able to cooperate on this. I wish all other tasks went as smoothly.'

He meant to engage her in some light-hearted conversation, but Edith Bicknell did not seem in the mood for it, and her expression had returned to its impassive state by the time they reached the school building. Bill stood back and waited for her to enter. She entered without acknowledging his polite gesture.

'Oh, by the way, Miss Bicknell,' he said, as she was turning to go to her office, 'Estella will also investigate the possibility of following a course in horticulture while in Bendigo. I should've thought of that long before this. Estella is a wonderful gardener. Never mind. I just have too much to think about these days. Well, good afternoon, Miss Bicknell.'

He turned and walked down the corridor, peering now and then into the classrooms. Gerda Vrouwendijk stood rigid, watching him go. She hastened to her office, where she paused, tapping her desk. She picked up the phone, dialled, and waited.

'Bruce Butcher in the Media Studies Department, please.'

The following morning, a few minutes before eleven, Charles and Aine arrived at the reception of Binawarra High School. With the office staff looking on, Mrs Charing hurried to alert Ms Bicknell. A minute later, Ms Bicknell entered the reception area, looking around. She stopped dead. 'The Magdalen!' escaped from her lips in a choking whisper. She composed herself and offered her hand. 'Nice to meet you, at last, Mr and Mrs Winterbine. Would you please follow me? We will talk in my office.'

As they made their way along the corridor and came into view through the classroom windows, teachers and students fell silent. Their eyes fixed on Estella Winterbine's reclusive mother with her long fair hair tied loosely at the back by a bright red ribbon so that her hair fell without touching her shoulders, and her white marble-like neck was exposed. Miss Bicknell ushered them into her office and to the chairs in front of the desk. She stood still for a moment, looking at them and then abruptly excused herself.

Gerda Vrouwendijk clumsily shut the office door behind her and hurried to the corridor window overlooking the recreational square. Clutching the windowsill, she breathed in gasps. She had not taken the lavish praise seriously, long heaped upon Aine Winterbine. The comparison with a medieval or Celtic princess had seemed hyperbolic. But now, if anything, those comparisons had fallen short, and she was taken by surprise. Her rigid control was shattered. There in her office, sitting in front of her desk, appeared the very embodiment of that ethereal princess she imagined in the mists of their common Germanic past, that primordial time when women created language and brought it to its peak in myth, fantasy and the narrative of feeling. Was this the princess prototype of that era when the sacred feminine had formed language only to see its divine vitality shackled by the unbending male mind? Aine Winterbine had the appearance of the Woman. Gerda clasped the ridge of the windowsill and composed herself.

She re-entered her office, made hurried excuses for her absence, and took her seat. Her eyes shifted from that face to the papers on her desk and back again. Shuffling the papers, she expressed her satisfaction that they had agreed to investigate the suitability of public relations work for Estella. Estella may be quiet, but with maturity, she would become more outgoing and talkative. She was a great deal cleverer than people thought, she stressed. Estella possessed many other qualities that pointed in this direction, and she enumerated them. In conclusion, her professional opinion was that Estella would find personal fulfilment in this sort of work.

All through this explanation, Gerda could not help bringing her eyes to rest on Aine's face. It was all she could do to keep her composure as those piercing blue eyes and the flawless, ageless face looked at her, at times seeming to look through her. People had spoken about her daughter as a goddess of beauty. It was a measure of how dull the descendants of the ancient Germanic tribes had become that they did not recognise the original outward form of the goddess in this reclusive woman hidden away in the bush of northwestern Victoria.

Fortunately, Charles was not slow to speak, and he took Gerda's gaze away from the goddess. He said they, too, were happy the arrangements could now be settled. They were confident they would arrive at an outcome in Estella's best interests. He thanked Miss Bicknell for her attentiveness to Estella's welfare. However, he continued, there was another matter they would like to discuss. It was an issue of great seriousness to them. Miss Bicknell, exhibiting polite surprise, asked him to go on.

'Well, Miss Bicknell, a few weeks ago, you asked our daughter a series of questions,' he began. 'She didn't understand their purpose. They sounded strange to us, too, and we sought an explanation from someone acquainted with such intellectual matters. That person was our parish priest. To our apprehension, he told us the purpose of such questions was to undermine a person's religious beliefs. Is that right?'

'Mr Winterbine, I would not put it in that way precisely. I mean, as an attempt to undermine religious belief. My job as a teacher is to encourage students to think and to prepare them for life outside the school. Your daughter will have her faith tested all through her life, as you have probably had.'

'Nobody has ever challenged our beliefs,' said Aine, 'and we have never doubted them.'

Gerda started at the voice. The anger she often felt at history's suppression of the spirit of the Northern Woman rose within her. Before her was the embodiment of that creating female spirit, but it had been misdirected; it had been stolen. It was a despairing thought that this beautiful, fair Northern European woman may be in permanent captivity.

'If that is true, Mrs Winterbine, then you are indeed fortunate. Most people doubt their beliefs.'

'That's what Fr. van Engelen said,' said Charles. 'Nevertheless, we have never doubted.'

'My purpose is to make your daughter think about the range of beliefs she holds. It is part of her education to weigh up the arguments against them and then go on to defeat them. That will strengthen her faith, won't it? Your daughter, I must admit, seemed to take it in her stride. I don't think I made any inroads. Am I right?'

'Yes, you're right,' said Charles. 'She remains devoted to her faith. And that's what we would like to talk about. Have you had any contact with Christian belief?'

'Yes ... a little.' Ms Bicknell did her best not to smirk.

'Well, we would like to give you our side of the story. That seems fair, considering that you put the arguments against Christian belief to our daughter.'

'All right.'

'As it was related to us by our daughter, the arguments you brought against Christian belief were abstract or theoretical. That's the way Fr. van Engelen put it. We couldn't follow the reasoning entirely, but we understood that if you can't see or feel something, you have no reason to think it exists. Is that right? Have we understood correctly?'

'There's more, but for the sake of what you want to say, we will assume that. But let me add that these are arguments against one form of religious belief.'

'Are there others?' said Aine.

'Well, some people think the spiritual arises within the person. In a way, the divine is in each of us.'

'We're not quite sure what you mean by that,' Charles said after consulting Aine with a glance.

'Why don't you go on with your explanation first,' said Miss Bicknell, 'and I will explain my point of view afterwards.'

'I was going to say that those sorts of theoretical arguments don't hold much weight with us. Fr. van Engelen called it a mode of thinking with its own problems. What did he call it again, darling?' he said, turning to Aine.

'Rationalism. He called it the method of rationalism.'

'That's right,' said Charles. 'By way of natural reason, as Father put it, we are convinced of the presence of God in all creation. Our contemplation reveals that to us. When Aine and I sit on the verandah in the evenings and contemplate the hills, we see God in nature. When I am with my daughter on that prominent hill just outside the town, we can see God as we contemplate the surrounding countryside. The force of our consciousness of right and wrong raises the idea of perfection, which is God. That may not be acceptable to the form of reasoning you have used, but it is acceptable t o us.'

'It's not acceptable to a lot of people.'

'Fr. van Engelen said the method of rationalism leads to belief in nothing,' said Aine.

'The end of the rationalist method is actually the starting point,' replied Gerda, her eyes shifting every time Aine spoke.

'What do you mean?'

'Finish your explanation first.'

'The indispensable ground for our belief is in the Scriptures,' said Charles. 'Jesus' message of love and redemption makes sense. It makes sense of our lives, at the heart of which is love. It's really that simple.'

'Other religions preach love.'

'Not as fully,' said Aine. 'To the extent they do, they share in Jesus' message.'

'And we have the authority of the Church to support and guide us,' said Charles.

'Are you happy with that? Are you happy with giving up your independence?'

'Everybody has to obey an authority,' said Charles. 'The school pupils are under the authority of the teachers. The teachers are under the principal's authority. The principal is under the authority of the Education Department. I have authority over my employee, Ken Bowery. No, Miss Bicknell, to simple people like us, it makes no sense to disregard all authority, as if we are the final judges. We have the Church's long-established authority to guide us in our daily decisions. The happiness of our love is due to God, the God we find in the example and lessons of Our Lord Jesus Christ.'

'Is that it?' said Miss Bicknell.

'Yes,' said Charles. 'We think if you expose yourself to the true message of the Scriptures, you might think differently.'

'I'll keep that in mind,' she said, unable to resist a touch of sarcasm. 'Mrs Winterbine, you stated that your parish priest claimed the method of rationalism leads to scepticism. That's right to a certain extent. However, the sceptical end of the rationalist method provides a basis for constructing a proper idea, a more human idea, of religious belief. The scepticism of what is outside us makes us contemplate what we truly are. In that contemplation, we find we have complete autonomy in a world of flux and uncertainty. We are left to associate with similarly autonomous beings and to impose an agreed order on the chaos. In doing this, we recognise the limitlessness of the human spirit, that spirit that continually arises within and out of our association. We recognise it as a divine spirit arising out of an association whose key mode is language and communication. Those in contact with that spirit are just as fervent as you are about their worship of the divine.'

As she continued to explain the idea of the divine spirit arising out of the autonomy of associated and communicating individuals, she felt Aine Winterbine's eyes boring into her. They grasped her in a way she had not experienced since the emotional crisis she had suffered in Amsterdam a few years ago. That was with another beautiful woman, but that woman, as bewitching as she was, was not to be compared with the vision she had in front of her. She stopped abruptly, hurriedly excused herself, and left the room. She passed through the door to the recreational area and walked to the end of the classroom wing, where she was out of sight of observers. She leaned up against the wall, gasping for breath and struggling against something she felt had her in its grasp. She clutched at the brickwork.

Five minutes later, now composed, she reentered her office and resumed her place behind the desk. Before Charles could speak, she said: 'How long have you had the name Winterbine?'

'What do you mean?'

'Well, Winterbine is a made-up name, isn't it? It was made up by the English and given to you sometime after settlement.'

'I have always had that name. It was my father's name.'

'Excuse me, Mr. Winterbine, I don't mean to offend. I have a legitimate purpose in asking you. You see, in what I have just explained about religious belief and feeling, language is of the utmost importance. We are communicating beings. Perfecting our being has to do essentially with the language we speak. I believe the natural and pure form of our language, our communication, is to be found in the origins of our first communities. It was a time when the process of language was unshackled, not put in chains, by certain historical events. It is hard to retrieve the purity of our language, but one way is to examine the surviving indigenous languages and regional dialects. They are the least affected by pernicious historical events. In that sense, they possess overriding rights. That's why I am asking you to look back at your real name. It may mean the road to rediscovering your true self. No one and no society can legitimately interfere. You have a legitimate right to free your language, and thus yourself, from the chains of a society that oppresses it and you.'

'Why are you telling us this?' said Aine. 'Have you said this to anybody else in the school?'

'I'm telling you in response to your questions about religious belief. This is not something I am concerned about promoting—at least now.' Her eyes dropped, and she picked up the papers in front of her.

'Miss Bicknell,' said Charles, 'Let me tell you a bit about myself. I had loving parents, but they were not perfect. They had habits that caused their early deaths. I mourned as much about their wasted lives as about their passing. Perhaps more. My two uncles, who lived close by us, wasted their lives in the same way. One ran his car off a bridge into a creek and drowned. I happened to be there on a visit with my wife and daughter. I had to help drag his body from the submerged car. I felt his humiliation. I felt the sorrow and humiliation of my aunts, who have been like a mother to me. I was determined I wouldn't succumb to the same way of life. I felt I had a duty to my parents to live differently. I also felt a duty to the parish priest, who became like a second father, and to my dear aunts who, with their hearts so full of generosity and kindness, loved me as much as my mother did. I did not want their efforts and care to count for nothing.

'In a strange set of coincidences, set in motion by that priest, I arrived here in Binawarra and met Aine at Bill and Joanne Huckerby's place. It turned out that Aine and I were meant for each other. After we had married, we returned to Binawarra for particular reasons. One vital reason was that here we were away from the influences that operated on my mother and father, and I could protect my wife and child from those influences. We came here with the name Winterbine, the name I took from my parents, and it is the name we have lived happily under for all these years. Not only do I have no interest in finding out what the past could have to do with my name, but I am also concerned about preserving the good things Providence has bestowed on us. It is my duty as husband and father to ensure that preservation. I will not fail that duty, Miss Bicknell.'

'I'm not suggesting you do, Mr Winterbine,' said Gerda, retreating before the Winterbine confidence.

'Miss Bicknell,' said Aine, 'your views on religion are opposed to ours. We kindly ask you not to expose our daughter to those views anymore. It is unnecessary for her education. We are happy to investigate the suitability of a career in public relations. That has nothing to do with our religious belief.'

'Of course, Mrs Winterbine. But I broached the subject as part of the counselling students undergo in deciding their direction in life.'

'Thank you, Miss Bicknell,' said Charles. 'We await news of the arrangements with the university.'

Without more ado, Gerda brought the meeting to a close. It was a relief. The exchange had unnerved her. The meeting did not go well. Despite the thrill of the discovery of Aine Winterbine, she realised the great obstacle was the indoctrination they had suffered from their religious overlords. So malignant was the confederacy of parents and clergy that they were regurgitating their lessons in no time. It was a prison where not only the daughter languished. It was all the more urgent to discredit the priest.

AINE HAD seen the aura of darkness she had been struggling with for years taking form within Miss Bicknell as its host. It was as if her words were coming from the mouth of the spirit that had taken control of her soul. The spirit abided in the waters of the dark well of her eyes. That the spirit had now revealed itself did not disturb her. The direct confrontation, in a way, relieved her. She was confident that with her many prayers giving her strength, she could confront its tangible expression. When Miss Bicknell shut the door behind her, she reached for Charles's hand.

'There seems to be something wrong with Miss Bicknell,' he said. 'Perhaps she doesn't feel well.'

'It may have something to do with her views. They are opposed to the way we think, aren't they?'

'They certainly are. I wonder whether Bill is aware of her thinking and efforts to promote it in the school. Surely Estella is not the only one she has spoken to about this.'

'We must leave no doubt about what we think, Charles.'

'Of course, darling.'

Chapter 15

Irresistible Bruce Butcher

BRUCE BUTCHER, senior lecturer in the Media Studies Department of Sandhurst University, cleared his desk on the second floor of the Humanities building. He wanted everything clean and tidy before he left for the day. In contrast to many of his colleagues, he was a well-organised academic. He was not so because he was particularly attached to neatness. It was a question of efficiency. He was clean, neat, and well-organised because the lessons had been there from his earliest memories. His father was a successful lawyer, and his mother a respected schoolteacher. Besides receiving constant parental guidance about efficiency, Bruce saw that his busy parents maintained their successful professional lives because they were well organised.

If Bruce had lacked anything in personal efficiency, he received firm correction during his stay in Holland as a postgraduate student at one of Amsterdam's universities. Some of his Dutch friends may have been boozers and rabble-rousers, but most were practical and well-organised in pursuing their social and political goals. Such, generally, were the qualities of the Dutch. A good example was his friend and political companion of those days, Gerda van den Donker. Gerda was astonishingly slovenly in her habits but meticulous and persevering in her professional and political life. And here he was now with an unexpected directive from her.

As he walked towards his car, he flicked open the page of the neatly listed instructions Gerda had given the evening before during her brief visit to Bendigo. It was clear enough, he thought. He had to supervise a prospective student, provide the best possible picture of the status and rewards of public relations work, and arrange meetings with the heads of several companies that depended on their public relations people. They were the written instructions.

The brief verbal instructions were that he was to ask no questions of the corporate people who may turn up in the department to talk to the students, and under no circumstances was he to lay a finger on the girl. The first instruction was no trouble. He willingly complied with the tasks the formidable Gerda van den Donker gave him. He was committed to her general political campaign and was well rewarded for the work she occasionally called on him to do. The second instruction had made him laugh.

'What? Do you think I'm hard up or something?'

'I don't care what your circumstances are. You are not even to think of laying the tip of your little finger on this girl,' said Gerda. 'I cannot emphasise enough how strict this instruction is.'

Bruce Butcher had laughed again, but he also understood. Such warnings from Gerda Vrouwendijk were never idle, and she was not hesitant in seeking retribution from those who failed. She was known for her unrelenting character among the core group in Amsterdam. In any case, it was not a problem. The university campus, on which he had just begun his second year, provided a glut of young female flesh that succumbed to his smooth manner, good looks, and political rhetoric.

Bruce Butcher's thoughts about himself were not baseless conceit. He was a handsome man along the same lines as Len Dawson, but more impressive. He was tall but not slight. His hair was long but not flamboyant. His hairdresser ensured there would be no bad hair days for Bruce Butcher. He wore an elegant 18-carat gold chain, visible under the bright, open-neck shirts, done up to the second-last button. In a word, he followed the glam rock fashion, but in a mature, understated way. The combination of popstar appearance with the status and articulation of a senior lecturer in media studies was seductive for the idealistic female students newly released from the confines of a private girls' school. These were the students Bruce specialised in. He focused on students from Catholic girls' schools. Deflowering one of these beauties provided a mind-blowing ecstasy.

With his idle ranking of the girls he had had over the past year on campus, he reached his restored British racing green MGB. He cast admiring glances over it as he unhitched the fold-back roof. As the weather was warm, he would drive the six miles into Bendigo with the wind blowing through his styled hair. It was a chance, too, for the public to see what authentic style was. With this thought occupying him as he drove and looked around, he arrived not too long after at his restored Hollywood Spanish-style house in a smart part of the provincial town. He approvingly surveyed the beautifully tended gardens. He insisted his gardener attend first to the line of bright red roses along the path leading to the front porch. These, he considered, would be the beginning of a period of arousal for the girls who visited him. He picked out the brightest as he walked up and down the path and snipped it off with his fingernails. This would be a special rose for a special girl.

Bruce Butcher had picked out Lilly Kelly from the new students attending his lectures on the sociology of communications. She was a fresh-faced kid with big blue eyes, a spotless complexion, and a gorgeous figure. She was smartly dressed, often in expensive brand dresses, and behaved with good bourgeois manners. He could see it a mile off; she was a girl from a well-to-do middle-class background and, in this case, most likely Catholic. He could not always put a finger on why he could see one girl was Catholic and the other not. There was something about the Catholics he could sniff out. Whatever it was, it was an enticing factor. When he noticed during the term's second lecture that she was looking at him with that familiar rapt expression, he knew there was a chance. He went to work.

During lectures, he looked in her direction with a sympathetic expression. When he opened the lecture room for questions, he gave her encouraging glances, and when she asked a question, he commented on its perception. He ensured she was a member of his tutorial group and encouraged her to come to his office if she had any questions about the course material. When she took him up on this invitation, he knew he was in with more than a chance.

He knew how to brighten his private meetings with jokes and ridicule of past customs that restricted the free flow of information in society. She responded to his jokes, often giggling. After two weeks of frequent meetings and chats with her, he felt he could move to the next level. It was quick, but he told himself all the signs were there. He rarely made a mistake—well, not often, anyhow. That afternoon, she was coming at his invitation to discuss her first assignment. She eagerly accepted the invitation, and he took that as the final go-ahead.

He checked the three-bedroom house to see that everything was in order. There were vases of fresh flowers here and there, and they gave off a sweet fragrance. Around the lounge room, he had placed or hung his favourite display pieces, and these would offer the starting point for the conversation leading to a climax of pleasure. In his bedroom, he folded the bedspread, and placed it on the nearby stool. He then turned down the clean, crisp upper sheet, exposing the light blue slips on the pillows. All was in order. He turned on the bedside light, which would give the room a soft glow by the time it was dark and he was ready to take her there. He checked his watch. It was a little past five-thirty. She would arrive soon from her student's accommodation, not too far away.

Lilly Kelly's parents had made a special trip to Bendigo to choose a suitable accommodation for the daughter they were proud of. She was the first in a family of tradesmen to go to university. Her parents wanted to

ensure she had the best possible start, including comfortable accommodation in a fashionable area of Bendigo. And why not, thought her father?
They had worked hard and made a success of their plumbing business. His
daughter would have opportunities that he and his wife had never had.
Lilly Kelly, conscious of her parents' hard work through the years, was
determined to do them proud. So she set out, telling her housemates she
was off to do some extra work with one of the lecturers. She carried her
small, fashionable leather briefcase with lecture and study notes inside. She
was flattered that one of the senior lecturers was taking a keen interest in
her progress.

Bruce Butcher opened the door to a smiling Lilly Kelly. He ushered
her into the lounge, uncorked a bottle of Moselle that he had placed in a
bucket of ice on the antique oak sideboard, and poured two glasses as he
chatted to her. Her eyes were caught, as he knew they would, by the various
ornaments and pictures around the room. His centrepiece was the huge,
framed reproduction of Pablo Picasso's *Guernica*. Lilly Kelly, seated on the
lounge settee, looked straight at it on the opposite wall. Taking his cue,
Bruce began an account of the painting's history, tying it in with methods
in modern communication.

Lilly listened attentively as she sipped her wine. The Spanish Repub-
licans, said Bruce, fought to free the oppressed Spanish people from the
tyranny of church and state. These idealistic freedom fighters, in solidarity
with fighters from all corners of the world, did not count on the evil
dictator, Generalissimo Franco. Franco, a fellow traveller with Hitler and
Mussolini, committed a grievous act of betrayal by taking command of the
Spanish army from a base in Morocco and launching an invasion of Spain
that snuffed out the beginnings of freedom for the Spanish people. Picasso
chose the rebel bombing of the village of Guernica to communicate to the
world the horror of war and the evil of the oppressors that kept Spain in
chains. Did Lilly see how important such individual acts of protest were?

Yes, she said, she could see that such individual acts of public communication were essential to maintaining freedom.

Bruce then passed on from the commentary on *Guernica* and the Spanish Civil War to other items around the room, each of them illustrating the same theme—freeing the individual from the oppression of others. As he passed from one object to another, he continued to link the objects with the concept of freedom and the necessity for people to seek out alternative means of public communication when the trusted means failed in their task. Without warning, he grabbed a camera from the oak sideboard and coming in front of Lilly said, 'Smile!' Lilly blinked from the flash and put the glass on the coffee table in front of her.

Next, Bruce Butcher was on the lounge beside her. She was grabbed and kissed roughly. The unexpected action left her confused and unresisting. It became rougher. Then it was still, and she was looking up at the ceiling. She sat up. Bruce Butcher was standing near the sideboard, glass in hand and smoking. He smiled and held out the packet of cigarettes. She stood up, arrange her clothes, and grabbed her briefcase.

Now Bruce came to offer comforting words, the usual words when he saw an expression of regret. While he walked around the other side of the settee, she ran, stumbling to the front door. Before he could do or say anything, she was outside. He carefully put his cigarette in the nearest ashtray and raced after her. He came out onto the porch and saw she was already down the street. He stopped. He felt his bare feet on the antique tiles that covered the porch. He returned inside and picked up the cigarette.

LILLY KELLY dropped her fashionable leather briefcase on the floor of her bedroom, gathered her towel and clean clothes, and rushed to the bathroom. After she had washed herself thoroughly and dressed in slacks and blouse, she wrapped the clothes in a plastic bag and put them in the garbage tin. She returned to her room and lay on her bed. Half an hour later she rang her parents. Her mother asked her what was wrong, but Lilly only cried. She asked again, but the response was crying. Her crying continued until her mother became frantic and handed the phone to her father, who also failed to get her to say what was wrong. Finally, Lilly said, 'I want to come home.'

Two and a half hours later, Lilly's parents arrived to find their daughter lying on her bed with her things packed up, ready to go. They tried again to get her to say what was wrong. Lilly just shook her head and said she wanted to go. Resigning themselves to her silence, they bundled her things into the car, and with Lilly's mother sitting in the back seat comforting her, they began the drive back to Melbourne.

BRUCE BUTCHER stubbed his cigarette out and lit up a second. Was this just a case of the inexperienced girl reacting to the first time? It happened, and most often, the regrets were temporary. The girl could be talked around, and he could enjoy himself some more. Or the girl went on to other adventures. Sometimes there would be more difficulty, and he would have to make more effort to appease the fragile feelings. He had a feeling this could be a troublesome case.

He fetched his address book and flicked through the pages. His eyes alighted on a postgraduate student he had been giving personal tuition. He found he was in luck. He checked the lounge room. He cleared away the dirty wine glasses and fetched himself a clean one. No need to check the bedroom. That was a bonus. And he could depend on his formidable recuperative powers. He then fell to considering what problems could arise if the girl went to somebody in the department. He poured himself a glass of wine.

The senior people in the department, he was convinced, would be held back either by their unspoken admiration for his tally of conquests, or they would not be keen because of their own pitiful efforts at seduction to point an accusing finger at him. Generally speaking, though, in 1975, people would not make too much of a fuss about any sort of sexual activity. What were society's sexual mores in reality? They were a pernicious fiction developed by the oppressive Church to keep their faithful psychologically unbalanced and under control. Any sensible person could see that in these enlightened times. The university authorities would make fools of themselves if they seriously tried to make an issue of sexual adventure. It was the sexual revolution, after all. If it turned out the girl did not like it ... well, she did not like it. Sometimes we don't enjoy dinner at an expensive restaurant. That's hardly a reason to hold an inquisition. In any case, he would just deny it. His alibi would arrive any minute. He picked up his camera from the coffee table. He had taken the last frame of Lilly Kelly. Good, he thought, he must get it developed. He had to bring his scrapbook up to date.

THE NEXT day, Lilly's parents waited until late morning before they tackled the cause of their daughter's upset. But no matter how they came at it, they could not get anything out of her. She kept repeating that she did not want to talk about it and would never go back 'there' again. When they asked her what she intended to do, she said she would stay in her room and never come out. Lilly's parents were sensible enough not to rage about lost opportunity, responsibilities, and ruin. They understood something serious had happened. After lunch, Lilly's father encouraged her to go to the doctor. She refused. He rang their long-time doctor, Dr. Gunn, a dignified and trustworthy man in his late fifties. He came immediately, understanding Lilly's father was not given to exaggeration.

The doctor spent more than an hour with Lilly. When he emerged, he told them he had examined her thoroughly. Physically, there was nothing to worry about. Emotionally, she was on the edge, though. It had taken some time, but she told him the problem. He could never reveal a patient's details without permission. On top of that, their daughter had sworn him to absolute secrecy. She would never speak to him again if he repeated what she had said. He had prevailed upon her to let him visit every couple of days to see how she was going. In his opinion, she needed his ongoing attention. It was the only way she could be helped. She might feel more like speaking when she was on the road to recovery. Until then, they should not say anything. The university had to be informed. He suggested they give him the authority to act on their behalf. He knew the university's routine. He would not get the run-around that they would likely encounter. Leave it to him, he said. He would provide them with rigorous representation. In their upset, they readily agreed.

Dr Gunn did not waste time. That afternoon, he rang the head of department and informed him that Lilly Kelly had to defer her course for medical reasons. Her parents had authorised him to speak on their daughter's behalf. When asked why she needed representation, he replied that Lilly Kelly's medical condition had to do with a staff member. There was a tense silence on the other end of the line. The department head asked who it concerned and what it was about. When Dr Gunn replied he could reveal neither, the head said it was impossible to do anything if he did not know what or who was involved. He added that if it was about sexual matters, there was little he could do. University students were at an age when they were active. It was not the university's fault if there were a few broken hearts on campus.

Dr Gunn met this evasion by saying that he could not reveal who or what was involved because of the shock the student had suffered. She could not and did not want to say anything. It was the department's duty to investigate what had happened. He added that he intended to pursue the matter relentlessly. The head repeated that he was limited in what he could do if he did not know who and what was involved. Student sexual activity was not a good reason to institute an investigation. Otherwise, he would be forever at it. Nevertheless, he would look into the matter and keep him informed. Next, Dr Gunn rang the university's administration about course deferment and filing a complaint against a staff member. It was a highly confidential matter, and he wanted to talk to someone in authority.

He was passed on to several people who gave him information about the deferment process, but stayed away from the complaint when they had a hint of what it was about. The last of these said it was a matter best handled by Ruby Waiting. Dr Gunn had hardly finished telling Ruby about Lilly Kelly's predicament when, without mincing her words, she asked whether he would have time to receive her as soon as she could get down to Melbourne. Dr Gunn, taken aback, said he would receive her whenever she wished.

'I understand, Doctor,' said Ruby, without preamble, 'that you have to maintain confidentiality because of the gravity of the case. That's why I have taken the time to come and speak to you personally.'

'You're right, Miss Waiting, it's serious, and I'm constrained by the student. Otherwise, I would be beating down doors.'

'Right, Doctor, then let's get down to business. You contacted the Head of the Department of Media Studies. You have informed him that a student named Lilly Kelly wants to defer her course because of an incident with a department member. And you cannot say what that incident was and who the staff member was. Correct?'

'Yes, that's the only information I can give you.'

'I've checked and found that Lilly Kelly is a first-year student staying in student digs in Bendigo. Her course selection and enrolment details indicate she intends to pursue a career in the media. Her final school results show she's a good student and, under normal conditions, would sail through her university work. If an incident has occurred involving a member of department and a student has taken flight at this early stage of the term because of it, I conclude it has to do with sex.'

The doctor said nothing.

'You know, Doctor, off the record, I know things about the staff of that department you wouldn't know.' He waited for her to go on. 'There is currently no notion of university staff standing in for parents while young people are on campus. Worse, some male lecturers think the female students are fair game. What used to be called seduction is simply having a relationship. Having sex in that relationship is a non-issue.'

'This is not a case of someone willingly having sex, whatever one wants to think about free love and that sort of thing.'

'Good,' said Ruby, 'we have that clear. A member of staff forced his attention on Lilly Kelly.'

'I will not confirm that publicly.'

'No, I'll keep confidence. This is an informal meeting. I need a clear understanding of what I'm dealing with.' The doctor nodded. 'Do you know the name of the lecturer?'

'Yes.'

'You're not going to tell me who it is?'

'No, I can't.'

'Did the student describe him?'

'Yes, I asked her for as much detail as she was willing to give. Miss Waiting, I have been the Kelly family's doctor for years. I was at Lilly's birth. She knows she can trust me, and she answered all my questions as best she could. I have documented the incident in case she has a change of mind.'

'Was the lecturer a good-looking, flamboyant sort of person?' The doctor said nothing. 'Was there much violence? I mean, is the girl injured in any way?'

'Apart from some tenderness, she is all right physically. However, emotionally, she has been dealt a terrible blow.'

'Did the incident take place in the lecturer's home?' The doctor did not reply. 'I must tell you, Doctor, a particular member of staff is very popular among the female students. He occasionally has students over to his home for extra tuition.'

'Miss Waiting, there is no way I can say anything that could lead to a break in confidence. It would only make matters worse.'

'I understand, Doctor. What action do you propose to take?'

'I'm still thinking about it.'

'Doctor, this is off the record again. Let me suggest you write a formal complaint and send it to the university administration with a thinly disguised threat of legal action. Send a copy to me and to the Head of the Department of Media Studies. That will at least give you ground for insisting that the student's opportunities at university are not limited more than can be helped. I can tell you now that a conspiracy of silence currently ensures that few male staff are brought to account for their predatory behaviour.

'Too many of them are active or want to be active. There is admiration for the predators and little sympathy for the prey. There is no enthusiasm for public discussion when things go wrong. But at least you can ensure Lilly Kelly's prospects are not harmed. If you pursue the matter diligently, you'll be able to achieve much. You may even negotiate hush money. It will not be called that, of course. It'll be called compensation, counselling, and material support. The condition will be that you do not go public. Please keep me informed of what you're doing. I'll give you support wherever I can. I'll start by emphasising how serious the matter is for the Head of the Media Studies Department. He'll know by now who the staff member is. The man has a record.'

'How is that possible? How is it possible he still has a job?'

'I've given you the reasons, Doctor. He is shielded. Things have changed since you were at university.'

'They certainly have.'

'It was a straight-out rape, wasn't it?'

'Yes,' he said, with a helpless sigh and passing his hand over his forehead. 'It was a cruel violation of an innocent girl who went up to university full of enthusiasm and hope.'

'Will she see me?'

'No.'

Ruby and the doctor covered the details of their discussion again to ensure they understood each other correctly. At length, Ruby did not think she could learn any more and thanked the doctor for seeing her at short notice. Dr. Gunn expressed his appreciation for her sincere desire to help. It would be a comfort to Lilly to know someone at the university was sympathetic. It was important, very important for her to know that, he said. With his undertaking to keep her informed of Lilly's condition and the progress he made with the university, Ruby bade him goodbye and started on the long drive back to Bendigo.

She had been keeping a secret dossier on Bruce Butcher and a few others, but had made little headway in bringing the problem into the open. Attitudes and the prevailing social conditions were against her. Even the university's feminists lacked the cohesion and the will to do anything. Most of them were behind the debunking of traditional sexual morality. They could hardly complain if some young women were expressing their sexual freedom by freely choosing their sexual partners among the male staff. That was the appearance. The exploitation and failure of the responsible authority were the reality. The feminists would act if there were an attempt to distinguish between men and women by gender. As long as the senior lecturer mouthed the slogans of feminism and loudly maintained the equality of the sexes, he would be left alone to let autonomous young women freely choose him as their sexual partner. The following morning,

Ruby made her way to the office of the Head of the Media Studies Department. He regarded her wearily. They had been through this before. He repeated the problem of not being able to do anything if he did not know who or what the problem was. Surely Ms Waiting could see that?

It was not as simple as that, said Ruby. Something had happened that caused a bright first-year student to flee from the university. The university was responsible for finding out what happened. Well and good, replied the head, but there still must be a starting point. There was none at the moment. And had Ms Waiting considered that this could be a problem the girl already had? Had she sought counselling? Was it just a young girl's regret at having given in to someone's advances? Besides, people thought very differently about sexual behaviour these days. The old prudish, restricting Christian morality of the fifties had been left behind.

When she stressed that the family doctor would persist and was already approaching the central administration, he came back with another standard reply: the university would do everything in its power to offer support and counselling for the student. Ruby asked him if he had started an investigation. Of course, was the reply. But he had only established that the girl was nowhere around the department the previous afternoon. She might have been somewhere else on campus or outside the university grounds, but he would continue his investigation. Ms Waiting should know he could only ask the staff and students if they had any knowledge of her whereabouts. If a blank came up there ... well, he had no authority to go outside the university. Ms Waiting must know that.

'Have you checked the whereabouts of Bruce Butcher?'

'Yes, I have spoken to him. He was forthcoming. He was in the department until fairly late and then went home. He said the girl called on him to pick up some notes and then went on her way. One of the postgraduate students was there from around six o'clock until late. She saw nothing of the girl. She said Bruce appeared to have just arrived home when she got to his house. It seems all above board, Ms Waiting. He had no idea the student was back in Melbourne. Such a pity, he said, if she throws in her studies. She was a good student.'

'You believe all that?'

'I have no reason to believe otherwise.'

'Bruce Butcher has a record of this sort of thing,' she said to goad him.

'What sort of thing?' he almost sneered. 'And if Bruce Butcher has a record, it's a record of accusations and innuendo. Nothing has ever been established.'

'You must think I'm stupid. The fellow has it written all over him.'

'Be careful your political prejudices don't interfere with your judgment, Ms Waiting.'

'What prejudices are those?'

'I will leave others to tell you that. But they're well known.'

'And yours?'

'I'm the Head of the Department of Media Studies. I have no political prejudices.'

Ruby had heard enough. She got nothing more than she expected. She would at least have a go at Bruce Butcher. He would not be allowed time to relax. She was not surprised to find she was expected.

'Hah! The administration's resident fascist,' he exclaimed when she appeared in the doorway. 'I've been informed the secret police are on to me.'

'But your political chums will protect you, won't they?'

'Be careful, Ruby. You're on the administration's business. You must conduct yourself with dignity. Slanderous sarcasm is quite inappropriate for a person in your position.'

'This visit is off the record, Mr Butcher. An official investigation has a way to go before it reaches this door if it ever does.'

'That says enough, doesn't it? I have nothing to do with it, whatever it is.'

'If the shoe fits—'

'Now, that's not very scientific, is it?' he said, with a grin and a look down his nose. 'Any investigation will have to do more than seeing if the shoe fits.'

'There are several features of this episode you must stay aware of,' she said, undeterred. 'Lilly Kelly was at your place yesterday afternoon; later that evening, she rang her parents extremely upset; she said something had happened involving a person from the Department of Media Studies; her parents came and took her home; she refuses to return to the university and to say what happened.'

'Oh, it was Lilly Kelly, was it? A very capable student. A lot of promise there.'

She ignored his baiting. 'Does your postgraduate student know she could be complicit in a crime?'

'Now, you're way ahead of yourself, you fat little fascist,' he said, turning red and sitting up. 'You've got a lot to do before you can make anything so absurd stick. I would be careful, too, of harassing one of the students.'

'The family's doctor is representing the Kelly family. He knows every-thing. The girl has told him, but until now, nobody else.'

Bruce Butcher flinched. 'So what?' He shrugged.

'So it seems you're safe for the moment. If the girl decides to talk, it could be very different.'

'It'll be no different. I'll maintain the truth of what happened and provide the same testimony to back me.' He paused and then pointed at her. 'You should keep off my back, I warn you. Every time something like this happens, you're over here like a homing pigeon.'

'That's because you're often in the thick of it.'

There was a pause while they stared at each other.

'You know, Fraulein Ruby, there is something contradictory in your accusations. If I were the evil person you speak of, how is it that I'm involved in sexually exploiting so many women? Surely, they would run a mile at the mere mention of my name?'

'That is precisely the nature of your evil.'

'Fortunately, you seem to be the only one who holds that opinion,' he sneered. 'Perhaps that says more about you and your attitudes, which are to the right of Genghis Khan, to put it mildly. What happened to you? While most women have joined in the fight for women's rights, you seem trapped in the last century.'

'You and your rhetoric are having your day. You should enjoy it while it lasts,' she said, turning to leave the room. But appearing to reflect, she turned back and came a few steps towards him. He looked up at her. 'I knew a nineteen-year-old girl once ... in a university in California. She idolised an academic she thought had a profound understanding of society and its ills until she learned that his circle of friends was privy to the most intimate details of their relationship and that there were other girls. So I promised I would do what I could to stop the liars and hypocrites stalking the halls of universities in our liberal democracies from damaging other nineteen-year-olds.'

He looked up at her with a crooked half-smile, nodded a couple of times, and seemed to be on the point of speaking, but reconsidered.

'But whatever my undertakings, don't think this present incident has gone away. Dr Gunn will see to that.'

'I will see to being an excellent lecturer and staff member,' he said stupidly as Ruby turned to go. 'And why don't you just jackboot it out of here!' he called after her. But she was gone.

He rubbed his chin nervously. While the girl refused to talk, he was safe. After that? Well, he had a pretty good alibi. There was still that photo of the girl. If anyone should see that ... he had the roll of film with him. Perhaps he should destroy it. That would be a terrible pity. There were some prized photos to go in his scrapbook.

ON THE evening of that same day, Gerda Vrouwendijk sat in her lounge room, going over her notes. A glass of wine rested on the coffee table in front of her. She held a cigarette poised between the fingers of her left hand while she reviewed Estella's program step-by-step. She had to make it perfectly clear what was expected of Bruce Butcher. If he grasped the seriousness of her warnings, she was confident he could handle the task. She put down her pen, took up her glass of wine, leaned back, and sighed. That spotlessly fair woman living in the bush—she was carrying within her the primordial spark. And there she was, trapped in history, locked in a curse. She would give her soul to rescue her spirit from its spell.

Chapter 16

Bob McKinnon overplays

ESTELLA SPENT the entire week in a daze. From the moment she watched Geoff and Ruby drive away, she had difficulty controlling her thoughts. No matter what she was doing, she ended up thinking about Geoff, and then about Ruby, and then about Ruby and Geoff. She retraced her climb with Geoff to the top of the Wombat many times. She went over every word he said as they peered over the landscape. She had experienced an intimacy with him she had never experienced with anyone before. His manly presence and quiet, familiar way of gently talking opened her heart.

No other man had talked that way with her. Everyone else, including Uncle Bill, spoke to some extent with her appearance in mind. From the first moment she laid eyes on him that day on the square, Geoff looked at her differently. But whichever sequence these thoughts took, they would always come to the same dead end: Geoff was in love with Ruby. She should not have such thoughts about him. It was wrong. He was Ruby's. Even saying he was Ruby's, raising the terrible possibility he could be hers, was wrong—and unnerving. She was not sure how Ruby felt about him, but he was still hers. Her haphazard thoughts brought tears to her eyes, which she struggled to blink away.

There were distractions, though. Len Dawson was waiting every second day, it seemed, to walk with her to school. She had to admit he had a different manner with her. He spoke calmly, without bravado. He talked about Jenny and what they had done on the weekend. He asked about her parents. It was all so ordinary and without guile that she sometimes found herself in conversation with him. That had never happened before. There seemed to be so many things happening for the first time. Amazing things. The change in Len Dawson was just one of those.

During morning recess, Len and Jenny would come and sit with her. They did their best to talk about the things she was interested in: books, gardening, and bushwalking. Len even suggested they organise a walk. She appreciated it. She appreciated the attention, and she appreciated the chance to get Geoff and Ruby out of her mind. At lunchtime, she returned home as she had been doing for almost a year, since her friendship with Jenny had deteriorated. She had no wish to change that routine because Jenny and Len, with the best will in the world, could not have kept up their conversation with her. Jenny could have, but not both.

Her growing friendship with Ruby had shown her what friendship was like with someone with similar standards and social outlook—even though she was not Catholic. Her mother and father had commented on that. There was no strain in their conversation. Perhaps her big-sister manner was part of it. Whatever it was, she found a growing affection for Ruby replacing her love for Jenny. That was another reprimand, for how could she dream about Ruby's boyfriend as hers? On Friday, as she was leaving for school, she met Terry Seddon, who had just pulled up to deliver an order.

'Len Dawson is spreading around the story that he has called the bet off. He's even told people he wasn't serious about it in the first place. Don't believe him. It's rubbish.'

'How do you know?'

'I know Len Dawson. He's a creep. Always has been, always will be.' He looked at her for a few moments. 'I heard he has been walking to school with you. What has he told you?'

'He told me he wants to be friends and that the bet wasn't serious. It was meant to annoy you. He said you don't like each other.'

'He's right about that. I can't stand the two-faced weed. You know you're already falling for it.'

'Please, Terry, understand that whether there's a bet or not, I'm not interested in Len Dawson. It will never happen. You must believe me.'

'I asked the pub bookie whether the bet was still on. He said as far as he was concerned, it was. He had the bets, and nobody was asking for their money. When I told him that Dawson said the bets were off, he winked and said that Dawson could say and do what he wanted. The bets were there and would be settled three months from the date stipulated. You see what I mean?'

'Are you sure of that?'

'Absolutely. He's at work, wearing you down.'

'He's not wearing me down.'

'You're walking to school with him. You're friendly with him. That's part of the wearing down process.'

'I'm just returning friendly conversation. I do that with anyone friendly towards me.'

'Be careful, Estella. Remember, if you're not a virgin at the end of three months, and Dawson is responsible, he has won. I'm sorry to be so blunt.'

'What ...what are you hinting at?' she said, feeling sick all over again and not wanting to understand.

'Don't put anything past Dawson. You can't imagine how a creep like that behaves. Don't even put yourself in a situation where you're alone with him. He has forced himself onto others. Not all the conquests he boasts about have been willing.'

'How do you know?' she said, looking around to see how far she was from the front fence.

'I know.'

'I must go to school now.' She looked to see if her mother or father had noticed their conversation.

'I'm sorry to upset you again. I'm only trying to put you on your guard.'

'I know. Thank you. I'll be careful.'

She left him, trying to shake off the sickening thoughts he had placed in her mind. Was it true? She remembered Len saying Terry was bitter because he had won out with Jenny. Were Terry's warnings a result of that bitterness? She could not know. Two things were certain, though: she would never succumb to Len Dawson no matter what he did, and she would continue to be pleasant to anyone pleasant to her. Besides, she had Len on probation. He must prove himself. By the time she approached the school grounds, she had shaken off the sick feelings. She was relieved Len did not join her.

She entered the school grounds from Huckerby Way and was walking up the dirt track when she heard quiet laughter coming from the bushes about fifteen yards away on her right. She walked on, glancing in the direction of the laughter. Len Dawson, Dennis Lorimer, John Sayer, and Don McGlashan walked from behind the bushes. They were talking and joking together and did not see her. They each had a cigarette in their hand, which they put to their mouths in unison and drew on ostentatiously while looking at each other. They noticed Estella, who had walked past th em.

'Hi Estella,' called Len.

'Hi Estella,' said the other three, grinning stupidly.

'Don't be idiots,' said Len, and then to Estella, as he came up beside her: 'Ignore them. They don't mean anything.'

'No, we don't mean anything,' they said together.

'Shut up!'

Estella walked on without stopping or saying anything. For once, they were not a nuisance. They just seemed to be having a bit of fun. Len continued to speak to her in a friendly, relaxed manner about trivialities.

He told her, with no obvious point, that Jenny and her mother planned to go down to Bendigo to buy clothes from an exclusive dress shop. He smoked as he walked, as did the others. She noticed the cigarettes were not the usual sort. And they gave off a strange, unfamiliar smell. As they neared the point where the path broke from the trees and bushes, the boys fell back. Len said they would follow shortly. Estella walked on.

At recess, Jenny came to sit with her. Estella might as well have been alone because Jenny kept breaking off from the conversation and looking around. Estella asked what she was looking for. She waved her hands, shook her head, and said, 'Nothing.' But she continued to look around. Estella asked if she was looking for Len and got an irritable reply. Jenny was immediately sorry and said so. Yes, it was Len she was looking for. He had probably gone off with those idiots he hangs around with.

'You know, there's one advantage to not having a boyfriend. You don't have to worry about where they are and what they're doing. Count yourself lucky. There's a lot of heartache in it.'

Estella said nothing, though she understood in a way. Geoff was not her boyfriend, but her feelings for him left her anything but comfortable. She was relieved when the recess bell rang. Jenny was not the companion she wanted at that moment. The thought that she had feelings for an older man, the man in love with the girl behaving like a big sister, would not go away.

FR. VAN Engelen picked up Frans's letter and read through it once again. He checked the sentences to make sure he could translate everything accurately. At length, he was satisfied with his preparation. He took his walking stick, and a few minutes later, he was sitting on a bench under the shade of some eucalypts. He did not have to wait long, for Miss Barker soon approached with her bags. She stopped before him as if to say a passing hello and then sat down.

'Well, Father, it is a fine day. We've got a lot to talk about. I see you have a letter there; from the looks of it, it's from Holland.'

She listened while the priest translated Frans's account of his clash with Cees van den Donker, of Cees's business activities, his anger at finding out that Frans was making inquiries about him, the difficulty he had in discovering where Gerda van den Donker was, and Anneke's assault.

'Father and daughter are in it together, whatever it is,' said Miss Barker.

'It seems that way.'

'That language institute appears to be the banner of something far more organised,' she continued. 'The anger caused by your brother's inquiring into Gerda van-whatever's father's businesses would seem to link them with the political activity. But how and why is all this connected with Estella Winterbine? The language link seems too slight and superficial to be of consideration. Why would that woman come all the way from Holland and London for such slight relevance?'

'Van-den-Donker. I thought of that, too. It makes no sense.'

'Did you know that Gerda van-den-thing has arranged for Estella to spend time at Sandhurst University to consider the possibility of following a course in public relations?'

'Yes, I heard.'

'What do you think?'

'I don't believe she's suited.'

'Nor do I. The important question is whether there's any connection here with that woman's political agenda. Or is it part of the charade? She has been appointed senior school career counsellor, after all. And the reasons she gives for the recommendation are at least plausible.'

'I don't know,' said the priest. 'Assuming it is part of the political agenda, what extra benefit could a course in public relations offer for Gerda's organisation? Again, it does not make sense to come all this way to prepare some unknown girl, no matter how beautiful, to promote her institute. Surely somebody who had some competence in linguistics would be more suitable. You don't need a course in public relations for that. And who but the truly fanatical would be taken by the claim that dialects and language customs possess rights?'

'You have a point,' said Miss Barker. 'Perhaps it's for a block of like-minded organisations? That would make more sense. But why Estella?'

'We have reached the same point, Miss Barker. We must wait for more developments. Either that or confront Gerda van den Donker with what we know.'

'That is, of course, an option. But is it reasonable? What would it mean for Estella's security? The foreigner with the moustache would bolt. What he would do before that is not predictable. The unmasking of the Bicknell woman would not only put you in the centre of it, but it would also raise sticky questions for people in Melbourne. Many would go to ground or pretend they knew nothing about it. To get this far, Gerda must have completed some clever work. It would not be easy for a Dutch national to successfully parade as an English teacher with a qualification in counselling. There seems a lot at stake. I suggest we keep an eye on things for the moment to see where Gerda is going. I'm confident Estella is safe in Binawarra. I have organised for Captain Shawcross to shadow her while she is with Miss Waiting in Bendigo.'

'You seem to have thought of everything,' said the priest.

'I do have experience in these things, if that's what you mean.'

'I have had that impression increasingly.'

Miss Barker hesitated. 'This business seems to go further than the interest of local authorities.' More hesitation. 'I have contacts—I would like to consult them. It could all be some petty action by a little group of idealistic fanatics without much effective power. It could, on the other hand, go fairly deep. It would be wise to find out just how deep before any action is taken.'

'As you wish, Miss Barker.'

'Good, Father, now let's arrange to meet again when there are more developments. I should have something from my contacts shortly.'

'How long have you been doing this?'

'It will remain confidential, of course.'

'You have my word.'

'Since the war. It's a long story, and I will tell you at the right time.'

'Whenever it suits you. I have often thought there was more to you than the appearance, Miss Barker.'

'I'm aware of that, Father.' She paused. 'You know, you're a good representative of the Church. Many people in this Protestant hollow have had their minds changed about the Catholic clergy.'

'I am very pleased to hear it, Miss Baker. The Second Vatican Council intended to reach out to our fellow Christians and remove the historical misunderstandings. It's a pity that some are misusing the Council for entirely different purposes.'

'I'm afraid that is part of the times. We're in a century of ideological warfare. And we are losing.'

'You are right, Miss Barker.'

'Don't get up, Father,' she said, standing and glancing around. 'I'll be on my way. Until next time.'

She hurried off in her usual stiff manner towards the end of the park. Fascinated, Fr. van Engelen watched her go.

THE SUN was high in a brilliant blue sky as Boris sat lazily at the wheel, heading towards Binawarra. He was enjoying the chatter and music on the radio as he drove with his side window open and his arm resting on the rim. The warm country air blew into the car, soothing an already self-satisfied feeling. He loved these hot Australian days. He felt himself come alive in the heat. While others were panting like dogs with their mouths hanging open, he was just getting ready for action. It was Friday, and a weekend of surveillance lay ahead of him. He had to be on the ball now. The Winterbine girl did not keep him all that busy; once he had established where she was, he could relax because she usually stayed in one place. It was Len Dawson and his busy routine that kept him on the go. He appeared to be teaming up with Stephen Calder. Calder would love to have a go at the Winterbine girl, no doubt. Anybody messing with a fourteen-year-old would not pass up the chance of the Binawarra beauty. So what was their business? He glanced at the plastic bag of marijuana on the seat beside him.

As the road began to rise, Boris noticed the sharp peak with the strange rocky outcrop rising on his right. The car slowed to a roll as he surveyed the peak. He stopped, put his head through the window, and squinted at the rocky ledge high above him. He got out, crossed the road, and walked to the fence, gazing up at the ledge. He lifted the fence wire, climbed through, and walked to the point where the peak rose sharply. Dusty rocks and stones of various sizes lay scattered across the eroded soil. He stared again at the outcrop, and then ran his eyes around the left and the right side. He drove up the rise to a clearing where the ridge coming off the back of the peak met the road. After parking his car, he struck out, following a bush track along the ridge, which rose steadily on a manageable incline. He reached the rocky ledge after about fifteen minutes of steady climbing.

It was a broad area of smooth flat rock, broader than it appeared from the roadside. The peak rose another twenty or thirty feet at the back of the ledge. He walked to the edge of the rocky platform and looked down. Some small stones were lying close by. He kicked these into the void and watched them float down until they hit the dirt and rocks with a rattle. He bit his lip while he peered down along the sheer drop. He looked around.

Opposite and a little further away, the great mound rose above him. Its overwhelming squatting bulk seemed turned and bent towards the peak. His brow knitted as he looked across at it. Could he see a figure looking down at him on the right side of the hill? He was not sure. He turned and walked away from the edge. When he looked back, whatever it was, it had gone. On his way into town, as the car picked up speed, he reached over and turned the radio off.

BOB MCKINNON wandered around the recreational area, feeling the tedium of lunch duty. There was nothing to amuse and distract him. There was no one he wanted to talk to among the students he could see. Len Dawson, always good for a bit of fun, was nowhere in sight. His usual sycophants were missing, too. They must be somewhere down at the lower oval having a smoke. He could not see Jenny Brougham either. Perhaps he had her down among the trees. He was too lazy to walk down there. Instead, he sat on a bench under the gums. A few minutes later, Ms Bicknell emerged from the classroom wing. She walked around, telling students to pick up rubbish or to stop ragging. What a party-pooper. Ms Bicknell, in her wandering supervision, eventually arrived in his vicinity.

'Are you keeping a check on the playing fields?' she called.

'Not at the moment, good lady,' he said, preparing for a bit of fun.

'Remain where you are. I will see to it.' She started to move off.

'I hear the Winterbine girl is off to Sandhurst University to investigate the suitability of a career in public relations.'

She did not miss the tone of voice and came over to him.

'Have you any remark to make? If you do, you should get it off your chest now.'

'Not so defensive, Edith. I'm in admiration. I wouldn't have thought of it, but you're right. The girl would be a fantastic drawcard for any organisation. Imagine someone looking like a goddess promoting a company's goods. That's what I call surefire. Congratulations.'

'Thank you.'

'Not at all.'

She began to move off again.

'But I'm wondering what company or organisation you have in mind.'

She stopped. 'If you don't have anything more meaningful to say—'

'I guess she's being groomed to front one or other hyperactive organisation,' he said, talking over her. 'The mystery is why you have come here to pick this one particular girl. Oh, her unparalleled beauty is one of the obvious reasons. What could the others be? How did you get to know about her? Who informed you? Mystery upon mystery. I'll have to wait for the next snippet of evidence.' He grinned at her.

'Estella Winterbine has been advised on a career path like all the other students. The reasons for public relations are there for all to see. It's all open and transparent. The principal has given his opinion. The parents were given time to consider. Estella has thought about it. The next step is to spend time at Sandhurst University, hearing about the course and the work of public relations. After that, it's up to her to decide. Ordinarily, I would not bother to explain all this, but you insist on being mischievous.'

'Oh no, not at all, dear lady,' he said, putting his right hand over his heart. 'I'm not being mischievous. On the contrary, I'm in awe of the way you're bringing this off.' He paused. 'Just where are you from? You speak impeccable English. You have the right accent. But, but ... once or twice, I have distinctly heard in your speech the pure vowel sound you find in most European languages, but not in English. It has betrayed you.'

'So science teachers are language experts now, are they?'

'I may be a science teacher, but my interests are not restricted to science, I assure you. It just so happens that I've spent a lot of time travelling around Europe. Naturally, I tried to learn a bit of the local language. It made things easier when I wanted to order a cup of coffee, you know, that sort of thing. Being inquisitive, I noticed particular differences between English pronunciation and the pronunciation of other languages. With some sounds, it's very obvious. With others, it is much less obvious. But if your ear is attuned to it, and mine is, you will pick it up.' He paused for effect. 'Amsterdam ...? Munchen ...? Köln ...? Brussel ...?'

'I must thank you for the language lesson. Much appreciated. Sadly, your imagination is running ahead of you. You confuse a manner of saying things with differences in pronunciation.'

'Nice try, but I don't think so.'

'Well, if that's all you have to irritate me with this afternoon—'

'No, there's one other thing,' he said with a glint of amusement. 'During the meeting at your house, I claimed that Rousseau's concept of the General Will can be exploited by any fanatical group that claims to have its authentic interpretation. Gauging your reaction, I should say you found that objectionable. But, for the sake of the meeting, I let it go. Now I'm coming back to it.'

'You're still not finished?'

'The Jacobins made wonderful use of Rousseau's pet theory about the General Will,' he said, ignoring her sneer. 'Easiest of excuses for guillotining their pesky opponents. They were the first but not the last to exploit that useful notion. The Nazis and the Soviet communists, with their utter contempt for the individual, are prime examples. Who knows at this point in time how many millions went to their deaths being, as Rousseau put it, forced to be free, and forced to obey the will of the collective? Rousseau is of particular inspiration for those radical groups who imagine they can re-establish the perfect society based on the dictates, not of reason, but of feeling and fantasy.'

There was a long pause while Gerda Vrouwendijk and Bob McKinnon looked at each other.

'Well,' said Gerda, with a big pretend sigh, 'you've subjected me to lessons of career choice, pronunciation, and political philosophy. I think I can be excused now, don't you?'

'Of course, dear lady,' he said smugly. 'A goddess, eh? Keep your wand and pointy hat well hidden, do you?' He laughed quietly as she turned. 'And the pentagram ...?'

She walked off as nonchalantly as she could, her expression changing to bitter resolve.

THAT EVENING, Estella sat with her parents after dinner.

'How is Miss Bicknell behaving towards you, darling?' Charles said.

'She's always friendly and interested in what I do,' replied Estella.

'Has she spoken to you about the trip to Sandhurst University?'

'She has.'

'What did she say?'

'She discussed the arrangements. She wants me to attend some talks given by people from international companies.'

'Do you know who to report to at the university?'

'Yes, she said I must report to Mr Butcher. He is a senior lecturer in media studies and responsible for organising the talks.'

'Ruby rang us today.'

'Did she?' said Estella, sitting up and taking her arm from around her mother's shoulders.

'Yes. There was now a four-way conversation between her, the Department of Media Studies, Miss Bicknell, and Bill about the arrangements. Bill told her that Miss Bicknell arranged the company talks directly with the Media Studies Department. She lamented that it all risks becoming a muddle with so many people involved. She also has reservations about Mr Butcher as your contact. She stressed that you are not to deviate from her program. Bill also says you're to take notice only of Ruby.'

'Yes, of course, Daddy. I wouldn't do anything without Ruby's permission.'

'Has Miss Bicknell discussed our religion again?' said Aine.

'No. She only asked me once if I had been thinking about what she said.'

'What did you say?'

'I said I had been thinking about it. And she seemed happy with that. She has not mentioned it since.'

'We spoke to Miss Bicknell during the week,' continued Aine. 'Her views about religion are opposed to ours. We've asked her not to discuss our beliefs with you. She agreed, but if she does resume, please tell her politely that you don't want to talk about it.'

'Yes, Mamma,' said Estella, who had no difficulty following her parents' wishes.

She put her head on her father's shoulder and closed her eyes. His solid shoulder and his slight manly smell were a comfort. Geoff came to mind. She could not help wondering what it would be like to have her head leaning on his shoulder. What would she feel? She opened her eyes and sat up. Her father turned to her inquiringly. She returned a faint smile and put her head back on his shoulder. There was a pressing, sick feeling in the pit of her stomach.

AS THE congregation entered the church on Palm Sunday morning, their first sight was of Fr. van Engelen prostrate before the altar with his arms stretched out in the form of a cross. Charles, Aine, and Estella, seated in the front pew, were not surprised to see the priest prostrate before Our Lord in the tabernacle. They shared his sorrow. They shared his apprehension of what was to happen a week from that day. Five minutes before the beginning of the Palm Sunday ceremony, Father struggled to his feet. He staggered. Charles hurried onto the sanctuary to give him an arm. The priest nodded gratefully.

'Today is Palm Sunday,' began Fr. van Engelen, after Charles had helped him to the pulpit, 'It is the beginning of Holy Week. It is the time when we witness the fulfilment of Our Lord's prediction, as we hear it in St Mark's Gospel. Jesus says: "Behold, we go up to Jerusalem, and the Son of Man shall be betrayed to the chief priests and the scribes and ancients ... And they shall mock him and spit on him and scourge him and kill Him: and on the third day he will rise again."

'This week we will follow in the steps of Our Lord's redemptive suffering. We will accompany Him into the severest mental, emotional and physical suffering to the point of abandonment. All this happened after he was welcomed into Jerusalem, sitting on an ass, and after the people had spread their garments and branches along the way, shouting: "Hosanna for the son of David, blessed is He who comes in the name of the Lord." Let us remember that this joyful acclamation of Jesus as Saviour is continually challenged by the mocking, spitting on and scourging of Christ's Mystical Body, the Church.'

The priest was hardly in a state to complete the long ceremony, which included the procession of the palms. Charles whispered that he would stay with him as support. The priest bowed his head and vested for the blessing of the palms. Charles remarked that the ceremony on that Palm Sunday was the most solemn the congregation had ever experienced, with Father van Engelen going before them, bent over as if he were carrying a cross.

Later that day, Aine knelt before her bedroom shrine. She had opened her missal at the Mass of Palm Sunday. Once again, she read over the psalm verses of the introit.

Lord, do not stand at a distance, if Thou wouldst aid me; look to my defence: rescue me from the very horns of the wild oxen that have brought me thus low. My God, my God, look upon me: why hast thou forsaken me? Why cannot my sinful words reach Thee, who art my salvation?

For some time, she contemplated these words as she brought before her mind images of Jesus's triumphant entry into Jerusalem and the terrible events that were to follow. Those images faded to be replaced by Miss Bicknell's eyes hovering, as it were, in a timeless space. The darkness stared at her soul from those eyes, not in a threatening attitude, but in wait, as if in a mocking pause. Then the figure of her daughter rose before her. The eyes turned. Aine bent her head in prayer.

Chapter 17

The darkness strikes

FROM EARLY morning on Holy Saturday, Fr. van Engelen had been anxious about the arrival of Fr. Hans de Jonge. The provincial had told him he would be driven up from Melbourne and arrive around mid-afternoon. Father was to be ready to receive him. But three o'clock came, and Fr. de Jonge had not arrived. Four o'clock came, and still no provincial. Fr. van Engelen planned to start a special Easter Vespers for his congregation at five o'clock, and he would not delay on any account. If the provincial arrived during the prayers, he would have to wait. By seven o'clock, Fr. van Engelen was back in the presbytery and not a sign of Fr. de Jonge. He hoped that something had happened to postpone his visit, but that was wishful thinking. He took up his daily office. Prayer and patience must be his course of action. At eight o'clock, there came a knock on the door. He opened to reveal Fr. de Jonge standing stiffly under the porch light.

'Goedenavond, Father.'

Fr. van Engelen had a quick look around outside as the provincial brushed past him, saying he had dropped in to ensure that all was in readiness. Dropped in? Fr. van Engelen replied that there was not much to prepare. Everything depended on him and his companions.

'Have you arranged for a table in the sanctuary, Father?'

'Oh, I'm sorry, I did not think of it.'

'I thought that might happen. That's all right. We have brought a portable altar table. With white linen draped over it, nobody will know the difference.'

Fr van Engelen was inclined to ask what that difference was, but his inquiry would sound facetious.

'Are you able to disassemble the altar rails? I assume the altar rails are still there?'

'Yes, they are there, and we cannot disassemble them.'

'Just as I thought,' said the Provincial, remaining standing. He fidgeted. 'Not to worry. The dancers can move through narrow spaces.'

'You mean the dancers will enter the sanctuary?'

'Don't be obtuse, Father. Of course, they will. We'll be at the church at nine o'clock for the preparations and for a brief rehearsal.'

'A rehearsal?'

'Yes. Don't worry. It'll just be a question of adjusting to the space and the length of the aisle.'

'The length of the aisle?'

'Father, will you stop parroting me. It sounds offensive.'

'I'm sorry,' said Fr. van Engelen, whose heart had sunk so low he had to sit down.

'Well, that's it. That's all I wanted to say.' He turned to leave. 'Don't move, Father. I know you're in a state of stress and fatigue. I will let myself out.'

Fr. van Engelen was too weary to move. How could he stand it? How was he to get through Easter Sunday morning?

SUZIE MCNAMARRA had been at Bob McKinnon's house from late afternoon. At around nine o'clock, Bob was stretched out on the lounge room sofa, lazily watching television, while Suzie, dressed in her underwear, was leaning over the back of the sofa and playing with his hair. She contemplated him as she ran her fingers through his hair and over his cheek. The phone rang.

'Oh, leave it,' said Bob, 'it can't be anything interesting.'

'I can get it. It's no trouble.'

'No, No. No need to give people something to gossip about.'

The phone continued to ring.

'Well, that's being insistent,' he said at last. He removed Suzie's hand from his head, got up, ambled to the phone, and picked up the receiver.

'Hello, yes ... that's right ...' There was a long break while he listened and then: 'Okay ... how did you know about me ... okay ... yes, I'll be there. Give me fifteen minutes.' He put the receiver down and looked at the floor. He glanced at Suzie. She frowned. Her hand on the back of the settee trembled. 'I'm going out for a while,' he said as if he had come to a decision. He sat on the lounge in front of Suzie, putting on his shoes and buttoning his shirt. 'Won't be too long,' he said, getting up. 'You can wait here if you want.'

'Where are you going?'

'Don't ask questions, and you'll be told no lies,' he said, resuming his jovial manner. 'Will you stay here?'

'Yes, but don't be long. It's Saturday evening, after all.'

'You're sounding like a wife, tut, tut.' He wagged his finger at her and was on the way to the door when he stopped. He contemplated her standing barefoot and in her underwear beside the lounge settee, one hand clutching the back of the sofa. 'What's a gorgeous young thing like you doing with an ugly, fat, self-indulged bugger like me?'

'It's not the weakness I like—'

'Oh, stop! You sound like a priest—you know, love the sinner, and hate the sin!' He flapped his hands about. 'I'll be back in a while. I shouldn't be too long.'

Suzie sat on the sofa and looked at the television, her arms limp in her lap. She picked up her dress, draped over the settee, and put it on.

Ten minutes later, Bob entered the smoky, noise-filled saloon bar of The Commercial Hotel. He ambled to the bar, glancing around a little nervously. A slender, neatly dressed young man with short fair hair was sitting in the corner. Bob let his eyes alight on him. The young man nodded.

He was no sooner outside on the footpath than the slender young man hurried by. Bob followed. At the end of the square, the young man slid into a car parked behind the trees on the park's border. Bob entered the passenger side. The car reversed, drove out of the circuit onto Melbourne Road, and headed at a moderate pace out of town. A minute later, it pulled off the road into the clearing at the crest of the road as it passed through the two peaks. The engine died, and the lights went out. Two figures silhouetted against the half-moonlit night got out of the front seats and into the back.

The entrance to the track running along the ridge to the top of Death Rock was about twenty yards further along in the clearing. Out of the darkness of the track emerged three men wearing balaclavas. One signalled the other two to stay. Keeping close to the trees and shrubs, he moved to within a few yards of the car. He stood there for fifteen minutes, observing the glint on the car roof as it moved almost imperceptibly. Then the window on the bush side of the car was wound down. Clothing was draped over the open window. The dark figure signalled to the other two. The two men came up beside him. They approached the car, reaching for the door handles. At the whisper 'go!' they wrenched the doors open and dragged the two occupants out. The young man, with his pants around his ankles, was held by the two men. Bob, barefoot and naked from the waist down, was choking in the grip of the arm around his neck.

'What ... what do you want?' he gasped as the arm relaxed its hold.

'Shut up, and nothing will happen.'

'What ...?' he whimpered. 'What do you want?' Cold steel was held against his temple. 'Stand still!' The man relaxed his hold a little more, but the pistol barrel pressed against Bob's temple. 'You move, and I blow your brains out, right?'

Bob shook his head. A blindfold was pulled over his head and adjusted over his eyes. He shivered, unable to control his convulsive movements.

'Stay still! I said.'

The next moment, his trousers and his sandals were pushed into his hands.

'Don't try anything, or it's the finish. Put your shoes on. Just your shoes.'

Bob crouched down in the vague light of the clearing, dropped his pants, and struggled to slip his sandals on.

'Pick up your pants.'

Bob felt around for his trousers, picked them up, and held them against his chest like a child awaiting orders.

'Come on.'

He was pushed forward a few paces, and his arms were taken by men on each side of him.

'What's happening? Where are you taking me?'

'Shut up, and nothing will happen,' came the same voice that was now behind him.

'Please don't hurt me. I'll do whatever you want.'

With tears dripping from under the blindfold, Bob was pushed and dragged to the track leading along the ridge to Death Rock. The leader signalled to the young man to pull up his trousers and follow. As they fell in behind Bob and his escort with a single torch to guide their way, he handed him an envelope. The young man put the envelope in his trouser pocket.

After being dragged and pushed, blubbering and pleading for about twenty minutes, Bob found himself on a hard, flat, even surface. His silent escort released him.

'Where am I? What do you want?'

'Just stand there.'

The night sky was clear, and the beams from the part moon gleamed in the smooth, shiny surface of the rocky platform. The leader beckoned the young man. He was thrown several lengths of rope with the direction to tie one around each of Bob's ankles and wrists.

'What's happening?' cried Bob. 'If this is what you want, I'm willing. You don't have to go about it like this.'

'Now, you two, finish what you were doing.'

As the young man approached Bob, the leader signalled to the other men to retreat. He accompanied them to the start of the track along the ridge, issued instructions, and waited until they had disappeared into the darkness. Five minutes later, he returned to Bob and the young man standing next to each other.

'If you want to look,' Bob said, feeling a hand taking hold of him, 'you don't have to go to this trouble.'

The leader shuffled Bob towards the edge of the outcrop, slipped the blindfold off his head, grabbed his right arm with both hands, hissed, 'Die Crusader filth, die!' and flung him into the dark. There was no cry, no words, just the thump and the short rattle of shifting rock and gravel a few seconds later. Then there was silence. The dark balaclava'd figure approached the young man standing paralysed in the centre of the rocky platform.

'You have done good work,' he said. 'Very good work. You have earned your money.'

He then grabbed him and, in a series of violent actions, ripped his shirt open and his pants down to his ankles, flung one arm around his neck, and put his hand over his mouth. The young man was marched, struggling to the edge of the outcrop, and with the same message whispered in his ear, 'Die Crusader filth!' he was lifted off his feet and thrown into the abyss. Again, there was no cry, no words, just the thump and the rattling of stone a few seconds later. Boris removed his balaclava and peered into the dark below. He took the torch from his pocket but thought better of it.

Twenty minutes later, he was at the fence at the bottom of Death Rock. He flashed his torch, but the long grass obscured his view. He crawled through the wire fence and only had to walk a few paces before the beam of the torch, which he flashed intermittently, revealed the two bloodied bodies lying next to each other. He held the beam on long enough to assure himself there was no life in them. He returned to the road and flashed his torch at the crest of the hill. A car arrived, picked him up, and then headed towards Bendigo. The empty car, standing in the clearing with its back window open, took in the full force of the cold night air that slowly wrapped around the peaks.

At one o'clock in the morning, a dark van nudged between the trees bordering the clearing. Eight robed figures, seven in white and one in black, assembled at the start of the track along the ridge. With a solemn nod, the black robe headed off, with the others following. They stopped some way in and lit candles. The glimmering line then resumed its way, a soft chanting mingling with the shrub and tree-lined track.

Twenty minutes later, the robed figures emerged on the rocky outcrop, keeping the same solemn glimmering line. At a signal from black robe, a cloth marked with a pentagram was laid near the edge. The seven white robes formed a semicircle around the cloth with black robe in the middle. Several more minutes of soft chanting followed while the black robe executed a slow spiralling, gesticulating dance. At a signal from Gerda, Lesley Conos and Faye Croft came forward. Lesley Conos produced a struggling rabbit. She and Faye Croft, each taking a fore and hind leg, held the wriggling rabbit in the centre of the pentagram. More chanting. At the end of the chanting, Gerda bent forward and grasped the rabbit around the neck. The rabbit wriggled furiously for a short time and then was still.

'The atoning and purifying male sacrifice,' she said, holding the dead rabbit aloft. 'Unblemished.' She turned and threw it into the dark abyss.

The eight women, holding their candles and chanting, made their way back down the bush track.

AT FIFTEEN minutes to nine on Easter Morning, Fr van Engelen left the presbytery to open the church. He greeted a group of adults and young girls in overcoats standing around. They returned a cautious greeting. He opened the doors and stood back, but the people pretended not to notice. He entered and knelt in the back pew. Some time later, he returned outside and was surprised to see the numbers had grown considerably. In the midst of them, he made out Fr. de Jonge dressed as the evening before in a spotless white shirt and neatly pressed black trousers. As he walked to greet him, a girl of thirteen or fourteen years discarded her overcoat to reveal a tight-fitting black leotard and a small pink gauze skirt. She was heavily made up, her lips coloured a bright red. Other girls of the same age began divesting themselves of their overcoats to reveal the same attire. The adults proudly took the coats.

'Goedemorgen, Father,' said the provincial, breaking in on Fr van Engelen's staring.

'Goedemorgen, Father,' said Fr. van Engelen, unable to take his eyes off the pubescent girls in black leotards.

'They are the dancers,' said Fr de Jonge, pleased with himself.

'Do you think that's appropriate clothing for a church?'

'Of course, why not? They're dancers.'

'Do you think pubescent girls dressed in immodest clothing are suitable for Easter Sunday Mass?'

'Immodesty has nothing to do with it. The girls give an air of freshness to the occasion. It's a foreshadowing.'

'That's what I'm afraid of,' said Fr. van Engelen, no longer able to hold back. 'They're going to give the Holy Sacrifice of the Mass the appearance of a pagan goddess ceremony, complete with vestal virgins!'

'Now, I will not stand for your spoiling tactics any longer!' said Fr de Jonge between his teeth. 'You have to get used to the processes underway. This marks the beginning of women's entry into the sanctuary. Face it!'

They had been speaking in Dutch, and it was only now that those standing around noticed the tension. 'If you can't say anything positive or encouraging, I would request you to go inside the church and leave us to get things organised.'

Fr. van Engelen agreed that it was probably the best thing for him to do. He could not stand there without raising objections. As he was turning to go, he recognised behind Fr. de Jonge two young seminarians dressed in tight white shirts and tight black trousers. They had their hair slicked back. One had his face coloured white, the other black. Undoubtedly, they were to mime the Gospel reading of the Resurrection. He said nothing. It would make no difference, and the provincial was standing there glaring at him. He returned to the pew at the back of the church.

During the next half an hour, Fr. van Engelen watched the preparations with increasing alarm. After the portable table had been erected, the seminarians entered the sanctuary, talking gaily and not bothering to genuflect as they passed the tabernacle. They rehearsed their Gospel mime, breaking off with much chatter as they discussed the effectiveness of certain moves. Fr. de Jonge came into the church during the rehearsals, and every time the seminarians looked in his direction after a sequence of miming, he would nod approvingly. After fifteen minutes of rehearsals, they left the church for the dancers to go through their paces.

Sister Elizabeth Parker, dressed in a grey outfit with a small veil and long black cape, brought her pubescent girls into the church and lined them up at the back. Fr. van Engelen counted eleven of them. One was dressed differently from the other ten. She wore a crimson red leotard and a small black gauze skirt. She was also more mature than the other girls. At a given signal, the ten girls in quick succession weaved and spun down the aisle, through the break in the altar rails, and formed themselves in a bunch facing the back of the church.

Following on the heels of the last girl, the red leotard and black gauze dress came weaving and spinning with greater flourish and grace than her companions. When she got to the bunched girls, she stopped, swivelled, stood on the toes of her left foot, lifted and bent her right leg, and then arched her back with her arms raised above her head. She fell backwards to be taken up in the arms of the ten girls and raised high into the air. When she was at the maximum height, she arched her back, flinging both arms behind her so they drooped towards the floor. She was now looking upside down into the tabernacle. She was deposited on the floor after which she spiralled around the altar several times. At the finish of her spiral dance, she rushed in graceful movements with the other girls following to the back of the church. The girls repeated their dance several times.

With the rehearsals finished, Fr. van Engelen made his way to the front and knelt in the foremost pew. Charles, Aine and Estella came into the church as the girls gathered after their last rehearsal. The Winterbines looked with amazement at the dancers. The girls looked back with equal amazement at the beautiful girl who had passed them, their eyes following her. They watched transfixed as she took her position in the front pew. Sister Parker, her eyes fixed on Aine, noticed the staring group of girls. She shooed them outside.

'I would like you to support me when I get up just before the start of Mass, Charles, if you don't mind,' Fr. van Engelen whispered.

'Of course, Father, just give me the sign.'

At that moment, about twenty minutes before Mass, Fr. van Engelen's congregation began to arrive. Bemused, each person had to run the gauntlet of the pubescent dancers and the miming seminarians with their entourages as they came into the church. There was a growing restlessness.

A couple of minutes before Mass was to begin, and the girls were lined up at the back of the church, ready to dance ahead of a vested Fr. de Jonge, the whispering and movement stopped. The congregation seemed to freeze. Then, when the sound of shifting feet was heard, Fr. van Engelen rose and stood in the middle of the aisle. Charles followed him, offering his arm. An eerie silence prevailed as all eyes turned towards the crippled priest. Fr. van Engelen moved forward leaning on Charles's arm. He came to the break in the altar rails. He steadied himself with Charles's help, dropped to his knees and fell forward, prostrating himself in the opening of the altar rails. He stretched his arms out in the form of a cross.

'Jesus, have mercy,' he cried.

Charles knelt behind him. Aine rose and knelt beside her husband. Now everyone—Fr. de Jonge, Sister Parker, seminarians, pubescent dancers, supporters and the congregation—watched spellbound as the tall, dark girl of peerless beauty, serene expression, modest dress and hands clasped together rose and, bowing her head, knelt behind her parents. For a few moments, all was in suspension. Then slowly, at first, the aisle filled with kneeling faithful. It gathered pace and grew into much bustling until every walkway in the church was blocked. The sound of movement died away, and Fr. de Jonge and his entourage were left staring. The scene was too much for some of the pubescent girls, and they began to whimper.

Fr. de Jonge's indecision did not last long. He saw the determination on the congregation's faces and knew his cause was defeated. He beckoned to his entourage to withdraw with him. After more shuffling of feet, silence came over the congregation. Fr. van Engelen gestured to Charles to help him up. Once again on his feet and steadying himself on Charles's arm, he bowed his head and began chanting the Church's ancient song of praise to God. The congregation joined him.

Te Deum laudamus: te Dominum confitemur
Te aeternum Patrem omnis terra venerator...

Fr. de Jonge stood outside with his people gathered around him and listened in silence to the chanting of the *Te Deum*. His face was red and set as he stared at the bluestone façade, all the while that ancient song of praise and thanksgiving filling the air to mock and triumph over him. He told his people he had to send them back to Melbourne to attend Mass. They must keep their strength and courage up. There would be obstacles for them to overcome. There would be selfish people, too attached to a dysfunctional past to see the new springtime in the Church. All these things were a suffering to overcome. But they must persevere.

As the last verse of the *Te Deum* faded into the joyous congregation, Fr. van Engelen turned. The miracle he had hoped for occurred. It had happened in the simplest, but most unexpected fashion and the Holy Sacrifice of the Mass was protected. It was now time to prepare for the Mass of Easter Sunday, celebrating Our Lord's rising from the dead in defeat of sin and death. Fr. van Engelen's relief was short-lived, for while he was taking his vestments off after Mass, one of Fr. de Jonge's seminarians entered the sacristy with the message that the provincial had summoned him outside.

'Would you please excuse us, sir,' said Fr. de Jonge to Charles, who had accompanied Fr. van Engelen, 'I have something important and confidential to say.'

Aine stood with Estella at a respectful distance, watching what was about to unfold. Out of her line of vision on the other side of the road and hidden partly by one of the gum trees, Sister Elizabeth Parker stood staring. Her girls had already been gathered up by their parents and whisked away. She fidgeted as she watched.

'You'll have to excuse me, Father,' said Charles, standing his full six foot four inches. 'It's important I stay. It is not only Fr. van Engelen who is concerned with what happens to him. We are all vitally concerned, those of us here in Binawarra and those who drive many miles to come to Mass here. We value Fr. van Engelen as a priest, and we value the way he conducts the parish. I want to warn you that we, as a congregation of faithful, will resist if you take action against him.'

'You warn me?' said Fr. de Jonge, after some moments of hesitation, his eyes dilating and his face reddening. 'Disobeying the Church's lawful authority is not consistent with faithfulness to the Church's teaching.'

'We are faithful to the Church and its teachings. Nothing else motivates us.'

'Are you really in a position to know you are faithful?' the provincial challenged, his head quivering.

'In this case, yes. How could the Mass that has been said for centuries be suddenly unlawful or against the faith or the truth?'

'You are taking the course of rebellion,' the provincial replied, making an effort to compose himself. 'Indeed, you're taking an unauthorised and incompetent lead in this. I will not discuss the matter with you. You are failing to render obedience to the Church.'

'We are faithful to the Church, Father, and will continue to be so.'

Fr. de Jonge frowned at Charles and turned to Fr. van Engelen. 'It appears, Father,' he said, speaking in Dutch, 'that I am even thwarted in having a private meeting with you. I'm sure that the seriousness of your rebellion is not beyond you. I will leave you now, but you must expect a disciplinary response.' He paused. 'I am obliged to take action that I have hitherto been reluctant to take. It concerns your medical condition, which I suspect is at the bottom of your rigidity and stubbornness. Please hold yourself available.'

'Fr. de Jonge,' said Fr van Engelen, 'it's not just me anymore, not just a personal decision. I have a duty to the people who come to Mass here. How can I abandon them? Nothing I have done has been done without painful contemplation of my duty as a priest.'

'I have explained your duty,' Fr. de Jonge snapped. 'There's nothing more to be done, other than to obey.'

He strode through the iron gates. Fr. van Engelen and Charles watched him march away. A car reversed from a parking spot and came alongside. A back door was pushed open, and Fr. de Jonge got in.

'Thank you, Charles,' said Fr. van Engelen. 'We priests take on a heavy responsibility. We do that willingly. But sometimes it becomes almost too burdensome, for we are also human. At those times, support is most welcome. I thank you for standing up for the faith and for giving me support at the very moment I felt like buckling.'

Aine, seeing that the meeting had ended, was about to go to join Charles and the priest when she heard, 'Aine, wait!' She and Estella turned at the same time to see Sister Parker hurrying across the road from the park, her black cape flowing behind her. A car screeched to a stop as the nun, with a suppressed squeal, side-stepped to dodge around it.

'You stupid nun!' Stephen Calder yelled, his voice carrying through the open windows of his utility and echoing across the park. Len Dawson, who was in the passenger seat, waved helplessly at Estella.

'You should be more careful, Elizabeth,' said Aine, as Sister Parker came up to them.

'It's your fault,' said Sister Parker breathlessly. 'You have upset me so much that I wasn't taking care. How could you?'

'I was sorry to see you taking part in that exhibition. I didn't know you were involved in that sort of thing.'

'That sort of thing?' Sister Parker exclaimed. 'This is the future, don't you understand? Why don't you let yourself be freed from your prison?'

'Please don't go on,' said Aine, 'I've heard it all from Margaret. If she has failed to convince me, you must understand you have no hope.'

'Still under the influence of that wretched Virginia Pearson.'

'Please, Elizabeth, you know how much Virginia has suffered. Let her alone. Besides, she is the dearest friend I have. We are of one mind.'

'She has brought it on herself, and she is bringing it on you,' said Elizabeth, her exasperation turning into anger. 'At least think of your daughter, if you won't think of yourself. Don't consign her to the same prison. Give her the opportunity to develop her extraordinary talents.'

By this time, Charles had joined them. 'And what talents are those?'

'The same that Aine has been prevented from developing—as you know all too well. You gloat over the forces that destroyed a brilliant career.'

'Estella will make up her own mind about matters she's not required to consider at the moment.'

'There's nobody I admire or love more than my mother,' said Estella. She was aware of the suffering her mother's friend had gone through. 'I will gladly follow her example.'

'Look within yourself, Estella. There you will find your salvation.'

'What are you doing in the Church?' said Charles.

'Reform, Mr Winterbine, I'm struggling to help the reform that the Church is badly in need of, reform that is being held back by ignorance and faint-heartedness. I will pray for you, Aine, and for your daughter. Good day.' She left them without waiting for a response.

BILL HUCKERBY beamed at his guests. Around the table in the Huckerby dining room sat Charles, Aine, Estella, Fr. van Engelen, and Miss Barker. Joanne was to the side on his left.

'This is the first time we have all been together, and what an occasion for us to be together—Easter Sunday, the day of the Lord's resurrection. I welcome you all. I can't tell you how overjoyed Joanne and I are to have you here.'

'We're all very glad to be here,' said Charles.

'Thank you, my boy, I know you are.' He stretched out his hand and shook Charles's hand warmly.

'Let's all remember that time, too ... how old are you, Estella, my dear, eighteen? ... that's right ... it was around nineteen years ago that Charles met Aine for the first time on our verandah outside. What an act of Providence! That meeting has brought us together. Let's celebrate it as the action of the Lord.' He sat down. 'Now, Father, you are the senior religious here. You can say grace. I ask the only heathen among us,' inclining his head towards Miss Barker, 'to indulge us in this.'

'Thank you, Bill, I will be glad to say grace,' said the priest, 'but may I also offer a prayer for you all, in particular for Miss Barker and a prayer in thanksgiving for our Mass today.'

With grace said, everyone sat back while Bill carved the roast and Joanne urged the guests to serve themselves from the bowls of vegetables and salad on the table.

'You know, Bill,' said Miss Barker. 'I may not be the heathen you think I am.'

'What, Flo? What have we now from that overactive mind of yours?' said Bill, while he worked away at the roast. 'Be careful, Father,' he said, turning to the priest at the other end of the table, 'she's a slippery customer this one. Her library is bigger than the town's public library.' The priest returned an amused smile. 'Okay, Flo, let's have it, full barrels!'

'Well, correct me, Father,' she said, 'but doesn't the doctrine of "no salvation outside the Church" entail this: that salvation comes only through the graces provided by the Saviour's death and that not only those living a life of grace within the Church, but those also living a life according to Christ's teachings, even though they are not formally a member of the Church, or have never even heard of the Church, may be saved?'

'Well, Miss Barker, you surprise me yet again. If a person lives a life of charity and virtue in the way Our Lord taught, while not hearing about the

Christian Gospel, or in all sincerity not having been able to accept Christ or the Church, he is saved, not despite, but by virtue of Christ's graces. We talk about a situation of invincible ignorance. The crucial point to remember is that no one is saved except by Christ through the Church he established.'

'Bill?' said Miss Barker.

Bill put down his carving knife and fork and contemplated the faces awaiting his reply. 'Invincible ignorance!' he said, shaking his head. 'You mean there is still a chance for me, Father? I will still get into heaven as an Anglican?'

'Yes, of course, Bill, but you will enter heaven as a virtual Catholic.'

'A virtual Catholic! Hah! Hah! That's a good one! Well done, Father.' He picked up the carving knife and fork. 'No doubt about you Romans, you have an answer for everything!'

Nobody could resist Bill's amusement, and they laughed heartily. Even Miss Barker had to drop her stern expression and smile, something that Bill did not miss.

'Hey, Flo, you're laughing, or almost. There, Father, that's an even bigger miracle than heathen Miss Barker getting into heaven as a virtual Catholic! A virtual Catholic! What next?' he muttered, shaking his head and attacking the roast.

The good humour lingered around the subject before moving on to Fr. van Engelen's predicament. It was Charles who brought it up.

As Charles answered Joanne's and Bill's questions, Bill became increasingly concerned.

'Do you mean they could transfer you out of Binawarra?'

'That's one possibility,' said the priest.

'That's scandalous!' said Joanne. 'How could they get away with it?'

'Could they really force you to undergo a psychological assessment?'

'Yes, of course.'

'That is a gross misuse of authority,' said Bill, appalled. 'That's contrary to administrative practice and good business sense. How do such people get into positions of authority? Is there no one to appeal to?'

'Bill, you must understand that I am a Catholic priest. I have willingly taken the vows of poverty, chastity, and obedience. There can be no reason for me to go against the first two, and there must be an exceptional reason for not obeying the directives of my superiors. Really, it can be only a question of faith. Nobody may order me to do something contrary to the faith. Humiliation, discomfort, disadvantage, and those sorts of things are not reasons for disobedience. Being a priest is not the same as being an employee of a business or a teacher in a school.'

There followed a thoughtful silence.

'You're going to stick up for Father, aren't you?' said Bill.

'Yes, of course', said Charles, with Aine and Estella following in their support.

'Well, so will we, won't we, darling?'

'We'll give Father whatever support we can give,' said Joanne.

Fr. van Engelen expressed his appreciation for their support, but everything must be left to him. There could be no other way. 'We'll see about that,' said Bill, swelling in indignation. After lunch, the guests were invited to retire to the verandah to enjoy the fine and mild weather. Joanne went to the kitchen to make coffee. As the others were settled on the verandah, the phone rang. Moments later, Joanne was heard hurrying down the hall.

'It's Sergeant Willis. He said it's urgent.'

Bill got up as quickly as his bulk would allow and disappeared into the hall. Joanne followed him. The others waited in silence. A few minutes later, Bill appeared, his face pale and lined. Joanne followed with a handkerchief held to her nose.

'What is it, Bill?' said Charles, rising.

'There's been an accident. Somebody's been killed.' He fell onto his chair. Joanne sniffled and held on to him.

'Who?'

'Bob McKinnon has been found dead outside Binawarra. On the roadside as you pass through the two peaks.'

There were quiet gasps from Charles, Aine and Estella, while Miss Barker and Fr. van Engelen looked on.

'Where exactly?' said Charles.

'I don't know. That's all Sergeant Willis would say. He could not say any more for the moment. News has gone down to Bendigo police. He was waiting for instructions. He said it was important for me to keep abreast of what was happening. There was something odd about it all, something that may cause trouble in the end. I asked him if there was foul play or something. He did not think so, but he'd leave that to others. I should stay by the phone.'

A sombre mood overtook the group. Charles offered to stay if they could be of support. Bill and Joanne pleaded for them to stay. Fr. van Engelen gave Miss Barker a look that was a silent plea.

'We'll be off,' said Miss Barker, helping the priest to his feet. 'I'm a phone call away if needed.'

Thank you, Flo,' said Joanne, accompanying them to the car. 'We'll give you a call if there are any developments.'

'What do you think of this, Father?' said Miss Barker as they drove away.

'It's tragic, very sad.'

'Nothing more than tragic?'

'Do you think there is more to it?'

'It seems just too coincidental, doesn't it?'

'I don't know. What connection could there be?'

'I don't know directly. We'll wait and see. But don't be surprised if there is a connection. A foul wind has been blowing through Binawarra since that woman arrived.'

She dropped him off at the presbytery and headed out of town. It was about two-thirty when she passed the empty car in the clearing on the crest of the rise and stopped behind Sergeant Willis's police car. The sergeant was standing against the boundary fence under the sharp peak, peering at the ground in front of him.

'Please, Miss Barker,' he said when he saw her. 'I must protect the scene from all intrusion. It's essential.'

'Calm down, Sergeant. I know. I'm here to help. I'm a nurse, you know. Has the doctor been?'

'No, he's away for the afternoon. I've left a message for him.'

'Let me have a look. Where's the body?'

'I don't think you should. It's not very pretty.'

'Don't be ridiculous, Sergeant. I've seen such things before, far worse than a simple death.'

'It's not a simple death. It's disgusting.'

'Disgusting? Where is he?'

'There,' he said, pointing, 'and don't say I didn't warn you. I would put a handkerchief over my mouth if I were you.'

He held the wire up to allow her to crawl through. She had gone ten yards when she saw the upper part of two bodies. She stopped, taking in the scene. She made her way to the base of the peak, keeping a proper distance from the bodies. It was not just odd. She looked up at the rocky platform and then at the bodies. She saw the dead rabbit partly hidden in the grass not far away. She rejoined the sergeant, who was relieved to see her come away from the bodies.

'Who found the bodies?'

'Three priests who were driving back to Melbourne after the Easter ceremonies. One of the young ones caught a glimpse of something light in the grass as they came over the crest. He must have been looking directly at the spot. Otherwise, he wouldn't have seen it. Nobody else before them saw anything. Anyhow, they were curious and got out to have a look.'

'Where are they now?'

'At the police station. They have to stay there until they can be interviewed.'

'How are they?'

'Shocked. Very shocked, the two young ones in particular,' said Sergeant Willis, shaking his head. 'It's not okay for young priests to see something like that. The older priest is trying to comfort them.'

'Have you been up there?' she said, looking up at the outcrop.

'No,' said the sergeant, alarmed.

'I'll have a look.'

'Please, Miss Barker, do not touch anything.'

'Do you think that dead rabbit means anything?'

'What dead rabbit?'

'Over there, not far from the bodies.'

'Miss Barker, dead rabbits are all over the place here. Leave it to the investigators.'

'Relax, Sergeant, I won't bother you anymore.' She walked towards the car in the clearing.

She glanced at the track leading along the ridge as she approached the empty car. She peered through the open window. Nothing. There was a car hire sticker on the back window. She returned to the track along the ridge and began the climb, looking around her. Scuffing of the track showed it had been negotiated in the last twenty-four hours. The brush beside the track was torn and trampled in places. When she arrived at the rocky outcrop, she saw the pair of trousers. Drops of wax lay around. She bent down to examine them. She walked to the ledge and looked down. The bodies appeared further from the cliff face than if they had merely fallen from the ledge. Three police cars arrived. She got out of sight and made her way down the track. Back on the road, she hurried to her car, but one of the policemen spotted her.

'Madam,' he called, 'can I ask you to keep on your way? This is now a police scene.'

Miss Barker waved her acknowledgment, got in her car, and headed straight for the Huckerby house. The Huckerbys and Winterbines were still sitting on the verandah when she pulled up outside.

'What is it? Do you have some information?' Bill said, getting to his feet. Before Miss Barker could say anything, he added, 'It's not good news, is it? I can see it all over your face, and I think somehow I will be involved.'

'Involved!' cried Joanne.

'You're right, Bill. But I fear it will be a lot of involvement rather than a little.'

'Come on, let me have it.'

'There are some very disagreeable aspects,' she said, looking at Charles and Aine.

Aine took Estella's hand. 'We'll go for a walk, Miss Barker. Charles will tell us later what we need to know.' She walked off with Estella in tow.

'How shocking! Did you know about his activities?' said Joanne when Miss Barker had finished.

'I had my suspicions,' said Bill, 'but as long as he did his job and made no issue of such things, it was not my business to inquire. He was a good science teacher.'

'Think, Bill,' said Miss Barker, leaning towards him, 'was there ever any sign that Mr McKinnon was in the habit of arranging for male prostitutes to come to Binawarra?'

'Male prostitutes?' said Joanne.

'Yes, Joanne, Flo is right,' said Bill. 'That's what it looks like. On the surface, it looks like some sort of sexual encounter gone wrong.'

'On the surface,' murmured Miss Barker, immersed in her thoughts.

'What? Do you think it could be something else?'

'I don't know, Bill. Let's leave it until we hear more. But you haven't answered my question. Was there ever any sign of this?'

'As far as I'm concerned, none at all. The only relationship I'm aware of was with Suzie McNamara. And he was discreet about that. There may have been somebody in Melbourne where, as you may know, he often went.'

'Indeed,' she said, 'I wonder if Miss McNamara knows.'

'By golly, that's a point,' said Bill. 'I should check. I suspect that young lady was fonder of Bob than she let on.' He went to the phone and returned a few minutes later. 'No, she had no idea where he was. The last she saw of him was last night when he was called out suddenly. I told her she should contact the police and tell them what she knew. She panicked right away. She asked me what was going on. I told her to contact the police. Then she was gone.'

'So she was at his place when he was called out,' said Miss Barker.

The phone rang. Bill rose to answer it and was back without delay. 'Darling, it's Suzie McNamara. She's hysterical. The constable had no reason to be tactful. He told her bluntly that Bob had been killed. Can't blame him. The young constable had no idea of the relationship between them. Would you speak to her, the poor girl? It's not my sort of thing, I'm afraid.'

Joanne was not long gone. 'The girl's completely overwrought. She asked me to come around. I told her I must stay here, but if she wanted some comfort, she was welcome to come over. To my surprise, she said she would.'

Five minutes later, Suzie McNamara's small car stopped outside, but there was no further movement. Joanne hastened to the car. Aine and Estella came around the side of the house to see Joanne struggling to help Suzie out of her car. She lost her grip, and Suzie crumpled at her feet, crying uncontrollably. Joanne and Estella half-carried, half-dragged her up onto the verandah, Joanne giving Bill a sign that he and Charles should leave them alone.

'We're not much good up there, are we, Charles?' Bill said when they arrived at the front gate. They looked on while the women crowded around the distressed girl sitting with her head in her hands. Comforting words amid the sound of weeping drifted from the verandah. They heard Miss Barker ask questions between long pauses. Eventually, Miss Barker left off questioning and joined them.

'The girl is overwrought,' she said. 'It seems there is no one in Binawarra she can turn to for comfort, not even among your staff. It appears she and Bob took sides against the Jane Cox faction. She said she would never go near them for anything, that they would be happy to see Bob dead.'

'That's very sad,' said Charles.

'It's more than sad,' said Bill. 'It has implications for the school. I had no idea there had been a split among that group of ... well, whatever they are. They've been in each other's hair in the past, but it has never come to a split.'

'Bill, it's time for you to start looking into what's going on in your school,' said Miss Barker. 'Politically. You're far too trusting.'

'What are you referring to?'

'I'm asking you to start weighing things up.' He did not respond. 'Anyway,' she continued, 'Joanne has told Miss McNamara she can stay with you for the moment.'

'The break must be serious if she wants to stay here,' said Bill.

'By the way, Charles,' said Miss Barker, 'Fr. van Engelen's superior and his two seminarians who came to Binawarra for the Easter Sunday Mass discovered the bodies. I wonder if Father knows. Sitting in the police station all afternoon waiting to be interviewed wouldn't be too comfortable.'

Bill accompanied Charles to phone the priest, leaving Miss Barker at the front gate to ponder the events. It was now past three-thirty. A few minutes later, another car pulled up.

'Good afternoon, Miss Barker,' called Ruby cheerfully. 'We thought we would find you all here. We went first to the Winterbines', then to you, and now here ... What's happening?' She broke off, seeing the women bunched around Suzie. Miss Barker related what had happened. 'Bob dead! We only spoke to him recently.' She paused. 'I was aware—but had no idea it would end this way.'

'There may be more to it,' said Miss Barker.

'What?'

'Let's wait until we get more information.'

'I'll join the ladies,' said Ruby. 'Geoff, wait here.'

'I have something that might interest you,' said Geoff after he saw Ruby settle among the women on the verandah.

'I would never expect anything frivolous to issue from your mouth, Captain Shawcross.'

'I met the man once, and I found him very odd. But I remember one thing about that meeting, and I'm surprised it did not come back to Ruby.'

'It depends on what your mind is attuned to, Mr Shawcross. Go on.'

'Ruby asked him what he thought of the proposal for Estella to pursue a career in public relations. His first reaction was to pick correctly that the proposal had come from Miss Bicknell. When Ruby asked him if he agreed with the idea, he began flapping his hands and saying that Estella did not have to do anything. She just had to be there, you know, because of how beautiful she is. But then he went quiet, completely changing his mood. He muttered something like "So that's it?" and left us in a hurry.'

'Excellent, Captain Shawcross! That's the link I wanted.'

'There's more,' he continued. 'Later that day, Bill told me that Bob had rung to warn him—something to do with the students. Not everything was as it looked on the surface, he said.'

'Well, indeed, indeed. I had my suspicions. As strange as he seemed, it was not in Mr McKinnon's character to take the trouble to go to that peak for his particular pleasures. Viewing the site and the bodies strengthened those suspicions. Miss McNamara's last words with him, and now this, suggest he might have got on to something about Miss Bicknell. Unfortunately, his well-known way of making the target of his subtle teasing suffer may have cost him his life. That, of course, and his lack of discipline.'

'Killing a fellow teacher because of teasing? It doesn't seem—'

'I've been here long enough to be aware of many things in this town, Mr Shawcross. Mr McKinnon was too open in many respects. No, all things considered, I'm as sure as I can be. Further developments will show whether I am right or wrong.'

'If you're right,' said Geoff, 'things have become dangerous.'

'Correct. It's not Miss Winterbine who is in immediate danger, though. It's those who look like they're disturbing Miss Bicknell's plans for Estella. You realise you're putting yourself in peril? You might be putting yourself on the frontline. Keep in mind that it would not have been Miss Bicknell who threw those two men off the cliff. It had to be someone with great strength. Our friend, Mr Rostowski, seems to be our leading candidate in all this.'

'Yes, it has occurred to me. It doesn't matter. I'm committed until Estella is out of danger.'

Miss Barker searched Geoff's face. 'Very good, Mr Shawcross; we are both committed. But I must remind you not to involve Miss Waiting more than necessary for her good and the success of the planning.'

'I'll be strict with her.'

'Good. What are you doing here? I thought Miss Winterbine's parents would drive her to Bendigo tomorrow.'

'You know what Ruby is like. She thought it would be good to come up today and see if Estella would come back with us this evening. It would give her time to settle in before the program tomorrow. It would save Mr and Mrs Winterbine the trouble.'

'That's a good practical idea. I'm sure Charles and Aine will be happy to agree. I have the photos of Miss Bicknell and her minder. Call around on your way to the Winterbines.'

At that moment, Bill and Charles appeared on the verandah. Miss Barker and Geoff then joined the group. Geoff noticed a shy, welcoming expression on Estella's face. That pleased him, considering how she looked when they had left her two weeks before.

'Geoff, good news,' said Ruby. 'Estella's mum and dad have agreed to her coming this evening.'

Geoff smiled in reply and sat down. Miss Barker took the opportunity to ask a few more questions of Suzie McNamara. What were the disagreements she and Mr McKinnon had with the others, and who exactly did they disagree with? The answer to the second question was direct: it was mainly with that revolting Jane Cox and that creepy Stephen Calder. She was not precise in her reply to the first question. It was about ideology, she said. It would not interest the people present. And with that, she began to cry all over again. Miss Barker then excused herself and left, leaving the women to comfort her.

Chapter 18

Estella goes to Bendigo

THE FOLLOWING morning in Bendigo, at about the same time Ruby Waiting was having breakfast with Estella, Bruce Butcher was getting ready to go to the university. He did not hurry, for there were no lectures that day, just some promotional work for the department. He took up Gerda Vrouwendijk's instructions and perused them once more. The verbal warning. He smiled. Who did that woman think she was? He dropped the instructions onto the coffee table and looked at his watch. He had a few minutes yet, so he poured himself a coffee and sat by the lounge room window overlooking his well-tended garden. The roses were coming on beautifully, he mused as he gazed outside and took in the full flavour of freshly brewed coffee. His mind was taken back to the days in Amsterdam when he had acquired a taste for 'proper' coffee and Dutch cheese. What a time that was! The political activity, the enthusiasm, the commitment—and the Dutch girls! When they were radical, they really went off, no mucking about. The Dutch seemed not to know what "prim and proper" meant.

On the whole, he had had a great life since starting at university. The revolutionary sixties in Sydney, graduation, and then a scholarship to a university in Holland—it had all turned out so well. And the girls! He wondered what it would be like to be an ugly man. He finished his coffee, took the empty cup to the kitchen sink, rinsed it, and laid it upside down to drain. He collected his case and walked to the front door with a last glance around. He ambled between the roses, admiring the delicate, untouched petals and breathing in their subtle fragrance.

ESTELLA SAT on the edge of the lounge settee and listened while Ruby explained the day's schedule.

'I'll give Geoff a ring now to come and keep you company until I get back,' said Ruby, getting up.

'Is Geoff coming over?'

'Yes, silly girl, don't look like that. He'll make sure you're not lonely.' She made the call and then collected her bag and some folders. 'Okay, Geoff will be here shortly, and I'll be back at the time arranged. Have a look at the books on my bookshelf. There may be something of interest there. See you soon, darling.' She blew her a kiss.

Geoff parked his car far enough away from Ruby's unit to give him space to survey the area. The trees lining the street on each side provided little cover. He checked each car with an inattentive glance as he walked. A van was parked on the opposite side of the street, down from the unit. He walked to the front door and knocked. A shyly smiling Estella showed him into the lounge room.

'You know, Estella, this is only the second time I've been here,' he said as he sat down. 'It's neat and cosy, isn't it?'

'Yes.' She waited for him to continue.

'Ruby generally comes up to St Arnaud. She's keen on getting away on the weekends. And she likes my mother. They're the same type, outgoing and confident.' He laughed lightly. 'I suppose you're wondering what happened to me?'

'No, you're good the way you are.' She looked away.

'Thanks.' He paused. 'We're both a bit on the shy side, aren't we?'

Estella's mouth opened a little, and she lowered her eyes. Geoff had turned towards the window and did not notice. He got up. Estella watched as he cautiously parted the curtains. He did not speak for a while.

'I'm just having a look around the street to see what it's like,' he said, glancing back at her.

The passenger door of the van opened, and Boris Rostowski stepped out. He crouched behind the van and fixed his eyes on the unit. He turned and hurried up the street. Geoff sat within reach of the phone. He tried to keep the conversation going with Estella, who was obviously wondering what he was doing. The phone rang. Geoff let it ring twice and then picked it up. 'Hello, Ruby Waiting's residence.'

'Yes, hello, this is the university,' said a voice with an accent. 'Is Ruby Waiting there?'

'No, Miss Waiting left for the university a short while ago. Can I take a message?'

'May I ask who I am talking to?' said the voice.

'I'm a friend of Ruby's. You can leave a message with me.'

'I will try to catch her at the university. Thank you.'

Geoff had suspected they would receive a call. Boris had seen him enter, so he knew who was in the unit. He must have seen Ruby depart for the university, too. So what was the point of ringing? He returned to the window. Estella watched all this with forbearance. A minute later, Boris came back to the van.

'I'm going to leave you for a short time. You'll be all right? I won't be long.'

Estella assured him she would be all right until he got back. Good, he said, but she should not open the door to anyone. That was important. She would do as he said. He hurried to his car and drove down several blocks until he was out of sight of the unit. He then swung to the right twice, so he was in the street parallel to Ruby's. He drove some way and, parking the car, made his way to the corner down from Ruby's unit. He eased into a position where he could see Boris's van. He waited fifteen minutes. There was no movement. Returning to the unit, he asked Estella if there had been any calls. There had been none. He sat near the phone and asked Estella how she liked Bendigo. They had chatted for five minutes when the phone rang again.

'I'm sorry to disturb you, sir, but is Ms Waiting there yet?'

'No, she's still at the university.'

'Oh, I am sorry. I misunderstood. I'll call back. Thank you, sir.'

Geoff had an idea there would be no more calls. He was right. There were no more. He settled back and resumed a pleasant meandering conversation with Estella, who seemed increasingly at ease. The more she relaxed, the more her sweetness shone, enhancing her striking appearance. Or was it the other way around?

IN THE meantime, Ruby had made her way to Bruce Butcher's office.

'Ah, it's our fat little fascist flunkey from the big boss, is it?' he said when she appeared in his office. 'What is it this time?'

'I want you to know that the administration has received Dr Gunn's letters and that a full investigation is imminent.'

'Letters?'

'Yes, letters. You see, Dr Gunn is not stupid. He knows what happened and is only restrained by the girl you have soiled and crippled emotionally.'

He flinched. A sneer formed on his lips. 'Soiled? You tied-up, emotionally stunted, politically backward, jackbooted little flunkey, only you would use a word like soiled, wouldn't you? Why can't you get it into your head that clean or dirty has nothing to do with sex? Sexual action has only to do with inclination and preference. If someone, hypothetically speaking, has not enjoyed a sexual experience, then fine. It's just like having a meal you didn't enjoy. You didn't enjoy it. It'll be better next time. An inquest is entirely inappropriate, an anachronism.'

'Do you genuinely believe that, or have you been using it as an excuse for so long that you have fooled yourself into justifying the violent rape of an innocent girl? That's a criminal mentality.'

'The personnel manager is a psychologist now,' he continued to sneer.

'You don't have to be a psychologist to tell the fundamental difference between right and wrong.'

He stared at her and gestured impatiently. 'Is that all, or is there something else? You're boring me.'

'Dr Gunn will not rest until he has justice.'

'Anything else?'

'Yes, I will bring Estella Winterbine to you at eleven o'clock, as Ms Edith Bicknell of Binawarra High School arranged. You are to stick to the program as stipulated. You are warned that this girl is under protection. To start with, she is staying with me with her parents' expressed approval. At the end of each session you have with her, I will be back at the department to collect her.'

'What is it with this girl? This is the second time I've been told she's under protection. She can't be that special.'

'Who else has said that?' said Ruby, unable to hide her surprise.

'Never you mind.'

'She is special, very special. Keep it in mind.'

'What's going on with you people? Do you think I have such a narrow choice that I have to take whatever pops up? There's plenty out there for me without worrying about some schoolgirl from the back blocks.'

'You are warned,' she said and left him.

At five minutes to eleven, Bruce Butcher was leaning back in his comfortable office chair, flicking through one of the Melbourne newspapers, reading the international reports. The North Vietnamese were mustering their forces in preparation for taking Saigon. The Khmer Rouge siege of Phnom Penh in Cambodia looked like it was in its last stages. He heard a tap on the door and footsteps entering his office. He lowered the newspaper. It fell from his hands onto the desk. He struggled to his feet, staring woodenly at the girl with Ruby Waiting. Dressed in a light brown skirt and cream blouse over which she had a loose-fitting dark brown woollen jumper for the morning chill, she stood motionless, regarding him distantly.

'This is Estella Winterbine, the student from Binawarra High School, who is on a vocational visit to the university. She is scheduled to be with you until twelve-thirty,' said Ruby, and then turning to Estella, 'Estella darling, this is Mr Butcher, senior lecturer in Media Studies. Any questions you have about the field of public relations, don't hesitate to ask him.' And turning back to Bruce: 'I will be back to pick up Miss Winterbine at the front office at twelve-thirty sharp. There's no need to keep her in your office while she is waiting.'

Ruby left Estella facing Bruce Butcher. He murmured a greeting and, with an effort to settle himself, came from behind his desk. He pushed the two armchairs in front of his desk closer together.

'Please ... please sit down, Estella,' he stammered. She sat, and he sat next to her. 'Now, the idea is for me to give you as clear a picture as I can of the work of public relations,' he said, getting up again and fumbling over his desk for several books and folders. 'The first thing to establish is what you know about public relations. What do you know?'

'Nothing, really, sir. It has been suggested I'm suitable for that sort of work,' she said, looking ahead of her.

'Okay, then we can start from the beginning.' He had gained his composure and was ready to apply the charm that bedazzled most young women who came into his office. 'And call me Bruce. We don't have to maintain the formality of the classroom here. You know, when you come to university, you are considered a free, independent adult, capable of making your own decisions.'

There was a pause. Bruce was now looking at the flawless, glowing skin around her perfectly formed ear, and the wisps of loose, luxuriant hair spun delicately around it. She turned and let her eyes rest on him.

'I would rather not, Mr Butcher. I wouldn't be comfortable.'

'Now, come on, you have to relax here,' he said, with a brief look of surprise. 'The old divisions of hierarchy don't count here. We are all equals. Call me Bruce.'

There was no reaction. The girl sat waiting with serene patience. There was no expression of annoyance, no missishness, apprehension, none of those things he had learned to overcome. Just serene patience. 'Okay, let's start with a general discussion of public relations work,' he muttered. 'Ask questions anytime you like.' He looked at her, but still got no response. He had the unusual experience of feeling embarrassed.

He clenched and unclenched his fists in a nervous movement. Gearing himself up, he launched into an account of the field of public relations in a snappy, entertaining way, throwing in his usual jokes, witticisms, and anecdotes. He walked around the office, gesturing and showing magazines from a small display he had on one side of the room. He acted out different promotional stunts to demonstrate the right and wrong ways to promote a company's image. He exerted himself as he had never done before to get an engaging response from the face whose eyes followed him impassively.

No matter what Bruce Butcher did or how many tricks he performed, Estella Winterbine maintained an unengaged interest. At no time during his talk could he say she looked at him as an individual, let alone as a man of charm. He was nothing more than an abstract talking head. When she addressed him, it was either with 'sir' or Mr Butcher. It was an irritating, deflating experience. He could not remember the last time a female student came into his office without being affected by his appearance and charming manner. When twelve-thirty came, he threw the pamphlets he was holding onto his desk.

'Well, that's the end of the first session,' he said, rubbing his hand over his face and looking at the unchanged, patient expression. 'Are there questions? You haven't asked any questions.'

'No, Mr Butcher, I don't have any questions. It's all new. I have to think about it.'

'Well, don't hesitate.'

'I'll go to the office now if you have finished, sir.' She stood.

'You can wait here. There's no need to go to the office.'

'Ruby told me to wait at the office.'

'Oh, Ruby said that—' he broke off, his irritation rising. He must not display any annoyance. Then it occurred to him that the girl had probably been warned about him. Yes, of course, that was it. That fat little fascist had warned her. He felt better. But then, girls had been warned about him before, and it had made no difference. Sometimes it had helped in his conquests. No, this girl was like a wet cloth. And now she was just standing there, waiting to be dismissed. The frustration returned. 'Okay, I 'll take you to the office.'

He deposited her with the department's secretary and was about to leave her when Ruby emerged from the stairwell. He saw Estella's eyes light up.

'Well, darling, how did you go?' he heard Ruby say.

'Well ... it was sort of interesting.'

'And how do you feel about public relations work now?'

'I don't know yet.'

'At this stage, what is it: public relations or gardening?'

'Gardening,' said Estella, smiling self-consciously.

Ruby noticed Bruce Butcher. She frowned at him. 'Come on, Estella, Geoff's waiting for us in the union bistro,' and then to Bruce: 'I will bring her back at two o'clock.'

Ruby put her arm through Estella's and walked towards the stairs, with Bruce looking on. Their chatter could be heard as they walked down the stairs. Bruce trudged back to his office. What was that 'darling' about?

No, impossible. It was a darling of close friendship. It was known that right-wing Ruby Waiting was seeing a Vietnam Veteran. That was probably the Geoff they were going to meet for lunch. He stood tapping the desktop with the knuckles of his clenched fist. He had been defeated. He had got a big fat nil in response to the best performance he could put on. Perhaps he was trying too hard. No, that was not it. The girl was simply unmoved by him. When asked about the morning, she said it was 'sort of interesting'. Sort of interesting? He would have preferred boring or stupid. That would have been a reaction, a reaction he could have engaged with.

Against his will and better judgment, he went to the cafeteria for lunch. He risked laying bare his interest, but he could not help it. He had to see how she reacted to others. What was he doing? He had just met this girl. Was he mad or something? He entered the Union bistro, looking around. There they were at the end of the hall. She had the attention of those closest. The girl would attract attention no matter where she went. He crept to the sandwich bar, served himself, and then sat where he had a clear view of them.

After five minutes, he pushed his sandwich away. With all his experience of female behaviour, Bruce Butcher could see what many would miss: the girl who behaved like a dead mullet towards him had feelings for the ordinary man sitting with her and Ruby. There was no mistake. He could see she was trying to hide it, but she betrayed herself; her face shone, and her eyes modestly sparkled as she listened to him. Those looks were of affection. He wanted to go but could not move. He could not take his eyes off them. The ordinary man the girl had feelings for was Ruby Waiting's boyfriend. It was too much. He dragged himself back to his office to await two o'clock.

THE LUNCH could not have been more enjoyable for Estella. At every point, Ruby was solicitous. She was truly taking the role of a big sister. Geoff, in his quiet way, offered his support. She did not quite know why he had accompanied them to Bendigo, but she was glad he was there, at least most of the time. His steady, thoughtful manner complemented Ruby's busy ways.

'And how did Bruce Butcher behave?' Ruby asked after Estella had spoken briefly about the session.

'He was friendly. He did his best to make it appealing. He went to a lot of trouble to explain everything.'

'I bet he did,' said Ruby, and then, responding to Estella's querying expression: 'Don't pay any attention to me. As long as he does everything according to the rules, we'll all be happy, won't we?'

'He asked me to call him Bruce, but I told him I wasn't comfortable with that.'

'What did you call him?'

'Mr Butcher and sir, the way I address teachers at school.'

'Good girl,' said Ruby, laughing.

Estella failed to see what was amusing her. Ruby, switching her attention to Geoff, wanted to know what he had to smile about. Before he could answer, she continued, 'You know, Estella, Geoff's mother always thought that he would be the best to manage the farm of the three children. He was a born farmer. She was disappointed when he joined the army. She was more than pleased when he retired, and his older brother and sister left the farm to him to manage.'

'I tried to explain why I wanted to join the army, but my mother typically was not inclined to listen.'

'Why did you join the army when you had the farm?' Estella asked, wondering why Ruby had begun talking about Geoff and his farm.

'I always thought I would come back to the farm. I was doing most of the work, anyhow. My brother and sister were busy building their professions. At the time, it was not certain how things would develop. I needed something to do if there was no agreement about the property. There was a chance we would have to sell it to split the inheritance. My mother was dead against that and had no trouble holding off that action. "Over my dead body," she used to exclaim.'

'I can just imagine, that old matriarch,' said Ruby.

'Why did I join the army?' he continued. 'I'm not sure why. I was fit. The work on the farm saw to that.'

'I must tell you he does not drink and has a shockingly healthy lifestyle,' said Ruby, interrupting. 'Good food, goes to bed early, all that sort of thing.'

'I also thought I would like to do something for my country. You know this area has an enduring Anzac tradition. The young men around here always selflessly answered the call to war.'

'Geoff,' said Ruby, interrupting again, 'the Anzac tradition is strong everywhere in the bush, not just here in north-western Victoria. It has only broken down in the cities, among those who have been educated, so to speak.'

'Anyhow,' said Geoff, glancing at Ruby, 'I joined the army. My father had been in the army during the Second World War, and that helped me decide. I consulted with the other family members and arranged for a farm manager to manage the farm in my absence. There, you just about have it. Of course, I wasn't absent all the time. Each leave, I spent at the farm.'

'He's left out the part about becoming a special services officer,' said Ruby.

'When I left the army,' Geoff continued, 'we had another family discussion. By that time, my brother and sister were willing to relinquish their interest in the property if I could buy them out. We settled on an arrangement, helped along by my mother, and now the farm is mine, with a fairly hefty debt. But I should manage. It's not a big burden.'

Estella listened intently to his explanation. His quiet, warm manner buttressed a mind of high principles. Generosity and duty, above all else, motivated him to join the army. He reminded her of her father.

'Are you still happy with the farm?' she asked.

'Like a pig in mud,' Ruby broke in.

'Yes, I can manage the work quite well and find it interesting. The thing I like is the wide-open spaces and the course of nature. You know, you can see it in your gardens, the steady, reliable movement of plants, seasons, animals, and so on. It makes the cities seem sterile and artificial. There is so much vibrant life on the land.'

'Geoff, you continually surprise me,' said Ruby, and then turning to Estella: 'I've never heard him talk as much as he has in the last two weeks. Getting something out of him before that was not always easy.'

'It's the company, I suppose.'

'You see, darling girl, you're good for him, too.'

'I meant both of you,' said Geoff, blushing.

What did Ruby mean by 'good for him, too?' Was there some way in which Geoff was good for her? Was that what she meant? Geoff was quick to say Ruby's company was also good for him. That was expected. Her heart sank. Fortunately, Ruby came to the rescue by leading the conversation away to other matters.

DURING LUNCH, Geoff scanned the bistro. As he expected, Boris entered about ten minutes after them. Boris watched them for a while. Then he turned his attention to a man who had come in after him. That man, too, observed their table. Boris was observing the man observing their table. That supported his suspicions that Boris was not stalking Estella; he was shadowing her, just as he was. Boris followed the man he had been observing when he left the bistro.

BRUCE BUTCHER returned to his office and tried to distract himself with the newspaper. But it was no good. His thoughts kept returning to the girl he had had in his office for one and a half hours of frustration. He must pull himself together. She was just another girl. Why should her lack of interest bother him? There had been plenty of girls who rejected his approach in the past. That was never a problem. He just moved on to the next one. Why should this country girl from some hick town be different? He flicked the paper he held in front of him and determined to fix his mind on the report about the Khmer Rouge. After reading the same paragraph four or five times, without getting much sense out of it, he gave it away. He suddenly remembered Gerda's warnings. They had entirely slipped out of his mind. That should be an incentive for him to forget about the girl.

Gerda Vrouwendijk's warnings ... nobody should complain if they were familiar with the consequences of failure, he had heard her say. The girl was under protection. That meant somebody was keeping an eye on him and the girl. That somebody would have seen him in the bistro. He must be careful. These thoughts turned over in his mind, while he attempted to distract himself by looking at timetables, lecture topics, assignment questions, book lists, and other such routine matters. Over this, the image of the girl's face insisted on imposing itself. The phone rang.

'Mr Butcher, it's Edith Bicknell here,' he heard a business-like voice say.

'Yes, Ms Bicknell.'

'I hope the sessions are proceeding according to plan.'

'They are.'

'I'm glad to hear it. I cannot emphasise enough how important it is for all concerned that our students enjoy the full benefit of a visit to the university. So much else hinges on the success of those visits. I'm sure you understand that.'

'I do, Ms Bicknell. There's no need to ring. The plan will be followed.'

'I'm glad to hear it. If something as simple as this failed, then we would have to review the whole plan.'

'You won't have to review any plan.'

'Then I will leave it in your hands. Good afternoon.'

Bruce returned the receiver to its cradle. That was a follow-up warning, and it was likely that whoever was shadowing the girl had prompted it. This was serious business, and he was playing with fire. He tried to impress himself with the seriousness of the situation to get his mind off her. By two o'clock, he had argued himself into a position of not caring. But as the minutes ticked by and no one appeared, he became agitated. Where were they? In this agitated state, he sat at his desk for another ten minutes. Then they appeared.

'I'm sorry we are late, Mr Butcher,' said Ruby, holding Estella's hand. 'Yesterday we experienced a big upset in Binawarra, and we have been talking about it.'

'No problem. I had other things to attend to, anyhow. I hope everything is all right,' Bruce said, his attention fixed on the girl's distress.

'Yes, it will be all right. By the way, did you know Bob McKinnon at Binawarra High School?'

'Not well,' he said, forcing his gaze away from Estella. 'I know of him. What has happened?'

'He was killed in odd circumstances.'

'Killed! How?'

'He was found at the bottom of a cliff with another person outside Binawarra.'

Bruce blinked. 'What other person?'

'I would rather not say.' She glanced at Estella.

'I understand ... it's bound to be reported in the local papers.'

With Ruby gone, he asked Estella with as much sympathy as he could muster whether she was all right to go on with the session. They could postpone it if she wished. She looked at him through teary eyes. She would be okay. At last, a reaction! It was a small opening, and he strove to get through. He knew what it was like to lose somebody suddenly. It came like a clap of thunder out of the blue. One minute they were there and the next gone, without any apparent reason. It was always worse when it was a sudden, violent accident. He saw her face tense up, and it sent a thrill through him.

'Did you know Bob well?'

'Not really. I only had him for a few classes. But he was always friendly. My mother and father were very upset yesterday and said we should say many prayers for him.'

He ignored the prayer bit and tried to pursue the angle of sympathy, but Estella composed herself and assumed the same impassive expression that had prevailed during the morning session. He tried his best to recapture and draw out the feelings, but she politely brushed aside any personal inquiry. He was blocked. There was nothing for him but to continue the program with his maddening frustration. His next task was to take her on a tour of the department. As they were preparing to go, there was a gentle knock on the door. They turned to see a trim, smartly dressed Asian gentleman in the doorway. He bowed with great dignity before wishing them a good afternoon in correct English with a slight accent.

'Mr Tanaka,' said Bruce, moving forward to greet him, 'we were not expecting you until tomorrow. Please come in.'

'I have come to see your beautiful town,' he said, walking into the office. 'I've dropped by to confirm tomorrow's meeting.'

'Of course, Mr Tanaka, everything is arranged. Our final year students look forward to hearing a man of your business eminence.'

'And is this one of them?' he said, coming to Estella and holding out his hand. Without thinking, Estella offered her hand, which he took and held while Bruce answered.

'This is a prospective student, Mr Tanaka. Estella Winterbine. We are showing her around the department.'

'I hope you will attend tomorrow, Miss Winterbine.' He raised her hand to his mouth, just brushing it with his lips.

'Yes, she will be there,' said Bruce, blinking at the action. He turned to Estella. 'Mr Tanaka is head of the Nippon Universal Corporation—'

'Good, I will leave you then.' Mr Tanaka returned Estella's timid acknowledgment with a courteous smile.

'You are not here by yourself, I trust,' said Bruce.

'No, I have my people below waiting for me.' He bowed again to Estella before turning to leave.

'We will accompany you downstairs,' said Bruce.

'As you wish.'

At every point in the walk from the office to his waiting staff downstairs, Mr Tanaka showed himself attentive to Estella. He stood aside to let her go first from the office. He waited until she came between him and Bruce before they walked to the stairs. At the top of the stairs, he stood aside again to let her go first, and at the bottom bade her leave the stairway in front of them. He did all this while talking to Bruce Butcher, but he did so, making it clear that his good manners and attention to Estella took priority. Once outside the building, he said goodbye with another respectful bow while his staff waited at a distance.

'That's a powerful international businessman,' said Bruce, as they watched his assistants escort him to his car. 'You're fortunate to be here during the visit of such a powerful man. I'm surprised he has taken up the invitation to visit us.'

Estella made no reply to this information. The way she stood waiting, her face devoid of expression, was almost more than he could bear. With renewed determination to suppress his feelings, he began a tour of the lecture theatres and seminar rooms, but now found there was something else to increase his frustration and irritation. Estella did not walk beside him. She was always that bit behind. It made it difficult for him to engage her in conversation. And even if he did get her into the correct position, she did not respond to anything outside the program. Even his effective, well-rehearsed rhetoric about personal freedom was ignored. At the end of the tour, he was exhausted. He had never tried so hard with such poor results. Poor results? There was no result. Her expression was unchanged. Back at his office, he motioned her to sit in the armchair in front of his desk, but this time, he sat behind it.

'Are you always so impassive?' he could not stop himself from saying. The next moment, he wished he had not said it.

'Impassive?' said Estella.

'I'm sorry,' he hastened to say. 'I meant from the point of view of public relations work. I mean, your temperament is not outgoing as far as I can see. That's usually required for this type of work.' He tried to sound sympathetic. To his surprise, it worked.

'I'm quiet, I suppose,' she said. 'But I'm only considering this work at the suggestion of Miss Bicknell. It would never have occurred to me otherwise.'

'Ms Bicknell will have good reasons.' His eagerness returned as he bent towards her. 'Perhaps she thinks the potential is there.'

'That's what she said. She said I'll be more talkative as I get older.'

'Yes, of course, that's right. As your teachers, we're here to guide you. Once you start your course, you'll see that we'll be of all possible assistance. It's not like school. You'll be able to contact me whenever you want. You'll be a free agent.'

'Thank you,' she said with a slight smile.

At last, some engagement. He must take it slowly, far more slowly than he was used to. This was a prize of unparalleled value. He was too used to having things his way. It was good for him to have to work for it. It would make the possession all the more satisfying. While these thoughts flashed through his head, the department secretary appeared at the door.

'I have Mr Essam Al Refai to see you, Bruce,' she said, reading from a business card.

'He's here, too!' Bruce exclaimed. 'Excuse me, Estella, I'll be back in a minute.'

Bruce returned with a man of such elegance and poise that he made Bruce Butcher look cheap and vulgar. He was tall and stood straight but with a relaxed, smiling manner. His thinning, grey hair was trimmed and neatly slicked back. He wore a spotless dark grey suit, an equally spotless white shirt, setting off a dark blue tie, and on his feet were gleaming black leather shoes. He was in his mid-fifties, of a healthy complexion with clear, friendly eyes. Not waiting to be introduced, he went straight to Estella and offered his hand.

'No, Mademoiselle, please remain seated,' he said, taking the hand she unconsciously raised, 'with whom do I have the pleasure?'

'This ... this is Estella Winterbine, a prospective student,' said Bruce. 'Estella, this is Mr Al Refai. He is head of the Parisian Worldwide Communications Company.'

'Ah, Mademoiselle, I am pleased to meet you,' he said, brushing his lips against her hand and letting it go. 'My company is in France, but I am from Cairo, Egypt. I love Paris and France, but I am Egyptian. Let's not be mistaken.' He smiled warmly.

'We were not expecting you until tomorrow, Mr Al Refai,' said Bruce.

'Not to worry, Mr Butcher. Everything is all right. I've just come along to see that everything is in order. The times are right? Tomorrow morning at eleven o'clock?'

'Yes, Mr Al Refai.'

'Well, Mr Butcher, my staff tells me you are among the few who can make decent coffee in this otherwise beautiful country. I would love a cup while I speak to this charming young lady here.' He took the armchair beside Estella, manoeuvred it into a respectful distance, and sat down.

'Of course, Mr Al Refai.'

Again, his fists clenched and unclenched as he left Estella with the Egyptian and made his way to the staff room. There was a limit to what he would swallow. Then he thought of Gerda Vrouwendijk. There were more important things than his dignity. He prepared three cups of coffee and hurried back to his office. He arrived to see a smiling Estella Winterbine chatting with the Egyptian. He handed each a cup, unable to help frowning at the Egyptian. Estella looked at the cup and was about to speak.

'Mr Butcher, you have a bright prospective student here,' said Mr Al Refai. 'She has been telling me all about her town. If she can speak as well on behalf of her future employers, she will be a great company asset.' He turned to Estella. 'You love your town, don't you, Miss?'

'Yes, it's a beautiful town. We're all very proud of it. Daddy has helped restore some of the historical buildings.'

'Daddy has, has he?' said the Egyptian, without a hint of amusement in his voice. Indeed, his expression was all polite interest.

'Yes. He's a highly respected carpenter.'

'I'm sure your father is delighted with a daughter who is so proud of him.'

Estella returned this comment with an appreciative smile that tested Bruce Butcher's composure. The Egyptian bent towards Estella.

'Here, give me your cup, Miss. I don't think you like coffee, do you?' Estella nodded and handed him the cup. He passed it to Bruce Butcher, who, scarcely able to control his irritation, placed it on his desk. Bruce looked on while the oily Egyptian chatted about the countryside around Bendigo. What a contrast with Cairo, Mr Al Refai said, but Cairo had its charms, and he hoped that Miss Winterbine would have the chance to visit his ancient land.

'You know, Miss Winterbine, you could pass for a young Egyptian woman,' he said. 'With your complexion, your posture, your manners, all those things, you would not be out of place among my acquaintances, apart from your appearance, of course, which every person must notice.' Estella politely acknowledged his remarks. 'I'm sorry to embarrass you, young lady,' he said, smiling. 'Tomorrow, I will come back to Bendigo to give a talk to interested students in the department. I hope you will attend.' He turned to Bruce for confirmation. Yes, Estella would be present. 'Good,' he went on. 'Now I have two of my daughters with me on this trip. They are a bit older than you, but I'm sure they would like you. On these trips, they do not meet many young women with whom they have much in common. Would you allow me to introduce them to you?'

'Yes ... of course,' said Estella.

The request also took Bruce Butcher by surprise. The arrangement with Mr Al Refai had been made on Gerda's recommendation. As the head of a big worldwide communications company, he was precisely the sort of speaker the department wanted. He was also the type of influential figure, heading the right sort of company that Gerda wished to cultivate. He was ideologically and organizationally desirable. There was, however, something else happening here. It dawned on him while he observed the Egyptian's manner with Estella.

He had never been part of this side of Gerda's activities, something he had limited knowledge of. His stomach turned. And here was the girl rising to it. How could she? How could he bear it? Mr Al Refai thanked Bruce for the coffee, took Estella's hand, and said he was looking forward to introducing his daughters to her. Having put Bruce out of the field of play, he departed, leaving him looking foolishly at Estella. Bruce consulted his watch. It was already past four o'clock. That irritating woman would be around any moment.

No sooner had that disagreeable thought passed through his mind than Ruby appeared at the door. Ruby threaded her arm through Estella's and, calling over her shoulder to a deflated Bruce that Estella would be back the next day at eleven o'clock, she led her out of the office. Bruce stood at the doorway and watched them go. Outside the department office, he saw the boyfriend waiting. The boyfriend waved at them and then looked in his direction. A flicker of recognition. Ruby's appointed minder, he thought, and you can bet a thick-headed soldier. He would make inquiries.

He walked back into his office, his feet like concrete blocks. The Melbourne newspaper still lay on the desk. He folded it with his thoughts fixed on the rejection he had suffered. The drive back into town in his restored MGB did not distract his thoughts from the humiliation of being passed over for some oily foreigner. The evening was no different. The dinner he usually made a ritual out of, with the choicest food and wine, had to be forced down. The television was on, but he could not concentrate. The vision of the girl smiling fetchingly at the Egyptian and ignoring him was fixed before his eyes.

THE MOOD in Ruby's unit was altogether different. Geoff had dropped them off, saying he would be back later to take them to dinner. Ruby sat Estella down. She was not to move until she heard everything that had happened that afternoon. She poured herself a glass of wine and Estella an orange juice. 'Now, let's hear it all,' she said, making herself comfortable and holding her glass of wine in front of her. She exclaimed, and laughed, and teased during Estella's narration, appearing delighted by Bruce Butcher's reaction to his visitors.

'So you continued to call him sir, and he was a bit grumpy, was he?'

'I didn't say grumpy,' said Estella, amused by Ruby's unrestrained delight. 'I said he seemed a little put out by the two visitors. He said he didn't expect them until tomorrow.'

'Don't worry, darling. He would have hated the presence of such impressive men. Did they really kiss your hand?'

'Yes, indeed.'

'What did you think?'

'I wasn't expecting it. They seemed to think it was normal manners. So I took it as an expression of their politeness.'

'Were they just being polite? Or was there something else?'

'They were polite and respectful, both men.'

'Be careful, darling. Boys will be boys.'

Estella, now used to being called 'darling' by the irrepressible Ruby, said she would be careful. As long as they were polite and respectful, there was no need for concern. For a moment, Ruby wore a doubtful expression, but it dissolved as she placed her empty wine glass down and rummaged in her briefcase.

'Here,' she said, taking a folder out and handing it to Estella, 'this is about the courses in horticulture at the technical college. I fetched it this afternoon.' Estella had a choice of pursuing different course strands: landscaping, floriculture, or tending parks and gardens. She could specialise to her heart's content. 'Have a leaf through the material while I freshen up.'

Estella picked out one of the strands and began reading, but despite its interest, her mind drifted. She could not help reflecting again on how much her life had changed since Ruby and Geoff had arrived on the scene. Ruby's companionship with all its affection, understanding, and encouragement had dispelled her hurt. It shed a new light on Jenny's behaviour. She understood now that Jenny was not just ignoring her. Jenny had her own problems, and those problems had to do with Len Dawson. Estella resolved to be more understanding and to avoid letting her behaviour hurt her so much. Then she recalled Jenny saying you couldn't control the heart, that the heart was a rebellious creature.

What was it that she felt for Geoff? Was the yearning feeling, the longing for his company, every memory of his being in her company, and the despair she felt at the realisation that Geoff belonged to Ruby—was that love? She thought of his inner strength, his honesty, and his warmth. He was not the cultured man that Mr Al Refai was, but he was just as respectful in his manners, with the difference that there was no artifice about him. And then it frightened her when the thought flashed through her mind that she saw things about Geoff that Ruby failed to recognise. She could not bear that thought. It was a betrayal. Ruby entered the lounge room. She hesitated, and then came and knelt by her.

'What is it?'

Estella could not help a moment of overwhelming feeling. She put her hand to her mouth. 'You've been so kind to me.'

'There, come on,' said Ruby. 'You've had a hard time, ostracised as you were. Everybody would feel bad about losing their best friend. It must have been very hard when they accused you of being cold when the very opposite is true. Geoff and I see the real you, and our friendship is genuine and heartfelt. It's only what you deserve.'

Estella felt an inclination to give her feelings release. But that would be wrong. That would be unfair and disloyal to Ruby. She must control herself. 'Thank you,' she said, trying to smile. 'I hope I'll always be worthy of your friendship.'

'Of course, you will,' said Ruby, puzzled. 'You know, you shouldn't try to be perfect. You're more than good enough as you are. It takes a lot of energy to be perfect. Come on now, go and get ready. Our escort will be here soon to pick up his ladies.'

Estella retired to her room. She returned to the lounge room fifteen minutes later to see Geoff holding the information sheets. He was studying them so intently that he did not hear her approach. She sat next to Ruby on the lounge settee, prepared to wait until he had finished reading.

'He's always like that,' said Ruby. 'The moment his attention is caught, he's gone. Have you ever noticed that men can only concentrate on one thing at a time?' She laughed.

'I'm sorry,' said Geoff, sitting up straight. 'Hello, Estella. These courses look interesting. What did you think?'

'I haven't had a chance to examine them.'

'They're not only about plant propagation and all that entails. They're also about running a horticultural business. Some of this stuff is right up my alley. If I should ever decide to diversify, this would be useful.'

'There you are,' said Ruby. 'You and Geoff can do the course together. You wouldn't be alone. You could even help Geoff.'

'If it turned out I went in a particular direction, and one of these courses was suitable,' said Geoff, hesitating, 'I would be happy to follow it with Estella. As long as she will put up with me.'

'Geoff, I would never be putting up with you,' said Estella.

'He's still not sure you like him,' said Ruby. 'I keep telling him you think of him as a big brother. I suppose it's understandable, though. You're hardly the ordinary girl down the street. Anyhow, I'm famished.' She got up and pulled Estella to her feet. 'Now, Geoff, no more uncertainty with Estella. She likes you, so relax.'

Not long afterwards, they arrived in the city centre. Ruby put her arm through Geoff's as they set off to walk to the restaurant. 'Estella, take Geoff's other arm. You look so lonely there, unattached. Geoff can flaunt having two beautiful women on his arm.' Estella took Geoff's arm and walked in silence as Ruby and Geoff chatted. When they got to the restaurant, she felt a wrench as she let his arm go. The feeling was soon forgotten because Geoff began questioning her about the two foreign visitors. At first, he appeared just interested. Then she had the impression that something else was motivating him. He took out a small notepad.

'I'm just trying to get it clear in my head how the Media Studies Department operates.'

'Why?'

'It's just something I'm doing for a particular purpose. I'll tell you later why.'

Although his interest seemed to cover more than the operations of the Media Studies Department, Estella was reassured. Whatever his reasons, they would be sound. Ruby switched the conversation to other subjects. There was one moment when Estella's raw feelings rose to the surface. The restaurant was where Geoff had taken her on their first date.

THAT EVENING, Gerda Vrouwendijk sat in her lounge room, arms folded and staring into the distance. Now and then, she broke the distant stare and glanced at her watch, only to resume the same faraway expression. For half an hour, she sat this way. Then, with a huff of impatience, she got up, walked to the mantelpiece, and grabbed the packet of cigarettes. She lit up, blew a puff into the air, and walked up and down, fidgeting. The telephone rang. She snatched up the receiver.

'Good evening,' she said, with forced calmness, 'Edith Bicknell.'

'Ms Bicknell, we have examined the property on offer,' said a formal voice. 'My client agrees to a value of five million dollars.'

'Five million US dollars.'

'Five million US dollars,' repeated the voice. As arranged, a prepayment of one million US dollars will be deposited in the vendor's New York account. The balance will be paid in stages as each condition is met. If any condition is not met, the purchaser has the option of retiring from the agreement with a full refund. If the purchaser breaks off the arrangement at any time for reasons other than the property failing to meet a condition agreed upon, the forfeiture will be one million US dollars and no more. There will be no further correspondence. Understood?'

'Understood,' said Gerda. 'The vendor will proceed after confirmation of the deposit in the New York account.'

'As agreed,' said the voice. 'We assume that negotiations with other parties will now cease.'

'Forthwith.'

'Thank you, Ms Bicknell. There is nothing further to add. My client looks forward to the next stage in the transfer.'

Gerda Vrouwendijk put the receiver back into its cradle as her lips broke into a smile of relief. She smoked her cigarette down to the filter and stubbed it roughly in one of the overflowing ashtrays. She dialled the exchange and asked for a number in Middelburg in the Netherlands. Fifteen minutes later, the phone rang. Gerda picked up the receiver and spoke in Dutch.

Chapter 19

Estella and Geoff

IT DID NOT surprise Geoff to see Boris's van still on watch as he walked to Ruby's unit the following morning. He had already seen Bruce Butcher recoiling behind the fence of the house on the nearest corner when he parked his car. Two people on watch ... well, three, including him. Things were gathering pace. He suspected, though, that the university lecturer was unaware of Boris's presence or who was keeping an eye on him.

'We are going to Sandhurst Technical College before we do our tour of the historical spots in the town centre,' he said to Estella as they walked to his car. 'I thought we should take the opportunity to learn a bit more about the courses in horticulture. Would you like that?'

After pulling up in the college's main parking area, Geoff handed her some sunglasses and recommended she put them on, together with her sunhat. He did not wait for her to ask why but said she might excite unwanted attention. He added that if she felt uncomfortable, she should not hesitate to take his arm or stand close to him. As he had anticipated, he had to discipline a few students whose uncontrollable mouths frightened Estella.

'I'm sorry that had to happen,' said Geoff, taking her hand. 'Sometimes there's no choice.' He glanced at her as they resumed their way. 'I hope it doesn't have to happen again.'

'Thank you. I hope not, too.'

Geoff let go of Estella's hand once they were in the department. They spent more than an hour listening to an explanation of the different course strands. Estella asked about landscaping and seed propagation, while Geoff was interested in the business aspects of horticulture. He noticed with pleasure her increasing interest in this subject. By the time they finished, there was no time to visit Bendigo's historical centre. As they headed back to the car, he said perhaps they could do that on Estella's next visit to Ruby.

'I would love to.'

'Well, you'll have to talk to Ruby ... you should put on your hat and sunglasses for the walk back to the car.

'I wish I didn't have to go to the university,' she said, putting them on. 'This visit has made me feel even less interested.'

'I can understand.' He took her hand to dissuade any further boyish attention. 'You only have to go through the motions for the rest of the day, and then it will be over.' They came around a corner on their way to the parking area. 'Hey, isn't that your contact at the university!'

Estella caught sight of Bruce Butcher disappearing into a side path. 'Yes, it is ... I wonder what he's doing here.'

'Perhaps he's following you.'

'Why?'

'Why would you think? You should be careful.'

'But I have done as Ruby said. I have done nothing to encourage him.'

'You should still stay on your guard.'

'Geoff, is there something going on that I don't know about?'

Geoff walked on, trying to decide what to say to a question he knew was overdue. He had seen Estella's many inquiring looks.

'Estella, I don't want to alarm you, but there is some sort of interest in you coming from— We're not sure what it's about. Bruce Butcher may be part of it. I don't know. It's best to be careful. We're here to protect you, anyhow. There's nothing to worry about if you keep close to us.'

'Protect me? Why? Ruby knows about this, does she?'

'Of course. But look, don't worry about it now. We didn't want to talk about something so vague and alarm you. Just relax and leave things to me. I have a little experience in this sort of stuff.'

Estella was willing to accept Geoff's explanation. She had many questions and felt unnerved by the thought that an unknown person or persons had an interest in her. But Geoff's protection reassured her. She was happy to put complete trust in him. With her hand in his, she could not have felt safer. Geoff continued talking about the courses as they drove to the university and what they meant for her and him. His conversation was easy and familiar and full of interest for her. She listened as much to his voice's tone as to what he said, all the time feeling her hand in his. By the time they parked the car, her heart was full to overflowing. He took her hand as they set off. They arrived to see Ruby waiting for them outside the downstairs entrance.

'Ah! You have your own knight in shining armour to escort you.'

Estella, becoming conscious of the public view of what she was doing, withdrew her hand.

'Don't worry, darling,' Ruby said, taking her arm. 'I know he's looking after you. He's like a faithful puppy dog, aren't you, Geoff?'

'We had a bit of trouble over at the technical college,' he said with a faint smile.

'I'm sure you handled it well. Come on, Estella, hurry. They're ready for the seminar. Geoff, we'll see you here at twelve-thirty for lunch.'

'Thank you, Geoff, for taking me to the college. I appreciate it very much.'

'We learned a lot, didn't we?'

'Not now,' said Ruby, pulling Estella along. 'Talk about it later.'

Estella had time to glance around and wave as they entered the building. They arrived in the department to find Bruce Butcher and Mr. Al Refai talking together. Bruce, showing no sign he had seen Estella at the technical college, looked sweaty and sullen while the cool, elegant Egyptian greeted them with polite familiarity. Bruce introduced Ruby to Mr Al Refai, who shook her hand with a respectful bow.

'Miss Winterbine,' said Mr Al Refai, 'my daughters are not here. It would be a little tedious for them to attend our talk. They have heard it before. I would like to invite you to lunch so we can chat in a relaxed setting. They are keen to meet you. Would there be any objection, Mr Butcher, Miss Waiting?'

'Miss Winterbine is under my care,' said Ruby. 'As long as she is willing, I have no objection. I only ask you to give me precise times and her where-abouts while she is in your company.'

'Naturally, Miss Waiting, I understand. My assistant will provide you with all those details after the seminar. At the risk of sounding presump-tuous, he has made the bookings.'

'Are you happy to accept the invitation?' said Ruby.

'Yes, thank you,' said Estella, feeling she had to be polite in the circum-stances.

'We will be honoured to have you as our guest.' Then to Bruce: 'You say your arrangement with this afternoon's talker has been cancelled?'

'Yes, Mr Tanaka cancelled without notice.'

'Then we can take our time.'

Still looking sweaty and sullen, Bruce Butcher took them to the senior seminar room while Ruby left them to attend to her business. Mr Al Refai gave an entertaining talk about his company and the need to present the right public face. He covered many aspects of marketing, social analysis, communication, and the need to create the right image and maintain absolute integrity and confidence in the public eye. When he finished, the students engaged him in a spirited discussion. Estella listened, fascinated. The students were so taken with him that the meeting ran to half past twelve, and when Bruce brought it to a close, they clapped their appre-ciation. Estella saw she was not the only one the elegant Egyptian had impressed.

Soon after, they were downstairs, where Ruby received the lunch arrangements from Mr Al Refai's assistant. Bruce had followed them, looking on morosely. Geoff arrived at this point. When he learned that Estella had been invited to lunch, he said he was sorry she would not be with him and Ruby but hoped she had a pleasant time. Estella wanted to say she preferred to be with them.

'Now, Estella, that's all organised,' said Ruby, breaking in on her thoughts. 'Mr. Al Refai will drop you at my unit no later than three-thirty. That should be plenty of time. His assistant has my address. I should be home by three o'clock. In any case, Geoff will be there before then. Remember, I promised your mum and dad to have you back in Binawarra by dinner time.'

With the arrangements fixed, Estella and Mr Al Refai followed the assistant to a gleaming dark limousine waiting not far away. It was the start of a level of formal attention that Estella had never experienced. At every turn, she received the calm, unostentatious attention that a caring host would give to an honoured guest. His daughters, Mr. Al Refai began, were traditional young Egyptian women. That was their choice, not his. He had given them the best education the West had to offer—schools and colleges in London and Paris—but in the end, they chose to follow Egyptian tradition. That made him proud. He remarked that she might find that she and they had some things in common. He had the impression Estella was a traditional young woman in the Western context. At the restaurant, the restaurant's owner ushered them with a great display of courtesy to a table where Mr Al Refai's daughters were waiting. The young women stood and bowed.

They were attractive, beautifully groomed young women wearing expensive but subdued, modest clothes. They were in their early twenties, not much more than a year between them. Their address was friendly but a little reserved. They did not possess the same relaxed, outgoing manner as their father, though they were as polished and elegant. Estella detected some uneasiness or embarrassment in their manner.

'You see, my daughters,' said Mr Al Refai, after they had settled themselves. 'Miss Winterbine could be a sister of yours.'

'Papa, don't be ridiculous. She's so beautiful,' said Aisha Al Refai. Tahani, the younger sister, nodded in agreement. Then, seeing Estella's cool reaction, Aisha changed the subject before her father could reply. 'Miss Winterbine,' she said in good English with a light accent, 'we would like to hear about your town. Papa has spoken about it. It sounds interesting, so different from what we are used to.'

Strangely, despite their formality, Estella found herself relaxing in their company. Their manners, their refined conversation and elegant way of talking, and their genuine interest in her kept the conversation going smoothly and pleasantly. Indeed, Mr Al Refai was right: they did have some things in common, more a way of behaving than anything. While the young women chatted, Mr Al Refai sat back and listened or attended to ordering their food. He did not consult her about what she wanted to drink. He ordered mineral water and freshly squeezed orange juice for the three young women and wine for himself.

'My assistant asked Miss Waiting what your preferred drink was,' he said as she raised the glass to her lips.

'Thank you, Mr Al Refai.'

'No thanks necessary. It is my duty to the young lady who is my honoured guest. This is standard hospitality in my country.'

The conversation about each other's social and cultural backgrounds flowed enjoyably to the end of the main meal. Estella was as interested in life in Cairo and Paris as they were in her secluded life in Binawarra. When the waiters had cleared the table, she excused herself. The older of the two daughters rose and accompanied her. They seemed to be in attendance on her. When they returned, a young man about Geoff's age was standing before Mr Al Refari, who, with his head turned and tilted, was gesturing with both hands. 'Didi!' she heard Aisha exclaim. 'Papa will not be happy.' As they resumed their seats, the young man glanced in their direction, distracted by the movement. He stopped mid-sentence. He looked at Estella, mouth half-opened, and then turned to Mr Al Refai.

'This is my son, Didi,' said Mr Al Refai to Estella, and then to his son, 'This is my guest from the student group at the university, Miss Estella Winterbine.'

Didi came around to Estella while Mr Al Refai motioned to the waiter to set another place.

'Pleased to meet you, Miss Winterbine,' he said, offering his hand with a warm smile. He was very much like his father in appearance, tall with the same pleasant, handsome face. But he lacked his father's refined confidence. He spoke English with a touch of an American accent and wore smart, expensive casual clothes. He was a contrast with the modest appearance and reserve of his sisters.

'I love my son very much,' said Mr Al Refai, 'but I have to tell you that I am not happy with him at the moment. He is a very bad boy.'

'I'm sorry, Father, to disturb your lunch,' said Didi, taking the seat next to him. 'I was unaware you had a guest.'

'Miss Winterbine, I am sorry to subject you to this embarrassment,' Mr Refai continued. 'My son's unannounced arrival is a breach of courtesy, and I apologise for it. Now let's resume our pleasant conversation.'

Didi accepted the public rebuke, looking around him like a boy caught red-handed in a juvenile prank. He glanced at Estella in a self-conscious way that amused rather than embarrassed her. As Tahini resumed the conversation, asking what Estella did for amusement in Binawarra, he sat back and listened, now and then making a cautious comment or asking a question to which Estella, surprising herself, openly responded. Eventually, the topic of religion came up. She was tentative at first, but soon realised the girls were interested. Didi left the questions about religious belief to his sisters, as did Mr Al Refai, who appeared content to observe the young people enjoying themselves. Aisha commented that she must sometimes find fashions in the West immodest.

'Yes, I do, very immodest. My mother and father often express their disappointment with the way girls in our town dress. I think they're right. There is something ugly in the way many girls expose their bodies.'

'That's how our society thinks about it,' said Mr Al Refai. 'Your attitude would not be very popular with your friends.'

'No, it's not.'

The daughters explained what they liked about Western fashions, and Estella found that she agreed with them to the extent she was familiar with the styles they discussed. They liked the elegance of Parisian high fashion; they disliked the vulgarity of other styles. Estella was so deep in conversation with the sisters that it seemed no time before Mr Al Refai said he was sorry he had to interrupt. 'It is nearly three o'clock, time to take you back to Miss Waiting.' He regarded Estella warmly. 'Miss Winterbine, we would like to thank you for your company. It has been most enjoyable. I am sure you are surprised at how much you have in common with my daughters.'

Estella was indeed surprised to find a similar outlook on life in them. The ease and comfort with which they drew her into their conversation surprised her more. She rarely, if ever, experienced such engagement with people her own age. It was a strange but pleasant surprise. Didi said a friendly but polite goodbye in the restaurant. He wished her well and hoped that their paths would cross again. He then hurried away. On arrival at Ruby's unit, the daughters said a warm farewell to her in the car while Mr Al Refai attended to opening the door. By this time, Ruby was at the front gate to greet them.

'I managed to get away on time,' she said, taking Estella's hand as she stepped from the car. 'I hope you enjoyed yourself.'

'I hope so, too,' said Mr Al Refai before Estella could say anything. 'We have certainly enjoyed her company.'

'Yes, Mr Al Refai, I enjoyed myself very much. Thank you.'

'More than you expected?'

'Yes, very much more. Thank you.'

'I hope we have the chance to meet again. We would like to visit Binawarra after hearing so much about it.' He kissed her hand and, with a last farewell, signalled he was ready to go.

THE MAN sat well hidden with the camera resting on his lap and gazed between the leafy branches at the cottage on the other side of the crumbling bitumen road. He had been waiting a while, but he was ready for it. A ridiculously well-paid commission ensured his patience. It was an irony, too, that he was more interested in the subject than in his fat fee. He had to stay out of sight. One glimpse of him, and she would be gone. And she had that knack, that almost unearthly ability to sense when she was being observed. That, he knew from experience. But he kept willingly still ... it had been a while since he had seen her.

He lifted the camera and peered through the telephoto lens. The detail of the gardens and the vine-lined verandah with its hanging plants appeared in sharp relief. He was close enough. He glanced into the sky. The light was still good. He laid the camera on his lap, letting his mind drift back into the past, thirteen years into the past. A faraway expression appeared on his face. He stiffened. Checking his surroundings so he would not brush against the shrubs or the low-hanging branches of the saplings, he got into position.

He need not worry that his noise or movement would alert her. Miraculously, the wind rose from the peaks and rustled the surrounding bush. A lone cockatoo with its hideous squawking swooped down from the same direction and perched in the top branches of a nearby gum tree, clattering the branches with its wings as it settled. He took advantage and clicked continually as the fair-haired woman in a long white dress walked up and down the verandah, tending the hanging plants. She descended the small flight of stairs to continue her desultory gardening. She came through the front gate and walked along the fence, stooping now and then to pluck from the colourful array of annuals. At length, she had a small bouquet. As she was on the point of passing back through the gate, she stopped to contemplate the bouquet and then selected a purple and yellow bloom, which she placed behind her right ear. It was a mesmerising gesture, one he could not resist. He replaced the telephoto lens, bundled his equipment into his bag, and broke cover.

'Wait, Aine!' he called, seeing apprehension pass over her face as she grabbed at the gate. He stopped in the middle of the crumbling and pot-holed bitumen road. 'I won't come any closer, I promise.'

'What are you doing here? I'll call the sergeant—'

'I haven't come to harass you, I promise. I'm here on a job ... not you ... I've accepted what you ...' The sentence petered out as he contemplated her. He raised the camera and clicked twice.

'What are you doing? Stop that!'

'Just a few photos for me—and Jannie. I'll go in a minute, I promise.'

She hesitated. 'If you keep your promise— How's Jannie?' she said, relenting and relaxing into a pose.

'Perfect,' he murmured and clicked several times from different angles. 'You're a natural, as I told you thirteen years ago.'

'No— Don't say any more—'

'Jannie's well. She would want me to say hello.'

'Give her my best wishes.'

'I will.' He lowered the camera. 'Do you mind if I take a few of you in the front garden? I won't come closer than the fence. Then I'll go.'

'What are you doing in Binawarra, Harry?'

'I told you. I have a commission. I didn't come here to pester you, I promise. I'm on my way back home. Jannie will love these photos of you—to see how you are. I'll go straight after—'

'I'll do it for Jannie.'

Aine passed through the gate and shut it while Harry approached the fence. 'Where do you want me to stand?' she asked while she took up position in front of the leafiest section of the garden below the verandah.

'Just where you are ... you know ... now don't look at the camera ... give me four different poses with your eyes directed in ... well, you know ...'

Aine did as he requested.

'I see a tragedy,' he said, lowering the camera after the fourth photo.

'That's all now,' Aine said, making her way to the verandah steps.

'What you threw away ... it's indescribable ... incomprehensible.'

'Don't say any more. Now, go, please. And remember me to Jannie.'

'Can I have the bouquet?'

Aine stopped and looked at the small bunch of flowers in her hand.

'Just put it on the fence post here.' He moved several paces away from the fence. He moved several more. 'Please ...'

Aine approached the fence. 'Now, please go,' she said, putting the flowers where he had indicated. She withdrew to the stairs.

'Thank you,' said Harry, picking up the flowers. 'They say the daughter is incomparable. She doesn't compare with her mother.'

Aine stopped as she mounted the stairs and swung around. 'Who is they?'

'What—? I'm only saying what everyone says about your daughter ... and what I've only ever said about you.' He paused. 'I'll never forget the look in your eyes as I held you in my arms.'

'Stop it! You're deluding yourself!' She stood behind the verandah railing as if seeking protection. 'Go, Harry. I'll call Charles.'

'Don't be alarmed. I'm going, as I promised.' He moved several paces away from the fence but stopped and turned. 'That look will stay here forever.' He tapped his left breast several times, then turned and, without looking back, hurried on to the vacant land. He disappeared among the tall gums and surrounding bush.

Aine remained several minutes staring at the spot where he had gone. She brushed her hair back and ran her hand over her mouth and cheek. There was no agitation in her movements nor moisture on her upper lip. Deep in the bush, the telephoto lens was recording her actions. When Charles returned from his errands, Aine was still standing at the verandah railing. She tried to raise a welcome smile.

'Is there something the matter?' Charles said as he ascended the steps and put his paperwork on the nearby table. He looked around.

'Charles,' she began, after some hesitation, 'I would like to withdraw for a while. I need to spend time in prayer. We must be vigilant.'

RUBY DID not let Estella rest. She sent her straight to her room to pack. They must get going without delay. Geoff sat in the lounge room, waiting for the young women to get ready. As he was thinking about Estella and the strange things happening around her, it occurred to him that Ruby need not take her back to Binawarra, only to have to turn around and drive back to Bendigo. When he caught Ruby in mid-rush from her room to the kitchen, he suggested he take Estella back home to save her the trouble.

'No,' she said, 'that's very kind of you, Geoff, and I'm sure Estella would find the trip back with you very agreeable. However, I have undertaken to look after her. I took her away. It's my duty to return her. Besides, I would like to drive with the dear girl. I want to make sure that my friendship with that exquisite creature is real.'

Estella entered the lounge room with her bags and caught the last sentence. 'My friendship is real. You must never think my appearance has anything to do with it.'

'Now, don't get upset,' said Ruby, putting her arm around her. 'I know your friendship is real. That was just one of my flippant comments. You must admit, though, that people will always take notice of you. It is a fact of life. It might cause you less anxiety if you admitted it to yourself.'

'Mamma says I should never dwell on my appearance. It is only temporary. One day, it will all be gone, and I'll be left with the person I am.'

'I know. You've already said that. But your mother is not really the one to talk about passing beauty,' Ruby replied, laughing. 'However did she manage to maintain the appearance of a twenty-five-year-old? She's beautiful, isn't she, Geoff? Like she stepped out of a medieval tapestry.' Geoff nodded. 'Anyhow, we haven't time to rattle on about that.'

Geoff took Estella's bags and disappeared through the front door. Ruby told Estella to follow while she made a final check. When she emerged, Geoff and Estella were talking beside Geoff's car further up the street.

'What are you doing?' she called.

'We're going in my car,' Geoff called back. 'I don't want you driving all that way up and back by yourself. Come on, get in.' He opened the front and back doors.

'Don't be ridiculous, Geoff. I've made that trip many times.'

'Well, not this time. Come on.' He stood, holding the door.

'You mean, you intend to drive us up to Binawarra, drive me back to Bendigo, and then drive home to the farm.'

'Yes. Get in.'

'You must be joking.'

'No. Get in. No arguments, this time.'

'You are a little mad, Geoffrey Shawcross,' she said, getting into the front and pouting absurdly.

Not knowing what to say about this pantomime, Estella got into the backseat.

'You can stay at my place for the night,' Ruby threw at Geoff when he had settled himself behind the wheel. 'It's too much, all that driving.'

'No. We're getting away early. So I'll have time to make the trip back to the farm. It won't be too late. I don't mind the drive. It'll give me time to reflect.'

'He doesn't want to spoil my reputation,' she whispered loudly to Estella, raising her eyebrows and rolling her eyes. She looked at him as he manoeuvred the car out from the curb and patted his shoulder. 'He's a good man, my Geoff, isn't he?' She turned and smiled at Estella.

Estella could not argue. His gallantry was just something more to arouse her admiration, and it was another wound in her soft heart. Geoff's obstinacy was soon forgotten. Before they were out of the town's built-up area, she turned to Estella.

'We've been discussing female beauty. What do you think it is?'

'Be warned, Estella,' said Geoff. 'Ruby is fixated on this subject.'

'I don't know,' Estella said, glancing at Geoff.

'Okay, what do you think when you see yourself in the mirror?'

'I don't think anything.'

'Not anything?'

'Well, I make sure I'm neat and clean.'

'No assessment? You don't compare yourself with others?'

'No. I don't want to think about what's said of me. It creates a false pride, an illusion.'

'You're serious, aren't you?'

'Yes. I told you. It's just on the surface. I don't like the attention, either.'

Ruby desisted for a while.

'Well, tell me who you think is beautiful,' she said, eventually. 'Take me as a starting point, for example. Am I beautiful—?'

'Yes,' interrupted Estella, not realising that Ruby had more to add.

Geoff laughed.

'This won't do! And you stop laughing,' she said, poking him in the ribs. 'That's the wrong starting point, obviously. Who can I think of to get an idea of who Estella considers beautiful?'

'Beauty is not just appearance,' said Estella. 'It's what I see inside a person that makes them appealing.'

'That's what Geoff thinks,' said Ruby, acknowledging Geoff's tilt of the head. 'But I still can't help thinking there is something more important about the outer appearance when talking about female beauty, something unique and distinguishing. Advertisers certainly recognise it. Take your mother, for example.'

'She's the most beautiful woman I have ever known, but it's not her appearance I see. It's the beauty of her inner being.'

'You mean you don't see that spotless pale complexion, the blue eyes—? She looks like a princess. She's what I imagine Galadriel, the Elven princess, to look like.'

'I've never thought of my mother like that.'

'Does your father?'

'I've never heard him mention those things, but I know he thinks my mother is the most beautiful woman in the world because of the way she is—as I do. He sees the purity of her heart. That's what makes her beautiful in our eyes. I try to be like her.'

'Many would be revolted at that.'

'Why?' Estella said, genuinely surprised.

'Many reasons—cloying, unreal, neurotic.'

'I don't understand. Why would anyone be revolted by the idea of inner beauty being more important than appearance?'

'Remarkable innocence,' said Ruby, turning to the front. 'I'd better give up. You baffle me.'

'It's not baffling,' said Estella, leaning forward. 'I like you because of your kindness, honesty, and concern for me. Those are the things I see and love. I can't just love appearance. The way someone looks must show those things for me to take notice.'

'That's pretty much what Geoff says, too,' said Ruby. 'You two have a lot in common. I mean your way of thinking.' She made the comment matter-of-factly, as if it carried no particular importance. But it was another strike in Estella's heart. A period of silence followed. They were now out in the country, and the fields and bush were rushing by in the glimmer of the late afternoon sun. Ruby turned to Estella. 'Do you think Geoff's handsome?'

'Come on, Ruby,' said Geoff. 'That's not fair. You'll embarrass the poor girl.'

'And not you?'

'No, I know I'm not handsome. And it's not important.'

Ruby fixed her gaze on Estella. Estella felt herself flush to the tip of her ears. 'I think of Geoff the same way I think of you. It's Geoff's character I see. You're both kind and honest. You've been good to me.'

Ruby gave her a piercing look that made her tremble. Then, Ruby turned away and stared at the road ahead of them. She remained that way as the car, negotiating the bends in the road, made her sway rhythmically. Estella kept her eyes on her. Eventually, Ruby turned and looked at Geoff.

'What is it?'

'I should take more time to find out what you're really like.'

'What do you mean?'

'Nothing.'

Geoff glanced at Ruby a few times, but Ruby gave no reply. Silence followed for another ten minutes, during which Estella felt the acute discomfort of her innermost feelings being laid bare. She looked at Ruby, but Ruby was expressionless. Geoff was quiet as usual. She couldn't know what he thought as he concentrated on the road in front of him. She wanted to say something but dared not. She might give more of herself away.

'Okay, we're not going to sit here in silence the whole trip, are we?' said Ruby. 'You two may be content to sit in silence, but I need to talk. Right, we're going to play a game, and I know the very game. We'll play the game that Emma Woodhouse and Frank Churchill played on Box Hill.'

'What game is that? And who are Emma and Frank whatshisname?' said Geoff.

'You've never heard of the game on Box Hill!' said Ruby in mock surprise.

Estella relaxed and brightened.

'No.'

'He has never read Jane Austen's *Emma*, has he?' she said, turning to Estella. 'He's probably never heard of Jane Austen.'

'The name rings a bell—from my school days.'

'You tell him, Estella, what that game is.'

'Frank Churchill told the people at the picnic on Box Hill that Emma Woodhouse instructed him to ask people to amuse the group by saying something clever.'

'That's right. We will enliven our trip by taking turns telling funny stories. I'm going to start by giving you an example, Geoff, and I'm going to be so ungracious as to tell a funny story that Estella told me.'

'Go on. I'm all ears.'

'Well, Charles and Aine Winterbine asked Bill Huckerby to choose a name for their newborn baby daughter. He chose Estella. He chose Estella because of the dark beauty named Estella in *Great Expectations*, you know, that novel by Charles Dickens.'

'What's funny about that?'

'The Estella in *Great Expectations* was beautiful, but she was the protégé of the embittered Miss Havisham, who wanted her to wreak revenge on the male population.' Ruby put her hand on Geoff's shoulder. 'She brought up Estella to be cruel and hard-hearted towards men. She wanted Estella to break men's hearts the way hers was broken. So beware.'

'Oh? But what's funny about that?'

'It's the irony, you silly boy. We'll have to educate Geoff about these things, won't we, darling?'

'Geoff may not like that sort of book,' Estella ventured.

'I must admit I've not read many novels,' said Geoff. 'There were other things to keep me busy. But I might like it if you like it.'

'You see the influence you're having,' said Ruby.

'Well, we seem to have similar ideas, as you said,' Geoff offered.

'Anyhow, we know our big girl here with her soft little heart wouldn't deliberately break anyone's heart. That's the funny part, Geoff.'

'Oh, I see,' said Geoff, smiling. 'You're right, too.'

'I hope nobody is ever unhappy because of me,' said Estella.

'Well, that depends because it's your turn.'

And so, the trip passed by with each taking turns, Ruby's stories being the wittiest, causing Geoff to smile and Estella to giggle. Geoff was only distracted from the amusement as they drove between the two peaks before entering Binawarra. Estella and Ruby were too preoccupied to notice the police tapes still securing the accident scene in the shadowy gloom beneath the sharp peak.

'I have not heard you giggle so much,' said Ruby as Geoff stopped in front of the Winterbine house.

'I haven't heard so many funny things in a long while,' said Estella. 'I used to giggle a lot with Jenny. She was always lively and funny. Mamma said she was good for me because I was quiet.'

'I can imagine,' said Ruby, getting out of the car.

'Estella,' said Geoff, as she was about to open the car door, 'what book would you recommend me to read?'

Estella reflected as she looked at Geoff's expectant face. 'J.R.R. Tolkien's *The Lord of the Rings*. I think that would appeal to you. It's a long story, though.'

'Okay, I might get a copy next time I'm in town.'

Estella took Ruby's hand and hurried to the front door, calling her parents. They appeared without delay. She hugged and kissed them, saying she had had a wonderful time and that Ruby and Geoff had been so kind. Charles and Aine expressed their gratitude and invited them to stay for dinner. The invitation was much appreciated, replied Geoff, but Ruby had to get back to Bendigo, and he had to get back to the farm. After more conversation and Ruby's insistent invitation to Estella to come and stay again, they prepared to go. Ruby then noticed Estella's bags next to the front door, where Geoff had put them.

'Come on, I'll help you with these to your room,' she said and was away before Estella, or her parents could say anything.

Estella followed Ruby to her room. Ruby placed the bags beside the bed and took a long look around. 'Do you say prayers before your shrine every day?'

'Yes, more than once.'

'What do you pray about?'

'I offer prayers of intercession for those I love. I praise God and His goodness and express sorrow for my failings.'

'Failings! What failings do you have?'

'Many.'

'Many! I told you, you shouldn't try to be perfect.'

'Your friendship has made me realise that I could have been more understanding with Jenny. Breaches of loyalty are serious.'

Ruby seemed to consider that thought. She looked around again in a troubled way.

'Who do you offer prayers for?'

'For Mamma and Daddy, Uncle Bill, and Auntie Joanne, you know, family. Sometimes there are special requests.'

'Do you pray for Geoff and me?'

'Of course.'

Ruby seemed lost for a reply. She walked to Estella's bedside table and picked up the book lying there. 'St Maria Goretti,' she said, turning it over in her hands. 'It seems so counter to thinking these days, to prefer to die rather than give in to advances.' She peered at the front cover. 'Do you mind if I borrow it?' she said, a little embarrassed. 'You can collect it next time you come to Bendigo.'

'Of course, Ruby,' she said and hugged her.

'You impetuous girl,' said Ruby, recovering from her embarrassment but not resisting. 'I haven't been hugged so much since I was a little girl. But don't stop. I like it. Come on, Geoff will be waiting.' She was already out the door and walking down the hallway.

Estella lingered, running her eyes along her shelf of fiction. She found what she wanted and hurried after Ruby.

GEOFF remained on the verandah with Charles and Aine after Ruby and Estella had gone to Estella's bedroom.

'What has happened about the accident with that teacher?' he said. 'Have there been any further developments?'

'No, the police are still investigating,' said Charles. 'Bill says they've interviewed him several times. Poor Bill. Miss Barker says he has been too trusting of his staff.'

'Nobody knows why the teacher ended up on that outcrop at that time of the night with that young man?'

'We haven't heard anything. It's all a mystery.'

'We had little contact with Mr McKinnon,' said Aine. 'Estella was never good at science subjects.'

'So nobody knows if that young man or others were regular visitors to Binawarra?'

'We don't know,' said Charles. 'Bill is very worried.'

'I can imagine.'

Ruby arrived on the verandah, looking surprised that Estella was not behind her. Aine and Charles thanked her again for looking after Estella. It was evident that she had enjoyed herself. She was like she used to be. A good friend is what she needed.

'Here, Geoff,' said Estella, as she came through the doorway, 'you can borrow my copy of the first book of *The Lord of the Rings*.'

'*The Lord of the Rings*,' exclaimed Ruby.

'Are you sure you can spare it?' said Geoff. 'I can always get a copy in Bendigo.'

'Please take it, Geoff. I can miss it for the moment.'

'Thank you, Estella, I'll look after it,' then turning to Ruby, 'I asked Estella to recommend a book to read, and she suggested this.'

'That's a good suggestion for an ex-soldier with all those chivalrous ideas swimming around in his head. I don't know why it didn't occur to me. *The Return of the King* is right up your alley.' Without waiting for a response, she embraced Estella. 'Goodbye, dear friend, we had such an enjoyable time, didn't we? Next time, though, there will be no program at the university. It'll be just us girls together. Oh, we might allow Geoff to join us sometimes.'

Geoff shook Charles's hand and then Aine's. He hesitated and then offered Estella his hand. She took it and felt his hand come around hers in a light but firm grasp.

'Goodbye,' he said softly. 'I'm glad you had a good time ... that you got some useful information about courses ... We enjoyed it, too, of course ...'

'Go on, Geoff, give her a kiss,' called Ruby, standing at the bottom of the verandah stairs. 'You're allowed.'

Geoff leaned over and kissed Estella lightly on her cheek. As he did so, their eyes met for an instant. She felt the rough stubble around his mouth and the light imprint of his lips.

'What courses are you talking about?' said Charles.

'I'll tell you about it later, Daddy,' said Estella. With some last warm farewells, Geoff and Ruby drove towards the town centre. The memory of Geoff's kiss stayed with her while she explained his reference to the courses in horticulture.

'He seems very attentive to you,' said Aine.

'They are both very attentive and very kind, too.'

Chapter 20

The investigation

A MINUTE LATER, Geoff pulled up in front of Miss Barker's house.

'Come in. I was expecting you this evening,' she said on opening the door. They followed her into the lounge room. 'Miss Waiting, I will ask you to wait here. There is no point in your being privy to information that does not concern you, indeed, may compromise you. There are magazines on the table. They will keep you amused. We will not be long.'

She then bade Geoff follow her into her library. Geoff spent five minutes giving an account of Boris's shadowing and the foreign visitors to the Department of Media Studies.

'You're right,' said Miss Barker. 'Our Mr Rostowski seems to be keeping a protective eye on Estella. Now, why? That's the question.' Geoff shook his head. 'Has the visit of the two wealthy foreigners anything to do with it? Did you see any connection between Rostowski and them?' Geoff shook his head again. 'Did there seem to be any out-of-the-ordinary connection between the lecturer responsible for Estella's visit and Edith Bicknell?'

'No. The man's name is Bruce Butcher. There was nothing in what Estella told me to establish a connection. The significant point about Bruce Butcher is that he has his eyes on Estella. I caught him twice shadowing her. Actually, it wasn't shadowing. It was more like stalking.'

'That may not mean much. He is not the first and will not be the last. It is likely to be nothing more than an attraction unless you can point to something specific.' Geoff nodded thoughtfully but made no reply. 'There must be a connection between the wealthy foreigners and Estella's visit,' Miss Barker continued. 'Is it just the avenue to a career in public relations? Or is it the path through public relations to some ultimate goal? Or is there something else we don't know about? And what is the connection with Gerda whatshername's father in Holland? We need more information, Mr Shawcross. And we must get it quickly. I have a sense that things are about to come to a head.'

'Estella knows something is going on. I couldn't hide my activities. I asked her to trust me and be careful—not to do anything away from my protection. She was happy to do as requested.'

'Was she? Indeed, she must trust you, Mr Shawcross. You're in a privileged position.'

'I appreciate that.'

'I mean a very privileged position.'

'What do you mean by privileged?'

'Just that. You should be aware of her affectionate nature. And you should be aware that she does not dispose of her affection indiscriminately.'

'I know, Miss Barker. I'm fully aware of it. She can rely on me absolutely.'

'I know, Mr Shawcross,' she said, subjecting him to one of her penetrating stares, 'and I will let things take their course.'

'What course?'

'Never mind,' she said with a wave of the hand. 'From now on, I want you to hold yourself in readiness. Can you do that, make yourself available on call?'

'Yes, but what do you have in mind?'

'I don't know yet. I need more time to consider everything. Now, another matter: I have learned from my contacts that you're handy with a knife, among other skills.'

'Yes, Miss Barker,' he said, first frowning but then realising there would be access to his military record with the right contacts. 'The knife was necessary in a jungle situation.'

'Did you have to use it often?'

'Occasionally, when I had no choice. I could play with it in my solitude, too.'

'I suggest you keep that weapon handy. It looks like Mr McKinnon was ambushed, taken to the peak, and thrown off that rocky platform. It is evident he was not suspecting anything when he went to his meeting with that young man.'

'The police were still busy there when we drove in. Have there been any developments?'

'Poor Bill has been questioned several times. I've managed to nail Sergeant Willis, who told me with much reluctance that police inquiries have pointed to a sexual episode gone wrong. There is no evidence of male prostitutes visiting Mr McKinnon at other times. Miss McNamara swears that his only relationship was with her, and that she was with him most of the time over the last six months. She admitted he went to Melbourne regularly, but as far as she knew, that was to see old friends. Mr McKinnon, she said, had a big mouth and matched it with little action. He was hated because of his big mouth and his liberal anti-collectivist views, as she called them. The police interviewed those whom Miss McNamara claims hated him, but could find no evidence that they were connected with his demise in any way. They could prove they were elsewhere that evening, anyhow. They were not reluctant to tell what they knew of his predilection for young boys, I should also add. So, the police conclusion is that it looks like an open and shut case of death by misadventure.'

'And you reject that, Miss Barker?'

'He was ambushed, taken to that cliff, and thrown off, as I said. It looks like the male prostitute was hired as a decoy. The police found a thousand dollars stuffed in one of his trouser pockets. He was killed to cover up the murder.'

'Other than speculation, do you have any firm proof?'

'Nothing firm, but that's the explanation that best fits the details. For example, I found clear signs—fresh signs—that somebody had been dragged along the track leading to that rocky outcrop. I would say that five or six people had recently walked along it when I saw it.'

'Okay, if he was murdered, why?'

'As I said, he was onto Gerda thingy's plans. What you heard him say is compelling evidence. In some way, he managed to understand what purpose Estella served in whatever plans she had. It has to do with more than a public relations function, though. All this trouble to have Estella act as a sort of image-maker for whatever association is involved just does not make sense. Even if the plan is to slot her into the multinationals of those visitors, surely that could be done openly. No, there must be something else.' She paused. 'Two other points remain unexplained. Well, to be frank, I don't know if there's anything to be explained. I found several drops of wax on the rocky outcrop, and a dead rabbit lay not far from the bodies. It looked like it had not been dead very long. The police did not find any wax the next morning when they examined the outcrop. And they dismissed the dead rabbit as having no significance. Do you have any ideas?'

'You come across dead rabbits in the bush.'

'There was something odd about this rabbit and its position. I don't know what. Anyhow, let's leave it for the moment. We shouldn't keep your Ruby waiting any longer, no pun intended. Let me think about everything, and I will be in contact.'

They returned to the lounge room to find Ruby holding a framed photo and examining it.

'Ah, that's what I like about you, Miss Waiting,' said Miss Barker. 'You are not afraid to satisfy your curiosity. Our dear Estella would wait until invited, wouldn't she?'

'Yes, she would. If I'm not mistaken, this is you.'

'That's right. I was eighteen when that was taken.'

'Miss Barker, you were a handsome girl.'

'Thank you, Miss Waiting, but that was a long time ago.'

'Sorry to be nosy,' said Ruby, replacing the photo on the sideboard.

'No apology necessary. I like that in you.'

'Thank you.'

BORIS HARDLY gave the police-secured accident scene a glance as he headed up the rise between the two peaks. Other matters occupied his thoughts. Gerda Vrouwendijk's plans were coming to a head, and the final task for him would be tricky. He turned his head as the soldier's car with his girlfriend passed him on the rise out of the township. They had already dropped off the girl and were returning to Bendigo. That confirmed the relationship between the three: the soldier was with the university woman, and the Winterbine girl was her friend. That presented extra security for the girl and meant less trouble for him when she was with them. He thought of the incident with the college students and was impressed by the way the soldier had dealt with them. He would avoid confronting him unless it were necessary. Ten minutes later, he was again in Gerda's lounge room, undergoing her close questioning.

'You should be happy,' he said after he had brought her up to date. 'Things are going just as you wanted.' He lit up.

'There's no relaxing,' she warned. 'I don't want any hitches at this late stage. You must still keep a close eye on the girl. The soldier may succumb to the girl's charms.'

'I doubt it. The man treats her like a child. No one could calmly hold that girl's hand the way he did.' He paused. 'What you have to worry about is Bruce Butcher. He is stalking her with long, lustful looks. Given half a chance, he could not help himself. The girl acts as if he were dirt on the ground to be walked over. Not funny for someone who imagines he's a playboy.'

'*You* have to worry about him. That's what you're paid for.'

'He will be no problem,' said Boris, leaning back in his armchair and blowing his foul-smelling smoke in Gerda's direction.

'Is he aware of your presence?'

'He may assume he's being watched, but he has given no sign he knows it is me. He is too infatuated with the girl to pay attention.'

'I'll warn him again. There's just one more contact to be arranged between the girl and the university, and then she will be out of his field of temptation.'

'Temptation?'

Gerda Vrouwendijk ignored the dig. She had no time for irrelevant comments. While she turned over the planning details in her head, she went to the kitchen to prepare Boris's coffee. His role would be critical in the coming weeks.

GEOFF WAS glad to have time to himself. He wanted to think. He wanted to get things into perspective. Ruby's unit was half an hour behind him now. He had just passed through Tarnagulla, leaving the faint streetlights of the historical gold town behind him to travel on in the dark. The dashboard lights had a comforting glow as he followed the road in the bright beam of the headlights, cutting its way through the dense dark. Gum trees bristled, waved, and swayed in and out of the beam as the car flew through the bends and up and down shallow gullies. Some wayward wallabies and kangaroos just managed to get out of the flashing light, while others stood there mesmerised. With the occasional evasive swerve, the car rushed on through the silent evening darkness. Out in the jungle of Vietnam, he had gotten used to such contemplative solitude. He needed it now.

It had been around two months since he had met Ruby at that party in St Arnaud. He had thought it was high time to settle down, to find a companion to share his life and the work of farming. He would put himself in situations where he might meet someone. As fate would have it, he was invited not long after by one of the partners in a farm equipment company to a party at the man's house. He was hardly through the door when he was introduced to Ruby, who seemed to take a liking to him, despite declaring that she had a good idea of what 'soldier-types' were like. Brazen and familiar, she engaged him in conversation before other guests took her off. He had kept an eye on her as she mingled.

He well remembered his first impressions of her. She was shortish and a little plump, but pleasantly plump with womanly curves. She had a pretty, lively face, full lips, and the most playful eyes he had ever seen. In temperament, she was his opposite: outgoing, talkative, confident, clever in her conversation, and not at all shy. She was popular among the men and showed total control when dealing with them. She would be a nice balance with him. She glanced at him occasionally. She broke away from her group to continue their conversation. Then she was taken away again. At the end of the evening, as she was leaving with two young men and a young woman, she said, 'You're not going to ask for my phone number, so I'm giving it to you. Give me a call.'

He gave her a call, and she took control. She arranged their first date and just about every date after that. They met once a week, provided she was free from work commitments. She was happy to drive up to St Arnaud, where she would stay Saturday night at his mother's place. He was not sure at first if she liked him, but she continued to go out with him and seemed to enjoy his company. She said he was a welcome relief from the social cripples she had to mix with at the university. Whatever she felt about him, he began to have feelings for her. It was not only her temperament and personality that drew him to her.

After learning that she held a responsible position at the university and observing her confidence and organisational skills, he decided that no one would be more suitable for the role of a farmer's wife. Helping to run the farm would be no trouble. She would never take any nonsense from the people that farmers had to deal with. So he set about courting her. He was prepared to take it slowly, and she seemed to appreciate his caution. She often exclaimed at how relaxed she felt with him. And that gave him the confidence to continue.

Everything was going fine until that day he met Estella Winterbine, though Estella made no conscious difference to his plan to court Ruby. He did not know what it was. She put a different atmosphere on things, a different dimension, something that was affecting him, and he could not work it out. He tried to trace the course of events since that day at Bill Huckerby's place. It was a little over three weeks since he had first seen her. He had never been in the company of such a girl, someone the average man could only regard from afar. That's what he did. He just looked. A girl who looked like Estella would not pay him any attention. She would have enough admirers to keep her busy. Gradually, he saw something, or rather someone, behind that serene appearance.

He discovered in Ruby's insistent questioning about female beauty that beauty was not just about appearance. Beauty had to do as much with the inner self as the outer self. He saw enclosed in the casting of peerless beauty a shy, sweet, soft-hearted girl of firm moral conviction. And she seemed to like him, to like him for the person he was. Feelings of protection arose. Then the gardens—he still could not get over the thought and work put into establishing the Winterbine gardens. That seemed to conflict with the picture of her as an incomparable beauty and a soft-hearted, vulnerable girl. And now he was up to his neck in protecting her from what could be a real danger.

He thought of their visit to Sandhurst Technical College and the vulnerability she exhibited when accosted by those stupid students. What could a soft-hearted girl of determined principles do alone in the face of such bullying? Nothing. She would have to be like Ruby—bold, outgoing, fearless, and unwomanly aggressive. But then, she would not be Estella. She would not be the sweet girl of pure principle that she was. She would be forced to change without outside protection. That would be a pity. More than that, it would be a tragedy. It would be the desecration of inner beauty. But there was more to it than his response to one particular girl. Any girl of such qualities would be in the same predicament. To be sweet, gentle, soft-hearted, and principled in the way only a female could be, a girl must have a guarantee of protection written into society. Surely? The world would be a lot worse if people like Estella Winterbine were not allowed to exist.

Ruby was right about something special in female beauty; that talk of genuine female beauty implied qualities that were not present when one applied 'beauty' to other things. He could see where Ruby had led his thinking. It was not a question of a choice of a guarantee of protection written into society. A healthy society was such that the guarantee was an unalterable moral obligation. A society that did not protect Estella Winterbine in its very structure was incomplete, a society not yet in mature development or one in decay. It was surely part of society's essence that those capable of protecting Estella Winterbine should do so. To do otherwise, to neglect or to shirk that duty, was cowardly and corrupt.

This thought stayed in his mind as the car raced through the evening to his farm on the other side of St Arnaud. When the car stopped outside the darkened farmhouse, he picked up the copy of *The Lord of the Rings* and stepped out into the chilly, silent evening. He looked up into the sky. The clouds were dispersing, leaving the stars glittering through swirling, darkened wraiths. He turned towards the slumbering range of hills Estella and her father called the 'Goanna'. He pledged to be at Estella's service until all danger had passed. As he approached the verandah, his kelpies came forward, giving him their little yelps of affection. He sat on the verandah steps and laid the book on his lap while he patted them.

Chapter 21

Bill Huckerby under attack

BILL HUCKERBY sat at his desk, leaning back in his swivel chair. It was Wednesday, three days since the accident. He fiddled with a pencil while the chair creaked to his unconscious movement. The last three days had been wearing, to put it mildly. The police had interviewed him three times, mostly to follow up on information he and others had supplied. They were polite and understanding, always apologising for the intrusion. He could not complain about their manner. But the death of one of his staff in such distasteful circumstances was a shock. It was a shock to everyone he spoke to.

Poor Bob McKinnon. Apart from his lifestyle, which he could never condone, he had liked him. Deep down, he was a decent bloke. Hiding behind that extravagant mocking manner was a man of common sense. He even showed understanding of his role as the principal of a country high school. Now he was hearing hints of a darker side. He heard things he had never been aware of. Bob often went to Melbourne until he established a relationship with Suzie McNamara. Everybody knew that. What he did there was not his concern. He never asked about it. It was not his business—nor anyone else's. Surely?

He rose and walked around to the front of his desk. He picked up some folders. He must get it out of his mind. He must get the school back into order. There was much restlessness around the place. He headed for the door and opened it to find Mrs Charing on the point of knocking. She looked embarrassed, but then her expression relaxed. She even seemed happy, or rather pleased with herself. That was a welcome change. Mrs Charing appeared to be one of the few on the school staff who had taken the news of Bob's death well. He handed her the files. Flo Barker appeared in the reception area carrying a copy of the *Binawarra and District Mail*.

'You seem pleased with yourself,' she said to Mrs Charing as she walked by her and into Bill's office.

Mrs Charing glared at her and then turned, her eyes closed and her nose in the air.

'I can see you don't have any good news,' Bill wearily said as he followed Miss Barker into his office.

'Be careful of that woman,' she said, sitting down.

'I hardly dare ask why.' He let himself fall into the chair beside her.

'Trust no one except close friends.' She handed the newspaper to him. 'Have a look at this.'

A headline splashed in big black letters across the entire width of the front page stared Bill in the face: **Sleaze and deviance in High School. Who knew about this? Who is protecting our children?**

'What in the world ...?'

'Read the whole lot before you comment,' said Miss Barker, going to the office's open door. 'Mrs Charing, will you please get the principal a cup of coffee. Nothing for me. And be quick, please.' Ignoring Mrs Charing's tossing her head, she resumed her seat next to Bill, who, mouth gaping, was reading the report.□

'Few people in Binawarra would be unaware of the tragic death of Mr Robert McKinnon, a senior teacher at Binawarra High School. Most would have reacted with shock. For how could such a thing happen to one of the school's teachers? That was three days ago. *The Binawarra and District Mail* has been investigating, and it grieves the editor that he finds himself obliged to report some unsavoury information. These are the facts of the case, as revealed in an interview with Sergeant Willis of the Binawarra Police.

'Mr McKinnon's body was discovered on Sunday, around noon, at the foot of one of the peaks just outside the town. He was naked from the waist down. His trousers were found on a rocky outcrop above. Around his wrist and ankles were lengths of rope of a strange make. A second body of a young male was found lying next to Mr McKinnon. He was also in a semi-naked state. There was an envelope containing one thousand dollars in the boy's trouser pocket.

'The police know the eighteen-year-old's name but are not yet prepared to release it. The post-mortem examination revealed that both man and boy died on Saturday evening.

'The evidence, according to police, points to an extravagant sexual episode of a ritual sort that ended tragically with both man and boy falling from the rocky outcrop. There were bruises and scratches around the boy's neck and shoulders that could only have resulted from rough play. If this is not shocking and sordid enough, there is more.

'Sources within the school itself say this was the tip of the iceberg. The editor is sorry to confront the people of Binawarra with information of so sordid a nature. He would not do it if it were not necessary. That Mr McKinnon was known among the school community for his unusual sexual preferences is of public interest. Those sources say that one does not have to go very far to find evidence of more than one person who shares Mr McKinnon's tastes.

'Sergeant Willis implied that more revelations would follow. The question that must be on everybody's lips is how this sort of thing has been allowed to flourish in the town's high school.'

Bill put the paper down and looked at Miss Barker. 'Has ... has that man lost his senses?' he stuttered. 'Who's he talking about?'

'Somebody has you well and truly in their sights. There's more. Go to the editorial.'

Bill flicked through to the middle pages with a sinking heart. The editorial heading read: **Our children are our precious resource.**

> There is nothing more precious in our community than the child. The child is our most precious resource. The child is our future. It goes without saying that all our institutions should protect our children. It is a gross dereliction of duty to ignore the welfare and security of our children. It pains us to point out that our high school seems to have fallen down in its moral duty. How could the presence of a person known for his questionable habits be tolerated in the sensitive, responsible position of educating our children? There needs to be an inquiry into the high school's management. Hard questions need to be asked. And answered. It must be done without fear or favour. If the school administration has become entrenched over the years, it needs to change. Let it never be claimed that a country school refuses to satisfy modern standards of accountability.

'The dam has burst, my good friend, hasn't it?' said Miss Barker.

'How could that man write such things? He knows nothing about the school. He knows nothing about the town, for that matter. If anything is known to the people here, it's his shameless touting for advertising. Who's going to take this seriously? Who will believe there is a deviant clique in the school, as he's suggesting? I would like to know who he means.'

They were interrupted by Mrs Charing suddenly appearing with Bill's coffee. Miss Barker lifted her hand until she had left the room.

'Unfortunately, when such things appear in print in an official-looking instrument like a newspaper,' she said, 'many people are deceived into assuming they are true. Some people gullibly accept in a newspaper what they would laugh at if told in the street. You must prepare yourself for some unpleasant reaction.'

'Flo, this is utterly outrageous.' He brushed his hair back with both hands. 'My administration is an open book. They can hold as many inquiries as they like. They will find nothing untoward here. All the books are in order. As for knowing about Bob McKinnon, I only vaguely knew of his libertine views, like everyone else, I imagine. And you never knew when to take him seriously. As long as he did not let those views interfere with his teaching and he did not try to influence the students, and as far as I know, he didn't, I had no authority or business to meddle.

'This year, I have had constant tussles with staff over so-called individual rights in organising the school's programs. I have had to review the administration on this basis. I would've been howled out of the school if I had attempted to put controls on any teacher's private life. This attitude prevails in the higher levels of the state's educational administration, and that's without the rhetoric I'm constantly subjected to from the teachers' union. How could anyone blame me for following prevailing attitudes on individual privacy?'

'Consistency and fairness are not high on the list if someone is bent on attacking and discrediting you, Bill,' said Miss Barker. 'You must prepare yourself for a campaign of dirty tricks and not rely on your opponents' goodwill or moral judgment.'

'My opponents? Who are they?'

'Who are your opponents? That's a pertinent question. I could name names, I suppose. That will not get you very far. Your real opponent is a mentality, a vision of the world in sharp contrast with the way you think and act.'

'You're not back on the political and ideological track again, are you?' he said, resting his head in his hand.

'Do you really suppose Bob McKinnon's sexual habits were distasteful to him? I mean in a moral sense. Do you really think he was aware of the wrongness of his actions but just couldn't help himself—sort of giving into temptation, like a fat man unable to pass up a cream cake?'

'Cream cake—? If he thought there was nothing wrong with what he was doing, he would not have been so secretive.'

'Bill, you are naïve. He kept it secret for prudential reasons. He knew those habits were not yet acceptable. Not only did he believe there was nothing wrong with his tastes and the satisfying of those tastes, but he also thought it immoral and oppressive of society to judge it morally wrong.'

'What? Did you hear him say that?'

'No, but if it quacks and waddles, it's likely to be a duck. I'm familiar with the thinking on such matters. It's all part of the discourse on sexual politics and the liberation of desire. Bob McKinnon did more than show all the signs. His mouth was his liability. It probably got him killed.'

Bill shook his head. 'Your images are too much. Two months ago, I would have accused you of hallucinating. You still sound outlandish, but I'm now so rattled I won't reject them out of hand. And I'm not even going to ask you to explain that last comment.'

'While you are watching television in the evening, I'm reading about such things. You should take the time to see what is developing around you, indeed, under our noses.' She put her hand on his arm. 'Look, my dear friend, I don't want to sit here arguing with you. In the long run, you must come to an insight on your own accord. For the moment, let's see what steps we can take to face your opponents.'

'But who are my phantom opponents?' he said, holding out his hands.

'Let me suggest that you go to the police station and ask Sergeant Willis whether he has been quoted correctly and if he has what the further revelations are. Don't phone him. Go in person and insist on knowing whatever concerns you and the school. Your reputation is at stake. Show yourself boldly to prevent the impression you have something to hide.'

'But I have nothing to hide!'

'Appearances are important.'

'I don't want to play games. People know me here. Not everyone agrees with my decisions in the school or the town's economic committee, but they know I'm open and have the town's interests at heart.'

'There will be people—there are people in this town prepared to do anything to discredit you. Their task is to formulate the right tactics. Nothing else. You're already condemned in their minds.'

'Whose minds? For what? Come on, Flo, that's not what people here are like!'

'Have you ever heard of the concept of "total war"?'

'No, I haven't,' he said, sighing. 'What's that when it's at home?'

'In brief, it means that any deviation from the prescriptions of a dominant ideology is not to be tolerated. The adherents of radical social or political theories will work until people, state, and society succumb to their theory. The classic cases are the Soviet Union and Communist China. Those who don't fit in are irredeemable outcasts. The jails of those nations are full of people who deviated from the prescriptions of the theory. The intolerance from theory is claiming many more lives than the intolerance of race or religion.'

'That's mumbo jumbo to me,' he huffed. 'Can't you put it a little more clearly?'

'Why don't you go along with my advice for the moment?' she said, seeing he was not in the mood to understand. 'It won't hurt. If I'm on the wrong track in the end, you can change course. Don't confront anyone openly for now.' The phone rang. She reached across the desk and handed him the receiver.

'Yes, Mrs Charing, please put her through.' He paused. 'Yes, darling, I have read it. Flo brought it in. She's here now ... Yes, it's shocking ... It's a mystery where he is getting this stuff from. It's outrageous ...'

Miss Barker rose and edged her way to the office door, keeping out of sight of Mrs Charing and her two assistants. She walked into view. Mrs Charing slammed down the telephone receiver. 'Mrs. Charing, I would like a coffee after all. No milk and one sugar, thank you.'

'Okay, Flo,' said Bill, putting down the receiver. 'I'll go and see Sergeant Willis. Perhaps you're right. Whatever else is involved, I should ask him what information he has and where he got it.'

'Do it now. Openly. Don't wait. Besides, I want to check something while you're away.'

'What? And why the haste?'

'Don't ask questions.'

'All right.' He shrugged. 'I suppose you know what you're doing.'

'Announce to Mrs Charing where you're going and for how long.'

'Why? I do that anyhow.'

'I will go now,' she said. 'Leave several minutes later. Okay? Several minutes later, understood?' She left for the sickroom, waiting until Bill had driven into town. Five minutes later, she returned to the reception area. 'I have misplaced something,' she said as she walked into Bill's office.

Mrs Charing was sitting at Bill's desk, flicking through one of his files. She slapped it shut and stood up.

'No need to disturb yourself, Mrs Charing. I'm looking for my watch.' She bent down and looked under the chair she had sat in. 'Oh, here it is.' She returned it to her uniform pocket. 'Thank you for the coffee, Mrs Charing.' She picked up the cup on the desk. Back in her office, she sipped the lukewarm coffee and fell to pondering what she had just confirmed.

'PLEASE COME into my office, Bill,' said the sergeant. 'I imagine you are here about our town's newspaper.'

'Roy, is it true you have more revelations to make?'

'No. The facts of the accident have been reported correctly, but the rest is rubbish.'

'Yes, Roy, complete rubbish, I assure you. I'm glad to hear you say that.'

'What have you done to Collins?'

'Nothing! I hardly know the man.'

'There's something going on there. I would watch out for him.'

'Why? Am I missing something? You're the second to warn me.'

'I know nothing more. I'm just commenting on what's in the paper. But, perhaps in confidence, I can say quite a few people aren't impressed with the editor of the *Binawarra and District Mail*.'

'You mean the *quid pro quo* advertising?'

'Not only that. His background, you know, he cleared out from his wife and children. Watch your back, Bill.'

Bill left the police station, reassured by the sergeant's support. He saw Charles talking to Fr. van Engelen under the trees in the park.

'This is a strange turn of events, Bill,' said the priest when Bill joined them. 'Someone wants to turn the unfortunate incident back on you and the school.'

'Do you also think it's aimed at me?' He sat heavily on the bench.

'It looks that way,' said Charles. 'Don't worry. We support you.'

'Thank you, dear boy. I know that. I've spoken to Sergeant Willis. He told me Collins has nothing more to reveal. It's all rubbish.'

'Malicious rubbish,' said the priest, 'it's a deliberate tactic, I would say. I advise you to prepare a response.'

'That's what Flo says.'

'Then you should follow her advice. She knows more about this than she may be telling you.'

'Oh no, not you, too, Father?' said Bill. 'How am I missing all this?'

'Miss Barker's a shrewd, perceptive woman.'

'How should I respond in your opinion, then, Father?'

'You could find out who the source in the school is. You should also discover who else allegedly shares Mr McKinnon's tastes.'

'Yes, you're right. The affair has so rattled me that I can't think straight. The idea that I have allowed deviant behaviour to flourish in the school is abhorrent. So, yes, I should make inquiries and address the school. That's what I should do.'

Bill was five minutes back in his office when Miss Barker appeared. She shut the door behind her.

'Well?'

'The accident report was accurate, but he called the rest rubbish.'

'As expected. Anything else?'

'He told me to watch my back.'

'Good advice. Now what?'

'I'm going to address the school. The barely disguised insinuations need to be refuted. I'll get in touch with Collins and ask him what he's up to. He should be aware of his reputation in the town. He'll only make it worse with scurrilous and inaccurate reporting.'

'Is that wise—contacting Collins?'

'Why not? I'm only stating what the case is, what everyone knows. And I have a right to defend myself and the school, surely?'

'It may backfire on you.'

'How? I will tell the truth. Most people are on to Collins.'

'Bill, will you get it into your head that your opponents are not concerned about the truth. You're already condemned, and they will seek the tactics to bring you down. You must play their game. You have no choice.'

'You want me to make up stories about my phantom opponents?'

'No, you must work out tactics to counter their moves. If you contact Collins now, you will extend the front on which he and they can attack.

They are determining the battlefield, and you're making yourself more vulnerable.'

'For heaven's sake, Flo, how?' He got up and walked to the window overlooking the front driveway. 'How am I to deal with these people if I can't work from the basis of the truth? None of those allegations has any basis in truth.'

Miss Barker looked at him long and hard while he stared out the window. He was not well. 'Well, I might be wrong. It's your decision in the end.' She paused to get his attention. 'Now there's something else—Mrs. Charing.'

'What's she got to do with anything?'

'Five minutes after you left the school, I returned to your office without warning. I found her leafing through that file on your desk.'

'Are you sure she was not just tidying up?' He walked to his desk, picked up the file, and looked at the heading.

'Positive. She was sitting at your desk, leafing through the papers. She slapped the file shut when she saw me. I pretended I didn't notice anything. What's in the file?'

'It's about the arrangements for the Anzac Day ceremonies.' He sat down and flicked through the papers. 'It's all here. Flo, are you sure?'

'That woman is spying on you.'

'Whatever for?'

'Perhaps the people she is spying for plan to disrupt Anzac Day. It's a big occasion for left-wing groups to promote their cause.'

Bill threw the file onto his desk and held up his hands. 'I'm stonkered. Totally floored. What's happening in this town?'

'Bill, she's spying on you. No doubt.' She pointed at him with both hands. 'Your job is to deal with her. Play her along. Don't let her know you suspect her. If we keep an eye on her, we may find out who she is linked to. I have my suspicions.' Bill frowned and eyed her narrowly as if something had just struck him. She ignored the expression. 'Set some traps for her to confirm she is rummaging in your administration and, second, to see where it leads.'

'All right. I do need to know what my secretary is up to, whoever she's in league with. This will also test how right that bee in your bonnet is.'

'It will. It will be an excellent test.'

'You know, Flo, I'm beginning to see a different side to you.' She sat back in her armchair and raised her eyebrows. 'I've known you for a long time, better than most people here. One thing is sure. That severe, cantankerous manner is a little exaggerated at times. Joanne says it's mostly bluff, and you deliberately make yourself look dowdy.' He wagged his finger at her, but without the usual joviality. She continued to look at him with her eyebrows raised. 'We have got on well because we know each other well.

'One thing I saw from the beginning is that you have a private life with which you don't want any meddling. I respected that, and so did Joanne. That's not a problem. Now I suspect all of a sudden that there is something more to it than just guarding your privacy.' He tapped the desk. 'Come on, Flo, what is it? What's going on? Your interest in this goes beyond the solicitousness of a friend. I may be dopey in many things, but one thing I do well is organising. You are directing me as if you are organising something.'

'When I came to this town by accident all those years ago,' she said in a steady voice after they had sat staring at each other, 'I was feeling a little lost. I wanted an escape, some relief from— I wasn't dissatisfied with my life. Its course had been set from the start of the war. I just needed breathing space. I found it here. I fell in love with the place. That would have been enough. But then there was a bonus, one I cannot speak too highly of, and that was the contact that arose first with you and Joanne, then with Charles and Aine, and lastly with Estella. It enabled me to continue with my life as it was. I won't tell you what it is, at least not now. I will only say you are right. The rest, you'll have to trust me on.'

'So all that gruffness is an act?'

'Not all. Some has to do with my experiences during the war. I am also naturally reserved; some would say severe. It's convenient in preventing people from getting too close. I admit I have little patience for the foolishness of some people. I am human, you know.'

'All those irregular trips to see family in Sydney—not true? I mean, about the family?'

'No. It was for other reasons. And it was not always Sydney.'

'Your reading interests, the library and all that, it has something to do with this clandestine life?'

'Yes, but it was the other way around. The interest, the library, and the person who gave it to me were the starting point.'

'I, we, could feel deceived.'

'You shouldn't. My regard for you and Joanne is genuine. Your friendship has been a consolation for me. You must view my extracurricular work as unrelated and private. You should not change your manner towards me.'

'All those books ... that library ... where ... who did it come from?'

'I would rather not say. And please don't ask. It's personal.'

'Would you be happy if I told Joanne all this?'

'I would rather you didn't, for the moment. It is better if we keep our cards close to our chest. One day, at the right time, I will tell you and Joanne everything. Remember, Bill, it's not just the work. It's also about my experiences. People here assume I suffered at the hands of the Japanese during the war. That's true, but not in the way they imagine. I was never in a prisoner of war camp. My experiences played a big role in my life after the war and continue to do so now. That's as much as I want to say.'

'Your reaction to Miss Bicknell's speech has something to do with your work?'

'Let's just say I was alerted to a certain mode of discourse.'

'A certain mode of discourse?'

'It had the sound of more than just the rhetoric of an idealistic left-wing teacher. It sounded as though there might be an agenda behind it. There were other things prior to the speech, I might add.'

'Prior to the speech? What?'

'Let's not get into that. It's important now to focus on your problem. Someone wants to discredit you, and they are using Mr McKinnon's death to do it. Second, Mrs Charing is spying on you.' He looked away. She waited patiently. She was confronting him with truths from which the small, ordered world of Binawarra had sheltered him.

'I will find it hard to regard you in the same way,' he said at last. 'All this secrecy, it's not something I'm used to.'

'Nothing's changed except that you now know I have a life outside Binawarra. It would be a great pity, Bill, if you lost that light-heartedness and joviality that always gives me a lift. You must know I rely on you a great deal.'

'In what way?'

'Let's just say you're my man-fortress when it counts.'

'Fortress! I'm big enough to be a fortress!' He could not help laughing. 'Flo, you are a mystery ... a mystery.' He shook his head and glanced at his watch. 'I need to reflect on it all before I say any more.'

'Good, that's as it should be.' Miss Barker resumed her business-like tone. 'The next step, as you said, is to address the school to clarify your position and refute the allegations in the *Binawarra and District Mail*.' Then, without warning, she rose, moved to the door, and jerked it open. Mrs Charing was standing there, holding some files.

'Mr. Huckerby, I am returning these files,' she said, flushing.

'Thank you, Mrs Charing,' he said, struggling to his feet. 'I will take them. Flo, I will talk to you tomorrow.'

BILL HUCKERBY stood on the rostrum before the assembled students and teaching staff. He shifted on his weary legs while waiting for the class coordinators to signal that all the students were present. When the murmur and movement subsided, he began:

'My dear students and staff, this is the first time I have had the unpleasant duty of announcing that a tragic accident has taken the life of one of our teachers. It is also the first occasion that I have had to deal with allegations—unsavoury allegations, as the town's newspaper put it—about the life and administration of this school.

'First, I want to convey the school's condolences to the relatives and friends of Mr Robert McKinnon. I have arranged for an expression of sympathy to be sent to his family in San Francisco. Bob McKinnon was a larger-than-life figure whose extravagant manner more often amused people than offended them. That manner could be misleading on occasions, for couched in that behaviour were often sensible insights. He was a conscientious teacher. In the eight or so years that Bob spent in this school, I never once had to question him about his teaching duties or program.'

Miss Barker was standing at the far side of the rostrum. From that position, she could observe teachers' expressions. Miss Bicknell, who stood on the other side of the hall next to Jane Cox, looked on, expressionless. Friend Jane was less discreet; she wore a look of amusement and glanced at intervals at Miss Bicknell. Not far away was Suzie McNamara, who appeared stricken as she kept her bulging eyes on Miss Bicknell and Jane Cox.

'You have read or heard about the report in today's edition of the *Binawarra and District Mail*,' the principal went on. 'There are suggestions with no basis in fact. It is true that Bob McKinnon's body was found with that of another male. Other claims about his habits are, at this stage, speculation. Just speculation. It remains to be proven. The thinly disguised allegations that those alleged private habits have infected the school, and some sort of network exists, is sheer fantasy—'

'Fantasy? Wrong word,' cried Suzie McNamara, coming forward to the first row of students. 'Lies and slander, that's what they are. Bob was tricked. I was there. It was a dirty trap. And I know who's behind this. Those lying bitches over there!' She pointed across the students at Miss Bicknell and Jane Cox. 'You're the ones who killed him. You hated him so much that you had him killed. He never saw anybody but me—' She put her hand to her mouth, heaving and gasping, while the audience gaped in consternation. Cries of dismay followed. Some of the first years began crying. Miss Barker, who had been awaiting this explosion, signalled to the first-form coordinator to take her students from the hall. The hall was now in uproar while Bill Huckerby stood transfixed.

'Please, please, some order?' he pleaded.

All eyes were now turned to Suzie.

'Miss McNamara,' Miss Barker hissed into her ear through the noise, 'this is not the time. Let the principal have his say. He's on your side.'

Suzie still had her hand over her mouth, her breast heaving, and her eyes rolling as if she was unaware of where she was. When she focused again, she caught sight of the cold look on Miss Bicknell's face and the mocking smile on Jane Cox's.

'You murdering bitches!' she cried, her voice nothing more than a thin screech. 'You—' She started in their direction.

Miss Barker grabbed her before she could go far and pushed her, stumbling and resisting, to the nearby exit.

'Please, please, settle down,' Bill appealed. 'Will the class coordinators bring order to the students?' The appeal broke the trance, and the teachers hurried to restore order. 'Thank you,' said Bill, after students and teachers had settled. 'This is most unfortunate. I appeal to you to show Miss Mc-Namara some understanding. She is grieving. We must make allowances.' He paused. 'Because of this regrettable incident, I will cut short what I was going to say.

'I'm appealing to each person here, students and staff, to come forward if you know anything about the allegations in today's local newspaper. It is our duty to clear up this matter immediately, for the sake of the school and the reputation of its staff. We do not want our school to aid and abet those who want to sensationalise a tragic occasion for their own motives. I will make myself available at all times to anyone who wants to discuss the matter. Strict confidentiality will be guaranteed. I will be in my office.'

Miss Barker led Suzie to the far end of the recreation area and sat her down on a bench. She stood beside her, rubbing her heaving shoulders. Eventually, Suzie's weeping subsided, and she wiped her eyes and nose. She came to herself and looked at the school nurse in surprise.

'I'm not a dragon all the time.'

Suzie turned away and stared at the ground. Miss Barker sat next to her. 'Why are you so sure that Edith Bicknell and Jane Cox had anything to do with this?'

'I know,' said Suzie, not shifting her gaze from the ground.

'Tell me.'

'It's got nothing to do with you.'

'I may surprise you. I have already spoken with Sergeant Willis.'

'I told him, and he just ignored me. The others ignored me.'

'Tell me.'

'They hated him. He got under their skin. He showed them how stupid they were, how stupid their ideology was.'

'In what way was it stupid?'

'You wouldn't understand.'

'Socialist ideas versus a libertarian vision?' Suzie turned in surprise. 'Miss McNamara, university-educated people are not the only ones with an understanding of political theory. Why would the disagreement over ideology lead to violence?'

'I don't want to talk about it. It's got nothing to do with you. They know what they've done. The police should find out.'

'Tell me, Miss McNamara. It's important. Is it Trotskyism or Mao—?'

'No!' she said, her breast heaving. 'I don't trust you! I don't trust anyone. You all had it in for Bob. He got it from both sides.'

'What sides? Tell me.'

But it was to no avail. Appearing not to hear the last question, Suzie jumped to her feet and ran, stumbling towards the main building, leaving Miss Barker sorely frustrated.

BILL HUCKERBY sat on the verandah, sipping his tea. It was around eight o'clock the following Saturday morning. It was a cold morning, and he had wrapped himself in a thick jumper and an old-fashioned dressing gown. He watched the curling strings of the early morning mist rise slowly into the sun's rays, lighting the fields. Joanne was in the kitchen, tidying up. The previous two days had been tense, but they had turned up nothing. He had been on edge in fear that someone would arrive at his office with revelations that would give credence to *the Binawarra and District Mail*'s report. He had been careful not to put anyone under pressure or to appear that he had it in for the person who was the source of the 'information.' In the end, there was nothing, and it was a relief.

He had thought it unlikely that Mrs Charing was the source. She did not have the intelligence or nerve to get involved in such machinations. That was until he followed Flo's advice. He set several simple traps to see if his files were disturbed during his absence. They were. Someone had rummaged through the file on the Anzac Day celebrations. That had set him to reflect. Perhaps there were other ways he was spied upon. He had looked around his office. His cassette tape recorder sat invitingly on the cabinet near his desk. In the tape compartment was a blank tape cued at the beginning. The thought that somebody might have used his own recorder to tape his conversations shocked him. No, he was mistaken. She could not have gotten away with it. Surely? Miss Barker appeared at the front gate. She was holding a newspaper. His heart sank.

'Stay where you are,' she called. 'Here, you read this while I go and say hello to Joanne.' She handed him the paper and disappeared into the house. Plastered above the front-page report was: **Uproar over killer allegations.** He lowered the paper. His first inclination was to throw it aside. He had a sense about what would follow. He braced himself.

'Sources at the town's high school have given this newspaper a disturbing account of the pandemonium that last Wednesday's school assembly degenerated into. One staff member frightened the younger students and caused a general uproar by hysterically accusing other staff members of 'murder.' The assembly followed the death of a teacher suspected of gross immoral behaviour. It appeared to be an effort by the school principal to scotch rumours and so safeguard the school's reputation.

'Some staff were heard to express reservations about the wisdom of bringing the school together to discuss such matters. They said it would have been more judicious of the principal to have organised a discreet meeting of the teachers. That would have avoided frightening the children and stirring up emotions that were already inflamed. Others who commented on the condition of anonymity said bluntly that the principal wanted to head off questions about his administration.

'The principal, Mr William Huckerby, claimed that the only known facts regarding the death of Mr Robert McKinnon were that he was found dead with another man and that nothing further was to be concluded. Yet Binawarra's police sergeant has informed this newspaper that the second body was that of a high-class male prostitute, a mere child. He also informed us of the circumstances in which the bodies were found, something too distasteful for adults and too shocking for children to be described in this newspaper.

'Still, others, wholly unconnected with the school, are saying that it is an indication of the principal's naivety or incompetence if it is true that he did not know about that teacher's activities—activities widely known in the school.

'The evidence, yet to be contradicted, is that the principal was aware of the nature of Mr McKinnon's tastes and habits and did nothing about it. There are still more revelations to come about this sad affair, and this newspaper will not be diverted from keeping its readership informed.'□

Bill lowered the paper with a mixture of anger and frustration. How could anyone have the nerve to distort and misrepresent the circumstances of Bob McKinnon's life and death in this way?

'There is no use being deflated and frustrated,' said Miss Barker, as she came through the front door holding a steaming cup in one hand. 'You must accept this as a struggle and go to meet it with your own tactics. I will have to drum this into you until you understand.'

'Flo, I'm not used to this. Nobody, surely, in this town is used to such lies and distortions?'

'People who don't know you or the school may be persuaded. Have you read the editorial and the letters?'

Bill flicked through to the middle pages. The editorial headline read: **There must be no cover-ups.**

'The unfortunate misfiring of the assembly organised by the high school Principal last Wednesday has once again revealed the mess administrations can get themselves into while attempting to ward off public interest. Two fundamental pillars of our democratic society are freedom of speech for its citizens and transparency in the actions of our appointed representatives and authorities. Only through the preservation of these sacred pillars can the public be confident in knowing the truth and holding authorities to account.

'Mr Huckberby must bow to public pressure and open the school to a thorough investigation. There are many important questions to be answered. How much did he know about Mr McKinnon's tastes and habits? Mr Huckerby's high praise of Mr McKinnon during last Wednesday's assembly raises the critical question of how much sympathy he had for him over those tastes and activities. Did he also know of the object of Mr McKinnon's regular trips to Melbourne? Was he aware of the secretive associations he was a member of? Was he aware of the extent to which Mr McKinnon had brought the influence of those associations into the school? There are many questions that the principal must answer. The safety and health of our children are at stake.'

'What associations?' cried Bill, 'I've never ever heard of this. There is absolutely no evidence of it. I challenge whoever is claiming this to come forward!'

'Read the letters first. There are two of them about the affair. There will be more.'

The letter writers expressed their shock at the reported 'goings-on' at Binawarra High School. What is society coming to when the school's trusted authorities allow this sort of thing to happen? Children were, indeed, society's precious resource. *The Binawarra and District Mail* should be unrelenting in their investigation.

'It will get worse, let me assure you,' said Miss Barker when Bill lowered the paper.

'It could scarcely get worse than this—and after all the time and energy I have committed to the school.'

'More of the same?' said Joanne, joining them.

'Much worse.' Bill passed the newspaper to her.

'How could he print this sort of thing?' she said after perusing the front-page report.

'That's what I keep saying,' said Bill. 'How do you deal with something so obviously skewed?'

'But what's he got against you?'

'This is politically motivated, Joanne,' said Miss Barker. 'There are people who want to destroy Bill. The immediate object seems to be to remove him from the headship of the school.'

'Bill has run the school so well. He has done so much.'

'Of no interest in the ideological campaign.'

'But the truth's got to mean something.'

'The truth is not the concern, Joanne. It is the power position. Bill must deliver the power position of the school's headship into the correct hands.'

'What's your evidence, Flo?'

'That's what I wondered,' said Bill.

'I'm not so sure that the removal of Bill is all they want.' Miss Barker seemed not to hear Joanne's last question.

'They?' Joanne looked at Bill, who held up his hands and shrugged.

'Whatever way it goes,' Miss Barker continued, 'we have to work out a way of dealing with this.'

'If I can't tell the truth,' Bill said, shaking his head, 'then all my experience, the experience of thirty years, counts for nothing.'

'Tactics, Bill. Tell the truth tactically. You must not say anything that your opponents can use against you. This report here on the front page should be a good lesson on how something apparently harmless can be manipulated.'

'But how do you know all this?' said Joanne. 'How can you be so sure?'

'Let's not worry about that now,' said Miss Barker. 'Let's worry about how Bill can catch up some ground.'

At that point, Charles drove up. 'You've seen the *Binawarra and District Mail*—,' he said when he had joined them. 'Bill, if there's anything we can do, just ask. Anything.'

'Thank you, lad, I know I can rely on you.'

'There's something else,' said Charles, 'which is really why I'm here. For the moment, Aine wants to spend her time in prayer, in isolation from—she's not clear from what exactly. Something is bothering her. I mean, deep down, as if something has happened. You know about the terrible dark episodes she has had. You know what happened all those years ago—' He hesitated. 'She has a message. That darkness, as she calls it, is materialising in the form of Miss Bicknell, or rather, it has taken residence in Miss Bicknell. Miss Bicknell, she warns, is a threat to us all.'

There was a long moment of silence. Miss Barker was the first to speak. 'Did she say why?'

'No, only that she saw a threat in Miss Bicknell.'

'How often has she seen Miss Bicknell?'

'We have seen her just once. That was when we went to see her about Estella's visit to Sandhurst University. When Miss Bicknell inexplicably got up in the middle of the meeting and hurried from her office, Aine said we should be cautious of her. We had asked her not to speak to Estella about ideas opposed to our religious beliefs. She had attempted to get Estella to question them. I don't know if she was upset or angry. She just left the room abruptly.'

'What's all this?' said Bill. 'When did she try to get Estella to question your beliefs?'

Charles gave a short account of Estella's interview with Miss Bicknell and their conversation with Fr. van Engelen. Stunned, Bill fell silent.

'Let me try to understand this, Charles,' said Miss Barker. 'Aine says that what she calls that debilitating darkness has materialised in the form of Miss Bicknell. What exactly does she mean?'

'She said she could see a dark abyss in Miss Bicknell's eyes. It was like an evil spirit living in the depths of her eyes. Her concern for Estella's welfare seemed to originate in that abyss.'

'Remarkable,' said Miss Barker, putting her closed fist to her mouth and tapping it several times. 'She saw that?'

'Yes, and—not what you'd expect—she said she felt her anxiety slipping away. Its materialised form has made a difference. The dark spirit is still fearsome, but she can now stand up to it through her prayers.'

'Why did you let Estella go to Bendigo?' said Miss Barker. 'That was at Miss Bicknell's instigation, wasn't it?'

'Yes, but we thought that was a regular part of the school's educational program, not tied to Miss Bicknell. Besides, Estella would be in no danger when she was with Ruby Waiting and Geoff Shawcross. Bill thought we should at least investigate the option.'

'I did, too. I didn't think— My God! I've just remembered something. When Geoff came over with Ruby that Saturday, he said that Bob McKinnon had hinted there could be trouble on Anzac Day. The funny thing is that Bob McKinnon had rung not so long before to warn me that people might try to exploit Estella. I asked him to explain what he meant, and he just replied—let me think—he told me to wake up. Not everything was what it seemed on the surface. I thought he was just up to his old tricks, pulling my leg, you know—'

'And you promptly forgot about it,' said Miss Barker.

'Well, how was I to know? I was never sure when he was serious.'

'Bill—'

'Okay, I admit it. I should have paid more attention.'

'Anyhow, as it turned out, Mr Shawcross told me what you said, at least part of it. You have filled it out.' She waved her hand. 'Forget about it for the moment. It's time to work out what to do.'

'Geoff remembered? You haven't linked Bob's death and his warnings to Miss Bicknell, have you?' said Bill.

'What do you know, Bill?' said Miss Barker. 'You know about Miss Bicknell's reference to a philosopher of revolution. That was not for nothing. You know about Bob McKinnon's warning to Geoff about Anzac Day. Mr McKinnon warned you about opening Estella up to exploitation. He meant Miss Bicknell, obviously. You know from Miss McNamara that there was a falling-out between him and the other left-wingers. You know Miss McNamara accused Miss Bicknell and Miss Cox of murdering Mr McKinnon. Was that just hysteria? Now there is a concerted attack on you in the local newspaper over charges of child sexual abuse. What conclusions are you going to draw? I urge you to pay attention to Aine's warning.'

'You're not seriously suggesting that Miss Bicknell had Bob murdered for some political reason, are you, and it has something to do with me? I just find that too outrageous to entertain.'

'I'm only saying the details lead in that direction.' She turned to Charles. 'Charles, the warning from Aine is one of the most astounding parts of this mystery. Aine has, without knowing what's happened, hit on the link between the incidents we are talking about and others that none of you are aware of. Now tell me, was that all she said? Was there any more to her warning, anything more specific?'

'No, she just said that Miss Bicknell is a threat to us all. She seems a little distant, preoccupied—I mean in spirit. I have not pressed her. We must be careful, she said. Aine and I must be particularly vigilant about Estella.'

'Remarkable,' repeated Miss Barker. 'There is a threat to Estella. I know a lot more about this than any of you could imagine. Aine is right, Charles. You must be vigilant.'

'What more do you know?' said Bill. 'Why haven't you said anything?'

'There are important reasons why I have not spoken about it. I assure you, though, that Estella is under protection. I am keeping a close eye on her here. In Bendigo, Captain Shawcross and Ruby were always with her. We can continue now, each of us, to keep an eye on her here. Charles, I would not have kept this to myself without providing the necessary protection for Estella.'

'I know Miss Barker,' said Charles. 'We trust you.'

'Thank you, Charles. Now, having come this far, we must keep all this strictly between us. I'm working closely with Captain Shawcross, and as long as those concerned don't know what we are doing, we have an advantage. We may be able to neutralise the threat if we can find out what Miss Bicknell's goals are. There is no use in going to the police at this stage. They will say they have nothing to go on. What's more, making our suspicions public will drive the people and their agenda underground. Finally, this affair goes well beyond the local police, believe me. No, we have no choice at this point. We must find out what's going on.'

She advised Bill to stay calm, especially in public, and stick to a short account of the actual circumstances. He was to garner support within the town from those who knew him well. He was to reassure them of the school's stability. Under no circumstances was he to contact the editor of the *Binawarra and District Mail* or to attack him in public. That would give Collins more opportunity to twist and misrepresent the circumstances. In the meantime, she would plan a counterattack.

'Counterattack?' said Bill. 'I can't stand this sort of thing. I should not have to do this. Why should I be forced to play their game?'

'Trust me,' said Miss Barker. 'You will have to defend yourself against some pretty shabby behaviour. There's more to come, most probably things that you would not dream of.'

The phone rang, and Joanne went to answer it.

'Bill!' said Joanne, hurrying from the hall. 'Somebody just abused me and made threats against you.'

'This just won't do,' exclaimed Bill, fiercely gesturing. 'I will not stand my wife being subjected to this sort of thing!' He made as if he was going to stand up, but Miss Barker took his arm.

'It's a nuisance call,' she said. 'It's not pleasant, I know. Don't respond. If anyone else rings up, put the phone down. Report it to Sergeant Willis later to cover yourself. It could work in your favour, you know, with your supporters.'

Bill remained furious. Miss Barker persisted in encouraging him to follow her advice. With the help of Joanne and Charles, she succeeded in keeping him on track. 'But I will not stand for my wife being abused,' he exclaimed again. Miss Barker excused herself and left Charles to comfort them. She resolved to get in touch with Captain Shawcross as soon as possible.

Chapter 22

Bruce and Didi in Binawarra

LATE THAT MORNING, Estella walked into town. She enjoyed the busy shopping crowd in the cosy atmosphere around the shops on a Saturday morning. As she walked along her regular way into town, her mind drifted back over the few days since she had returned from Bendigo. Ruby had already rung her twice to ask her how she was going. That really pleased her. She had come across Len Dawson twice outside school and was again relieved to find he had changed his manner. She had to admit he could be pleasant, even charming, and she thought she had a glimpse of what the other girls saw in him.

She had taken steps to repair her relationship with Jenny. To Jenny's wonder, she admitted that she was inclined to think too rigidly about relationships. Perhaps she could understand that the heart sometimes could not be controlled. Jenny said she was pleased to hear her change of mind, but responded with what seemed like distrust. Estella resolved to persevere. She would be more understanding now that she understood what pain and joy love could bring.

Geoff was never far from her thoughts, but now she was confident she could deal with it. He was for Ruby, and that was that. She would hide her love in her heart, and as long as he showed her the concern and affection of a big brother, she would be happy. She could manage like that. Yes, she could be satisfied with the love in her heart—like Miss Barker. In this way, she would look forward without trepidation to the times she would meet him in the company of Ruby.

After completing her few shopping errands and having a short chat with the women from the Country Women's Association, she looked around the park for Fr. van Engelen. He was not there. She would later pay a visit to the Blessed Sacrament to see if he was there. She sat on a bench among the gardens and looked at the bustling crowd around the square. She had been there for five minutes when a familiar face close by the coffee lounge caught her attention. She started when she recognised the staring eyes of Bruce Butcher. With a hesitant movement, he headed across the road towards her.

'Hello, Estella.'

'Good morning, Mr Butcher,' she said, not knowing whether to stand or stay seated.

'Stay where you are,' he said, sitting at one end of the bench. She moved along to the other end. He flinched. 'So this is where you live.'

'Yes.'

'Pretty town.'

'Yes, it is.'

'Pretty town for a pretty girl.'

He flushed and then hesitated, seeing Estella's discomfort. 'I came to see where you lived. I was curious.' She did not reply. 'The slimy manner of that Egyptian does not fool you, does it?'

'I beg your pardon.'

'I wouldn't trust him if I were you.'

'I don't know what you mean.'

'I know. That's why I'm here. To warn you.'

'About what? Mr Al Refai and his daughters were very friendly.'

'I know. That's the plan.'

'What plan?'

'Take it from me. There's a plan—'

'Good morning, young lady,' said Boris, standing before them. 'It's another fine morning in Binawarra, is it not? An early morning chill and then a change into this mild sunny day. It's like paradise here, isn't it, at this time of year? I will miss my visits to Binawarra if they have to end.'

'Good morning, Mr Rostowski,' said Estella, again not knowing whether she should remain seated. It was strange to be in the company of two mature men talking to her with such familiarity. Now Bruce Butcher was looking suspiciously at Rostowski.

'I have planned a walk into the hills on that side,' said Boris, pointing to the west along the range from Death Rock and the Wombat. 'A wonderful place to walk, this.' He stopped. 'I am not interrupting your conversation, am I?'

'Oh no,' Estella assured him. 'Mr. Butcher has just arrived. You're not interrupting anything.'

'You are from out of town,' said Boris.

'Yes,' said Bruce, tapping the bench beside him and looking away.

'Mr. Butcher is from the university,' said Estella. Boris's inoffensive comment deserved a more polite response.

'Ah, the university? I believe your university runs excellent courses in marketing. I am in the sales business, Mr Butcher, and have always been interested in marketing theory. Theory has its limits, but with some things, it's helpful. The trick is to distinguish what is helpful and what is not. I'm sure you understand.'

'The university is well known for the comprehensiveness of its programs,' said Bruce. He straightened himself. 'And I understand the limits of theory in the practical world.'

'I'm sure you do.' Boris looked from Bruce to Estella. 'Yes, well, I will leave you now and continue my walk around the shops before I take my morning coffee over there.' He pointed to the coffee lounge. 'It is pleasant to sit there and gaze at the people coming and going. You have a view on all that is happening.' He gave Estella and Bruce a bow and began to walk away. 'Mr Butcher, I mean to have a closer look at your department's activities,' he said, turning. 'It's wise to keep abreast of what is happening in one's area.'

Estella and Bruce watched him walk to the coffee lounge, apparently forgetting his intention of continuing his walk.

'Who is that man? That's a Balkans accent,' said Bruce, after Boris had disappeared into the coffee lounge. 'I would recognise it anywhere. What's he doing here? Do you know him well?'

'No, only to say hello to. He comes to Binawarra on business. He's always friendly,' said Estella, to counter the inexplicable antagonism Bruce displayed towards Boris.

'Always friendly?'

'Yes.'

'And you're always friendly back?'

'Yes. He's polite.'

'Just because he is polite and friendly?'

'Mr Butcher, I have to go,' said Estella, getting up. She was a captive audience at the university, but in Binawarra, she did not have to put up with him. She walked away.

'I wouldn't trust that man if I were you,' he called after her. He punched his fist on the bench as she walked on without saying anything.

Estella did not react, but she was conscious of the warning thrown after her with such vehemence. Miss Barker warned her to be careful of Mr Rostowski. Was that a coincidence? Was it somehow connected with Geoff's information that someone was following her? Could it be Mr Rostowski? But he was so kind. She walked onto the path along the shops, still not turning to see whether Bruce was following.

As she was now heading towards the church, she decided to pay a visit. Dipping her hand in the holy water font at the entrance and making the sign of the cross, she walked to the nearest pew, genuflected, knelt, and took her rosary from her bag. After she blessed herself with the rosary's small cross, she looked around. The priest was busy in the confessional. Of course, he heard confessions on Saturday morning. Taking advantage of the occasion, she returned her rosary to her bag and began her examination of conscience, starting with her duties to God. When she came to her duties towards her neighbour and then to herself, she could not help but ponder her feelings towards Geoff and the consideration she owed to both Geoff and Ruby.

Was she selfish in not restraining her feelings? Did she lack charity towards Ruby by interfering with the relationship between her and Geoff? When she first met them, it had been clear that Geoff had nobody but Ruby on his mind. Now she was there, he was paying her attention, even if it was a big brother's way. That way was impeccable. He was warm, considerate, and solicitous. Unconditionally. He did not feel any other way about her. That's the way it appeared, anyway. It was the source of her joy and pain. But now, in the seclusion of her conscience and kneeling before the Blessed Sacrament, she had to acknowledge that her appearance had an effect on men—on most men. She tried to put it out of her mind. She tried to ignore it, but she had to face facts. Did she lack charity? Was she selfish? Was she guilty of disloyalty towards Ruby by not keeping Geoff at a distance? Was she blameworthy in acting in the very way she silently condemned other girls for? She tried to avoid doing it, but it happened before she knew what she was doing. Or did she know?

Her heart sank as she considered the terrible possibility that her appearance could be determining Geoff's feelings for her, as it seemed to be with Bruce Butcher. No, no, it was not so! Geoff was different. The door of the confessional opened, and an elderly man emerged, holding the door for her. She acknowledged the thoughtful gesture and entered. She knelt before the curtained grille and made the sign of the cross. After confessing some sins of omission and selfishness, she paused, deciding how to broach the subject of Geoff and Ruby.

'Is there something on your mind?' said the priest in a whisper. His bowed head, turned slightly away from her, was visible in the subdued light through the transparent purple curtain. He had his rosary beads in his hands. His fingers were placed on the beads as if he had been interrupted in his prayers.

'Father, I am in love with a boy, I mean, a man. He's a man—' She stopped, for now she was speaking the thought out loud for the first time. She couldn't help but take a breath. Fr. van Engelen's head lifted and turned a fraction towards her.

'Take your time,' he said as he bowed his head again.

'I am in love with a man who belongs to someone else,' she said, trying to compose herself. 'Is it wrong for me to continue in his company?'

'In what way do you keep company with him?'

'I meet him with the girl he belongs to?'

'Belongs to? You do not meet him alone?'

'No, or only by her arrangement.'

'Is the man married to the girl?'

'No, Father.'

'Is he engaged?'

'No.'

'In what way is he committed to her?'

'He seems to have chosen her.'

'Has she chosen him?'

'I don't know. She likes him a lot. She receives his attention.'

There was a long pause during which the priest made no discernible movement. 'In all our relationships with our fellow man, the example of Our Lord's love must be before our eyes,' he began at last. 'We must always act with charity, with consideration, unselfishness. We must never take advantage of someone, and we must always be ready to give of ourselves.

That means we must never be deceitful, manipulative, treacherous, or mean—all those things which spoil a friendship. The love of God, in brief, always dictates how we treat our fellow man.

'When it comes to relationships between young men and women, there are other things at play. In general, young women should always be aware of their physical attraction and never misuse this God-given fact of nature. They must be modest in their dress and manners. Young men must never treat young women as objects of desire. They must treat them as a person, despite the feelings that are often aroused.

'When it comes to the heart, it is left to our prudence, our moral judgment, as to how we should act. Most of us, even people dedicated to a religious life, experience deep affection for someone at some point in our lives. The circumstances determine how we should behave. A religious knows that such affection must be contained, and any circumstances avoided that may cause a challenge to their commitment. The Church talks here about avoiding occasions of sin. The same applies to married men and women. The heart is sometimes difficult to control, but the heart and its affections are not the problem. The problem is keeping in sight the duties our circumstances in life dictate. The married man or woman who has feelings for someone else must be governed by the duties of their state, even those whose marriage has turned sour.

'When unattached young people experience affection, it can often be painful. Affections can spring up and just as quickly subside, leaving one person broken-hearted. As long as there is no formal commitment, there is no wrong in changing affection. Affection is not something one can dictate in male and female relationships. One must learn to overcome disappointment in this, as in other areas of life. We are governed in the affairs of the heart by charity as in all our relationships. If you like a man who is not formally committed, you are not doing anything wrong in keeping his company, provided you always act in charity.' He paused. 'Does this man arouse you sensually?'

'No ... no, I don't think so, Father,' she said, at first not comprehending.' I just feel an overwhelming love for him.'

'We all must be aware of our sensual nature and its propensity to govern our actions. Our sensual nature must always be linked to genuine love in a committed, consecrated relationship for it to remain healthy and for it to be truly enjoyed. Again, God's love and Jesus's suffering on the cross must be brought before our minds when sensual thoughts and feelings threaten to harm ourselves and our relationships.' Again, he paused. 'Other than this, you should be at ease with those who respect you and return your friendship.'

'But I can't help feeling disloyal towards my friend who has been so good to me.'

'It is right to be scrupulous about your behaviour in such circumstances, but it is not right to be overscrupulous. You must let Providence guide his heart, your friend's heart, and your heart, too.'

'I will never stop loving him.'

'You are young. You can never anticipate how you may feel in a year.'

'It won't change, Father.'

'Be that as it may, you are not committing any sin in merely keeping company with a man who is not committed formally to someone else. It is best to relax and let things happen in their natural way. You must let happen what will happen.'

'Yes, Father.'

'Good, for your penance, say the first Joyful Mystery of the rosary, keeping in mind Mary's constant purity of mind to help you maintain your own purity of mind. Now say a sincere act of contrition, and I will give your absolution.'

She said her act of contrition and listened to Fr. van Engelen recite the formal absolution in Latin. She waited for the point when he raised his voice, saying, '*Ego te absolvo*'. She bowed her head.

'Now go in peace,' he said, with his head bowed further over, 'and offer sincere prayers for me and all the world's priests who the devil attacks without cessation. Also, pray for all those religious congregations in which the devil has already made himself at home.'

She came out of the cool, soothing, subdued light of the little stone church into the brilliant sunlight of the shopping square. Across the road, all through the park, the gardens seemed to be bursting with the vigour of life. The sounds and bustling of the country shopping square were comforting and consoling. She would linger to enjoy the atmosphere and wait for Fr. van Engelen, who usually came after Saturday confessions, to sit in the park. She had nothing particular to say to him, but she needed to talk to the kind Dutch priest whose ability to see into her feelings always left her wondering. She had been sitting for ten minutes when he hobbled from the church. She rose to meet him. He waved his walking stick as soon as he saw her.

'You are such a kind-hearted girl,' he said when she came offering her shoulder as support. 'You and your mum and dad are such a consolation to me. I am very blessed.' He lowered himself awkwardly onto the bench. 'Well, I haven't heard anything about your trip to Bendigo. Tell me all about it.'

She related how good Ruby and Geoff were to her. She spoke about her sessions at the university, her meeting and lunch with Mr Al Refai and his daughters, and later his son. She related all the details, for she knew he would never speak to her or even make assumptions about what she told him in the confessional.

'Miss Ruby sounds like a good friend to you,' he said when she had finished. 'She's mature, sensible, and down-to-earth, just the right sort of person you can rely on. Your parents like her and Mr Shawcross very much. That's a great compliment to them.'

'Geoff has been just as kind as Ruby. What do you think of him, Father?'

'I have not had much to do with him, but he seems a decent young man. Miss Barker speaks highly of him, and that's no small thing, as you would know. She has said you should put your trust in him. He will not fail you.' Estella was taken aback. 'Yes, I am aware of Geoff's efforts. Miss Barker and I have discussed it.'

'Have you? How many people know about—whatever it is? Geoff told me to be careful and to trust him.'

'What have your parents said?'

'The same thing.'

'Then, that's the best advice while Miss Barker and Mr Shawcross try to discover what's behind the threat. Try not to be alarmed. You are in good hands. And say some prayers that it will all work out all right, as I'm sure it will.'

It was a revelation that Geoff and Miss Barker were working together. She could not help concluding that whatever was going on was more serious than she had thought. As these thoughts passed through her mind, she glanced towards the busy end of the shopping square and was astounded to spot Didi Al Refai wandering around the shops. She watched him advance towards them, sometimes having to sidestep someone at the last moment as he looked around.

'Is it someone you know?' said Fr van Engelen.

'Yes, it's Mr Al Refai's son. I wonder what he's doing here.'

They watched Didi as he approached. When he was almost abreast of them on the other side of the road, he stopped at the wrought-iron front gates of the church and peered at the front. With a glance to the left and right, he passed through the gates and walked to the steps at the entrance. After another pause, he entered the church.

'He is Muslim, isn't he?' said Fr. van Engelen.

'He's from Egypt.'

'His background, at least, is Muslim. Why do you think he has entered our church?'

'I have no idea, Father.' Then, on reflection, 'Well, during our conver-sation, Aisha and Tahini asked about my religious beliefs. They seemed interested, including Didi.'

The priest did not reply, and Estella recognised the familiar drift in his expression. A minute later, Didi emerged from the church, looking around him. She was amazed that he had not yet seen her. He passed through the front gates, looking at the ground, and walked in the direction he had c ome.

'He has not seen you,' said the priest. 'Are you going to let him know you have seen him?'

'I don't know. I don't want to disturb him. He may be on business or something.'

'Somehow, I suspect you would not be disturbing him.'

They watched him as he walked on. When he was level with the coffee lounge, he stopped and turned his attention to the park. He stood there, taking in the surroundings. He even looked in their direction, but still did not focus on them. He crossed to the park, where he continued his absent-minded stroll. Now he was heading in their direction again. Bruce Butcher appeared from behind some bushes. Didi did not evince any surprise at seeing him. They exchanged words—at least Bruce Butcher was spoke and gestured at Didi.

'Who is that?' said the priest.

'Mr Butcher from the university. He conducted the sessions I had at the university,' she said, surprised that Didi and Bruce Butcher were acquaint-ed.

'Have you already seen Mr Butcher this morning?'

'Yes, he spoke briefly with me.'

'What about?'

Estella did not want to tell him. She had no desire to talk about Bruce Butcher's interest in her. The priest acknowledged her reluctance. They continued to watch Bruce Butcher and Didi. Then Didi walked away while

Bruce was still speaking. When he was several paces away, he turned slightly, held up his hands, and shrugged, leaving Bruce staring after him. He must see them now, thought Estella. But wonders of wonders, he did not notice them until he was just about on them.

'Oh, Estella!' he exclaimed. 'I hoped I would run into you. This must be your parish priest.' He offered his hand. 'Please do not move, Father. My name is Didi Al Refai. Everyone calls me Didi. I met Estella in Bendigo when she was at lunch with my father.'

The priest held out his hand, which Didi shook firmly. Didi's exclamation and polite greeting were in the same boyish, slightly embarrassed manner Estella had observed in the restaurant. Again, there was the contrast with his polished, confident father and his smartly dressed conservative sisters.

'I just had a look inside your church,' he said, shifting. 'I suppose you saw me. It's a beautiful old church. Estella told us all about it—and the town. It's just as charming as you described it.'

'Are you here on business, Mr Al Refai?'

'Estella has been speaking about me or us?'

'She told me about the meeting with you and your father and sisters.'

'Good.' He shifted again. 'No, Father, I'm not here on business. Estella impressed us so much with her talk about the town that I had to come and see for myself. I said I would, didn't I?'

'I don't remember.'

'Or perhaps I didn't. I certainly thought it.' He gave her his boyish, embarrassed look. It was not unattractive. 'I hope I don't seem forward, Estella, but I would like to invite you to have lunch with me. There's a cosy coffee lounge down there. I won't keep you long, I promise.'

'My parents are expecting me.' But she did not feel reluctant to accept the invitation.

'For anything special?'

'No.'

'Then, please, I would be honoured. Just lunch and a chat. I'll drive you home after.'

Estella glanced at Fr. van Engelen. He was also somewhat disarmed by Didi's open self-conscious manner.

'Do you think I could?' she said to him.

'If you like, I can give your parents a call to tell them where you are.'

'All right—'

'Didi. Call me Didi. I'm not that much older than you, at least in maturity, my father would say.'

His smile and self-deprecating joke disarmed her further. 'All right, Didi,' she said. 'Thank you for the invitation.' She got up and offered to help the priest to his feet, but Didi had anticipated her action.

'It's my pleasure, but let me help, Father.' He offered his hand to the priest and then, seeing his unsteadiness, added: 'Let me also help you across the road.'

Without resisting, Fr. van Engelen leaned on Didi's arm, and they began the slow walk across the road. Estella walked on the other side of him, casting several curious glances.

'I assume you are Muslim,' said Fr. van Engelen when they were on the footpath in front of the church.

'I suppose I'm what one would call a secular Muslim. I have spent so long in America, in Los Angeles to be precise, that the American way has rubbed off on me. I guess you can see that.'

'You have an American accent.'

'Yes. Is that a good thing or a bad thing?'

'Well, an accent is neither a good nor a bad thing morally,' said the priest, responding to Didi's playful question. 'However, to answer what's behind that, America is a religious country, despite the image of Hollywood.'

'Yes, you are right. Perhaps I have been influenced by Hollywood America. I don't know. I have been working in the film business—not very successfully, to my father's annoyance. That's why I am in Australia, to talk to my father about— well, he's not happy with me. It's a coincidence I tracked him down in Bendigo and met Estella there.'

'Is your father happy about America's influence on you?' Fr. van Engelen asked as they halted in front of the presbytery.

'I think you have guessed the answer. Although my father's business concerns are centred in Paris, he likes the English way of life. He likes to consider himself a refined English gentleman with the traditions of Egyptian hospitality. He is not happy with the American influence on me, and that influences the finance he will make available to me. I suffer from his prejudice.' He smiled.

'And your sisters? Estella has told me she liked your sisters very much. She felt she had something in common with them.'

'My sisters like France and Parisian elegance, but are traditional Egyptian girls. They disapprove of the way I live. Their looks continually scold and shame me. Estella is what one would consider a traditional young woman in Western terms. That's where the connection is, I think.'

'You are right,' said Fr. van Engelen. 'Estella maintains the traditional ways of European Christian civilisation. She is serious about the principles that underpin a Christian way of life.'

'No need for the hint, Father,' said Didi, smiling. 'I've been taught to recognise a lady and to respect her. I will treat Estella with the respect and dignity she deserves, the same respect I give my mother and sisters. Besides, one does not possess a beautiful rose by crushing it.'

'An appropriate image, Didi, one that most young men seem to have lost sight of these days.'

'I have been immersed for many years in the vulgarity and tastelessness of Los Angeles, but my father's lessons are not forgotten. I'm guilty of a lot of stupidity and rightly reprimanded for it, but some things are beneath my dignity.' He turned to Estella, who had been following this exchange. 'Estella, talking about you as if you weren't here is not very gallant, is it?'

'I don't mind,' she said. 'I appreciate Father's concern and am interested to hear your views.'

'Estella is quiet, Father, but from the first minutes in her company, I had the impression that she is alert and discerning. Are you all right to walk to your door?'

'Yes, thank you, I'm all right. I will leave you now to have your lunch. Nice to have met you, Didi. Look after Estella. She's precious.'

'I will, Father, thank you. Nobody needs to worry. The day after tomorrow, I must return to Los Angeles.'

As Didi and Estella walked towards the coffee lounge, Fr. van Engelen reflected on the meeting with the young Egyptian, whom he judged to be superficially influenced by Hollywood and American pop culture. He entered his parlour and sat at his desk. He was puzzled. He could see where Estella's meeting with Mr Al Refai senior fitted in, but where did the son, Didi, fit in? Didi was either a superb actor or what he appeared to be: open, polite, and considerate with a childlike ingenuousness. Estella did not feel threatened by him. On the contrary, he could see she liked him. Indeed, he was likable. He dialled Miss Barker's number.

'Miss Barker, when you have time—'

'Two hours, Father, at the usual place.'

DIDI USHERED Estella to a table by the front window of the coffee lounge and, making sure she was happy with the spot, drew out the chair for her. He handed her the menu. 'Orange juice, and let me guess, a salad sandwich with salmon, sardines—?'

'Yes, I would like that—salmon or sardines, any sort of fish. It doesn't matter.'

'It was not a difficult guess. I remember what you ordered at the restaurant in Bendigo, and I can see you have a healthy lifestyle. I try to stick to a healthy diet, too. It does not always work. The temptations of my surroundings are often irresistible.' He shrugged and smiled.

The conversation proceeded in the same vein. There was no particular subject that Didi followed. He passed from one thing to another as he was reminded of it. He asked questions about Estella and her family, which led him to speak more about himself. One thing struck Estella during their meandering conversation. He talked about his life in Los Angeles with embarrassment and regret. His father had provided all the means necessary for him to make a go of it in the film business, but he botched it time and time again, either because of stupid mistakes and trusting the wrong people or because of his unworthy habits. He was ashamed to talk about it with a girl like Estella.

'I'm like the man with a toothache who cannot pass the candy shop. I wonder why people like me are determined to waste their lives.'

The regret appeared genuine. He spoke as if owning up to some unpleasant addiction and not just revealing facts about himself. It was strange, she thought. He was a handsome young man with plenty of opportunity and family wealth, but at the same time, self-conscious, uncertain, and unhappy.

'I've told you enough about myself,' he said, waving his hand. 'That's boring. What about you? What are you going to do with yourself when you finish school? My father thinks you would do very well in public relations work. You have the poise, the dignity, and the manner that suits. He would encourage you to go on with it. That's what he said to the people at the university, to Bruce Butcher, I assume.'

'Do you know Bruce Butcher?'

'I met him when I went to the university to find my father. He told me he was at the restaurant. I had not seen him before that.'

'He spoke to you in the park.'

'Yes, that was strange. He pounced on me and asked why I was in Binawarra. I said that was my business. He said I shouldn't interfere with the university's plans for you. Much planning was involved in recruiting students, and interference could spoil things. I knew what he was talking about, he said mysteriously. I said I had no idea what he was talking about and that I was in Binawarra for reasons that were none of his business. I walked away then. You saw that, I guess.'

'Yes, I did.'

'I have the impression you don't like him.'

'He makes me feel uneasy. I don't know why he's in Binawarra on a Saturday morning.' Then she remembered what Bruce said. 'Well, actually, he did say.'

'Why?'

She hesitated. 'I really don't want to talk about it.'

It was the only time during the conversation that Didi gave her an examining look. But it was brief. 'That's okay,' he said and brushed aside the subject.

He returned to Estella's plans. Was there something besides public relations as an option? Estella told him about her gardening interests and the possibility of following a course in horticulture. This information aroused his interest, and he spent some time questioning her. 'I must see them. I am not a gardener, but I like garden design, and I like visiting famous gardens. When I am in England, I visit some of the famous gardens there. You would like Sissinghurst in Kent. Wandering around there is like being in another world. A good, well-planned thriving garden is like that, don't you think?'

Bruce Butcher walked by outside, staring at them. He passed out of sight and a few seconds later appeared inside. He continued to stare while he made his way to a table on the other side of the room. A waitress approached, and he picked up the menu without looking at it. He kept his eyes on them.

'He's creepy, isn't he?' whispered Didi, leaning forward. 'I don't blame you for feeling uneasy. What's he up to?'

'You are taking advantage of this pleasant location,' said Boris, appearing from nowhere. 'You are in the right place to look out over the square. I have been sitting there behind you.' He looked at Didi and then at Estella.

'This is Mr Didi Al Refai,' said Estella. 'He's visiting Binawarra. Didi, this is Mr Rostowski.'

Didi rose and shook Boris's hand. Boris wished him a pleasant stay in Binawarra, adding that every visitor should take advantage of the bushwalks in the vicinity. Surprisingly, that was all Boris had to say. He had arrived at their table with the impression of lingering, but now excused himself and left the coffee lounge with more purpose than Estella had seen. Didi's attention passed from Boris back to Estella's gardens. Eventually, he looked at his watch and reluctantly said he must take her home, as promised. As he was calling the waitress for the bill, Miss Bicknell walked into the coffee lounge, looking around.

'Hello, Estella, this is a fine place to be sitting on this sunny day,' she said after she had spotted them. 'Edith Bicknell is my name,' she went on, turning to Didi. 'I am one of Estella's teachers.' Didi rose again and introduced himself. 'Oh, you must be related to Mr Al Refai. A son or a nephew? I arranged for Estella to attend Mr Al Refai's talks at the university. Two men with that name in the neighbourhood seems too much of a coincidence.'

Didi politely replied that he was Mr Al Refai's son, but he had nothing to do with his father's business with the university. It was a sheer coincidence that he met up with his father in Bendigo that day.

'And now you are here visiting Binawarra.'

'Yes, I heard all about Binawarra from Estella.'

'Will you be here for very long, Mr Al Refai? There are marvellous hikes to be made here. There's no one better to tell you about them than Estella here.'

'No, Ms Bicknell, I will return to Los Angeles the day after tomorrow.'

'A few days are much too short to see the sights here.'

'You are right. Unfortunately, I only have the morning in Binawarra. I will return to Melbourne after I drop Estella off at her house.'

'Oh, much, much too short. You have seen nothing. But I wish you a safe return to Los Angeles.'

Didi thanked her, and she turned to leave, but then, spying Bruce Butcher, joined him. How did Miss Bicknell come to be in the coffee lounge? She seemed keen to give the impression she had come across Didi and her by accident, but her oddly talkative manner belied that impression. And now she was talking to Bruce Butcher, who had little interest in what she had to say. Didi paid the bill and ushered Estella out of the coffee lounge. As they were leaving, she glanced at them. Bruce's eyes were following her. She walked beside Didi, pondering the chance meetings that morning, scarcely able to concentrate on what he was saying. She was not used to it.

'My car is parked at the end of the square up there,' Didi said, pointing to a group of boys standing around a red, low-slung sports car. The boys parted to let her and Didi through. He opened the door for her. As she slid onto the black leather-covered seat, she heard one boy say something to Didi.

'Yes, it's the latest Ferrari. And, yes, it will do two hundred miles an hour, but not around here, of course.' He slid into the driver's seat. 'I won't tell them I have hired it for a few days,' he said, shutting the door and buckling up. 'And I won't tell them you don't know what a Ferrari is.' He laughed as he snapped the car into gear. 'It's a change to have a young lady in a Ferrari who is not the slightest bit impressed with it.' He laughed again, this time ironically, as he drove off.

'What a beautiful little house,' he said, pulling up outside the Winterbine house.

'Little house?' said Estella, taking his offered hand when he had opened her door. 'It's not what we call a little house here.'

'I didn't mean it was little physically. I meant, it is charming. I use the word little to mean charming.'

'Yes, it is charming.' His immediate embarrassment intrigued her. 'My mother and father have done a lot of work on it.' She stood next to him as he surveyed the house and front gardens.

'I've just got time to have a look at your garden. That is, if you are happy to guide me. I don't want to be a nuisance.'

'I'm happy to show you around. First, I'll tell Mamma I'm home.'

Estella disappeared through the front door while Didi remained at the bottom of the verandah steps. A minute later, Estella appeared with her mother. Didi looked at her in undisguised astonishment.

'I'm pleased to meet you, Didi,' Aine said, holding out her hand. 'Estella said you like people to call you Didi. Thank you for providing lunch for Estella and bringing her home.'

'It was my pleasure,' he said, shifting. 'I met Estella in Bendigo, where my father gave a talk to the students.'

'Yes, Estella has told us. I believe you would like to take a look at our back garden. You're very welcome. Most of the work is Estella's.'

'Thank you, Mrs Winterbine.'

'Then I will leave you with Estella to guide you. You are welcome to visit whenever you are in Binawarra.'

He thanked her again and then followed Estella around the side of the house. 'Your mother,' he said, coming up beside her when they were at the back, 'your mother is very ... well, unusual. I was not expecting that.'

'People say I look more like my father.'

'I can imagine. That pale complexion and the piercing blue eyes—' He was examining her face. 'I can see the influence of your mother's features in your face. Your father must be a big man.'

'Yes, he is tall.'

'Amazing. You and your mother are different.'

It was a passing remark because immediately afterwards, Didi looked eagerly at the pathway in front of him. Then, amused again by his openness, she led the way. Didi spent the next half-hour exclaiming over everything he saw. It was not possible that Estella had done all that on her own. And the imagination of it all! When they arrived at the archway covered in pink roses, he passed through it and then came back. He sat on one of the stone benches. Estella sat on the other.

'This is romantic. That was your purpose here, wasn't it, to make something with a romantic atmosphere?'

'Yes, there are different moods all around the gardens.'

'I can see that. These gardens say a lot about you. They say much more about you than you say yourself or your appearance says. Anybody who wishes to know you well must see these gardens.' He looked across at her, and for a moment, warmth appeared in his eyes. 'Anyhow, it's time to go,' he said, getting up.

'You don't want to see the vegetable garden?'

'Not this time. Next time, if you allow me to visit. I must get back to Melbourne. I have an important meeting at five o'clock.'

It was an abrupt end to their tour, but Estella did not question it. It was up to him as to how much he saw. Didi walked in silence as they made their way back to his car. He looked a little distracted. By the time they had reached the car, his mood had changed. She asked him if he was all right.

'Of course, I am. Why do you ask?' he said as he opened the door of the gleaming Ferrari. 'Say goodbye to your mother for me. I won't disturb her,' he continued, without giving her a chance to answer. He took her hand and kissed it. 'I'm glad I bumped into you. I was hoping to see you.' He lowered her hand and let it go. 'Perhaps I will see you again someday.'

'You're welcome to visit whenever you are in Binawarra. My mother's invitations are always sincere.'

He lingered a moment and seemed on the point of speaking, but then got in the car. He revved the engine once and, with a beep of the horn, took off, engine roaring, tyres screeching, and gravel and dirt spraying everywhere. Estella had to take a few paces back. A few seconds later, he had disappeared into the trees along the road that led up between the Wombat and Death Rock.

Estella sat on the verandah steps. Three men had been seeking her attention. Mr Rostowski was always polite and friendly, but she could not help thinking now that his attention had a purpose. He appeared at specific times, usually when she was with another male. She did not often come across him when she was alone. And today, although he was casual in his manner, he gave the impression he wanted to know who Bruce Butcher and Didi Al Refai were and what they were doing in Binawarra.

She had gradually become aware of the activity around her since— well, since she met Ruby and Geoff. And was that a coincidence? Whatever the case, bits and pieces of a puzzle were coming together. Bruce Butcher and Mr Rostowski were interested in her, however different their interest might be. And that interest appeared to have a purpose, a purpose belonging to the same puzzle. Their curiosity about Didi's presence in Binawarra also seemed part of the puzzle.

Didi was different, though. Although his presence featured in the puzzle, she was sure he was outside it. He wore his heart on his sleeve. He liked her, really liked her. He was intrigued with her, not because of her appearance but because of who she was. And his poorly hidden feelings did not make her uncomfortable. On the contrary, she liked it. The openness in his manner, in his conversation, connected with her, as it must with most people. One could not help being drawn by a person whose kindness and goodwill were so undisguised and so well expressed. She had been with him for over two hours, and not once did she feel weary of his company. In this openness of speech, he was the opposite of Geoff, whose precise thoughts she was hardly ever aware of. Geoff was far more complicated.

She wondered if they would meet again. During their conversation, he said several times that he intended to return to Binawarra, but on leaving, he expressed doubt. It was that restlessness—but it had been a pleasant meeting, and she was happy he had made the trip to see her. It was yet another improvement in her relationships with other young people. First Ruby and Geoff, and now Didi, yes, it was a significant improvement.

'Has your visitor gone?' said her father, appearing at the front door. 'I'm sorry I missed him. Your mother said he seemed a nice young man.'

'He was, Daddy.' She got up, put her arms around him, and rested her head against his shoulder.

Chapter 23

Truus's decision and Bill's counterattack

THAT SAME SATURDAY morning, Anneke van Engelen lingered at the florists outside the Trefcenter. A soft voice at her shoulder interrupted her thoughts.

'Goedemorgen, Mevrouw,' said Anneke, turning to see Mevrouw van den Donker's youthful face, shyly seeking her attention. 'We only seem to meet at this flower stand.'

'I've been watching for you. I wish to talk to you if you have a moment.'

'Of course, Mevrouw.'

'But not here,' she said, glancing around. 'There's a little coffee shop in the Trefcenter. Would that suit?'

'Yes, of course,' said Anneke, looking around and then following her.

'I spoke to you a little over three weeks ago,' she said when they were seated. 'I asked you about your uncle. You told me he was severely injured and somewhere in Australia.'

'That's right.'

'Can you tell me where?'

'Why ... why do you want to know?' she half-stammered.

'You don't want to tell me.'

'I'm sorry, Mevrouw,' said Anneke, 'my uncle told me it was better you don't know. He's afraid it might cause trouble with your husband. You know, because of your husband's attitude to the Catholic Church.'

'Did he tell you that?'

'Yes.'

'You mean you have been speaking to him about me?'

'Yes.'

'Oh.'

'My father rang him one night to discuss something. I spoke to him, too. I told him then I had seen you and that you had asked after him. He asked about you, too, by the way.'

'And he told you not to tell me where he was in case I contacted him?'

'That's right.'

'He was afraid it might cause trouble with my husband?'

'Yes. He was very concerned. He understands it's not easy for you. I'm sorry to be blunt, Mevrouw.'

'That's all right, Anneke. It cannot be a secret about our marriage. Please do not feel sorry for me. It's something of a relief to be by myself in the silence of the surrounding fields and canals. Others don't have it so easy.'

'It was solely out of concern for you.' She paused. 'There was something else.'

'What?'

'He said you were interested in the Church. That was the reason he was afraid of your husband's reaction if he should find out.'

Truus van den Donker fell silent and sipped her coffee. Anneke saw one solitary tear run down her cheek. Truus brushed it aside. 'Anneke, let me tell you the full story of what your brave uncle did, something a girl like you from a happy home would not have experienced. A few days before the allies arrived in Amsterdam at the end of the war, I was being pushed along by a stampeding crowd on Dam Square. German soldiers had fired on the people. I had Gerda in my arms. Just at the point where I thought I was going to fall, a hand reached out and grabbed me. That hand belonged to your uncle. He saved my baby and me from certain death.

'Afterwards, he comforted me until my husband found me. My husband had become very bitter about our circumstances by then and was not very friendly to your uncle despite his actions. We didn't know your uncle was a priest. He looked half-starved and was dressed like a dirty beggar, but there was something about him. The point is, Anneke, your uncle, without any worry about his own safety, saved my child and me from death and could only look with compassion on my husband, despite his offensiveness. I don't know whether it was the war that affected Cees, or if it would have happened the way it did, but my husband became worse in his bitterness and meanness. I bore the brunt of that. He was furious when he learned that your uncle was a priest and that he owed our lives to a papist. He confronted your father and uncle about it when they met by chance on Abbey Square.

'When I saw your uncle four years later, on market day, he was just as kind and tender. He touched my heart. That brief conversation was enough affection for some time. You see, Anneke, when you have nothing but bitterness and meanness to accompany you day in, day out, genuine unconditional concern can strike deep. Unfortunately, my daughter turned out to have the same character as her father. I had little tenderness from her. It is long since she went her own way, and I'm ashamed to admit that I do not miss her company.

'When I met your uncle on Marktplein in 1960, eleven years later, I saw how moved he was by my circumstances. I told him he was one of the few people in all those years who had treated me with genuine kindness and sympathy, and the fact that he was a Catholic priest was significant. I told him I had been inquiring into the Catholic Church and its teaching and had found that many things I had been taught were false or misrepresented. I learned later that he had gone to Papua and New Guinea. His kindness has stayed with me all those years. I saw him briefly again six years ago when he was back in Middelburg on sick leave. He hadn't changed—just as kind to me.'

'I'm very sorry to hear about your difficulties,' said Anneke. 'My uncle's sympathy for you hasn't changed.'

'Thank you, Anneke, I appreciate your concern.' She sniffled and wiped her nose. 'But let me get to the point. I had to face the fact some years ago that my marriage was finished. I have little contact with my husband—I believe he has a woman in Paris. He wouldn't make too much of a fuss if I left him. Some anger in the beginning, but that would subside, provided his business interests were unaffected.

'I'm independent because of the inheritances that came to me from relatives killed in the war. I haven't touched that money, and Cees has not needed it, not yet at least.' She stopped as if to gather courage. 'Anneke, I would like to be of help to your uncle, if he is a cripple and needs caring for. I don't know his circumstances. He may have enough help. But if he does not have the necessary attention, I want to offer myself. Please do not misunderstand. He is a priest, and that will never change. I am married, and that commitment will end with my death or Cees's death. My offer is unconditional. Let's say that I'm motivated by the charity the Lord exhorts us to. We believe in the same things, so we are both aware of what that means. Would you please pass that on to your uncle? Tell him I will come to him as a committed Christian and give him whatever help he needs.'

'Mevrouw, I don't know what to say ... Your generosity ... Are you so prepared to offer yourself like that?'

'Will you tell him?'

'It's an extraordinary offer, Mevrouw. The sacrifice is more than most nuns and religious brothers would be prepared for. And I don't know if it's possible.'

'Your uncle strengthened my faith. Even if I'm not Catholic or never become a Catholic, my faith as a Christian is stronger. Regarding its possibility, I know women are attached to presbyteries as housekeepers and cooks. It will be no different.'

'That's true.'

'Will you tell him?'

'Yes ... yes, of course, I'll pass the message on. But aren't you afraid of your husband's reaction?'

'Not anymore. While I was talking to your father on market day, Cees came and interrupted our conversation. He was very rude to your father and to me, for no reason. There's often one drop that causes an overflow. It happened that day. I thought it was pointless to persist in a situation of so much anger, bitterness, and meanness. I told Cees when I saw him later. He just shrugged and said I wouldn't have the nerve. As long as I did not interfere in his business, I could try what I wanted. That response decided me. It seemed pointless to persevere in an atmosphere of contempt. It is time for me to go. I am fortunate to have the means.'

'I assume your husband knows nothing about this?'

'No, I haven't seen him for a while. He is in Paris on business. That's what he said, at least.'

'Will you tell him when he gets back?'

'No, I will not tell him anything. He has lost the right to know what I'm doing. He tells me nothing and has told me nothing for years. Gerda knows more about his activities than I do. I sometimes have the impression she is connected with his business in some way.'

'What way?'

'I don't know. Over the last few years, there has been more contact between them than ever before. The contact was more than saying hello. Anyhow, Cees and Gerda are not the types for a simple chat. There's always a purpose.'

'You don't know what?'

'I have no idea. He rang me before he left for Paris to say Gerda would visit in a few weeks. He wanted her to stay with me. He didn't have the time to look after her, he said. That was strange because Gerda usually stays at the house in Middelburg.'

'He didn't say why she is coming, did he?'

'No. If it's got to do with his business, he would not tell me. He wants her out of the way for a particular reason, not because he cannot look after her. I know him well. There is always a reason.'

'How long will he be in Paris?'

'I don't know. Why are you interested?'

'I'm trying to understand,' said Aneke evasively. 'Uncle Jos will ask me about you. He would never agree to an arrangement that interfered with someone's marriage.'

'Please tell him that my offer, should he accept it, would not affect a marriage that was destroyed years ago. Please tell him that.'

'I will, Mevrouw. My father is due to ring him. I will talk to him then.'

'Thank you, Anneke. I appreciate it. Please give me a call when you hear from him. Here is my telephone number.' She handed her a piece of paper with her address and telephone number. 'I trust you'll keep this to yourself. I don't want Cees to know what I am doing, or even that I have had contact with you. He seems to have as much animosity for your father and you as he has for your uncle.' She bowed her head for a moment. 'I will never understand how he could take such a dislike to a person who saved his wife and child from being crushed to death.'

Anneke cycled home, weighed down by Truus van den Donker's sad circumstances. She was relieved to find her father alone. 'I have something to tell you about Meneer and Mevrouw van den Donker,' she said, sitting beside him on the lounge settee.

'That poor woman!' Frans said when she had finished. 'To be driven to such a point— It's difficult to believe that man could be so hard-hearted, especially to someone as soft as that woman.'

'Do his trip to Paris and Gerda's visit have anything to do with Uncle Jos's inquiries?'

'It's hard to say. I don't know enough about the situation Jos is in. I wouldn't be surprised if it had. I will call him tomorrow after Mass. As for her request, I don't know. Uncle Jos is more or less isolated in his country parish. He is there for disciplinary reasons.'

'I assume it's because he won't go along with the Terror that has erupted since the Council.'

'Yes, that's right. So he is probably in a position where he could use a housekeeper.' He scratched his head. 'Mevrouw van den Donker's offer is amazing. How would he react? He would need permission, probably.'

The next day, Frans rang his brother and passed on Truus's message and the information about Cees and Gerda.

'Yes, Frans, that information about Meneer van den Donker and his daughter is important, and it has something to do with a situation that is getting bigger by the day. Please continue to pass on whatever you hear about those two.'

'And Mevrouw van den Donker's message?' said Frans, before his brother could go on.

'I don't know, Frans. It's heart-wrenching to hear of that poor woman's suffering. What she's offering is possible in principle. My question is whether this is right for Truus, whether she is ready for such a commitment.'

'Truus ...?'

'She asked me to call her Truus. You know that.'

'Forgive my frankness, brother. Is there something personal in this?'

'You know my sympathy for Mevrouw van den Donker is more personal than usual for a priest. But Frans, you also know there is no danger of it being any more than that.'

'Okay, I understand. What am I to say to her? Can I give her your address?'

'Tell her that her offer deeply touches me. It's a credit to her faith. I will have to think about it. You can say in principle it's possible if that's what she really wants. But there is much to consider, not least of all permission from my superiors.'

'Will you write to her yourself?'

'Yes, that's a good idea. What's her address?'

THE FOLLOWING morning, Miss Barker listened closely to a summary of Fr van Engelen's latest conversation with his brother Frans.

'Let's review what we know at this moment,' she said when he had finished. 'Gerda van den Donker is parading here as a teacher of English with a specialty in counselling. The truth is that she is Dutch, is a linguistics expert, and heads an association called The Institute for the Rights of Regional Dialects and Language Custom. My inquiries tell me this is a small, obscure left-wing group that has only shown up on the intelligence radar in recent years. No direct link has arisen so far with other radical organisations, but the evidence suggests, only suggests, links with a few radical groups in the Netherlands and Germany. Again, there is no direct link with acts of violence, but a few unsolved political deaths point loosely in their direction, among a couple of other comparable organisations. The problem is establishing a reason for the killings, if that's what they were. There is none at the moment. Why kill someone because of a concern for preserving a regional dialect?'

'If the fanaticism is deep-rooted enough, then there are no boundaries,' commented Fr. van Engelen. 'That's inherent in rationalistic ideologies, as you are aware.'

'That's an explanation. But I can't help but suspect something else is involved. I just cannot put my finger on it.' She tapped her mouth with her fist in her characteristic manner. 'Let's go on. Gerda has focused on Estella, either to exploit her or to recruit her to the cause, or perhaps both.

She has come all the way from London to do this. She has guided her towards a career in public relations and arranged talks with powerful heads of international companies who appeared in an obscure country town to speak to her. Either Gerda or the university has extremely useful contacts, or something special is attracting them here. Is it Estella's beauty? But that seems a trivial pretext. After all, those men can have their choice of women. Can you conceive of something extra that Estella has to offer, Father?'

'It may be just her beauty, her untouched beauty.'

'I can't imagine it. Estella is the last to be seduced by men old enough to be her father, no matter how wealthy they are. The odds are overwhelmingly against them. It may be a lot of trouble for nothing.'

'Perhaps something untouched and hard to get is the challenge?'

'Those powerful men could not be so trivial, surely?'

Fr. van Engelen shrugged and made no reply.

'Two other events seem related to Gerda's activities,' Miss Barker continued. 'Mr. McKinnon dies in strange circumstances after he hit on the reason Miss Bicknell has directed Estella to a career in public relations. Second, the town newspaper, otherwise an unimpressive country newspaper, has launched a concerted attack on Bill, linking him with the death of McKinnon and a group of alleged sexual deviants in the school. Suddenly, the newspaper is in demand. How is this linked to Gerda? McKinnon's demise can be explained, but why the attempt to destroy the high school principal?'

'To remove him? He may be an obstacle.'

'But why? Or is this a move to get rid of an ideological undesirable?'

'Perhaps. Perhaps both,' said the priest. 'The aim to disrupt the war veterans' celebration is ideologically driven.'

'Okay, that sounds reasonable. Now, where does Didi Al Refai fit in?'

'My guess is nowhere,' said Fr. van Engelen. 'It is a sheer coincidence he met Estella. He was intrigued enough to visit Binawarra. He said himself it was a coincidence. I asked Estella if he dropped her off straight after lunch.

He did, but stayed half an hour looking at her gardens. Then he left, saying he would leave for Los Angeles today. He made no further arrangement with her.'

'Let's assume you're right,' said Miss Barker. 'We'll remember he is the son of the powerful company head who has taken an interest in Estella. Now, about Boris Rostowski, he is in league with Gerda, but why? Why is he keeping an eye on Estella? As far as I can gather, he only speaks to her when she is with another male. And he is always polite and respectful, according to Estella. It appears he is keeping a guard on her.'

'The idea that his surveillance is to preserve Estella for—it seems absurd,' said the priest.

'I agree. We're missing something crucial. If I'm right that Rostowski murdered Mr McKinnon and that prostitute, then the stakes are very high.'

'Very high—and very dangerous.'

'Now about this latest information, Father, we learn that Gerda's father is in Paris on business and that Gerda is expected home in a few weeks. Mr Al Refai's headquarters are in Paris, and a few weeks will take us beyond the Anzac Day march. If these things are all linked, we are heading for a climax, aren't we?'

'It would seem so.'

'It's now vital we stay alert to whatever unfolds and keep Estella closely watched. We can do our bit, but to ensure effective protection, I will ask Captain Shawcross over to Binawarra for the next few weeks. We must also keep Bill on an even keel. He's not used to this sort of nasty political infighting, and he is not well.'

'Not well?'

'No, not at all. His blood pressure is too high, and his weight has become a serious problem. He's in the danger zone for a heart attack or stroke. The stress he is under may put him over the edge. Perhaps, Father, you can speak to him, I mean, from the religious point of view. He'll bluster but will listen, nevertheless. He needs to reconcile things.'

'I'll try.'

'All right, that's it. I'll be off.'

Without more ado, Miss Barker was on her feet and walking towards Melbourne Road while Fr van Engelen hobbled back to his presbytery.

BILL HUCKERBY sat at his desk, trying to ignore the sick feeling that had been with him for a few weeks. He suspected Miss Barker's warnings about his health were right, but there was no time to attend to it. Now he had to concentrate what energy he had on the problem caused by Bob McKinnon's death and the scandalous lies spread by the town's newspaper editor. He had thought long and hard about Flo's advice. He had taken it seriously, considering her experience. Her recommendations, however, were not him. He would flounder if he tried to manipulate circumstances the way she suggested. His instinct was to deal with it the way he dealt with all problems: go and meet it head-on. Let the truth be his weapon. He had never compromised his principles when it came to the crunch. He would not do it now. He had been accused; he would react with the truth. He took Flo's advice to plan a response, but he would do it in his own way. Let the cards fall where they will.

'Ms Bicknell is here to see you,' said Mrs Charing, interrupting his thoughts.

It occurred to him that he hardly ever saw Mrs Charing before she addressed him. She seemed to slink into his presence. And that was another issue. He would have to deal with her treachery. There was no other word for her behaviour. He had given her much consideration and understanding, but that now had to end. 'Show her in, please, Mrs Charing.'

'I have received an excellent report from Sandhurst University about Estella Winterbine's recent visit there,' said Miss Bicknell, declining the offer of a seat. 'I have a copy for you here.' She placed an envelope on his desk. 'Her supervisor was impressed with her presence, quiet confidence, and ability to articulate her thoughts clearly and directly. The two company heads who met her were fulsome in their praise. She is young, they said, but in a few years, with more maturity and confidence, she will make an outstanding representative for any major company. They would have no hesitation even now in offering her work and training. This was my assessment, if you remember.'

This speech, Bill observed, was delivered in an officious, almost arrogant manner. Now that he thought about it, she always spoke in this way.

'That is indeed a marvellous report, and I do remember your assessment. Your judgment has been vindicated.'

'Thank you.'

She never addressed him with a title. There was no 'Bill' or 'Mr Huckerby'. That was odd for a teacher responsible for advising students on careers. Good manners were essential in job interviews.

'I assume there are further recommendations.'

'It is not me who is making the recommendation. An invitation has arrived from the university for Estella to attend a work experience program. Several companies offer this program to students who show potential. It is an offer that should not be ignored.'

'No?'

'No.' She hesitated. 'Do you have an objection?'

'Miss Bicknell,' he said, searching for the right words, 'your eagerness to steer Miss Winterbine in this direction does not go unnoticed. Is there an object in view?'

'Whatever do you mean?'

'I mean, you seem to be guiding Miss Winterbine— It raises the question of why.'

'I am treating Estella Winterbine no differently from others,' said Miss Bicknell, stiffening. 'You have all the details. It's all open. I'm surprised that you are questioning me in this way. If you don't have confidence in my handling of this, I will pass it on to someone else.' Her gaze remained steady.

'No, no, Miss Bicknell, these are routine inquiries to keep abreast of what is going on.' He shifted a little. It vexed him that he had no substantial grounds to question her further. He only had Flo's hunches. It was not enough, despite suspecting that Ms Bicknell was bluffing. 'You are recommending that Estella attend this work experience program?'

'Yes, but it is up to you to approve it, and her parents must approve it. The program is supervised, of course. The contact will again be Bruce Butcher at the university. The students are to meet at the Grand Pacific Hotel in the city, where the representatives of several companies will take care of them. The companies will bear all the expenses. Estella has to do nothing more than take herself and her clothes for a two-night stay. The students will be brought back to Bendigo on Sunday evening.'

'Two nights' stay? When is this planned for?'

'It is two full days, the 25th, Anzac Day, and 26th April, Saturday. The students are to return on Sunday evening, the 27th.'

'Anzac Day!'

'Yes. The companies intend to treat the students well, giving them more or less a fully paid holiday for that long weekend.'

'Very generous.'

'These are big companies that pick the most promising students for this program. It's a great compliment to Estella.'

'Yes, you are right.' He hesitated. 'Leave it with me, Miss Bicknell. I will discuss it with Estella's parents. There is time to think about it.'

He picked up the report when she had left the room. She was right. It was an excellent report, and it all seemed in order. He had nowhere to go. Everything so far was above board. It made him doubt Flo's judgment. She may be right about the political agenda, but was everything the result of Edith Bicknell's manipulation? Then he remembered Aine's stark warning. In any case, he had other things to do at that moment. He picked up the phone, checked the number he had written down, and dialled.

Sometime later, he called Mrs Charing into his office and asked her to inform the teaching staff that there would be a meeting after the final bell. He would not keep people long. He then phoned different people in the town. At the end of a half hour, he was satisfied that he was making the proper response. Everyone he spoke to understood his situation and was critical of the editor of the *Binawarra and District Mail*. Perhaps he had got too excited. It was a small bushfire, and he would soon have it under control. He thought with embarrassment of the troubled state he had been in the previous week. He had handled difficulties in the past. He would handle this one, too.

'Well, Bill, you're looking happier than the last time I saw you,' said Miss Barker, strolling by a glaring Mrs Charing, 'but not healthier. Working out a few strategies?'

'Yes, Flo, I am.' He put the phone down. 'Come on, follow me. Don't worry about the door. Mrs Charing, I'll be back in a minute.'

'This is a departure,' she said when they were alone in the staff room. 'What are you up to?'

'You know, Flo, I haven't realised it before this. You have a very suspicious mind.'

'Could it be that I pay more attention to what's happening around me than most people—than you, for example?'

'And you always have an answer,' he said with an accusatory smile. 'Come on, take your cup of tea. I will explain.'

Back in his office, he shut the door and put his finger to his mouth. 'Please sit down, Flo,' he said in his everyday voice. 'I want to talk to you about the newspaper reports.' Putting his finger to his mouth again, he pointed to the tape recorder on the shelf behind his desk. He examined it and then pointed at the buttons. The recording button was pressed. 'The best way to handle the newspaper reports is to meet them head-on and respond with the truth. Nothing the paper has said is right about the school or me. I welcome any inquiry by a competent authority.'

'I'm glad to hear it,' said Miss Barker.

Bill explained his intentions, with Miss Barker punctuating his explanation with polite, meaningless comments. After twenty minutes, he invited her to follow him again.

'Just going to check something with Miss Barker, Mrs Charing. I'll be back in a few minutes.' They walked to the sickroom, remained there a minute, and then returned to his office. Once inside, Bill shut the door and checked the tape recorder. 'As I thought,' he said, opening the cassette compartment. 'A fresh tape cued to the beginning. What a fool I've been. To think that woman has been taping my conversations. And for how long and how often, I could only guess.'

'Well done, Bill, that's the way to go about it.'

'She may have taped our recent conversations. Have you thought of that?'

'Not likely,' said Miss Barker. 'She had to have a warning, as she did in this case.'

'For once, Flo, that occurred to me, too. Besides, there would be signs by now.'

'You're getting the picture.'

'It was the only way I could check to see if she was spying on me.' He sat at his desk. 'I don't imagine you'll agree with everything I plan to do. About the newspaper, I'm going to meet Collins head-on with the truth, show him that the dissemination of lies will work against him.'

'Oh, Bill, the dissemination of lies by newspapers shows that it works for them. Come on, tell me, what have you done?'

'If I can't work with the truth and rely on the goodwill of our fellow citizens, things have come to a sorry pass.'

'Things are at a sorry pass. The people who greet the truth with goodwill are becoming a voiceless group.'

'I will triumph or go down with the truth.'

Miss Barker looked at her friend and shook her head. 'The time you grew up in, Bill, has passed. I admire your courage. I suppose I should expect nothing more from you. But will you be happy with a fruitless sacrifice? They will destroy you, mark my words. You are facing heavy artillery with a popgun.'

'I will persist in holding the belief that braving danger with honesty and principle will contribute to the right order of things in the end.'

'A very Christian perspective, and I cannot argue with you over that. It leaves me with no choice but to support you as best I can.'

'I appreciate that, Flo.'

'Now tell me what you have done.'

'I phoned Collins and challenged him about the lies in his paper and the source of those lies.'

'He claimed the immunity of confidential sources, no doubt.'

'Correct.'

'And he would stick to his position no matter what pressure he suffered,' said Miss Barker.

'That's about it.'

'Did you threaten him?'

'Of course not. I told him people would see through his lies. People already had a good idea of what he was like. His exclusive not-so-secret advertising deals speak for themselves.'

'He will present that as a threat.'

'How?'

'You wait and see. It will be best to learn from experience. I must go. I must keep my cover. It's even more important now that you have wandered onto the battlefield with your popgun.' She got up. 'You know, Bill, talk about the right order of things is Catholic thinking.'

'I wouldn't know. That's the way I see it.'

'We'll talk again, no doubt,' she said as she opened the door. She looked around to see where Mrs Charing was. She was nowhere in sight. 'You should keep an eye on your weight,' she whispered. 'You'll need to stay as fit as you can now.'

She left him reflecting on his undertakings. There was no going back now, no matter how dire Flo's warnings were.

Two days later, Bill spread the Wednesday edition of the *Binawarra and District Mail* on his desk. He had prepared himself for the worst, and now he saw he would not be disappointed. The front-page headline said it all: **School restless as cover-up continues.**

'The unresolved tension at Binawarra High School continues to disrupt the school's routine. Teachers are waiting for action following startling revelations about the senior teacher who died in questionable circumstances. The malaise among the teachers is causing confusion among the students.

'Sources at the school claim that, instead of finding out what the teacher and others were involved in, the principal is spending his time shoring up his administration. He has spent long hours on the phone seeking the support of powerful figures in the town. The same sources said it would be better to come clean about the problems and take steps to sort out an entrenched administration rather than perpetuate the problems.

'One staff member said that, to the professional eye, behavioural problems usually associated with sexual abuse could be observed in at least one student. This could be the tip of the iceberg. It is now imperative to uncover any corrupt clique in the school and its links with outside groups.

'Evidently, the affair still has a long way to run. The embattled principal rang the editor of this newspaper to refute the charges. At the same time, he made some thinly veiled threats against Mr Collins (see editorial). Yet the charges have not been refuted, and this newspaper stands by its information and the claim that more revelations are to come.'□

'Sheer fantasy,' Bill exclaimed. 'What behavioural problems? Where is he getting all this stuff?' He turned to the middle pages for the editorial. The heading read: **Threats to freedom of the press.**

'Matters have come to a sorry pass when the principal of a high school will brazenly try to muzzle the local newspaper. Incredible as it may seem to our readers, Mr William Huckerby, principal of Binawarra High School for more years than anyone cares to remember, rang the editor of this newspaper to force him to 'call the dogs off.' Unseemly personal threats accompanied this attempt. They were not physical threats but, perhaps far worse, threats to the editor's reputation and credibility. Moral blackmail.

'The editor of the *Binawarra and District Mail* wants to make it plain that no threat whatever will cause this newspaper to deviate from its responsibilities. We will not desist until the situation at the high school is brought out into the open and an independent investigation into the school's administration takes place.

'There is a string of questions requiring an urgent answer. What was Mr McKinnon really up to in the school? Who are his associates and sympathisers? Who was protecting him? What students were the victims of his predatory behaviour? How deep does the problem go? Are there substantial links to groups outside the school? The boy who died with Mr McKinnon came from Melbourne. Were there others?

'This newspaper will not rest until these questions are answered. The beacon of press freedom will guide the editor and his staff.'

'Call the dogs off?' said Bill aloud. 'I never said any such thing.' He rested his head on his hands and stared at the wall. How can revealing actual circumstances be construed as a threat? Flo was right. Collins was pursuing a campaign, a barefaced campaign. How could anyone fall for it? The letters to the editor showed some people were swallowing it whole. There were eight letters, all agreeing with the editorial that an investigation ought to be held into the school's running. One letter wanted the investigation extended to the schools in the neighbouring towns. 'People's minds will not rest,' said the letter writer, 'until they are satisfied the evil has not spread to other schools. Our children must be protected, whatever the costs.'

'This is just whipping up mob hysteria,' he said aloud again. He caught himself turning to see whether the tape recorder was on. 'Keep calm,' he muttered. He pushed the paper aside and wiped the perspiration from his forehead.

'I will be with the school nurse for ten minutes,' he said to the three ladies in the office.

Miss Barker was sitting at her desk with the newspaper laid out before her when he entered. She held her hands up in a helpless gesture.

'I know, you warned me. But it doesn't discourage me.'

'There are particularly hurtful letters to the editor, aren't there?'

'Yes, yes, there are.' He sat on the sickbed and wiped his forehead again. 'Have you got something for a headache?'

Miss Barker produced two tablets, filled a glass with water, and handed them to him.

'I have such a pain in my head,' he said, giving the glass back to her.

'What are you going to do?'

'I'm going to draft a response and insist the newspaper print it. I will challenge those who claim to have evidence to produce it.'

'It may be wise to wait and see what happens. Collins and whoever is behind this may not have played their full hand. It may backfire on you if you throw your cards on the table too soon.'

'This is not a card game, Flo. I will come back from a position of principle each time. Excuse the pun. I won't play their sordid game. You know how I feel.'

'Has anyone come forward?'

'I spoke to the combined staff twice and each time encouraged anyone with a complaint or vital information to come forward. No one has appeared.'

'What about Jane Cox and Edith Bicknell? I suggest they told Sergeant Willis about McKinnon's sexual tastes.'

'I gave them ample opportunity to come forward. They have not yet done so. Now I will talk to the senior teachers individually. I will draft my letter after I complete these interviews. But I must get back. I set a trap for Mrs Charing.'

'What are you going to do if she walks into it?'

'I will dismiss her on the spot.'

'You should reflect on that, too. Collins will use it against you, especially if it is done hastily and without apparent cause.'

'Let him. He may win these battles. We will see who'll win the war.'

'You may end up a crippled victor. The vanquished may retreat in defeat but whole in body. Ever hear of a Pyrrhic victory?'

'Flo, you have an answer for everything.' He forced a smile. 'But your support now is indispensable.' He got up to go.

'Do you have any idea which student is referred to here?' She pointed to the editorial, which was open in front of her.

'You mean with the behavioural problems.' Miss Barker nodded. 'No idea. It's made up. Outrageous. Why? Do you suspect someone?'

'I've been thinking about it. Whose behaviour could be represented as problem behaviour? I mean in a psychological sense. Don't forget, Bill, we're not dealing with people of goodwill and honesty. It's about manipulation for tactical reasons.'

'My God, do you have someone in mind?'

She hesitated. 'No, I don't want to say yet. Let me reflect further.'

Back in his office, he checked the tape recorder. Yes, it was on. He then called for Mrs Charing and instructed her to call the subject coordinators to his office when they were free. He wanted to see Miss Bicknell at the first opportunity. Over the following three periods, he spoke to the coordinators. They had nothing to tell him. They were aware of Bob McKinnon's particular tendencies. They thought everybody was. They were vaguely aware of his trips to Melbourne, but many teachers regularly went to Melbourne for the weekend. There was nothing remarkable in that.

Some were not aware of the close relationship with Suzie McNamara. There was no evidence of Bob molesting any students. They agreed that he had been a conscientious teacher. They also saw no signs that other teachers shared Bob's sexual and political views. On the contrary, most did not want to hear about it. They were content to let the Lefties argue with Bob about his ideas. Did they take Suzie McNamara's accusations seriously? Not at all. She was obviously in a state of shock. People knew about the deep antagonism between Jane Cox and Bob McKinnon, but murder? Ridiculous! As for behavioural problems, one could classify several students in that way. They were not willing to say if it had to do with sexual abuse. Were they willing to state that publicly? They were.

The interviews took him through to lunch, and as he left his office, he reminded Mrs Charing that he wanted to see Miss Bicknell at the first opportunity. When he returned, he heard she would be the first to see him. He checked the tape recorder. It was not recording. Then he checked the files. The files on his desk had been disturbed, and the filing cabinet drawers opened. Talk about revelations! And to think he had given Mrs Charing special attention because of her marital problems. Miss Bicknell arrived five minutes later.

'Sit down, Miss Bicknell,' he said, pulling the armchair in front of his desk into position. Reluctantly, she sat down. 'Let me get straight to the point. The town's newspaper editor has levelled certain charges at me. What do you know about those charges and their origins?'

'I have been at this school and town for a little over two months. I am not familiar enough with the town and its citizens to comment authoritatively.'

'I would like to know what you do know, Miss Bicknell. Did you know of Mr McKinnon's sexual tastes?'

'I heard vague reports about him.'

'Vague, only vague?'

'Yes.'

'Who made the comments?'

'They were general observations by different people.'

'Who in particular?'

She hesitated but remained calm. 'I am reluctant to name names because various people made the comments. I should not name some people and omit to name others. That would not be fair.'

'Miss Jane Cox, did she say something?'

'She might have.'

'How did you react to Miss McNamara's accusation?'

'I don't react to ridiculous nonsense like that.'

'And Miss Cox?'

'You should ask her.'

'Miss Bicknell, why are you so cagey?'

'Am I being cagey? I thought I was answering your questions. I should leave others to make their own answers.'

'This is straightforward, Miss Bicknell. The newspaper has made charges which I completely reject, and they are based on sources in this school. Are you one of those sources?'

'No. I have only ever spoken to the editor of the *Binawarra and District Mail* in passing—as good as not having spoken with him at all.'

'Are you sure?' he said, remembering that Fr. van Engelen had seen her coming from his office several times.

'I beg your pardon. Of course, I am sure.'

'Do you know who is feeding the editor with his information?'

'No, of course not.'

'Let me be honest, Miss Bicknell, I find that difficult to believe.'

'Am I to conclude that you don't trust me or have no confidence in me?'

'I'm not saying that. I find it difficult to believe that, as the person with special responsibility for the students' psychological health, you are not aware of the concerns of one or more of the teachers. Remember, it was your qualifications in counselling that particularly recommended you for your position.'

'I am not privy to the thoughts of all the teachers. I depend on them telling me their concerns.'

'Then nobody has mentioned these concerns? You have not heard that companions or sympathisers of Bob McKinnon are in the school, or that he had connections with outside groups? You don't know if there has been any abuse of the students?'

She hesitated again. She was in a corner.

'As I said in the beginning, I have not been in the school long enough to know in detail what is going on. It would be unfair of me to drag someone's name into this affair. You must ask those who have been here longer and let them speak for themselves.'

'Miss Cox, for example?'

'You could speak to Ms Cox. She has been here some time, I understand.'

'I am to conclude, then, that in addition to not being the source of the charges, you have no evidentiary support for them?'

'They are your conclusions.'

'Again, why so cagey?'

'Your lack of confidence is deeply troubling. I must have the principal's support and confidence to do my work effectively. Without that, I will be forced to review my position here.'

'That seems an extreme reaction, Miss Bicknell?'

'It is a reaction based on the mode of questioning you are subjecting me to.'

'I simply want some straight answers to some straightforward questions. I'm not getting them. And I don't know why.'

'I have given you what are fair answers under the circumstances.'

'All right,' he said. 'There are no further questions at this point. I may come back to you.'

'You make it sound like I am a suspect in a crime,' she said, showing some indignation.

'I'm just trying to get to the bottom of serious allegations, Miss Bicknell. I regret I must ask uncomfortable questions.'

'Your questioning raises serious questions about professional confidence.'

'I also regret you have taken that view,' he said, not believing she was serious.

'By the way, Miss Bicknell, who do you think the anonymous source is talking about when he, or she, is referring to one of the students with behavioural problems?'

'I would rather not say at this point. It is a sensitive matter.'

'So it's your opinion that there is a student with behavioural problems caused by sexual abuse?'

'I'm not saying that.'

'What are you saying?'

'I will comment when the person is named.'

'All right, we'll leave it there.'

Miss Bicknell left him without further comment, and he settled at his desk to weigh things up. He was convinced that he had her on the back foot. He was confident, too, that if that student were named, all hell would break loose. No student in his school had problems caused by sexual abuse. That he was sure of. The interviews had gone well. No one had yet supported the newspaper's allegations. A false accusation like that would backfire monumentally on the accuser. He had three more staff to interview, and he did not expect anything different from them. On the surface, it looked like Mrs Charing was the source of Collins's charges. But where was she getting it from? The accusations went well beyond anything on the recordings, and she did not seem smart enough to make up such charges out of the tapes' scant material. Someone else was using the tapes, probably. Who?

His interviews took suspicion away from the school staff, despite Flo's insinuations. Was it Collins for mere mercenary reasons? Perhaps. But again, like Mrs Charing, he did not seem to have the necessary information. If he had known anything about Bob McKinnon's activities, why would he have left reporting it until now? He was opening himself up to charges of journalistic negligence. The other possibility was that a disgruntled staff member was lying and causing trouble. If that were the case, the affair would peter out. Whatever the case, without real open support, Collins would have to back down in the face of a challenge to put up or shut up. He started to relax. He should have taken this action sooner instead of letting anxiety get the better of him.

GERDA Vrouwendijk returned to her office to ponder the meeting. Despite the principal giving the impression he had the affair under control and would soon get the better of his accusers, she was happy that things were still swinging her way. He was suffering enormous damage, and he appeared not to realise it. The longer the accusations and suspicions dragged on, the more the mud would stick. She was confident in her worst-case scenario that the principal would be irreparably damaged by the time the *Binawarra and District Mail* had to call off its attack for lack of evidentiary support. And she still had ammunition to fire off.

Moreover, Joyce Charing was so exuberant about the success of her sneakiness that she was becoming indiscreet. She was banking on that indiscretion becoming so obvious that the principal would be forced to take action. The focus would stay on her for a while. Whatever happened,

Mrs Charing had served her purpose, and the affair was on an unstoppable course of its own. Indeed, even if something occurred to force her, Miss Bicknell, to withdraw, the affair would carry on without her. She had one more crucial task ahead of her in Binawarra.

BY FRIDAY morning, Bill was satisfied he could launch his first counter-attack. None of the senior staff would support Collins's charge, and he now had enough evidence of Mrs Charing's treachery. He would refute Collins's charges and neutralise what seemed to be his primary source in the school. He read through his neatly compiled notes. He wanted everything to be perfectly in order.

'Mrs Charing,' he said, emerging from his office, 'I will be with the school nurse.' Shortly after, he entered the sickroom. 'Are you ready?'

'I hope this works for you,' said Miss Barker, unable to hide her amuse-ment. 'It's a nice little deceitful plan.'

'No, it's a justified trap.' A minute later, he entered his office with Miss Barker in tow. 'Mrs Charing, I don't want any interruptions.' He closed the door and checked the tape recorder. He winked at Miss Barker. They talked for ten minutes before he rose and beckoned her to follow him. 'I will be gone for the next half-hour, Mrs Charing.' He walked through the reception area and out the front door while Miss Barker returned to her sickroom.

Mrs Charing watched the principal's car pass through the gates. She went to his office, took the cassette from the tape recorder, and replaced it with a fresh one. She rummaged among the files on the desk. She returned to the front office, put the cassette in her drawer, and, without paying attention to her two office colleagues, proceeded to copy pages from the file.

'Mrs Charing, the principal wants you to stop what you are doing.' Miss Barker was beside her with one hand on the photocopier's lid and the other on the file.

'I beg your pardon,' said Mrs Charing, overcome by surprise. 'What right do you have—?'

'Miss Barker has my authority,' said the principal, walking out of breath into the reception area. 'Please stand back, Mrs Charing. Now, Miss Barker and ladies, you are witnesses to this.' He picked up the file and examined it. He opened the copier's lid and took out the page that had just been copied. 'Mrs. Charing, you are copying this material without my authorisation.' He took his notes from his trouser pocket. 'Furthermore, you have been taping my confidential conversations. By my count, you have made three unauthorised recordings this week, the third being just now.' He named the day and the time of each recording. 'Miss Barker, will you check Mrs Charing's desk drawers and her handbag. Move back, Mrs Charing. I advise you that if you do not cooperate, I will be obliged to call the police.'

Shocked and dismayed, Joyce Charing moved away while Miss Barker checked her desk drawer and handbag. The tears began to flow. There was nothing of interest in the handbag, but the search of the desk produced that morning's tape and some pages from other files that had lain on the principal's desk.

'Bob McKinnon's private details,' said the principal, examining the pages. He turned to the pale and weeping office secretary. 'Mrs Charing, I am immediately terminating your employment. Miss Barker, will you escort Mrs Charing from the premises and stay with her until she has left the school grounds? Mrs Charing, you are not to venture onto school property until the matter has been thoroughly investigated.'

Mrs Charing, shaken by shock and humiliation, went to say something, but she could only open her mouth. Miss Barker handed over her handbag.

'No, Mrs Charing,' said the principal, seeing her reach for her desk drawer. 'You are to take your handbag. Nothing else. We will check your desk later, and any property belonging to you will be returned as soon as convenient. Please accompany Miss Barker.'

Bent, sobbing, and stumbling, Mrs Charing followed Miss Barker, but at the front doors, she swung around. 'You will pay for this, you fat, lazy fool! Don't think for one moment that I will lie down and have you walk over me again.'

'Walk over you, Mrs Charing? You have had more consideration than any other person on staff!'

'Hah!' she cried, wiping her face and smudging her make-up so that she looked quite wild. 'You wait. You haven't heard the last of this! You and all the other bullies will pay. You men are not going to trample over women in this way!' She disappeared through the doorway.

'Good heavens, what other bullies?' said Bill, surprised at the sudden intensity of her anger. 'I had no idea she was like that.'

'She's gone,' said Miss Barker, returning to Bill's office ten minutes later. 'I had to wait until she composed herself before I let her drive away. She was in a dangerous mood, not because of shock but of anger. You did not expect her last reaction, did you?'

'No. Did you? I have never seen anything like it in her.'

'I had my suspicions. I would take her warning seriously if I were you. She may have something up her sleeve. Is there anything in your administration that she could use against you—manipulate against you?'

'Absolutely nothing!'

'Don't relax too much. Be on your guard.'

'Now you're worrying me. You've been uncanny in your assessment so far. What on earth could she have on me?'

'We will have to wait and see what they draw out of their hat next.'

'They?'

'Yes, Bill, she's just a tool in this.'

Chapter 24

The property scandal breaks

THE FOLLOWING morning, Saturday, Joanne reached for the phone, her hand quivering.

'Joanne, it's Flo. You haven't seen today's edition of the *Binawarra and District Mail*?'

'No, don't tell me it's something else?'

'It's not good. I'll come around. Don't let Bill know yet. I want to be there when he reads this. He will need support.'

'Can it be any worse than the allegations about a sex scandal?'

'In a way, yes. Wait until I'm there to hear what Bill has to say. This is something I know nothing about. And, Joanne, do not answer any phone calls before I get there.'

Five minutes later, Miss Barker's car pulled up outside. Next thing, Bill cried, 'Oh no!' He shuffled through the front door, holding the *Binawarra and District Mail* up in front of him. Joanne and Miss Barker followed him into the lounge, where he fell into an armchair. He held out the paper to Joanne and put his head in his hands.

'What!' she gasped, staring at the front page. The editorial heading read:

High school sacking unleashes property scandal.

'There have been sensational developments at Binawarra High School, just as this newspaper thought the situation there could not get any worse.

'Yesterday, the principal's hard-working secretary, Mrs Joyce Charing, was sacked on her feet and escorted from the school premises, bag in hand. The humiliating treatment of Mrs Charing was so sudden and clean that many of the staff did not know about it until school had finished.

'Mrs Charing told a reporter from the *Binawarra and District Mail* that despite the shock and humiliation, she had no doubt about the reasons and was calm enough to give a full account.

'She spoke of a property scandal that would shock the town's citizens. There was something seriously wrong with the power-sharing in the town, she said. She had no hesitation in laying the blame squarely at the feet of a small clique of men who had managed to concentrate political power in their tiny, unrepresentative group over the years.

'Conscious of its public responsibility, this newspaper reports Mrs Charing's allegations:

'* Mr Huckerby has long been using the school's time, property, and money to advance his private business interests.

'* Those business interests centre on property purchase and development in Binawarra and nearby towns.

'* Mr Huckerby has amassed a property portfolio over the years, most of which has been to the disadvantage of the ordinary mums and dads who want to buy or sell a house.

'* In the worst case, Mr Huckerby squeezed the town council to acquire the plum properties that make up the old Miners Emporium at a fire sale. That building now has a National Trust classification, and its value has skyrocketed.

'When questioned about the seriousness of the last allegation, Mrs Charing said she had all the evidence. Her only object was to see that the abuses of power in the town stopped.'□

'This is a lie, a total fabrication,' exclaimed Joanne.

'I can't believe that woman has behaved in such a deceitful manner,' said Bill. 'Of course, it's a lie. To think that she has been assembling evidence against me all that time—false evidence. She has got to be the source for the sex scandal allegations.'

'I wouldn't be too sure about that,' said Miss Barker. 'Is this all Mrs Charing's work here? Is this her voice? Is Mrs Charing clever enough to mount a case like this? Since when has she been politically active?'

'Never, come to think of it. No, she's not bright enough. That's the one thing that stopped me from holding her responsible until now. Yes, you are right, Flo. Who, for heaven's sake, is behind it?'

'First, fill me in on your property dealings.'

'That has been my way of ensuring our future,' said Bill wearily. 'I'm an economics and accounting graduate, qualified to be my own financial adviser. The simple truth is that we have invested in property. We have competed in the market with everyone else. There have been no special exclusive deals. The record will show that. It will show we have acquired eleven properties through the usual channels.'

'Yes, Flo, this is all true,' said Joanne. 'The Miners Emporium had nothing to do with the council. Frank Fonori, who happens to be the mayor, was the owner of the property, not the council. Frank wanted to sell because he was in financial trouble. The price he needed was above the market price. He knew that, we knew that, and the property agents knew that. It was no use advertising for a price he wouldn't get. Things looked grim for him. So now Bill did what he has so often done for people in this town.

'He had a good look at what we could do. He talked with Frank, and he talked with the bank about finance. There was much discussion, some of it taking place during school hours, no doubt. But if I added up the private time and energy Bill has devoted to the school and the town economic committee—in brief, Bill and I agreed to a price that would stretch us a little, but just for a while, for Frank and his family's sake. We were confident it was a reasonable investment. That's what happened. It has turned out that that property has soared in value. Few could have anticipated that.'

'Poisonous calumny following on from the sex scandal allegations,' said Miss Barker, more to herself than to Bill and Joanne.

'Yes, more poisonous than the sex scandal allegations,' said Bill, 'for in that case, the claims about Bob McKinnon's tastes appear accurate. There is no truth here, except that we have acquired several properties, all above board. Joyce Charing has really got herself into a muddle.'

'And how dare that contemptible Alan Collins print the accusation that our investments have been to the disadvantage of ordinary mums and dads?' said Joanne. 'The fellow has no conscience. Neither has Mrs. Charing—either that or she is demented.'

'There is evidence she is a little unbalanced,' said Miss Barker. The phone rang. 'I will get that while you read the rest.'

Joanna flicked through to the editorial. The heading: **Immediate investigation imperative.**

'On the heels of serious allegations about a sex scandal in Binawarra High School come fresh allegations against the principal. So far, Mr Huckerby has shown that his object is not to answer the sex allegations but to shore up his administration by covering up and seeking support from powerful figures in the town. New allegations link him now to many of those powerful figures. We mentioned in a previous editorial that the more people in authority try to evade public scrutiny by attempting to pull down the screen of secrecy, the more they implicate themselves and the greater the mess they end up in.

'The principal now has to acknowledge that the whole affair has gotten out of hand, and for the sake of the school, students, parents, and the town, he should step aside while a thorough investigation is carried out. This is the only moral course open to Mr Huckerby, and we appeal to him to take it, for the good of all.'□

There were again eight letters to the editor. They all dealt with the allegations about the sex scandal. The authorities had to step in and get rid of entrenched authority figures who protect their interests to the detriment of the people. One letter caught Joanne's eye.

How can any parent stand by and watch their child depart for school without trepidation these days? Once upon a time, people could trust official authority. That trust seems to have disappeared. I have heard the principal of Binawarra High School is a practising Christian. Is this not another sign of how much hypocrisy the Christian religion naturally engenders in those who follow it? I have heard the principal has close connections with other religious figures in the town, particularly with the Catholic priest. Should not these links also be reviewed? Is it not time for the people in the community to make up the balance between Christian belief and its influence on our lives?

'How can these people be taken in like this?' she said to Miss Barker, who had returned from a brief telephone conversation.

'It is the natural influence of public media, as I've said. People's thirst for information makes it that way. It is a thing to be exploited. The modern media have become an irresistible drawcard for any cunning scoundrel seeking to earn big money. Here, however, a real political purpose looms behind Collins's attacks.'

'How can one individual like Bill stand up to that alone?'

'Not very well,' and turning to Bill: 'That was Charles on the phone. I asked him to come around for support.'

'Thank you, Flo. I could do with Charles's company.'

'Did you note,' said Miss Barker, who had never seen Bill look so dispirited, 'that Fr. van Engelen has been dragged into it? I've been wondering about his position. I suspect that letter is phony and designed to advance the campaign. An important part of this campaign will be an attack on Christian belief.'

'Who is "they," for heaven's sake?' said Bill, 'Who is doing this with Collins's help? It has not originated from him, that's for sure. He has had several years to have a go at me. Why would he have left it till now?'

'You're right, Bill. He is conducting a campaign at the behest of someone or some people. And there is no doubt he has a price on it. That's his interest. His record speaks for itself. I doubt, too, whether he is writing these pieces without at least some help, especially the editorials.'

'Who is writing them, then?' said Joanne.

'Bill, didn't you say Fr. van Engelen has seen Miss Bicknell entering the premises of the *Binawarra and District Mail*?'

'Yes, it was a passing comment, but somehow I remembered. She has denied all involvement.'

'Let me ring Father now,' said Miss Barker, checking her watch and going to the phone. 'Father sends his sympathy and says he will be in touch later today. He confirmed he had seen Miss Bicknell enter the newspaper's office. He has seen her with Collins in the shopping centre. He also said he had seen Mr Rostowski entering the building.'

'Who's he?' said Bill.

'You have never noticed that tallish, thickset man of Middle Eastern appearance in the town? He is a salesman for a gift and stationery wholesaler. He has been visiting the town for around six months.'

'No, I haven't noticed him.'

'Neither have I,' added Joanne.

'Is that significant, I mean, his contact with Collins?'

'Yes, because there has also been contact between him and Miss Bicknell.'

Bill and Joanne gaped uncomprehendingly.

'You've been on to this for some time, haven't you, Flo?' said Bill.

'On to what?' said Joanne.

'Let me just say a link between those two has yet to be explained,' said Miss Barker. 'Miss Bicknell, whose teaching qualifications are in language and literature, seems the chief candidate for crafting the editorials.'

'You still haven't answered my question, Flo,' said Joanne. 'Onto what?'

'I would rather not go into that now, if you don't mind, Joanne. The priority is to confront this latest attack.'

Bill nodded his assent, and Joanne agreed to follow Miss Barker's advice.

'Good. Bill, I still advise you not to respond publicly to Collins's attacks. Whoever is behind Collins wants to leave you so damaged you cannot function. You see, in the long run, you'll be able to refute the charges. They must know that. They aim to exploit what they have as much as possible. So let them play all their cards to reveal the full measure of what you have to counter, and then only counter what is necessary. You do not want to give them any more than they presently possess to exploit. In the meantime, you can continue to explain yourself to the people who know you well. Your response will come back to those who want you damaged, but they cannot use it without risking their credibility.'

'Flo,' said Bill miserably, 'I am just not used to the vindictiveness of these attacks. What could I have done to offend them so much?'

'I have told you; it has to do with ideology. It has to do with getting rid of you. Don't let yourself sink into self-pity. Take up the battle. You have support, much support.'

'Yes, you do, darling,' said Joanne. 'Charles will be here soon.'

'Good. I suggest I stay here today to field any inquiries,' said Miss Barker. 'This latest attack will bring more media people out of the woodwork. Mark my words. There is a story to be sniffed out here.'

Miss Barker's resolute manner put Bill and Joanne somewhat at ease. They agreed to her fielding any inquiries or nuisance phone calls. Miss Barker then went over the steps Bill had taken so far and the plan he had worked out. On further discussion, they agreed that he should refine his letter to the editor in response to the sex scandal allegations and send it off on Monday. He should explain to friends and supporters how he bought the Miners Emporium. On Tuesday, the eve of the Wednesday edition of the *Binawarra and District Mail*, he should send his rebuttal of Mrs. Charing's allegations with evidence to make it clear how muddled Mrs. Charing had been.

'In fact, what you suggest fits in with what I had planned,' Bill said as they removed to the verandah. 'The crucial point for me was the lack of support from senior staff for the sex allegations.'

'That is your strongest point there,' said Miss Barker.

At that moment, Charles arrived at the front gate with Estella.

'There's a cheering sight!' cried Bill. 'Good to see you, my boy,' he called to Charles. 'And you, too, of course, Estella.'

'We're glad to be here,' said Charles, shaking Bill's hand. 'We're with you until this outrage has finished.'

For a moment, Bill was overcome. Estella hugged him.

'You see, with friends like this, we will beat these heartless people, won't we?' said Joanne.

'They're our family,' said Bill with a quick sniffle. 'Where is Aine?'

'Aine wants to stay withdrawn,' said Charles. 'She is thinking of you and praying all will work out.'

'Thank her for me, Charles, won't you? I appreciate the prayers. I need them right now. I need the good Lord to help us through this trial.'

Joanne and Estella slipped away to the kitchen to prepare morning tea. Miss Barker remained with the men but added little to the conversation, allowing Charles's sympathetic manner to have its calming effect. Her mind turned to re-examining the details of the newspaper attacks and how they could relate to Gerda Vrouwendijk, Mr Rostowski, and Estella. In this way, two hours passed, only interrupted by the phone, which she vetted. The nuisance calls she dealt with smartly; the calls of support she passed on to Bill. The support also worked to revive Bill's spirits. The most important call was from Frank Fonori, who, flabbergasted at the nonsense Collins had printed, said he would correct any misapprehension about the purchase of the Miners Emporium. How could that woman get it so wrong? And how could Collins publish that slander without making the obvious checks? At around eleven o'clock, a car pulled up outside.

'It's Reg Charing, for heaven's sake,' said Bill, getting up to greet him.

'Stay where you are, mate,' Reg called as he got out of the car. 'I'm coming up. I'm sorry about all this,' he said without greeting the others. 'My wife has gone completely off her rocker. It had to happen. I kept telling her she was up the creek about your property, but she wouldn't listen. The woman's a drunk, totally incapable of making sense most of the time. It's a wonder she lasted so long at the school. How could you miss it?'

'Please take a seat, Reg,' said Joanne, as everyone looked on in astonishment.

'Oh, I'm sorry, Joanne. Hello, everyone,' he said. 'I had to come and see you. I'll tell you another thing. She's being manipulated, willingly, very willingly. She wants to get back at men. She hates men, me most of all men. You're second, Bill.' He laughed nervously. 'The woman belongs in a lunatic asylum. She should be dried out, too. The wine companies' turnover will go down, though, if she stops drinking. I had better warn them.' He laughed again as he looked from one to the other.

'Who is manipulating her?' said Miss Barker.

'Jane Cox,' said Reg, looking cautiously at the formidable school nurse, 'the sexy Jane Cox.'

'Jane Cox?' said Miss Barker and Bill together.

'Yes. She's been on the phone with her for these last weeks. I could see Joyce was up to something. I had no idea what this time. Usually, it's clear where her lunacy is taking her.'

'There is no doubt about this?' said Miss Barker.

'Absolutely none. I wouldn't tell you if I didn't know.'

'Is there anybody else involved?'

'Probably, but Jane Cox is the only one who rings. She's using her to get at you, Bill. I get the idea from snippets that they're planning something for Anzac Day. This has to be the explanation or something like it. Otherwise, why would a sex bomb like Jane Cox mix with a frump like my wife? But she's very cunning in keeping it to herself this time. Anyhow, I'm not interested in finding out where her madness is taking her. I'd go mad if I let myself get involved. Bill, I'll support you in this. Don't you worry about that! The woman should be scheduled or sectioned or whatever you call it—not fit to walk the streets unattended.'

Joanne thanked Reg for his support, and Bill, startled by Reg's passionate condemnation of his wife and support for himself, uttered his thanks, too. Miss Barker said nothing further. Joanne invited him to stay for a cup of tea, but he refused, saying that his weekends were his only escape. He intended to leave for Melbourne at once.

'Jane Cox,' said Bill, after Reg was back in his car and heading out of town, 'so it's Jane Cox who is behind all this. Why? What have I done to her? She has never complained.'

'Perhaps not to your face,' said Miss Barker. 'She is the sort of person who does not dare to take up the fight alone. She needs someone to work with or direct her. Others are involved, and we must find out who.'

'What fight are you talking about now?'

'Bill, don't be so naïve, the general left-wing fight, of course. As a traditional Christian male, you will always infuriate people like Jane Cox. It's like a red rag to a bull.'

Bill sighed and ran his hand over his head.

EARLIER THAT morning, a powerful motorbike carrying a helmeted and black, leather-clad rider, stopped at the entrance to the circuit. It rolled nearer to the picnic shelter while the rider glanced around. After scanning the gardens, he dismounted, wheeled the motorbike to the side of the picnic shelter, and, removing his helmet, sat in the shade of the shelter. He brushed his close-cropped hair back as he fixed his eyes on a man wandering along the side of the park and looking around. Another man approached and stopped the wandering man. They stood exchanging words for a few minutes. The second man poked Bruce Butcher in the chest. Bruce grabbed Boris's hand and flung it away, mouthing at him. As he walked away, Boris spoke some words. In reply, Bruce looked around and gesticulated before heading towards the far end of the shopping area. Shortly after, Boris followed.

Geoff mounted his bike, and with one jerk of the starter lever, the powerful engine roared into life. He pulled away from the curb and rode towards the hills. At the foot of the Wombat, he covered the short distance along the dirt track to the picnic area where he and Ruby and the Winterbines had picnicked. As he untied the camping gear strapped to the saddle, he glanced at the spot where he had sat observing Estella. Things had changed since then, but he did not want to think about it, at least not at that moment. With the camping gear slung over his shoulder, he began the steady climb to the top of the Wombat. He stopped below the crest where he had sat with Estella and dumped his pack on the ground.

He stood scanning the town to get his bearings. Satisfied, he set up his binoculars. He fixed his gaze on Anzac Square. After some minutes of running his eyes over the square, he caught sight of Bruce Butcher standing outside the old Miners Emporium. Bruce was looking around the park and the shops, as he had been earlier, when Boris confronted him. Boris was nowhere to be seen. Geoff focused on the Winterbine house. There seemed to be no life there, but as he was about to turn away, Aine walked into view on the verandah. She stood contemplating the gardens. She looked in his direction. The binoculars caught her pale face turned towards him, clearly visible. He started and took his eyes away. When he looked again, she was gone.

He picked out the back of Miss Barker's house. The curtains were drawn. He shifted his gaze to the Huckerby House and focused on Bill, Joanne, and Miss Barker. He watched them deep in conversation, with Bill throwing his hands up and shaking his head, and Miss Barker responding in the firm manner he was now familiar with. Charles and Estella arrived. He watched the warm greeting between Charles and Bill and saw Estella's sudden embrace of Bill. He concentrated on Estella, observing her movements. He followed her until she disappeared into the house with Joanne. He took his eyes away from the binoculars and forced her out of his mind.

He leaned back against the hillside, keeping his eyes on the Huckerby house. He had his people in view, or at least situated. He rested on an elbow in the soft grass and stared up at the cloudless blue sky for a while. Estella and Charles left the Huckerby house at one o'clock to return home. He focused the binoculars on the shopping square. He could not see Bruce Butcher or Boris. He scanned the main streets again. He took a small pack from his bag and chewed on a sandwich. It would be a long afternoon, but he did not mind. He liked the solitude of the Wombat and the chance to reflect.

An hour later, Boris emerged from the square and started along Melbourne Road, just failing to break into a trot. Glancing behind him several times, he turned into a motel and disappeared. A few minutes later, a car emerged, turned to the left, and drove further on into Old Melbourne Road. It travelled a little way before parking. From its obscured position, it had a clear view of the Winterbine house. Not long after, Charles and Estella appeared and drove to the presbytery.

Boris followed, stopping at the entrance to the square. Five minutes later, Charles and Estella reappeared, supporting the crippled priest. They helped him into the car and then drove around to the Huckerby's house. Boris followed for a short while but then turned back, drove around the shopping square, and entered the lane behind Gerda's house. He was no longer discreet about his connection with the Dutch woman. What did this change mean? Geoff trained the binoculars on the shopping square.

The square was not busy, but people were walking around, many patronising the two pubs and several coffee shops. He was on the point of directing his binoculars towards the Huckerby house when he noticed a small gathering of people at the near end of the park. Partly hidden by the trees and gardens, they were looking at something. They moved into view, one person supporting Bruce Butcher, who was bent over and holding his head. Another pointed towards the police station, but Bruce waved him and the others away. Realising he did not want their help, they left him to himself.

Bruce staggered to a car parked nearby and leaned against the bonnet. He crumpled and fell. Now, he was out of sight, and nobody came to his assistance. A few minutes later, he struggled to his feet, steadying himself. He clumsily unlocked the driver's door, eased himself in, and slumped against the steering wheel. More minutes passed as Geoff kept him in view. Then the car pulled out, turned, headed out of the shopping precinct, and continued at a cautious pace along Melbourne Road. Geoff watched as the car passed out of sight beneath him. Boris had gotten rid of Bruce Butcher.

Geoff returned to scanning the town, after a while arriving at the Huckerby house. He observed Estella's calm demeanour as she listened to the conversation between her father, Miss Barker, and Joanne Huckerby at one end of the verandah. He shifted his gaze to the other end, where Bill sat with Fr. van Engelen. The priest and Bill leaned towards each other, with Bill doing more listening than talking. He refocused on the lane where Boris had parked his car. A few minutes passed, and Boris's car emerged and drove to the other side of the town. It stopped between the trees outside Stephen Calder's house. Boris got out, carrying what looked like a brown paper bag. Len Dawson ran into view and took the paper bag. After a short exchange, they disappeared.

A little after three o'clock, a car turned into Eureka Street and proceeded until it came abreast of the Huckerby house. It stopped. A minute passed before two men got out. One took a camera from the back seat and aimed it at the Huckerby house while his companion stood beside him, holding a microphone. After a few minutes of filming, the man with the microphone stood several paces away, facing the cameraman with the Huckerby house in the background.

BILL HUCKERBY was delighted to see Fr. van Engelen arrive with Charles and Estella. After exchanging greetings, he took him to the end of the verandah and asked what he thought of the distasteful circumstances he had been sucked into.

'What's going on, Father? How is this part of God's providential order in the world?'

'I am sure Job asked the same questions when he sat in the dust, reduced to poverty with dogs licking his ulcerated limbs,' said Fr. van Engelen.

The priest had been counselling Bill for some time when a shout interrupted the intensity of their exchange.

'Bill!' Miss Barker cried. 'Hurry! Inside!' They looked up and saw two men alongside a car parked on the other side of the road. 'Come on, Bill, before they see you. You, too, Joanne, don't give them what they want.' She was already pushing Joanne towards the door.

'Who are they?' said Joanne, following Bill into the hall.

'No doubt, they're from one of the television stations,' said Miss Barker, gazing across the road. 'Let me handle this. None of you move. Don't give them any opportunity to misuse your movement.' She stood at the verandah railing and looked steadily at the reporter, who was now speaking into the camera. When he and the cameraman turned to head across the road, she walked to meet them.

'Can I help you, gentlemen?'

'Is this the Huckerby house, the high school principal's house?' said the reporter.

'Who is asking?'

'Is it?'

'Young man, I asked you a question, and I do not expect a question in reply. Identify yourself, or the town police sergeant will be called to ask you the same question.'

'Are you afraid to answer the question?' said the reporter, not very confidently.

'I am a resident of this town. You are not. You have arrived here without notice, in secrecy, and attempting to hide your identity. That would indicate you are up to no good. Unless you identify yourselves, I will call the police sergeant. He will not take kindly to outsiders harassing the town's citizens, which seems to be your object.'

The cameraman raised his camera and pointed it at Miss Barker. Miss Barker remained unperturbed. The reporter gave a sign to lower the camera. 'We are from the Premier Network.'

'Your name, young man.' There was hesitation. 'What possible reason could you have for not giving your name?'

'I'm Rob Meakin, and this is a nameless cameraman,' said the reporter with a smirk.

'What can I do for you?'

The reporter signalled to the cameraman to start filming. 'Is this the Huckerby house? And who are you?'

'This is the Huckerby house. My name is Miss Barker, and you will call me Miss Barker. I am a close friend of Mr and Mrs. Huckerby. Mr Huckerby will not be available for the moment.'

'When will he be available?'

'It is not likely he will be available for the foreseeable future.'

'What is his response to the accusations that a group of pedophiles are preying on innocent children in his school?'

'Whatever the accusations, they are groundless. The police investigations have failed to produce anything that would give them any credibility. You are referred to the local police sergeant. There is no further comment.'

'What has he to say about the accusations of corrupt property dealing and undermining the democratically elected town council?'

'Whatever the accusations, they are groundless.'

'Why won't he explain himself? Is he afraid to confront these accusations in public? Is he afraid to give an account of himself to the people?'

'Mr Huckerby is a respected member of the town's community. You are welcome to ask the people of the town. They will testify to Mr Huckerby's long commitment to the welfare of this town and his private works of charity.'

'Why is he hiding?'

'He is not hiding.'

'What does he have to hide?'

'He has nothing to hide. His refusal to answer the particular questions of a particular reporter for a particular television network in no way means that he has something to hide or that he is hiding. You flatter yourself, young man, if you think when Mr Huckerby is ready to say something publicly, he must say it through you.'

The reporter looked over Miss Barker's shoulder. The heads of Charles, Estella and Fr. van Engelen were visible. He signalled to the cameraman again.

'There's a cleric of some sort sitting at that end,' said the cameraman after he had lowered the camera.

'Get a long close-up.'

Miss Barker glanced around while the cameraman aimed at the priest. The use the reporter could make of Fr. van Engelen had not occurred to her. The cameraman moved along the front fence to get a closer shot of the priest. Father looked steadily at him, making no effort to get out of the line of vision. That was the right response. Apparently satisfied with what he had, the reporter walked back to the car with the cameraman in tow.

GEOFF FOLLOWED the car with the reporter and cameraman as it headed over town and stopped outside the house that Jane Cox was sharing with Pat Dillon. Jane, dressed in sloppy grey tracksuit pants and a dark sweater, opened to the reporter's knock. There was an exchange for a minute. She disappeared into the house, reappearing a few minutes later dressed in a white miniskirt, a pink top, and pink high-heeled shoes. Another discussion followed. Jane remained on the porch while the reporter and cameraman took up positions at the front of the property.

At the reporter's signal, Jane strolled around the garden, stopping to pick flowers. The camera followed her. The reporter then repositioned her in front of a lush hibiscus tree. The interview lasted around five minutes, after which the cameraman took shots of the reporter in different poses and expressions.

The threesome drove in the reporter's car to the town square where Jane was filmed in reflective poses among the gardens; then to Bob McKinnon's empty house with its signs of abandonment; more filming of Jane from different angles as she stood on the front footpath looking at the house; next the high school where she was filmed walking along the front fence and stopping at the gates. The reporter continued the interview with the camera at an angle that took in the principal's office. Shots of Jane were taken from different angles. The final fading shot was of Jane from behind as she walked away from the front gates of the school. While the cameraman packed up his gear and returned to the car, the reporter stood chatting with her.

At six o'clock that evening, Bill, Joanne, and Miss Barker sat in front of the television. They did not have to wait long. The newsreader introduced the report with switching shots of the high school, young people in the town's square, an attractive miniskirted female, the surrounding hills, and the Huckerby House.□

'There is upheaval in the sleepy town of Binawarra. Sensational allegations of sexual impropriety concerning the high school principal, the existence of a group of sexual predators in the school, and today's disturbing accusations of corrupt property dealings by the principal and influential figures in the town have shattered the serenity of this picturesque Victorian town. Mr Alan Collins, the editor of the town's newspaper, has broken a series of stories on the affair, which keeps getting bigger. [vision of Alan Collins outside the premises of the *Binawarra and District Mail*] He says he will persevere as any responsible journalist would in getting to the truth. The Premier Network sent its gun reporter, Rob Meakin, to investigate.'□

ROB MEAKIN [in front of the high school]: We are not often called to a lovely, peaceful town like Binawarra. It goes to show that behind the serene curtain of the quaintest country town, human corruption writhes and wriggles as much as it does in the big city. [vision of the reporter in front of the Huckerby house]. At the centre of this corruption is the principal of the high school. We tried to approach Mr William Huckerby, but he refused to give his side of the story. Instead, he sent a not-too-popular family friend to answer our inquiries. [vision of Miss Barker's stern face in close-up] Miss Barker, is Mr Huckerby prepared to answer the accusations about sexual impropriety in his school and corrupt property dealings?□

MISS BARKER: Mr Huckerby will not be available at the moment.

ROB MEAKIN: Most people believe the principal has a duty to answer the allegations and reassure a concerned public. When will he do this?

MISS BARKER: It is not likely he will be available to speak to you in the foreseeable future.

ROB MEAKIN: What does he have to say about the accusations that a group of pedophiles is preying on innocent school children?

MISS BARKER: Whatever the accusations, they are groundless.□

ROB MEAKIN: What has he to say about the accusations of corrupt property dealing and the undermining of the democratically elected council of the town?

MISS BARKER: Whatever the accusations, they are groundless.□

ROB MEAKIN: Why won't he explain himself? Is he afraid to confront these accusations in public? Is he afraid to give an account of himself to the people of this town? Why is he hiding?

MISS BARKER: He is not hiding.

ROB MEAKIN: What does he have to hide?

MISS BARKER: He has nothing to hide.

ROB MEAKIN [vision of the reporter in front of the Catholic church]: As you see, our attempts to clarify this sordid affair met with evasion by Mr Huckerby's representative, but we did notice a curious thing at the Huckerby house. [vision of Fr. van Engelen sitting on the Huckerby verandah] The town's Catholic priest was present this morning at the Huckerby residence. Our inquiries have revealed a close connection between Mr Huckerby and the Catholic priest. This raises questions for some people. Mr Huckerby is a member of the Anglican Church. What is this close relationship between a member of the Anglican Church and the celibate Catholic priest who is under disciplinary supervision? [vision of the reporter in front of the offices of the *Binawarra and District Mail*]. The editor of the *Binawarra and District Mail*, who broke the story about the accusations, said he stands by what he wrote. □

COLLINS [at his office desk]: I have published the reports and the evidence. It's up to Mr Huckerby to refute them publicly. I can't understand his reluctance to face the tribunal of public opinion. In a democracy, the final tribunal is public judgment. Mr Huckerby has a duty to submit himself to the public's judgment.□

ROB MEAKIN: [vision outside Jane Cox's house] If the principal of Binawarra High School lacks the courage to appear in public to answer serious accusations, one of his staff is not afraid to speak up. [vision of Jane Cox walking from the front door of her house. The camera follows her around her garden, zooming in on her face and trim figure.] Jane Cox is one of the senior teachers at the high school. She said she is deeply concerned about the unresolved state of affairs. The students' welfare is at stake. So, she is prepared to shed light on the accusations but must be silent on some aspects for obvious legal reasons. I asked this Gloria Steinem look-alike to explain as much as she could without exceeding the legal boundaries. [vision of Jane Cox's pretty, suntanned face in close-up in front of the hibiscus tree]□

ROB MEAKIN: Ms Cox, what can you tell us about the accusations of sexual impropriety in the school?□

JANE COX: There are certain undeniable facts. They are in the police report. One of the senior teachers, whose sexual preferences were well known, was found dead in very distasteful circumstances and with a boy of eighteen. A boy of eighteen is hardly more than a child. The senior teacher had evidently arranged for him to come to Binawarra on the night they were both killed. The indications are that the senior teacher was—□

ROB MEAKIN: Please, Ms Cox, remember the legal boundaries.□

JANE COX: I was going to say that the indications are that— [break in the vision]

ROB MEAKIN: I'm sorry, Ms Cox, you cannot say that.□

JANE COX: I'm sorry. I am only saying what the evidence points to. I know it's not very nice.

ROB MEAKIN: Okay, let me ask you this: was there a close relationship between the principal and that senior teacher?□

JANE COX: Absolutely. The principal spoke highly of him. During a school assembly, he praised him for his good humour, his judgment of character, and the help he gave him in his work as principal. He said never once did he have to question him about his activities. He said that in front of the whole school. I think he sometimes accompanied him to Melbourne.□

ROB MEAKIN: What for?

JANE COX: Oh, everybody knows the teacher was in the habit of spending the weekend in Melbourne. We are aware it wasn't for family because he wasn't married, and all his relations were in San Francisco. I believe he was a major figure in San Francisco's alternative lifestyle groups.□

ROB MEAKIN: And the principal went with him sometimes?

JANE COX: I believe so. But you had better check that.

ROB MEAKIN: [vision of Jane Cox walking in the park in the town square] This attractive Gloria Steinem look-alike told me other things, but we cannot reveal them for legal reasons. There was one delicate subject, however, that I had to ask Ms Cox about. [vision of Jane Cox standing in front of the high school with the principal's office in the background] Ms Cox, there have been suggestions that sexual abuse is evident in the behaviour of some of the students. Can you tell us something about this?□

JANE COX: According to the scientific literature, there are typical manifestations in children and youth of past sexual abuse. Suspicions should be aroused when a student is overly timid, anxious, silent, withdrawn, and displays eccentric tastes and behaviours. Often, the victim takes flight into some weird religious group. I won't say how many or who fits this pattern well, except for one case who— I cannot say more. The proper authorities need to investigate the school.□

ROB MEAKIN: Before we end, Ms Cox, do you have a comment about the suspicious property dealing by the principal?□

JANE COX: Nothing would surprise me, but you should ask the person who is making the accusations.□

ROB MEAKIN: Mrs Charing is too upset to speak about it.

JANE COX: I'm not surprised. The way such a trustworthy woman was dismissed was appalling. No wonder she is upset. I would not be surprised if someone had got at her.

ROB MEAKIN: That's serious.

JANE COX: You should turn your attention to those running this town.

ROB MEAKIN: Thank you, Ms Cox, for talking to us. We know it may put you in an awkward position with the principal.□

JANE COX: I only want justice served—for the students and the town.

ROB MEAKIN: [vision of Jane Cox walking away from the school gates] This is a story that won't go away. There are many questions to be answered by the principal of Binawarra High School, and as long as there are courageous teachers like Ms Cox, the principal will have no rest. We will keep our viewers informed of the developments. This is Rob Meakin reporting from Binawarra.□

Bill turned the sound down and held out his hands. 'What can I say? Would it do any good to fly into a rage?'

'It is nothing more than we should have expected, Bill,' said Miss Barker. 'Actually, on the whole, and despite the clever editing, it was not as bad as it could have been.'

'You are joking, of course, Flo,' said Joanne. 'The whole report was a tissue of lies and distortions. It's outrageous! Anybody not acquainted with the facts might swallow it.'

'I know, Joanne. But they have not pushed the fabrication beyond the reports in the *Binawarra and District Mail*. It would not surprise me if the reporter had investigated and not found anything to support the accusations of sexual impropriety. You know well what sort of answer he would get if he asked ordinary people around the town. No, he was beating up Collins's report to draw an audience. The focus on Miss Cox's attractive features was clearly for this purpose. And he barely touched on Mrs Charing's allegations. Why? Why didn't he try to develop this juicy side of the story? Because he knows he would be on thin ice if he made accusations against a town council that weren't irrefutable. The television station is a commercial enterprise, first and foremost. Binawarra and its council are in the Premier Network's market area. No, he would be cautious there. It is likely that he knew or had discovered that the council did not own the Miners Emporium. That would be fairly easy to establish. The rest of Mrs Charing's accusations would be deprived of their foundations.'

'I hope you're right,' said Bill, with a big sigh.

'We should hold course for the moment. I still believe the aim is to damage you by keeping the slander running.' She stopped to consider. 'It might be worth sending the General Manager of the Premier Network a copy of your letter to Collins. The television station will back off if they know the checkable facts. It would not be worth getting this wrong. They would make every municipality in their market wary of them.'

'I can only say I hope you're right, Flo,' Bill repeated. 'I feel like I have aged twenty years in the last week.'

GEOFF LET the pushbike roll to a stop on the dark dirt road approaching the picnic area below the Wombat. He propped it against a nearby tree, keeping his eyes fixed on a clump of bushes ahead. A figure emerged from the bushes and crept along the track towards the fire glimmering through the trees in the picnic area. Geoff followed the figure silhouetted against the orange glow. It stopped on the edge of the bushes and crouched. Ten minutes passed by without Boris moving. Geoff could not see what was holding his interest. He skirted around to the right, away from the Wombat, keeping Boris's position in view as he moved through the undergrowth. The soft crackling of the fire and the subdued voices of those around the fire covered any slight noise he made. It did not take him long to get into a position where he had a clear view.

Stephen Calder and Len Dawson were sitting with two girls. They had blankets wrapped around them. They were chatting, laughing, and drinking from cans. After twenty minutes, they retired to their cars. The girls were no more than fourteen or fifteen. That seemed the signal for Boris to move. Geoff watched the shadowy figure walk back down the dirt track. He mounted his bike and cycled after him. He reached Melbourne Road to see Boris driving at a modest speed towards the town. He followed him to Miss Bicknell's house, where he parked in the lane.

Boris was inside for no more than ten minutes. As Geoff expected, he then drove to the other side of the town and parked close by Jane Cox's house. The Premier Network reporter's car was parked in the driveway. Next, with Geoff following, he drove past the Winterbine house, slowing to have a look, and then, apparently satisfied, continued to his motel. Geoff was also ready to call it a night. He returned to the picnic area under the Wombat. As expected, Stephen Calder and Len Dawson and their girls had gone. He was glad to see the fire still burning. He threw some wood on it. When it was crackling comfortingly, he reviewed what he had seen, but his mind drifted to the problem of Estella—his problem with Estella.

Chapter 25

Under siege

THANK YOU, CHARLES, for driving me down to Melbourne,' said Fr. van Engelen, as they passed between the two peaks on Monday morning. 'I know it must be an inconvenience to you.'

'Please don't worry about it, Father. I said I would support you to the end in this nasty business.'

'God bless you, Charles. I rely so much on you and your dear wife.'

Shortly before two o'clock that afternoon, Charles helped the priest into the Collins Street rooms of the psychiatrist with whom Fr de Jonge's assistant had arranged an appointment.

'I am very sorry, sir,' said the receptionist, distressed. 'I tried to contact you before you left, but you had already gone. I'm afraid the doctor has taken ill. He has been rushed to hospital.'

'Taken ill?' said Charles. 'When did it happen?'

'Late this morning. He'll be in no condition to have appointments for some time. We apologise for the inconvenience.'

'No need for apologies, Miss,' said the priest. 'We wish him well and will offer prayers for his speedy recovery. Come on, Charles, it is left to us to drive back to Binawarra and await further instructions.'

BILL HUCKERBY scarcely had any time for himself that week. Nuisance phone calls had harassed him during the weekend. People had even parked outside their house and taken photos. He and Joanne did as Miss Barker advised. They kept to themselves, out of sight, and put the phone down as soon as they recognised a bogus call. On Monday, as agreed, he sent off his letters of explanation to the editor of *The Binawarra and District Mail* and to the state management of the Premier Network. In the afternoon, the postman brought the first batch of hate mail. A bigger batch arrived on Tuesday, and they kept up a steady flow until the end of the week. He could not believe how nasty people could get with someone they had only read about in the newspaper or seen on television.

Education Department high-ups contacted him on Monday, as he expected, and warned that the whole episode was doing irreparable damage to the department's reputation. It had to stop. Officials would arrive in Binawarra to sort things out. They arrived late morning and went into conference with him, after which they launched an independent investigation, precisely along the lines he had already taken. It was a relief that he did not have to concern himself with it. By the following afternoon, they had interviewed the teachers but had turned up nothing. How had the affair gotten out of control? What had he done to stop it?

Bill was exasperated. Couldn't they see he could not control the local newspaper's gossipmongering? He must control it, they insisted. The task of a modern school administrator was to deal with the media. When he asked how he should deal with an editor who insisted on telling lies, they replied that perception and not the truth was the concern of management. He must do something to influence perception. What that was, what action he chose to take, he had to be discerning about. Bill returned home that night, frustrated and with his spirits dragging along the ground. How right Flo was proving to be. Where had his head been in recent years? How hadn't he been aware of the shift from the concern with truth to the concern with perception? And what was to become of society if perception was the central issue of debate and social conflict? How would he educate young impressionable minds if their primary moral concern was shallow, ephemeral image and not enduring standards of behaviour?

The next day, on the way to school, he collected a copy of the Wednesday edition of *The Binawarra and District Mail*. He threw it on the passenger seat as he got back into the car, not daring to look at it. Once in his office, he spread the newspaper on his desk and prepared for the worst. The front-page headline still gave him a jolt: **Officials intervene and psychiatrist examines priest**. He should not be surprised that Fr. van Engelen was dragged into it. Flo had warned him. He only wondered how Collins had got wind of Father's appointment with a psychiatrist.

'The inevitable has happened. Department officials arrived in Binawarra on Monday to force the embattled high school principal, Mr Huckerby, to step aside while they investigated. Some teachers were heard saying that it would have saved a lot of worry and heartache if Mr Huckerby had done the right thing from the beginning. The school's staff hope that he will cooperate and not prolong the investigation needlessly. Some have expressed the wish that the principal take leave of absence. Already, one senior teacher fears for her position.

'Ms Jane Cox, the senior teacher who appeared bravely on the Premier Network's main news bulletin last Saturday, remains steadfast in her claims that there are real problems in the school and that at least one student is showing the signs of abuse. She hopes the officials will take quick and appropriate action.

'In another startling development, this newspaper has learned that the local Catholic priest, Fr. J. van Engelen, was ordered by the Superior General of his order to submit to an examination by a psychiatrist. This may seem unrelated to the sexual abuse allegations hanging over the principal until one learns that the priest is a close friend of the principal. He is also responsible for the religious supervision of some young people in the town and the surrounding area.

'This newspaper has learned that Fr. van Engelen's invalid state resulted from an assault suffered in Papua and New Guinea, where he headed a parish of young families. Shortly after, he was sent to the order's smallest parish in Australia for disciplinary reasons. The local superior told our reporter that the order would not comment on Fr. van Engelen's condition or why he was in Binawarra. Another veil of secrecy.

'This is a story that just will not go away, and this newspaper assures its faithful readers it will see it through to the end.'□

Bill looked up from the paper and stared into space. Checkmated! No matter what he did now, it would go against him. If he talked to the staff, he would be harassing them. If he avoided them, he would be attempting to cover up. If he spoke to Jane Cox, he would be guilty of harassing her. If he did not respond to her claims, it would either be an admission of guilt or an attempt to evade the issue and hush her up, or both. If he spoke to Edith Bicknell, he would be leaning on her and forcing her to resign. If he did not speak to her, it would again be a cover-up. He felt like he was being squeezed into a little hole in the ground, just waiting for someone to finish him off by stomping on him.

And now they had dragged that poor priest into the miserable affair. He knew about Fr. van Engelen's injuries, and he knew well the circumstances of the assault. He had wheedled it out of the priest over time until Father showed him a copy of the police investigation. The report concluded that it was a vicious assault and attempted robbery. The police could establish no other motivation. Father was silent on the matter, only saying he accepted the police report.

What sort of person could so willfully distort the priest's tragic circumstances? Bill was among the few who knew the extent of the priest's medical condition, a condition that left him in constant pain. If only they knew how incapable the priest was of Collins's disgusting insinuations. As for the psychiatrist's examination, that was an extreme disciplinary measure his superiors imposed because of doctrinal differences. It had nothing to do with anything in Binawarra. He flicked to the middle pages to plough through another weaselling, hypocritical editorial about the triumph of democracy over those in power positions who would abuse its freedoms. The arrival of officials from the department to sort out the mess should be a salutary lesson for the embattled principal of Binawarra High School. On page 6, in the bottom corner, was a grudging admission that the transaction regarding the Miners Emporium was above board.

That is hardly fair, thought Bill. Going from a front-page story and an editorial comment to a little ambiguous report squeezed into a corner of a minor page would not compensate for Joyce Charing's outrageous charges. Why weren't there any letters of support? Surely it was unlikely that not one person had written to the editor defending him or Fr. van Engelen. He got up from his desk and staggered as he walked to the window. He felt so sick and lethargic. Was his lethargy due to his feeling ill or his failure to make headway against the slander? He could not know. All he could feel was nausea and the weakness that beset his limbs. He steadied himself against the windowsill while he fixed his eyes on the Wombat and Death Rock beyond it.

At eleven o'clock, Aine and Charles arrived to lessen his preoccupation with his nausea and lethargy. They insisted on confronting the officials from the Education Department. They would not take no for an answer. Regarding the couple down their noses, the officials tried to brush them off as people incompetent to deal with the very serious issues relating to Binawarra High School's principal. Despite the haughtiness, Charles and Aine insisted on forcing the sour-faced officials to listen to a long, vigorous defence of Bill, the school, and Fr. van Engelen, condemning the allegations against Bill and the priest as contemptible lies and slander to which the officials were obliged to put a stop. The officials made several more attempts to brush them off. The last was the flabby insistence that the high school's problems had nothing to do with laymen. Each attempt was met with an exhortation that the officials respond to their unalterable moral obligations. Aine and Charles left the two officials purple-faced and severely regarding Bill.

'Wonderful,' said Bill, as he accompanied them to the front door. 'I'm so grateful for your support. It has given me the courage to fight on.'

Charles and Aine left Bill at the front steps and drove to St Philomena's presbytery. Miss Barker opened the door to them.

'Come in,' she said. 'The time has come to present ourselves openly in solidarity with Bill and Father. We will meet here from now on.'

They followed her into the parlour, where Fr. van Engelen sat looking at the fireplace.

'Thank you, Aine and Charles, for your support. It is appreciated,' he said with calm resignation.

Things were moving inexorably to a conclusion, said Miss Barker. Bill, Charles, and Aine had taken the proper steps in stating their case against the visible accusers and those behind them. The malice of the accusers would run up against the facts in the end. In the meantime, their group had to keep a ready eye on what was happening around them. Estella must stay under supervision at every point. Miss Barker then announced that Captain Shawcross had been in Binawarra since Saturday, and he was keeping her abreast of what the leading players were up to.

'Is he really here?' said Charles. 'I haven't seen any trace of him.'

'And you won't. Do not ask any more questions. His effectiveness depends on remaining out of sight. I stress that events are leading to a conclusion. Only when the main players break into the open can we call in the proper authorities. Until then, we must be prepared for surprises. Please tell me if you notice anything suspicious. I need to know where Mr Rostowski is.'

ON FRIDAY morning, the still-annoyed department officials called a meeting with Bill.

'Mr. Huckerby,' said the junior official, 'there is a matter we must resolve before we return to Melbourne this afternoon.'

'You have my cooperation, needless to say.'

'Ms Bicknell has told us she has arranged an advantageous career opportunity for one of your students.'

'That's true,' said Bill, who had been in a state of indecision about the work experience weekend. 'I have delayed approaching her parents about it. I know they are not keen for their daughter to pursue a career in public relations.'

'But the whole point of these vocational occasions is for the student to have direct experience in a particular job to make an informed decision,' said the official. 'On all accounts, the work experience that Ms Bicknell arranged is an excellent opportunity for a student who had an outstanding report on her first exposure to public relations.' He paused. 'You know, Mr Huckerby, it is precisely in the competence of the school to offer sound guidance to parents and students.' Bill was squeezed again. 'Ms Bicknell is understandably deflated by your lack of confidence in her and an apparent reluctance to cooperate in this unique opportunity arranged through Sandhurst University. Ms Bicknell believes she has been marginalised in the very position you put her in. It would be a shame to lose a teacher of such qualifications and connections.'

What could he do? He was checkmated again. He did not have the strength of body and spirit to struggle against it. With much reluctance, he agreed to recommend the weekend. He would make sure Estella remained under official supervision the whole time, even if he had to go himself on the weekend. Oh, how sick and tired he was!

LATE THAT evening, a van drove into the darkened lane behind Gerda Vrouwendijk's house. Three men alighted and hurried inside. Over the two hours, under Gerda's supervision, they packed her belongings and took them to the van. Shortly after midnight, the van emerged from the lane without lights. Once on the main road, it switched its lights on, drove around the shopping centre, and headed out along Melbourne Road.

Geoff stopped at the end of Anzac Square and watched the van depart. Satisfied they were leaving town, he pedalled back to the house. The lights were still on. He propped the bike against a tree and crept to the lane entrance. Nothing there. He returned to the front and waited. Fifteen minutes later, Boris drove up and stopped, leaving the engine running. Gerda Vrouwendijk appeared, switched the lights off, and strolled to the car. Geoff followed them, and when satisfied they had gone, he returned to the house. It did not take him long to find a window he could open. He climbed in, took a small torch from his jacket pocket, and walked around the house, looking in each room and opening cupboards. There was the debris of Gerda's slovenliness around the place: full ashtrays, empty cigarette packs, takeaway food wrappings, and the like. Only one room, the smallest bedroom, was free of such debris. It was spotless. That was curious. There hung a faint odour in the air, like incense. He returned to his bike and pedalled to the picnic area.

He stowed the pushbike among the bushes, donned his helmet, and mounted his motorbike. With a few short revs, he was on his way along the dirt track. He came out onto Melbourne Road, and with a roar of the powerful engine, he raced up the incline and disappeared at a rate between the Wombat and Death Rock. Maintaining a breakneck speed, he caught up with Gerda and Boris as they approached the junction with the Calder Highway. He slowed and followed at a distance all the way into Melbourne, at times turning his lights off so as not to alert the vigilant Boris.

Boris dropped Gerda off at a house in West Heidelberg, not far from Fawkner University. Geoff then followed him to a house in a back street of the outer northern suburb of Upfield. At a knock on the door of the darkened house, a swarthy, thickset man appeared. Boris brushed by him, and the front door closed, robbing the dimly lit street of the fluorescent light that leapt out as the door had opened. Seconds later, the slit of light under the front door disappeared, and the curtained windows of the front room glowed weakly. It was now past three o'clock in the morning. Geoff, astride his motorbike at the top of the street, looked around him. The clouds were low and pressing, and the moisture of rain hung in the air. He rode to an overnight truck stop on the Hume Highway.

He sat, eyes closed, leaning against the cafeteria wall while sipping his tea. His endurance was now being extended, as it often had been in Vietnam. He had been on the go since early morning the previous day, indeed, without much of a break since he had arrived in Binawarra. Now the fatigue of those days was bearing down on him. His object was the protection of—who was Estella, and what was she for him? He saw meaning in Miss Barker's looks and comments. He pushed it aside. He had to make critical decisions before he gave in to shutting down for some rest.

Whose movements took priority at that moment? The Dutch woman's or the Balkan's? What was Rostowski going to do now that Miss Bicknell had left Binawarra? Her plans had not been abandoned. Her manner and her organisational steps did not bespeak defeat. No, this was a stage in the plans. That meant that whatever she had planned for Estella still had to happen. Boris's role was not yet finished in Binawarra; he had to be there to keep an eye on Gerda's prize. The conclusion was that he must head back to Binawarra as soon as possible. But first, he had to get an idea of what the Dutch woman was up to in Melbourne.

He dozed fitfully without being disturbed until seven o'clock. After freshening up, he rode back to the West Heidelberg street. He parked his bike out of sight around the corner and prepared to keep watch. After two and a half hours of walking up and down the adjacent street and around the block, avoiding the residents' attention, he arrived again at the corner to see Miss Bicknell emerge from the house with a tall, handsome woman a few years older.

The woman was dressed stylishly, wearing a headscarf and flowing garments in different shades of purple. They got into the car parked in the driveway, and drove off. Geoff pursued them. He did not have to pursue them for long, though. They came onto Highdale Road and drove straight onto the grounds of Fawkner University. He followed them around the right-hand side of the university to one of the parking areas. He rode on to the next parking area. Chatting casually, they walked between the native plants, bushes, and towering eucalypts to one of the university colleges. He went after them. Dressed in his dark clothes and unkempt, he would not look out of place.

He followed the two women into a passageway, hanging back until they exited at the other end. He hurried to the exit. Remaining out of sight, he watched them cross a bridge over a moat and enter a building fifty yards further on. He reflected. What more could he learn by pursuing them? Nothing really. Whatever Gerda was doing with this handsome woman, who had something familiar about her, the central action was back in Binawarra where Estella was. It was time to head back there.

AT HALF past ten, Joanne picked up the phone and listened.

'Joanne, how's Bill?' she heard Miss Barker say. 'Has he seen this morning's edition?'

'No, Flo, he is so dispirited that he has just been sitting around as if he has no energy left. This is hitting him very hard. He won't admit it, but I know him well enough.'

'It's to be expected, Joanne. Nobody can take such relentless battering and not be wounded.'

'He sees all his life brought to nothing, and he is powerless to do anything about it.'

'I understand,' said Miss Barker. 'Ideological prejudice is turning out to be the most merciless and unrelenting of all.'

'What's to be done, Flo?'

'We must stay with him and support him. There will be an end to the campaign. In fact, it's not too far off. In the meantime, we must ensure he is not too damaged.'

'Oh, Flo!'

'Joanne, I'm coming around. There are other developments besides what's in this morning's newspaper. Give Bill a cup of tea and try to pep him up. I will need his concentration.'

Twenty minutes later, Miss Barker handed Bill the newspaper and took a chair beside him on the verandah.

'They are opening a third front,' she said.

In thick black letters, the headline read: **Time to question the Anzac Myth.** 'Oh, no!' cried Bill, folding the paper into his lap, 'is nothing sacred?' He turned to Miss Barker, who returned his question with a shake of the head.□

'Every year on the 25th of April, Australians and New Zealanders come together to celebrate their role in war. We say we remember the bravery of our soldiers who gave their lives to defend our freedom, values, and way of life. We celebrate without reflecting on those values and way of life. But should we reflect on them? Ms Jane Cox of Binawarra High School thinks we should.

'Few will forget Ms Cox's television interview, during which she spoke out about the problems at the high school and the principal's attempt to ward off public scrutiny. She was vindicated when Mr Huckerby was forced to step aside. Ms Cox now has something to say about Mr Huckerby's attitude to Anzac Day.

'Our nation, she said, is unwilling to look at what's behind Anzac Day. We are unwilling to see that Anzac Day is a celebration of white superiority. She was not merely speaking of people of a different colour.

'The Anzac boasts of bravery and self-sacrifice in the military conflict, but what really happens, Ms Cox asks? Her answer is clear: the aim of the men of the Anzac legend is to subjugate other races and cultures while at the same time relishing the excitement of the conflict and the rape of women. The rape of women and their continuing subjection are among the primary objectives in all wars. War, in truth, should be defined as male conflict. Wars ensure the supremacy of the white male and the social system he has created, whose pillars are business profits and the traditional family. Indeed, the traditional family is the original social unit of male supremacy.

'Ms Cox pointed to the sexual abuse affair and the cover-ups at the high school as justification for speaking out. Were people aware of the principal's efforts to glorify the deeds of the nation's soldiers and trumpet their superiority over others? Perhaps only the school staff and students were aware of the jingoistic flag ceremony conducted on every patriotic occasion.

'This year, she said, the principal intends to include Vietnam veterans in the Anzac parade, soldiers who fought in an unjust war. How could he show so much contempt and insensitivity by promoting those who symbolise the disgrace of that unjust war?

'Her speaking out would probably mean her forced resignation. She was willing to accept that. On Anzac Day, she would hold a vigil for the women raped in wars. She hoped other women would make the courageous decision to join her in solidarity.'□

Bill lowered the paper and sighed. 'There does not seem an end to it. Just when they have twisted and distorted and lied about the final bit of information they could dig up about me, they come out with something new. How could people swallow it?'

'But how many are swallowing it now, Bill?' said Miss Barker. 'Your enemies have just about exhausted their firepower. There's a growing feeling in the town that Collins has had more than a fair go. And Jane Cox is right: she has shot herself in the foot. Collins and people outside Binawarra may celebrate her, but the townspeople will not want her now, and not least her swollen feminist rhetoric. Her tactics and aims are too clumsy and transparent, and we are too sober-minded. I have the impression she is happy to go. You know, the media notoriety will open doors for her.'

'Flo, how can you stay so calm and analytic about this?' said Bill, brushing his hand over his forehead.

'Yes,' said Joanne, 'how can you keep so calm?'

'That is not relevant now. There are other things far more urgent. I have surprising news for you, Bill.'

'What now?' said Bill, turning to the editorial page.

'Don't worry about the editorial. It is a repetition of Miss Cox's views. This is more important. Miss Bicknell packed up last night and exited the town. She has gone.'

'What?' said Bill and Joanne together.

'I checked with the real estate agent, and he says rent has been paid for four weeks in advance, plus cleaning. He found the keys and a letter poked under his front door this morning. Miss Bicknell excused herself and said events had necessitated her immediate departure from Binawarra.'

'How did you know?' said Bill.

'Again, don't worry about that. We must understand the move and plan to counter whatever the purpose is.'

'Perhaps she has seen the futility of her plans,' suggested Bill, not very convincingly.

'No,' said Miss Barker, 'it is the contrary. Her plans, whatever they are, are now on the point of bearing fruit. We must keep an eye on everything.'

'But how are her plans in Binawarra going to bear fruit if she's not around?' said Bill.

'I don't know yet. That is what we must keep a lookout for.'

'But she is not here,' stressed Joanne. 'How will she do it?'

'Consider carefully,' said Miss Barker, as much to herself as to Bill and Joanne. 'She has set many things in train, and they now have their own momentum. She has completely removed you from the field, Bill. She has the editor of the *Binawarra and District Mail* dancing to her tune. Now she has Jane Cox fronting the media on her behalf. Everyone has fallen in with her plans. She is a very cunning woman. She is also a very ruthless woman. I am sure she had Bob McKinnon murdered because, somehow, he hit on her objective and the reasons for it. Now, that objective is Estella.'

'But why? Why resort to murder?' said Bill. 'It's baffling. It doesn't make sense that all this trouble is for something connected with Estella.'

'I know,' said Miss Barker grimly.

'Did you know,' said Bill, 'the department has instructed me to encourage Charles and Aine to let Estella attend a work experience program next weekend?'

'No, I know nothing about it.'

'Yes, it seems it was the last thing Miss Bicknell arranged before her departure. She complained about my reluctance to recommend that Estella go. I was questioning her professionalism. Anyhow, the department officials leaned on me to give the weekend my blessing. I don't have a choice.'

'What are the arrangements?'

'It's all straightforward, as a matter of fact. Several companies have organised the weekend for students with the best prospects. It is all outlined in the invitation. The students will be under supervision the whole time. The school has no part to play in this. I can't see how it will suit Miss Bicknell's plans or how she can manipulate it to her advantage. There'll be too much supervision.'

'Can I see a copy of the invitation and the schedule?' said Miss Barker.

'I will show you on Monday morning. I suppose I'll hear then about Miss Bicknell's resignation.'

Chapter 26

Len and Estella

AT HALF-PAST seven that evening, Larry Burgess was walking along Old Melbourne Road, wondering if he had understood correctly. Was he really on the way to pick up Estella Winterbine to take her to a party? Was it really true she had rung him and asked him to take her? It was true, and he still could not believe it. He was under no apprehension, though. Estella had said she wanted to be friends like before, but still— Just about every male in Binawarra would die for the opportunity to go out with her, no matter the arrangement. As he approached the Winterbine house, he tried to suppress his rising anxiety. He relaxed a little when he caught sight of Estella standing alone on the verandah waiting for him. He drew breath as he opened the gate and had a clear view of her, enshrouded in the soft glow of the verandah light, dressed in a long light mauve skirt and a blue blouse imprinted with a brown cross-like motif. The long, wide sleeves ended at wrists adorned with fine, elegant bangles. Her hair fell loose around her shoulders, and she wore no makeup. A delicate silver chain around her neck hid behind her blouse.

'Thank you, Larry, for taking me. I appreciate it,' she said as she came down the stairs.

'Hello, Larry,' said Mrs Winterbine, emerging from the doorway. 'We are relying on you to look after Estella. Please make sure you walk her home, too.'

'Of course, Mrs Winterbine.'

With Mrs Winterbine's acknowledgment of Larry's undertaking and her wishing them an enjoyable evening, they set off for the walk to Tricia Barry's house. Estella put Larry at ease by chatting about her experiences in Bendigo and her friendship with Ruby. About halfway there, she put her arm through his.

'Do you mind, Larry?'

'Of course not, Estella,' he said, blushing.

They arrived at Tricia Barry's house, where Len, Jenny, and their friends greeted them on the front porch. They stared at Estella with her arm through Larry's. Len gave Larry a momentary frown. When they were settled in the lounge room, Estella found herself next to Jenny on the settee, with Len in the armchair beside her. Tricia, Dennis Lorimer, and John Sayer occupied the armchairs opposite. Larry stood alone beside the settee, but, upon receiving a dismissive nod from Len, joined the people near the record player. Estella, who did not see the nod, was going to call him to join them, but thought he might be content where he was. She wondered where Tricia's parents were.

'Oh, they're out for the night. So they won't bother us,' she said. Sniggers around the room greeted this news.

Jenny led the conversation, and Estella was happy to listen to her babbling on. It was like old times. At length, she became aware that the music was soft and to her liking. That may be for her sake. If so, she appreciated it. Despite the beer and wine consumed, there was no loud, raucous behaviour. Somebody even gave her a glass of orange juice when she sat down. She relaxed and gave her attention to the conversation. Len maintained the pleasant manner he had adopted with her since that day on the way to school when he said the bet was a joke. The bet! Nobody had mentioned it, and with so much to distract her, it had slipped her mind. It must have been a joke, as Len said. As she listened to his friendly conversation and noted his attention to her comfort, she was ready to accept it.

In this way, the group laughed and talked for some time. Len gave a signal now and then to turn down the music. Disgruntled noises came from the people dancing, but they did as they were told. Larry came and asked Estella if she was all right. Estella said everything was all right, but he should join them. At another dismissive nod from Len, unseen by Estella, Larry said he would listen to the music. She found that strange. Then Len's conversation took on a confidential, even intimate, tone. He made pointed remarks when Jenny's attention was elsewhere.

'You know, Estella, I did not understand why you were so interested in reading and gardening until recently,' he said when Jenny left the group to help Tricia with the food and drinks. 'But I have come to understand there is a lot to garden design and that great literature is not only entertaining but informative.'

'There is a whole history connected with garden design,' she said, not knowing what else to say to this unexpected admission.

'I know,' he said, lowering his voice and leaning towards her. 'I will make sure I read more about it.' Dennis Lorimer, and John Sayer joined the others in dancing, leaving Estella alone with Len. 'I suppose if I had thought about it earlier, I would have realised how interesting it was. But, you know, things happen. You get distracted and caught up in superficial activities. You know, the people you mix with …'

There was no mistaking it; it was a criticism of Jenny. It was harsh, made with Jenny's declarations of love fresh in her mind. Her first reaction was to be sorry for her lifelong friend. To have given herself so fully to Len and be demeaned in this offhand manner was horrible. As Len's criticism became more open, and he hinted he was drawn more to her interests and way of life, his former duplicity emerged. At length, his breach of trust so revolted her that she could hardly maintain her composure. How could he believe he was fooling her? Did he really think she was that gullible?

She looked around for Larry and saw him looking at her from across the room. Len, taking her silence and calm expression as an encouraging sign, was emboldened to continue. She tried to signal to Larry to join them, but he was not used to her ways and stood back, indecisive. Jenny returned and sat beside her. Tricia and Dennis Lorimer also returned to their seats. Len made some friendly remarks to Jenny about the music and dancing. Estella excused herself and got up. The others, not noticing anything remarkable, said nothing. She walked over to Larry.

'Larry, please take me home,' she whispered.

'But ... why? What has happened?' he said, seeing Estella's agitated but resolute expression.

'Please, I don't want to talk about it. I want you to take me home. I will see you on the porch outside.'

Puzzled, Larry joined her a minute later. He followed her through the front gate. When he came up beside her, she took his arm. He looked at her but said nothing. They had got around fifty yards down the street when they heard a call.

'Estella, wait!' Len was running after them.

'Don't stop, Larry,' she said. But Larry stopped.

Seconds later, Len was with them. 'Where in the hell are you going?' he said, panting.

'Estella wants to go home,' replied Larry, seeing that Estella would not answer.

'Why?'

'I don't think she feels well.'

'I'll take her home, then. You go back to the party.'

'No, I want Larry to take me home.'

'It's not necessary. I can take you. I invited you. I should take you home. Larry, you go back to the party. Go on!'

'No, Larry, stay! Please.'

'Go!' commanded Len.

'Larry, I want you to take me. You told my mother you would.'

'Larry! Get back to the party!'

'Larry, please—'

'Come on, Estella,' said Len, grabbing her arm.

Estella jerked her arm free.

'I said, come on,' said Len, grabbing at her again.

Estella brushed him off again.

'Bitch!' cried Len and grabbed her with both hands, trying to draw her to him.

Estella struggled. 'Larry, help me!'

Larry stood paralysed. Len released his grip with a groan. A dark figure brushed beside Estella as Len went reeling back, losing his balance, and tumbling along the ground. The dark figure picked him up and shook him.

'Look after her, Larry,' the dark figure ordered. 'Take her home. Now!'

Larry watched, stupefied, as Len spun back again along the path. 'Move!' the dark figure repeated. Larry's trance was broken, and he hurried to Estella. He took her arm and led her away. He turned around once more to see a ferocious blow send Len tumbling over. Len was, at last, getting the thrashing he deserved.

Outside the Barry house, Geoff picked up Len and held him by his shirt. He shook him. 'You will never go near Estella Winterbine again. Is that clear?'

'Yes, let me go,' whimpered Len as he peered into the glinting, angry eyes half-hidden by the dark beanie pulled down to the man's brows.

He was lifted off the ground and thrown against the fence. The momentum took him over the fence and face down into the garden dirt. Len got up to see the figure disappearing into the shadows of the street. He felt his ribs and flinched in pain. Wiping his face and brushing the dirt off his clothes, he limped towards the front door as his friends appeared. They looked at him in astonishment. Bent over, he passed them without saying anything. Across the road, hidden by the trees, Boris had been a witness. He had been on the point of intervening when he saw someone save him the trouble. It was too dark to see who had appeared from nowhere to deal out the punishment, too dark even to confirm that it was the soldier. The figure disappeared into the shadows. Boris followed Estella and Larry at a distance to see if the figure would appear. There was no sign of him. He looked around as he went, wondering where the man had gone.

With Estella and Larry just in view along the straight stretch of road, Geoff had turned into the darkest driveway he saw. He had seen Boris arrive outside the Barry house. He ran through to the back fence, climbed over into the backyard of the next house, and emerged on the road parallel with the street Estella and Larry were in. He ran along several blocks, which brought him to Gold Nugget Way. There he turned to the left and edged his way towards the junction. Estella and Larry appeared, walking slowly. He could see, or rather sense, that Estella was upset, very upset. Bent down against the front fence of a house, he watched as they crossed over and continued in silence. A minute later, Boris appeared. He looked around as he crossed the intersection.

AS ESTELLA felt the dark figure brush by and saw Len reeling backwards, she knew it was Geoff. If she could have wished for anyone, as Len grabbed her, his face contorted, it was Geoff. And there he was. There he was, breaking the threatening hold and flinging the danger away from her. She glanced back as Larry took her arm and saw Geoff's violent treatment of Len. She did not want to watch any longer and turned away, giving herself to Larry's care. Her mind connected the releasing violence with all she had experienced since the moment she had seen Geoff on Anzac Square. And the more she thought about him and how he looked after her, the more she despaired. After they had crossed over Gold Nugget Way, her head drooped. She slowed. Some fifty yards further on, she came to a stop.

'What's wrong?' said Larry. In the scant light, he saw the pain. 'I'm sorry,' he said, ashamed and embarrassed at his loss of courage.

'No ... I—,' said Estella, as she turned to him. She came a little forward and bent her head, so it rested on his shoulder. Larry felt the slight movement of her head as she released a few quiet sobs. At first, he did not know how to react, but then he put his arms around her. To his surprise and reassurance, she welcomed his comfort.

Geoff watched from behind trees in the front garden of a house not far away. He was happy to see Estella's friend looking after her at last. There was a wrench at his heart as he watched the young fellow with his arms around her. Up the road in the dark, Boris also looked on. He hastened a few steps forward but then stopped. Estella lifted her head, brushed her eyes, said something to Larry, and they resumed their way. They passed so close to Geoff that he could have reached out and grabbed them. He remained motionless and felt another tug at his heart as he caught a glimpse of the sorrowful expression on the face of the seventeen-year-old.

Shortly after midnight, Geoff approached his farmhouse as quietly as he could so as not to disturb his farm manager. He parked his bike and walked to the front verandah steps while the kelpies leapt with subdued yelps around his legs. He sat down and surveyed the clear night sky as he patted his dogs. Apart from Estella's unpleasant experience, the rest of the evening had passed routinely. Boris had given up his surveillance and returned to his motel. The party was still going on at eleven o'clock. Len Dawson and his friends were settled there. He checked Jane Cox's house several times. She was home when he last checked at half past ten. The Premier Network reporter's car was parked at the front. He assumed they were both inside for the night. There was no sign of Stephen Calder anywhere.

He had sneaked into Miss Barker's house and brought her up to date. She was not perturbed by Estella's experience with Len Dawson, remarking that it was one of many unpleasant experiences Estella was sure to endure during her youth. She was fortunate that he was present to protect her. Geoff was no longer oblivious to Miss Barker's meaning. How perceptive that woman was. As for the rest of his information, she noted it without comment. She recommended he rest for a couple of days. He might need his energies in the coming weeks. She would make sure that Estella was safe. He was dismissed with the warning that he had to be ready at a moment's notice.

Now he sat there on the verandah steps contemplating Estella. He had gone from regarding her as an untouchable object belonging to another realm to feelings of protection, then finally to feelings of affection. How did it happen? Or how did he let it happen? When did it happen? Despite her mature appearance, she was much too young for him. For him! How could he be entertaining such thoughts? And what about Ruby? He really liked Ruby. But was he in love with her? He thought he was. In contrast, his feelings for seventeen-year-old Estella were different. He did not want to think about it. It was a feeling he was unused to. He was used to working things out calmly and decisively. This was no good. He got up and shooed the dogs away. They retreated to the side of the house, where they watched him in his indecision.

He walked over to the nearby fence and looked up at the clear night sky. The quarter moon gave a dim silvery glow to the surroundings. He looked towards the Goanna. It seemed in readiness. He looked away, and the evening scenes passed before his eyes. He saw Estella fighting off Dawson. Later, she broke down and cried on the shoulder of the friend who had let her down. The contrast between her softness and her affectionate nature with such a determined spirit and unbowed principles, shone from the scenes he contemplated.

Again, a person like Estella could not exist without society's protection. Was that why he had roughed up Len Dawson so violently, far more than he would have usually done? He had wanted to hurt him and had to keep himself in check. He must shake off this churning of his thoughts. He shivered. Miss Barker was right: he had to ready himself. There were signs that something was going to happen. That Rostowski—now there was someone who seemed ready for violence. He could smell it. He would be ready to protect Estella as much as necessary. This, he knew how to do. About that other, he sighed and told himself that he should let events take their natural course. He had no control over it.

A CAR WITH its headlights out rolled to a stop outside St Philomena's presbytery at three-thirty on Sunday morning. Two men and a woman got out carrying cans and brushes. One man jumped the fence and painted PERVERT in thick white letters over the front of the presbytery, while the other two painted PERVERT LIVES HERE over the front footpath. Then they were back in the car and driving off.

Late on Sunday morning, Charles, Aine, and Estella arrived with brushes, brooms, buckets, and a good supply of turpentine. They set to work removing the paint. Fr. van Engelen leaned on his walking stick and looked on. He ignored the ringing phone. People avoided walking by the presbytery, and those who came by hurried on. Charles tried to cheer him up. They would see that nothing happened to him. Estella looked at Fr. van Engelen, who seemed to understand her thoughts. He gave her a look of resignation.

That whole day, Bill and Joanne stayed inside. The phone was off the hook. The front curtains were drawn to shield them from the people driving by and gawking. The Premier Network car pulled up twice, but nobody got out. Bill kept walking from the lounge room to the front windows, peeking through the curtains and then walking back again. Joanne was worried about him. He was not behaving normally. The affair was like a sword in his chest. Fortunately, Flo came during the afternoon. Her encouragement was priceless.

***

AS BILL Huckerby expected, the department officials turned up at ten-thirty on Monday to seek an urgent meeting with him. Miss Bicknell had resigned. Did he know that? Sadly, with the principal's loss of confidence in her, she could not stay a moment longer in the school. The department accepted her request for immediate release with understanding and sympathy. All this just added to the principal's problems, they said. Then Mrs Charing's replacement interrupted them to announce that one of the parents demanded an interview. When Mrs Anderson was asked to usher the parent in, she said, embarrassed, that the parent wanted to see th e officials in private. The senior official followed her into the reception area. He returned a minute later.

'Mr Huckerby, Mr Barry has requested a private interview with us. Would you kindly leave? We will call you when needed.'

Bill walked to Miss Barker's sickroom. He was sorry to find she was not there. He sat on the bed and waited. Fifteen minutes later, Mrs Anderson arrived to fetch him. He returned to his office and was requested to resume his seat in front of the two officials. They regarded him more severely than before.

'Mr Huckerby,' the junior official announced, 'things are going from bad to worse. Mr Barry has informed us that one of your teachers has a relationship with his fourteen-year-old daughter.'

'Who?' said Bill in dismay.

'You know nothing about this?'

'No! I would have intervened if I had any inkling that—'

'Perhaps you should have been alert to this.'

'How could I? Nobody else knew.'

'You are the principal. It is your duty to be abreast of these things.'

Squeezed again!

'I found not a jot of evidence in the school during my interviews with the teaching staff. Who is the teacher?'

'Mr Barry said he would not talk to you because of the current scandal. He did not believe he could have confidence in you.'

'But we have found nothing—' Bill realised what he was admitting.

'Mr Huckerby,' said the senior official, 'we have no other option but to suspend you until this business has been resolved. We will ask the deputy principal, Mr Seaver, to take full control from this point on. We request that you remove yourself from the premises. My colleague will escort you to your car.'

Bill collected his personal items. 'Who is the teacher concerned?' he asked again, on the point of leaving his office.

'You are now suspended. That is no concern of yours.'

The junior official accompanied Bill to his car and waited until he had driven from the school grounds before returning to his office.

STEPHEN CALDER sat opposite the department officials and regarded them with an impudent curiosity.

'Mr Calder,' said the junior official, 'we will get straight to the point. Mr Barry, one of the—'

'I know who he is,' snapped Calder. 'What's this about?'

'Mr Barry has accused you of having a relationship with his fourteen-year-old daughter.'

'Who told him that?'

'Mr Calder, we ask the questions—'

'You won't ask questions that deny my rights,' Calder said, leaning a little forward.

'Mr Calder, we have a duty, and the authority, to ask you questions about a serious matter,' said the official, eyeing his size and belligerent posture.

'You don't have a duty or the authority to deny me my rights.' He straightened and leaned back into his armchair. 'I want to know who or what the sources of this allegation are. Did his daughter tell him?'

'No, and we cannot reveal his source. He has not told us as yet. Mr Calder, this is serious. Mr Barry claims he has the evidence and will cause much trouble if the business is not handled to his satisfaction.'

Unperturbed, Calder held their gaze. 'You should be careful who is doing the political manoeuvring.'

'What do you mean?' said the senior official, frowning.

'Exactly what I say.'

'You will have to explain yourself.'

Calder hesitated. 'Let me paint a hypothetical picture for you, Gentlemen. Say you discovered that one of the teachers here was having a relationship with a fourteen-year-old student, and say that relationship happened outside the school. Say that fourteen-year-old girl was not only willing but claimed she was in love with the teacher and enjoyed having sex with him. What then?'

'Mr Calder, it's a crime to have sex with an underage girl.'

'Underage? Most intelligent people these days know that society's decision to set the limit for lawful sex at sixteen is totally arbitrary. The empirical evidence is that females of fourteen and under have sex and enjoy it. The indisputable physiological evidence is that a girl of fourteen is not only ready for sexual activity but also desires sexual pleasure. The sixteen-year age limit resulted from a society still tied up by oppressive Christian morality. Few people in academia, especially those in the social sciences, would regard that moral code seriously. Sex is something to be enjoyed by those willing, no matter who they are—and what age.'

'It is still a crime,' said the senior official, shifting in his seat.

'I know nobody who disagrees with me about this, and all my contacts are in academia, the media, or the unions,' said Calder. 'In fact, some old student buddies are now in the department.' He paused and regarded them with a malicious grin. 'You know, I can name at least three people in high positions in these areas who have indulged in sexually forbidden activity—arbitrarily forbidden, that is.' He named three names, leaving th e officials gaping.

'What do you expect us to do with the complaint, Mr Calder?'

'I know more about Mr Barry than you do.' A crooked grin appeared on his face as he paused for effect. 'Mr Barry is a broad-minded man. He leaves his daughters to their own devices. I know that. He is so broad-minded that he would not think twice about having an affair. Indeed, Gentlemen, I know of at least two women he has had a relationship with. I know because I have enjoyed them, too. It seems to me that an acute case of hypocrisy has struck Mr Barry. If the accusations are true and I am not admitting any- thing, his daughters are simply following his example. They are enjoying people they enjoy being with. Game, set, and match, Gentlemen.'

'Daughters? We were speaking about one daughter.' Calder gestured dismissively. 'I ask again, Mr Calder,' said the senior official, with increas- ing alarm, 'what do you expect us to do?'

'You should treat Barry sympathetically.'

There was a long silence while the dismayed officials and Stephen Calder regarded each other. Finally, Calder broke the silence by naming the two women. The officials did not respond.

'Mr Calder,' said the senior official, 'we will consider the complaint further and call on you if needed. Thank you for your co-operation.'

Stephen Calder swaggered out of the office without acknowledging the officials and headed for the staffroom, where he made a cup of coffee and sat lazily in an armchair, grinning.

'MR BARRY,' said the senior official, in a confidential tone, 'you should take this as a preliminary meeting. Be assured, we will do all in our power to provide you with satisfaction and to ensure that justice is served. Feel free to contact us at any time. Now, let me inform you of our meeting with Mr Calder.' Mr Barry, looking relaxed, nodded. 'Firstly, Mr Calder has rejected the accusations.'

'I have the proof.'

'He is prepared to challenge the charge.'

'On what grounds?'

'He would not say. He would only say that he has a defence against the charges. That, of course, would come out in an official inquiry.' The official hesitated. 'He said he would call upon character witnesses. He has friendships with many people who would speak on his behalf.' The official then named the two women.

Mr Barry blanched. 'Oh?'

'But that's just routine, I might add,' said the junior official. 'I'm sure you have your own support.'

'Yes, of course.'

'But look,' said the senior official, 'let's try to resolve this question without causing too much inconvenience for anyone. That won't serve any purpose, will it, Mr Barry?'

'No ... not really.'

'Good. You will receive every consideration, I assure you. Your daughter will be counselled and provided with the means to overcome any psychological discomfort. It goes without saying that the department will reimburse any out-of-pocket expenses incurred by you and your daughter. You would help if you could give me a preliminary estimate of immediate expenses.'

'Yes, of course,' said Mr Barry. 'I will be in touch tomorrow.'

'We are finishing our inquiries in Binawarra today, but I will give you my direct number. Please call me on that number so we can discuss the matter further. Is that all right?'

'Yes, yes, of course.'

After seeing a mollified Mr Barry off, the senior official turned to his colleague. 'Check the accounts for a surplus somewhere. A few thousand dollars will do, I believe. Bury it among sundry expenses. The junior official nodded. 'And keep this to yourself, do you hear?'

Later that afternoon, Stephen Calder walked into the offices of the *Binawarra and District Mail*. Without acknowledging anyone, he breezed into Alan Collins's office and shut the door. Collins looked up. He dropped his pen and pushed the document he was reading aside.

'I have a short message to give you,' said Calder, 'and I don't want you to say a word.' In front of him on the desk, he spied a mug with a bunch of pencils. He extracted a pencil, snapped it in two, and threw the bits in front of Collins. 'If ever you feel inclined to print something about me that may cause me inconvenience, you should know I will not sit back and take it like others.' He extracted three pencils one after the other, snapped them in two, and threw the bits on the desk. 'I have ten pieces of damaging information about you and your paper for every piece you could print about me.' More snapping and discarding of pencils. 'I know something about you that hardly anybody else knows.' Collins shrugged. 'I have many contacts in the unions,' Calder went on. 'If you do anything to disturb our campaigns, I will have your business shut down. Finally, I will personally deal with you if you cause me undue trouble.' He snapped the remaining pencils one after the other and threw them on the desk.

'A little melodramatic, don't you think?' said the newspaper editor, looking at the bits of pencil scattered in front of him. 'I'm not without my resources. I, too, will not sit back and take it.'

'We'll see. You are warned. I will take pleasure in mucking up your face.' He turned and strolled from the office and out of the building.

Collins cleared the broken pencils from his desk and reached for the sheet of paper he had set aside when Calder walked in. It was a proof of the front page of the next edition of the *Binawarra and District Mail*. The headline read: Sexual abuse and the glorification of war.

Chapter 27

Estella and Larry

ESTELLA HAD NOT long set out for school the following morning when she saw Larry ahead, staring at the ground in front of him. He looked up when he heard her footsteps.

'Hello, Larry, I'm glad to see you.'

'Are you?'

'Yes, of course.'

'Even after Saturday night?'

'Especially after Saturday night.'

'Really? It was pretty gutless of me.'

'Larry, in the end, you stayed with me. You gave me comfort when I needed it.'

'I promise you I won't let that happen again. I won't let Len Dawson or anyone else intimidate me.'

'Your dependability and friendship mean so much.'

'You have it.'

Estella put her arm through his as they walked on. They crossed over Melbourne Road and continued up Diggers Road towards the high school. They both knew it would be better to enter the school by the front gates.

'Who was that?' said Larry.

'I would rather not say at the moment.'

'Why?'

'I would rather not say that, either.'

They were nearing the front gates when Larry spoke again. 'Whoever it was, he got across to me. He made me realise what a wimp I've been.'

'Did he do that?' said Estella, stopping.

'Yes. The speed and decisiveness of his action—the man obviously wasn't afraid. He gave Len what he deserved. I was totally ignorant of it before that. I didn't understand that someone like Len Dawson needs to cop it that way. Other ways don't work.' He paused. 'You know about the bet, don't you?'

'Len told me it was a joke,' said Estella, expecting Larry to confirm that the bet was real after all.

'I know. He told us to spread the word. Estella, I'm really sorry. I was there when it all started. At least I had nothing to do with the betting.'

'Larry, I can't tell you what it means to hear you admit that it was wrong.'

'I'm sorry, Estella. I see now how rotten it all is. The man who gave Len his medicine wouldn't get into something like that. I could hear it in his voice.'

'Oh? What did he say?'

'He said, "Look after her. Take her home. Now!" So unlike Len. It's hard to understand how Len could fool us.'

'You are right, Larry. He is a man of principle. I'm glad you see it.'

'Can I meet him sometime?'

'Of course. He will be happy to be friends with you. I know he will.'

AT MORNING recess, Estella went to her usual spot under the trees. She had seen the unfriendly looks of Len's group, Jenny's, in particular, as she passed them. She took her position under the tree. Larry was not far away by himself, hesitating. She waved him over.

'Larry, I'm so relieved you are here to be with me,' she said when he sat next to her. 'They don't look very friendly, do they?'

'No, they're not. You must be careful, Estella. You don't know them as well as I do. I mean, you can't imagine what they are capable of. Len knows he's lost the bet. You've hurt and humiliated him. So he won't hold back now.'

Len stood clutching his side, giving signs of discomfort as he shifted position. A brownish abrasion was visible on his temple. He had the leering, mocking expression Estella had been so familiar with. He seemed to be making remarks about her and Larry, for there were contemptuous glances and sniggering.

'He's working them up,' said Larry. 'I know how he does it. I can't believe I didn't see through him before.' He turned to Estella. 'There was never any chance he would succeed with the bet, was there?'

'No, Larry. I would rather die than submit to him.'

'I believe you.'

'I appreciate that.'

'It's only what you deserve,' he said. Then, after a pause, 'I want to apologise for being part of the way you have been isolated these last couple of years. I hope I can make up for it. With the friendship you want.'

'You already have. As long as I have your trust and friendship, you will have my affection.' She paused. 'But why couldn't you see how deceptive and manipulative Len is?'

'Two months ago, I wouldn't have been able to answer, but now I'm seeing it through your eyes,' he said, gesturing his self-guilt. 'I didn't then. And I don't know why. You sort of get immersed in the group's connectedness, and you automatically begin to think like it. Len comes across as a pretty impressive fellow. That confidence, that big mouth—he says things nobody else would dare to say. You soak up his mentality. His mentality becomes the group's. While you are a part of Len's group, you share that mentality. It's like being enslaved. I started to break free from it when you spoke to me outside the hall on the first day of school, and Len took on the bet.' He stopped and shifted on the bench. 'I am sorry, Estella, it sounds so crude and cowardly now.'

'Is that why Jenny is so tied to Len? I mean that the group influences her feelings towards Len?'

'It has to. Otherwise, how do you explain it? Jenny is stunning and classy. It's a mystery she was blind to his tactics and the trouble he would give her.'

'Does he cause her trouble?'

'Yes, a lot. We all hear about it, the boys, I mean—well, heard now for me. You're not the only one he's tried it on with. Only he didn't succeed with you. Jenny can't cope with it. She's now suspecting everyone. She didn't suspect you, though.'

As Estella reflected on Jenny's recent behaviour, she was not so sure. They looked across at the group. Jenny saw them looking and glared. She said something to Len, who cast a look of contempt at them and spat out a comment. Jenny continued to glare. Finally, she broke away and rushed over to them.

'You are such a hypocrite! You ... you phony goody-two-shoes,' she said to Estella, stumbling over her words as she came and stood in front of them with hands on her hips. 'And, and ... you're a fake ... and all that talk about honesty and purity ... and all the while you were working your dirty little tricks!'

'What do you mean?' said Estella, her voice wavering.

'You know. As if you didn't. You're nothing but a big tease.'

'She means Len has told her you gave him the come-on,' said Larry.

'I did no such thing. You must know how I have always felt about Len Dawson.'

'You're a fool to swallow anything Len tells you,' Larry said. 'He's a liar. That's his talent. Face facts and stop letting him use you.'

Jenny glared at Larry, first in astonishment and then in anger. 'How dare you talk to me like that, you ... you non-event!'

'I wasn't a non-event when you used to play with Estella and me.'

'She's got you taken in, too,' said Jenny, her lips quivering. She turned to Estella. 'You make me sick! You're so two-faced.'

'Jenny, I would never—'

'I am not falling for your tricks anymore—' Her breast was heaving, and she stared wildly, her long blond wavy hair whipping around her face as she jerked her head this way and that. It was no use. She could not control herself. She turned and ran, sobbing back to Len and the group. Tricia Barry put her arm around her.

Larry saw the hurt on Estella's face but thought it best to keep quiet. It was getting to the end of the recess, anyhow. 'You like that man who took on Len, don't you?' he said to change the subject as the bell sounded. Again, pain passed over her face.

'I admire him very much.'

'He must like you to be around at the very moment you needed help.' It was a calculated comment, for he could not contain his curiosity. They walked towards the classroom block.

'He has a girlfriend. I think he wants to marry her. He treats me like a sister,' she said, staring at the ground in front of her.

'I got the impression it's more than that.'

'You are mistaken.'

Larry disagreed but did not comment. 'How old is he? Late twenties?'

'Yes, how do you know? It was too dark to see, wasn't it?'

'It was dark, but I could tell from his build, voice, and manner.' Larry stopped at the entrance to the classroom block. 'From the tone of his voice and the way he dealt with Len, I would say he regards you as more than a sister.' Larry could not help pursuing the subject. He was intrigued that Estella was showing some emotion over a man.

'You are mistaken, Larry,' she said again.

Larry had seen enough, and he followed her quietly.

ESTELLA ENTERED the classroom, still pondering Larry's last comment. As she passed the rostrum, she noticed Miss Cox with a woman she didn't recognise.

'This morning, we will have a special class on social issues,' said Jane when the class had settled. 'This is an important part of our personal development program. We will discuss the moral problems confronting you as autonomous adults in modern society. At my request, Ms Eva Reiner, who has special expertise in the approach we are adopting this morning, has kindly come up from Melbourne for this special period. Please welcome Ms Reiner.'

'Thank you, Jane,' Ms Reiner said, resolutely coming forward. 'Now, this is quite simple, really. As Ms Cox said, it is about personal development, your personal development as autonomous moral agents, enjoying and asserting the fullness of your human rights. We will acquire a deeper understanding of the everyday ethical issues we face by simulating the kind of thinking that should engage you as you confront them. I will raise different issues, and we will then split into groups to discuss them. Let's get started.

'The first topic is relationships. You are all at an age when you have boyfriends and girlfriends. This is only natural, and it's an important stage in your life. The question is: how serious should those relationships be at your age and time of life? Okay, let's hear your opinions.' She went around the class in random order, listening to the different opinions. At length, she stopped to summarise.

'We can isolate the following group opinions. Firstly, relationships should be as serious as you want. It's your decision. Secondly, you should keep relationships in perspective, as there is so much to experience before you get serious about someone. Thirdly, you should not take relationships too seriously and always be ready to move on when you have lost interest. Are there other views?' She looked around the classroom and let her gaze alight on Estella. 'What does that young woman think there?' Everyone turned towards Estella. 'What's your name?' Estella gave her name. 'Well, Estella, what do you think? Do you have an opinion that differs from those I have just mentioned?'

'It depends on what those opinions really mean,' she said hesitantly.

'Well, give your opinion. Tell us what you think.'

'People our age should be careful about entering into serious, committed relationships. We need the time and experience to know our true feelings. You need to know the other person well before you commit yourself.'

'So well that you are ready for marriage?'

'Yes, that's what I think.'

'You mean no contact before then? No going out and spending time alone with someone you like?'

Len and his friends smirked at each other.

'You can spend time with someone you like without entering into a serious relationship.'

'You mean no touching?'

'You can enjoy the company of someone you like without touching if that means more than holding hands or walking arm in arm.'

There were muffled sniggers during this exchange, and the class broke into laughter at Estella's final comment.

'Please, please, patience,' said Ms Reiner, holding up her hands. 'You will have the chance to discuss and debate this and other opinions. Please form into three like-minded groups.'

There was much bustle and chatter as the class moved about. When the students had settled, Estella found herself sitting alone.

'It looks like you're in a group of one,' said Ms Reiner, raising her eyebrows. 'Join the group nearest your views.' She split the three groups into six discussion groups. She and Ms Cox moved around, offering an assessment of the discussions and suggesting directions the students had not considered. Fortunately, Estella found herself in a group across the room from Len's group, and, better still, she was left alone. After some time, Ms Reiner called the class to attention.

'Right, we will go a little further in our discussions. I presume you are all normal, healthy young people with normal sex drives. What part should sexual activity have in your relationships? Before I continue, I assume everyone knows what I am talking about. Is there anyone who has not experienced sexual desire?'

There was a brief pause before another muffled snigger moved in a wave through the class. Estella held her hand up. More sniggering.

'Estella, you have not experienced sexual arousal?' said Ms Reiner.

'That's personal information,' said Estella. 'It's not necessary for the discussion.'

'Of course, you can defend that sort of information as personal, as belonging to your private life, but your fellow students are entitled to ask why you think it's necessary to keep it private, wouldn't you think?' She did not wait for an answer and turned to the class for their opinions about sexual permissiveness. The class delighted in offering a range of views. Again, Ms Reiner came last to Estella. 'What do you think, Estella?'

'I don't think premarital sex is right,' said Estella. She had the sense that Ms Reiner would continue to put pressure on her. So she might as well be forthright.

'Never?'

'No, sexual activity belongs to a loving relationship.'

'So there are no loving relationships outside of marriage?'

'No, a relationship is consecrated in a formal union if it is truly lasting and loving. Sexual activity follows that as an expression of that union.'

'Consecrated? Formal union? That sounds like religious language.'

'It is the teaching of the Catholic Church.'

'Don't you have an opinion of your own?'

'That is my opinion. I agree with the teaching of the Church. If I didn't, I would not be a part of it, and I would behave differently.' She glanced around. 'Besides, if my opinions are learned, they are no more so than those I have heard here.'

Ms Reiner blinked and regarded Estella. 'Now, Estella, I don't know whether you realise it, but all you have said raises the previous question. If you express such a view about sexual activity and marriage, we must assume you have experienced sexual arousal.'

'I haven't,' said Estella, not agreeing with Ms Reiner's conclusion and suspecting this was the answer Ms Reiner was looking for. Her response, as she expected, was met with sniggers and snorts.

'You are a virgin, then?' said Ms Reiner.

'That's not a subject for discussion.'

'Then how can you judge?'

'About what?'

'About sexual activity.'

'You can have an opinion about something without having experienced it.'

'Now, really, that's the question. Can you hold a reasonable opinion about sexual activity if you have never experienced it?' said Ms Reiner, addressing the whole class. 'How do we defend that view and the other views expressed here? Divide now into discussion groups.'

The class divided into four groups, leaving Estella alone on one side of the room.

'Is there no one else who is a virgin and has not experienced sexual arousal?' said Ms Reiner, surveying the room. Her question was greeted with more whispering and suppressed laughter.

Larry was not laughing. He had not laughed. He rose and sat next to Estella. 'I'm a virgin.'

Estella leaned towards him. 'Thank you, Larry.'

'Are we to understand that you, too, have never experienced sexual arousal?' said Ms Reiner, frowning at Larry.

'That's a private matter, as Estella said.'

'Yes, he has, and we know how,' called Len from the back. 'By looking at photos of Miss Winterbine. He's Miss Winterbine's devoted handmaiden!'

The class erupted in laughter.

'Please,' Jane Cox intervened, suppressing a smile, 'please keep the noise down.'

'The difference between me and some of you I'm looking at,' said Larry, when the laughter had died down, 'is that I admit it.'

'That will do now,' said Ms Reiner. 'We will now proceed to debate and defend our opinions.'

The rest of the class followed along the same lines. Whatever the subject, whether it was homosexuality, contraception, or divorce, Estella ended up sitting alone with Larry. Eva Reiner and Jane Cox encouraged Larry to express his true opinion, but Larry maintained solidarity with Estella. Estella was relieved when the final bell sounded.

'The point of this class,' said Jane Cox as the students were getting ready to go, 'is to encourage you to think as independent adults and to be aware of your rights as autonomous moral agents.'

'Does that mean autonomous in sexual matters?' Len called above the noise of the student bustle. The noise stopped.

'Especially in sexual matters,' said Ms Reiner. 'Gone are the days when teachers preached a restrictive, oppressive sexual morality to the young. You all must understand that you are the sole arbiter of what you do sexually. The young women here must realise that they have an indefeasible right to remain in control of their bodies.'

'So we ourselves choose when and with whom we have sex?'

'Yes,' said Ms Reiner, now cautious, 'but it is sex with consenting adults who have reached physical maturity.'

'So a fourteen-year-old girl who has reached full physical maturity has the right to decide independently whether or not she has sex?'

Eva Reiner and Jane Cox glanced at each other. 'It is unlawful to have sex with a girl of that age.'

'But according to what you just said, that law has to be arbitrary, doesn't it? Isn't it depriving a fourteen-year-old girl who wants to have sex of her inalienable human rights?'

There was a heavy silence as the students looked from Len to the two teachers and back again.

'This is a complex legal question,' said Ms Reiner. 'There is no time to go into that in these few short moments. You can leave it until the next class on personal development.'

Len smiled smugly as he and his retinue exited the classroom.

'Larry, I'm so grateful for your support,' said Estella when they were in the corridor. 'It wouldn't have been easy.'

'They were picking on you. It seemed deliberate, as if the class were specially organised for you. Do you know why?'

'Not really. I presume it's just because they know I think differently. Anyhow, I'm used to being isolated like that.'

'I'm not so sure,' said Larry. 'There seemed more behind it.'

With their classmates behind and in front of them, they were walking through a part of the corridor that narrowed with cupboards and storage rooms on one side and a bare wall on the other. Estella heard a faint sizzling and felt heat near her neck. Then Larry grabbed at her hair.

'Estella, your hair is burning!'

Before she knew what was going on, Larry had smothered the incipient flame and doused the burning with a can of drink. Estella brushed her hair and wiped the drink from her head and clothes. Larry turned to Len and his smirking mates. 'You cowardly sneak! I didn't realise until now how utterly gutless you are.'

'The devoted handmaiden protects his untouchable lady,' Len sneered.

Larry marched up close to him. 'You weren't so brave on Saturday night, were you?'

Len's mates moved to either side of Larry as he and Len stared at each other.

'Have you told your pals about the thrashing you got and how you whimpered like a baby?' He nudged Len with his chest.

The mates came in closer to hem Larry in. The other students fell silent. 'Did you tell them what I did before that ape grabbed me from behind?' He gestured with his hand.

'You filthy liar!' cried Larry, giving Len a vigorous shove.

Len's mates tried to grab Larry and push him away, but he brushed them off and came eyeball-to-eyeball with Len. Larry had never been known for belligerence, and, indeed, it had never entered his head to respond physically to Len's taunts. But now, as he stood staring into his mocking eyes, he felt a boundary had been passed. He grabbed him by his shirt, shook him, released him, and swung his fist in the direction of his face.

As fate would have it, the first punch Larry had ever released in anger collected Len across his left eye, sending him sprawling. The next moment, Len's mates had Larry around the neck, and one was punching into him. Larry struggled free for a moment, but then succumbed to the wild punching from both sides. After giving Larry several violent kicks to the body and head as he lay on the floor, they got Len to his feet, staggering and feeling the grazed skin around his eye. Estella knelt beside Larry, whose eyes were beginning to swell. He groaned. Shocked, she lifted his head. She became aware of Len standing over them.

'You're nothing but a bush scrubber, not worth urinating on,' he said, swaying and holding one hand over his eye. Then, in an unexpected movement, he reached down and tore the silver chain from Estella's neck.

Estella clutched at her neck while she held onto Larry. 'Give me that!' She stared at him.

Len seemed surprised at her burst of anger and then, in his usual sneering way, dropped the chain and medal on the floor in front of her. When she reached for it, he stamped his foot on it. He waited for her reaction. 'Come on, beg for it,' he said. She gave him the same angry look. He walked off, followed by his smirking retinue.

The students dispersed, expecting the commotion to bring one of the teachers.

Estella scooped up the medal and broken chain. 'Larry, are you all right?' she said.

Larry continued to groan, his swollen eyes shut. 'Help me up,' he said after a while. 'I should go to the sickroom.'

Supporting himself on Estella's arm, he made it to the sickroom, where he let himself fall awkwardly onto the bed. Estella sat next to him and took his hand. A few minutes later, Miss Barker burst through the door. She glanced at Larry and was going to say something, but noticed Estella's wet hair and uniform.

'Your hair is singed. You had better tell me what happened.'

Estella related the course of events while Miss Barker attended to Larry's grazes and bruises. When Estella had finished, and Larry was patched up to her satisfaction, Miss Barker left the room. Estella sat on the bed and took Larry's hand again. He opened his eyes and rubbed his forehead.

'I'm sorry,' said Estella. 'This is because of me.'

'No, Estella, you're not to blame,' he said, in a voice just above a whisper. 'Len had that coming to him. Someone at the school had to stand up to him. He has gotten away with it for too long. I stuck up for you. That's what your friend did.' He closed his eyes. 'What's his name?' he said after a minute.

Estella hesitated. 'Geoff,' she said, relenting, 'Geoff Shawcross. He was in the army until a couple of years ago. He has a farm north of St Arnaud.' Silence followed for some minutes.

'You know,' said Larry, 'I'm glad to have these cuts and bruises as a sign of doing the right thing at last. Don't feel sorry for me. I'm proud to have copped it. You should be protected against scum like Dawson.'

She bent over and kissed him on the cheek.

'I'm glad to have your friendship, Estella.' He put his hand on his forehead, closed his eyes, and seemed to drift off.

Another five minutes had passed in silence before Miss Barker returned with the deputy principal in her wake. 'I've explained to Mr Seaver what has happened,' she said. 'I have recommended you both return home and take the next few days off.'

'I accept Miss Barker's recommendation,' said Mr Seaver, after contemplating Larry. 'We can't have this sort of violence in the school, but I will leave it to Mr Huckerby to deal with it when he returns.' Then, turning to Miss Barker: 'Ah, Miss Barker, I forgot to tell you the department officials reversed their decision about Mr Huckerby. They suggested that he, too, take time off to rest. He will return to school next Monday.'

'What decision?'

'The suspension ... you know. You did know?'

'Suspension? When?'

'Today. It was lifted shortly before you came to me. I had only just spoken with Bill.'

'Suspended and unsuspended? Strange business, don't you reckon?'

'Strange?' he said, surprised. 'Well, Miss Barker, I would rather not discuss it here. However, let me say that the officials were being suitably cautious. They thought it best to take such action to avoid compromising the principal. It was for his sake. Later, they considered that, perhaps, the circumstances, after all, did not warrant such action. Simple. And I agree.'

Miss Barker found the explanation unconvincing, but there was no time to discuss it. She dropped off Estella and Larry, staying at both houses to explain what had happened and that the school had authorised time off for them. She had a suggestion about how Estella and Larry should spend their time resting. First, though, she had a few things to arrange. Back at her house, she dialled Ruby's number, hoping to catch her in her office. She was in luck. After a little more organising, she drove to the Huckerby house

.

'How are you, old friend?' she said to Bill as she arrived on the front verandah where he was sitting. 'It has not been easy, has it?'

'That's an understatement, Flo. I feel like a steamroller has been rolling over and over me.'

'The end is in sight. Keep up the resistance. Now, tell me what happened this morning. Bring me up to date.'

'It won't take long to tell you. Those city-types from the department said a parent accused a teacher of having a relationship with his fourteen-year-old daughter. That, they said, implicated me, and they had no choice but to suspend me. They escorted me from the school premises like a common criminal, from the school I had poured my heart into all these years. But to floor me all over again, no sooner had I finished telling Joanne than the phone rang. That snooty official dumbfounded me by saying that they had reconsidered and decided that the circumstances did not warrant my suspension.

'The matter, on further investigation, did not seem as serious as they thought. I should leave it to them to resolve. The parent was happy with that, too, they assured me. He said he was sorry for the hasty decision but hoped I would understand the difficulty such cases presented for the administration. Although I was free to return to school, he recommended I take some time off, perhaps until next Monday. They would have their report ready by then, and, apart from a few recommendations on procedures, it would scotch the rumours and insinuations doing the rounds. What do you think of that?' He held out his hands.

'I'm not surprised.'

'Oh, okay, astound me again,' said Bill, with a sigh.

'I know who the parent is. I know who the student is. And I know who the teacher is. Mr Barry's complaint has a solid foundation.'

'Don't hold me in suspense, Flo.'

'I am not going to tell you anything more.'

'What! Why?'

'It won't do you any good now. For one thing, you will be blocked in your efforts to find the right evidence. You'll waste your time and likely get into trouble by appearing to confirm the charges Collins has been running against you. I'll only say this: a cover-up is underway, and it works in your favour. It will stop further agitation within the school and starve Collins of ammunition.' She stopped and rubbed her chin. 'I would not be surprised if he has got at Collins,' she said, more to herself than Bill.

'Who? Stop talking in riddles. My brain can't stand it.'

'Never mind. You have other things to consider, more important things.' Bill raised his hand in submission. 'Good, there has been a bit of trouble at the school. However, it does not appear connected with Miss Bicknell and her campaign, at least on the surface.'

She outlined the incident with Estella and Larry, waving aside Bill's alarm. 'You should leave dealing with that until this crisis is behind us. Len Dawson and his type need to be dealt with. But it should be considered. He wields a lot of influence among the young in this town. Now, I have a plan.'

'This should be good,' said Bill, waving his assent.

'I suggest Estella and Larry go down to Bendigo for the rest of the week. Getting out of the school environment and away from the people making things difficult for them will do them good. It's necessary, especially for the boy who has suffered quite a beating. I spoke to Estella and Larry, and their parents. They are happy with the plan. I spoke with Miss Waiting, and she is willing to have them. The added advantage is that we can keep Estella under close supervision. Miss Waiting and Mr Shawcross will see to that. Captain Shawcross will lead the veterans' march in Binawarra as arranged. He will return to Bendigo early afternoon to take Estella to Melbourne for the work experience weekend.'

'You seem to have it all under control,' he said with relief. 'I'm grateful. I am still as rattled as a broken engine.'

'Your task is to rest and get your strength back.'

'Yes, your plan is a good one,' he said, after some consideration, 'but I want no major interruption to their study. Let me talk with Seaver. I will get back to you this afternoon. I must say now Miss Bicknell has departed the scene,' Bill went on, 'I feel more confident that the work experience arrangements do not present a danger for Estella.'

'Miss Bicknell may not be in Binawarra, but she is in Melbourne. We must not relax our vigilance.'

'In Melbourne? How do you know? No, don't tell me. Geoff Shaw-cross!'

RUBY HAD scarcely pulled up at the front of the Winterbine house before Estella appeared and ran to meet her.

'Are you sure it's all right for Larry and me to come and stay with you?' asked Estella, taking Ruby's arm.

'Larry and you, Eh? That's a change.'

'Larry is a good friend. He's always been a good friend.'

'I know, silly girl,' said Ruby. By this time, they were at the front door, where Aine and Charles were waiting.

'We're very grateful you have fitted in with Miss Barker's plans,' said Aine.

'No, it's my pleasure. You've got no idea what Estella does for my confidence,' she laughed. 'But seriously, I agree with Miss Barker. It will help Estella and her friend to get over the bullying episode. Let's look at your hair,' she said, taking hold of Estella and turning her around. 'Oh, hardly any damage. You've got so much hair. A little bit gone from here is hardly noticeable.'

'Fortunately, Larry was there to help,' commented Charles.

'He was very brave,' said Estella.

'He certainly was. Now, are you ready? We must get going.'

After some tight hugs and a promise from Estella that she would ring her parents the next day, Ruby was off to pick up Larry.

'Where is Geoff? Are we going to see him?' said Estella, after they had collected Larry and were passing between the peaks.

'Of course, impatient girl,' said Ruby, with a disconcerting smile. 'He'll be looking after you and Larry during the day. He will be at the unit before I leave for work tomorrow morning.'

LATE THAT afternoon, Geoff sat in the picnic shelter at the end of the plantation, surveying the shopping area. After some time, he returned to his car and did a quick run past Miss Bicknell's empty house, Jane Cox's house, the Huckerby's, and finally the Winterbine's. He checked the motel parking area. Boris and his car were nowhere to be seen. Somehow, he was not surprised.

'I'm not surprised, either,' said Miss Barker when they were seated in her lounge room. 'This is a hiatus. Gerda van den Donker has gone from Binawarra, and Rostowski is being briefed for the next step. Now that step involves one of two scenarios: either Gerda's plan has moved into a new phase, or she is on the point of striking, whatever that means.'

'Or she has given up,' said Geoff, to offer a third possibility.

'It's an unlikely possibility. So far, she has shown meticulous planning and expert manipulation. If the plan is about to bear fruit, it's hard to see what and where it will happen. The work experience weekend does not seem to provide a framework for the resolution of any plan. It will be under the supervision of the university and the companies.'

'Perhaps all the more reason to be attentive,' said Geoff. 'The final thrust can come in a feint movement, a move that appears innocuous or mundane.'

Miss Barker thought for a moment. 'You could be right. But what could it be with the work experience weekend serving as a distractive move?'

'On the evidence, the only object would seem an abduction.'

'By whom and for what purpose? It does not make any sense in the framework of the details. Any of those in the framework would be exposing themselves.'

'The Egyptian businessman?'

'Why would he need to abduct Estella? If he wanted her to work for his companies and had designs on her, it would surely make more sense to be open about his wish to employ her.'

'There is a purpose we do not yet know about,' said Geoff.

'Are you suggesting that, or is that what you think?'

'I am inclined to think that the plan is still running, that Estella is the target, that the weekend could be its fulfilment, and that there is a factor here not yet known to us.'

'You must stay close to Estella every available minute between now and the end of the work experience weekend.'

'Yes,' said Geoff. 'Tonight, I will check on the whereabouts of Miss Bicknell and Rostowski. Has there been any overseas airline booking for her?'

'No.'

'Would she be using another name?'

'No, I doubt it. An Edith Bicknell exists. I checked, and she is registered as having arrived in Australia from London in early January. If Gerda is the head of that language institute in London, it makes sense that she will return to London as Edith Bicknell. No, if she leaves Australia, it must be as she came in, as Edith Bicknell, and it must be to London. Gerda came to London from Holland under her Dutch name. If she is to be in Holland shortly, she must also return under it.'

'And Rostowski?'

'There is no record of Boris Rostowski. It is an alias. It will be harder to track him if or when he leaves Australia. You must try to find out his real name. All this assumes the abduction is to take Estella out of the country. The question is more urgent than ever—why?'

Geoff arrived in Melbourne at the start of peak-hour traffic and headed to the Upfield address. Boris's car was not there. So he drove to West Heidelberg. Slowly passing the street, he spied Boris's car. Someone was sitting in it. Half an hour later, Miss Bicknell arrived with the same woman he had seen her with on the previous occasion. She wore the same stylish scarf and long, flowing garments. Boris followed them into the house. Another half-hour later, he appeared and drove off. Geoff hesitated. Should he follow him? Who was more important? Boris probably had his final instructions and was leaving to continue his surveillance on Estella through to the weekend. If Boris turned up the following morning in Bendigo, that would be confirmation. He could then conclude that he or Miss Bicknell still had a contact in Binawarra. On the other hand, if he stayed, he might learn more about Miss Bicknell's connections and intentions. He settled in for a long wait. He did not have to wait long. Miss Bicknell and her attractive companion appeared shortly after Boris's departure and drove off.

He followed them south through the eastern suburbs. As he neared the end of Blackburn Road, he saw the buildings of Joseph Banks University rearing up on his right. Miss Bicknell's car crossed the Princes Highway and turned into a side street. Shortly after, it swung into a narrow, darkened street. Two women approached the stationary car. Within minutes, they were back on the Princes Highway, heading towards the city. At Punt Road, they drove up around the central business district, eventually finding a parking spot near a pub close to John Batman University. He drove past them as they were entering the pub. Five minutes later, he was at the bar ordering a beer and looking around. The place was full of scruffy bohemian types. The women, now numbering six, occupied a corner of the room. Sometime later, he decided he could not learn any more. The women had ordered dinner, and it looked like they were settled in for a prolonged sitting, a celebration of some sort. It was time to set off back to B endigo.

As he walked to his car, two women got out of a car parked just ahead of him. He thought he recognised them. He turned his head away as he passed. He need not have worried, though. They were too busy chattering to take notice of him. He walked on to the next corner and turned to look. They were walking towards the pub. He hesitated. He had a feeling. He stood in indecision before walking back to the pub. At the entrance, he stopped. No, he should not risk it. Returning to his car, he moved it into a position from where he had an unobstructed view of the women's car.

Two hours later, Lesley Conos and Faye Crofts appeared with Edith Bicknell and the tall, attractive woman. There was no sign of the other women. With Geoff following, they drove towards the northeastern suburbs. Eventually, they turned off the main road. Geoff followed, but as he turned, he noticed a car behind him in the rear-view mirror. He drove on for a while, avoiding the impression he was following the car ahead of him. Not far ahead, the lights of the residential area came to an end. He swung into a side road, letting the car behind him pass. He waited and then came out to resume his pursuit. The cars were no longer visible.

At the end of the residential area, he caught a glimpse of flickering lights in the distance through the trees. He switched his lights off. There was a half moon, which enabled him to follow the road. After driving along a weaving and undulating unsealed road, he found himself on a ridge. He slowed further. On his right, he caught the glint of the moon in the water far below. It must be the Yarra River. When he thought he might have lost the women, he came around a bend and saw dim lights and the silhouette of a large building with a high Gothic tower looming in the dark. He stopped. He would go the rest of the way on foot. He made his way along the ridge to a dirt driveway. As he approached the brick entrance with its iron gates, the building and tower flecked with moonlight rose out of the surrounding bush. The gates were locked. To the side, on the brick wall, was a plaque. 'The Convent of the Blessed Mother,' he made out. What was Edith Bicknell doing in a convent? Perhaps he had lost her and her companions.

He walked back along the brick wall at the end of which a high cyclone wire fence, topped with barbed wire. Not far further, the fence swung around and continued down into the bush. He followed it through the thick bush down to the river. There seemed to be no life anywhere, just the tower, whose ominous shape he could make out between the trees. As he was making his way back to the road, he caught sight of some light. It was, at first, just a flicker. Then there was more. An intermittent line of lights proceeded from the building towards the river. He must get closer. He headed back down to the river. The end of the fence jutted out over a rocky ledge with the water ten feet below. That made it difficult. He had to climb over the barbed wire or swing himself under the fence. Choosing the second, he would end up in the river if he failed. And was it worth it? He might be in the wrong place.

He launched himself at the lower end of the fence, managed to grab the galvanised piping, and swung his legs under and up onto the ledge on the other side. He got a hold with one foot and gradually pulled himself along the piping onto the ledge. He made his way through the bush with caution towards the lights. He came out onto an open parapet in full view of the tower. If he went any further, he would be seen by the robed and veiled women, holding candles, and chanting while forming a circle in a paved clearing near the river. He could not risk it. Escape would be difficult if detected. And if they caught him, he would have an embarrassing time explaining why he was trespassing. He moved back into the line of trees. Just as well, for at that moment, dark hooded figures holding candles appeared on a balcony in the Gothic tower. They stood observing the nuns' activity in the clearing below the parapets and rocky stairway.

For some minutes, he stood trying to make out what the nuns were doing. The chanting stopped, and flames appeared in a large bowl in the middle of the clearing. He edged forward to get a better look. A bright light flashed in his direction, and he heard a muffled cry. He retreated into the trees, turned, and dashed to the rocky ledge and the fence under which he swung himself more easily the second time. He half-ran, half-stumbled up the slope. But then he stopped. He could not hear anyone in pursuit, either from below, the side, or the front of the building. He waited. Still, there was no sound or movement. All was in darkness. Not even candlelight could be seen through the gloomy veil that hung around the tower. Baffled, he made his way back to the car. Perhaps Miss Barker could make sense of this if it had, indeed, anything to do with the Dutch woman.

AFTER THE drive, a cup of tea, and a chat, the young people were ready to retire for the night. Ruby had installed Larry in the guest room, and he was already nodding off.

'Do you mind if I say my prayers before I go to bed?' said Estella, who, already in her nightdress, was standing beside the bed Ruby had set up in her room.

'Of course not. Make yourself at home. I will attend to some things in the kitchen. Don't forget to say a prayer for me!'

'I won't.'

'I read that little book about Maria Goretti,' said Ruby as she got into bed.

'How did you react?'

'It's an astounding story. That a girl of that age could choose to suffer such terrible violence—I hardly know what to say. It seems so counterintuitive these days.'

'Do you want me to explain— I mean to try to explain why?'

There was a long silence in the darkened room. 'No,' said Ruby softly, 'leave it for another time. Good night, darling girl. I'm so glad to have you stay with me.'

'Good night, Ruby. I am, too.' She felt a pang of guilt.

Fifteen minutes later, after the lights had gone out in Ruby's unit, Boris quietly pulled out of his parking spot fifty yards up the road. Gerda Vrouwendijk's virgin was in no danger. In the early hours of the morning, Geoff arrived in Ruby's street. He stopped down the road and gazed at the darkened windows. Then he continued to a park where he would spend the rest of the night trying to sleep.

Chapter 28

Estella and Geoff in Bendigo

FR. VAN ENGELEN woke from a fitful sleep to the crashing of broken glass. He dragged himself from the ragged bed with which he seemed to merge in his dishevelled state and crawled to the attic window. Gestapo soldiers were forcing the priest and the resistance fighter to their knees in front of the SS officer. The sumptuous Dutch Renaissance merchant houses behind the officer glittered in the glassy, sunlit water of the canal. The SS officer contemplated the bent heads and then calmly lifted his Luger and fired twice— It was dark as Fr. van Engelen opened his eyes. Only the fast-fading sound of a car engine impinged on his half-wakeful world. He fetched the dustpan and broom. With much awkwardness and pain, he swept up as much glass as he could see in the parlour light. He did his best to cover the broken pane with an old sheet. Satisfied he could do no more until the morning, he sat in the armchair and dozed, images of the bloodied burst heads of his comrades appearing before his mind.

Later that morning, Charles stood on the front footpath looking at the graffiti. He glanced at the broken window and shook his head. 'This cannot be tolerated any longer,' he said to the priest standing on the porch and leaning on his walking stick.

'It's difficult to know what to do, Charles. It's perhaps best to wait until the whole affair blows over.'

'No, Father, we're not going to wait. I'll repair the window shortly, and Aine will tidy things up.' He marched across the park to the police station.

'Somehow, I expected a visit from you, Mr Winterbine,' said the sergeant. 'I agree with you. It has now got to a dangerous stage. I will talk to Collins. Please leave it with me.'

'Thank you, Sergeant,' said Charles, 'but I would appreciate having a word with Mr Collins beforehand.'

'Of course, Mr. Winterbine, I would be reluctant to agree to anybody else talking to him under the circumstances, but I know you well enough.'

Without ceremony, Charles asked Collins if he was aware of the second attack on St Philomena's presbytery. Yes, someone had mentioned it. 'Have you had a look?'

'No.'

'Then I want you to have a look,' said Charles. 'Come with me.' Collins looked at him in surprise. 'I said, come with me, Mr Collins.'

Collins looked warily at the six-foot-four-inch Charles Winterbine, who nobody had ever seen angry. They walked in silence across the park. Charles stopped in front of the word 'pervert' on the footpath. He pointed to it.

'This word here may apply to other people, but it certainly does not apply to Fr. van Engelen. It is there as a result of your incitement.'

'I report the news,' said Collins. 'That is my duty and my right in a liberal democracy. Besides, my hand did not write that word nor throw the rock.'

'This happened because of your incitement. You provided the bullets for others to fire,' said Charles, holding the editor's gaze. 'Mr Collins, your duty is to report the truth, and this word is far from the truth about our parish priest. This discriminatory treatment of Fr. van Engelen has no place in a democracy. I am a simple carpenter, but I have enough sense to know that your reporting is not what the people expect in a just democracy.'

'That's your opinion,' said Collins, 'and in a democracy, you're allowed to hold it.'

'You did read the statement my wife and I handed out last week, providing the facts about Fr. van Engelen?'

'I received it.'

'Did you read it?'

'No.'

'Then I ask that you read it and print it. Our system of justice, in what you are proud to call a democracy, demands it. You published lies and disgusting insinuations about our parish priest. You have a duty to correct it. Next week, after the Anzac Day ceremonies are over, I will organise a town meeting to discuss your newspaper and its reporting. The people of this town will respond to the truth and feel the injustice that Fr. van Engelen and Mr Huckerby have endured. We are not people you can manipulate indefinitely.'

The editor of the *Binawarra and District Mail* looked at Charles Winterbine. The vision of the most handsome couple in Binawarra addressing the town meeting and the reaction to the beautiful, reclusive Aine Winterbine were sobering. 'I have heard what you have said, Mr Winterbine.' He turned and walked off.

On entering his office, he called for his production team. He reached for the proofs of the next morning's edition and laid out the front page and editorial page on the desk. For the second time, he told his team they had to work hard to make changes to the next day's edition. Their newspaper must not give the impression that outside intervention had held it up.

WHEN THE sun rose, Geoff drove to a motel on the outskirts of Bendigo. He showered and rested before ringing Miss Barker. Silence was Miss Barker's reaction.

'Are you sure you followed the right car?' she said.

'No, I'm not. So, you find it baffling, too?'

'I must admit that I don't have a ready explanation if it was Gerda van den Donker.'

I can't be certain it was that weird place they went to. There was a tall, attractive woman in long, flowing, ritual-like clothes with Ms Bicknell each time. Not her type at all, at least in looks. I'm pretty sure she was part of the circle of women.

'You've never seen her before?' asked Miss Barker.

'I'm not sure. There's something familiar about her, but I can't place her.'

'Describe the two women you recognised.' She listened attentively and broke in before he had finished. 'Lesley Conos and Faye Crofts. Two silly, incompetent teachers. It gets stranger by the minute. Are you sure it was a convent?'

'The women looked like nuns, and the place was called The Convent of the Blessed Mother.'

'Looked like nuns? You weren't sure?'

'They looked like nuns. That's all I can say.'

'And you're not sure where it was exactly?'

'No, I'm not familiar with that part of Melbourne. It was in the outer north-eastern suburbs.'

'Aine was in a convent northeast of the city, if I remember correctly. Describe the ceremony again.'

Geoff did his best to describe what he had seen from a darkened, obscured position.

'Leave it with me,' she said after a long silence. 'The Convent of the Blessed Mother ... that doesn't go with an esoteric ritual. We'll be in touch.'

LARRY WOKE that morning feeling as if he was in another world. It began from the moment he got in the car with Ruby and Estella. Ruby took control, talking nonstop. She was a bit like Jenny Brougham, bubbly, witty, joking, and engaging, with the difference that Ruby was mature, confident, and possessed an air of authority. She subjected Estella to an affectionate kidding which, to his amazement, brought out a side of Estella he had not seen before. She smiled and giggled at Ruby's quips while they played guessing games. It was all very entertaining, without the sneering and ridicule of Len Dawson's jokes.

During the drive down to Bendigo, he felt more connected with the two girls than he had ever been with Len's group. He thought Ruby could not be more than twenty-five, looking at her from the back seat. She was attractive, too. It was not only her bright, sparkling manner. She had a lovely, regular face and a cuddly figure. She was an impressive girl. At eight o'clock and clad in his dressing gown, he followed the homely noises to the kitchen.

'You've slept in, Larry,' Ruby threw at him, without stopping what she was doing, 'but that's all right. You're allowed. You're on holidays. Now, what would you like for breakfast? But mind.' She wagged her finger, 'I'm not going to do it all for you. Come on, give me a hand.'

Estella's smiling face greeted him when he walked into the dining room, holding his plate of eggs, toast, and bacon. She wore quite a different expression from what he was used to. He settled in for a leisurely breakfast and a lazy chat with her, but was shooed off to his room as soon as he had finished eating and told to get ready as Geoff would arrive soon. When he returned to the lounge room sometime later, the sight of a robust man in his late twenties standing near the front window and looking through the curtains confronted him. He recognised the man's build. It was the dark figure who had suddenly appeared to rescue Estella and give Len Dawson the hiding of his life. Estella was sitting on the lounge settee, gazing at him. Geoff looked around when he heard the movement behind him. The ordinariness of Geoff's appearance and the calm, shy expression took Larry by surprise. Was this the man the goddess Estella Winterbine liked? He glanced at her. Yes, there was that look, an expression he had never seen bestowed on any other male. Geoff approached him, his hand outstretched.

'Geoff Shawcross, Larry,' he said, taking his hand and firmly shaking it. 'Estella told me you know it was me last Saturday. Sorry to be a bit rough with you, but we had to move quickly.'

'That's all right. I understand.'

Ruby joined them, and they chatted about what they would do during the day, settling on a casual tour of the historical sights in the town centre.

'Larry, Estella told me that the incident on Saturday night has made an impression on you,' said Geoff, after Ruby had left for work and Estella had gone to get ready. 'I don't want to give the wrong impression. I do everything I can to avoid violence. Unfortunately, there was no other choice on Saturday night. Estella was—I know about the bet, by the way.' He paused. 'Len Dawson had to be warned off. Perhaps I was a little rougher than I should have been.'

'No, you weren't,' said Larry. 'He deserved what he got. You don't know the half of it. He's an animal. It makes me sick now to think about the bet and my role in it.'

'Being a soldier,' said Geoff, 'is about defending what is right and just. Men who bully women are the worst sort of males.'

It struck Larry how calm and unassuming Geoff remained while he said this. When he heard Geoff had been in Vietnam with the Special Services, he did not know whether to express admiration or surprise. Geoff seemed to read his thoughts. One of the requirements of being a Special Forces soldier, he said, was mental toughness, and that included having a sense of the righteousness of the soldier's role and the objective sought. It's that mental toughness that is needed when one must endure extended periods of physical and psychological discomfort.

At that moment, Estella entered the lounge room. Geoff's attention shifted to her, but in a way that did not ignore him. It was quite odd. Although Geoff and Estella communicated with him on one level and with each other on another from the moment they left the unit, he never felt left out. Estella spoke to him about the sights they visited, apparently to make him feel comfortable. Geoff told him some aspects of Bendigo's gold-mining history that might interest a young man.

When they came to the Alexandra Fountain in the centre of Bendigo, Estella took Larry's arm as they walked around it, listening to Geoff's account of its history. While they studied the allegorical figures of dolphins, nymphs, and unicorns, Estella gave him a friendly, encouraging smile. When she turned her attention to Geoff, she acted differently. She did more than listen to him. More than admiration beamed from her eyes. What about Ruby? As they moved off along Pall Mall towards the grand building of the Bendigo Post Office, he listened to their conversation. These two are in love with each other. They have to be. And from their tentative manner, each seemed not to know it of the other.

'Geoff, what was it like in Vietnam?' he asked as they stopped in front of the 160-foot clock tower of the Post Office.

'Why do you ask?' Geoff said, turning to him.

Larry did not know exactly. There was something about this ordinary-looking man that Estella Winterbine was in love with, a SAS captain who had fought in what some teachers called a dirty and unjust war.

'Well, the thought occurred to me that while you were there, we were living our lives, not really aware of what you were going through.' He looked up at the clock high above them. 'All this is so different.'

'Yes, it is, Larry. It is very different. It's a different world.'

'Do you think much about the violence of war?'

'I try not to, but inevitably there are flashbacks.'

'Did it make you more appreciative of what life is like here?'

'Yes, of course. You'd have to be a dill not to be.'

'Did it make you think more about people in general?'

'Yes, it did,' said Geoff, who seemed to understand what motivated Larry's questions. 'The ugliness of war makes you reflect on a lot of things. It certainly forced me to reflect on how I behave and how others behave.'

'Do a lot of people lead a pretty meaningless life here in Australia?'

'Yes, Larry, I do believe that. People take so much for granted. Worse still, some seem hellbent on ruining what we have built up. It has made me take more notice of our history, too. For example, take this post office. It's here because of the people who dug for gold. It's here because of the wealth they generated and because those people, despite the dramas on the goldfields, wanted to have something to reflect the good fortune they enjoyed as a community.'

'I've hardly thought about such things before these last few days,' said Larry, taking in the whole building. 'You know, what happened with Len, Estella, and the rest of it—' He glanced at Geoff, embarrassed. 'You seem to know a lot about the area.'

'My mother's doing,' said Geoff, giving Larry a knowing pat on the shoulder. 'She's always been a keen student of the goldfields area. When we visited Bendigo years ago, she would drag us three kids around, looking at these things. We found it boring at first, but as I got older, I also started to find it interesting. You don't think much about it, but if you look, you see yourself in the history of the place. You see what's shaped you as a person.'

'And if you don't bother to look at it?' said Larry.

'It's your loss, I'm afraid,' he said, stopping. 'You know, Larry, if you're trapped in the stinking hot jungle waiting to kill or be killed, all sorts of things pass through your mind. These sights came back to me so often. I couldn't help it. They were a cause of sadness and consolation, sadness because I might never see them again, consolation because I had seen them and benefited from knowing about them.' He put his hand on Larry's shoulder. 'Come on, let's not get too serious. It's time for a cup of coffee. We can have a look at the Shamrock Hotel over there on our way. That boom-style building is more than anything a symbol of the wealth generated by the goldfields.'

Larry glanced at Estella. She was regarding him with a warm smile.

'I knew there was a lot more to you,' she whispered as she retook his arm to follow Geoff.

They found a coffee lounge and sat for a long time, chatting about what they had seen. Estella said she could not have guessed that Geoff was so interested in the area's history. It was something that had not yet arisen in their conversation, he replied. The look she returned caused him to blush. He rose, saying it was time to keep their appointment with Ruby. As they returned to the car, he slyly scanned their surroundings, as he had been doing. A look here, a glance there, was enough for him as he chatted to his two companions. Twice during their tour, he had seen what he was looking for. Twice, he caught a glimpse of Boris.

On the way to the university, while Estella was talking to Larry, he thought back over the morning. When he arrived at Ruby's unit earlier, Estella had greeted him in her usual shy, friendly way, but now she seemed a little cautious. She was almost clinging to Larry as they walked around. It was in her nature to show her appreciation for what Larry had done in defending her against Len Dawson. But it seemed that was not the only reason. It was as if she were seeking safety in his company. What for? An answer to that, he could not bear to contemplate. He thought of Ruby. He was feeling differently about her and differently about Estella. The conflict caused an anxiety he was not used to. He became aware of Estella looking at him.

Estella had noticed Geoff's thoughtful expression. It was familiar enough, an expression that reflected his effort to work something out in his mind. What was he working through now? When he had entered Ruby's unit earlier that morning, he greeted her with the same quiet warmth. But then she detected a trace of apprehension in his face. Why? And he went at once to the window as if he was evading something. When Larry entered the lounge room, he relaxed. While they walked around the centre of Bendigo, he remained relaxed. Only, now and then, he seemed cautious, even apprehensive of her. Now, this pensive expression—what did it mean? When they got out of the car, they looked at each other. Estella flushed and looked away. Geoff began to walk to the student union.

'We may be too early, Geoff,' she said as she hurried up beside him, leaving Larry to follow.

'No, I don't think so,' he said, a nervous smile breaking his thoughts.

'OH, GOOD, I've just arrived,' Ruby called out as they entered the bistro. She held her hand out to Estella. 'Come on, you come and sit next to me and tell me all about the morning. I'm sure you've had enough of those males.' She winked at Larry.

If there was one thing about Ruby, Larry thought, she was no fool. Those bright, intelligent eyes—very attractive. Now, as she was kidding and cajoling Estella, he could not believe she did not see the feeling passing between Estella and Geoff. If he, dull boy that he was, could see it, surely she could see it? She gave no sign. Instead, she continued to dominate the conversation.

'You're a lucky boy, aren't you?' she said, turning her attention to him.

'Why?' he said, shifting under her gaze.

'Why? Why, Auntie Ruby, if you don't mind! How old are you?'

'Eighteen,' he said, realising that he was about to be subjected to her kidding. He saw a smile on Geoff's face.

'Well, I'm twenty-four, old enough to be—so mind your manners!' She gave him a stern look and then smiled at Estella.

'You must keep on your toes with Ruby, Larry. She likes to boss,' said Geoff.

'Geoffrey Shawcross!' said Ruby, in mock indignation. 'And I thought you were a shy, inarticulate soldier! But I have seen quite a different person these last weeks.' She narrowed her eyes and stared with a squint. 'Or have you been tricking me?' She turned to Estella. 'What's your view, darling? Has he changed, or was he always like that?'

'He has always been the same,' said Estella, flushing again.

'Stop teasing,' said Geoff.

'Teasing?' She turned to Larry. 'Am I teasing, Larry?'

'I don't know what I should say,' said Larry.

'You men! You're good for nothing.' She turned back to Estella. 'They're good for nothing, aren't they?' She gave her a quick smile, but Estella also had no answer.

'Stop teasing,' repeated Geoff.

'Okay, Geoff,' she said, feigning contrition, 'but I still want to know if Larry knows how lucky he is to have Estella as a friend.'

'I do know,' said Larry. 'Definitely.'

'I hope so. This darling girl attaches more to friendship than most people. Anybody misusing that friendship will have me to deal with.'

'I won't let Estella down ever again.'

'I hope so.' She fixed her eyes on him. 'And I think you mean it.' She glanced at Geoff.

'I do,' said Larry.

Estella and Geoff exchange glances.

'Good, lesson over.' She looked around and, without skipping a beat, said, 'Now, look who's over there keeping an eye on us.' At the other side of the bistro, Bruce Butcher slouched in his chair, staring at them. He turned away when he saw he had been spotted. 'We can't have that,' said Ruby, jumping to her feet.

They watched her march over to him. He looked at her while she spoke. When finished, she nodded, wagged her finger, and then turned on her heels. As she sat down, Bruce Butcher got up and hurried out of the bistro.

'Good,' she said. 'That's got rid of him. We can't have him around spying on us and making Estella uncomfortable.'

Geoff had seen something else. While Ruby was getting stuck into Bruce, Boris appeared at the bistro entrance. As Ruby was returning to their table, Bruce glanced at the entrance. He stared a moment, then got up and left.

Before leaving them after lunch, Ruby ordered Larry to rest before they went out again. 'You don't want Miss Barker to deal with you, do you?' she warned, but then tempered her bossiness with sympathetic words and a brief but gentle caress over his swollen eye, drawing a curious look from Larry. When Larry retired to his room, leaving Geoff and Estella alone, Geoff, forcing himself to remain relaxed, asked if there was anything special she wanted to see on their second outing.

'I'll leave it up to you, Geoff,' she said, unable to hold his gaze. 'You know more about the area than I do.'

He contemplated her and opened his tourist guide. After a while, he closed the guide and looked at her. She returned an inquiring look.

'Have you seen Rostowski lately?'

'No.'

'When was the last time you saw him?'

'I'm not sure—three weeks ago, I would say.'

'He has been following your movements closely.'

'Has he?' she said, alarmed. 'Why?'

'We don't know exactly, but whatever it is, it won't be long before we find out.'

'Geoff, it frightens me. Please tell me what's going on.'

'Estella, Rostowski is a dangerous man. I want you to keep right away from him until I find out what he's up to. From now on, I'll be close by except for Thursday evening and Friday morning, when I will be in Binawarra for the veterans' march. I will return as soon as it's over. Until then, Ruby will be with you.' He paused. 'You will be careful?'

'I promise.' She hesitated. 'Thank you for saving me from Len Dawson. I haven't had a chance to say anything before this.'

'I'm glad I was there. Well, I had been keeping an eye on you. I know more about Len Dawson than you're probably aware.'

'How?'

'Miss Barker, a little questioning in the pub—'

'It's so humiliating.'

'I know. I understand. That's why I handled Len Dawson more roughly than I should have.' He understood what he was saying and was not sorry. Estella lowered her eyes. There was silence for a while. 'I'm glad it had a good effect on Larry,' he said to break the painful silence.

'I am, too. We've become good friends again, like we used to be. Deep down, he's really a thoughtful boy with a good heart.'

'I see that.'

There was another period of painful silence.

'Have you been reading *The Lord of the Rings*?' she said.

'Yes. It was hard going at first, but I'm now interested.'

'Where are you up to?'

'Where Boromir tries to take the ring from Frodo, and the Orcs kill him.'

'What do you think?'

'I can see why you like it.'

'Why?' she said.

'Because of the struggle between good and evil, because those struggling on behalf of good are conscious of what's right and what has to be done to achieve what is right, no matter what the sacrifices.'

'Do you like it for the same reasons?' She knew the answer.

'Yes. In a way, the story reflects all struggles to do the right thing, no matter how big or small.'

'I agree.' She could not look at him. She had one last question. 'Which character do you like best?'

He thought for a moment. 'I don't know. There's Frodo's tenacity, and I am fascinated by the Elves, especially Galadriel. But I suppose because of my experience as a soldier, I identify with Strider, with Aragorn.'

Estella's cheeks glowed, and a lump came to her throat. She rose, excused herself, and went to the bathroom. Geoff watched her go. He wondered what he was doing. What was he getting into? It had grown gradually, but now came onto him so fast that he risked losing control. And he was sitting in Ruby's unit. He got up, went to the window, and separated the curtains. He looked up and down the street. He could not bear it.

Despite Geoff's attempt to leave the unit without any noise, Estella, listening at the bathroom door, heard the front door shut. She was relieved. She needed to cool down. She returned to the lounge room and picked up the tourist guide he had been reading. Oh, what was she going to do? Every time she convinced herself that she could be in Geoff's company, resigned to the fact that he was meant for another, something happened to bring on the full force of her feelings. Only now, to make it worse, Geoff's behaviour towards her was changing. It was not too long before Larry appeared.

'Where's Geoff?' he said, looking around.

'I assume he went for a walk.'

'Oh,' said Larry, seeing her embarrassment. He hesitated. 'I'll go and see where he is.' He spied Geoff down the street, standing on the curb edge, looking in the gutter. Geoff looked up when he heard him approach. There was some embarrassment, followed by a friendly gesture.

'I'm just having a look around,' Geoff said. 'But come on, we'll have to get going if we want to see the sights. Are you okay?'

Larry was eager to get going, too. They spent a pleasurable afternoon going from one historical point to another, with Estella and Geoff avoiding eye contact. They arrived back at the unit at about four o'clock to find Ruby waiting. Geoff left them. When Ruby heard that Larry had only spent half an hour resting, she bustled him off to his room with many threats and imprecations. Larry could not help laughing.

'Oh, I can see you've been getting together with Geoff,' she said, pinching his arm. 'Becoming mates, no doubt! You men. Now rest for a while!' She shut the door with a bang.

Larry lay on the bed, smiling. He had never met a girl like Ruby. After half an hour of wakefulness, he heard a peremptory knock and the shout: 'You can come out now!' He joined the others with a smile. Ruby nodded and gave him a wink. Shortly after, Geoff appeared to take them to dinner. When they got out of the car and were walking along Pall Mall, Larry felt Ruby take his arm.

'You can be my escort tonight,' she said with a cheeky expression. 'Estella can go with Geoff,' and when Estella hesitated, 'Come on, take his arm. He will not bite you. Geoff, take her arm. Come on. Her arm is not a sausage!' Larry could not help laughing at the ridiculous picture she was making of the cautious couple. Geoff turned and gave Larry a helpless look. Estella attached herself to Geoff with a self-conscious smile, and they walked on. Ruby looked archly at Larry. She must know, he thought. When they returned to the unit, Geoff left straightaway. Ruby remarked that his abrupt departure was undoubtedly related to his surveillance activities. She seemed to restrain herself from further comment. Estella said nothing and kept her eyes down.

As he drove away, Geoff was relieved that his departure did not draw comment. He could do without it. He reflected that there had been no sign of Boris anywhere. That supported the conclusion he was following Estella only to be sure of her whereabouts. That established, there was no need to hang around.

AT AROUND the same time, but nine hours earlier by the clock in Holland, Truus van den Donker was looking at the envelope just delivered. The sender was St Philomena's Church, Binawarra, Australia. She sat by the front window in the lounge room, holding the envelope and staring at the flat, dripping fields stretching out into the misty, poplar-lined vista around the village of Vrouwekerke.

She had expected the letter, but now she hesitated. What if her attempt was repudiated? She feared that it was more than a possibility. Indeed, it was probable, she told herself. He was a Catholic priest who had submitted himself to the strict rules of his order. She understood he would not deviate from those rules. Whatever the case, she had no choice but to accept whatever happened. She opened the envelope.□

Dear Truus,

I am sorry that I have taken so long to respond to your request. You will understand, I am sure, that it is something I have had to weigh up in your best interests.

I am sorry to hear you accept that your marriage is beyond saving. I know how you have suffered through the years. I know the disappointment you feel. I pray that you will come to terms with it and go forward in the way the Lord wants.

About your offer to help me in my present circumstances, I appreciate your generosity and selflessness. I know it to be just like you. My brother, Frans, was careful to explain what you have offered and what expectations you have. This shows me you already understand the Catholic way of life. And what you have offered is entirely compatible with the traditional structure of a Catholic parish.

However, being a sober-minded person from Zeeland, you will understand that there are practical issues. Assuming that your decision to live apart from your husband is made on strong prudential grounds, which you must justify before the Lord, there is the practical question of whether or not my superiors would allow me to have a housekeeper. For reasons I cannot go into here, I am almost sure they would not allow it.

There is, however, nothing to stop you from coming to Australia to live independently in our parish. Frans assures me that you have independent means. We are a small parish following traditional Church teaching with members who would make you feel welcome. You would be able to enter into the life of the parish and offer me whatever help you like, as do others, and you would become part of a large church family. You would not be alone. There are, however, practical problems to consider, like the language and a different cultural environment.

Please weigh up all these things and let me know. Whatever you decide, you can count on my sympathy and help. I will keep you in my daily prayers.

Yours in Christ Jesus,

Jos van Engelen

Truus laid the sheets of paper on her lap and stared again through the window at the moist green fields that were emerging as the mist dissipated. For a while, she was only aware of relief. She had all she could wish for in the reply. She should not have feared repudiation. Fr. van Engelen's letter revealed him just as she had always known him. He would always act with sympathy and with her best interests at heart. She had been so used to the long years of repudiation that she automatically doubted the good intentions of even the kindest person.

During the rest of the day, as she cleaned the house and did outdoor chores, she came back to the letter she had left lying on the dining room table. She must experience the thoughts and words of a person of such compassion. At the end of the day, she was in better spirits than she had been in a long time. As the light faded and she prepared her evening meal in her small kitchen, she came to a decision. She would contact Anneke van Engelen to talk about English lessons. She would also investigate how she could get to Australia. Of course, she would discuss that with Anneke, too. Oh, how she wished her daughter had been like Anneke van Engelen. The Van Engelen family seemed so blessed. Then she remembered the shocking, starved appearance of the young priest who had saved her and Gerda from being trampled to death. And now he was crippled. She could not help releasing a few tears for someone she loved with all her gentle h eart.

MISS BARKER arrived at the Huckerby house carrying two copies of the *Binawarra and District Mail*. All rugged up against the early morning chill, Bill was waiting for her on the verandah. She handed him a copy.

'Your expression is encouraging for a change,' he said as he sat down and flicked the paper open. He ran his eye over the headline and then over the reports. He raised his eyebrows and glanced at Miss Barker when he saw the headline about a government report on the development of local tourism. As he reflected on the role that he had played in chairing town meetings on tourism and its benefits, a wry smile passed over his face.

'That man has no shame, has he?' said Miss Barker.

'Flo, how can people like this live with themselves?' He fixed his eyes on the minor report dealing with the violence against Fr. van Engelen. 'You must have a special mind to write this sort of thing,' he said. 'This waffle about breaches of the democratic order covers his refusal to state that Fr. van Engelen is innocent of his filthy insinuations.'

'You're starting to catch on. Charles has already spoken to me about arranging a town meeting next week. It's a good idea.'

'Yes, excellent,' he said, flicking through to the editorial page. 'Ah, he's not going to let up on Anzac Day yet. This is just a clumsy repetition of Jane Cox's view. I hope he knows by now that I am not the chief organiser of the ceremonies. He will have to deal with Frank Fonori in the end. He'll find Frank a little different to deal with.'

'Mr Fonori has already been in contact with him.'

'Good. You see, it was bound to run out of steam in the end.'

'Bill, I repeat. You are neutralised. You and Fr. van Engelen have had your reputations sullied forever. The school is disrupted. And Miss Bicknell's plans still have to run their course.'

RUBY BUSTLED around in her cheery manner, ensuring her guests had an adequate breakfast. She stood behind Larry as he tucked into a plate of fried eggs, toast, and sausages. 'Glad to see you have an appetite,' she said. He felt her hand touch the side of his face. 'Is it still painful? You had a fair whack there.'

'It's a lot better.'

'Good. That's the idea of time off to rest, isn't it?' She sat at the end of the table. 'Yesterday, you had off. Today will be for study.' She outlined the day's program, which Geoff would supervise. Geoff arrived sometime later, and Ruby departed. When Estella and Larry were settled, he said he had a few things to attend to and would be in and out during the morning. He guessed from Estella's look of relief and avoidance of eye contact that she could do without him for the moment. He, too, wanted the space to work things out. He was suspended between two women. He had been courting one, and he had growing feelings for the other, which refused to be controlled. He kept on telling himself that Estella was too young—far too young. She was only seventeen, for heaven's sake! What had got into him?

All he could do when he left the unit was walk around the streets, trying to concentrate on preparing for a possible ambush of Estella. It was hard.

Within a few minutes, he spotted Boris's car, which left him to walk on with his struggle. When he returned, he went straight to the kitchen. As he prepared morning tea, he could hear Estella and Larry talking. Estella's voice was soft and feminine. He sat with them during their break and listened while they discussed what they had done. Larry asked if he would take them to the local library after lunch. Yes, it would be okay. He left them again when they were settled. He trudged the same path, but now Boris was gone. As soon as they were ready, he returned to the unit, where he set about preparing lunch. Estella came to help. They stood at the kitchen bench, making sandwiches.

'We had a good morning studying,' said Estella, breaking the silence. 'Larry and I are doing almost the same work.'

'That's handy.'

'Yes, it is. We could exchange ideas. It's very helpful.'

'He's a good lad.'

'Were you able to get those things done that you wanted?' Estella asked.

'Yes, yes,' he said, blushing, aware that with his fair complexion it was obvious to all.

'That's good,' said Estella, keeping her eyes on what she was doing.

They worked in silence.

'Do you have your broken chain with you?' asked Geoff.

'Yes, yes, I do.'

'Leave it with me. I reckon I can fix it.'

A few minutes later, the sandwiches were ready, and they took the plates to the dining room table.

'What's that look for?' said Geoff, putting the plates on the table.

'What look?' said Larry.

AFTER LUNCH, they returned to the library where Geoff wandered around the shelves while Estella and Larry continued their study. They returned to the unit late in the afternoon. When Ruby arrived home, Geoff hurried away. He returned at six o'clock to take them to dinner. Larry expected Ruby to repeat her mischievous teasing when they arrived in the city centre. He smiled to himself to see how right he was. She grabbed his arm and told an unwary Estella to take Geoff's arm. Geoff was on to her this time and scowled. Ruby again looked archly at Larry. When the discussion came up about the next day's program, Geoff suggested they go for a walk in the Whipstick State Forest during their time off.

'What sort of a walker are you?' said Ruby to Larry.

'I don't know,' said Larry. 'It's not something I do.'

'Then you're not like these two, I hope,' she said. 'They don't walk through the bush. They run! Uphill, too.'

'No, I've never been bushwalking the way Estella and Mr Winterbine do,' said Larry.

'Good, then I will come, too. You and I can stay together when those two want to rush around the place.'

'I take it, then, that you approve?' said Geoff.

'Of course, silly boy! What do you imagine I've just said to Larry?' said Ruby, feigning indignation.

'One never knows with you,' said Geoff.

'Oh, Geoff! You mean you don't know when I'm serious? That's serious. What about you, Larry, do you know when I'm in earnest?'

'I reckon I'm getting the idea,' said Larry.

'I believe you are, too, you nuisance,' she said, giving him a wide-eyed glare. Larry smiled, and Ruby poked him in the ribs. That Ruby, no wonder Geoff was attracted to her or had been. He wished she were closer to his age. As much as he admired and liked Estella and was glad of their friendship, he would never be as at ease with her as he was with Ruby. And Ruby seemed to see it as well. He was curious to see how things would work out in circumstances that were becoming more complicated by the hour. Geoff was supposed to be Ruby's boyfriend; something was going on between him and Estella; Ruby was playing her own game and, at the same time, giving him winks and nods. It was very odd and intriguing.

'Well, that's decided, then,' said Ruby. 'I don't have to ask Estella. She's at home in the bush and probably suffers withdrawal symptoms this very minute. So the two students can study through to lunchtime and then pack up. Larry can get his things ready to go back to Binawarra. I'll be back at the unit between one-thirty and two o'clock. Just time for me to get changed. Agreed?'

They settled the plan, and it went as Ruby had arranged. At lunchtime the next day, Larry went to pack while Geoff and Estella made sandwiches and chatted. As Larry busied himself with packing, he listened to their cautious conversation. They were not aware of how it sounded. Surely, anyone who heard them talking would catch on? Ruby was back at the unit by one-thirty, looking harassed. She hurried to change, and then they set off for Whipstick State Forest. Very soon, Estella and Geoff separated from the other two. After Ruby and Larry had dropped behind several times, Ruby told Geoff and Estella to go ahead. 'Stick to the official tracks, though. We don't want to get lost forever. Some prospectors got lost and died of starvation out here,' she said, her face red with the exertion. 'When we've had enough,' she called, reconsidering, 'we'll turn back and meet you at the picnic spot, okay?'

Geoff acknowledged the plan with a wave. As he and Estella walked on, he told her what Ruby had referred to. At the news of the discovery of gold in the Mt Hope area, many had rushed to stake a claim. It was a dry, hot summer, and some were ill-prepared. They succumbed to heat and starvation on the way through Whipstick Forest.

'That's tragic,' said Estella.

'There were many such cases,' said Geoff. 'I have often thought about the diggers' trials. Some claim greed was the sole motivation for everyone who rushed to the gold fields. That's not true. Many just wanted to set themselves up.' He broke off for a moment. 'Those poor, weak, ill-prepared diggers who died along the way were an important part of what built and peopled all the fine towns in the gold mining areas stretching from Bendigo through to Stawell. They should not be forgotten.'

Estella's eager agreement and admiring glance were not lost on Geoff. They walked on, leaving Ruby and Larry far behind them. As they followed the track into shallow gullies, through thickly treed areas, and up rises with a view of the surrounding bush, Estella pointed out the different sorts of eucalypts, birds, and other animals native to the area. They became so engrossed in their conversation as they stopped to look around and search for traces of kangaroos, wallabies, and echidnas that they relaxed in each other's company.

Estella lost her reserve. She even took Geoff's arm several times as she pointed out some bird or unusual tree. Geoff was relieved he could forget the danger hanging over her. Here she was under no threat. Boris, as he expected, had not been seen since the first day. He put all that out of his mind and let himself enjoy Estella's company. In his haste to move into a better position to see a rosella, he jagged his right arm against a spiky branch, breaking the skin above his wrist. 'It's nothing,' he said, reaching into his pocket for a handkerchief to stem the blood.

'Let me,' said Estella, 'I have a clean handkerchief.'

Geoff held out his arm while Estella wound the white lacey handkerchief around his wrist and tied it tightly. A few bright red specks appeared in the white material.

'Thank you,' said Geoff. 'That will stop it.'

More than two hours had flown before they arrived back at the picnic spot where Ruby and Larry were perched on a weather-beaten wooden picnic table.

'At last!' cried Ruby. 'We thought you two had taken off for good! We were about to send out a search party.' There was an edge to Ruby's voice, and Larry glanced at her. Estella's lips parted. 'And look, Larry,' Ruby continued, jumping from the picnic bench, 'her cheeks are hot enough to warm your hands on.'

'I'm sorry if we kept you waiting,' said Estella.

'No need to be sorry, silly girl. You're allowed to have fun. Geoff's had a good time, too, I see.'

'We weren't too—?'

'What happened to you?' Ruby interrupted, seeing the handkerchief wrapped around his wrist, and without waiting for an answer, said, 'Come on, we must get back. I have a meeting at the university.' Geoff remarked as they set off towards the car park that it was the first he had heard. 'Geoff, I don't have to tell you everything, do I?' she said. 'I won't be long. Make sure Larry's ready to go by the time I get back.'

The mood in the car was subdued as they drove the few miles back into town. Geoff swapped a few comments with Ruby, who seemed to have her mind elsewhere. Estella looked out the window, glancing now and then at Ruby. Only Larry appeared undisturbed in the pleasure of the afternoon. He glanced at Estella now and then.

After Ruby had left for the university, they sat around without saying much. Geoff began flicking through the tourist guide. Estella wondered whether Ruby was upset with her for staying away so long with Geoff. Larry turned on the television but, after a few minutes, turned it off, saying it did not go with their afternoon of pleasure. Estella's feelings were mixed. The afternoon's enjoyment with Geoff left her with a brimming glow that she did not want disturbed. But there was that same constant check on her feelings and the possibility that she had upset Ruby. Geoff glanced at her. She was sure Geoff was struggling with similar feelings.

When six o'clock approached and Ruby was due back, Larry, who had felt increasingly out of place in the subdued conversation and silent exchange of feelings, made sure his things were packed and the guest room tidy. As he completed his preparations, he became aware that the mood had changed, and Geoff and Estella were now talking without reserve. He took his bags to the front door when he had everything ready. He lingered there at the open door, reluctant to join Estella and Geoff. Ruby would arrive any moment, anyhow. Twenty minutes passed, and still no Ruby. Geoff appeared in the hallway, with Estella close behind.

'I wondered what has held up Ruby,' he said.

'I wonder, too,' said Estella.

'Why don't you take your things to the car, Larry?' said Geoff, handing him the keys. 'At least there won't be any delay when Ruby arrives.'

Larry took the keys, picked up his suitcase, and headed for the car, leaving his school bag for a second trip.

'It's been a wonderful day, Geoff,' said Estella. 'I've enjoyed it so much.' They had walked with Larry to the front door and had moved some paces back towards the lounge room.

'I enjoyed it, too. A walk in the bush always seems to clear my head.' They stopped at the entrance to the lounge room.

'It does that for me, too,' said Estella, unaware of her heightened breathing. 'It's the green and brown expanse of the bush and the natural surroundings. It seems to concentrate my thoughts outwardly and not so much on myself.'

'I know how you feel. It's a pity it has to end. There are so many other interesting walks around here.' Geoff looked steadily into her eyes.

'I know.'

'Perhaps next time when you come to Bendigo?'

'Yes ... yes.'

More conscious of the glow deep in Estella's eyes than of what he was doing or saying, Geoff placed his hands on Estella's arms. He drew her to him. She did not resist. He felt his lips on hers, then his arms around her, holding her tight. Then her arms were around him. He hardly knew what was going on. There was a blur of feminine sweetness over consuming love for the girl in his arms.

Estella had been no more aware of her movements than Geoff had been of his. She was only aware of being drawn into his eyes. She felt her breathlessness. Then Geoff was holding her, and his lips were on hers. A wave of love rushed through her, and she sank in his arms. Then an unfamiliar feeling sent a slight shudder through her body. Her mouth slipped to the side of Geoff's, and she let out an almost inaudible groan.

At that moment, Larry came through the front door. He stopped. His mouth fell open. He should not have been surprised, but he was. He was more. He was shocked. The girl they had been calling the Ice Maiden was, before his very eyes, locked in a sizzling embrace with a man more than ten years older. Suddenly, Estella pushed herself away from Geoff. She stared wide-eyed at him.

'What am I doing?' she whispered. 'What am I doing?'

Geoff stood stupefied, arms hanging by his side. She burst into tears and ran down the hallway. Geoff came out of his trance as the door shut with a bang. He hurried to the closed door.

'Estella, I'm sorry,' he called. 'I'm sorry. I don't know what came over me.' It was the truth. He had had no intention ever of touching her. It had never entered his mind to embrace her, let alone kiss her. Had he gone completely mad? 'Estella!' he called again. There was no answer. Larry was standing in the kitchen doorway and staring curiously at Geoff when Ruby came striding through the half-opened front door.

'Who has left the door open—?' She stopped when she saw Geoff at the door of her room. 'What's happened?'

'I'm sorry, Ruby,' he said, looking stupidly at her. 'I have upset Estella. I'm sorry. I don't know what came over me.'

'What have you done?' she said, coming up to him. He stood staring at her. 'Geoff, tell me. What have you done?' She looked at the closed door.

'He kissed her,' said Larry, seeing that Geoff would not say anything sensible very quickly.

'Kissed her?' She raised her eyebrows and gave a little shake of the head. 'Estella, are you all right?' she called, standing up against the closed door. There was no answer. 'Right, you two, get on your way. I will handle this. Come on, move.'

'I'm sorry, Ruby,' said Geoff, as he brushed past her. 'I really had—'

'Let's talk about it later,' she said, striding after him. 'You've got to get Larry home.' She turned to Larry. 'Have you got everything?' Larry nodded and picked up the rest of his things. 'Good.' She followed them outside. 'I'm not blind, you know,' she said to Geoff. 'That girl has fancied herself in love with you for a while, probably from the beginning. I thought something would happen in the end, but not this, not now, not in my unit, and not in full view of Larry, for heaven's sake!'

'I'm sorry, Ruby. I have betrayed you, and I've betrayed Estella.'

'Don't talk nonsense, Geoff. I must take some of the blame, anyhow.' She turned to Larry. 'Well, Larry, your stay in Bendigo has been topped off with this little melodrama. I hope you had an enjoyable time. I enjoyed having you. You're welcome to come with Estella and stay anytime.'

'I had a good time, Ruby, thanks,' said Larry, still in a state of bemusement. He went to get in the car but was tugged back by Ruby, who stood on her toes to give him a quick kiss—on the lips. More bemused than ever, he got in the passenger seat to see her addressing Geoff through his open window.

'Geoff, I'll see you tomorrow as arranged, okay?' Geoff nodded. 'Goodbye, then.' She hurried back to her unit.

As they drove off, Larry examined Geoff's face. The distracted expression on the face of the man who had acted so decisively the Saturday evening before filled him with awe.

'You are the first person to kiss Estella Winterbine,' he said after five minutes of silence. 'And what a kiss! You'll be famous in Binawarra.'

Geoff frowned and glanced at him, but said nothing. It was going to be a long drive back to Binawarra.

'I don't know what came over me, Larry,' said Geoff, rousing himself. 'I've never done anything like that before. In fact, it's the first time for me, too. I mean, the first time I've kissed a girl. Like that.'

'Amazing. Who will believe it?'

ESTELLA SHUT the door and leaned against it, sobbing. The shame of what she had done, the awareness she had ignored, and the lingering feeling of being held and kissed by Geoff bore down on her. She could feel his arms around her, still feel being pressed against his solid body, and feel his lips on hers. She trembled. She stumbled over to her bed and threw herself half on her knees and half over the bed. The shame burnt into her mind. How could she betray Ruby like Len had tried to betray Jenny? How could she do the same thing to Ruby that caused her to run away from Len in moral revulsion? There could not be worse hypocrisy. She could howl endlessly at her failure to control her feelings. Then she heard Geoff calling at the door. He was the last person she could face. She took her pillow and buried her face in it, begging for God's forgiveness.

She did not know how long she lay there in the dark before she heard the door open and Ruby call to her. She lifted her head and saw Ruby silhouetted against the dim yellow light flowing into the room. She turned her face into the pillow again. The next moment, Ruby was sitting on the bed, stroking her head. 'Don't be upset, Estella darling,' she said. 'I know what happened, or more to the point, how it happened. It's nothing, nothing to get so upset about.'

Estella sobbed without lifting her head. Then she took Ruby's hands and kissed them. 'I have betrayed you after all you have done for me. Can you ever forgive me?'

'There's nothing to forgive,' she said, taking her hands away. She drew Estella to her so that her head rested on the pillow on her lap. With gentle caresses, she brushed the hair away from her face and kissed her on her temple. 'Now you just lie there and listen to what I have to say. Not a word until I finish, okay?' Estella nodded. 'Let's look first at the reality of the situation.

'Geoff and I are not married. We're not even engaged. We are hardly what you would call girlfriend and boyfriend. I'm very fond of Geoff, but the truth is that even after a few months together, we have not got that far. There has been no real commitment between us.' She paused. 'I have always had my doubts about Geoff. Oh, I was aware that he had ideas about marriage. As much as I liked him, I had a suspicion I was not really what he was looking for. When you came on the scene, I became aware that you saw things about him I was oblivious to. That was not a good sign. The two-hour jaunt in the bush this afternoon—and now this. It's not great for my self-respect, but clearly, Geoff has shifted his affection to you, as he is free to. Considering it coolly—that's what I'm famous for—I was right to doubt we were suited.' She caressed her. 'Do you understand?'

Estella was relieved to hear Ruby repeat what Fr. van Engelen had said. She was relieved to hear that she and Geoff were not as committed as she thought. Nevertheless, she could not suppress the feeling that she had interfered in a growing relationship. After all, what had they been doing during those months together? What would have happened if she had not come between them? And as much as Ruby boasted about thinking coolly, her reaction had not been entirely neutral.

'Now about you—do you think I was blind to what was happening?' Ruby continued. 'No, Estella, it did not take me long to see you were attracted to Geoff, and you began to fancy you were in love with him.' Estella looked up at Ruby. 'Estella, it's normal for girls to fix on someone a lot older, to have a crush like that. I had been in love with a hundred boys and men before I reached twenty-one. That's life. It's normal.' She paused. 'The wonder is that it was Geoff.'

'It's not a crush,' Estella said.

'Dear girl, remember that this is the first time you have felt affection for a male. You must wait and see how it goes. You may change. Geoff may change.'

The thought of it brought out another sob. 'No.'

'Estella, you have to face reality.'

Estella wiped her eyes. Still kneeling, she hugged and kissed Ruby. 'You have made me feel a bit better, but I still feel I have betrayed you.'

'You know, I have told you before, you're too scrupulous. Come on, get up, you silly thing. Get that out of your mind. You haven't betrayed me. You have helped me clear up the way I feel about Geoff. I'm serious about my work. I am an office person, an administrator. I would not make a good farmer's wife.' She took Estella's arm and smiled. 'I'm sorry for teasing you and Geoff. I could not resist it. The two of you—' She stopped. 'Perhaps I went too far and ... never mind.' She walked Estella to the kitchen. 'Come on, that's all behind us now. You can help me get dinner for us, just the two of us. We'll have a quiet evening without the men. You know, you were right about Larry. He's a nice young man. If I were younger, I might be interested.' She smiled at Estella as she opened the refrigerator to see what could serve as an evening meal.

Chapter 29

Anzac Day

THE FLICKERING flames lit up the sombre faces in the dissolving darkness before dawn. Fr. van Engelen, supported by Charles, moved to the front of the Cenotaph. 'Lord Jesus, we are here to commemorate the bravery of those young men who, in imitation of you, willingly sacrificed themselves so that all people may live freely and peacefully. We ask you to accept their sacrifice. We ask that their blood purify their souls. Lord, have mercy on their souls, forgive them their sins and bring them to life everlasting, Amen.' Then making the sign of the cross, 'In the name of the Father, and of the Son, and of the Holy Spirit. Amen.'

As Charles helped the priest to the side, one of Geoff's soldier mates raised his bugle and played the Last Post. Then, as the last mournful strains faded into the chilled silence of Anzac Square, Ray Foley, the Returned Soldiers League President, spoke:□

'They shall grow not old, as we that are left grow old:□
Age shall not weary them, or the years condemn.□
At the going down of the sun and in the morning
We will remember them.'
'We will remember them,' echoed the people.□
'Lest we...'

'Remember our bodies!' It was a high-pitched scream from nowhere, and it echoed eerily in the dark around the square. 'Remember our defiled bodies!' came a second scream from a different voice. It, too, pierced the serenity of the square.

Out of the shadows of the nearby trees emerged two black-robed figures with paper bags over their heads. On the bags was written 'the desecrated feminine' in bright red letters. The robed figures walked into the semicircle of the bemused onlookers and threw off their robes to reveal two naked female bodies over which had been scrawled strange, unfamiliar symbols in red and black. They began waving their arms and gyrating. 'The sacrifices of the universal soldier,' they sang mournfully. 'The sacrificed bodies, the victims of male wars, have mercy on us. In the name of Mother Earth, have mercy on us—'

Miss Barker, breaking the spell that the grotesque bodies had cast, marched over to the two women. 'Enough of that malignant nonsense!' she cried and tore the paper bags from their heads.

Lesley Conos and Faye Crofts stopped gyrating and waving their arms and gaped at her. They looked around for their robes, but Miss Barker scooped them from the ground and held up her hand in an arresting gesture. The two junior teachers cringed and clutched themselves in the chilly air.

'I will tell you what sacrifice I remember,' Miss Barker said. 'I remember the love of my life walking out in front of a troop of Japanese soldiers so that I could live. I watched while those soldiers shot to death a man whose only thoughts were about helping people. You are desecrating the memory of a man who had more moral worth in a strand of his hair than in a thousand of you self-indulged parasitic types.'

Lesley Conos and Faye Crofts retreated. Miss Barker followed them. Out of the shadows emerged a group of darkly clad men and women, with Stephen Calder leading. Behind him, Geoff could make out Jane Cox, Joyce Charing, the Premier Network reporter, and Len Dawson. He signalled to his fellow soldiers. They walked forward and reached Miss Barker just as Stephen Calder came face to face with her.

'I would not come any further,' said Geoff, taking the robes from Miss Barker.

'Who says so, fascist soldier boy?'

'We do.' Geoff stood his ground as Stephen Calder came eyeball to eyeball with him. 'Now get out of here and leave these people in peace.'

Calder was the first to blink. 'You'll keep, fascist soldier boy.' He drew back with the comrades following.

'Hey!' called Geoff, noticing the two shivering junior teachers. Calder turned and clutched clumsily at the robes thrown at him. With menacing looks, the group retreated behind the nearby trees.

'Flo, are you all right?' said Joanne, coming to her and taking her hand.

'Yes, Flo, are you all right?' said Bill, bemused.

'Nobody's made of rock—certainly not me.' She turned to the Returned Services League President. 'May I add a few words, Mr President?'

'Of course, Miss Barker,' said Ray Foley, who, like all those present, remained startled by the warmth of her intervention.

'Let us remember those young men,' she began, with her head bowed, 'those virgin soldiers, whose bodies still lie in the dirt of the cliffs of Gallipoli, in the earth of Palestine, in the fields of The Somme, who fell from the skies over Germany, who lie in the sandy islands of the Pacific. Let us not forget those five hundred diggers who succumbed in Vietnam and whose sacrifice was rewarded with vilification. Last, let us not forget those thousands of young men from the United States of America whose bodies came to lie all over the Pacific as they and their fellow soldiers pushed the Japanese army all the way back to Tokyo. Their blood in the white sands of the Pacific Islands was a price for Australia's freedom.' She moved aside to take her position beside Bill and Joanne Huckerby.

As if suddenly becoming aware of his cue, Ray Foley came forward again. 'In the going down of the sun and in the morning, we will remember them.'

'We will remember them,' said the others.

'Lest we forget.'

AT NINE-THIRTY, Captain Geoff Shawcross stood at the head of the group of fifty veterans who were readying themselves to march around Anzac Square. Behind him were his four fellow Vietnam veterans. He had difficulty concentrating and fidgeted foolishly. Thoughts of what he had done had been plaguing him all morning. He could not understand his actions. It just was not him. No matter how often he went through it, he could not explain it. It was true that Estella did not resist, at least not immediately. He was not sure why. She liked him. He could at least be sure of that. However that may be, it still did not explain his actions. It certainly could not excuse them. He had somehow dishonoured the sweetest girl any man could meet. He sighed. He now had to admit that he was in love with her. He felt stupid when he remembered what he had said about Estella being too young for him. He got a signal from Ray Foley. He made a supreme effort to compose himself.

'Okay, blokes, let us be proud of what we are and what we have done,' he said over his shoulder.

'Yes, sir!' they responded. That bucked him up.

They moved forward to the drumbeat. Along the shop front and the park side, the townspeople waved flags and cheered as the procession of veterans passed them by. At the first turn on the square, Geoff could not resist giving his mates a thumbs-up. But he knew there could be trouble.

Calder and his group stayed in the Commercial Hotel bar during the morning.

As the procession turned the second corner to march up the right-hand side of the square, Geoff caught sight of them mingling with the people outside the hotel. He braced himself. As they drew abreast of the coffee lounge, three women rushed forward. Lesley Conos, Faye Crofts, and Joyce Charing, dripping with red dye, flung themselves at the Vietnam Veterans, shouting, 'Give us back our bodies! Give us back our defiled bodies!' Geoff and his friends tried to push them away without violence. Then they withdrew, leaving the soldiers with red stains over their uniforms.

'Keep calm,' Geoff called. 'We have only a short distance to go. Most of the people are welcoming.'

Calder and his friends remained motionless between the welcoming townspeople until Geoff was within several yards of them. They came forward *en masse*.

'Capitalist white racist filth! Shame! Sieg Heil! Fascist pigs! White oppressors! Warmongers!' were repeated over and over.

Amid the spitting and screaming, Geoff smelt animal manure. The screaming followed to the end of the square, where Geoff turned to face them. They retreated among the people and disappeared into the pub.

'I'm sorry, blokes,' he said, wiping his uniform. 'Nobody was expecting this.'

'Are you all right?' said Bill, who had followed Charles through the staring townspeople. 'I apologise for this. There were indications—I had no idea, though, that it could be this bad.'

'Come on, we'll get you cleaned up,' said Joanne, arriving with Miss Barker.

Without further discussion, they set off for the Huckerby house. Half an hour later, after Joanne had sponged, rubbed, and sprinkled the uniforms with eucalyptus scent, the group returned to Anzac Square for the barbecue. Caught in conversation with two of his veteran friends, Geoff fidgeted, knowing he would have to leave soon.

'Quick, the pub, your mates are in a fight!' came from the other side of the square.

Geoff dashed across the park and arrived in the bar to see one of his mates on the floor and Stephen Calder punching into another. Calder's mates were pushing another two around. He went to tackle Calder but was hit from behind. He reeled around to see Len Dawson with several others. He felled Dawson, forcing the others to draw back. He turned back to Calder, who was rushing at him. Moving deftly aside, he helped Calder headlong into the nearby table and chairs. He was grabbed from behind again. He shook the assailant off but was rammed up against the bar by Calder. Seeing Calder as the ringleader, he grabbed hold of him, swung him around off the bar, and put him out of action. Calder and Dawson now lay groaning on the floor, their comrades at a standstill, looking down at them. Soon, men from the town filled the bar, appealing for order. Sergeant Willis and his constable shouted for attention. Most of Calder's comrades took advantage of the confusion to slip outside. After some brief but targeted questioning, the sergeant ordered those caught in the brawl over to the police station, where he and the constable would take statements.

'You'll keep, you fascist scum,' Calder shouted at Geoff as he was helped off, wincing in pain.

Geoff did not react. There were other things on his mind. He asked Miss Barker to ring Ruby and explain what had happened, and that he would not be there in time to take Estella down to Melbourne. They should go without him, but Ruby had to stick strictly to the arrangements. Fifteen minutes later, Miss Barker was back. 'Miss Waiting was very disappointed you couldn't go. This change has made her nervous.'

'Did you stress that she should keep strictly to the arrangements and keep a careful lookout?'

'Of course.'

'The demonstration was clearly meant to get me out of the way. Rostowski knew I was protecting Estella.'

'I agree. Miss Waiting wants you to go down to her unit as soon as you are ready. She will call you after she is satisfied she has delivered Estella safely.'

'That was my plan.'

'Miss Waiting also wants you to stay in the unit with her during the weekend. You must do this, Mr Shawcross. No place for scruples. You need to be within reach if anything develops. Miss Waiting is fearful and understandably so. She will feel more secure if you are there.'

'Yes, I understand,' said Geoff. 'You're right.'

'Keep by the phone so that I can contact you. There has still been no booking out of Australia for Miss Edith Bicknell. And we still don't know Rostowski's real name.'

'Have you found out anything about the Convent of the Blessed Mother?'

'Not yet, but I'm following a hunch. This could be a lot deeper and sinister than I suspected.'

ESTELLA WAS sorely disappointed that Geoff could not take them to Melbourne. She wanted to be with him. On the other hand, she was relieved she did not have to look him in the face. Despite Ruby's efforts to put everything in the proper perspective, the shame would not go away. Her disgust at Len Dawson's behaviour remained her great accuser. Against her disgust was the continual sense of Geoff's body and lips on hers.

Ruby distracted her during the morning despite her nagging feelings. She went through the preparations with her, ensuring she packed everything she needed. But now that they were in the car, leaving the outskirts of Bendigo and heading through farming country, the conflict returned in force. She did her best, but she could not help it. The sniffles started, and a few tears rolled over her cheeks. Ruby did not say anything, merely putting her hand on Estella's arm now and then. Estella sobbed and sniffled until she could compose herself.

'There, you've had a good cry. You'll be better now.' Ruby caressed her arm. 'Come on, wipe those tears away and put on a happy expression. You don't want to appear out of sorts in front of those influential businessmen, do you?'

Estella shook her head and did what Ruby suggested. She was right. She had to present herself with dignity, no matter how she felt. She wiped her eyes and cheeks.

'Fortunately, you don't wear make-up,' said Ruby. 'Mascara would be all over your face, making you look like a clown.' She got a helpless laugh out of Estella. 'There now, no more upset. Just let things take their own course. We know what sort of person Geoff is. He will never think badly of you. Give yourself time. Besides, he blames himself for what happened.' She paused. 'Miss Barker has stressed that we are to stick exactly to the program. You understand that?' Estella nodded. 'Good. Then there'll be nothing to worry about. You'll have a great weekend, and Geoff and I will pick you up on Sunday afternoon. You'll be together again with all those who love you.'

Ruby was right, as always. Estella was determined to handle the weekend sensibly. She brightened, and they spent the rest of the trip avoiding the subject of Geoff. Around one o'clock, they drove into the centre of Melbourne. Ruby found the hotel in St Kilda, where a handsome young man dressed in a smart dark grey suit approached them as they got out of the car.

'You are accompanying Ms Winterbine for the public relations weekend?' he asked. With Ruby's affirmative, he continued, 'I'm here on behalf of the companies to welcome you and to make sure everything goes well for the young lady.'

'Where's Bruce Butcher?' said Ruby.

'He is in the hotel foyer, greeting other guests. Would you like to talk to him?'

'No, if it's not necessary. Lead on.'

Taking Estella's suitcase and overnight bag, the young man accompanied them to the hotel foyer.

'Very exclusive,' said Ruby as they entered. 'You'll be comfortable here.'

'We will do everything we can to ensure Ms Winterbine is comfortable,' said the handsome young man. 'We have some pleasant surprises in store to make doubly sure there are no worries.'

'There you go, darling, you can relax and enjoy it all,' said Ruby, holding Estella's hand.

While they gazed around the hotel foyer, Ruby's eyes came to rest on Bruce Butcher sitting with young people not far away. He turned to look at them, but quickly averted his eyes.

'We will proceed to the hospitality room on the first floor,' said the young man, leading them to the lift. 'Ms. Winterbine will meet company officials and other guests there.' He turned to Ruby. 'Madam, you are welcome to come, but if you want to leave now, you can be sure Ms Winterbine is in safe hands.' He waited, expressionless, for her answer.

'I don't suppose it's necessary to go to the hospitality room,' she said, thinking she should leave the others to do their work without her meddling. 'No, I'll leave you here, Estella.' She took Estella for a quick kiss, but the taller girl pulled her into a hug.

'Thank you, Ruby,' she said. 'I don't deserve your friendship.' She kissed her on the forehead before releasing her.

'Now, none of that. Have an enjoyable time, and we'll see you on Monday.

Ruby watched Estella disappear into the lift. She blinked back some tears while she went to find a phone. Geoff picked up the receiver after one ring.

'Everything's all right,' she said after Geoff's breathless inquiry. 'I delivered her into the hands of the organisers.'

'Right inside the hotel?'

'Right inside the hotel. I left her with a young man who took her to the hospitality room on the first floor.'

'Did you see the hospitality room?'

'No. Should I have seen it?'

Geoff frowned. 'Are you sure about the young man?'

'Yes, Bruce Butcher was there with him. It's all in order.'

'Okay, I'll see you when you get back to Bendigo. I will stay the weekend with you.'

'I appreciate that, Geoff,' said Ruby, relieved. 'I would feel safer. We can talk, too, clear away a few misunderstandings.'

ESTELLA FOLLOWED the young man out of the lift and into a plushly furnished room. The room was empty. 'Oh,' said the young man, putting the luggage down. 'They must have gone elsewhere.' He looked around. 'Just wait here. I will be back in a tick.' He returned a minute later with two familiar faces.

'Miss Winterbine, we are glad to see you,' said Aisha Al Refai, offering her hand. 'We are so happy that you agreed to attend the weekend.'

'Yes,' said Tahani, holding out her hand. 'We are here to take care of you. Father says we are to give you special attention.'

Any anxiety and sadness Estella felt dissolved at the sight of the friendly faces. 'I didn't know you would be here. It's a nice surprise.'

'Well, there will be more nice surprises,' said Aisha. 'As Tahani said, we are to give you special treatment. Father sees great potential in you. You will experience what it is like to work for a great international communications company. Now come with us. We have our own program. We will see the others later.' She picked up Estella's bags, giving one to her sister. 'Come on,' she encouraged with a warm smile.

Estella followed the beautifully groomed young women to the lift. They descended several floors to the basement car park, where a black limousine was waiting. Two attendants jumped out, one taking Estella's bags and the other opening the door for her. A few minutes later, they were driving along St Kilda Road towards the city centre.

'Where are we going?' said Estella.

'You will see. Just relax,' said Aisha. 'How are things in Binawarra? It's a public holiday today, isn't it? You celebrate your soldiers, right?'

Estella explained the significance of Anzac Day and the ceremonies people attended, while Aisha and Tahini expressed keen interest. During this time, the black limousine made its way above the city and turned onto the Tullamarine Freeway.

As it was picking up speed, Estella caught sight of Ruby's car in the left-hand lane up ahead. She tried to catch her attention as they sped by, but their car was going too fast, and the darkened windows obscured her face.

'Is that someone you know?' said Tahini, who sat opposite her.

'Yes, yes, she's the friend who brought me down from Bendigo.' She turned and watched Ruby's car fall behind them.

The sisters did not comment. The limousine sped on with Estella's thoughts lingering on Ruby and Geoff. Then she was aware of the car turning off the freeway. She looked around at the high cyclone wire fences and the aircraft buildings.

'What are we doing here?'

'You will see,' said Aisha.

The car drove through a security gate onto a restricted area, negotiated several roads around large buildings, and arrived at an open area in front of huge hangars. A hundred yards away was a plane with four jet engines.

'Have you flown before?' said Tahani.

'No,' said Estella, awed by the surroundings.

'We thought so. That is why we have arranged this.'

The car pulled up at the foot of the stairs leading up to the aircraft. The attendants jumped out to open the doors. Estella looked up at the plane as she alighted.

'Come on, leave your bags,' said Aisha. 'Now, don't be shy.' She took Estella's hand and started up the stairs.

They were greeted at the top by a young man in uniform. He bade them follow. They entered the aircraft, passed through several partitioned areas that looked like business offices, and came into a lounge area richly decorated and furnished in polished wood and materials of soft fawns and greens. In one of the leather lounge chairs sat Mr Al Refai, glasses on and reading some documents. He had a black and gold fountain pen poised in his hand as he concentrated. As soon as he was aware of their presence, he rose and took off his glasses. 'Miss Winterbine, welcome aboard. I am so pleased that you could attend our familiarisation session.' He took her hand and brushed it with his lips. 'I hope you are well.'

'Yes, thank you, Mr Al Refai,' said Estella, the sight of him reminding her of how handsome and elegant he was. 'This is all a surprise. I didn't expect to go anywhere.'

'It is meant to be a surprise, Mademoiselle. We are going to show you what it's like for talented people to work at a successful, pre-eminent international company. I hope my daughters have spoken about this.'

'Yes, Father, we mentioned it,' said Aisha, who appeared in charge of the arrangements. 'We will wait until we have settled in before we go into detail.'

'Well done, my daughter. You see, Miss Winterbine, I am well supported by my capable daughters. Have you told Miss Winterbine where we are going?'

'Not yet.'

'Let's sit down now,' he said, resuming his seat. In the background, Estella heard doors closing. 'Would you like a cup of tea or orange juice, or something else?'

'I would like a cup of tea if that's all right,' said Estella.

He pressed a button on the console near his armrest. A second uniformed young man appeared, and Mr Al Refai instructed him to bring them tea.

'Mr Al Refai, the plane is almost ready to take off,' he said. At that moment, they heard the jet engines firing up.

'Bring us the tea when we are airborne.'

The engines were now humming, and the plane seemed to be trying to edge forwards. Mr Al Refai sat back and inquired about Estella's parents. The plane began moving. Estella could not help gazing through the windows as they taxied along the tarmac and away from the airport buildings. The great expanse of the runway area came into view.

'This is your first plane trip, isn't it? Well, just relax. There's nothing to it. No need to be apprehensive.'

'Father, we should prepare for take-off,' said Aisha.

Just as they had finished preparing themselves, there was a roar from the engines, the brakes were released, and the jet aircraft jerked forwards, gathering speed. Estella clutched her armrest and stared at the ground rushing by. The front of the plane lifted and seemed to hover for a moment. Then it rose sharply, leaving the ground disappearing below them. Estella felt her stomach cramp.

AT AROUND six o'clock, Ruby parked her car outside her unit. 'She's all right,' she said to Geoff, waiting at the open door. 'Everything seemed to be in order.'

'That demonstration was planned,' he said, following Ruby to the lounge room. 'Its purpose was to tie me up.'

'Geoff, are you sure?' She sat down and leaned back into her armchair.

'As sure as I can be. I'm going down to Melbourne. I don't trust it.'

'You mean tonight?'

'Yes. I must.'

'Geoff, you can't be serious. What could happen in the hotel?'

'I don't know. That's why I want to be there.'

'You're not letting your feelings get the better of you, are you?'

He looked at her and grimaced. 'I don't know. I'm sorry.'

'Geoff, don't worry. And for heaven's sake, stop saying you're sorry. I told you I understand. We'll talk about it later, at the right time. Not now. Come on, let's have something to eat. We can calmly discuss your fears. We'll go through all the points to see if going down to Melbourne is warranted.'

Geoff had been through it. He had been through it a thousand times during the afternoon while comforting his army friends and waiting to be interviewed. He had been through it on the drive down to Bendigo and while waiting for Ruby. Nothing surer than that demonstration had been manipulated to keep him away from Estella. And Ruby had not accompanied Estella to the hospitality room— No, he would go down to Melbourne after dinner. When they were seated at the table, he felt little inclination to go through it all again. He let Ruby talk, but could not help making it obvious she was having little impact on him.

'Geoff, don't worry. She'll be all right.' The phone rang. Occupied more by Geoff's intense expression than the ringing phone, she picked up the receiver.

'Just listen carefully to what I have to say. It's about someone you hold dear,' she heard an unfamiliar female voice say. She turned and signalled to Geoff. 'Be at the Myer department store cafeteria at nine-thirty sharp tomorrow morning. Alone. Strictly alone. You know where the Myer department store is?' Ruby said she did. 'Pick up a tray at the food selection line. Move along with the people. Someone will talk to you. Do not turn around. If you do, the information will stop. After that, go and sit near the wall closest to Little Burke Street. Sit facing the wall. When you have done this, an envelope will be put on the table behind you. Wait one minute before taking the envelope. Do not attempt to do anything before this meeting. You will risk everything. Have you got all that?'

Ruby had frantically noted the information on the pad beside the phone. The caller rang off. She sat down on the edge of the chair. 'Your suspicions were right, Geoff,' she said, sinking back into the chair. 'My God, she hasn't been abducted, has she?'

Geoff took her notes and asked her to repeat what the caller had said. He listened, studying the notes as she spoke. He rang Miss Barker and related everything, including the course of action he intended to take. She agreed with him. But he should wait until she had made some inquiries. Thirty minutes later, she was back on the phone.

'Miss Edith Bicknell took off for London this afternoon. It was a late replacement booking, and she arrived at the last moment. Mr Shawcross, Miss Waiting's call might be a hoax or a ploy to put us on the wrong track, but I'm inclined to think the caller is genuine. Now the question is: how has she been abducted, which seems to be the message of the call? Why? For money?'

'No, money does not fit into it. There's something else here.'

'You're right. I've been considering that ideology has something to do with it, however oddly. Now it's dawning on me that ideology could be connected with something just as important. Think again, Mr Shawcross. What did Mr McKinnon say to you that day? What exactly did he say?'

'I told you. He said something like Estella was a goddess, and she only had to be there, but stopped and then exclaimed, "A goddess? So that's it".'

'But that's not what you said. You left the "goddess" out. My goodness, another picture is forming here,' she said, unusually animated.

'What? What significance do goddesses have?'

'I'm not sure. Leave it with me. I need to speak with Aine. There's something else. Now, the caller— If my suspicions are right, there has been trouble within their camp, and this contact is a countermove. How else could they have that information?'

'I don't know, Miss Barker. We have to wait and see what the caller says.'

'Agreed. I need time now to reflect. You put your mind to it, too. When you have something firm, give me a call. Otherwise, call me between midnight and one o'clock. Don't worry. I will not be asleep.'

Geoff drummed on the armrest. Ruby waited.

'I'm going now,' he said, getting up.

'I'm coming, too.' She stood up, wringing her hands.

'No, you're not used to this. You might find it difficult, even frightening. I can't afford to have a handicap.'

'No, Geoff, I'm responsible for Estella's position. I should have gone to the hospitality room. I should've been more attentive.'

'Don't blame yourself,' he said. 'We are dealing with cunning people whose tactics are to throw people off the scent by seeming to act normally. They probably anticipated that you might go with Estella to the hospitality room. You just made it a step easier for them.' He came closer and took hold of her hands. 'Ruby, you have to know what happens in this sort of action. You must be ready with countermoves, sometimes violent countermoves.'

'All right, but I'm still coming.'

'Things may happen unexpectedly. I don't want to be impeded if I must act suddenly. I may also have to sit still for long periods. You're not used to these circumstances.'

'I won't get in the way, I promise. If you must act quickly, ignore me.'

'Ruby, it doesn't happen like that. You must be accounted for if you're there.'

'Geoff, I don't want to be alone,' she said, clasping his hands. I'm frightened, and I fear for Estella.'

This was something else. He had gotten used to her supreme confidence and the trueness of her decisions. Now she looked so miserable and helpless. He relented. Ten minutes later, they were in the car speeding out of Bendigo. He spent some time instructing her about what to expect and what to do if he had to act suddenly. It was only a warning, he said. Nothing may happen, but they must be ready. He saw with relief that she listened and nodded when he had finished. There was no time for teasing or making jokes.

Teasing and making jokes were the last things on Ruby's mind. As they fell into a depressive silence, she reflected again on how mistaken she had been about Geoff's character and abilities. She felt her cheeks burning with embarrassment when she remembered the manner and spirit with which she undertook to rid him of his social ineptness. She felt so stupid as she glanced across at the calm, determined expression on his face. Not long ago, that expression had been a sign of cognitive emptiness and social ignorance. It had represented the necessary task of redeeming him socially. Now she was getting a hint of what that expression meant and the mode of cognitive activity behind it. What a fool she had been. They were on their way to a potentially dangerous situation to rescue the girl they both loved, and she was helpless where it counted. And there was Estella, who had seen the real Geoff from the beginning! How could it be?

How could that innocent, childlike beauty, long isolated socially, see so unerringly into Geoff, the person? It was not often that Ruby could not control her emotions. The self-blame and her helplessness in aiding a girl she loved as a sister brought tears to her eyes. Her self-condemnation went deeper still as the full awareness of what she had rejected dawned on her. Had her misjudgment of Geoff meant that she had stupidly and cavalierly put aside a chance of true love, of finding a reliable partner? He had had marriage in mind—but it was too late to dwell on that now. Fortunately,

Geoff was too preoccupied to pay attention to her emotions. She turned her head, looked into the dark through the side window, and sought relief in the few tears rolling over her cheeks.

Ruby was right, at least about Geoff's concentration. She had jumped to the conclusion that Estella had been abducted, but the caller had not been explicit. It seemed to be the case. He should prepare himself for something else, though. And was Miss Barker right about the possible dissension in the ranks of the people who had been circling Estella for the last few months? Again, the evidence was not explicit. He had great respect, however, for Miss Barker's intuitive judgments. Whatever the case, he had to be careful not to put Estella in greater danger than she was already in. That she was in danger seemed to be the caller's message. What sort of danger? These thoughts, and not least the lie and structure of the hotel, were continually sifted as he raced through the dark along the highway towards Melbourne. When they arrived outside the St Kilda hotel, Geoff circled it twice before driving into the parking area. He turned off the lights and engine and peered at the hotel's entrance for several minutes. Ruby did not speak. He looked around the car park. It was more than half full.

'A lot of people must be staying here,' he said. 'That would provide cover. You wait here.' He opened the door. 'Keep the doors locked and stay out of sight. Keep your eye on the hotel entrance and tell me if you see anyone you know.' He was gone the next second.

Ruby slid down the seat so she could peer over the dashboard. Half an hour passed before Geoff returned. She did not know he was there until he unlocked the door and slid in.

'See anyone you know?' he whispered. Ruby had seen nobody she knew. 'There is a basement car park,' he continued. 'If Estella has been abducted, they probably took her to a car waiting there.'

'I saw the lift go up.'

'Did you see it go down?'

'No, but I saw it linger on the first floor before I looked away.'

'Okay, then the hospitality room was genuine. That was in case you accompanied Estella there.'

'But the young man made a point of inviting me to go there.'

'Made a point?' Ruby shrugged helplessly. 'How involved are you in the arrangements for this weekend?'

'Hardly at all. The companies invited interested students. It was up to them to accept. The university's input is minimal. It is one of encouragement. Bruce Butcher's role is voluntary.'

There was another long pause before he spoke. 'Go to the reception and ask for Bruce Butcher. Say who you are, from the university, and you have a message for him. Don't comment on the information they give. Act as naturally as you can. And try not to look anxious.'

Ruby did as she was told and was back within five minutes. 'The receptionist said Bruce Butcher's group had left the hotel at seven o'clock. They had never been booked to stay there. They had booked the reception room and the restaurant—nothing else. The reception had been instructed to take messages for him. I left the message that he should contact me.'

'As I thought,' said Geoff.

Ruby remembered the young man saying there would be pleasant surprises in store for the guests. But Geoff seemed not to be listening. She sat back and waited. He started the car and headed out of the parking area. A half-hour later, they were in West Heidelberg parked in a back street. Another half-hour passed while Geoff kept his eyes on a house with no lights. He then drove to a street in Upfield. 'Rostowski's car,' he said as he brought the car to a stop. They waited there for nearly an hour. 'He may still be there, or he may not. You're tired.'

'I'm all right, Geoff. Just do what you have to do.'

'Can't learn anything here,' he said, starting the car and backing out of the street.

They drove to a motel on the Hume Highway. 'Come on,' he said, after he returned from the motel office with the room keys, 'it's too late to go back to Bendigo. You need some sleep in preparation for the meeting tomorrow.'

Ruby did not object. She went to the bathroom to freshen up and prepare for bed while Geoff rang Miss Barker. It was well after midnight when he put the phone down, and Ruby was tucked into bed. Geoff turned the lights out after encouraging her to get a good sleep. She would need to have her wits about her. He sat at the small table by the window of the room. Ruby's last vision of him before she drifted off was the profile of his determined face shining in the dim lights of the motel parking area.

DURING THE ten minutes the plane was climbing, Mr Al Refai left Estella to herself while he discussed business matters with his daughters. Estella had the impression he was giving her time to settle and get used to the new experience. She began her daily rosary. At length, she felt less anxious. She told herself to relax and enjoy the company of the two young women with whom she seemed to share a similar outlook. As the plane levelled off, Mr Al Refai gave her a few warm, encouraging words, excused himself, and headed to the front offices.

'We can be at ease now,' Tahini said, helping her to be comfortable.

Aisha sat next to her on the lounge settee. Tahani placed a folder of documents on the coffee table in front of them and sat in the lounge chair opposite.

'We are going on a little trip north, a thousand miles north,' began Aisha, 'to Brisbane where we will have dinner. After dinner, Father has meetings with company heads to discuss potential acquisitions. These are media properties he is considering. The dinner will be for us to relax and enjoy ourselves. You are our special guest. Father hopes that you will enjoy it, as it should be enjoyed. He also wants you to attend the meetings as one of his assistants. We will be there, of course, to help you. The idea is for you to have direct experience in a business situation where image and presence are an important part of the negotiation.'

A steward with cups of tea, plates of biscuits, and small pastries arrived to interrupt Aisha's explanation. She waited while he set them on the table and withdrew. She then spent the next thirty minutes going through the documents, which were descriptions of the business activities and interests of the Parisian Worldwide Communications Company or glossy promotional sheets. Estella, said Aisha, needed to be aware of the company's size and interests to enjoy the benefits from the meetings. At the end of the explanation, Mr Al Refai joined them as if on cue. Was Estella comfortable? was the first solicitous inquiry. Did she want anything to eat or drink? Dinner was still an hour away, at least. Estella, who scarcely had mental space to consider anything except what was happening at that moment, replied that she was happy to wait.

'Now, my daughters, have you finished briefing Miss Winterbine on the immediate plans?'

Aisha recounted what they had covered, adding that Estella had been attentive and seemed to understand the significance of the material discussed. Estella found that last comment curious because the background information about the company and its activities was straightforward enough.

'Very good,' said Mr Al Refai, seeming to read her thoughts. 'Miss Winterbine, it is no small thing to have a grasp on this sort of extensive business set-up. You would be surprised how much it is beyond the comprehension of many young people. I know you will take to it like a duck to water, as the English expression goes.'

He went on to tell her entertainingly how his company had developed from a small firm in Cairo to an international business enterprise in one of the world's great cities. It was a contrast with the dry, business-like account of his daughter. He was as warm, charming, and engaging as he had been during his visit to Bendigo. He spoke long about the hardships of the early years and how his family went without before the rewards of his hard work were felt. Estella found herself drawn into conversation while the two sisters sat back and looked on with faint smiles.

'Well, Miss Winterbine,' he said at length, looking at his watch and getting up, 'soon we will land in Brisbane. It is time for my daughters to prepare you for the meetings.' He gave her a little bow and headed towards the front of the plane.

'Come with me,' said Tahani. Aisha nodded that Estella should be at ease.

Estella followed Tahani into a passageway leading to the back of the plane. Not far along the passage, Tahani opened the door to a small but luxuriously furnished cabin.

'This is your room for the trip,' she said. 'By the time we finish tonight, it will be quite late, and you will be eager to freshen up and rest while we fly back to Melbourne. You have everything you need here.' She opened the door to a small bathroom and pointed out where she would find soap, toothpaste, and other toiletries. Next, in the same business-like manner, she opened a dresser's drawers to reveal an assortment of clothes. Out of the drawers, she took a selection of expensive lace underwear, stockings, and tights and laid them on the bed. From the wardrobe, she took two hangers on which hung a dark suit and a cream satin blouse. She hung these on the back of the cabin door.

'Father would like you to wear these clothes to the meetings. You will find that they fit you well.' Estella was about to object. 'Estella, it is vital that one dresses correctly when representing the company's interests. One of the most valuable lessons for people entering the public relations field is the crucial importance of dressing to convey the right impression.' She took Estella's arm. 'It is only temporary to give you an idea of the work.'

Estella understood the reasons for wearing suitable clothing. After all, she was always concerned that her clothes were neat, clean, and modest.

She was not blind, either, to the impression the impeccably groomed sisters projected. But she was not comfortable wearing someone else's clothing.

'Someone else's clothes,' exclaimed Tahani. 'Estella, these are new clothes. They are yours. They are part of the work experience.' Estella was about to object again, but Tahani was ahead of her. 'You must understand that you are experiencing an international company with enormous expenditures. The cost of expensive clothing is negligible in relation to its effectiveness. Come on, put them on. You will feel better once you are dressed and see how appropriate they are for the coming meetings.' She gave an encouraging smile. 'You have your shoes there.' She pointed to an elegant pair of black shoes beside the bed. 'And, yes, I know you do not usually wear stockings or tights, but on formal occasions, they look smarter. You have a choice.' She gave yet another encouraging smile. 'Now, put everything on. Everything.' She directed Estella's eyes to the expensive underwear. 'It all goes together. When you are ready, come to the lounge.' She left Estella staring at the clothes.

It took Estella some minutes to get used to the idea. She understood all the reasons Tahani gave ... but these expensive clothes ... she felt uncomfortable. She examined them, item by item. Even with her limited knowledge of fabric and high fashion, she could see that the clothes were of the first quality. She was curious to see what they looked like. She held the dark skirt against her and saw that the hem fell beneath her knees. It was a beautiful style. She examined the suit jacket. Also very smart. She noted that the blouse was of the finest, delicate satin and did up to the neck. She sat on the bed and looked at the underwear. It was discreet and feminine. At length, she thought it might be all right under the circumstances. It would do no harm to wear the clothes in restricted circumstances. She resigned herself and began to change.

The last to go on were the shoes. She put them on, stood up, and walked around in the confined space. She sat down on the bed, took one off, and examined it. She had never seen such elegant, well-made shoes, let alone have them on. She shook her head in admiration. She was not used to wearing high heels, but these were as comfortable as she could wish. There was no denying it. They were a pleasure to wear. She straightened herself in front of the mirror and could not help staring. It was like looking at another person. The clothes were a perfect fit, and she presented as a picture of smart, modest elegance. She could not have chosen clothing that complimented her more. She looked at her own clothes, the skirt, blouse, and jumper, lying on the bed. For the first time, she was aware of their quality. With pleasure and a slight discomfort, she returned to the lounge.

Aisha and Tahani stood up and looked at her in silence. Tahani walked around her and untied her hair while Aisha disappeared towards the front of the plane. She returned seconds later with Mr Al Rafai. As Tahani was ruffling and stroking Estella's hair, Mr Al Refai's staff assembled around him. Estella looked away.

'Father!' said Aisha, frowning.

With a nod, Mr Al Refai dismissed his staff, and he came forward, taking her hand.

'Miss Winterbine, you are an attractive young woman now dressed to represent the Parisian Worldwide Communications Company. In this work, one always appears to one's best advantage. Appearance is power. Look at my daughters. What do you see? You see elegant young women who demand respect wherever they go. You will do the same. Your beauty has a natural dignity. You must learn how to maintain that in all circumstances. It is a powerful weapon.' He let go of her hand. 'My daughters will help you with this.' He smiled, letting all his charm put her at ease. 'Now it is time for you to relax and prepare for an enjoyable evening during which you will be our special guest.'

After he had withdrawn, Aisha approached, carrying a small jewellery box from which she took two bright pearl earrings set in gold. Beckoning Estella to bend forward, she fixed them to her ears. Tahani took her left hand and slipped a fine gold bracelet onto her wrist. 'There you are,' said

Aisha. 'You are complete.' She stood back. She glanced at her sister and nodded almost imperceptibly

A black limousine was waiting at the bottom of the aircraft stairs when Estella and the Al Refais emerged from the plane at Brisbane airport. Soon they were on their way into the city centre. Wherever they went, there were admiring looks and people attending to Estella's every need. Mr Al Refai's easy charm took over as they were shown to their seats in one of Brisbane's chicest restaurants. He and his daughters returned to the conversation about her life in Binawarra. When the subject of her gardens came up, she mentioned that Didi was surprised and delighted by them. There was a sudden tense silence.

'Do you mean that Didi has been in Binawarra?' said Aisha, struggling to contain her surprise. Her father's eyes narrowed.

'Yes,' said Estella, surprised they did not know. 'He came to have a look at Binawarra, he said. He came across me in the shopping centre while I was chatting with Fr. van Engelen. He invited me to lunch, and after, he took me home, where he had a look around the gardens. My mother thought he was nice.'

'Oh, Didi can be a very charming boy,' said Tahani, with a touch of sarcasm. 'The gossip magazines are there to tell us endlessly about the playboy, Didi Al Refai—' She received a gesture from her father.

'Miss Winterbine,' he said, turning to her, 'my son is a very charming young man. He is kind and honest. That's his appeal, we think, with young women. He is, however, quite irresponsible. He has many lessons to learn before he plays a fruitful role in our company.'

Estella did not know why Mr Al Refai should repeat so emphatically what he had already said in Bendigo and what she already knew. Whatever Didi had done, she thought he was kind and considerate. That's all he meant to her. Geoff came to mind. There had been so much happening—she bent her head forward.

'Are you all right?' said Aisha, leaning towards her and placing her hand on her arm. She glanced at her father and sister.

'Yes, of course,' said Estella. 'It's nothing.'

She blushed at the fib and forced a smile. Her companions seemed eager for that response, and they relaxed again. She had a responsibility to be pleasant and happy. That was the least she could do in return for the efforts to ensure she was enjoying herself. The pleasant conversation resumed without further mention of Didi. She was sorry when Mr Al Refai reminded them of the meetings. They were taken to a plush conference room with a magnificent view over the city and the Brisbane River.

Mr Al Refai sat on one side of a polished Tasmanian Oak conference table with Estella on his right and Tahani on his left. Aisha took her seat beside Estella. She placed some files in front of her. Estella had to be ready to hand them to her father when requested. She was not to worry. 'I am here to help,' said Aisha. It was simple, anyhow, and she would not make a mistake.

Very soon, the first people arrived. Tahani showed them to their places on the other side of the table. They seemed surprised to see Estella sitting next to Mr Al Refai, but the meeting soon settled down to its business. Estella found it engrossing. In a manner that displayed complete control and mastery of the business details, Mr. Al Refai led the conversation, asked questions, made light jokes of unreasonable demands, told amusing anecdotes, referred to the competence of his assistants, and altogether had everyone at ease. During all this, he gave Estella a sign when he wanted the next file.

He took her hand when the meetings were over, and they were standing, ready to leave. 'Miss Winterbine, you did extremely well.' And when Estella replied that she did not have to do much, he said, 'Your task was relatively straightforward, I know, but you completed it with no mistakes or help from my daughter. You would be surprised at how easy it is to mess up such a task in an important meeting. The company executives complimented you as they left. They wanted to know more about you. I'm not the only one to see your potential in business.' He paused. 'Did you find it interesting?'

Estella told the truth. She found it very interesting, fascinating even. Mr Al Refai beamed. She was happy he was satisfied with her. On the way back to the plane, she reflected on how enjoyable the company of the father and daughters was. They were competent and accomplished people, but also pleasant, polite, and friendly, showing attention to her every comfort. The people who surrounded them were the same, always gracious in their attention without overdoing it. And the clothes she was wearing! In a way, she was sorry she had to give them back.

When they were back on the plane, Mr Al Refai wished Estella a pleasant rest and retreated to his office with his business assistants. At a signal from Aisha, Tahani accompanied Estella to her cabin. Estella was surprised to find her suitcase unpacked and her clothes put away. The bed had also been turned down. A long white nightdress with a dressing gown lay across the bed.

'Your clothes have been put away in the drawers and wardrobe,' said Tahini, anticipating her question. 'It has been a demanding evening for you, and the plane will not be ready for departure for a while. So you can get a much-needed sleep. Here, let me help you undress.'

Estella felt unusually sleepy. She offered no resistance as Tahani helped her off with the suit jacket. Tahani hung the jacket on a hanger and put it in the wardrobe. Then she helped her off with the skirt. Estella hesitated, but seeing that Tahani was attending to the clothes, she continued to undress. In this way, she could put on the nightdress without discomfort. Tahani left her, saying that if she needed anything, she should press the button on the side of the bed. When she laid her head on the pillow after coming from the bathroom, she fell asleep while saying her prayers, which rarely happened.

She did not wake up when an official from the immigration department checked the papers of the plane's occupants. She did not wake when the engines fired up, and the plane started moving. She remained unaware of the sisters' concerned voices as they discussed a change of plans with their father. She stayed asleep when the plane took off and, after climbing for ten minutes, slowly turned and headed in a northwesterly direction.

AT TEN o'clock that evening, Fr. van Engelen cautiously picked up the phone. He was relieved to hear Fr. de Jonge's voice and not some nuisance caller. The relief was momentary, however.

'Father, I have been weighing up what action to take in the face of your stubborn disobedience. To add to the problems, there is now the suggestion in your local newspaper that you are connected in some way with the Binawarra High School principal, who is guilty at the very least of neglect in dealing with sexual abuse in his school.'

'The newspaper allegations are completely false,' said Fr. van Engelen, wondering how the provincial had got to hear of the local goings-on. 'Mr Huckerby is a man of great Christian charity and integrity. He has been slandered.'

'It is not for you or me to judge these matters,' said the provincial. 'The charges remain and are yet to be decided upon. In the meantime, I have no other choice but to suspend you until the matter is resolved.'

'You mean you're suspending me because of the grubby scurrilous scribblings in the local paper?'

'Don't be offensive, Father. These are public charges and cannot be ignored. I must be cognisant of the order's standing in the public eye. You are suspended from this moment. I have arranged for one of our Melbourne priests to go up to Binawarra to say Mass on Sunday.'

'This Sunday, you mean?'

'Yes, of course.'

'Without any warning to my congregation?'

'Your congregation?' said Fr. de Jonge.

'They are faithful Catholics who come to Binawarra to attend Mass in the rite they are used to.'

'And they will be attending Mass.'

Fr. van Engelen paused. He was on a knife-edge. The provincial did not need much more provocation. He must be careful of what he said or did—or do it knowing the consequences. 'I cannot allow that,' he said, at last. 'My parishioners have a right to some warning. It will not hurt to announce the changes during my last Mass on Sunday.'

'I am warning you formally, Fr van Engelen. We have reached the end with your flagrant disobedience. One more act of disobedience will mean more than suspension.'

'I will do what I believe is right.'

'Have it your way, Father. You now leave me no alternative. You will be informed of my decision in writing.'

Fr. van Engelen put the phone down, fearing he had indeed reached the end. Expulsion from the order loomed. It would be an extreme and unusual action for the provincial to take, but he would feel justified. Fr. van Engelen was deliberately setting about frustrating the implementation of the decrees of the Second Vatican Council, he would explain to his fraternal colleagues. It could not be more serious. His senior priestly colleagues would support him as they had done so far.

At ten o'clock the next morning, two members of the Melbourne house arrived to lock up the church. They posted a notice on the front doors stating that the church would be closed until further notice. They apologised to Fr. van Engelen. They were just following instructions, they said. They handed him a letter and added that the Binawarra police had been informed. The worn-out priest opened the letter on the spot and read what he was expecting. He was formally expelled from the priestly order he had entered as a youth in 1928. He had ten days to vacate the premises.

GEOFF BROUGHT the car to a stop in Little Bourke Street. 'Wait until twenty past nine and then make your way as instructed to the Myer cafeteria,' he said to Ruby, who was staring ahead of her. 'You know where it is from here, don't you?'

'Yes, it's just around the corner,' she said, her fingers clutched and rubbing her palms. 'Geoff, I'm nervous.'

'Try to stay calm and do exactly as you have been instructed. I'll not be far away. But don't look around for me. Okay?' She nodded.

From the back seat, he took an old dark jumper with fraying hems and the smell of kelpies. He pulled it on. He slipped a beanie over his head and then put on wraparound sunglasses. He got out and came around to Ruby's side. 'You okay?' he said, bending down.

'I'll be all right,' she said feebly. 'You're a sight, Geoff, like some grubby university student.'

'That's the idea,' he said, and with one last word of encouragement, he was off.

Ruby sat thinking about Estella. She was frightened for her. It occurred to her that if she had Estella's faith, she would pray for her. Estella would do the same for her. If there was a God, she prayed that He would please keep Estella safe. The prayer gave her support, and she felt strangely relieved. She forced herself to concentrate on the details she had noted on the piece of paper. At a quarter past nine, she prepared to go. Ten minutes later, she entered the Myer building and made her way to the escalator. She went to the fourth floor, where the escalator deposited her in the Book Department. She headed for the passageway to the right and braced herself as she walked to the cafeteria. At the start of the self-serve line, she took a tray and moved with the people along the food display. Within seconds, she heard movement behind her and a familiar voice at her shoulder.

'It is an irony, is it not?' said Bruce Butcher. 'Do not look!' he hissed when she jerked her head his way. 'That's better. Well, here I am helping you when I could be killed doing it, and you're doing your best to have me locked up.' He stifled a bitter laugh.

'Where is she?' whispered Ruby out of the side of her mouth as she pretended to examine the dishes.

'I told you not to talk. Don't say anything! Now listen. When you go to pick her up, you'll be told that she did not sign in.'

'But you saw her,' Ruby could not restrain herself from saying. 'You saw me with her and that young man welcoming the students.'

'I caught a glimpse of you and Ms Winterbine with a fellow unknown to me. I assumed you had your own plans. After all, you said nothing to me, and I was there waiting for you.'

Ruby felt sick to her stomach as the ever-growing extent of her carelessness dawned. 'But ...' she said, trembling, 'but he took her to the hospitality room. I was with her when she entered the lift.'

'Inquiries will reveal that nobody saw Ms Winterbine in the hospitality room,' he said between his teeth.

There was a frightful pause while Ruby tried to gather her thoughts. She threw him a glance and saw an expression of bitter defeat. He did not appear to enjoy her discomfort or even to be aware of it. Despite the caution to keep quiet, he seemed to be waiting for her to speak.

'Well, where is she?' she said, at last. 'Why are you meeting me like this? Why didn't you phone me yourself? Is Ms Bicknell involved?'

'Well!' he exclaimed. 'Ms Bicknell ... Ms Bicknell ... yes, well, Ms. Bicknell! There's a one ... Oh! Oh! Oh!' Ruby could not help turning to this manic mumbling, but he pushed her face away. 'Shut up and listen carefully,' he went on. 'I'm dead if I'm caught passing on this information.

Ms Winterbine's life could be in danger. At the very least, she is in what you people call moral danger. Big moral danger. Oh, what am I saying, what am I saying?' He shook his head, muttered a few incoherent words, and stopped. 'You have to look in the direction of the Parisian Worldwide Communications Company,' he resumed in a rush. 'More I cannot or dare not tell you. They would kill me if they found out.'

They were coming to the end of the serving line. They stopped. Several people in front could not make up their minds. As Bruce seemed to be waiting for her to speak again, she spoke up. 'Where will we look? And why are you telling me this?'

'It's an international company. You could start with the headquarters in Paris. I'm telling you too much,' he groaned.

'What—? You mean she's overseas?'

'I don't know, but it's more than likely. Tell your soldier friend. An ex-SAS captain should have handy contacts. You must get cracking now if you don't want your darling returned as soiled goods or, even worse, if you don't want to see her leading their sort of life.' He could scarcely contain his bitterness and resentment.

'I see,' said Ruby, 'if you can't have her, nobody can.'

'What normal man would not be turned off at the thought of that oily sleazebag having such a girl? It's an outrage.'

'The promulgator of left-wing ideology is racist, too? Is there any limit to your hypocrisy?'

'I'm ready to swallow your sneers and barbs, but you and your soldier friend will feel her desecration as much as I will. Yeah, your boyfriend—he's also come under her spell.' He gave another bitter, ironic laugh. 'The girl has the power of a witch. Who would have thought I would be here telling you all this? I will end up being her Sydney Carton! Don't you think so?'

'Hardly,' said Ruby, whose wonder now overcame her fear.

'You don't think so? But what a good joke! You should be satisfied. The girl has bewitched me into experiencing disgusting bourgeois virtue—of giving my life for her. Now I know how you live! It's a prison.' They were silent while Ruby waited for the person in front to pay. 'Any police inquiries will draw a blank before you can get to her,' he went on. 'I advise you and your SAS mate to go after her yourselves. With the utmost haste.' The line moved, and Ruby paid for her cup of tea and cake. 'Wait a bit, but don't look at me,' he said as she began to walk off. He came up beside her. 'If you succeed in rescuing the girl, and later I am found dead, remember I was her Sydney Carton.' His face twisted as if he were trying to make up his mind. 'Sorry about Lilly Kelly. Now follow the rest of your instructions. There is still the envelope.' He was gone.

Ruby didn't know what to conclude as she sat down. Was he genuine? He must have been. He did not sound like the Bruce Butcher she had known. In his way, he had expressed regret for what he had done. It was unbelievable. A few minutes later, Geoff sat next to her with the envelope in his hand.

'They've gone,' he said, opening the envelope. 'He was with a group of young people.' He unfolded the sheet of paper. 'The head of the Parisian Worldwide Communications Company has a private jet.'

'Is that all?'

'Yes, but it's crucial information. Tell me what he said.'

Ruby related the essential points of their conversation. But she omitted Sydney Carton and the admission about Lilly Kelly. It was not likely, anyhow, that Geoff had read Dickens's *A Tale of Two Cities*.

'Okay, so that confirms her abduction. It also confirms Miss Barker's judgment that there was dissension in their group. Indeed, it's betrayal. Bruce Butcher has put himself in genuine danger, as he is aware. But he has not given a clear picture of the reasons for Estella's abduction or how she was taken. His obsession with her has forced him to focus on only one thing. There has to be more to it. There's got to be more. I don't believe the rape of Estella is Mr Al Refai's or the Dutch woman's key motive.'

'How can you say that so calmly?' said Ruby, horrified.

'Ruby, I must remain calm. I've got to think my way through this. I cannot afford to let my emotions govern my actions. Come on. I want to ring Miss Barker, and then we'll get back to Binawarra.'

Chapter 30

Estella in Wonderland

MISS BARKER was at the Winterbine house shortly after six o'clock. Aine, barefoot and in a long white dress, opened to her before she could knock.

'Something has happened to Estella, hasn't it?' she said before Miss Barker had a chance to say anything.

'Yes, I'm sorry to say.'

Aine pulled the door behind her and sank into one of the verandah chairs.

'Miss Waiting dropped her off at the hotel as arranged,' Miss Barker continued, taking the seat beside her, 'but later received a phone call saying that Estella did not arrive.'

'I was afraid—do you have any idea where she is?'

'No, not at the moment. There's more to it, but I would like to wait until I hear from Mr Shawcross before we speculate. He is investigating. Will you wait?'

'Yes, of course, Miss Barker, I trust your judgment,' said Aine, looking at the bushy vacant lot opposite. She cast a look at the front door. 'Miss Barker, there is something—a few things I should tell you. Charles is showering. Do I have your confidence?'

'You know you have.'

'Thirteen years ago, I was encouraged to consider a career in modelling. Do you remember?'

'Yes, I remember well. I remember the fashion shoot on the square with that Mr Harry, the personable fashion photographer. He had a tall, pretty girl as his assistant.'

'That's right. That was Jannie. She was one of his favourite models. She and Harry encouraged me.'

'A tall, pretty girl?' said Miss Barker, raising her hand. 'If I remember correctly, she had an accent.'

'Yes, she was Dutch, came to Australia when a teenager. She was also with me as a postulant in the same convent.'

'A postulant in the same convent,' repeated Miss Barker, with her hand still raised. 'Where was that convent?'

'It was in the northeast of the city. This is what I wanted to tell you. She and another postulant who eventually became a nun urged me to develop my talents and seek my true inner self, words to that effect. Ms Bicknell spoke in a similar way about Estella. Then Harry, whom I hadn't seen for quite a while, turned up at our house wanting to take photos of me. I was alone. He said he was in Binawarra on a special commission. He gave the impression it had nothing to do with me. I think now he wanted to hide his purpose.'

'You did not question him about it?'

'No, I assumed he took the opportunity to come by because of—' She bent her head and put her hand to her forehead.

'But you later thought the commission had something to do with you?' said Miss Barker, taking Aine's hand away from her forehead. 'Why?'

'As he was leaving, he said people were saying my daughter was incomparable, but in his opinion, she did not compare with me. He was only here a few minutes. I threatened to call the police.'

'And you drew a connection with Ms Bicknell and Estella?'

'Yes, but I don't know what it is exactly. That talk thirteen years ago about developing the divine within suddenly came back to me.'

'Have you seen that girl, the tall, pretty one, recently?'

'No, I haven't seen Jannie de Kam for some time.'

'Aine, tell me more about that time in the convent and why Jannie de Kam encouraged you to become a model. Tell me as much as you can before Charles appears.'

MISS BARKER reassuringly waved when she saw Joanne and Bill sitting on the verandah.

'The news can't be that bad,' said Bill, seeing the newspaper in Miss Barker's hand. 'No expression of doom.'

'Glad to see your spirits have picked up.'

'The old boy is bouncing back,' said Joanne.

'Old boy, by Jove!' cried Bill. 'Let's have a look at that wretched rag.' He took the newspaper and flicked it out in front of him. The headline: 'Vietnam Veterans in wild pub brawl.'

'I suppose we could not have expected anything less.'

'No, the report is not too subtle in placing the blame on the Vietnam veterans,' said Miss Barker. 'There's no mention of the outsiders who participated in the demonstration and later disappeared from the bar. The editorial is what you should read. Our Mr Collins is sticking with it, and his selected correspondents still agree with him.'

Bill turned to the editorial page to read: **Will Anzac Day divide the community?** 'Anzac Day is what brings the nation together as one people. People like Collins will not change that, no matter how hard they try.'

'I suspect it's going to be a fight, though,' said Miss Barker.

'We'll win this one.' He returned to the editorial.

'The violent brawl involving Vietnam Veterans in one of Binawarra's hotels raises once again the stark reality of a conflict that has divided the nation. Many claim that capitalist, imperialist motives were behind the entry of our troops into a local conflict the allies had no business in. Others thought it in the tradition of the Anzac to go and fight for the 'freedom' of the Vietnamese. Was this misguided? Many ordinary people thought so. But there is a deeper issue underlying these questions.

'Does the Anzac tradition glorify the male inclination to resolve social problems by violent conflict? This was the question Ms Jane Cox, a senior teacher at Binawarra High School, courageously raised. Is the deeper problem the male urge to dominate through violence and then use the authority through domination to oppress the weak and vulnerable? If this deeper problem is underwriting the Anzac tradition, then it behoves every person of conscience to reflect on that tradition.

'The Education Department report on the charges of sexual abuse in Binawarra's High School is still awaited. But whatever the outcome of an official report, something that is rarely conclusive, it is surely the responsibility of the townspeople to ensure that male authority does not provide the grounds for the abuse of impressionable young people. As this newspaper has consistently maintained, this issue is far from finished.'□

'He is still after me,' said Bill. 'And I'm determined he will not succeed.'

'I'm glad to hear that determination, but once again, I warn you to tread carefully,' said Miss Barker.

'Charles's idea of a meeting is just what the town needs. It will present a forum for everyone to have their say. We will see then how much support this unconscionable person who parades as a newspaper editor has.'

'Yes, you are right. But we must attend to other matters.'

'What's happened?' said Joanne, alarmed at Miss Barker's tone.

Miss Barker gave a brief account of Estella's disappearance.

'Oh no!' said Joanne, 'surely, she has not been abducted?'

'My God!' said Bill, turning pale. 'I was convinced the work experience weekend was safe and legitimate.'

'It was legitimate. These are devious people. Don't blame yourself, Bill. And let's not get too anxious before we hear from Mr Shawcross. We still know nothing about the nameless informant.'

'What will we say to Charles and Aine?' said Bill. 'This is terrible. How right you have been!'

'I have already spoken with them. They are upset, of course, but will wait for my advice. I'll return home now and wait for Mr Shawcross's phone call. We'll know more then. I am just informing you so we can be ready to act.'

As Miss Barker was preparing to go, the phone rang. Joanne hurried to answer it. She reappeared seconds later. It was Geoff.

AT ELEVEN o'clock, Miss Barker, Fr. van Engelen, Bill, and Joanne assembled in Charles and Aine's lounge room.

'What we feared has happened, despite our attempts to guard Estella,' said Miss Barker. 'I'm sorry, Aine and Charles. We have been outsmarted—for the moment.'

'It's not your fault,' said Charles, holding Aine's hand. 'We know what steps you took to guard against an unclear threat.'

'We will continue to say our prayers for her safety,' said Aine. 'I'm sorry I could not provide what may be vital information before this.'

'You were not to know, Aine,' said Miss Barker. 'There was no reason for you to make the connection with your friend.'

'What are you talking about?' asked Bill.

'There is possibly a utopian vision motivating all Edith Bicknell's plans,' said Miss Barker, 'at least a variety of the utopianisms seizing the leftist mind these days.'

'Utopian Vision? We've gone from radical political philosophy to utopian visions?'

'It's all interwoven, Bill. None of us could have guessed it. Information from Aine and Mr Shawcross's chance recall of something Mr McKinnon said led us to this possibility. But let's leave that for the moment. Our immediate task is to plan recovery action.'

Bill gave a helpless gesture while Miss Barker summarised the current situation. Estella had disappeared. Miss Bicknell and whatever she represented seemed to have motivated her disappearance. Mr Al Refai and his company appear to be the actual agents of her disappearance. The informant hinted that Mr Al Refai's private jet would be involved. To go where? Paris? They did not know yet. What is the object? It still was not clear, although the informant said Estella was in moral and physical danger. There was a knock on the door. Aine brought Larry into the room. Surprised to find himself in the middle of a meeting, Larry gave the school principal a cautious nod.

'I have asked Mr Burgess to tell us about the incident between him and Len Dawson,' said Miss Barker. 'It doesn't seem to fit into the scenario, but I can't help but think there's a connection. Mr Burgess, we know how the fight occurred. Did anything odd happen beforehand?'

'No, we were in class before that. It happened because Len was still furious about the previous Saturday night when Geoff gave him a hiding for his attempt to—to assault Estella.'

'What's this?' said Charles. 'Assault Estella?'

'What's possessing the young people in this town?' said Joanne after Larry had explained. 'That is despicable. How can anyone make such a bet about a girl like Estella?'

'Was there nothing before the class that was in some way related to the incident in the corridor?' Miss Barker pursued. 'Concentrate. Anything? Anything at all?'

'No,' said Larry, 'I sat with Estella at the lower end of the recreation area. We were alone. Len and the others were standing not far away, glaring at us. Then we went into class. It was Ms Cox's class, and she had invited an outside teacher to talk to us.'

'Who?'

'A lady named Eva Reiner. It was a special social issues class.'

'Eva Reiner! A well-known radical like Reiner in the school—it could not be coincidental. What did you discuss?' Larry described the class discussion. 'A Marxist propaganda session, as I would expect from that woman,' said Miss Barker. 'It was well done of you, Mr Burgess, to stick up for Estella. You have said enough, though. Thank you for your help. You can go now.'

'What's this about?' said Larry, remaining where he stood. 'Has something happened to Estella?'

'You are alert, young man,' said Miss Barker, 'but it is not your business.'

'If Estella is in trouble, I want to help. I will do anything you want, including keeping my mouth shut.'

'I'm sure you would,' she said, looking Larry up and down. 'All right, but you must have your parents' permission. So here's what I want you to do.' She explained his allotted task. 'Now be off with you and ask your parents. Tell your mother to call me if she has questions.' Larry left them, full of eagerness.

'Young Burgess has provided me with further confirmation of what seems part of the object of the two groups working with each other: the seduction of Estella. When Father raised this possibility some time ago, I dismissed it as improbable. Now, for whatever purpose, it has all the appearances of being so. In retrospect, there has been a concerted effort by Miss Bicknell and her colleagues to change Estella's moral outlook, first through argument and then through ridicule and shaming. On the evidence, the efforts were futile. This is further supported by our informant's explicit warning that Estella is in moral danger.'

'We pray that Estella will continue to resist the attempts,' said Aine.

'No one is stronger in their consciousness of what's right and wrong,' said Fr. van Engelen.

'Mr Shawcross and I think there's something odd about all this,' Miss Barker continued. 'Some things don't add up. Estella would have recognised the moral danger well before this if it had been a straightforward seduction. It doesn't add up unless—it's a tentative unless—unless the utopian vision of the "goddess" holds the key.'

'Whatever are you talking about now, Flo?' said Bill. 'What goddess?'

'This is something not yet widely known, but soon will be. Indeed, I don't know enough at this stage to speak with authority about it. But there are things to consider before the ideological motivations. For example, how are the Al Refai and Bicknell groups related? Is there a common aim? If not, how do the different aims merge? We must keep these considerations in mind as we plan our action.'

'What do you propose?' said Bill.

'Well, before I go into that, I must stress that our informant also said Estella's life might be in danger. We know less about this than the moral danger. I suspect that a failure in the plan will put Estella into physical danger.' She stopped to consider her words. 'All right, what are we going to do? We must move with haste. Despite the information about the private jet and its likely destination of Paris, Mr Shawcross and I have decided the most reasonable place to begin our search for Estella is in Middelburg, Holland, Miss Bicknell's hometown.'

There were cries of astonishment. Miss Barker left it to Fr. van Engelen to explain.

'Well, that clears up a lot,' said Bill when the priest had finished. 'It's also an extraordinary coincidence. To think that you and Gerda-whatever ended up in the same place!'

'Father's presence may be the hand of Providence,' said Charles.

'To protect our daughter and us,' added Aine.

'I don't know what to say to that,' said Miss Barker. 'I hope you're right. Now I intend to take the plane to Holland this afternoon.'

'This afternoon,' said Bill, 'how have you—?'

'Bill, I will explain later. Let me go through the plan first. The first step is to begin the search in Middelburg. Fr. van Engelen will contact his brother to tell him I'm coming. He is already aware to some extent of Miss Bicknell's activities. Mr Shawcross will remain here and try to track down Mr Rostowski, the man who has been shadowing Estella for the last few months. This man has also been Miss Bicknell's support and the one to do his dirty work. Mr Shawcross will stay on his trail if he finds him. If he doesn't, he will join me in Holland. Now comes a tricky part of the plan. I want Charles and Father to leave for Holland tomorrow to join me in the search. Father may provide invaluable information about the local conditions and the connections with Gerda van den Donker. You have indispensable knowledge of everything that has occurred. Can you spare the time, Father?'

'Miss Barker, here is another coincidence,' said the priest. 'I have just been expelled from my order for disobedience. I can go, but how am I to pay for it?'

'What has happened?' said Charles.

'Charles, let's hear about it later,' said Miss Barker. 'Father, I will pay for you and Charles.' She held up her hand to stop any objections. 'I am a woman of means. Again, no explanation for the moment. Just know I can absorb the expenses. Charles, you know your daughter better than Father and me. You will be needed in the search.'

'Miss Barker, I don't know if I can leave Aine at this point and if I can be—'

'He will go, Miss Barker,' said Aine.

'But I have no passport.'

'Leave it to me. The necessary paperwork will be ready for you tomorrow at the airport. I will arrange for Miss Waiting to keep Aine company. Indeed, you will keep each other company.'

'Flo, you seem to have thought of everything,' said Bill, dabbing his brow with his ample handkerchief. 'Is there something we can do?'

'Bill, you, and Joanne have an important role besides supporting Aine. I will leave some contacts with you. They will be for the planning and the money to pay for it. I will also leave cash. You will discuss with Mr Shawcross, Fr. van Engelen, and Charles how much they need. You can do that later, not now. Father will also leave his contact numbers in Holland. Now, are there questions?'

'Are Geoff and Ruby aware of all this?' said Bill.

'Mr Shawcross, yes, Miss Waiting, not fully. Mr Shawcross's function in this is critical. Much of the planning has been his. If we get to Estella in time, it will be his doing.'

At that moment, Larry Burgess walked unannounced into the lounge room. 'Mum says it's all right, Miss Barker. She says I can go.'

'Did she have any objections?'

'No, she said I would not get into trouble if I were with you.'

'All right, young fellow, I want you to come to my house at one o'clock.'

'Will you be ready by then?' asked Joanne after Larry had left. 'Surely you need more time.'

'Joanne, I am usually set to move with little delay. In this case, there was a likelihood of having to travel. We knew Gerda van den Donker was expected in Middelburg around this time. I prepared myself as much as I could. Everything is now booked, and my contacts are alerted. I will leave the keys to my house with you as I do when I go to see my family in Sydney.' She gave them an ironic smile. 'Now, let's talk about the details.'

Miss Barker spent the next half hour discussing the planning. When satisfied that everyone knew their role, she let Aine conclude.

'Charles and I appreciate the great trouble you are all taking to find out what has happened to our daughter. We pray that you will succeed. However, we want to say that even though we would be devastated if anything happened to Estella, we are more concerned about the moral danger. The welfare of our daughter's eternal soul is more important than anything. Please pray that she perseveres, no matter how insidious the temptation. Geoff and Miss Barker are right. Estella would not let herself into anything obviously wrong. I fear she is subject to severe temptation. We pray that she remains aware that luxury and flattery are major paths to sin. I once found myself on that same path when—'

Charles took her hand as if signalling that she need not explain.

AT ONE o'clock, Larry knocked at Miss Barker's front door. To his relief, she welcomed him curtly but kindly and instructed him to take two bags through the back door and put them in the car.

'They are very expensive-looking bags,' Larry commented.

'Do you think so?' was all Miss Barker said while she walked through to the kitchen.

Larry put the bags in the car and returned for further instructions.

'Wait for me near the garage,' said Miss Barker.

Ten minutes later, Miss Barker emerged wearing a full-length coat. Her hair was pinned around her head like a tight-fitting helmet. She carried a round box in one hand and an elegant beauty case in the other.

Stop staring, young man,' she said as she put them in the back seat.

'Sorry, Miss Barker.'

'You surprised me this last week,' said Miss Barker as she turned onto Melbourne Road. 'I must congratulate you on the mature way you faced up to adversity. You have won the friendship and affection of Estella.'

It was an unsolicited compliment, and it pleased Larry. Then, contrary to his expectation, the drive down to Melbourne passed by quickly. Miss Barker kept the conversation going with inquiries and comments about his future. It seemed no time before they were approaching the airport.

'Now listen carefully,' she said after she had parked the car. 'I want you to go to the international terminal and look for Miss Waiting and Mr Shawcross. They are probably in an unobtrusive spot. They won't be together. Tell them I will check in at the Qantas counter when you find them. Tell them not to approach me. If they have a message, they should pass it on to you. Have you got that?'

'Yes, Miss Barker.'

'While looking for them, keep an eye out for Mr Rostowski. If you see him, stay out of his sight. Hurry to tell Mr Shawcross. After I have checked in, I will sit in the lounge area. You must not behave as if you know me.'

Larry made his way to the international terminal. As he passed by the counters of the foreign airlines, he noticed Boris checking in. He moved out of his vision and waited. He watched him go outside the terminal building and light up a cigarette. He strolled to the counter and asked the dispatch clerk where the flight went from that check-in point. Singapore, Bahrain, Beirut, and Cairo was the short answer.

'I'm looking for Mr Rostowski,' said Larry, as innocently as he could. 'Was that the last man, Mr Rostowski?'

The dispatch clerk frowned. 'I don't know,' he said, looking at the documents beside him. 'Well, here it is. That was a Mr Saladin, N. Saladin, not Rostowski, okay?'

Larry thanked the man and went on his way. Five minutes later, he heard his name called and turned to see Geoff shielded by some ornamental plants.

'What are you doing here?' Geoff said.

'I came with Miss Barker. And I just saw that foreigner.'

'Rostowski? Where?'

'He just checked into a flight to Singapore, Bahrain, Beirut, and Cairo. But he did not check in as Rostowski. The name was Saladin, N. Saladin.'

'Really?' said Geoff, digesting the information. 'Well done, Larry. You've saved us a lot of trouble.' Larry beamed. 'Where's Miss Barker?' Larry passed on Miss Barker's message. 'Okay, tell her we're here. Tell her what name Rostowski checked in under, where he is going, and if she follows him, I'll take the first available flight to Holland. Ask her if everything has been arranged as discussed. I will fetch Ruby in the meantime.'

Larry walked towards the Qantas check-in counters, keeping to the side to avoid being seen if Boris should wander back into the terminal. He waited there for twenty minutes, but no sign of Miss Barker. He was fidgeting and leaning against the wall when a tall woman came to check in at the Qantas counter. She was dressed smartly in a light-coloured casual suit. She had a scarf wrapped fashionably around her short, dark hair and glided away from the check-in counter in brown high-heeled shoes. She was an older woman with an attractive oval face, enhanced discreetly with make-up. She came towards him.

'Follow me,' she whispered as she passed without looking.

'Miss Barker?' said Larry.

He followed her into the lounge and sat down when she sat.

'Is that really you, Miss Barker?'

'Did you find Mr Shawcross?'

'Yes.' He gave her Geoff's message and the information about Boris.

'Mr Saladin ... well, well, well. Excellent, Larry,' she said. 'You're proving your worth. Tell Mr Shawcross I will switch my booking to Cairo or wherever our Mr Saladin is going. He should travel to Holland and Middelburg as discussed. All is still as planned, except for the change to my flight. I will attend to that now. Tell Mr Shawcross that he and Ruby must not come near me. I don't want to run any risk of alerting Saladin.'

Larry, flattered by the praise and happy to hear his name, found Geoff talking to Ruby, not far away from the ornamental plants.

'Larry, I'm so glad to see you,' said Ruby. 'And terrific work. I'm relieved something is going right to make up for my blunders.'

Larry saw she was not quite herself. 'Has something bad happened to Estella?'

'Yes, Larry,' she said, looking at Geoff.

'If he has come with Miss Barker, then he is to be trusted,' said Geoff. 'Larry, it looks like Estella has gone missing. We are trying to find her. Where's Miss Barker? What did she say?'

'Gone missing? How?' Larry said, but saw that Geoff wanted an answer. He passed on Miss Barker's message.

'Okay, but where is she?'

'She's either rebooking her flight or in the lounge. You won't recognise her.'

Geoff stood reflecting. Larry looked at Ruby, who shrugged. There had been a change in Ruby, he observed, especially in her attitude to Geoff. It was as if they had switched roles. Geoff was focused on the problem at hand, while Ruby seemed to be waiting for instructions. No, it was more than that; what precisely, he could not decide.

'Go and tell Miss Barker that I will return home to prepare myself,' said Geoff. 'Ruby can take you home in Miss Barker's car. Ask if there is anything else before we make contact in Middelburg.'

Larry went off to find Miss Barker. He ran into her fifteen minutes later, walking to the lounge. He passed on Geoff's message.

'Look the other way!' she whispered.

As Larry turned, he saw Boris strolling towards the customs door.

'All right, he's gone through,' she said. 'Where are they? I will talk to them myself.'

Geoff and Ruby were standing where Larry had left them. When they saw him approaching, they made ready to listen, taking no notice of the tall, elegant woman walking several paces behind him.

'Well, Larry?' said Geoff when he was within earshot.

'Move a little further to the side,' said Miss Barker.

'Miss Barker!' said Geoff and Ruby together. They followed her to the side.

'Is that really you, Miss Barker?'

'No time for that, Miss Waiting. Everything is in place, Mr Shawcross, as we discussed. The only change is that I'm following Saladin to Cairo. I suspect that his stay there will be short. Here are my keys, Miss Waiting. You can drive Larry back to Binawarra, and I suggest you stay in Binawarra for the weekend. Charles and Aine are expecting you. You can bring Mr Shawcross, Charles, and Fr. van Engelen to the airport tomorrow. Understood?'

'Understood,' said Geoff. 'I hope Saladin does not recognise you on the plane. You may be at close quarters.'

'He'll never recognise her!' exclaimed Ruby. 'Miss Barker, you are a handsome woman.'

'Thank you, Miss Waiting,' she said, indifferently. 'I will be in First Class. It is not likely we will see each other until we collect our bags at Cairo airport, if then. I will have plenty of opportunity to avoid him.'

'That is an amazing woman. That dark wig suits her,' said Ruby, as Miss Barker's tall, elegant figure glided towards the customs door.

'Have you got everything?' said Geoff. 'Is it all understood? Larry knows where Miss Barker's car is.' Ruby said she understood. 'Well, I will be off now. I will call you later tonight at Estella's house. Okay?'

'Geoff, I'm so relieved you know what to do,' said Ruby. 'I have been like a brick to you. I'm sorry. I had the wrong idea about you. What a fool I've made of myself.'

'You have your skills, and I have mine,' said Geoff. 'Don't blame yourself. I have told you we're dealing with clever, organised people. And, Ruby, please don't change. She shouldn't change, should she?' he said, turning to Larry.

'No,' said Larry.

'You look after her, won't you, mate?'

'Of course.'

'You men are bearable sometimes,' said Ruby, standing on her toes and pulling Geoff forward to kiss him. She took Larry's arm. 'Larry will look after me. We understand each other, don't we?'

'I suppose we do.'

Ruby glanced back after they had gone several paces, but Geoff's mind had already moved on.

ESTELLA opened her eyes and, at first, did not know where she was. The jet engines were humming in her ears, adding to a pleasant drowsiness. She concentrated on the hum, and then it came to her. She was in bed on Mr Al Refai's plane. It was pitch dark outside. She fiddled around for her watch and then for a light switch on the console beside the bed. She was alarmed to see it was seven o'clock in the morning. She had slept more than seven hours! Where was she? They should have been in Melbourne hours ago. She put on the dressing gown hanging on the cabin door and headed for the lounge. Several dimmed lamps lit up the lounge. Aisha was stretched out on the settee, and Tahani was lying back in one of the lounge chairs.

On the table in front of them were cups, a teapot, pots of jam, and plates of rolls, toast, and pastries. The sisters had on similar dressing gowns.

'Oh, you are awake,' said Tahani, who saw her first.

'Where are we?' said Estella.

'Now, don't be alarmed,' said Aisha. 'Here, come and sit beside me.' She made room for Estella on the settee. 'We are nearly at Singapore. We are in descent now. It's around four o'clock Singapore time.'

'Singapore!' exclaimed Estella. She looked at Tahani, whose expression bespoke unease.

'Everything is all right,' said Aisha. 'Let me explain. Shortly after we returned to the plane, Father received an urgent message from Head Office in Paris. Critical business negotiations appeared on the verge of failing. After much discussion, he decided there was no choice but to return and take the matter in hand. It was too late to do anything else but leave. Father says to assure you that we will bring you back home as soon as he has attended to the business. That will mean a couple of days in Paris. It will not be much longer than the proposed work experience weekend. We sent a message through to Melbourne advising the change in plans.'

Estella could barely absorb what was happening.

'Don't be anxious,' said Aisha. 'Everything is all right. We will do everything we can to make sure you are comfortable. Father understands that the change in plans may cause some worry. He will talk to you later about a sightseeing program in Paris.' She paused. 'Let me assure you that we only heard about the change when Father came from the business lounge just before take-off.'

'Yes,' said Tahani, 'we knew nothing. You must believe that.'

'Of course,' said Estella. 'I've hardly been out of Binawarra, and now I'm on the way to France. It's a shock. Don't you need a passport to go overseas?'

'Yes, but Father will look after that for the short term,' said Aisha. 'He is a prominent business leader with great responsibility. The officials will be cooperative, he said. He will talk about that later. Come, have some breakfast. You must be hungry.'

'Do you mind if I freshen up first?'

'Of course not, but you can stay in your dressing gown. Nobody will bother us for a while.'

Estella returned to her cabin and knelt to say her morning prayers. She included a prayer for her safe return. When she had finished, she sat on her bed and fiddled with the Miraculous Medal on the silver chain around her neck. She had never been in such a situation. She had no idea, really, what to make of it. The sisters were solicitous as usual. That reassured her. But to be on her way to France ... suddenly ... she must suppose it was all right and that Mr Al Refai knew what he was doing. Well, if they had sent a message to tell her parents where she was, there couldn't be any harm. What harm could there be, anyhow, with people who were so kind and attentive to her ?

Ten minutes later, she was back with the young women. Tahani no longer looked uneasy. Aisha instructed the steward to bring more tea, toast, rolls, and pastries. He arrived five minutes later, and Tahini served Estella. That was a gesture of solicitude that further calmed her. As she sipped her tea and took small bites from a French pastry, she told herself there was nothing to worry about. She would leave everything in the hands of those looking after her so well.

Not long after, the plane landed in Singapore. As they taxied to a stop, Aisha asked her to return to her cabin. There would be people in and out of the plane. She would be more comfortable there. Estella was glad to be by herself. Paris! What a marvellous thought. French was one of her best subjects. She loved the sound of the language, and France's history fascinated her. But now to be experiencing France and hearing French before she sat for her final exams!

Amid these pleasant thoughts, Geoff intruded. The happenings of the evening had blocked her memory of him. She felt a pain in her heart as the episode in Ruby's unit came back to her. She felt shame mixed with the pleasure of being held in Geoff's arms; the kiss and the passionate embrace lingered. She thought of Ruby's unfussed reaction and her assurance that it was not betrayal and that Geoff blamed himself. Oh, how did they end up in that embrace? She could not think how it had happened. One moment she was talking to him, and the next moment, in ecstasy in his arms. How could she ever get over that embrace? It was her first kiss. Now she understood some of the things Jenny had said and the warnings Fr. van Engelen had given. She had felt the force of it. It had crept up and almost consumed her. She got up and walked up and down in the restricted space of the cabin.

What did Geoff think about it? Did he feel the same way? He liked her a lot, that was sure, but did he love her in the same way she loved him? Was he thinking of her? She sighed. She must get him out of her mind for the moment. She should put the 'Geoff problem' on hold while she was with the Al Refais. Yes, she had a duty to do that. She should gracefully accept and enjoy all the benefits the father and sisters were offering her. It was temporary, and she would be back home soon enough. In this way, she managed to calm herself. The new experience of so much distance between her and home helped her put her affairs aside.

Half an hour later, Tahani came to tell her they had the lounge again to themselves. After dressing, she joined the sisters. She asked Aisha where their father was, for she had not seen him yet. Aisha explained that he was busy with his assistants. He had a lot to prepare for the important meeting he had as soon as they landed in Paris. Besides, he thought it best to leave the young women to themselves so they could be at ease without any men bothering them. Estella said Mr Al Refai would not be a bother. The comment drew an exchange of glances between the sisters.

When the plane was in the air again, Aisha announced they would watch some movies during the long flight to Paris. In between them, she urged Estella to spend time resting in her cabin, sleeping if she could, to overcome the effects of jetlag. They would land in Paris early afternoon, and there would still be time for them to see quite a lot. Not long after, the steward prepared the lounge for the first movie. Estella was delighted to hear they would be watching *My Fair Lady* with Audrey Hepburn and Rex Harrison. She loved the music but had never seen the film. A few enjoyable hours followed while they watched the film and discussed it.

When they had finished lunch, Estella returned to her cabin with some glossy magazines on Paris that Tahani had given her. She was to rest for at least three hours, said Aisha. Estella was glad to oblige. She lay on the bed, leafing through the magazines until sleep got the better of her. A knock on the door awoke her.

'You have had a good long sleep, almost four hours,' said Aisha, coming into the cabin. She wore a long black dress, gold embroidered down the middle and along the edges. 'That's good. Now, if you are ready to have a shower and get dressed, I have some special clothes for you.' She held a long, dark blue dress with gold embroidery. It was like the one she wore. 'This is a traditional Egyptian dress, the galabia,' Aisha continued. 'Father asks that you wear it to blend with our party when we arrive. It will make things easier as we complete the formalities. You would also give us much pleasure if you dressed like us. Do you like it?'

Estella held the dress up to have a closer look. 'It's beautiful. My mother often wears long dresses. She would like this, too.'

'So you will wear it?'

'Yes, of course. I have long dresses with traditional folk motifs.' She held it against her. 'It's my size, too. Is it really a traditional Egyptian style?'

'Very much so,' said Aisha, looking as animated as Estella had seen her. 'I am so pleased you like it. Tahani will be, too. You can wear your black shoes with it. Take your time.'

Aisha left Estella to shower and dress. An hour later, Estella, dressed, was satisfied with her appearance. The dress came almost to her neck with a little embroidered slit that revealed the gleaming skin of her upper chest and the silver chain as she moved.

'It suits you,' said Tahani when she had returned to the lounge. Tahani wore a dark green embroidered galabia. 'You will bring a tear to Father's eyes when he sees you. He loves us in traditional clothing.'

Aisha was right. Mr Al Refai, again as if on cue, arrived a few minutes later, exclaiming about such beautiful young women in his lounge. Estella saw that he was indeed moved as he let his gaze linger on her.

'You could be a young Egyptian woman,' he said, taking her hand as he usually did. 'You know, Miss Winterbine, you have paid us a great compliment by wearing the galabia.'

'Thank you, Mr Al Refai,' she said. 'It is no burden, I assure you. My mother would like this, too.'

'You and your mother are very special people. I believe she would not be shamed standing next to you.'

'My mother is very fair. I have a lot from my father.'

'So I have heard,' he said. 'Now I will leave you to relax. There is still much to do. I apologise again, Miss Winterbine, for the change in plans. It could not be helped. We will do everything to make up for it.' He kissed her hand, a gesture she had come to like. 'I will come back and talk with you before we land.' He smiled and left them.

Estella wanted to ask him how he knew her mother was fair. But her mind was distracted by Aisha announcing they would watch another film, *The Sound of Music*. Estella was again delighted by the choice of film. She asked whether it was just a coincidence that they were showing two musicals.

'Not really,' said Aisha. 'Father likes musicals, at least these sorts of musicals. We do, too.'

'We have similar tastes,' Estella could not help commenting.

'Yes, Father said that, too.'

Another few hours passed enjoyably. The sisters had lost all their reserve. They called her by her Christian name and invited Estella to call them by their personal names. The undisguised desire to make her comfortable at every turn gave her a sense of family intimacy. The privilege flattered her. Mr Al Refai appeared at length, dressed in fashionable casual clothes. There would be few men of his age so handsome.

'Miss Winterbine, I cannot tell you how pleased I am to see you so relaxed. I feared that the change in circumstances might have caused worry.'

'I did feel a little anxious,' said Estella, 'but Aisha and Tahani have made me feel welcome.'

'I am proud of my daughters,' said Mr Al Refai, looking at each of them. They smiled slightly and then looked embarrassed. 'They are accomplished, well-trained, and responsible young women. I am lucky to have them among my closest assistants. Now that brings me to a matter I had intended to discuss with you later. Miss Winterbine, to be brief, I would like you to come and work for me.'

'Work for you?' said Estella, taken by surprise. She looked at the sisters, but they remained expressionless.

'Yes, Miss Winterbine. Your presence at the business meetings in Brisbane was secretly a little test. Please don't be offended.' Estella was not offended and said so. 'I am glad to hear that. You passed it with flying colours. Not only did you understand what was going on and made no mistakes, but you also made a big impression on my business contacts. This is paramount in negotiations over modern media properties. Media properties, Miss Winterbine, are among the most important and influential worldwide assets currently. There will be enormous growth in this sector over the next twenty-five years. Our company must stay at the forefront, and to achieve that, we must have the best people on staff. You have amazing potential in this area.'

'But what sort of work would I do?' said Estella. A few weeks earlier, she would have rejected the idea. But after experiencing Mr Al Refai and his daughters' level of organisation and solicitude, and being invited into the family circle, she was not sure she should reject the offer out of hand. At that point, the daughters excused themselves and disappeared into the business lounge.

'My daughters have to make arrangements for our arrival in Paris,' he said, seeing Estella's eyes following them. 'About the work you would be doing, I would rather leave the details for another discussion. In general, however, it will be work in my inner circle. It will be a combination of public relations and administrative tasks. You see, Miss Winterbine, a big corporation like ours, concerns itself not only with producing a product for different consumers. It also has a social and cultural function. Keeping this role before our minds is important. Our company cultivates relationships with all sorts of associations and organisations in the social and cultural fields. In many cases, we provide funding for them, and in a few cases, quite a lot of funding. Now I need people of special abilities to maintain supervision over these connections. You have great potential here. I would like you to consider the idea seriously. Your few days in Paris will bring you into contact with the actual forum of your work and the conditions you will be enjoying.'

'I don't know what to say, Mr Al Refai,' said Estella, who wondered how many more surprises she would be exposed to.

'You don't have to say anything now. You just have to think about it while you enjoy yourself. You may also like to consider the circumstances of your employment. There will be a training program that will span several years as you develop in the role. You will be given individual tuition in modern languages, particularly French and Spanish. You will end up speaking these fluently. You will be provided with an apartment in Paris with a generous clothing allowance. You must always appear in the best and most fashionable clothing. That is part of the work. You will have a generous salary with an entertainment budget. You will be accustomed to flying to all parts of the world. I know how attached you are to your mother and father. They will have the opportunity to visit you whenever they want. And you will have the opportunity to go to Australia. Indeed, that will be part of your working area. Australians will be proud to see one of their fellow citizens working in such an important international role.

'These are briefly the rewards. With all important positions like this, a contract is signed between the company and the employee. You must see the contract as an expression of mutually acceptable conditions and responsibilities. But let's not get too far ahead of ourselves. We will discuss the contract further when we get to that point. So, just enjoy the next few days. And keep in mind that much of what you will be doing will be a part of your work. My daughters will oversee your activities while I attend to other business. You are not to worry about anything, all right? Let my daughters look after you. They have looked after you till now, and they will continue to do so.'

Estella could do no more than acknowledge the enormous compliment and express her acquiescence in the arrangements. Mr Al Refai waved aside any expression of gratitude, saying that the offer was what her talents warranted. In the next breath, he began talking about the films she and his daughters had seen. He spoke enthusiastically about both pictures, praising the music and quality of the films. He lingered over the elegant, ethereal, childlike beauty of Audrey Hepburn. He had met her at a function in Switzerland. She was just as beautiful and charismatic in person as she was on the screen. They chatted in this vein for some time before the sisters returned. When Aisha asked Estella what she thought of working for their father, Mr Al Refai excused himself and returned to the business lounge.

'I don't know what to think,' said Estella. 'I never expected such an offer.'

'It is a genuine offer,' said Tahani. 'Father means all he says. He has no doubt you will excel in a public relations or promotional role. I believe you would too. Nobody would forget you once they saw you, especially dressed in the finest clothing Parisian designers have to offer.'

Aisha gave her enthusiastic support, then resumed her businesslike manner as she discussed the program for Paris. During this discussion, Estella became aware of the plane's slow descent, eventually bursting through the clouds to reveal her first sight of France. The young women crowded around the portholes while Aisha and Tahani took turns to point out recognisable landmarks. Estella felt a thrill when Aisha directed her attention to Paris's skyline.

AROUND THE same time, Geoff was doing a mental check of all he needed as he drove into Binawarra. He had a dry suit, climbing equipment, heavy clothing and shoes for the cold, binoculars, knives, and other odds and ends. He was not familiar with Holland, but he knew it was cold and watery. His first stop was the Huckerby's. He reviewed the planning Miss Barker had discussed with Bill and Joanne. He made notes and checked all the contact numbers. Satisfied that the arrangements accorded with Miss Barker's plan, he drove to the Winterbine's. Charles greeted him with surprise. Ruby and Larry were also surprised to see him. He told them he was returning to the airport to catch the midnight flight to London, from where he would fly to Amsterdam. He wanted to get moving as soon as he could. Nothing was known yet of the whereabouts of Mr Al Refai's private jet, but he was sure Middelburg was the logical place to start their search.

'How on earth will you get to the airport?' said Ruby.

'I'll drive down to Bendigo, leave the car outside your flat, and then take a taxi to Melbourne Airport.'

'No, you won't. I'll go down with you.'

'But it will be so late. You'll get too tired. It will be dangerous.'

'No matter, this is something I can do.'

'I'm coming, too,' said Larry. 'I'll keep her company—stop her from going to sleep.'

'If Larry accompanies Ruby, it should be okay,' said Charles. 'It will ensure you make the flight. It will be tight even now.'

'I may not be able to handle thugs and kidnappers, Geoff,' said Ruby, 'but I can go with you to the airport and drive back without difficulty. Remember, I'll only be driving back if we go in your car.'

Geoff relented. He called Fr. van Engelen to ask if there had been news from Holland. There was. Gerda van den Donker was already in Holland, staying with her mother on the outskirts of the village of Vrouwekerke, not far north of Middelburg. His niece, Anneke, had been in contact with Truus van den Donker that day. It appeared that Gerda had arrived late morning. That was all he needed. He gave the signal for Ruby and Larry to go to the car. Then, telling Aine and Charles that he would do all he could to find Estella, he departed.

Fortunately, he agreed to Ruby's going because he made it to the airport with just enough time to check in and go to the departure lounge. When the plane was airborne, he sat back to take a breath and review all that had happened. Events had reached such a momentum that he needed time to fathom the relationship between them. He needed to think about Estella. He needed to understand what was going on. He was in love with her, but could not consider his love legitimate or allowable.

THE MERCEDES carrying Estella and the two Al Refai sisters drove onto Place Vendome in the middle of Paris's swankiest district. It made a turn around the square and came to a stop in front of The Ritz. Attendants hastened to open the doors and help the young women with their luggage. They were taken from the reception to a suite whose broad, curving window opened onto a panorama of the historical square. Estella was breathless as she looked around the luxurious suite done out in soft pastel pinks and rose. The sight of more luxury in a hotel room than she had ever experienced was just the last of a series of splendours she had seen on the drive from the airport. Sights that had been photos and illustrations in books all came into view on a sunny day in what must surely be the most romantic city in the world—the magnificent cathedral of Notre Dame, the Place de la Concorde, the Champs-Élysées, the Arc de Triomphe, and the Eiffel Tower,

'We will leave you for twenty minutes to freshen up,' said Aisha. 'We will be back to collect you for a tour of the nearby sights and shops. There are two attendants for this room. Don't hesitate to call them for anything you want.'

Estella stood by the window, looking around the square and trying to absorb it all. If this were the arena of her work—no, it could not be. This was special. Forcing her eyes away from the sights, she prepared herself for the sisters' arrival, who returned in stylish casual slacks and tops.

'Do you like your room?' said Tahani, smiling.

'I've never experienced anything like it.'

'It is a standard you will enjoy if you work for Father and succeed in the job,' said Aisha. 'But come on. We have a lot to see, and we must purchase suitable clothing for you. We are pleased you wear the galabia in our company, but you need different clothing for business and other occasions.'

They spent the next couple of hours visiting celebrated fashion shops and boutiques in Rue St Honore, Avenue de l'Opéra, and Boulevard Hausmann. For much of the time, Estella was in awe as she slipped on one expensive garment after another. Aisha took charge, appearing to have an uncanny sense of what suited Estella and what she liked. All the dresses or skirts she tried on fell elegantly below her knees or were full-length. The blouses, shirts, and T-shirts were also modest. At each fitting, there were noises of admiration as the boutique directors and staff looked on.

Her French was good enough to understand much of what they said. To her delight, they began speaking to her. In the whirl of clothes changing, expressions of admiration, and French conversation, she sometimes found it hard to recognise the person she saw in the full-length mirror. At one point, she looked up to see a young woman in an evening gown of such glamour and sophistication that she put her hand to her mouth. The high heels made her even more imposing.

'You are beginning to see yourself as others see you,' said Aisha, amused by her reaction. 'You must get used to the power of your appearance, as Father said. Nobody could look more arresting in such a gown, not even Audrey Hepburn.'

With Tahani's eager assistance, Aisha selected clothes for Estella's stay in Paris. The choice included a dark formal business suit, an evening gown for a formal occasion the following evening, an off-white pantsuit with a matching blouse, and several pairs of slacks with shirts, all with matching shoes. Aisha directed Estella to keep on the pantsuit as that was suitable for the walk to the Place de la Concorde and the Jardins des Tuileries. Arranging for the other clothes to be delivered to The Ritz, the three young women set off towards the Place de la Concorde.

Estella's awe was scarcely lessened as she walked between the two sisters, looked around at the buildings, and listened to the historical explanations they gave. Admiring stares and the occasional comment came her way. At the Place de la Concorde, they paused to survey its grand expanse, with the obelisk of Luxor rising majestically in its middle. They crossed to the Jardins des Tuileries and began a slow, reflective walk towards the Palais du Louvre. The wide, pale paths, the green, treed lawns, and the dreamy, meandering people in the park induced an almost soporific mood in Estella. It was all so romantic, so elegant, and refined. That mood was only enhanced when they reached the Palais du Louvre and stopped to gaze at the buildings. Estella did not know the names of the architectural styles, but she saw everywhere in the buildings the result of refined, confident minds and a delicate imagination. She could not imagine a more beautiful and romantic city scene than the one exposed to her. The sisters left her alone in her silent contemplation.

Savouring the atmosphere, they retraced their steps to the Place de la Concorde, crossed over, and walked up the Champs Elysees to the Arc de Triomphe. By the time they climbed the stairs of that monument to enjoy the view of the most brilliant sights of Paris between the roads thrown out as if from a Catherine Wheel from the Place de l'Etoile, it was time to return to the hotel. Aisha and Tahani left Estella in her suite, instructing her to wear the new pantsuit when they returned to collect her for dinner. Their father would like it very much.

The suite attendants checked that everything was to Estella's liking. She was shown where she could find slippers and a dressing gown if she wanted to change and relax. Estella was glad to change out of the pantsuit. The attendants seemed to understand that she wanted to have a nap and did not disturb her until she awoke and began moving around the suite. When the sisters returned, Aisha attached delicate gold earrings to her ears. Tahani had several large gold bangles for her wrists. When she got into the waiting limousine outside the hotel, Mr Al Refai exclaimed. It was just as Aisha said. He looked at her in her new clothes with undisguised admiration and pleasure. He listened with keen interest to the sisters' account of their activities. When Estella said she was in a daze from all the new experiences, he looked so satisfied that he seemed on the point of tears. The next surprise was dinner at the restaurant on the second level of the Eiffel Tower. They were ushered to a table beside the glass wall, where they had a view of Paris's night skyline. It stretched out, glittering and shimmering into the distance like a magical fairyland. Estella gazed in wonder. Mr Al Refai, seeing her entranced expression, pointed out some of the major sights that lay before them.

'Miss Winterbine, this will be your playground if you join me,' he said. 'The fashion shops and their designers you visited this afternoon will be a grand wardrobe from which you can choose at will.'

Estella expressed her appreciation for the honour given to her. She did not know what else to say. It continued to overwhelm her. It was no honour, Mr Al Refai said again. It was what her talents deserved. He then changed the subject and did not return to the job offer for the rest of the evening. Instead, he let Aisha and Tahani lead the conversation, which meandered through their life in Paris, their work, and Estella's interests. Mr Al Refai was content once again to listen.

When Estella returned to her hotel suite, she reflected on a day full of surprises, enjoyment, and the warmest company. She could not help lingering a while before the window overlooking the ancient square with its glorious history and its elegant buildings. She could not help returning to the full-length mirror several times, where a dazzling image stared at her. It would be a change when she was back in Binawarra.

Chapter 31

The Castle of Heavenly Bliss

CHARLES HELPED Fr. van Engelen from St Philomena's Presbytery to the front of the church, where a makeshift altar had been erected at the top of the small flight of bluestone stairs. He bowed before the cross on the white linen cover of the altar and turned to face his bewildered congregation.

'Dear brothers and sisters, I have sad news for you, and I ask you to remain calm while we wait until the good Lord shows us the way. I have been expelled from the order of the Missionaries of the Wounded Heart.' He held up his hand to arrest the movement and murmuring. 'Please, let's pray our Mass fervently this morning and implore Jesus and His Holy Mother to rescue our congregation from the present difficulties. I will be away for the coming week on an urgent mission. Please offer your most fervent prayers for the success of that mission.'

As he turned to begin Mass, he caught sight of Bill and Joanne Huckerby by the front gates. He had to pause to compose himself. And there was Charles next to him, ready to serve Mass. It was a difficult time, but he thanked God for his consolations.

MISS BARKER manoeuvred to keep the crowd between her and Boris as they walked to the luggage collection at Cairo International Airport. Minutes later, she slipped into the back seat of a taxi and tapped the back of the seat. The driver jerked his head around. 'I want you to drive to the side and wait until I give you instructions,' she said, glancing back. 'I will pay you well if you follow my instructions.' The driver gave her an eager signal with his thumb. Ten minutes later, Boris appeared, paid his porter, and hailed a taxi.

'Follow that taxi,' she said as Boris passed them. 'Stay out of sight.'

They followed Boris's taxi through the roaring chaos of Cairo traffic into the city centre. Finally, the taxi skidded to a stop in a teeming shopping precinct. Boris emerged and disappeared into a shop. Miss Barker told the driver to wait. The driver had to contend with the convulsing traffic and the blaring horns, but he followed her instructions. Five minutes later, Boris reappeared. He led them on a winding tour of narrow, crowded streets. Unperturbed, Miss Barker's taxi driver stayed in pursuit. After half an hour of this madness, the taxi headed out of the city's labyrinth. They came to a less wild side, turned onto a main road, and drove alongside a vast cemetery that looked like a city of mausoleums.

'What's that?' said Miss Barker.

'It cemetery,' said the driver. 'Many people live there. Housing shortage. Called City of Dead.'

'City of Dead?' said Miss Barker, hoping it was not an omen.

The road rose as they approached a great ancient fortress. They lost sight of Boris's taxi while they drove along the high brown walls. When they came to the parking area, Boris was already walking towards a tourist entrance between the battlements. Miss Barker ordered the taxi driver to wait and hurried after him. She followed the tourists around a huge mosque with its imposing domes and towering minarets and arrived in an open courtyard with a panoramic view of Cairo's ramshackle skyline and its polluted air. Behind her towered the mosque she had skirted around.

Boris had disappeared. She scanned the area. It would be a fruitless search. She would return to the taxi and await his reappearance.

'Miss Barker, I have to congratulate you.' She swung around to face Boris, who had emerged from behind a group of tourists. 'I have been over there in the shade, trying to work out who you were.' He pointed over his shoulder. 'I had no idea who could be following me just after arriving in Cairo. My taxi driver alerted me because, stupidly, I was not paying attention. So I came here to discover who was tagging me. I thought I must be mistaken because all I saw in the courtyard were tourists.' He stopped to convey his admiration with a nod of the head. Miss Barker responded with a patient smile. 'Then it was obvious that the tall, elegant lady was on a search, probably looking for me. I could not for the life of me recognise you. Only as I approached you did I see— Incredible! Not too many people fool me, and fewer fool that Dutch woman. We had no idea. Your appearance here dressed as an attractive, classy woman says much.'

'About what? And which Dutch woman?'

'Are you aware of where you are?' he said. He waved his arm around to indicate he meant the surrounding buildings.

'What does my presence here mean, Mr Saladin?'

'Hah, very clever again! You have found out my name. Miss Barker, you have a real talent.' He shook his head. 'This, my dear lady, is called the Citadel. For centuries, Egypt's rulers had their seat here. The great Islamic warrior and ruler, Salah ad-Din, built it to meet the threat of the filthy infidels from Europe with their equally filthy religion. You know him as "Saladin."'

'That explains your surname. What does the "N" stand for?'

'Nasser.'

'The celebrated Arab nationalist. It's my turn, Mr Saladin, to say your adopted name and your comment about this place are illuminating.'

'Salah ad-Din, the valiant warrior, met and defeated the blasphemous Christian Crusaders after their initial successes. We are now in the time of the resurgence of Salah ad-Din and Islamic pride.'

'Then what are you doing in league with an unbalanced godless left-wing fanatic like Edith Bicknell?'

'Oh, I would love to hear you say that to that woman's face! You have no idea what I must suffer.'

'Do people live in that cemetery we passed?'

Saladin's face darkened for a moment. 'Miss Barker, you have been cunning enough to come this far without us having the slightest suspicion of your game. Are you cunning enough to get out of it? As you have seen, the streets here are dangerous and chaotic.'

'Most tourists enjoy their stay in Cairo with no problems.'

'Tourists, yes, spies, no.'

Miss Barker had known as soon as Boris spoke to her that it would be fruitless to stay in Cairo. Worse, with her cover blown, it would be more than dangerous. 'We are not in the blasphemous West, Mr Saladin. There is a death penalty in Egypt. Bringing about the death of an innocent Western tourist would not be viewed too kindly, despite your type's hatred of Westerners, or Crusaders, as you call us.' He tilted his head and grinned. 'There were police guards at the entrance,' she said, deciding it was better to confront him. 'What if this defenceless woman tells them you have threatened her, and she fears for her life?' She turned and walked away.

At the exit, she asked a policeman the way to the pyramids. He gave her a brief explanation in faltering English, pointing to the waiting taxis. She thanked him and, glancing at Saladin at the corner of the mosque courtyard, hurried to her taxi. 'The airport as fast as you can,' she ordered. 'There's triple the fare if there are no delays.'

The taxi driver drove at a frightening pace but got there without mishap. An hour and a half later, she relaxed in a KLM jet flying to Amsterdam. It was then just after ten o'clock on Sunday morning.

ESTELLA HAD been to Mass at Notre Dame Cathedral, as Mr Al Refai had arranged, and was waiting for breakfast. She stood at the window, observing the early morning activity on the square.

'May I disturb you?'

She turned to see Didi Al Refai standing at the half-opened door.

'Oh, hello, Didi.'

'I'm sorry to intrude,' he said, coming into the room. 'I asked permission. I was told you were respectable and waiting for breakfast. I ordered breakfast to have with you. Is that all right?' He took her hand and gave it a gentle shake.

'Yes. I'm glad to see you.'

'Are you?'

'Yes, of course, I am. How did you know I was here?'

'I spoke to my father from New York. He told me that a mix-up with arrangements left you isolated in his jet. He said he had planned a few enjoyable days to make it up to you. I had to come to Paris to visit my mother. So I got on a plane. And here I am.'

'Just like that?' said Estella, disarmed by his boyish frankness.

'Yes, um, I'm sorry. Of course, not everyone has the luxury of flying where they want when they want.'

'Please sit down, Didi.'

'That galabia suits you,' he said. 'It would have pleased my father.'

'Thank you, it did. My mother wears dresses like this. I told your father that.'

'Oh, yes, your beautiful fair mother, she would look stunning in that style.' There was a short, nervous movement of one hand, which then went into his pocket. 'Are you enjoying your stay?' He sat in the nearby armchair.

'Oh, yes,' she said and then thought it curious she had so little reserve with him. 'Your father and sisters have been so kind.'

'I expect they have been.'

The attendants arrived to set the table for breakfast. Didi asked about her parents. They were well. To her surprise, he continued to speak about them and her life in Binawarra. When they finished breakfast, she excused herself to change for the day's sightseeing.

'Do you mind if I stay here and wait? I'll come with you today.'

'That would be nice,' she said, going to the bedroom. 'I won't be long.'

Didi watched her close the door. A painful expression passed over his face. He walked to the window and gazed down at the square that was so familiar to him. Ten minutes later, Estella emerged from the bedroom and smiled at him on the way to the bathroom. He grimaced. How arresting she looked in those chic Parisian slacks and top. But she looked different. The innocent rustic aura she projected in her usual clothes had faded. Again, he gazed through the window.

'What are you doing here?'

He turned to see his sisters.

'I knocked beforehand. I didn't come in uninvited.'

'It will not please father if you disrupt his plans,' said Aisha.

'Doubtless.'

'Father has organised a day of sightseeing for Estella,' Aisha continued. 'He does not want you around with your scheming ways.'

'My scheming ways!'

'Yes, the gossip papers are full of your exploits, not Father's. Anyhow, Estella is not your type. She will not succumb to your methods.'

'My methods! *You* talk about my scheming way and methods!' He sat down in a nearby chair. 'Why do you judge me so poorly? Anyhow, you're right. You probably won't believe me, but I also recognise this girl's uniqueness. I only want to go with you today. I won't say anything. I won't interfere.'

The sisters looked at their brother as if uncertain about his sincerity. Before they could respond, Estella came from the bathroom and expressed her pleasure at seeing them. Her eager, unreserved manner dissolved the tension.

'Is it a coincidence that Estella is dressed like Audrey Hepburn, same style of clothes, same fashion designers?' Didi whispered when Estella had gone to fetch her bag and sweater.

'Coincidence or not, those clothes suit her. And she is just as— ' Tahani stopped at an impatient gesture from Aisha.

Estella had no more time to devote to Didi or his sudden appearance, for the sights and atmosphere of Paris monopolised her attention as soon as they left The Ritz. The morning rushed by as they walked from the Palais Royale to the Palais du Louvre, crossed over to the left bank, and strolled along the multitude of booksellers with their fascinating array of books. Aisha had to prod Estella gently to keep moving when she lingered too long at an attraction. The only pause in their touring came with a stop at a coffee lounge on Boulevard St Germain, one of Didi's favourites. At one o'clock, they approached the restaurant on the Champs-Élysées where Aisha had arranged to meet her father. Mr Al Refai was already at a table outside, gazing thoughtfully at the passing activity. When they joined him, Estella remarked on the view of the boulevard and its shops, the elegant buildings, the Arc de Triomphe, the Place de la Concorde, the Jardins des Tuileries, and the Palais du Louvre in the distance.

'And over there, you have the Eiffel Tower,' said Mr Al Refai. 'We will end today's sightseeing with a trip to the top. There you will have a stunning view over this incomparable city.' He paused. 'Are you enjoying yourself, Miss Winterbine?'

'Very much, Mr Al Refai. I could not have dreamt I would experience all this.'

'This is just the start.'

'It is truly a wonderful place,' said Estella. She looked at the others, noticing Didi's sombre expression. She met his eyes, but he turned away. The job was not mentioned again. Mr Al Refai asked her what she had seen and thought of the different places. He let her talk, only responding when her eager narration called for it.

'Miss Winterbine, we are very pleased that you seem so much at ease with us now,' he commented yet once more when they had finished lunch. 'In the beginning, you were shy and not so talkative.'

'You have been very kind,' she said. 'You have offered your friendship. That has put me at ease. I feel like I am in your family.'

Silence greeted this artless reply before Mr Al Refai said they truly valued her friendship. The sisters and brother expressed their agreement.

CHARLES AND Fr. van Engelen had taken off on a flight direct to Amsterdam at one o'clock. Ruby had arrived back in Binawarra and was fidgeting on the verandah. She still blamed herself for Estella's disappearance. Aine had tried to console her, but Ruby was not ready to be consoled. She had much to ponder—so many reasons for blame and regret. It was best to leave her alone. Aine returned to her prayers, kneeling before her bedroom shrine. Prayer was her weapon, her only weapon, against the evil that hovered over them.

When she closed her eyes, the darkness that had beaten and oppressed her all those years now rose before her. It rose majestically as if it had already savoured a victory. As close as it was, revealing the spirit within it, it no longer overwhelmed her. From that day in Miss Bicknell's office, when Miss Bicknell had revealed her soul, it had ceased to bow her, and she faced it without fear. Now, as if in mockery of her new courage, the darkness projected an image of Estella. Oozing, spreading stains disfigured her daughter.

BILL AND Joanne Huckerby were watching the evening news on the Premier network. They half watched, for the worry of Estella's disappearance preoccupied their thoughts. They felt so helpless, and Bill blamed himself for not heeding Miss Barker's warning. The news about the 'pub brawl' in Binawarra drew their full attention.□

NEWSREADER: Our reporter, Robert Meakin, returned to Binawarra to report on the significance of Anzac Day.□

ROB MEAKIN [before the cenotaph on Binawarra's Anzac Square]: Six hours after a select group stood around this cenotaph to remember our fallen diggers, a wild brawl broke out in one of the pubs over there. Senior teacher at Binawarra High School, Jane Cox, said the violence of the Vietnam Veterans illustrates the problems deep in the mentality of Anzac Day glorification.□

JANE COX [face in close-up]: Why would soldiers who had remembered their fallen comrades go straight to the local hotel and start a brawl? The answer is there behind the so-called manly virtues of courage, honour, and patriotism that are allegedly celebrated on this special day for war veterans. Vietnam veterans start pub brawls with anti-war demonstrators because it's in the male's nature to resolve differences by violent means. It's an inclination developed and encouraged by our patriarchal society.□

ROB MEAKIN: [with the camera still on Jane Cox's face]: Perhaps this was an isolated occasion. Not all—

JANE COX: Lame excuse! No, the problem of male violence manifests itself everywhere. It's not only about Anzac Day. The recent problems in Binawarra High School are a painful illustration. The authorities may sweep it all under the carpet in the end, but certain features of this case cannot be ignored. The school principal is obsessed with veterans' affairs and the military. He brings that obsession into the school as if it were a major part of the curriculum. You get an idea of the orientation of that celebration when you witness his flag ceremony. That flag ceremony acts before anything else as a symbol of the superiority of white European male civilisation over all others. But that's on the surface. Do people really think there is no link between the male domination exhibited in veterans' ceremonies and the male domination evident in cases of sexual abuse?□

ROB MEAKIN: I would ask you to be careful—

JANE COX: Careful! We should be careful with our children. Our children come first. Our children are our primary concern. They are our only concern. They are our precious resource.

ROB MEAKIN: There are laws—

JANE COX: The law is not only an ass. It is a male ass! People should see the link between the fetish preoccupation with military celebrations and the incidence of sexual abuse in the school.

'What is she saying?' cried Bill, getting to his feet.

'Children who suffer sexual abuse are known to manifest certain behaviours,' continued Jane. 'There is at least one student who has long manifested those behaviours, and her family has a close friendship with a man in a position of authority and power.

'She means me!' said Bill, turning pale. 'She means Estella and me!'

'Bill, please, don't get upset,' said Joanne, alarmed by Bill's colour. 'She may mean someone else.'

Jane Cox's voice droned on in the background.

'No, it's unmistakable. Flo has seen it, too, but was reluctant to say it. She means me. She's accusing me. How is it possible? Look at her! My God, how could anyone imagine I would harm that girl, a child I have treated as my granddaughter?' He staggered and clutched at the chair behind him.

'He just doesn't get it,' Jane Cox was saying. 'It's frightening. He just doesn't get it. He will never get it. People like that must be removed.'

'Bill, please, calm yourself.' Joanne turned the television off. 'It's not worth thinking about. Consider who's making the allegation. We know what she's like.'

Bill swayed, and his eyes rolled. 'How could anyone imagine I would harm that beautiful girl?'

'Bill, we all know how much you love Aine, Charles, and Estella. There's no doubt about that. The people who matter know you.'

He tottered, his eyes showing their whites. He put his hand out, crumpled onto the side of his chair, and rolled onto the floor. Joanne ran to the phone and called the doctor. Next, she called Aine. The doctor came without delay.

'It's a stroke,' he said. 'We must get him to the hospital.'

Shortly after, Aine arrived with Ruby.

ESTELLA LOOKED down through the dusky haze at the lights twinkling along streets and around buildings. Those elegant, whimsical products of the finest imaginations lit up into a fairyland scene.

'All that will be yours,' said Mr Al Refai, bending towards her. 'It will be at your feet once you join us.'

'It is so beautiful,' said Estella. 'It surpasses anything I have seen in my books.'

'I do not mean to give you empty flattery, Miss Winterbine,' he said, looking her full in the face. 'Your appearance is a match for what spreads out before you. You are made for the fame of Paris. You will thrive here like nowhere else.'

He had taken Estella from one side of the highest floor of the Eiffel Tower to the other, pointing out the city's famous landmarks. Didi and his sisters stood to the side. The two sisters smiled as she passed them. Dejected Didi forced out a smile. Mr Al Refai turned to gaze below as if he was giving Estella time to contemplate all that lay before her. She understood she would have to respond soon to his job offer.

'Well, it is time to go,' he said. 'But I have another surprise for you. After a light dinner, we are going to Holland.'

'To Holland?'

'Yes, it will be the last occasion before we take you back home. I will be hosting a reception tomorrow at a magnificent reception centre on the coast. It will be exclusive to some of my most valuable business relations. This glittering occasion will truly give you an idea of your work. These occasions require much finesse and composure. These qualities are natural to you, and you will come to understand how effectively you can deploy them.'

'Oh,' said Estella.

Mr Al Refai seemed not to expect her to say any more, for he led them to the lift. While they descended, he said, as if reading her thoughts, that they would go to the plane at Paris airport directly after the reception. That pleased her, but she wondered why Didi appeared so bleak.

MISS BARKER stood on the footpath outside Middelburg railway station. It was around five o'clock. It had been a long day, and she had had little rest since leaving Melbourne. She ignored the distinctive medieval skyline of Middelburg and hailed a taxi. The taxi took her to a hotel on the canal running along the front of the station. She checked in, showered, and thus refreshed, considered her options. Despite it being wise to have an early night, she rang Frans van Engelen and arranged to meet him at a restaurant on Marktplein.

She arrived at the restaurant, took a seat inside near the window, and ordered a glass of wine. She relaxed and looked around the square. Over on her right was *Het Stadhuis*, Middelburg's famous Gothic town hall. Her eyes lingered over its pleasing proportions and Gothic embellishments. Two men deep in conversation came into view, walking from Vlasmarkt. Nasser Saladin! How in the world had he got to Middelburg before her? His casual manner showed he was familiar with Middelburg. Estella must be here somewhere. As they passed by, still in animated conversation, the waiter came with her wine.

'Excuse me, waiter, I have to leave for a short while, but I will be back,' she said as he placed the glass in front of her. He looked at her doubtfully. 'I will pay now, but please keep the table reserved. I am meeting someone here. Do you know Mr Frans van Engelen, by chance?'

'Yes, Madam, everyone here knows Mr. van Engelen. He is a well-known notary.'

'Please ask him to wait. I won't be long.'

She left the wine untouched and hurried after the two men walking down Lange Delft. She had to be careful. She was alone. The deserted road curved slightly to the left, so she had to hang back as Saladin and his companion continued to Damplein. On arriving at the square, they turned and walked out of sight. She hurried to the edge of the square to see the unknown man shaking Saladin's hand. He then ambled to the other side of the square while Saladin disappeared through the nearby Gistpoort, an archway that led to the Abbey complex. She hastened after him. As she reached the Gistpoort, he turned right at the end of a short thoroughfare. She peeped around the next corner. Saladin had passed under another archway and was walking across Abdijplein. She paused under the archway.

Saladin continued across the square and through the Balanspoort, the entrance on the opposite side. With the ancient cloisters of the Norbertine monks on her left and the medieval buildings of the provincial government on her right, she made for the Balanspoort.

The Balanspoort was divided into two archways, a small and a large one, separated by a red brick pillar. As she passed under the small archway, a man darted from behind the pillar and seized her. He shook her violently, leaving her dazed. A second person was in front of her, grabbing her head and forcing it into an ample cloth soaked in some sort of anaesthetic. She lost consciousness with the self-rebuke that she had been stupid enough to walk into an obvious trap. The cloth was taken away. She gasped for air. Supported on both sides, she was walked staggering out from under the Balanspoort and onto the square outside. 'If anyone says anything, say she's drunk,' she heard. A car came to a skidding stop. The door opened, and she was pushed in. The door slammed shut. The cloth was again over her mouth and nose. She lost consciousness.

GEOFF STOOD on the same spot as Miss Barker outside Middelburg railway station. Paying little attention to his unfamiliar surroundings, he went to the public phone next to the taxi stand. He dialled Frans van Engelen's number and got a female voice without an accent—or rather with an English accent.

'Hello, Geoff. I'm Marijke, Frans's wife. You're expected. Frans has gone to meet Miss Barker in town. But don't worry, I'll send Anneke to pick you up.'

Ten minutes later, a blond head in a car pulled up next to Geoff. She waved at him to hop in.

'You!' she exclaimed as he opened the door and slid in.

'Yes, it's me. I will explain.'

'Wait,' she replied, taking off at once. 'Sorry to hurry you. I don't want to hold up the taxis.' She crossed the bridge over the *Kanaal door Walcheren* and passed the hotel where Miss Barker had checked in.

'Anneke, my contact with you seven years ago was coincidental. But I don't want to discuss it now. I'm here to track down a possible abduction.'

'Well, I'm glad about the coincidence,' she said drily. 'It was my saviour.'

'I would appreciate it if you kept my part in those events to yourself. It has nothing to do with my present task. I'll tell you more about it at the right time.'

'Of course, Geoff. I owe you more than your confidential request. I, too, want to keep it secret. Nobody here knows anything about those traumatic events—except Nienke. I want to keep it that way.'

'Of course. I understand. And thank you.'

'Did you know who you were coming to meet?'

'Yes, of course. I quickly realised that Fr. van Engelen was your uncle. Now, is it possible for me to see Miss Barker before we go to your house?'

'That's where I'm going.' She drove to the Abbey complex and parked near the entrance to Nieuwe Burg. They walked down to Marktplein. 'The restaurant is just around here. Pappa, what are you doing?' she said, catching sight of her father sitting bewildered at one of the outside tables.

Frans stood and greeted Geoff. 'I arranged to meet your friend, Miss Barker, here,' he said. 'When I arrived, the waiter told me she had gone. She left a message that she would be back, and I should wait for her. I've been here for half an hour. She hasn't appeared.'

Geoff questioned him closely. After some consideration, he thought it probable that Miss Barker had been lured away from the restaurant. Abruptly leaving meant that she had seen something or someone she recognised. She had either walked into a trap or was still in pursuit. The latter was not likely. She wouldn't take unnecessary risks and said she would be back shortly. No, this had Saladin and Miss Bicknell all over it.

He suggested they go to Frans's house and leave a message in case Miss Barker returned. He was not confident. Impressed by Geoff's quiet, firm ways, Frans fell in with his wishes. They took him to a house on the outer canal and settled him into their guest room. Geoff updated them on Fr. van Engelen's initial request. Central was a possible abduction.

'What's going on?' said Anneke when Geoff had finished. 'Why have they abducted her, and what is the connection with Gerda van den Donker? And how can you be sure that the girl is here in Middelburg or on Walcheren?'

'Well, we don't know for sure. All the evidence, though, suggests that she won't be far away from Gerda. Miss Barker's disappearance seems to confirm that we're warm.' He thought for a moment. 'Is Miss Bicknell or Gerda whatshername still with her mother?'

'Van-den-Donker,' said Anneke. 'It means "of the darkness," by the way. As far as we know, she's at her mother's farmhouse outside Vrouwekerke. Let me check. Don't worry. I have an excuse to ring her,' she added, seeing Geoff's doubtful reaction. The call was brief. 'I told her that Uncle Jos would be in Holland shortly, but she should not breathe a word of it yet. She was very pleased to hear the news. She said she did not see many people to tell and that she would certainly not tell Gerda. Gerda is still there. She has set herself up in one of the rooms—it is like an office with some odd posters on the wall—and spends most of her time there. She has made quite a few phone calls, many in English. Gerda gave her a clear signal that she wanted her privacy while on the phone. Gerda has left the house only once, late last night, to go to her father. And she wasn't long away.'

'Where does her father live?'

'Not far away along the canal,' said Frans.

'Miss Barker went in the opposite direction, didn't she?'

'More or less,' said Frans.

That did not mean much. The crucial point was that Miss Barker had gone missing, and Gerda was holed up in a farmhouse on the outskirts of a small village north of Middelburg, obviously making plans and waiting for something. It occurred to him that if Estella had unwittingly gone with Mr Al Refai in his private jet, it was most likely to Paris, in which case Estella was still to arrive on Walcheren.

'Did Miss Barker say where she had been before arriving in Middelburg?'

'No, she said nothing. Only arranged a meeting,' said Frans.

That was critical. She had followed Saladin to Cairo but had flown on to Holland almost at once. Something happened in Cairo. But what? Did she come across Saladin? Was she being pursued? Well, she seemed unaware of it when she arrived in Middelburg. Otherwise, she would not have strolled to the restaurant and taken a seat. No, she happened on someone or something unexpectedly.

'I want to take a walk around the town centre. I want to see the street where Miss Barker was last seen. Would one of you show me?'

'I will go, Pappa,' said Anneke, 'I'm probably a little fitter.'

She was right. Frans had no objection and told Anneke to be careful.

'Make sure you wear dark clothing,' Geoff said, pleased that she was attuned to his plans. A half-hour later, they were on their way along Seissingel.

'How deep is that water?' he asked as they approached the bridge over the canal.

'A metre to a metre and a half, I would say. Why do you ask?'

'Just to know. Is that a sort of park on the other side?' he said, indicating the sloping grassy banks running down to the reed-lined water's edge.

'Yes, it's called the *Bolwerk*, in English, the rampart. It marks the defences of the old town and runs quite a way in both directions.' They were about to cross over the bridge. 'Mr van den Donker's house is not far away. Do you want to see where?'

Geoff stopped to think. He did not want to show himself if Saladin or Gerda were with him at the house. 'Is the house visible from the Bolwerk?'

'Yes, but probably not much else.'

They crossed the bridge and took the tree and shrub-lined pathway to the right along the top of the Bolwerk. Anneke stopped and pointed out a house on the other side of the canal. Geoff peered through his pocket binoculars. The lights were on in the lounge room, and the curtains were open, but there was no sign of anyone. Did that mean nobody was home?

'Most likely,' she said. 'If there were anyone there, you would see them in the lounge room. It's still cold in the evening, and most people would sit where the heating is. Mr van den Donker has probably gone out for a while, and not far, either, because his car is in the driveway.'

Geoff pondered his choices, then asked her to lead on. They walked back to the bridge and turned right into Seisstraat, which led towards the town centre. They came out from Vlasmarkt onto Marktplein and headed over to Lange Delft. They walked as far as Damplein. Anneke supplied whatever information she thought relevant, but nothing suggested a lead. Miss Barker could have gone anywhere from Damplein. There seemed to be narrow streets and gloomy entrances everywhere. He asked where Mr van den Donker's office was. It was a short distance away but shrouded in its dismal medieval frontage. It was not telling him anything, so Geoff decided to return to the house to consider further action.

As they were walking along Vlasmarkt, Anneke stopped. 'You know, there are several cafés or pubs, as you call them, around here. Meneer van den Donker frequents some of them. Let me take a quick look.'

She set off while Geoff walked to the bridge over the inner canal. He looked around, crossed the bridge, and stood to the side in Herengracht, the road running along the canal. Ten minutes later, he caught sight of two figures emerging from the shadows and coming towards him. He watched them for a moment and started. He hastened along Seisstraat. When he reached the traffic lights at Klein Vlaanderen, he glanced behind him. It was a mistake. He had alerted Boris. He crossed and hurried to the path leading to the right along the Bolwerk. His position had improved little after he had gone some way. If he stayed on the path, Saladin would continue to pursue him. If he took cover in the bushes, it might not take Saladin long to flush him out. A confrontation would put Saladin, Gerda, and their group on their guard, jeopardising Estella's safety. As it was, Saladin could not be sure who he was. He scrambled down the grassy slope to the water's edge and eased himself between the reeds into the water. It was about three feet deep and cold, freezing cold.

He scarcely had time to crouch down behind the reeds before Saladin appeared, followed shortly after by his companion. They were mere silhouettes and shades as they poked among the bushes and trees. He heard them talking but could not discern the language they spoke. There were limits to his endurance. He pushed through the water under the cover of the reeds. As he reached the dark shelter of the Seis bridge, Saladin came down the slope to the water's edge and looked around. His companion stayed on the path and sounded as if he were giving advice. At length, Saladin joined the other man where they stood talking. They ambled back towards the bridge. Shivering in about four feet of water, Geoff crouched up against the slime of the brick arch as they disappeared from his sight. He had to get out of the freezing water. He waited.

Voices drifted down from above. He edged closer. They spoke English. An occasional car passed over the bridge, muffling their words. Only snatches were comprehensible. It sounded like they were reviewing plans. 'Okay, but discreet,' one spoke up in a thick Dutch accent. 'Make sure secure. Absolute. No mistakes. *Morgen dan*— ' The voice was walking away. A few more words, and there was silence. Geoff moved to the other side of the bridge and kept his eyes on the road. He guessed well. The figure of a man appeared, walking towards Van den Donker's house. It had to be him. But he must now get out of the water. He pushed through the water to the bank on the Seissingel side and climbed up the steep grassy slope. He crouched and waited for a car to pass before looking around and stepping onto the footpath.

'*Allemachtig!*' came from behind him. 'Is that where you got to?' He turned to see Anneke hurrying from the bridge. 'You must be frozen. Quick, we had better get you home. I will tell you later what I saw.'

A long hot shower soon took the chill out of him, and with a fresh change of clothes, he was in the lounge room listening to Anneke. Marijke had joined them and listened with interest.

'I had a look in a couple of cafes in the Lange Viele district and was coming to join you when Meneer van den Donker blundered out in front of me from Schuttershof lane with a man I did not recognise. I was just a few paces behind them. It's a wonder they didn't see me. I edged to the wall and stayed with them. Then I caught sight of you standing near the bridge. You took off too quickly, and that seemed to alert them. You gave yourself away when you looked around at the lights on Klein Vlaanderen.'

'You're right,' said Geoff. 'I was caught off guard. I had to elude them. I thought it was too dark to be sure it was me. The other man was Nasser Saladin, Gerda van den Donker's minder.'

'Well, when Saladin took off after you and Van den Donker followed, I knew something was up. When they followed you along the Bolwerk, I followed, too, but not too far, just enough to see what they were doing. They began rummaging in the bushes, Van den Donker showing little enthusiasm. They soon gave up, obviously having no idea where you had got to. I hadn't, either. When they came back along the path, I hid in the bushes. As they passed, I heard Van den Donker say in bad English that you were probably a local youth having fun. I did not hear Saladin's response. Anyhow, they stopped on the bridge to talk. I couldn't hear what they were saying, but from their body language, they were making arrangements. Then they left each other, Van den Donker to go to his house and Saladin to his car, which was parked close by. He drove over the bridge just before you appeared, turned right, and headed off along Sandberglaan, which takes you to the north of Walcheren. It would be the route you took to go to Vrouwekerke.'

'All this is more evidence that the resolution of Gerda van den Donker's plan is on Walcheren,' said Geoff. 'But what and where? In Middelburg itself or to the north near Mrs van den Donker's village? Have you got a map of the area?'

Marijke fetched a map and laid it out on the dining room table. Frans pointed out where the village of Vrouwekerke was.

'Is there anywhere to hide someone without arousing suspicion?'

'Nowhere obvious,' said Frans. 'At least, nothing I can think of.' He looked at Anneke and Marijke, who nodded.

'It's not as if they have subdued and abducted Estella by force and are keeping her imprisoned,' said Geoff, almost to himself. 'That does not seem to be the purpose. Estella, we think, has gone willingly. Where would you take someone willing but unaware of the threat?'

'There are plenty of hotels and holiday accommodation here. This is a resort area. Do you know Cees van den Donker has big investments in restaurants and hotels here?'

'Yes,' said Geoff. 'Does he have property in that area? It's probably something luxurious and exclusive.'

'I don't know offhand. I will have to check tomorrow.'

'Okay, but search for accommodation that caters to the really wealthy. The Egyptian businessman is very wealthy.'

Frans, Marijke, and Anneke pointed out on the map places they knew were for wealthy visitors. 'There could be more,' said Frans, 'but those are the ones we are aware of. They are mostly on the coast near Domburg.'

'May I borrow the map? And a bike?'

'You mean you are going there now?' said Frans.

'It is urgent, Mr van Engelen. I must keep going.'

'I'll come with you,' said Anneke. 'You need someone to guide you. You may get lost.'

'Anneke, I do not want you taking risks,' said Marijke. 'It's bad enough that one young woman has gone missing.'

'I will be careful, Mamma.'

'I will make sure she is in no danger, Mrs van Engelen,' said Geoff. 'It's just reconnaissance work.' He turned to Anneke. 'It won't be too strenuous for you? I will cover as much ground as possible. It may be late when we return.'

'We are used to bike riding in Holland, Geoff. If I get too tired, I will rest. You can go on.'

Ten minutes later, Geoff and Anneke were cycling out of Middelburg towards Vrouwekerk, about five kilometres away. The night was dark and overcast, and as they rode with only the swishing of the tyres on the bike path in their ears, Geoff scanned the area. All he could make out were the flat fields extending into the darkness and the lights twinkling from the surrounding farmhouses. A peculiar peacefulness enveloped the scene. When they approached Vrouwekerke, Anneke motioned for Geoff to stop.

'That farmhouse along that side road is Mevrouw van den Donker's house.'

They walked in silence to the intersection of the side road with Middel-burgseweg. Geoff stopped beside the row of trees along the bike path. He could see a farmhouse attached to a big barn. A car was parked on a white gravel driveway. The curtains were not drawn on the lounge room window, and a soft light lit the gardens and pot plants in front.

'Whose car is that?' asked Geoff.

'Mevrouw van den Donker's.'

'Is there nothing else here, I mean, houses?'

'No, it's a short road. Over there, you see the houses belonging to the village proper. Mevrouw van den Donker owns the farmland around here but leases it to other farmers. She only occupies the house.'

'Wait here,' he said, 'and keep an eye on the front.' He disappeared into the dark.

Anneke waited a couple of minutes. Then, with her beanie pulled down so that her blond hair was hidden, she positioned herself in the dry ditch that ran along the road in front of the house. Someone was in a lounge chair, but she could not see who. She waited. She made out Geoff in the faint light at the side of the lounge room. He mimed picking up a stone and throwing it at the house. She had to do it several times before the front door flew open, and Gerda appeared, looking around. Anneke bobbed down. The door shut. A minute later, Geoff was beside her.

'There are only Gerda and her mother there, no sign of anybody else,' he whispered. 'They're watching television. Come on.'

After a brief discussion, they headed for Domburg, the most celebrated of all Zeeland resorts. They turned onto the coast road that proceeded eastwards to Vrouwenpolder, the village before the Veerse lake. Geoff did not need to see Domburg's bright, busy centre, so they turned right before entering the village and cycled around to the main road to Oostkapelle. They viewed some old mansions and hotels on the way. They did not seem to qualify. Then Anneke led Geoff along a side road to the dunes to show him some mansions that had been converted to holiday accommodation.

'Do you have access to the dunes here?' he asked after viewing the houses.

'Yes, the road leads right up to them. There's a pathway through the Manteling, an ancient forest of oak trees. It brings you out at the top of the dunes.'

'What can you see from there?'

'A lot from some spots. The land is flat, you know.'

'Come on, let's have a look.'

As a fierce wind blew from the sea against their faces and flapped and ruffled their clothing, Geoff scanned the countryside shrouded in darkness in places and brightly lit in others.

'It's a charming scene, indeed, a suitable place for an exclusive holiday resort. That's the North Sea, isn't it?' he said while he looked up and down the coast.

'Yes. Did you see that light there?' she added, pointing.

He looked in the direction of her finger and at first discerned nothing. Then he saw a light flickering not far out to sea and less than a mile eastwards along the coast.

'You have sharp eyes,' he said, taking the binoculars from his pocket. He concentrated his gaze on the light and saw it was blinking in a regular manner. 'Can we get closer than this?' Anneke thought they could. 'Let's get going, then. As fast as you can. I'll follow you.'

Anneke set a cracking pace as they cycled back to the main road and headed eastwards. North of Oostkapelle, she took a left towards the dunes. On his right, as he followed her, was a castle intruding on the forest fringe. Light was showing in a few windows. On his left was bush, evidently a continuation of the forest.

'Let's go—and be careful,' he said as they placed their bikes in bike racks in a small parking area lit by one miserable light. They walked along a sandy path through the bush and arrived at the top of the dunes. The light had stopped blinking. Through his binoculars, Geoff could make out a medium-sized vessel, like a coastal trader, moving out to sea. He looked around. If the blinking light had been sending a message to someone in the dunes, they were gone now.

'What's that place there?' he said, pointing at the castle whose towers, turrets, and high-hipped roofs were silhouetted against the scant light coming across the expanse of land from the main road.

'That's a reception and conference centre. As far as we know, it does not offer holiday accommodation, not even for the wealthy. That's why we did not mention it. But it is very exclusive, top-shelf. The ordinary person could not afford their wedding reception there.'

'A conference and reception centre,' said Geoff. 'That's maybe what we are looking for. Does it provide accommodation for those hiring it?'

'I don't know,' she said evasively. 'I would imagine so, though. I don't know much about the place. I have heard it hosts business meetings and conferences for big multinationals and non-government organisations.'

'Then it must have accommodation. Apparently, nothing's on at the moment. It looks closed.'

'Yes, there's not much life there. That's odd because it's called *Kasteel Zaligheid*. That means in English "Castle Bliss" or "Castle of Heavenly Bliss." I would translate it the second way.'

'Castle of Heavenly Bliss,' Geoff repeated. 'There's got to be an entrance from the dunes. There's a path here.'

'You're right. The path runs along the top of the dunes,' said Anneke, following Geoff as he took off.

They came to a path that led down the dunes to a security fence. At the fence, they found a sign on a gate in several languages. In the dim light, Geoff could make out: 'Private property. Trespassers will be prosecuted.' He stood staring at the sign while Anneke waited, fidgeting.

'Okay, we'll come back here tomorrow morning,' he said. 'We can't see anything now. I'll be able to make a better assessment during the day. We could be onto something here.'

About twenty minutes later, they passed Mevrouw van den Donker's house. It was just as they had left it earlier, light on in the lounge room and her car in the driveway. Geoff shrugged and said it was time for bed.

Anxiety began to grip him as he rode beside Anneke in the dark. Although he thought his speculations pointed him in the correct direction, he had nothing substantial to go on. What if he were wrong? What if he were right off track? He felt his heart being squeezed as the terrible thought came to him that he might not get to Estella in time.

ESTELLA RETURNED to her hotel suite to find preparations complete. Her new clothes were in bags waiting to be taken to the car. Aisha asked her to change into the galabia again. That would be more comfortable for the four-hour trip. She changed and joined the Al Refais in the restaurant. She wondered why Didi did not appear. By seven o'clock, they were ready to set off. Estella and Tahani were to go in one car while Mr Al Refai and Aisha would take another. Estella would have time and space to rest. They were about to board when Didi appeared.

'I hope you have a pleasant stay in Holland.' He took her hand.

'Aren't you coming?'

'No, I don't think I will.' He looked away. Estella wondered about his uneasiness. As he raised her hand to his lips, a bright flash lit up the surroundings. Didi swung around.

'Come on, a better shot, Didi,' called the photographer, lining up the camera again.

'Quick, get in the car and duck down,' Didi said, shielding her. He threw open the car door and pushed her in. There were more flashes.

Estella sat, startled, with her hand over her face. Tahani draped a scarf over her head. 'Leave it like that until we go,' she whispered. 'Do not let them see your face.'

The next moment, the car moved off. They drove around the square as Tahani made Estella comfortable with pillows and a rug. The car then picked up pace and made its way through the Paris traffic. Tahani advised her to sit back and rest. Estella needed little encouragement. An irresistible drowsiness came on her. Before she drifted off, the last images in her head were of Mr Al Refai's contented manner and his son's dejected expression.

She slept soundly as the car headed north, followed by Mr Al Refai and Aisha in the second limousine. She did not awake when customs waved the two cars through at the border with Belgium, north of Lille. She slept on as the cars continued to make their way northwards through some of the prettiest medieval towns in Belgium. She did not awake when the cars were again waved through customs outside the border village of Sluis as they drove into Holland. She only stirred as the cars rattled over the ramp onto the ferry at Breskens to cross over the river Schelde and disembark at Vlissingen, the modern sea entry to the Province of Zeeland.

'It's only a short trip across the river,' said Tahani, who had seen Estella stir. 'We are nearly there. We will stay in the car.'

Estella was not inclined to move. She was awake but still felt inexplicably drowsy. She shut her eyes again. Several decks above her, Didi stood against the port side rails of the ferry, looked at the flickering lights along the Boulevard at Vlissingen, and listened to the rhythmical wash of the water against the boat.

She remained half-awake as the cars disembarked at Vlissingen, drove along the *Kanaal door Walcheren* to the outskirts of Middelburg, skirted around the town to the left, and came on Walcherseweg. When Walcherseweg became Middelburgseweg, she didn't notice they passed two cyclists heading back into Middelburg. None of the occupants of the two cars stopped to wonder what those two cyclists were doing there so late at night.

GEOFF SKIDDED to a stop and looked around at the passing cars.

'What is it?' said Anneke.

'Those limousines ... they have French number plates, don't they?'

'Yes, but what about it?'

'Come on. I'm going after them.'

'But it's so late, Geoff. Do you have to?'

'You go home.' He turned his bike around. 'I want to know where they're going.'

'I'm coming, too, then.'

Geoff saw she was tired, but he had no time for arguing. He told her where he was headed if she dropped too far behind. 'And be careful! You don't know what you are dealing with, and I told your mother and father you would be safe.'

She assured him she would be all right. What could happen, anyhow, if she just rode after him? He gave her a doubtful look and then set off, pedalling flat out. Anneke watched him fade into the dark, marvelling at his endurance and determination. He had arrived more than ten hours earlier from Australia and had had no sleep in the meantime. She had seen signs of it seven years before when he came to her rescue. She cycled after him. A few minutes later, a red Ferrari passed. Also, French registration. Three expensive cars with French number plates? It was not usual.

The lights in the lounge room were out when she arrived at Mevrouw van den Donker's house. The road into Vrouwekerke was deathly still. She bent over the handlebars, breathing heavily. She considered turning back but thought a short rest might give her enough energy to go on. Geoff may need her assistance. He may not find his way to *Kasteel Zaligheid*.

Geoff did remember the way. As he was running through the route in his mind, a red Ferrari with French number plates glided past. He felt a thrill. He had to be right. He slowed when he got to Mevrouw van den Donker's house and cycled on, seeing no sign of life. Not long after he had left Anneke, he was standing on the main road looking across the open grassy space at the castle enveloped in the gloom below the dunes. His spirits dropped as he saw no visible change. Lights still glowed from several windows. But then, had the soft light streaming from two windows in the main tower been there before? He strained but could not see any cars. He surveyed the area around the castle.

A high wire security fence ran along the border with the main road, and inside the fence lay a narrow ditch half-filled with water. He found that it ran the entire length of the main road border as he walked to the right-hand side of the property. A public road led down to the dunes, with the thick oak forest on the right. A line of trees was on the left, breaking into clusters of trees and shrubs. A wide canal ran to the main road just beyond the line of trees. Beyond the canal, about fifty yards across a grassy stretch, he could make out the glittering water of a moat. Two towers jutted into the night sky. It was strange; all the windows on this side of the castle were darkened.

He cycled to the left-hand side, where he found the same high wire fence, also tree-lined, but no water-filled ditch. The castle complex was at least a hundred yards across an open space. He could not see any moat but assumed there was one. He stared at the castle. It was too dark to see anything distinctly. Then he thought he saw a shadow pass over one of the lit windows of the main tower. He focused his binoculars on the window. Nothing. Just the glow. He wondered where Anneke had got to. She should have caught up by now. He felt a pang of anxiety.

ANNEKE SAT on her bike among the roadside trees opposite Mevrouw van den Donker's house. She did not feel any better for the rest. There was no point in going after Geoff. By the time she arrived at *Kasteel Zaligheid*, he would be gone. She stared at the house. There was no sign of life. Then, as if materialising out of the dark from the direction of Vrouwekerke, Nasser Saladin appeared. He hurried to the front door and knocked sharply. Gerda opened, and he disappeared inside.

For a while, she continued to stare. She propped her bike up against a tree, crossed over, and went around the barn side of the house. A light was on in one of the back rooms. She edged along the wall. She could hear muffled voices. The curtains were not drawn, so she took a short peek. It was long enough to see Gerda and Saladin sitting in armchairs and talking. Mevrouw van den Donker was right. The room had been turned into an office, now messy with papers. A desk was against one wall. Behind Gerda on the other wall were three poster-size photos of a fair-haired woman in a long white dress.

She listened for some time but understood nothing in the muffled conversation. Geoff would be on his way back by now. But one more peek. She poked her head around the window and came face-to-face with Saladin. She froze. He ran for the door. She rushed to the barn side of the house, thinking he would take the shortest route around the other side. But she was wrong. As she came to the front, he was already running towards her. She got across the road and mounted, but he bore down on her, tearing her from the bike.

'What are you up to?' he growled, snatching the beanie from her head, and seeing with surprise that it was a young woman.

'*Laat los, schoft!*' She struggled to free herself.

'I said, what are you doing? I will let you go when you tell me.' He squeezed her wrists.

'*Laat me los, schoft.*' She kicked at his legs.

There was a swish of tyres followed by a skidding stop and the rattle of a bike sliding over the rough ground. Saladin, making choking sounds, released his vice-like grip. As Anneke backed away, rubbing her wrists, she saw Geoff with his hands around Saladin's throat. Then, just as it seemed Saladin was recovering from the surprise to put up resistance, Geoff pushed him back into the ditch. He signalled to Anneke to get going. She did not need a second invitation. They were both on their bikes and pedalling away as fast as they could when Saladin got to his feet and struggled out of the ditch. He clutched his neck as he peered into the dark.

'Who were they?' said Gerda when he came to her at the front door, rubbing his neck. She had not seen the struggle. Nor had she seen him falling clumsily into the ditch.

'I don't know. They were Dutch, a young man, and a young woman.'

'Dutch, how do you know?'

'The girl spoke in Dutch.'

'Then they're probably thieves. It's a growing problem here. Forget about it. You have your instructions. You can go now. Don't fail. We are at a critical stage. In the unlikely event that the Barker woman has backup, it's your job to keep them away until the job has been completed. And don't leave any trace.'

In a very bad mood, Saladin retraced his steps to his car parked on the outskirts of the village. It was fortunate for the young man that he had caught him off balance. He would not have gone easy on him.

Chapter 32

The surveillance

MISS BARKER opened her eyes to a room lit by a bedside lamp. She tried to shake off the drowsiness as she propped herself up on one elbow and looked around. She was in what appeared to be a hotel room. It was neat, clean, and comfortable, but very much economy class. She sat up. There was an ordinary table with two chairs in the middle of the room, and on the table a tray with a cup and saucer, a plate, a knife, a butter boat, pots of jam, and a plastic bag with sliced bread. There was a note on the plate.

'Miss Barker, please make yourself at home. Here are some things for a snack. There is a kettle in the cupboard next to the sink. Breakfast will be brought to you at eight o'clock.'

This is a very comfortable abduction, she thought. But that did not diminish the danger—Saladin's voice still ringing in her head as she was walked, staggering to the car. She glanced at her watch. It was after four o'clock in the morning. She noticed a long slit of a window on one side of the room. She peered into the darkness. She could make out slight wind ripples gleaming in the water below, about ten feet down. It was a canal of some sort. About fifteen yards across, a grassy bank appeared in the gloom. She could not see anything else and was too tired to look further. She lay on the bed. The next moment, knocking roused her from a deep sleep. Sunlight was streaming through the windows. Now she noticed two narrow curtained windows by the door. There was fiddling as a key was pushed into the lock, and then the door opened. Saladin entered, holding a t ray.

'Here's an English breakfast for you, Miss Barker,' he said. 'I will leave you to eat in peace. I will be back in an hour.'

She settled down to eat, again musing that she was being made very comfortable for someone who had been abducted with a certain amount of unpleasant violence. After eating, she showered and dressed. Refreshed, she had a further look around. The window frame over the water was recessed into the wall, narrowing her field of vision. Still, she could see below a moat about fifteen yards wide. Beyond the grassy bank and out to the left stretched an expanse of land spotted with shrubs and bushes. Between the flora, sheep and deer wandered. In front of her were rows of geometrically arranged hedges, separated from the grassy area by a long hedge about three feet high. About a hundred yards away, there was a high wire fence, and beyond that, a forest. Further, on her right, another wide canal ran along a driveway to the border fence.

The two narrow curtained windows next to the door looked out on a cobblestone courtyard. Opposite was a modest hipped-roof building with a small, slim tower. Over to her right, a lowered drawbridge gave access to a two-story grey brick castle with a slate hipped roof and a tower on the left. There were pretty dormer windows in the slate roof. She concluded that the building she was in and the one opposite were on the castle's bailey. Now people were coming and going. They looked like service staff. She thought about crying out but quickly reconsidered. They would have been told to keep away. And she did not want to attempt to extricate herself until she was sure she had a good chance of getting away. No, she would bide her time and hear what that strange man, Saladin, had to say. Good to his word, Saladin came back shortly after nine.

'You are making me very comfortable,' she said. 'I would have expected to be tied up in a dungeon somewhere and abused in a way consistent with your record.'

'My record!' He laughed and shook his head. 'No, Miss Barker, not even a good try.' His expression of superiority indicated that he thought he had the better of her. 'Miss Barker, you are a temporary guest. I admire your courage and talents. You deserve to be treated with respect, and as long as you cooperate, that will happen.'

'If I do not cooperate?'

'Then you will be tied up and your mouth taped. What else would you expect?'

'What is going to happen to me?'

'You will stay in this room until an hour before dawn tomorrow morning. Then you will be delivered to a spot where you were helped into our car.'

'Why?'

'Miss Barker, I will not treat you like an idiot. You know some things and have guessed others. Let us say that certain things must happen. You will be removed from the scene until they take place. After that, it does not matter what you do or say.'

'You are joking, surely.'

'Not at all.'

'I know too much.'

'Indeed, you know quite a lot, but proving it to the world is another thing. You will not be able to demonstrate any convincing connection. People will say you are raving if you try, especially if no one complains. Come now, Miss Barker, I am curious. Tell me what you think you know. There are things I will confirm if you are right.'

'You have abducted Estella Winterbine for one or more purposes, purposes that only she could satisfy.' He shrugged. 'What are those purposes? What has the Egyptian businessman to do with it?'

'You cannot guess? Come on. It's very simple.' He waited, but Miss Barker said nothing. His arrogant expression said he was going to boast. 'It's very simple. It's only the execution that is clever and audacious. As much as that wretched Dutch woman irritates me, I must admit she is very clever.' He paused for effect. 'She would not be pleased to hear me say it, but she has to be the world's greatest madam.'

'You're not going to tell me that all this is about procuring a girl for a wealthy businessman?'

'In a way and crudely put, I suppose, yes.'

'I cannot believe it. There's got to be more.'

'There is. But, Miss Barker, you obviously don't understand. This is not a case of someone paying a brothel madam for a beautiful girl. The Winterbine girl is in a unique category. You must consider it in the same category as purchasing a Rembrandt or a Van Gogh. Some men believe that one of nature's most exquisite works is the beautiful, young, unblemished female. The most outstanding examples of beauty, elegance, style, innocence, self-respect, virtue, and exclusivity may compare with the Mona Lisa. Such a beauty will be treated like a great work of art. The girl will be feted like a princess and more. It is not just about money and sensuality. Such men would be highly indignant if accused of anything so low and vulgar. They abhor crudity in any form. They will bestow honour, respect, and unlimited admiration on the chosen girl. Few girls, not even those you call moral, can resist such seduction.'

'Then Fr. van Engelen was right. A Faustian contract. It did come down to seducing the maiden thought out of reach. It is still difficult to believe.'

'I suppose this is something only men understand, even priests.'

'You're making the mistake of projecting your attitudes onto other men.' She stopped to consider. 'But why does such a man need someone like Gerda van den Donker to procure his works of art?' Saladin shook his head and did not answer. 'Then what's in it for her? What's in it for the left-wing fanatic?'

'What about money? Could that not be a reason? Gerda Vrouwendijk needs to finance her activities.'

'Her activities? She does not see that as abusing the very people she pretends to fight for, women?'

'I will not pretend to be capable of fully explaining her point of view. A lot of it makes no sense to me, certainly from my perspective, but she obviously thinks that it is all consistent. I suppose she's of the opinion that if she and other women can take great bags of money from stupid men, then they should do so. People like her put no value on the sex act other than the pleasure it gives. I mean, there is no moral value in having sex, no matter who or what it concerns.'

'You appear to know how to explain it, after all, Mr Saladin. How does that sit with your knowledge that Miss Winterbine and her parents place great moral value on such things?'

'My knowledge? It is your Western ways we are talking about,' he replied with a dismissive flick of his hand. 'Don't blame me. I have a business contract with Gerda Vrouwendijk. I do what I am paid handsomely to do. I am only talking to you because I have never met a woman like you before.'

'You mean, a Crusader woman like me.'

'If you want.' He lounged in his chair and continued to regard her with the same superior smirk. 'You know, Miss Barker, as clever as you have been, when it came down to it, you crumpled like a piece of paper. That's the undeniable difference between men and women. You will always be subject to the power and authority of men. Your Western liberalism is so much corrupt and effete thinking, particularly concerning your weak, self-indulged, homosexualised men.'

'You mean your Muslim culture sees the proper relationship between men and women?'

'Yes, put simply.'

'Mr Saladin, your type, whether Muslim or Western, makes the same mistake. You identify Western liberalism with European and Christian civilisation. I am not about to give you lessons in European culture. Still, you must know that those of us who have imbibed the ethos of European civilisation think that the prevailing materialist liberalism is corrupting. It's corrupting an ethos that has its origins in five thousand years of history.'

Saladin hesitated for a moment. 'Five thousand years? Well!' More hesitation. 'Whatever. You all remain infidels whose systems are opposed to Islam. It's either you or us, as it always has been. We are in what you call the endgame. The endgame has started. The aircraft hijackings are a taste of the future.'

'And what is a good Muslim doing in league with a bitter, unrelenting representative of Western ideology?'

'If your representative is foolish enough to pay me handsomely to attack and harm the Crusader world, then— '

'Is Gerda van den Donker aware of your views?'

'No, she has no time to think about it. Because I am willing to be the weapon in her hands, she regards me as a savage brute who has no real understanding of her actions. I do not do anything to discourage that view. I can only applaud in silence for being given the means and occasion to harm the enemy. Miss Barker, it is your privilege to hear this from my mouth.'

'Why does the Egyptian businessman really need Gerda van den Donker to procure his girls?' said Miss Barker, after a period of silence.

'You really want to know, don't you?'

'I do.'

'In a way, it's not the right question. But you will have to work that out for yourself,' he said. 'Now, I have things to attend to. Be patient, and you will be released unharmed.'

'Wait,' she said as he turned. 'What was that dead rabbit doing near the man and boy you killed?'

'I killed them, did I?' He nodded again in acknowledgment. 'What rabbit?'

'Do you know anything about the Convent of the Blessed Mother?'

'What are you talking about?'

'Mr Saladin, I suspect there is a part of Gerda van den Donker that you know nothing about. A very important part.'

'What?' The superior expression faded, and, for an instant, he looked unsure of himself.

'My turn to say that you will have to work that out for yourself. Your help to Miss van den Donker may be just as harmful to your world as the Crusader world.'

He hesitated. 'Don't play games with me, Miss Barker.' He walked to the door.

'There's just one more thing,' she said as he opened the door. 'In the true European ethos, men and women are considered spiritually or metaphysically equal. It is in the temporal or concrete sphere that men and women have different roles. There is no real inferiority in splitting a communion of people into different ranks whose relations represent a partnership in metaphysical equality. Men and women are from nature partners, and in an ideal society, they would do everything to preserve the partnership.'

'A nice academic speech, Miss Barker,' he said with a crooked sneer.

'You say I crumpled when it came down to it. But a partnership is an ongoing thing. How do you know I am not working in partnership? A wound in one arm concentrates the energy in the good arm.'

Saladin again looked unsure of himself, and he seemed to be reflecting. 'I'll be ready for your partner if he turns up.' He forced out a laugh. It was not convincing.

'Your type of Islam is not really a religion, sir. It is a cultural and political framework. Your invocation of Allah is merely the blasphemous excuse to carry out your barbarism.'

He stopped, rigid in the open doorway. 'There are limits, Miss Barker. Be careful not to defeat the privileges my respect for you has given.' The door shut, followed by the sound of a key in the lock.

Miss Barker sat pondering. She did not trust him. She sniffed at his assurance that she would be released unharmed. It was to keep her quiet.

She would remain quiet, but for her purposes. Her hope was Captain Shawcross. Where was he? If all had gone according to plan, he would have arrived in Middelburg not too long after her. He would have contacted Mr van Engelen, who would have told him about the meeting and her disappearance. That, she could be sure of. After that? He would go searching for her. That was the problem. She could not know what information he or Frans van Engelen had to work on. She did not even know where she was. She was in a castle, though. There could not be too many castles on Walcheren. Would there be anything to give Geoff a clue that she may be locked up in a castle? Would Gerda van den Donker lead him to her if she were on Walcheren?

She went to the window above the moat. All that was visible beyond the high fence were trees. If she set up a signal in the window, somebody among those trees would have to look within a narrow margin to see it. There was nothing else. What sort of a signal? She considered what she had. Clothing of any kind would not be useful. They would not stand out. Only her high-heeled shoes might work. They were not the sort of shoes she usually wore. If Mr Shawcross had been observant as usual, he would have noticed them. She placed them on the windowsill but did not harbour much hope.

ESTELLA OPENED her eyes to the sun's rays streaming into her suite. It was an open space with a curtained four-poster bed on one side and a sitting area on the other. A French-style lounge suite upholstered in exquisitely patterned material dominated the sitting area. Near the entrance was a doorway to a small but luxuriously appointed bathroom. Alongside the bathroom and between two windows, a fancy, wrought-iron spiral staircase wound mysteriously to an upper level.

In the bright light, she could now see that she was in a round building with four long windows evenly spaced. She walked to the nearest window and had to suppress a gasp as she looked down at a sheer drop into dark green water about thirty feet below. Her suite was evidently on an upper level of a tower within a castle. She stood at the window, contemplating the scene. It was so calm and peaceful, and a welcome change from the hectic pace of the last few days.

The grassy field below with its grazing animals, the garden designed in English-style, the calm, gleaming waters of the moat, the slumbering forest of oak trees beyond, and the flat green fields disappearing out of sight had a mesmerising charm. The view from the other three windows was no less enchanting. On one side, she looked down on the castle's bailey with its twin wings sporting a slim tower each and separated from the main castle by a moat. Beyond the bailey were a grassy lawn and a white path leading into the forest that squeezed between the castle grounds and the sandy dunes. On the other side, she looked along a wing and over a grassy area to the inviting fields beyond. It was so different from the Australian bush with its ruggedness and hilly expanses. This flat, peaceful country, with its lush, friendly flora, had a cosy doll's-house aura.

'I am happy to see you awake and relaxed,' said Aisha, looking around the half-opened door. 'May I come in?'

Estella hastened to welcome her. Aisha said breakfast would be served for the three young women in Estella's suite after she had showered and dressed. It did not take long for Estella to be ready. Soon, an attendant had tidied the suite, and two waiters arrived to serve the three young women. They lingered long over their choice of food. Estella had never sat so long at breakfast with such delightful company.

SOMETIME before Estella awoke and began to survey her surroundings with growing pleasure, Geoff was already back, anxiously surveying the castle. He must establish as soon as possible whether Estella was there. Time was critical. If she was not there, he had to look elsewhere. And now the task was more difficult. He had to conduct his reconnaissance alone and without being seen, for Anneke had to return to class. From the castle and its surrounding grounds, security had a clear view of anyone approaching its borders. He calculated that he could risk two passes along the main road before he sparked interest. After that, he would have to restrict himself to the forest.

He approached the right-hand side of the castle first. He had an idea that if Estella were somewhere in the castle, it would be on the other side. He did not know why. It was a gut feeling. So eager to get the inspection of this side out of the way, he quickly moved among the trees, stopping here and there to observe. Where he found a tree he could scale, he climbed to the highest point and peered through his binoculars. As expected, he could not confirm much more than he had seen the previous evening.

He made his way to the top of the dunes, which were a little lower at that point than elsewhere. His view over the castle and its grounds was obscured. He would not risk passing the castle gate along the dunes but would arrive at the higher point from the other side of the castle. He returned to his bike and cycled casually along the front border, glancing to his right as a tourist would. The hedge separated what looked like a garden from the grazing animals. He rode beyond the castle property, stowed his bike among the trees, and made his way through the forest, stopping to examine the castle from different perspectives. On this side, he had an unimpeded view of the castle building. He found a tall oak tree he could climb and settled between its branches. He ran his binoculars over the building complex whose division he could now see clearly.

The castle consisted of a two-story building with a high hipped roof facing the dunes. Two wings, also with hipped roofs, branched out on either side towards the main road. As he rode along the main road, he had seen that between the wings, there was a tree-filled courtyard. On the front corner of the main building, at his side, was a broad, high tower with windows at three levels. At the junction of the tower with the wing was a section of the building, about six feet wide by four feet deep, protruding from roof level to below the water level. It, too, had windows at three levels. It looked like a stairwell, but he could not be sure.

On the opposite corner of the main building was a companion tower. In front of the main building, separated by the moat, was a bailey with twin buildings, each with a slim tower. Whatever else could be said, *Kasteel Zaligheid* was an impressive, fairy-like castle with alluring grounds. As he scanned the castle and its grounds, he noticed purposeful activity. His view of the courtyard between the buildings on the bailey was obscured, but he could see people coming and going. People were also on the grounds in front of the bailey. They seemed to be preparing for something.

One aspect did intrigue him. During that time, no one approached the castle's entry at the foot of the dunes, and nobody left. There was no sign of cars or Estella. The more his scanning failed to produce anything, the more anxious he became. He was losing valuable time. He climbed down from the oak tree, worried and dejected. A minute later, he arrived at the main road to see Frans and Charles waiting for him among the trees. Frans had picked up Fr. van Engelen and Charles at Schiphol as arranged, but had left the priest to rest at his aged mother's house.

'Good. You don't need a rest, too, Charles?' said Geoff. 'We have some demanding surveillance to carry out.'

'Don't worry about me, Geoff,' said Charles. 'I'm fit enough. Just tell me what needs to be done.'

'I'm afraid I have met a check here. I've looked hard but cannot find any sign of Estella, nothing at all. You know, too, that Miss Barker has gone missing?'

'Yes, yes, I know. Don't give up. Our prayers will be answered in the end. I have great confidence in you.'

'Should we persist here?' said Frans. 'What are the probabilities?'

'I'm inclined to,' Geoff said, gazing through the trees at the castle. 'Whatever information we have, it seems to point here.' He paused. 'I have a feeling about this place.'

Charles had fixed his gaze on the castle while Geoff was talking. Without saying anything, he moved stealthily between the trees towards the dunes. Geoff and Frans followed.

'There's someone at the second window on the middle level of the main tower,' he said, pointing. 'It looks like a woman.'

Geoff raised his binoculars and focused on the window. 'My God, you're right,' he exclaimed, focusing on someone's arm in a white sleeve. The person seemed to be resting against the window frame. The arm disappeared. 'How do you know it was a woman?'

'I don't know exactly. There was something about it,' he said. 'I could only see the outline of an arm, but the manner of the arm belonged to a woman.' They contemplated the castle. 'Geoff, I, too, have a feeling about this place. If Estella were taken somewhere she would enjoy and not suspect any danger, it is this. It seems to fulfil all her romantic fantasies.'

Geoff did not underestimate the power of Charles's observation and intuition. He had seen enough of the Winterbine family to understand. His confidence was up. He then split them into three areas. He would continue on that side of the castle, taking his position again in the oak tree. Frans would go to the other side. Charles would install himself on the highest point of the dunes, being careful to stay out of sight. He should keep alert to any vessels lingering close to the coast. They arranged to meet and confer at the roadside again at twelve-thirty.

AISHA WAS at the window in Estella's suite, surveying the castle grounds below. Estella stood at her side, partially hidden for want of sufficient room at the window.

'It's such a beautiful place,' said Aisha. 'The castle and the surrounding nature are brilliant. I wish we could spend more time here.'

'It would be wonderful,' said Estella.

'If you work for Father,' said Tahani, still on the lounge settee, 'you will have opportunity enough.'

'Come on. It's time to get ready to meet Pappa for morning tea,' said Aisha, frowning at Tahani.

Estella followed the sisters down the tower stairs and across the opulent foyer to a large, lavishly decorated room where they found Mr Al Refai and Didi in earnest conversation. Didi had his head half-bowed while his father gestured. They stopped and looked at the young women when they heard them enter.

'Good morning, young ladies,' said Mr Al Refai, his face brightening, 'and especially good morning to our lovely guest.'

Estella acknowledged the greeting and stared in surprise at Didi.

'I came after all,' he said, with more embarrassment than usual. 'There is nothing like the Castle of Heavenly Bliss to put one at ease.' But Didi looked far from at ease.

Estella felt his discomfort and had an impulse to console him. Alas, Mr Al Refai's outline of the day's schedule prevented any such action. After morning tea, Estella was to spend a short time with him alone, and after that, she was free to wander in the castle or around the grounds until lunch. After lunch, she should rest in preparation for the evening's reception and the drive back to Paris airport. It would be a busy, exciting time. When morning tea was over, Aisha, Tahani and Didi rose as if on cue and left the r oom.

'We are now nearing the end of your work experience weekend with us,' said Mr Al Refai to Estella, sitting in a lounge chair next to him. 'You have been exposed to the environment in which you would work if you join us. You have had some experience of the sort of business meetings you would attend. Your response has been excellent, all that I would want.'

'Thank you, Mr Al Refai. I am pleased I have done well. It seems a small thing in response to the enjoyable time you and your daughters have given me.'

'In saying that, you could not please me more. This evening, you will experience a lavish reception for some of my most valuable business contacts. In this, you will shine, I assure you, as few people could.'

Estella smiled in appreciation of the continuing praise, keeping her eyes fixed on his handsome face with its kindly eyes and healthy complexion. She felt a warmth for him that was spilling into affection. He paused, apparently sensing the rising emotion within her. There was a flash of satisfaction in his eyes that his kindly manner immediately covered. She saw it. She, in turn, had a flash of understanding, and it brought an abrupt halt to her expanding feelings. He reached across and laid his hand lightly on her arm. She recoiled.

'Now, I want to explain an important part of the promotional work you would be engaged in.' He took his hand away. The chill of perspiration cooled her neck and forehead. 'I explained to you that we cultivate contacts with all sorts of organisations, and we provide funding for some of them,' Mr Al Refai continued, immersed in his thoughts. 'It's vital for a modern communications company to maintain a presence in the community. We have the responsibility of giving voice to their concerns and providing the information they want and need. There is a big future in communications, especially given the increasing development of countries whose populations have long been poor and uneducated.'

'I am thinking of China and other Asian countries. In the future, great opportunities will arise for businesses in communications. An understanding of culture and language is absolutely indispensable here. This is where you will be of great value. I propose making you responsible for maintaining close relations with organisations dealing with language and culture. The promotion of language and culture is paired with media opportunities. People need media to convey their message. There is an important organisation in London called The Institute for the Rights of Regional Dialects and Language Custom. 'The people in this organisation see a close connection between the liberty of the person and the maintenance of natural speech patterns and customs. They have worldwide connections. Naturally, we have a great interest in their work. We provide funding and promotion for them. It will be your responsibility to work closely with them. What do you think? Would you be as interested as I think?'

'I don't know,' said Estella, unable to concentrate. 'I need time to consider everything that has happened.'

'You have an interest in culture and languages. I can see that. I see how much you have enjoyed your stay in Paris.'

'I am interested in languages, history, and culture. But I am not sure of the work. I need time to consider it and to talk about it with my mother and father.'

'Of course, you do,' he said with much sympathy. 'I do not mean to pressure you. You have time to reflect, and you will be given every consideration.'

'I appreciate that, Mr Al Refai. I am grateful for your confidence in me.' She had the uncomfortable sensation of listening to herself talking.

'It is what you deserve. I am not a person for empty flattery.' He smiled and patted her arm. She shuddered and recoiled. 'If you have any questions, please ask them. It does not matter when. I will be here all afternoon, attending to business. You can interrupt me whenever you want. All right?'

'Yes. I appreciate your understanding,' she replied woodenly.

'One last thing: I spoke to you about a contract. You understand, it's normal for an employee to agree to certain conditions in return for a very generous salary, an expense account, a clothing account, and an apartment in the centre of Paris. The conditions will be straightforward, and I do not suppose onerous. Among them, you will agree to be on call whenever you are required. That does make social relationships difficult sometimes, but I do not believe you will be bothered with that, will you? Your work and pleasurable surroundings will be great recompense. All right?' He smiled again and, without waiting for a response, continued, 'Enough of business! I leave you to enjoy yourself now.'

'Yes, Mr Al Refai, thank you,' she murmured, becoming aware that the repetition of her employment rewards coupled with the contract had come stressed lightly but pointedly. As Mr Al Refai's handsome, sympathetic face bent towards her, she was suddenly reminded of Geoff, her feelings for him, and all that had happened between them. Those feelings ran into the reasons for her thoughtless enjoyment, for the pleasure from the attention and flattery of an elegant, cultivated man, the sort she had never encountered in her isolated country town, where the grubby coarseness of the boys constantly impressed her. The dawning of how far along the path the relentless attention had drawn her came close to overwhelming her. It had taken her far away from Geoff and his world of quiet integrity.

A growing sense of betrayal filled her, and she struggled to compose herself. Mr Al Refai was so preoccupied with his own thoughts that he failed to see any sign of her inner turmoil. He escorted her to the door where Aisha was waiting. With a faint smile, she let herself be led away. The bubble had been pricked, and the lavish opulence of her surroundings bore down on her. As the young women were about to turn into a hallway, she glanced back and saw Didi enter the room where she had left his father. A frown disturbed his boyish face.

CHARLES STOOD where Geoff and Anneke had stood the night before and gazed over the Dutch countryside. The flat, lush countryside broken here and there by lines of trees and clusters of buildings with church spires peaking above them radiated peace. He and Estella would enjoy exploring Walcheren. But the task of finding her took priority over such thoughts. He fixed his eyes on the castle while recommencing his prayers. Some figures passed by the windows on the second floor. One stopped at a window. It was the same person he had seen at the tower window earlier, a young woman. She moved aside, and another young woman appeared beside her. He started, trembling. Framed in the window and dressed in clothes he had never seen was his daughter.

Relief filled him. She stood there willingly with someone, unaware of any threat. He watched, transfixed, with growing apprehension. She moved to another window, seemingly at the invitation of her companion. Then another young woman appeared at the window. Estella was with two young women. He watched them go from window to window and then disappear. He waited. A few minutes later, they appeared at the front entrance. He rushed along the path and down the dunes.

ESTELLA, AISHA, and Tahani were stopped by Didi, calling to them. 'Would you mind if I had a few words with Estella?' he said. 'I'm returning to Paris, and I would like to say goodbye. Just time for a short walk.'

Aisha hesitated but, seeing her brother's forlorn expression, relented. 'Five minutes. That's all. And as long as Estella is happy to go with you.'

Estella assured Aisha of her willingness. As she and Didi set off, a welcome sense of safety reassured her. She waited for him to speak, but he said nothing until they had passed over the bridge between the bailey and the castle grounds and were on the white crushed gravel path to the dunes.

'Have you enjoyed yourself?' he asked.

'Yes, I have. Your family has been very kind.' It was the truth despite her present anxiety and the yearning to return to Geoff and her parents.

'Estella, you must never forget, no matter what happens, that the family friendship is sincere. My sisters like you very much and would never want to hurt you.'

'I understand,' she said, wondering at the strength of his assurance. 'I will always appreciate it.'

'You must understand, too, that my father's consideration of you is genuine. He means what he says when he praises your talents. He will do everything to ensure you're happy and content with your work if you choose to work for him. You will always be treated with respect. My father places a high value on his honour.'

'I understand that, too.' She stopped. They were not far from the gate to the dunes. 'Didi, is there something you are trying to tell me?'

Didi took her gently by the arm and walked to the gate without speaking. He opened it and ushered her through. They climbed to the top of the dunes. The wind blew from the sea and ruffled her hair as he stopped and faced her.

'Estella, my father will give you everything you could want except the love of a husband.'

'Didi—' she started to say, brushing the hair from her face.

'No, let me say what I want to say. It's not much.' He took her hand, raised it to his lips and kissed it tenderly. 'From the beginning, I saw something different in you. I don't mean your beauty. There are enough people to tell you how beautiful you are. No, I saw how empty my life was and how full yours was. I have everything a son could wish for, and I am a sad, empty person. You have your mother and father and your garden. And you, I mean your inner self, it shines like gold. It's full to bursting with goodness and beauty.' He kissed her hand again. 'I have nothing to give you except my love and a promise.'

'Didi—' she started to say again. She put her hand on his.

'No, Estella, just a little more, and I will be finished.' He looked at the sand under his feet. 'You don't have to give me an answer now. In fact, I don't want you to answer until I can prove myself to you.' He looked her full in the face. 'I love you, and I want to be yours, and I want you to be mine. I am asking you to marry me. No, don't mention all the reasons for refusing,' he said as she opened her mouth. 'I know what they are. Just give me the chance to prove I have changed, that I am suitable to be your husband. It does not matter what situation you are in, how old you are, whether there is someone else, or whether I am of a different culture or religion; just give me time to prove I am worthy of you, of your love, and then you can refuse me. Just time enough to prove I have turned away from the miserable, meaningless life I have been leading and have put in that emptiness some decency and manliness.'

Estella felt his love and sadness. She could not say anything. She could never love him the way she loved Geoff, but she had much affection for him. The comfort and honesty he showed in her present anxiety deepened that affection. He came forward and embraced her. She could not resist. Indeed, the impulse to comfort him, in turn, was irresistible. Without thinking, she put her arms around him. His mouth was on her cheek, and his lips were moving towards her mouth. She was inclined to accept the kiss, but as his soft lips touched hers, she turned her head away.

'I'm sorry. You see, I cannot help myself.' He released her. 'I'm going to return to Paris now. I will see you—'

'Didi, will you please bring Estella back here! You know you are not supposed to be there.' Aisha and Tahani were standing at the open gate below them.

GEOFF STARTED violently when Estella came into view from the castle bailey with a young man. He felt profound relief. Then he saw that the young man was holding her attention, and she seemed to be listening sympathetically. It was not the demeanour of a person under threat. He stiffened against the tree trunk as they passed through the gate and ascended the dunes. Where was Charles? They must act. He froze as the young man took hold of Estella's hand and kissed it. Then another kiss. Then he embraced her, and she did not resist! His heart was squeezed, and a lump came to his throat. He dropped the binoculars. He did not want to see any more. He could not understand it. Estella would not give her affection to someone without reason. He was confused. Whatever—he must put it aside. They must grab her while she was out of the castle grounds. Where on earth was Charles? Then a black limousine from nowhere passed through the front gates and drove to the main road. No time to think about that. As he scrambled down the tree, he heard Charles's voice.

'Geoff, I have seen Estella.'

'Yes, I have seen her, too. Quick, she is outside on the dunes. We must grab her.'

They rushed through the trees, fighting overhanging branches and forest floor refuse until they reached the path leading up the sandy slope. They came out together on top just in time to see Estella walk out of sight. Geoff took off but stopped. 'No, it's too late. She will be well inside the castle grounds by the time we get there. It's too risky now.' If only Charles had stayed where he was, another fifty yards closer. He was not to know.

DIDI SHRUGGED and said he had finished and would leave for Paris immediately. He gave Estella's hand a final squeeze and left her to his sisters. Estella wanted to say something. Despite her enduring love for Geoff and the impossibility of that ever changing, she wanted to wish Didi well. She wanted to send her affection with him wherever he went. But she could not bring herself to say it. She was strangely tongue-tied. A heavy, ominous guilt hung over her for not being able to speak her affection—for not detaining him longer. Then it was too late to say anything. All she could do was watch him walk, head bowed, across the lawn to the garage hidden among the trees. She stopped before the bridge across the moat and watched until the red Ferrari drove to the front gates, where a guard opened for him. Then he was gone.

'Come on,' said Aisha, 'we will continue our tour of the castle.'

'Yes, come on,' said Tahani, taking her arm, 'we can enjoy ourselves without the presence of troublesome men.'

MISS BARKER crouched at the window looking onto the courtyard. She was waiting for the young people to return. She had caught a glimpse of a young man and a young woman through the curtains when they were about to pass over the bridge. They were out of sight when she got to the window. Now Estella came into view without the young man. She seemed a little subdued but otherwise unaware that she could be in danger. Ms Bicknell's purposes were yet unfulfilled, as Boris had said. There was still time. Surely, if Geoff had worked out that the castle was a likely place for her to be, he would have the castle under surveillance.

She had to bank on that. She must concentrate. She must anticipate what he would do. But she had so little to go on. Whatever the case, if he had seen Estella, which seemed likely if he had concluded that she was in the castle, then he must also have realised that she would not be far away. She must prepare herself for a possible rescue attempt. She had a rough idea of what he would attempt. In the meantime, she must rest for whatever might happen.

FROM THE shelter of the trees, Geoff and Charles watched the red Ferrari drive past them and turn right at the main road. It had to be the younger Al Refai at the wheel. And the young man with Estella on the dunes also had to be Didi Al Refai. Only someone so privileged would behave like that and drive such an expensive car. When Geoff thought about it, it looked like he was saying farewell to Estella, and the Ferrari's departure probably meant he was leaving to return to Paris. What was the relationship between Estella and him? And the car that had gone before him, who was that? Suddenly, there was much action in the castle. He would maintain surveillance until twelve-thirty as planned, then break for lunch. Charles returned to his place on the dunes, and Geoff climbed into his oak tree. Fifteen minutes later, another car departed. Three cars had departed, and none had entered. Something was up.

Sometime later, one of the tower's windows on the top level swung open. He directed his binoculars. He drew a sharp breath as he, at last, brought a clear view of Estella into focus, standing at the window looking out. She seemed distracted. He recognised that look. It was the expression she wore when she was troubled. She bent over, rested her elbows on the window, and gazed into the water more than fifty feet below. Why was she troubled? Because she had, at last, felt the danger? Because Didi Al Refai had left? He could not know.

Estella had not initiated contact on the dunes if he thought about it. It had all come from Didi Al Refai. Whereas she had moved towards him in Ruby's—no, he must stop dwelling on it. He needed to stay calm. He let the binoculars drift over the tower and then to the side wing, examining every crack and crevice. If he had no choice but to break in and get her out of there, how best to do it without alerting the security? Men were roaming around the grounds in front of the castle. But no one was beyond the moat that circled the castle and ran along the driveway to the entrance. The moat was evidently considered security enough. That was a weak point.

He stopped to examine the stairwell. The right-angled corner with the wall would give him support if he tried to climb to the roof from the moat. The binding material between the bricks was probably crumbly, too. He would have little trouble tapping in climbing supports. That would give him fairly easy access from the roof to the tower's top level and the open window where Estella was. That was the simple part. How to time it and get her down—that was the difficult task. Now he entered his routine of continually reviewing the possibilities. The freezing temperature of the water in the moat was not the least of his worries. He had a dry suit. Estella would have nothing but the flimsy clothes she was in. Those clothes! They were not the usual clothes she wore. The fashionable light slacks and top made her look different.

THE BLACK limousine pulled up in the driveway of Truus van den Donker's house. Mr Al Refai walked to the front door and knocked. Gerda Vrouwendijk opened at once.

'I thought it was essential we were not seen together,' she said. 'I had trouble getting rid of my mother.'

'There has been an important change,' he said, pushing his way past her.

'I don't like changes,' she replied. 'We had an agreement. I didn't expect you to change anything once the agreement was fixed.'

'I'm a flexible Egyptian businessman, not a tied-up fussy Dutch woman. Now, where can we sit while I explain?'

There was no hint of the generous, open character that Estella saw. Gerda showed him to her makeshift office, where he sat in the armchair she indicated, without bothering to look around. She took the chair opposite him under three poster-size photos of a fair woman in a long white dress. He stared at the photos.

'Well?' she said, noticing with satisfaction that her guest could not resist the photos.

'This won't take long, Ms Vrouwendijk,' he said, taking his eyes from the posters. 'Something quite unexpected has happened. My son has fallen in love with the girl. He wants to marry her. In such a case, the agreement terminates, and you keep the first payment. You are royally rewarded for your trouble.'

'Fallen in love?' she snorted. 'Your son's falling in love means nothing. You're not going to forgo this girl because your son tells you he has fallen in love, are you? If he gets anywhere with her, and he most probably won't, he will forget her like all the others. You'll lose, and we'll lose. It makes no sense. Besides, in terms of the agreement, it is not a reason to terminate it.'

'In normal circumstances, Ms Vrouwendijk, I would agree. My son has a very poor record. In this case, however, he has given certain commitments which amount to self-abasement to demonstrate to the girl and me that he has changed and will respect her for the rarity she is. I am severe with my son, but I love him. I am prepared to give him a chance. I am confident the girl will not be receptive unless he can demonstrate that he is serious about changing. She's not in the category we have discussed. She is above that. And it is in the agreement's terms.'

Ms Vrouwendijk's lips curled in contempt. 'You have succumbed, too, have you?' He said nothing. 'It just demonstrates my point. This girl possesses irresistible inner power. You will waste it by abandoning her to your misogynist son. More seriously, marriage to your son will lock it up. The girl's influence and power will only blossom in the agreement we have discussed. It is an agreement, I stress, that gives her favours to you in a way that unleashes the full effect of her talents. A deadening, virtuous bourgeois marriage will tie it all up forever. You can't turn your back on it. I will not allow it.'

'You will not allow it? Dear lady, you overreach yourself. I am the one with the power. You have a little organisation that depends on me for much of your financing. So don't talk to me about not allowing anything.'

'A little organisation?' said Gerda with snarling contempt. 'You have an agreement with me.' Mr Al Refai waved his hand. 'Where is your son now? Pursuing his self-abasement in the luxury of the castle?'

'He has left for Paris to get his affairs in order. Ms Vrouwendijk, I will not be the object of your sarcasm. If there's nothing else, our conversation is at an end.'

'See these photos here?' she said, pointing over her head. 'She's a beautiful woman, isn't she?'

'Very beautiful,' he said, glancing at the photos.

'Do you know who she is?'

He shook his head without looking at the photos. He began to rise.

'Wait. Have a closer look. Look carefully at the mouth and the cheeks.'

Mr Al Refai turned his unwilling attention to the photos. At first, he saw nothing that meant anything. Then something caught his attention. He came closer, straining to see.

'It's the girl's mother,' he exclaimed. 'I heard she was beautiful, but I had no idea— What does this mean? Whatever it is, it makes no difference.'

'I will give you the privilege of an explanation,' said Gerda Vrouwendijk, her eyes dilating from her agitation. 'An unexpected outcome of this mission was the discovery of this woman hidden in a primordial state in the pristine bush of country Australia. The daughter is the less-than-perfect product of this perfection. This woman is the figure of the redemptive woman, the being that will re-order society and return it to its primordial state, where language and communication are back in the hands of its originators, where true freedom for the human spirit in its original state will prevail. The trouble is that this woman is imprisoned, like us all, in the social fetters forged thousands of years ago. She does not know it. She languishes in exile in her fetters, not seeing the way out or the way back. The daughter provides a way out for her—only if the daughter's talents are unleashed. Once unleashed, the mother will see the way and follow to take her rightful place. So, you understand how important it is.'

Mr Al Refai stared in bemusement at the twisted animated face in front of him. 'You cannot be serious,' he said at last.

'Don't patronise me, Mr Businessman.'

'Far be it from me to be so ungallant. But I advise you to be careful,' he said, getting up. 'You will end up being scheduled for a period of rest if you broadcast that madness too far abroad. Stick to your proven talent of language research.' It was an offhand comment that was worse than a blow to her face.

'I wouldn't have expected any other response from a man.'

He ignored the clenched teeth and slightly shaking hands as she uttered these words. 'Ms. Vrouwendijk, the bottom line is that the agreement lapses for the moment. If there is a change in my son's undertakings, we may resume our talks. In the meantime, Miss Winterbine will still be offered training and employment in my company, with a different orientation of goals. I bid you good morning. Don't bother seeing me out.'

She did not. She sat in her chair for a few minutes and then went to the phone. She dialled furiously and waited. 'The son has left for Paris. Follow him at once. He will not be far ahead of you. He's likely held up at the Vlissingen-Breskens ferry. Report to me as soon as you reach Paris and establish where he is.'

Twenty minutes later, Nasser Saladin pulled up behind a line of cars waiting for the ferry at Vlissingen's inner harbour terminal. He got out and looked around. Gerda was right. A red Ferrari was near the head of the first row of cars. Judging from the number of cars and the activity around the docking area, he estimated the ferry was probably five to ten minutes away.

He walked to the kiosk at the train terminal, not far across the parking area. While waiting to be served, his eyes ran idly over the newspaper and magazine racks. He became attentive when he saw a headline and photo on the front page of a London tabloid. He took it from the rack and perused the front-page report. The headline: **Egyptian playboy is at it again.**

> Didi Al Refai, who has more money (daddy's, of course) than he knows what to do with, and more girls than he could possibly service in a lifetime, is, according to friends in the playboy's circle, in love again. There are reports of a mysterious girl of incomparable beauty who has captured little Didi's heart. The playboy has been so secretive about this and gone to such lengths to shield the girl from public scrutiny that friends say it can't be anything but serious. The unclear picture printed here is the only one our photographer could get before the girl was pushed into a limousine outside one of Paris's swishiest hotels. Is this the girl to capture his heart and billion-dollar inheritance? The frantic efforts to keep her identity secret don't lie, and the curiosity to know who she is will only grow.

Saladin paid for the paper, food, and drink and then went to a nearby public phone. After making two calls, he returned to his car just as the first line of cars was driving across the ramp onto the ferry. He got in and threw the paper on the passenger seat. He glanced at the photo of Didi, obscuring the Winterbine girl's face as they stood beside the car outside The Ritz. He drove forward with the other cars, his face tensed in thought.

ESTELLA WAS roused from her thoughts by Aisha appearing at the top of the spiral staircase to call her to lunch. Reluctantly, she left the window and descended the stairs with her.

'Father will not be joining us this time,' she said. 'He will be busy this afternoon with urgent matters. He offers his apologies and says he looks forward to seeing you this evening. We will have a quiet afternoon together.'

Estella was happy to have some quiet. She saw, too, that Aisha looked fatigued. Perhaps the program had also been too intense for her. There had hardly been a let-up since they left Melbourne, which now seemed an eternity ago. And it was just three days. So much had happened. So much crowded in on her now. And what Didi said— She could not bear the thought of it. The lunch followed in a subdued mood. The same two waiters served it with the same faultless attention. But none of the young women seemed inclined to conversation. Talk was desultory. Estella was glad when lunch finished, and Aisha suggested she return to her suite to rest alone. They, too, would take the opportunity for a rest.

Back in her suite, Estella sat in an armchair and picked up one of the fashion magazines Aisha had given her. The pictures of elegant Parisian fashion no longer held her attention. She rose, walked around, and then ascended the spiral staircase to the next level. The room resembled a lookout, with chairs and tables arranged so one could look through the windows and enjoy the view. She sat in a deck chair and looked at the sheep and the deer grazing below. She ran her mind over all that had happened in the last few days.

She had been treated like a princess. No trouble had been spared to make her comfortable. No expense was spared to entertain and amuse her. There had been high praise for her talents and an exciting job offer. She had lapped it up. She had gone from misery and isolation a few months ago to an abundance of pleasure and happiness. It had been a steep stairway to bliss with only her bitter-sweet love for Geoff to trouble her. She thought of Didi's words on the dunes. What did he mean when he said he could give the love of a husband, while his father could offer everything else? Why the contrast? And then her sudden recoiling from Mr Al Refai's touch. She could not bear to think of where those questions led. It would spoil her opinion of the father who had been so considerate. Surely not? Surely, she had misunderstood Didi's meaning. She knew she had not. She shouldn't kid herself.

What would her mother say? Now, for the first time since Friday night, she focused her attention on her mother. She half closed her eyes while her head tilted back against the chair. Those familiar, intense blue eyes in the pale, unblemished face rose before her mind. What would she say about all the joy, attention, and privileges if she were there to talk to her? She concentrated on that face and the counsel she had given in the past. Estella did not know whether her eyes were closed or not, but the image of her mother's face seemed to leave the confines of her mental world and appear starkly outlined against the happenings of the last few days. She seemed to be present in body before her. She did not say anything. She just looked at Estella in sorrow.

Next moment, Estella was on her feet, leaning against the window and looking straight down into the reflecting dark green water of the moat below. She shuddered. She deserved the rebuke. She had let herself down by allowing the pleasures and praise to distort her judgment, luring her away from all that gave her comfort and meaning. Oh, what would Geoff say and think if he knew? Allowing Didi to embrace her and her inclination to let him kiss her shamed her. How could she—no matter how much affection she felt for him? She tried to tell herself that it was brotherly love, but gave up. She had betrayed Ruby, and now she had betrayed her love for Geoff.

Twice she had behaved that way in a matter of days. What was happening to her? Why was she losing connection with principles that had been second nature and so dear to her? Shame and despair passed through her. She wanted to be back in Binawarra. She wanted to be away from the temptation. The only thing she could think of at that moment was prayers in reparation for forgetting all that was right and precious to her. She fetched her rosary.

ANNEKE VAN Engelen left the school at lunchtime and hurried to the florist outside the Trefcenter. She did not have to wait long. Truus van den Donker emerged from the supermarket, anxiously looking around. Their eyes met.

'Mevrouw, I was hoping to find you here.'

'I was hoping to catch you, too, Anneke,' she said. 'I have been here every day. How is your uncle?'

'He's well considering his injuries. He is staying with my grandparents. I didn't know how badly he was injured, quite crippled now, but in good spirits. He asked after you. He would like to see you when you have a spare moment.'

'That's why I wanted to talk to you,' she said. 'Tell him he is welcome to visit me anytime at my house. I'm prepared to come to him, too, but I would like to talk in private.'

'I understand. What about Gerda?'

'It is time for her to know that your uncle saved her life. That's another reason I would like him to come to me. My daughter needs to be confronted with the truth.'

'How is it going with her in the house?'

'A little awkward. She has more or less taken over. She's preparing something she does not want me to know about. She has asked me to leave a couple of times. I am here now because she wanted the house to herself.'

'Why?'

'I don't know. I think she has had meetings there. At least, there have been indications somebody has visited.'

'You have no idea who and what it is about?'

Truus hesitated. 'Anneke, I can't help thinking you have an interest in what Gerda is doing. Looking back, it seems more than coincidental that you and your father made contact with me. And Cees was so abusive to your father on that day at the market.'

'You're right, Mevrouw, there is something, I confess. Someone is in danger, gone missing, and your daughter is mixed up in it.'

'What? Who?'

'I don't have time to explain. It's a long story, and I don't know all of it, but I assure you it's real. Please trust me. You will help if you keep me informed about what Gerda is doing and who she has contact with. The situation has reached a crisis point.'

'Is my husband mixed up in it, too?'

'It looks very much like it.'

'I will keep you informed,' said Truus. Her tone was one of resignation. Then she added, 'Is Fr. van Engelen aware of all this?'

'Yes, he is part of the effort to find the girl. It looks like the people visiting Gerda know where she is. Will you keep us informed?'

'The girl? Do you mean my husband and daughter are involved in the disappearance of a girl? Whatever for? Are you sure?'

'We are sure. Please trust me. By the way, does your husband own *Kasteel Zaligheid*?'

'Yes. Why? What has that to do with it?'

'My father has found no record of it belonging to his companies.'

'Anneke, I don't know anything about Cees's business affairs. I know about *Kasteel Zaligheid* because I heard him boast about it when it was acquired. He thought it was a wonderful joke that he managed to purchase such a grand symbol of papal corruption in Zeeland.'

'That's another confirmation,' said Anneke. 'Mevrouw, we think the girl may be there. I will explain everything later. I must get in contact with my father and then return to school. If you have any information, please leave a message at my parents' house.'

AT THREE-THIRTY, Geoff climbed down from the oak tree and headed for the meeting among the trees near the main road. By this time, Frans had brought Fr. van Engelen to join them.

'Are you all right, Father?' said Geoff, as he came to greet him.

'Quite all right, thank you, Geoff. You have discovered where Estella is, I have heard. What about Miss Barker?'

'There's no clear sign yet, but we must conclude she is also somewhere in the castle; either that or she has already been done away with.'

'Heaven forbid! We continue to pray that your efforts will free them both,' said the priest.

'Any news from your side?' said Geoff, addressing Frans.

'Anneke met with Mevrouw van den Donker in Middelburg. She said Gerda sent her away from the house as she had done a couple of times. She had the impression that Gerda was meeting someone.'

'That must have been around mid-afternoon when Anneke was with Gerda's mother,' said Geoff. 'A car left the castle not long before to return around forty minutes later. Mr Al Refai was the driver. Something is going on. There was also the hasty departure of Didi Al Refai. We must act. We can't afford to wait any longer. The whole thing smells of danger.'

'What ... what do you have in mind?' said Charles.

'When is Anneke free to join us?'

'Any time from now on,' said Frans.

'Will you ask her to come here as soon as she can? The rescue attempt will involve us all. Anneke's part will be crucial, and I need to discuss it with her.'

'I will make sure she gets the message.'

'Thank you. Charles and I will continue to monitor the castle and the sea passage. I don't think, though, that anything will happen before dark. Father, you should go with Mr van Engelen so you can rest. You can return this evening for what I have planned. You'll be needed. Mr van Engelen, please bring my two bags when you return. There are also a few other things I may need. This is what I would like, and this is a rough plan of what we will attempt. Timing will be critical.'

Chapter 33

The rescue

NASSER SALADIN crawled around Place Vendome, keeping an eye on the red Ferrari ahead. It parked outside The Ritz. The driver said a few words to the doormen and then disappeared inside. Saladin parked his car and hurried into the hotel foyer. He made several phone calls and returned to his car. Twenty minutes later, a car pulled up beside him. With an exchange of nods, they drove to a narrow street not far away. Two men on a motorbike joined them. They conferred. Five minutes later, taking a two-way radio receiver from one of the men, Saladin exchanged cars. At that moment, reporters and cameramen were gathering outside the hotel.

He waited in a back street, engine running. A street map of the area was spread on the steering wheel. 'He's just appeared,' came on the receiver. He readied himself. 'There's a large group of reporters and cameramen following him to his car. He's ducking and weaving.' There was a pause. 'He's heading for the Place de la Concorde.' Saladin set off. 'He's going to try to outrun them.' He jerked the wheel around to make a turn. 'We're close behind.' Another pause. 'He has taken off through the red light! The motorbike is keeping pace. He's gone right!'

Saladin flung the receiver and the map on the seat and slammed the accelerator to the floor. With tyres squealing and people leaping onto the footpath, he negotiated two narrow streets and came up beside the freeway, looking for a slip-road. One had to be close by. There it was. At a mad pace and with the car drifting as he swung onto it, he glanced to his left. No sign of the Ferrari. Then it appeared in his rear vision mirror, coming up behind him at a frightening speed with the motorbike on its tail. He had time only for a sharp manoeuvre to his left as he braked.

There was screeching of locking wheels and a violent collision with the back left-hand side of his car, sending him jerking and lurching to the right. He struggled to keep control as the car swung sharply to the left. The driver of the Ferrari was too late to break the momentum of the accelerating car. He went into several careening swerves, first to the left and then to the right, and then smashed with a thunderous clap into a pillar beside the road. Saladin came to a stop and looked behind at the steaming and smoking wreck. The men on the motorbike were looking into it. He got a signal. The bike took off and raced past him. He took off, too, and saw with a glance in the rear vision mirror that the reporters and cameramen had caught up. He grabbed the receiver off the passenger seat and shouted, 'Place de l'Etoile!'

Within five minutes, he had exchanged cars. Sometime later, while he was racing at high speed along the freeway north towards Holland, several men in a workshop in an industrial area outside Paris worked feverishly to disassemble a car's engine and cut up its body.

THE RAYS of the afternoon sun streamed at an angle into Miss Barker's room. Her tan high-heeled shoes were lit up on the windowsill. If anyone was surveying the castle buildings from trees opposite, the chances were they would see the shoes now. She peered at the trees. She saw only the front-line trees. Her eyes could not penetrate the sombre shade of the forest. She pushed her face against the window, so the sun lit up part of it. She could only hope that someone was looking directly at her window.

Geoff had established that Estella was on the top level of the tower. There she remained except for two occasions when she descended to the lower level. Within minutes, she was back. Nobody was with her, and nobody had come there since before lunch. She had taken up a position in the one chair between bouts of walking from window to window. She was uneasy. There had been a significant change in her bearing from when he caught sight of her with Didi Al Refai.

To distract himself from his painful thoughts, he ran his binoculars over the castle buildings, one by one. He was passing over the first building on the bailey when he caught sight of something in the window. It had not been there before. At least he had not seen it. He focused and saw it was a pair of shoes, high-heeled shoes. They were familiar. And then Miss Barker's face appeared in the sunlight. He blew out a breath of relief. Until then, he had had grave fears for her. Now he could firm up his plans.

A difficulty was alerting Miss Barker to his presence. Any signal to her would risk alerting unwelcome eyes. The security people were few and unobtrusive, yet continually present. It was unlikely that their surveillance covered the area around his tree, but he could not risk being too obvious. The only tactic was to climb as high as he could in the tree and sway the top branches in a way only human hands could do. He carried out his plan, keeping an eye on the window. After some time, a hand waved in the same rhythm as the branches. He stopped his waving, and the hand stopped. Good, she knew he was there. It was past four o'clock. He climbed down from the tree and went to meet Anneke.

AISHA CALLED Estella from below. There was a change in the usually calm voice, and Estella hurried down the spiral staircase. Aisha, her face contorted and her eyes red and swollen, rushed to Estella and threw her arms around her. She rested her head on her shoulder and burst into tears.

'What's happened?' said Estella, panic rising within her. 'What's wrong?' Her guilt-ridden mind was imagining some sort of merited retribution.

'No, no, no,' said Aisha. 'Something terrible has happened. It's got nothing to do with you.'

'What is it?' said Estella, relieved but then sorry for her selfish reaction. She held Aisha tightly, her body shaking with emotion. It was a stunning change. Aisha, the older, confident, and more mature sister, clung to her like a little girl. 'Tell me what's wrong.'

'No, I can't tell you. Father says we are not to say anything.'

She continued to cling to Estella without speaking. There was an occasional sob. At length, she disengaged herself and wiped her eyes.

'No matter what has happened, our affection for you is sincere,' she said. 'We would never want you to do something you did not want to do.' She held her hand up when she saw that Estella was going to speak. 'No, I have a brief message from Father. Tonight's function has been cancelled. The preparations have ceased, and most of the staff are leaving. We are sorry about it. We regret any inconvenience we have caused. We have come to appreciate you even more since—' She broke off while she caught her breath. 'We are returning to Paris immediately, Father, Tahani, and I. You will stay here until this evening, when you will be driven directly to the airport. I am sorry, I cannot say anything more.'

'I understand,' said Estella, taking her hand. 'I will not cause you difficulty. I will wait as you wish until tonight.'

'Father would like you to stay in your quarters if you don't mind until the car is ready to take you. Please.'

'I will do as you say.'

'Thank you. An attendant will bring you afternoon tea and dinner. He will call on you regularly to ensure you are comfortable.'

'Thank you.'

'Now, I must go.' She kissed Estella on both cheeks and hurried from the suite.

Estella climbed back to the upper level and took her seat in front of the same window. The sun was going down in a clear sky. The calm, peaceful atmosphere belied the turmoil in the castle. A limousine was departing. She got up and watched the car until it turned right onto the main road and drove out of sight. She turned from the window, her eyes brimming from Aisha's sudden overwhelming sorrow. Why would she not say what it was about?

GEOFF AND Anneke hurried off the footpath when they heard the car. They were just in time to hide among the trees when the limousine appeared and turned right in front of them. The windows were darkened, but Geoff thought he could make out three people in the back. He raced through the trees to where he had a clear view of the tower's windows. He focused his binoculars. Estella was standing at her window. What was happening?

'Is she still there?' whispered Anneke.

'Yes, thank God,' he said, lowering the binoculars. 'You know what to get?'

'Yes, I'll get everything you want.'

'Good, go now and try to catch the limousine. See where it goes. I have an idea it will stop at Mrs van den Donker's house.'

'Why?'

'I don't know,' said Geoff. 'Things are going wrong.' At that moment, a group of bike riders passed along the side road. 'The staff are leaving. Something's definitely up.'

'It seems so.'

'If the staff is leaving *en masse*, something has to be amiss. Follow the limousine to see where it goes. If it stops, don't do anything, for heaven's sake. Just observe and then go and get the things I have asked for. Okay?'

Within five minutes, she had caught up with the limousine, just as it arrived on the other side of Oostkapelle. As the two cars emerged from Vrouwekerke, the limousine turned into the side street and parked in Mevrouw van den Donker's drive.

GERDA SHOWED Mr Al Refai quickly into her makeshift office, but she could not hide him from her mother sitting in the lounge room. Truus turned her gaze away as he walked by the living room door. When she heard the door close, she rose and stole into the hall. She stood listening.

'I don't want to hear a word from you,' Mr Al Refai said, refusing the seat offered him. 'My son was gravely injured this afternoon in a car accident in Paris. At least, that is the public report. My associates, however, tell me there is something suspicious about this. It happened after you had told me you would not allow a change to our agreement. I am returning to Paris to supervise an investigation. Let me tell you, Ms Vrouwendijk, if you and your organisation have anything to do with this, you will pay dearly. You must pray that my son survives his injuries.' He turned, looked around, and, seeing the photos of Aine Winterbine, ripped them from the wall. 'If your mad ideas are behind this, I will see your organisation destroyed to the last comma.'

'I will excuse the behaviour of a grief-stricken father,' said Gerda, holding his gaze. 'I will defend my innocence and the innocence of my organisation—to the last drop of my blood and energy.'

He looked at her with contempt. 'That may be the cost. You have said it.' He trampled over the photos and left the room. Gerda followed him and watched the limousine depart. She returned to her office, disregarding the inquiring looks of her mother. She picked up the photos, smoothed and caressed them on her desk, and went to the phone. 'Tell Boris to call me as soon as he makes contact. It's urgent. I will be on the second number for the next hour.' She returned to her room, stuffed some papers into her bag, and hurried to her car, all the time ignoring her mother.

Standing at the front window, Truus van den Donker watched her daughter depart. She rang the Van Engelen number. Anneke had just arrived home. After passing on her information, she went to Gerda's room. She entered the room fearfully and looked around. There was nothing unusual except the poster-size photos of a beautiful fair woman lying on Gerda's desk.

A LITTLE after six o'clock, the group assembled among the trees not far from the corner of the main road with the castle grounds. Each, as instructed, wore dark clothing. The sun had set, leaving a lingering light for them to see by. The outline of Geoff's determined face was just visible to his small team.

'Now, you are all aware of the plan and the role each will play. We are to move when I give the signal. There is lessening activity around the front of the main building, which supports the impression that the castle is in the last phase of shutting down rather than preparing for a reception. Whichever way it goes, we won't be able to act before ten o'clock. When we do go, we need to go with speed and surprise. Anneke and Fr. van Engelen will take the watch on this side of the castle. Charles and Mr van Engelen will take turns keeping surveillance from the dunes. We must be prepared for anything that happens from the seaside.'

'What could happen from the sea?' said Charles.

'I don't know. Anneke and I saw signalling last night. We don't know what it could mean or whether it was meant for the castle. We don't know. But we must cover all options. Something's happening. The people responsible for abducting Estella have left the castle, and Estella has remained in the castle tower the whole afternoon. It's absolutely imperative that we keep a lookout so we can deal with every move. Okay, let's take up our positions, and please report anything suspicious or out of the ordinary.'

They split up and went to their positions. Geoff took out his torch and checked the equipment. Satisfied he could act with what he had, he prepared himself. Not far away, by the trees bordering the main road, Anneke could see his outline as he undressed, put on his dry suit, strapped knives to his right calf and left side in their sheaths, and put his dark clothes back on over the dry suit. As before, she was impressed not only by his physical strength but by his strength of character. She knew by then he was in love with the girl in the tower. She saw him tying something around his left wrist. The coincidence was ironic.

AS SOON as the phone started to ring, Gerda hurried from her room. Truus edged her way to the kitchen door and listened.

'I want you to remove both tonight,' Gerda whispered in English. 'The plan must be aborted. I will return to London tomorrow. Ring again when they have been extracted. The Barker woman must be dealt with. Prepare for it. The girl is not to be harmed, not even a scratch. Make sure you take all her clothes with her, carefully packed. Understood?' She put the phone down and returned to her room.

Truus stood at the kitchen sink, turning over her daughter's conversation in her mind. She understood little of what Gerda had said. But there was a tone of urgency in the whispering. London was mentioned. She continued to do the washing-up while considering what to do. At least ring and pass on the message to Anneke. She would have to wait for her opportunity. Gerda's room was too close to the phone. The difficulty was removed when Gerda came to tell her she would be out for a while, but would return if anyone rang.

'How long are you going to use my car?' she asked as casually as she could.

'I will return to London tomorrow,' said Gerda, preoccupied, and disappeared through the front door.

As soon as the car's engine faded into the night air, Truus rang Anneke's number. She was not surprised to hear from Marijke that Anneke was out for the evening. Was there anything she could do? Take a message? No, she said undecided. She put the phone down and fell to thinking. She had never done anything audacious in her life. She had followed Cees meekly to Amsterdam during the war, and then back again. She had put up with all he and her daughter had dished out over the years. Her first difficult step to independence had come with her offer to look after the priest she loved. Now, circumstances quite different but more demanding faced her. Something was going on, and she may have vital information.

GEOFF HAD stationed Fr. van Engelen among the trees near the main road to keep an eye on the traffic while the others focused on the castle. He wanted him rested because his spiritual comfort may be needed once he had extracted Estella. Just before eight o'clock, a bike came to a stop at the corner of the castle grounds. A woman in a thick coat and a scarf around her head walked a little way along the castle fence, stopped and walked back again. She looked along the side road. She turned, came back and stopped. 'Anneke, are you there? Anneke, are you there?' the priest heard. He took his stick and struggled among the trees to the edge of the road. 'Is that you, Truus?' She started. 'Please, don't be alarmed. It's me, Fr. van Engelen. Come in between the trees. We don't want to be seen.' She wheeled her bike in among the trees and stood facing the priest who had been on her mind since her rescue on Dam Square. She took a deep breath.

'Anneke's not far away,' he whispered.

'I have some information for her.'

There was a rustle among the trees, and Anneke appeared. Not evincing any surprise, Anneke listened to what Truus had to say and then fetched Geoff.

'Ask her to recount every detail, every detail exactly,' Geoff said after Truus had repeated her information.

'Gerda received what appeared to be an urgent phone call,' Anneke said when Truus again repeated her message. 'She thought a troubled Gerda gave urgent instructions to whoever she was talking to. Gerda told her she was leaving for London tomorrow.'

'Leaving tomorrow?' said Geoff. His thoughts were interrupted by Frans's voice crackling through the two-way radio receiver.

'A merchant ship has approached close to the coast and is slowing. There appears to be activity on the deck. Over.'

'Keep an eye on it and keep me informed. Watch to see if they drop a dinghy overboard. Over.'

Tensed by the unfamiliar circumstances, the group watched Geoff in helpless silence.

'It's much earlier than I had wished,' he said, 'but we have no choice. It's time to move. Anneke, will you thank Mrs van den Donker and ask her to return home? Tell her to stay there in case Gerda turns up. I don't want her here.'

'I will attend to Mevrouw van den Donker,' said Fr. van Engelen.

While Geoff conferred with Charles and Anneke, the priest accompanied Truus to her bike. 'I am sorry that your husband and daughter seem to be at the centre of this problem,' he said, laying his hand on her arm in comfort.

'I suppose it had to come to a head in the end,' she said. 'It was not only the way they have treated me. It's dawning on me how much they hid from me. It confirms me in my decision.'

'We shall talk about it when you want to.'

'Would you come to my house tomorrow morning? I want Gerda to see you and to know what happened.'

'Gerda knows me very well, I have to warn you.'

'What? How?'

'Truus, it is part of the story. Gerda has been living in the same country town as I have during these last few months. It's part of her duplicity, I am afraid. But let's leave it until tomorrow. I will be there at nine o'clock.'

Truus nodded sadly and rode off. The priest, his heart aching for the sorrow Truus van den Donker had suffered through the years, returned to his position among the trees and began saying his rosary. He could hear Geoff talking quietly to Charles and Anneke.

'Have we understood?' Geoff said. They understood. 'Well, let's get our little group of amateurs into action. Charles, whatever happens, don't move from the fence until I call you. Come on, Anneke, let's go.'

Geoff and Anneke crept to the corner of the fence. With wire cutters, Geoff clipped an opening and handed the tool to Charles, who retreated to his position among the trees. With a coil of rope around his neck and carrying a cloth bag over his shoulder, he climbed through and held the wire open for Anneke. Anneke, with a canvas bag in one hand and the two-way radio in the other, followed him. They jumped over the narrow ditch. After walking a few paces, Geoff took her by the arm. He crouched down.

'This is it, Anneke. You are not afraid?'

'No. I'm with you, Geoff. I owe you.'

'Okay, you have the two-way radio receiver. Now keep in contact with your father and speak only in Dutch. No English.'

'Ja, Meneer.'

He looked at her in the dim light and could see her old waggishness on her pretty face. It suited the action that she was relaxed enough to make light of it. She had reasons to feel the trauma of seven years ago revisiting her.

'Ask your father to keep us informed of everything that happens on the boat. Everything. But keep the volume down.'

'Ja, Meneer,' she said again.

'I'm off now. You know what to do. Keep down and stay at least ten yards behind me.'

'Yards?'

'Metres, then. Remember, you will act as my lookout while I concentrate on my task. I don't want anyone to see two figures together roaming over the fields. You're slight enough to escape notice if you are by yourself. Okay? Now, do as I have told you this time. No deviation,' he finished. 'It's serious.'

'Ja, Meneer,' she repeated and smiled at him.

He gave her an encouraging pat on the shoulder and slunk off. They made their way unhindered by animal or obstacle to the hedge that separated the open grassy expanse from the garden. As Geoff crept along the hedge, he heard Anneke talking softly to her father. He turned, and she shook her head. He continued until he reached the moat. He waved to Anneke to stay down. He looked up at the tower. The upper level was now in darkness, and the windows on the second level were glowing faintly. That would make it difficult if Estella were not on the upper level and the window was shut and fastened. The two-way radio crackled. Anneke crawled over to him.

'Pappa says someone is on the dunes about fifty metres along from him and he is signalling to the ship with a torch.'

'Right, we have to hurry,' he whispered. 'Keep with me now and stay down behind the hedge. Tell me if there is more activity on the ship.'

He stared at the stairwell wall. He was fairly sure he would find enough gaps between the old bricks to get a sufficient foothold and handhold. But he could not be certain. Should he take his equipment to fix the climbing supports in the wall or try without them? Time was at a premium. Then Frans's voice came over the two-way radio. He waited.

'Pappa says they are getting a rubber runabout ready.'

'Okay, I can't wait any longer. You know what to do.'

He placed the bag on the ground and took out a harness. He would risk it without the climbing supports. He then stripped down to his dry suit and lightweight climbing shoes. He fitted the harness over the dry suit and eased himself into the water with the coil of rope around his neck. The water was freezing. He breaststroked to the wall and felt along it. He was relieved to find the cement between the bricks eroded by time and weather. He pushed himself through the water to the junction of the stairwell with the wall of the wing. It was slippery under the water, but he finally got a foothold and reached up, his fingers searching for a hold. He got one. He bowed his head and pleaded with Estella's God. He eased himself out of the water and moved successively from foothold to handhold towards the top of the stairwell.

He was fortunate that the angle of the stairwell with the wall provided firm support and even more fortunate that the long, narrow windows in the stairwell were close enough to give him an extra boost. As he arrived level with the window on the second level, he looked in. No one. At least he could not see anyone. The thought that Estella could be somewhere else gnawed at him. But she was there not long before, and he had not observed any movement from the upper level. He must go on.

When he reached the rooftop, he looked down at Anneke crouching behind the hedge on the other side of the moat. She waved urgently. The rubber runabout must be on its way. He edged up the sloping roof to a point level with the tower's upper floor. The first window was only a couple of yards away now. There was a ledge around the tower under the windows, wide enough for him to walk along. He climbed onto the ledge and inched along it. The window was ajar. As the window opened towards him, he had to go by it before he could open it fully. He did so, turned and opened it, and in a loud whisper called Estella's name.

ESTELLA HAD grown despondent during the afternoon as the full meaning of her behaviour became painfully clear. Shame possessed her. It had been a painful irony that while Didi was praising her for her inner life and resolving to restore his, she was letting hers flow away. The praise and luxury now covered her body like a stain. She was aching to cleanse herself of it, aching to go home, to be with her parents, to be in her garden, and to be with Ruby and Geoff again. They seemed so far away in time and distance. These despairing thoughts had occupied her in her loneliness.

When the light faded, she remained sitting in the dark, staring through the window. She had no inclination to move. At length, she sought consolation in her prayers. Now, as she knelt beside her chair and was finishing her rosary, she heard scraping outside the window. Then a shadow passed over it. Frightened, she sprang to her feet. The window opened slowly. She waited, trembling. A feeling of unreality took hold of her. Then Geoff's voice called her name.

'Oh!' she said, sharply drawing breath.

At her cry, the window was pushed open, and a figure in dark clothing climbed through. She put her hand to her mouth and swayed as she recognised the silhouette against the scant light from the spiral staircase, but she did not know whether she was dreaming. How could it be? The next moment, Geoff had caught her.

'Estella, it's really me,' said Geoff holding her. 'Don't be afraid. Listen carefully and stay calm. I'll explain everything later. You are in grave danger. I must get you out of here.'

'What's happening?' she said, reviving as she understood she was not talking to a phantom. 'What danger?'

'Estella, I beg you. Leave all the questions until I get you out.' She nodded, hearing his urgency. He looked at what she had on. Fortunately, her clothing—light slacks, a jumper over a top, and light casual shoes—was as suitable as could be expected in the circumstances. Without resisting, she let him take her jumper off. He took the coil of rope from around his neck and undid the harness. He manoeuvred her arms through the loops and did it up. He attached the rope. 'I'm going to lower you to the moat. Understand?' She nodded. 'The water is extremely cold. Don't attempt to swim across the moat by yourself. Wait until I join you. Understood?' Shock was setting in. Her eyes were dilated, and she was nodding mechanically. 'Estella, concentrate only on what we are doing. Everything will be clear once you are out of here. Your father is waiting for you, too.'

'My father?' she said, breathing in gasps.

'Yes, you'll be safe and among people who love you. Just concentrate for the moment. Don't mind anything else.' He led her to the window. 'Now, remember, hang on to the wall when you reach the water. Wait until I am with you before I undo the rope, and we swim across the moat. Understood?' She nodded distractedly. He put on the gloves he had tucked inside his dry suit and helped her onto the ledge outside the window. She did not appear afraid. Instead, she stared at him unseeingly while he held her steady with the rope. 'Now crouch and lower yourself over the edge. I have hold of you, so don't worry.'

She did as instructed. The rope tightened as she climbed over the edge. His face disappeared. There were slight jerks as he lowered her. The harness was tight around her armpits and back, and she steadied herself against the wall. She felt no fear from the height or what was happening. She was too overwhelmed to have any fear. Geoff's comforting voice drifted down to her, only making it worse.

She could hardly reconcile his presence in the tower. How did he come to be there? He must have been present somewhere to have known where she was. Then the realisation pierced her to the core of her being; he must be aware of what she had been doing. He must be aware of her terrible betrayal. Did he see her let Didi embrace her? He must have. What danger was he saving her from? Why had he seen it and not she? These questions turned over and over in her mind in the eternity of time it took to slide down the tower wall. Then she gasped as she plunged into the freezing water. She tried to clutch the wall, but she could not hang on. She swayed around at the end of the rope, her head dipping into the water.

Geoff felt the slack on the rope and came to the window. He drew in the slack. Anneke ran to the water's edge. 'Don't!' he called in a loud whisper and was relieved to see her hang back. 'Stay where you are.' He did not want Anneke risking herself. She still had much critical support to give. He looked around for something to anchor the rope on. He fastened the rope to the back of the deck chair and mounted the window. He turned and, securing the chair lengthwise across the window frame, let the rope take his full weight. The chair locked into place. He descended as quickly as he could.

Amid the numbing cold and the despairing realisation of how her betrayal contrasted with Geoff's kindness and loyalty, Estella felt him untie the rope and take her by the chin. Now they were moving through the water. She did not know where she was going or what to do. She abandoned herself to his guidance. As she was lifted from the water, she heard a girl's voice with a slight accent.

'The runabout has landed on the beach, and men are approaching.'

'Tell your father to return to his car and park it at the front, and be ready now.' Geoff half-carried and half-walked Estella along the hedge. He waited until Anneke had relayed the message. 'Give me the blanket.' He undid the harness, took the blanket from Anneke, and wrapped it around Estella. 'Estella, take off your clothes. Quick! We have dry clothes for you.' He tightened the blanket around her to show she had protection. She did not move. 'Estella, take your clothes off. Quickly! Anneke will slip a dry woollen dress over you once the wet clothes are off. You need to warm up.'

'Geoff, she's in shock. Come on. You take them off. I'll hold the blanket.' Geoff hesitated. 'Geoff, there's no time.'

He let Anneke take the ends of the blanket so that he and Estella were enclosed in it. He slipped the top off over her head, took the dress from Anneke, and put it on her. In one movement, he pulled her slacks down to her ankles and then the rest of the dress over her. The change seemed to bring Estella to herself. She looked at Geoff, leaned against him, and began weeping.

'I'm sorry,' she said and put her arms around him.

Geoff felt her clinging to him, murmuring, her body shivering and shaking. 'Come on. We must hurry.' Again, she did not move. In one movement, he scooped her off the ground and started towards the boundary fence. Anneke picked up her clothes, stuffed them in the bag, and followed. Charles appeared out of the darkness.

'Thank God!' he said, seeing his daughter in Geoff's arms.

'Here, take her,' said Geoff. 'Put her in the car and keep her warm, but wait for me. Only move off if you're in danger. Anneke?'

Anneke nodded. Charles took Estella into his arms, but Geoff had disappeared into the murky darkness before he could say anything. Charles hurried with Anneke to the opening in the fence. Soon, Estella was in the back of Frans's car between Charles and Fr. van Engelen. She clung to her father while he and the priest consoled and reassured her.

GEOFF REACHED the moat, skirted around the hedge at the water's edge, and came to a point opposite the building on the bailey. A light was on inside. No sound or movement was coming from the bailey courtyard. He found some pebbles and pelted them at the window opposite. One struck the mark, and Miss Barker's face appeared peering into the dark. Thank God she was still there. She waved and gestured her relief. He signalled that he was coming across the moat. Then, he heard voices coming from the direction of the bridge over the moat to the bailey. Miss Barker nodded igorously and pointed to his left. She disappeared. He had planned to swim across the moat and climb up onto the courtyard at a point nearest the door of Miss Barker's quarters. There was no time for that now. He concentrated. It was likely they planned to take Miss Barker to the ship lying offshore. There was only one choice. He understood why Miss Barker pointed to his left.

He ran to where the moat joined the canal alongside the driveway to the front fence. He eased himself into the water and swam to the other bank. Now he was on the castle's ground side. He pushed himself through the water until he came to the small bridge to the bailey. The voices became clearer. There were three men at a guess. He waited. They were coming towards him. He climbed out of the water and crouched on the grassy slope beside the bridge. He turned and looked across the moat. Anneke had taken up position. He braced himself. He felt the knives strapped to his calf and side.

Nasser Saladin had dispatched one of his companions to fetch the girl from the tower while he and his two companions took care of Miss Barker. As the three men were passing over the bridge with Miss Barker, who offered no resistance, a loud cry rang out from the tower. 'Ambush!' Saladin swung in the direction of the voice. Geoff leapt up over the side of the bridge and, in one movement, landed a blow on Saladin's temple. Saladin jerked to the side and dropped heavily. His companions, stupefied by the sight of him lying twitching on the ground, let go of Miss Barker. Taking advantage of these fatal instants of inaction, Geoff grabbed a second man in a continuous movement and flung him over the railing. The water splashed up over the bridge while the man spluttered and gasped for breath in the freezing water. Grabbing Miss Barker's arm, Geoff dragged her to the water's edge and pushed her in. 'Quick, across the moat. There's a blanket on the other side.'

He turned to face the third man, who had come to his senses and was rushing onto him, holding a knife outstretched. With a duck and a feint to one side, Geoff drew his knife from the calf sheath and, in an upward lunge, slashed the man's neck and pierced his shoulder. Blood gushed, and the man dropped back, groaning and holding himself. Geoff plunged into the water and caught up with Miss Barker, who was making slow progress. He helped her the rest of the way and out of the water, where Anneke draped a thick blanket around her.

'Are you all right?' he said. 'Do you want to discard your wet clothes? Anneke has dry clothes here.'

'No, no,' said Miss Barker, recovering now with the blanket wrapped around her. 'Do you have Estella?'

'Yes, she's safe.'

'Then we should get out of here,' she said, between her clattering teeth. 'Thank you, young lady,' she added.

'Yes, go, follow Anneke,' said Geoff, looking across the moat to see what Saladin and his companions would do.

The man with the slashed neck and pierced shoulder had disappeared. The man in the water had crawled out and was sitting shivering on the grassy slope, catching his breath. Dazed, Saladin was staggering to his feet and looking around as the man from the tower arrived at his side. He said something to his companion, who pointed at Geoff. Puffing, muttering, and gesticulating, Saladin limped along the bank towards Geoff, trying to get up to a run with the man from the tower cautiously following. But it was no use, he had been dealt a disabling blow, and it would take some time to recover. Geoff held his ground. If Saladin attempted to cross the moat, he would immobilise him for good. But Saladin knew he was in no state to continue the fight.

'You will keep, Crusader boy,' he snarled, his pent-up hatred seeking release. 'I have not finished with you and your girlfriend, no matter what else happens.'

'I have one message for you and those you take orders from,' said Geoff. 'You will get at Estella Winterbine over my dead body.'

'That's the way I want it, Crusader scum. The infidel is never destined to triumph over Allah's servant.' He stared wildly and made meaningless gestures at Geoff.

'You have established the battleground,' returned Geoff. 'You will not survive another attempt.'

'Hah! You kaffir dog—' but nothing else would come from his mouth as he swayed and staggered a few steps back. His companion supported him.

Geoff held his mad gaze and then made off. He arrived at the fence to find Anneke's and Frans's cars parked as arranged. He went straight to Frans's car. Estella had recovered from the shock, but she clung to her father with her face turned into his chest. When she heard Geoff speak, she looked up and was about to say something, but stopped when she saw her handkerchief tied around the wrist resting on the open window.

'Thank you, Geoff,' she said as she bowed her head.

'She'll be all right, Geoff. Give her time,' said Charles. 'We can't express enough gratitude for what you have done.'

It was a duty of friendship and esteem, said Geoff, leaving them to go on their way. Anneke noticed the handkerchief when he got into the car.

Are you all right?' she said as she prepared to follow her father's car.

'Me? Of course,' Geoff answered, and then coming to himself, 'We should be asking Miss Barker.'

'Oh, I'm quite all right, Captain Shawcross,' she said. 'I had never given up hope.' She reached over and gave him a friendly pat.

'I got vital support from everyone,' said Geoff, glancing back over his shoulder, 'especially from Anneke.'

'I understand, Miss van Engelen. Your role is much appreciated.'

Anneke acknowledged Miss Barker's thanks and drove to her hotel in Middelburg. While they waited for her to shower and dress, Geoff remained subdued and thoughtful. Anneke left him to his thoughts, only passing a few comments, to which he barely made sensible replies. Miss Barker appeared after twenty minutes, refreshed and dressed smartly as if nothing had happened. They drove to the van Engelen house on the Singel where they found that Estella had retired.

Charles took Geoff's hand and shook it again, expressing his profound thanks for what he had done. Aine had received the good news and sent Geoff her most profound gratitude. It was the answer to their prayers. Estella was too upset to be in company and had gone to bed. In the morning, she would be better, and they could talk. Geoff was happy that she was resting. He excused himself and left to shower and put on clean clothes. While Miss Barker and Fr. van Engelen discussed the course of events, each filling in the different parts of the story they knew best, Charles returned to Estella. He found her sitting up in bed, clutching her knees, and staring at the blankets in front of her. She looked up, her face pained.

'Aren't you relieved that it is all over?' he said, putting his arm around her. 'It seemed to have reached a dangerous point at the end. Geoff was very brave.'

'I know. I owe him so much—' She took a deep breath. 'I didn't see what was happening. And I should have. I should have realised where I was being led. Or perhaps I did. Yes, maybe I did. I was blinded— I never thought I would be—'

'No, Darling, don't be hard on yourself. Put it out of your mind for now. Have a good sleep. We can discuss it after you are rested and better able to put it in the right perspective. You've been through a frightening ordeal. Perhaps you don't yet realise how frightening.' He paused. 'Do you want to see Geoff for a moment? We owe it all to him.'

She shook her head. 'May I see Fr. van Engelen?' she whispered at length.

'Of course, darling, I will ask him to come in.'

'I would like to go to confession, Father,' she said when the priest entered the room.

'As you wish, Estella,' he said, taking a nearby chair and positioning it so that he was looking directly at her. 'I would like to talk to you first, in a way that belongs to a conversation rather than the confessional.' She bowed her head. 'Miss Barker and I have been explaining to my brother, his wife, and his daughter what led to your abduction.' She looked up. 'Yes, it was a meticulously planned abduction. Although we were aware of a general plan and those involved, we were never sure about the details. I will tell you what we know.'

Fr. van Engelen related the course of events and the connection between Miss Bicknell, Mr Rostowski, and Mr Al Refai. Estella listened with growing consternation. It corresponded with all that she had experienced. The praise and the pleasure were aimed at seducing her in every way, and it had been succeeding. How could she have fallen so easily? She should have been shocked at what Fr. van Engelen was telling her, but all she could feel was despair for refusing to face what was happening under her nose.

'Was Didi Al Refai in the plan, too?' she was almost afraid to ask.

'No, as far as we know, he had nothing to do with it. It was as he said. He met you by chance.'

That was a great relief. She was reminded of the frequent assurances by the Al Refai sisters that they would never do anything to hurt her, would never make her do anything she did not want, and that their regard for her was sincere. She thought they were being honest. But how could they cooperate in the plan to seduce her? She knew the answer. They had left her to make her own decisions about what she did. They were right. They and their father had forced her to do nothing. She had been left to exercise her free will.

'Can you tell me what is upsetting you?' said the priest.

'The depth of my betrayal.'

'Who do you think you betrayed, especially?'

'Geoff,' she said, relieved to have said it aloud at last. 'And he was the one responsible for getting me out of there. I cannot look him in the face. I would die of shame.'

'Estella, Geoff is not the type to change his mind about someone he holds in high regard. I am sure he understands how cleverly you were drawn into the trap. If you are honest with him about what happened and you really love him, it will not change his feelings.'

'Oh, I can't.'

'Do you want to tell me what happened?' he said. 'It is your business in the long run ... so, only if you want to ...'

Estella, at first wondering at the delicacy of Fr. van Engelen's manner, understood. In that respect, at least, she could put him at ease. She related how she was drawn in by the praise of her appearance, the expensive, elegant clothes, the luxurious circumstances, and the promise that it would all be hers if she accepted Mr Al Refai's job offer. She had let Didi embrace her, knowing it was an embrace of love. Her pitiful self-deception began to dissolve after the incident with Didi. And when Geoff appeared in the castle tower, having risked great danger, it hit her how deep her betrayal was. She may not have succumbed completely, but the turning of her mind had already been achieved. The wrong had been done. She did not deserve Geoff.

'But was it? You saw through it all in the end, didn't you? You resisted.'

'Father, I must be honest with myself. It was just not the praise and luxury and Didi's embrace. I was attracted to a handsome, elegant man who was years older, but it was not an attraction of love. I suppose ... I suppose you would call it seduction ... but it was willing. How can you call willingness an abduction? A week ago, the very thought of such an attraction would have disgusted me. How could I ever explain to Geoff—I can't explain it to myself? I am such a hypocrite.'

'Temptation. You were drawn strongly by temptation, but in the end, you did not give in to it. You must understand that we are all tempted. Even Our Lord had to rebuke the devil for his efforts to tempt Him. And don't you recognise the same sort of temptations, the same pattern? They are the false promises of power, pleasure, and adulation. You must be happy and grateful to Our Lord that you were able to overcome them.' He leant forward. 'Estella, it's important for you to understand that you are a maturing young woman who is facing the sort of emotions that most of us must face, even those in the religious life. It's the way of our lives and the way of the world.' Estella glanced at the priest. His words were comforting, if nothing else.

'Our moral life is about dealing properly with those emotions,' the priest continued. 'Particular temptation will not end for you, or for me, or for your loved ones until we all depart this life and have to give an account of ourselves.' He paused. 'You can also be too scrupulous, you know. That is also a fault. You must be careful of that.' He paused again. 'There is something else. You must pay due tribute to the selflessness of those who set out to rescue you, particularly Geoff. And in the end, it was not only moral danger that surrounded you. It appears there was a break in the partnership between Miss Bicknell and Mr Al Refai. When Geoff reached you in the tower, people were on the way to take you and Miss Barker to a ship lying offshore. Do you appreciate that?'

'Daddy said that it had become dangerous. I had no idea. I thought I would be taken to Paris.'

'We don't know yet what happened, but certainly, you were not being taken to Paris. You must understand the reasons why Geoff took the action he did. You may be able to mitigate the motives of Mr Al Refai, but do not let your scruples blind you to Gerda van den Donker's plans.'

'Oh, no, Father, it's because of Geoff's goodness and bravery that I feel undeserving.'

'Do you love, Geoff?'

'More than anything.'

'Then you should let him decide whether you're deserving or not. He came to rescue you, to do you a service. Unconditionally.'

'I will never forget it.'

'He does not know the depth of affection you have for him. You must tell him.'

There was a long silence. Fr. van Engelen waited. At last, she said she felt better having spoken about it, but she could not rid herself of the shame and betrayal.

'I can't look him in the face.'

'You must give yourself time. And trust those around you. You have had a bad experience.' He looked at her sympathetically. 'Now, tell me, how much of what you have told me do you want to remain confidential? You know, everyone is concerned about you.'

'I will leave that up to you, Father. I trust you.'

'I will treat what you have said with respect and discretion.'

'Thank you, Father. Now, will you hear my confession?'

Fr van Engelen shifted his chair, bowed his head, and closed his eyes. For a minute, he remained in prayer while Estella waited. Then, making the sign of the cross, he inclined his head towards her with his eyes still closed.

Chapter 34

Return home

GEOFF WAS up early the next morning. The tension and exertion of the previous days had helped him to sleep soundly. But once the sleep was over, that was it. His mind was churning. It was a great relief that he had rescued Estella unharmed, but the relief let loose the many postponed feelings and thoughts now crowding him. He was glad for Charles and Aine's sake that she had come to no moral harm. He understood their primary concern. He had suspected, though, that the physical danger was the greater threat. Estella's inner self was strong. She might be fooled about people's intentions, but once aware that they were leading her down the wrong path, she would retreat. Fr. van Engelen had confirmed this. No, his suspicions were correct.

Gerda van den Donker's plans were an all-or-nothing enterprise. What, for example, would they do with Estella once it became clear that she would not cooperate? She had too much on them. Mr Al Refai and his family might have been reluctant, but Gerda would not hesitate to preserve her interests. And the psychopathic Saladin had no hesitation in being her weapon. As it turned out, they had outsmarted Gerda and extracted Estella from danger. He was profoundly relieved and glad of it. There were two things that his mind now dwelt on.

First, the physical danger was not at an end. Saladin's threat was not idle. He had a vivid image of the face contorted by hatred looking at him from across the moat. There could be no doubt. Saladin would attempt to complete the task. Indeed, it was likely to be sooner rather than later. He had said nothing about it yet to anyone, including Miss Barker. He had to work through what he would do, and he did not want to upset Estella anymore. At the right time, when they were back in Binawarra, he would discuss it with Miss Barker. In any event, he would have to maintain secret surveillance over Estella and the Winterbine house. That could be difficult, especially considering the second issue that would not leave him in peace.

He thought back over all that had happened. His affection for Estella had steadily grown until she replaced Ruby in his feelings. She returned that affection. How much, he was never sure. Then the kiss. No matter how much he questioned the reality of it, it was indisputable that she embraced him with passion. Then she backed off. He could not quite understand why. Ruby seemed sure the kiss cemented the relationship. He was in love with her despite all the objections he could think of. But was she really in love with him?

The image of Estella in an embrace with Didi Al Refai kept returning. His heart sank not because he was jealous but because there might have been something between them that was closing him out. Perhaps Estella's embrace with him, Geoff, had been a temporary show of affection, and her genuine, enduring affection was for Didi? He would be right in the end: a girl like Estella would not fall in love with an ordinary bloke like him, a man so much older. It just did not happen. But theirs was a truly passionate embrace, and with Didi, it was something else. He could see that. Estella seemed to be receiving his attention passively, and he did not think they had kissed. She kissed him, though. And she would not have kissed him passionately if she did not feel the same sort of affection. And so, Geoff tormented himself without let-up. He rose and dressed, intending to go for a walk while the house awoke to the new day.

When he arrived downstairs from the attic room where he had slept, he got no further. Anneke and her mother were busy preparing breakfast, and they engaged him in conversation. Their first words were again of praise for what he had done and the courage he had shown. Many questions followed. They were so interested that they halted their preparations. When Marijke turned, at last, to the breakfast, Anneke gave him an understanding look.

'You must give her time, Geoff,' she said, accompanying him to the lounge room. She's confused and upset. She's blaming herself for letting herself and everyone down.'

'But she shouldn't,' he hastened to say. 'They are cunning, resourceful people.'

'I know. I'm sure she will come to realise it.' She stopped. 'You are better at problems of action, aren't you?'

'Yes.' He shook his head.

'I would like to visit your country,' she said, with an abrupt change of subject. 'Your courageous, selfless action has forced me to confront matters I have refused to reconcile.'

'I understand. And I would advise it. Whatever your decision regarding those matters, we would make you very welcome,' said Geoff, mindful that the crucial role she had played the night before might have influenced her resolution. 'I have the highest respect for Fr. van Engelen,' he added.

They did not get far with a subject Anneke seemed keen to talk about because Charles appeared. Frans followed him. Not long after, Miss Barker was at the front door, having walked over from the hotel. She needed a brisk morning walk, she said, after Anneke showed her into the lounge room. She had resumed her severe appearance with her greying hair tied tightly into a knot at the back of her head. She wasted no time in fixing the agenda. They had a brief conference during which she urged a return home as soon as possible. There was no resisting her, and soon she had their agreement.

AFTER A night of tossing and turning and only falling into a deep sleep at around five o'clock in the morning, Estella awoke to her father's gentle caress and soothing voice.

'Come on, darling. It's time to have breakfast and discuss what we are going to do.'

She sat up, glad her father had been there to wake her. She had such a disturbing sense of dislodgment. She pulled him to her so she could put her arms around his neck. He let her hug him.

'Darling, I know how you must feel. Fr. van Engelen told us briefly what you have been through. You must not blame yourself too much. You are young and did not see the trap you were being lured into. And if you made mistakes, remember that we all make mistakes. That's only human. The important thing is that you are safe and out of all danger.' He brought the tray he had placed on the dresser to her. 'It's time for breakfast. We can talk further later.' Estella took the tray. 'We have been discussing what to do next,' he continued. 'Miss Barker says you should return home immediately. You'll adjust and recover more quickly once you're back in your trusted environment. She is arranging the necessary papers.'

Estella expressed her pleasure with the plans, and Charles left her to finish her breakfast. No sooner had she got out of bed than her thoughts returned to Geoff's appearance in the tower. Before the self-blame and misery could take hold, there was a knock at the door. The door opened, and a smiling face appeared.

'Estella, may I come in?' said Anneke. 'I am Fr. van Engelen's niece.'

Estella now had a good look at the pretty, confident young woman she had seen the previous evening. She expressed her heartfelt gratitude for her part in her rescue. Anneke said that she was only supporting Geoff.

'I've been to the shops to get some clothes for you,' she went on, laying packages on the bed. 'Miss Barker, Geoff, and your father told me the sort of things you wear. This will do for your return to Australia.'

Seeing that the clothes were the right size and to her liking, Estella thanked Anneke and apologised for being such trouble.

'No apologies necessary. You have had a difficult time. Uncle Jos told me in private what you're feeling. You should not blame yourself too much. You should rather be grateful you have so many people who love you enough to do everything possible to safeguard you.' She paused. 'Geoff loves you very much. It's obvious. He would do anything to protect you.' She put an arm around Estella's waist. 'I would be happy to have a man like Geoff love me.'

It was too much for Estella. Anneke's words struck deep despite her resolve to steel herself. The misery and self-recrimination rose in full force. She sank onto the bed, her hands covering her face. Anneke sat beside her.

'Uncle Jos has told— He thought I would have a keener understanding of your feelings. He was right. I would feel the same way.' She hesitated. 'To tell you the truth, I was once in a similar position, but unlike you, I let my emotions blind me to what I was getting into.'

Anneke's story was brief, without mentioning Geoff, and it left Estella gaping in astonishment.

'Shocking, isn't it?' said Anneke.

'I ... I don't know what to say,' said Estella, wiping her eyes and sitting up.

'It's not necessary to say anything. I'm telling you something I've never told anyone because you should understand you're not alone. You should be aware of what girls can get into and the damage we can do to ourselves. I have a similar background to yours. My parents were always an example. Yet I deluded myself so much that I ended up doing something I will regret for the rest of my life. It will be on my conscience until the day I die. Perhaps I've ruined my life forever. Be thankful that you received enough grace to turn away.'

'It's terrible,' said Estella.

'This is just between us,' said Anneke. 'It would devastate my parents if they knew.'

'Of course,' said Estella. 'I'm grateful for your trust.'

'It was to help you understand. A young woman like you will not escape the attention of powerful, attractive men like the media magnate. So you should prepare yourself.'

'Thank you, Anneke. I appreciate it. It must be difficult to admit—'

'It is ... It's a relief to tell someone who understands.'

'I do. I understand how—'

'But you were preserved from making a mistake. Anyhow, that's our secret.' She paused and stroked Estella's arm. 'You must remember your experiences have made you sensitive. You must give yourself time to recover and see things in their proper place. And don't forget that if you really love Geoff, you will not make him suffer by letting him think that you don't appreciate his love and his desire to protect you.'

'Oh, I don't want that.'

'Then no more tears for him. Remember, true love is patient, suffering, and unselfish. St Paul ...'

It was enough to restore Estella's composure. As terrible as she felt about her actions, she must compose herself in Geoff's presence and honour and respect his feelings for her. She must contain her doubts and misery. She must put the images of the handsome father and son out of her mind. That was only right. She thanked Anneke again for the comforting words.

'I'm going to make the trip to Australia—to visit Uncle Jos,' said Anneke, in an apparent attempt to put the conversation on a lighter footing. 'Geoff said I would be welcome.'

'Yes ... yes, you will be most welcome,' said Estella, taking her hands. 'I will show you around—Geoff and I will.'

'I will count on it—you and Geoff showing me around. Now, I will say goodbye to you here. I must return to my duties.'

'Thank you, again, Anneke.'

As Anneke cycled slowly to marktplein where she intended to stop and have a thoughtful coffee, she resurrected the events of seven years ago, events that she had savagely repressed. It was time to reconcile them and move forward. It would be difficult, even traumatic, but she must follow the same advice she and everyone had given Estella. Geoff's wrist, with the handkerchief tied around it, sent an irresistible message.

AT FIVE minutes to nine, Frans van Engelen dropped his brother off at Truus van den Donker's house. As the priest approached the door, Truus's face appeared at the lounge room window and then disappeared. The next moment, the front door opened. An expression of surprise and sadness passed over her face. She came forward to help him.

'I'm a fine mess, aren't I?' He smiled and indicated that he was grateful for the support.

'I didn't realise ... in the dark, I could not see.'

'Oh, don't worry, Truus, it helps me to keep in mind my sins,' he joked. 'We all have our cross, high and low. Don't feel sorry for me. I have a lot to be thankful for, so many things the good Lord has given me. My body was broken, but my spirit wasn't, not by a long shot. So, no sympathy!'

But Truus could not help being pained by the sight of the crippled priest. Each time she had seen him through the years, he had either been starved, exhausted or crippled. And yet he always appeared calm, strong-minded, and cheerful. He was such an encouragement for her in her loneliness. She supported him into the lounge room, where he sat looking at the fields beyond the road outside.

'Gerda is busy with a guest in her room. She has packed and is ready to fly back to London. The man has been here several times since she arrived.

I'm sure they will be finished soon. Then I will tell her what happened in Amsterdam.'

Fr. van Engelen had no time to answer. They heard a door open and then voices. Truus hurried to the lounge room door.

'There is someone here I want you to meet.'

'There's no time,' Gerda snapped. 'I have a tight schedule—' She stopped, and her mouth opened as her mother moved aside to reveal the priest.

'Goedemorgen, Gerda. Good morning, Mr Rostowski.'

Saladin stared stonily at the priest but did not speak. He glanced at Gerda.

'Do I know you, Meneer?' she said in Dutch, after regaining her composure.

'I should think you do. Quite apart from my patting you on the head when you were a little girl and you staring at me on Marktplein fifteen years ago, we spent the last three months together in the same country town where you posed as a teacher named Edith Bicknell. I must say, on reflection, it's a mystery why you never made it your business to find out where I came from. Even a few words in Dutch from me would have revealed a regional accent that is unmistakable for a person of your talents and qualifications. That might have jogged your memory.'

Gerda stared hard at him. Enlightenment passed over her face.

'I don't know what you are talking about, Meneer,' she said, her jaw tightening.

'Mr Rostowski knows, don't you, sir?' said Fr. van Engelen to the sullen Saladin, who sported a bruise across his right temple.

'Go to the car and wait for me,' said Gerda. He did as ordered. 'I repeat, Meneer,' said Gerda, struggling to sound convincing, 'I don't know what you are talking about. Now, if you will excuse me, I have a busy program t oday.'

'You know now, of course, that Estella Winterbine is in safe hands, and that in due course there will be an investigation.'

'Any investigation will reveal that I have been in Holland since January, conducting research into regional dialects,' she said. 'It's the central activity of the institute of which I am the head. It's also a painstaking process that means spending a lot of time listening to and observing people in their daily routines. There is, of necessity, much solitude in such research. Meneer, I wish you luck in your investigations, whatever it is all about.' She turned to follow Saladin.

'The investigation will take its course,' said the priest. 'That is outside my competence. I have only these questions for you. Why is it that you were never influenced by the kind heart of your mother? Why are you so lacking in feeling for people? Why are you so prepared to use people to achieve your aims, whatever they are?'

'How dare you, manipulative misogynist cleric that you are,' she said, exploding. 'How dare you address me in this way? Look to your own political activity! The world will be all the better for ridding itself of your type. It can't come soon enough.'

'Gerda!' said her mother.

'And when are you going to extract yourself from the cramping provincial attitudes that keep you a miserable prisoner?' she said, turning on her. 'Your inner self is the open door to the freedom you reject.'

'Gerda,' said Truus, ignoring the invitation, 'the reason I asked Fr. van Engelen here was to tell you that he saved your life and my life just as the war was ending. You owe your life to this man.'

Gerda looked from her mother to the priest and back again as if she could not comprehend what had been said. Truus related what had happened.

'It's a lie,' cried Gerda, reddening from confusion and anger. 'Why didn't you tell me before this? And why hasn't my father told me? Lies, foul oppressive bourgeois lies!'

'Your father educated you in your hatred of Catholics and the Catholic Church. He could not stand the thought that a Catholic priest saved his wife and baby daughter. He forbade me to say anything about it to you.'

Gerda's anger and outrage turned to disgust. 'I don't believe it. Why would a Catholic priest lift a finger to save a Protestant? No, you have been fooled. It's a trick to convert you to their foul beliefs, to imprison you like a mindless animal. Look at you. If you have been miserable and pathetic, that was your choice. You had the choice to extract yourself like Father and me. Why did you insist on being stupid and pathetic in your life? Why should I have sympathy for someone who freely chooses to remain a slave?' She paused and regarded her mother and the priest. 'He evidently has you in his clutches.'

'Fr. van Engelen has been very kind to me through the years. His consideration has been selfless. Please don't talk about him that way.'

'Selfless! You're a bigger fool than I thought. Selfless! That's the tactic to suck you in, don't you see, you imbecile. It's all manipulation, to fool you so that your mind comes under their control.' The priest and her mother returned expressions of sadness. It infuriated her all the more. 'I can account for all my actions, Meneer *de pastoor*,' she said bitterly, 'but whatever is involved there, I am going to make you pay for your pernicious influence, here and in Binawarra, if it's the last thing that I do. I will make you pay for putting an obstacle in the way of my efforts to free people to their true selves.'

Truus interrupted Gerda's railing by leaving the room. Gerda blinked at the priest. A few seconds later, Truus returned holding one of Gerda's poster-sized photos.

'Do you know who this is?' she said to the priest.

'Yes,' he said. 'But what does this mean, Juffrouw van den Donker?'

'How dare you interfere in things you don't understand!' Gerda shouted, snatching the poster from her. 'I should have known the part you would play. Offering freedom from your cramped prison is like casting pearls before the swine. The opportunity for redemption has passed you by, and you are left to struggle in your self-administered chains.'

'Why do you have a photo of Aine Winterbine?' said the priest, alarmed. 'What does she mean to you?'

'That's for you to find out,' she spat at him, as she left the room. Next minute, she was back at the door holding her bags and the rolled-up posters. 'I will tell you this much. Perhaps you misjudged the Winterbine mother. Perhaps she harbours the seeds of a freedom all women want and need. She only has to be released from the prison of the coarse and rigid male mind. It's not to be wondered that your so-called Saviour is a man. If he was unblemished, he was a fitting sacrifice to atone for the centuries of male crime.'

She ran from the house with her bags, bashing against the front doorway. She stared ahead, not once looking at her mother, as the car took off and disappeared behind the trees along the Middelburgseweg.

THE LOUNGE room was full of friendly chatter as the Dutch family and their guests eagerly engaged in conversation. Geoff tried to join in the cheeriness, but no matter how much he tried, no matter how cosy the room was with the aroma of freshly brewed coffee, he could not relax. He could not get his mind off Estella. He kept wondering how she was and what she was thinking. He was painfully aware that neither Charles nor Anneke had said she wanted to see him when they returned from her room. Then amid the chatter, she was standing there. Silence fell on the group.

'Come on, my girl,' said Miss Barker, sitting with her second cup of coffee, 'you need to cheer up. We're celebrating your return from danger. You are not like the prodigal son, but we could not be happier about your deliverance.'

Estella forced a smile. 'I would like to thank everyone very much for your concern, for all the risks you took in rescuing me,' she said. 'I hardly deserve it. I have been so foolish and naïve.' She glanced at Geoff, but lowered her eyes when his eyes met hers.

'Now, now,' Miss Barker continued, 'you're not going to punish yourself anymore.' She wagged her finger. 'I'm not as patient as the others, you know.' Estella put her arms around her. 'Hey! You'll spill my coffee, silly girl.'

Releasing Miss Barker, she hesitated and approached Geoff. Geoff got to his feet. They stood facing each other. A poignant silence again fell on the room. 'Geoff, I'm really grateful. I owe my safety to you—in more ways than one.'

'I did it for you,' Geoff found himself saying.

Before he could say any more, Estella put her arms around his neck and hugged him. He did not know what to say or do. It was unexpected. She let him go with, 'Thank you,' and then sat next to her father on the lounge, threading her arm through his.

'Miss Barker has done wonders and arranged everything,' Marijke said. 'We will be sorry to see you go so soon. It's a pity you don't have time to see our beautiful island.'

'We will return someday,' said Miss Barker, with surprising decisiveness. 'Circumstances are forcing our early return. And, of course, you are always welcome to come and visit us. I have a certain reputation in our little town, but I assure you that you will receive the same hospitality and warmth we have experienced here.'

Charles was quick to support Miss Barker's invitation and her gratitude for the help and hospitality. Even in their short time, they had seen that the Dutch way of making guests comfortable had its own character. After many such sentiments had been warmly exchanged, the guests prepared themselves for their departure while Frans went to pick up his brother. Around midday, Frans returned with Fr. van Engelen. After expressing his pleasure at seeing Estella more like herself, the priest went apart with Miss Barker. Then he announced that he would not return to Binawarra until Friday. After a light lunch and many warm farewells, the group was ready to leave for Schiphol.

There was little conversation after they had passed customs and sat in the departure lounge. Miss Barker seemed to think it was no longer necessary to speak, and she sat immersed in her thoughts. Estella sat with her father with her head on his shoulder. Geoff was strangely agitated. He got up to walk around to ease the agitation. As he passed a kiosk, he purchased a newspaper and returned to his seat next to Miss Barker. Laying the newspaper on his lap, he stared before him. He became aware of Miss Barker leaning towards him. She grabbed the newspaper from his lap.

'Oh, no, no, it's not true!' Estella cried, sitting straight.

Geoff bent over to see what had provoked her cry. The headline: **Egyptian playboy dies as fast as he lived.**

'Well-known, filthy rich playboy, Didi Al Refai, was killed in a car accident in Paris yesterday, trustworthy sources have reported, though it has not been officially confirmed. According to observers, the Egyptian playboy had been driving with needless recklessness to evade a small group of reporters and cameramen.

'The playboy's grief-stricken father is making accusations against the press and 'sinister people,' who, he claimed, bore ill will towards him and his son. He has sworn to get behind the real causes of his son's fatal accident.'□

Miss Barker and Geoff looked at Estella and then at each other. She had her hands over her face, and her head was bent forward. For a short while, there was the muffled sound of rapid breathing. Then she turned and leaned against her father. Charles, who had not been paying close attention, put his arm around her. Miss Barker frowned as if not quite comprehending.

She glanced again at Geoff. Geoff thought his heart could not sink any lower. Miss Barker seemed on the point of speaking, but for some reason he could not guess, remained silent. He was thankful not to be challenged, and, deciding he could not change anything, resigned himself to whatever might happen.

Estella's first reaction was disbelief. Didi could not be dead. But he was. The horrible thought struck her that she might be somehow responsible. She could not think why, but the feeling was overwhelming. Why did Mr Al Refai claim sinister people were behind Didi's death? She remembered the sudden change, almost disintegration, in the relations between the people at the castle. She thought of what had happened between her and Didi—a declaration of love and a marriage proposal. His proposal had been linked to an undertaking to change. She never doubted his sincerity. Later, it dawned on her that Didi's declaration had a second object. He wanted to save her from his father's temptation. Now, in the light of what had happened—it was all rushing by her in a jumble of events—she could not stop the thought that Didi might have got in the way of the plans for her. No, it could not be true. People could not be so cruel.

Whatever her feelings, she did not want Geoff to suspect that she loved Didi. She desperately hoped he had not seen the embrace on the dunes. If she could not look Geoff in the face because she had been seduced from her principles, she certainly did not want to add to it by arousing the suspicion that her affection for Didi had risen for more than a moment. It had reverted immediately to sisterly sympathy. And Didi was dead. She cried inwardly for him, but her love for Geoff was everything. She fought to hide all that was happening inside her. It was a relief when the boarding call came. She could no longer control her appearance. Fortunately, she and Geoff were designated to different rows. After the plane took off into the night, she escaped with her raw feelings into the silence of the slumbering aircraft. Her last glance at Geoff told her he was in as much turmoil.

THE LONG flight passed comfortably enough for the foursome. While other passengers found the time in their seats tedious, Charles, Miss Barker, Estella, and Geoff welcomed the chance to sit back and take a breather from the drama and exertion of the last week. Charles urged Estella to try to sleep. She was so exhausted, both mentally and physically, that she did not need much urging. Before she knew it, she had drifted off, with her dozing interrupted only by meals and stopovers. The anxiety and shame returned when the plane was several hours out of Melbourne. While they waited to pass through customs, she still found it painful to look at Geoff. Just a glance at his sympathetic expression as he stood next to Miss Barker was enough for her to feel the dagger of her betrayal. Only when Ruby greeted them with her open affection did her spirits revive.

'I'm so relieved and glad that you are all right!' Ruby said, holding her. 'I was so careless in dropping you off at the hotel. Geoff, you are a hero, a knight in shining armour. Nobody else could have done what you have done. How I misjudged you! Can you ever forgive me?'

'There is nothing to forgive,' said Geoff. 'Your friendship and what it has meant has been precious to me.'

Ruby seemed to understand the allusion. 'Come on,' she said, linking up with Estella, 'we're going to catch up on everything like sisters do. And no self-blame!'

Charles was happy for Ruby to take charge. When they arrived at the car, Ruby put Geoff behind the wheel and the women in the back.

'I hope I'm not being too pushy, Miss Barker,' she said.

'Of course not, Miss Waiting, You're a girl after my own heart.'

While Estella was making herself comfortable, Charles whispered to Ruby, 'How is Bill? Aine has told me, but Estella does not know yet.'

'He has improved quite a bit. It turned out to be a mild stroke, a little paralysis in the left side of his face and left arm, but the doctor says he's likely to make a full recovery. He will be in hospital for a few more days.'

'What a relief. I would still like to keep it from Estella until we get home.'

'Of course,' she said, not moving. 'There is something else that may upset her.'

'What?' said Charles, alarmed.

'Jenny Brougham and Len Dawson have cleared off.'

'Cleared off?

'Yes, they are nowhere to be found. Jenny's parents are frantic. Mrs Brougham has been around to talk to Aine. They called the police, and, from inquiries among their school friends, it seems the two have gone to Melbourne. The police sergeant said they cleared out as some young people do. There's little he can do about it except inform the police in Melbourne.'

'That's sad,' said Charles. 'That boy is not a good influence.'

Ruby had done well, arranging the drive back to Binawarra. Geoff needed to do something instead of sitting stupidly, not knowing what to say. Ruby kept questioning Estella about her experiences, filling in the details she knew. It was done in a hearty, positive manner, emphasising that nobody could be blamed for what had happened and, indeed, that, in the circumstances, Estella would have had no way of knowing what lay behind Mr Al Refai's kindness. She, Ruby, had found him a handsome, charming man she could trust. Few girls would have seen through it all.

Estella did not quite agree with Ruby's opinion of Mr Al Refai and his treatment of her. It was not as devious as Ruby made out. Mr Al Refai never forced her to do anything. He held out the temptation to give in to or turn away from. His charm, his kindness, and respect for her were sincere in their own way, regardless of how very wrong aspects of his proposal were. He would not have been any different once she had rejected his offer. She hoped she was not naïve in thinking so. She would be stupid to forget what Anneke had told her and warned her about. Perhaps that was the most seductive thing about Mr Al Refai. He always appeared so kind and sensitive to her feelings.

She appreciated Ruby's attempt to put her at ease and lessen her culpability. And Ruby did largely make her see that few people would have seen through Gerda van den Donker. She reinforced Anneke's warning of the temptation hidden in Mr Al Refai's kind, generous manner. In this way, Ruby raised her spirits. Although Estella could again appreciate Ruby's familiar warm understanding and encouragement, she saw something different in her; Ruby was now more subdued and cautious. Her mind, though, did not linger on that observation. When the Wombat came into view, it seemed a good omen. Only as they passed between the Wombat and Death Rock did she feel a chill. The car became silent, too. It was all over in a moment, and the next thing Estella was hugging her mother.

'Come on, Geoff,' said Charles, seeing him hanging back. 'Aine wants to thank you. We all want to thank you.'

'I would like to say some prayers in thanksgiving for Estella's safety,' said Aine when they were all assembled in the lounge room. 'I hope Miss Barker, Ruby, and Geoff will allow us this short time to offer thanks to God.' There was no objection. 'I appreciate it. You are our dear friends. Charles, would you lead us in the Fifth Joyful Mystery?' While Charles led the prayers, Geoff kept his eyes on Estella, who kept hers closed as she repeated them.

Morning tea passed in light conversation as if Aine and Charles were determined to spare Estella further upset. Geoff understood. He was pleased she seemed to be recovering. But he was aware that she still avoided looking at him. At length, he could not bear it any longer and rose, saying it was time for him to return to the farm.

'Geoff, we understand you have your duties,' said Charles. 'Aine and I would like you to come and spend a day with us as soon as you have completed your chores. Will you do that?'

Geoff thanked them for their hospitality and was about to say that he gladly accepted their invitation when Estella approached him.

'Geoff, I'm so grateful,' she whispered, embracing him. 'I'm so sorry.'

Geoff held her limply, his tongue paralysed as it often used to be.

'It's time for me to go, too,' said Miss Barker, breaking the trance. 'Mr Shawcross, you can drop me off at my house.'

Geoff wondered why Estella said she was sorry. What was she sorry for? That she should be grateful to him, he could understand. But sorry? That she had let everyone down? She had been amply reassured about that. Was she sorry that she could not love him the way she had loved Didi Al Refai?

'I want you to come inside for a while,' said Miss Barker when he had stopped outside her house. 'You must take your mind off things. Stop tormenting yourself. It will work out, trust me. Besides, there are a few things we must discuss. This matter has not yet finished.'

THE FOLLOWING day, Thursday, Ruby entered Bruce Butcher's office at Sandhurst University.

'I expected you. I see from your expression that you, or rather your SAS friend, succeeded in retrieving her.'

'Yes, we found her. She has been rescued.'

'Where was she?'

'You don't know?'

'No. There are several places they could have taken her. I told you. I'm a small cog in this business. There is much I don't know.'

'Your role as a small cog has proven critical. I don't know how we would have found her in time if we had not known she had gone when we did. So we have you to thank. It is ironic, as you said.'

'Where was she?'

'In Holland, in the provincial town of Middelburg.'

'Ms Vrouwendijk's hometown. You know all about Gerda, I assume?'

'We know a lot about Gerda van den Donker.'

'She was being spoilt in the Castle of Heavenly Bliss, no doubt.'

'Yes, what do you know about it?'

'Only that it's one of the places Gerda Vrouwendijk has at her disposal to advance her utopian vision, whatever that is exactly. The Castle of Heavenly Bliss, so appropriately named, serves as the pot of honey or the gilded cage for some of her victims.'

'You call them victims?' she said with irony.

'In the long run, they are victims, however willing they are to be in that gilded cage. It is a place of unequalled luxury if you have not seen it. It's only for the very wealthy or for people with access to loads of public money.'

'You're very frank about the activities of your ideological friends.'

He shrugged. 'In war, all weapons are equal. Besides, this business has made me question whether I am their ideological friend.'

'Why?'

He waved his hand dismissively. 'The women are—' He stopped himself from going further.

'You should be happy that Estella Winterbine did not succumb to the pot of honey. That's what you wanted.'

'Are you sure she resisted? Few women could resist the material and ideological temptation— Oh, what am I saying?'

'Positive. I believe you know more than you are admitting.' She looked keenly at him, but he returned a steady gaze. 'Perhaps, you don't. What has the Convent of the Blessed Mother got to do with this?'

'Convent of the Blessed Mother?' he said, raising his eyebrows. 'What are you talking about?'

'Never dabbled in Gnosticism or the occult, you and Gerda?'

There was a long silence as he seemed to be considering. 'When we were together in Amsterdam, it was left-wing ideology that drove us,' he said. 'What Gerda has been up to after that, I don't know. My materialism is too strong for that New Age stuff.'

'She will never be yours,' said Ruby, after a moment of silence. 'She's in love with someone else.'

'Yes. That boring virtuous soldier. What's wrong with the girl? Most girls like to throw themselves away on dangerous, exciting blokes like me.'

'You have no understanding of—he returns her love.'

Bruce Butcher sighed. 'Is there any justice in the world?' He knocked on the desk a couple of times with his knuckles and looked away. 'I know she would never be mine. I may be obsessive, but I'm not that stupid. I'm relieved she has been saved from that sleazebag. And my reasons for saying that are not racist. I told you. An attack of bourgeois morality suddenly afflicted me. I was outraged a girl like that could be used and soiled by a man with nothing more to recommend him than his great wealth. I'm disgusted that I was concerned about the girl's virtuous state. What a degeneration I have undergone!'

'Natural moral feeling can sometimes shine through the hardest heart.'

'Oh, please!' he sighed. 'The trouble with your type, Ms Ruby, is that you are too eager to condemn my type as evil and corrupt.'

'No, Bruce, it's the other way around. It's your type that thinks my type is corrupt. My type thinks your type is deluded. The evil and harm have their origins in your delusions.'

He stared at her and raised his eyebrows in a gesture of boredom—or was it resignation?

'It may not mean much now,' he let slip.

'Whatever our differences, you did an honourable deed,' Ruby continued, without seeing any significance in his comment. 'Through your intervention, we saved someone very precious from moral and physical danger. We owe you a debt for the turn of your conscience.'

'Does that cancel out the other?'

Ruby hesitated. 'If I had been outside this business, I would have said no. The seriousness of what you did to Lilly Kelly is not diminished.'

'And now?'

'It makes a difference that you saved someone I love as a sister. I have trouble balancing the relationship between the gratitude we all feel and the penalty you incurred for destroying that poor girl's life.'

'We both love the same person. Another irony, isn't it? Me, who you so detested.' Ruby had no answer. 'Do you remember I said I was acting like her Sydney Carton?' Ruby nodded. 'As much as it sounds ridiculously like bourgeois melodrama, I ask you not to forget if anything happens to me.'

'You're serious, aren't you?'

'Yes. Perhaps you now have an idea of how ruthless Mistress Gerda can be.'

'You have a lot on Gerda and her activities. Why don't you go to the police?'

He laughed loudly. 'You mean, compound the disgusting Christian seduction of my conscience by turning to its state apparatus? I couldn't live with myself. And others would not allow me to live, that's for sure. They would get me in the end. We are a vindictive lot, you know. We don't forget easily.'

'Whatever you have done, and however I have regarded you in the past, I wouldn't want to see these people prevail and do you harm.'

'Ruby, I am happy to hear that. It will suffice. It's a sort of a victory for me.' He paused. 'There's nothing more to say, really. I can only hope that Gerda has not traced your action back to me. I might get away with it. I can only hope.' Another long pause while he was in thought. 'I will make it up to Lilly Kelly. I will try to redress the wrong I did her, at least materially. I will pretend she is the person I am obsessed with instead of Estella Winterbine. I have written her into my will. Remember that.'

BRUCE BUTCHER opened a bottle of his best red and sat on the lounge settee. He poured a glass, took a few sips, and leaned back. He was looking at Picasso's *Guernica*. The bottle gradually emptied as he sat staring at the writhing mass of lines. When the last glass was empty, he fetched another bottle. On the way back to the lounge, he stopped. He put the bottle on the coffee table and went to his bedroom. He took a photo album from the back of one of the wardrobe shelves.

Back on the settee, he slowly flicked through the album pages while he sipped his way through the second bottle. So many beautiful girls, most more than willing. Why should he become obsessed with the one girl, then? It was a mystery. He came to the last photo. It was Lilly Kelly. She did look young. He wondered what she was like. Really. He should know if she was to replace Estella Winterbine and if he was to redress the wrong he had done. He stared at the photo until the second bottle was empty. He got up, swaying. He steadied himself on the lounge and went for a third bottle. He lurched as he came back but steadied himself again on the back of the settee. He had hardly finished the first glass when his eyelids drooped. They shut, and he lurched to the side. He jerked himself upright, splashing the contents of the glass around him. He put the glass on the coffee table, or meant to, for it fell over inexplicably. He leaned back and gave in to his drunken stupor.

He did not see the eyes peering through the back window. He did not hear the rustle and scraping of feet, going from window to window, until the slightly open bedroom window was found.

Chapter 35

The final attempt

ESTELLA'S HEART ached when Geoff left to take Miss Barker home. She had seen his withdrawal since the night of the rescue. And he had hardly responded to her last hug. It seemed that her fears were true. She had let him down too much. The constant company of her reassuring mother and father and spending the night in her own bed helped her regain her sense of connectedness. They began a novena to St Joseph in thanksgiving for her safe return and deliverance from temptation. The communal prayers and the long talk with her mother about the circumstances of the temptation helped to put everything in perspective. Her mother stressed the fallibility of the person suffering the effects of original sin and the constant struggle necessary to lead a good and happy life. She related Jesus' story of the publican who stood at the back of the temple and struck his breast, saying to himself, 'Lord, forgive me, I am a sinner,' while the Pharisee loudly broadcast his virtue.

'It was the publican sinner that was more justified in his prayers,' Aine said. 'We must accept that we sometimes err. We must own up to our faults and sins and then, with the joy of God's forgiveness, resume our lives full of resolve.'

It was what she needed. Her mother's quiet comfort and caresses were all-important. She suspected that her mother was fully aware of the strength of her love for Geoff and of the shame she felt at having failed so dramatically in the face of a powerful temptation. By the end of the morning, she was ready to think of Geoff without shame. She was ready to face him, understanding that perhaps he really did not think less of her.

'Aaah, you are a lot better, I see,' said Charles when he came in for lunch.

During lunch, Charles raised the subject of going back to school. It was then that Estella realised she had not yet seen Uncle Bill and Auntie Joanne. She asked where they were. There was a brief pause. She was immediately alarmed. Charles hastened to reassure her that he was all right now.

'All right, now?'

'Darling, Uncle Bill suffered a minor stroke last weekend,' said Aine, taking her hand. 'He's still in hospital, but the doctor says he should fully recover. He will be home on Saturday.'

'A stroke ... how?'

'It appears that Uncle Bill collapsed after being falsely accused of something very bad,' said Charles, 'behaviour that is against everything he holds dear. It's also about people he loves as if they were his and Joanne's family.'

'What? Who?' said Estella, knowing he was talking about them.

Aine briefly related what Jane Cox had publicly implied.

Estella was first astonished, then disgusted, and finally indignant. She could never have imagined that someone could even think of such a thing, let alone accuse someone so dear to them.

'But Uncle Bill has shown us nothing but kindness,' she said. 'Everybody in Binawarra must know that. Auntie Joanne and Uncle Bill are more like grandparents to me than anything else.'

'Yes, that's right,' said Charles. 'Unfortunately, we must accept the existence of people whose malice is incomprehensible. We must pray that they will eventually recognise their malice and its effects.'

Estella wanted to do something about it immediately. It was not fair. She wanted people to know the truth and how wrong and vicious the accusation was. There was no time to think about her troubles while this disgusting charge hung over Uncle Bill. She had to wait until the next day when Joanne came to visit. She rushed to greet her. Bill was getting better. He would be his old self in no time, said Joanne.

'He's very teary. The doctor says that's normal. It would be nice if you visited him,' she said to Estella. 'It would give him a boost. He wants to say how happy we are that you're home safe and sound.'

'Of course, I want to visit him as soon as possible. When can I go?'

Estella could go whenever she was ready. After some discussion, it was decided that Aine and Charles would go early in the afternoon, leaving Estella for a later visit. That would cheer Bill enormously and send the right message.

It now struck Estella forcefully that her worries were slight compared with Uncle Bill's circumstances. This realisation was like rubbing the sleep from her eyes. She knew deep down she had Geoff's affection and support. She should not be silly and fanciful about it any longer. She should acknowledge it. Yes, she would put her self-doubts and childish scruples aside and tell him how she felt. She would tell him all she had been through, exactly as Fr. van Engelen had suggested, exactly as Ruby and Anneke had encouraged. She looked forward to the strength of his presence, to the strength of his inner life, a strength that his quiet reserve belied for those who did not know him well. She reflected then, as she had not before, that Miss Barker's good opinion of Geoff was immediate and sure.

AT AROUND five o'clock, Miss Barker was interrupted by the phone on her desk. She put down her book and picked up the receiver.

'Miss Barker, I've been trying to find Geoff,' said Ruby, in a rush. 'I've rung the number at the farm, but he is not there. The caretakers don't know where he is. Do you know? It's urgent.'

'Steady, Miss Waiting. Keep calm. He's here in Binawarra. What's happening?'

'Thank God he's there. Is he looking after Estella?'

'Yes. Miss Waiting, what has happened? Tell me.'

'Bruce Butcher is dead.'

'Killed?'

'Yes, it is so shocking that I can hardly talk about it. I became suspicious when I learned that he had not turned up at the university. You know, the warnings from that Balkan brute. Anyhow, I went to his house to see if he was there. When I got no answer, I called the police. They were reluctant at first, but eventually forced their way in. They found him murdered. His body had been mutilated. They would not let me in.'

'The Goddess has wasted no time. When do they estimate he died?'

'I don't know. They found him about an hour ago.'

'Thank you, Miss Waiting. I must act at once. There's no time to lose.'

'I'm coming up to Binawarra.'

'No, Miss Waiting, it's better to stay where you are. It may not be safe for you to drive up here alone. We must keep a grip on what's happening. Leave it to Mr Shawcross and me.'

'Please ring me as soon as you know anything,' Ruby pleaded.

AS SOON as Estella put her arms around Bill, his tears began to flow. 'I'm so sorry to see you here, Uncle Bill. Auntie Joanne says you'll be much better in a few days. I'll look after you the way you cared for us when I was young, and Mamma was sick. I'll read some of your favourite stories.' A smile came to his teary face, and then a laugh.

'You're swapping places with this fat old fool, aren't you?' he said, wiping his eyes.

'You're not at all a fool,' she said, taking his hand and squeezing it.

'Not a fool, eh? That's rich,' he exclaimed, laughing all the more. 'I can't tell you what your few words have done for the spirits of this fat old codger here. Just wait till I lose the numbness in my side! With the support of you and your mum and dad, I will be fit in no time!'

A half-hour later, Estella left to return home, happy that her visit had done some good. The light was fading as she passed through the hospital gates for the twenty-minute walk home. She made her way along a stretch of road beside a bushy area, her thoughts still on Uncle Bill. Without warning, a figure in black dashed at her from between the shrubs and trees. She was flung around and dragged into the bush. A moist cloth was rubbed over her mouth. She gasped for breath until she lost consciousness.

GEOFF WAS on watch from a house a hundred yards down the road. He should have anticipated this tactic. He raced towards them as Saladin pushed Estella into a car hidden among the trees. He was not far away when the car shot from the trees and came veering towards him. He jumped over the front fence of the nearest house as Saladin swerved up onto the footpath and then back onto the road. He swung round and ran after the car. He turned into Goldminers Road, where he met Miss Barker hurrying towards him.

'Saladin may be in the neighbourhood—'

'He's got Estella. In a car. A blue Ford. I'm going after him. Call the police. He'll be heading out of town.'

A minute later, he was racing along Melbourne Road. He gunned the engine as he tore up between the peaks, but then slammed on the brakes, coming to a skidding stop some yards beyond Saladin's car parked in the roadside clearing. His stomach twisted. He jumped off the bike and felt along his right calf. He sprinted up the bush track with the long grass and low overhanging bushes brushing against him as he went. The light was fading. He desperately hoped that he would not be too late. Again, he offered a prayer to Estella's God.

ESTELLA REGAINED consciousness as Saladin dragged her out of the car. He righted her and bound her hands in front of her as she stood groggily, trying to understand where she was. Then he grabbed her from behind and held a knife to her throat. The razor edge cut into her skin.

'Cooperate, or I'll slit your throat!'

She held her head back to reduce the blade's pressure as he walked her along a bush track. As her mind cleared from the effects of the drug, she knew where she was going. He was going to kill her. That had to be the end of the failed plan. But she was not overtaken by fear. A feeling of inevitability arose in her. She was powerless to do anything. The distance between her and any earthly help seemed unbridgeable. Her mother and father, Geoff, Ruby, the Huckerbys—they were hopelessly out of range. She was in the hands of Providence, and amid Saladin's rough and violent treatment, she said prayers of supplication. She said prayers of contrition. She, Estella, had made mistakes, big mistakes, but now she would persevere until the end, no matter what he attempted to do to her.

She would be true to Geoff. She would love him and no other, ever. Oh, how she wished she had not lost heart! She wished she could have overcome her shame and told him she loved him. The thought of it was unbearable. And so, the prominent feeling that accompanied Estella as she was pushed onto the rocky outcrop was regret, deep, painful regret, that she had not been able to say to Geoff that she loved him like she loved no other. She knew that he loved her. She could see that now. Oh, why did she not acknowledge his love as he leaned on the car window, looking at her with her handkerchief tied around his wrist?

It was too late now.

Geoff's love-filled eyes stayed before her mind as Saladin pushed her towards the edge of the outcrop. She was looking down into a darkening abyss when Geoff burst from the bush. Saladin swung her around, so they were facing the panting, scratched, and dishevelled former SAS soldier. For a moment, Estella saw a mixture of love and despair on his face, but then his eyes changed in a way she had never seen and took on an intense focus as he edged towards them.

'Aah, the Crusader arrives on cue,' Saladin mocked. 'How does it feel to be wound in like a fish, flapping helplessly on the end of the line?' Geoff continued to edge towards him. 'That's right, come a little closer. You need to have a good view as I slit your beloved's throat and hurl her over the edge like a worthless animal carcass. Stop now!' He moved the blade of the knife up under Estella's chin. It cut into her skin.

Geoff stopped. He was just a few paces away from them. Saladin had judged the distance well. He could not get to Saladin's knife arm without Saladin carrying out his threat. He continued to watch every movement, thinking of ways to hold his attention. Every second was bought time.

'Are Islamic soldiers always so brave?' he said, his voice just above a whisper. 'Do you need to kill innocent people? Why don't you take me on? Just me.'

'It is not a question of bravery. You Western infidels are like filthy animals that must be slaughtered. It might as well be a goat or a sheep I am about to slaughter. Your turn will come when your girlfriend is finished.' He laughed. 'It will be over her dead body that I deal with you. Hah, hah! You won't be so effective when you meet me head-on.'

'Is this where you dealt with Bob McKinnon?'

'That filthy pervert, yes. His death was too clean and easy. But why should you worry?'

'I was curious. You seem to make easy victims a specialty.'

'Is there anything else you want to know before I kill you both?' Saladin sneered. But he did not show any haste to do the job.

'Are you doing this on Gerda van den Donker's orders?'

'That woman does not order me to do anything I do not want to do.'

'But she has ordered it.'

'She has requested it in return for a large amount of money, a big, big amount of money that my brothers and I employ to carry on our task, the task given us by the almighty.'

'And Miss Barker?'

'Ah, you know about my respect for Miss Barker? No, Miss Barker will escape this time. She has had her warning not to meddle anymore. After you and your girlfriend, my job here is finished.'

Geoff saw that he was relaxing, confident that he had him and Estella at his mercy.

'You don't imagine you will get away with this, do you? The police are already being alerted. They're probably not far off right now.'

Saladin laughed again. 'Surely, you don't think I can't outwit your stupid police sergeant, do you? Your beloved here pointed out all the walking tracks in the neighbourhood. Very accommodating. I checked them out long ago. I will simply disappear from this mountain. I will be long in Cairo by the time your police discover where I went—if they ever do.'

'Cairo?' Geoff tensed. He could see him further relaxing.

Estella had been following the exchange in a state of stupefaction as if she were not part of the proceedings. Geoff, whose steady demeanour did not falter, never once looked at her. Uncomprehending, she watched the intense expression in his eyes as they focused on the man holding her. Then he glanced at her. She saw love in his eyes. It was too much. Her heart ached in longing for him. Now that she was seconds away from death, she cried ou t.

'Geoff, I love you!'

Her heartfelt cry rose out above the rocky peak of Death Rock and shot across to the Wombat, where it dwelt for a moment, gathering and murmuring within itself. It then came back across the valley and hit the peak in a series of forceful echoes before fading back towards the Wombat. Saladin looked up for an instant. It was enough.

Geoff rushed forward and, with his left hand, clenched Saladin's knife wrist in a bone-crushing hold. With his right hand, he grabbed Saladin's left wrist. They were now locked in a deadly embrace. Estella felt the pressure of Saladin's arms lessen as Geoff prized them apart. Then there was a gap. She slipped out from under his arms.

'Hold me!' Geoff shouted. She grabbed hold of his belt. 'Keep me steady! Steady!' He felt the backward pressure. It was enough. He released Saladin's left wrist and grabbed his throat. Saladin had never reckoned on the strength of the hands of a Mallee farmer and now felt the tissue around his neck being torn and crushed. He let out a muffled cry. His knife arm lost its strength as he instinctively reached to prevent his throat from being torn apart.

Geoff released his hold on Saladin's throat and, with both hands, took hold of the hand around the knife handle. With one movement, he brought the knife plunging down with such force that it passed straight through Saladin's chest wall and into his heart. Blood gushed. Saladin's eyes glazed, and choking in his blood, he began to fall backwards. He was already dead when Geoff released him. He disappeared into the darkness. A thud and the rattle of stones drifted up seconds later. Geoff turned, cut the rope around Estella's wrists, and took her into his arms.

'As long as you want me, I will never leave you,' he whispered.

'Geoff, never leave me,' she said, shaking and holding him. The relief of being at last in his arms and the awareness of what had happened, that a man had been killed, was more than she could cope with. 'Hold me,' she said, as he seemed about to release her. They stood there in an embrace for some time.

Charles was the first to arrive at the ledge. He stopped and said a prayer of thanksgiving when he made out Estella and Geoff in the fading light.

Estella let go of Geoff when she was aware of her father standing beside her. He took her in his arms. Geoff nodded at the edge of the rocky outcrop to indicate how the struggle had ended.

'It's all finished now, darling,' Charles said. 'Geoff has released you from the last of it.'

'Yes, Daddy, he has. I love him dearly.'

'We know, darling.'

Estella put her arms around Geoff again. She kissed him several times on the cheek and on the lips and then rested her head on his shoulder. Sergeant Willis appeared, out of breath. His constable was not far behind. He shone his torch around and expressed relief that Estella was all right. He asked a few questions and, receiving short answers from Geoff, walked to the edge and looked down. He flashed his torch and then instructed his constable to secure the area.

'I understand, Mr Shawcross and Miss Winterbine, that you are not yet ready to answer any more questions. I will give you time to recover from the shock and excitement. Would you please drop by the police station later? In the meantime, I'll alert the Bendigo office.'

He left with Geoff's undertaking that he and Estella would come to the police station shortly. Miss Barker arrived puffing. She shone her torch around. She let out a cry of relief. Tears appeared in the torch's glow before she switched it off. The next moment, she had Estella in an embrace.

Two hours later, at the Winterbine house, Charles took Geoff aside while Aine spoke with Estella. They sat on the verandah. It was a clear evening sky, with the stars glinting over the country town as the crescent moon rose. Geoff sat down, wondering about things. He had heard Estella talk about Providence, about God's mysterious and masterly supervision of the affairs of people, and he could not help wondering if anyone could ever explain to him that everything that had happened to him in the last few months was merely random or coincidental. Someone seemed to have a hand in it all. He glanced at Charles. He had an idea of what Charles was going to say.

'Geoff, we are eternally in your debt, as I have said many times. Aine and I will never be able to thank you enough for what you did. Only God could have sent someone like you to protect our daughter. Twice, you rescued her. We will offer our rosaries and our Mass for the next month in thanksgiving for His deliverance through you.'

'I've done it out of love and respect for your family,' said Geoff, no longer embarrassed.

'I know, Geoff, and that's what I wanted to talk about. We were aware some time ago that our daughter's affection for you was growing. We knew it had to be serious. She had never expressed a liking for a boy until you. And once her affection is given, it is usually strong. We also saw that you returned that regard. Now, there is a significant difference in your ages and maturity. The age difference is not so important, but the differences in maturity are. You might be ready for marriage. Although Estella won't likely change her mind or her affections, she is too young to enter a relationship with the idea of marriage. That's what she will be thinking of. But she needs time to be sure of herself.'

'I understand, Charles,' said Geoff. 'I'll do whatever you want. My love for Estella will never change. I can wait. I'm prepared to wait. I've waited so long already. I told Estella that as long as she wants me around, I will never leave her.'

'Thank you, Geoff. We appreciate that.' He patted him on the arm. 'After all that has happened, it would be cruel to separate you now. So, under certain conditions, we will allow her to be with you for the next two weeks. After that, we ask you to take a break from her until she finishes schooling. It will give you both time to examine your feelings. Then, at Christmas, we can see how things are.'

'I understand,' said Geoff.

'Estella will be upset to hear this. Aine is talking to her about it. But she will do as we request. She has always been a good daughter. She knows that we would never ask her to do anything unnecessarily hard. She will remind us that we married when Aine was not yet nineteen. That was different. Aine is, in some respects, quite different from Estella. She is calmer and considered, while Estella is passionate and romantic. You must have seen evidence of that behind that quiet exterior.'

'Yes, indeed.'

'Aine and I were also around the same age when we fell in love. Most importantly, we shared the same religious beliefs. That is not so with you and Estella. Even with those advantages, we were not without problems and difficulties.'

'I understand, Charles. I will do whatever is required for you and Aine to be sure Estella is doing the right thing.'

'You have taken into consideration Estella's religious beliefs?'

'Yes, it is part of Estella. I would not want her to change anything. I will make it my business to learn more about it,' Geoff added, thinking Charles was reluctant to request that of him.

'You understand how Catholic teaching regards the sanctity of marriage?'

'Yes. I promise to respect that teaching.'

'Estella will always attempt to do the right thing, but she is a passionate girl and two young people who love—'

'Charles, I promise you I will respect her and her beliefs.'

'I don't want to speak out of turn, Geoff, or repeat things you already know, but for Estella and us, true love means an abiding commitment. Estella could not love without thinking of a permanent commitment. That's why it's important to make sure that your feelings for each other are sound. That's why Aine and I thought it important to talk to you and Estella now, despite the shocking events of this evening. There is no point in starting without an understanding of the duties, as well as the joys, of a loving relationship.'

'I'll respect all that you want and believe. I am now just happy to have Estella's love. It's like a dream, a dream that I would have never dared to dream.'

'Thank you, Geoff. We could not ask for more. You'll be apart for only a short period.'

That was all Charles had to say for the moment. It was a necessary formal talk, but now that they had an understanding, he and Aine wanted him to feel part of their family. At that point, Aine brought Estella to the verandah. She looked at him as if to see how he had reacted to her father's talk. She seemed relieved when Geoff returned a look of affection. Aine, receiving a signal from Charles that he had completed his talk with Geoff, said they would leave them to have some time together while dinner was being prepared.

'Geoff, we are so happy to have you among us,' said Aine, and as they left, added, 'Estella wants to tell you what happened to her.'

Geoff understood that it was important for Estella to get it off her chest. They sat in silence, holding hands for a while. Estella struggled to find a start, but the words flowed once she had started. She did not go into exhaustive detail, enough to reveal what was necessary—everything crucial for him to know. And that was difficult enough. Some aspects of her feelings would be admitted unnecessarily if she told all. Anneke's admission partly influenced this decision. Also, there was Didi. She did not want to be hurtful, though she was not comfortable holding back her true feelings. Geoff listened without interrupting, holding her only when she related something difficult.

When she had finished, he told her in the same brief way how he felt, how much he loved her, and how he came to feel that way. Whatever had happened with the Egyptian businessman and Gerda van den Donker made no difference. He loved her for what she was, not for what she thought she had done in error. Nobody was perfect. Her love determined his happiness. Nothing else. He told her he accepted all the conditions her father had placed on them. He understood. He would do anything as long as he had her love. In this way, the half-hour before dinner rushed by. When Aine called them to dinner, they went with reluctance. They walked into the hallway, knowing that the way ahead would be entirely new, but only Geoff thought for a moment of the fickleness of youthful passions alluded to by Charles.

While Geoff and Estella sat down with her parents for the first time, the crescent moon rose high in the clear starlit sky, shedding a silvery glow over the high peak and the Wombat. Below in the valley, in a section sealed off by the Binawarra police, lay Nasser Saladin's body with the hilt of the knife protruding from his chest and forming the outline of a cross in the shimmering light.

Chapter 36

Truus decides

On the Thursday after the Van Engelens' guests had left, Truus van den Donker parked her car in Herengracht, where Geoff had stood the previous Sunday.

'I appreciate this, Truus,' said Fr. van Engelen, after she had helped him out. 'A last look around before I return. These are the streets of my childhood. So often I walked along here or rode my bike.'

'They are familiar to me, too. We often came this way to go into town.' She held out her arm, and they set off towards Marktplein.

'Perhaps I passed you sometimes,' said the priest.

'I would have been very young.'

A smile lit up her face. It reminded him of how innocent and pretty she looked all those years ago in Amsterdam.

'I have been melancholy each time we met,' she said, appearing to read his thoughts. 'I suppose I can smile now. I have a different view of things. Your influence has been lasting, that of your family, too. Your niece, Anneke, is such a beautiful girl, kind and confident. Marijke, too. I am serious about my Christian faith. But I want it to do to me what it has done to you. I don't want it to twist and destroy me as it has done to Cees and Gerda. What Cees believes is not religion, as far as I can see. And I wonder whether Gerda ever believed anything.'

'It seems you are right. I am sorry.'

'Don't be sorry. At least I face it now.'

They walked on in silence. Fr. van Engelen could not help reflecting on their different ambitions and experiences. He was a priest. He had great joy in his priesthood, but he always knew there would be hardships. There would be times when the load would be almost too much, and he had to abandon himself to God's graces. Truus, on the other hand, had married for love and a happy family life. He could understand the deep disappointment. He tried to make light conversation about the familiar buildings they past, and she responded, understanding his sympathy. When they got to the junction of Kromme Weele and Vlasmarkt, he stopped. They were standing in front of one of the sex shops that had proliferated all over Walcheren. Pornographic books and magazines of all sorts, with graphic colour photos, were on full display together with implements for sexual stimulation.

'Frans had written about this,' he murmured, turning away, 'but I could never have imagined the visual violence.'

'Hey, dirty old man,' a boy of about fourteen yelled as he cycled by with a friend.

'Come on,' said Fr. van Engelen, 'we had better move on.'

When they reached Marktplein, they sat on the iron bench he had sat on fifteen years before with Marijke and Frans. Truus let the priest watch and enjoy the comings and goings of the busy market for a while. Then, without speaking, she went off and bought him a croquette with mustard.

'You haven't had this for a long time, I imagine,' she said, handing it to him. 'You would not have got it for yourself.'

He thanked her, and they sat in silence again, eating and watching the people pass by.

'I have made a decision,' said Truus. 'I will visit Australia to see how it is.'

'A visit first would be wise.'

'But I have not changed my mind. My life with Cees has been a life of lies. What has happened has just made it worse. I must get away from it. I'll take it slowly. I know that it will be a momentous change.'

'You will always have my encouragement and my prayers. Do you have a time in mind?'

'I will bring my affairs in order and discuss the plans with Anneke. I'll ask her to give me lessons in English—'

'So, Gerda was right, the papal agent has got you in his clutches!' They turned to see Cees van den Donker standing over them. 'It took thirty years, but he succeeded in the end. And you wondered why I didn't trust him. You fool!'

'You don't really believe anything so absurd, Meneer van den Donker,' said the priest.

'Don't I, Meneer *de pastoor*?'

'I married you because I loved you and wanted to share my life with you,' said Truus. 'You repudiated me from the beginning. I will never understand why.'

'You repudiated yourself. You could not see my vision. I did my best. You would not go with me. You wanted to spend your life in ignorance—in your provincial ignorance. I abandoned you to your own wishes. You have no one but yourself to blame for your misery.'

'Did you want her to follow you and your daughter into abduction and political murder?' said the priest.

'Political murder?' He appeared surprised. 'What are you talking about? The Vatican is the only organisation that does such things.'

'Meneer van den Donker, the plot to abduct Miss Winterbine has failed, as you well know. It's not necessary to tell you that an investigation will follow. The relevant authorities have already been alerted. You will not get away with any further attempts on the people involved. What happens to your wife is of interest.'

'What happens to my wife? Yes, that's an interesting point. What will happen to my wife, celibate priest?'

'I only have this to say, Meneer: you are under scrutiny. You are advised not to move against anyone who could be a witness.'

'Meneer *de pastoor*, I am a businessman. I invest in particular types of property, and I have been successful. My business activities are open to scrutiny. An investigation will uncover nothing untoward.'

'And if there is an investigation into *Kasteel Zaligheid*?'

'*Kasteel Zaligheid*?' He laughed nervously.

'You are the owner of *Kasteel Zaligheid*, are you not?'

Cees scowled at his wife. 'There is no discoverable connection between me and that medieval castle. I know nothing about what goes on there, and it is none of my business.' His chin went up. 'Your brother will tell you I am not stupid.'

'If you are not stupid, you will realise the game is up.'

'The game is up, is it?' He mocked.

Fr. van Engelen made no further reply. Cees seemed uncertain.

'Cees, now is the right time to tell you I have made certain decisions,' said Truus. 'I'm taking action to end our marriage. It has not been a genuine marriage. Looking back, I have concluded you never loved me or intended to be in a normal marriage. You showed that in the way you rejected me, in the contempt you showed me all through the years. It is now at an end.'

'You will not get anything out of me, rest assured.'

'I only want what is mine. I won't bother you as long as you leave me alone.'

Cees looked from Truus to the priest and then back again. 'Had some legal advice, have you? And what are you going to do with this papal cripple here?'

'What I intend to do is none of your business. And your offensiveness and insults must stop.'

'You were always an ignorant fool.'

The weak, abusive reply was a sign he accepted his wife's conditions.

Truus held out her hand. 'Come on, Father, I will help you back to the car.'

Twenty minutes later, they were walking along the far end of Boulevard Evertsen at Vlissingen. They took their places on a bench that faced out to sea. The cold wind blew through a patchy sky, indolently gusted over the sand on the beach, and ruffled the water into splashing, peaking foam. Far over to their left, the Vlissingen-Breskens ferry, the same ferry on which Didi stood contemplating the water, made its way through the white spray of the Schelde River towards the docks in Vlissingen harbour.

'This is one of the enduring sights of my youth,' said Fr. van Engelen. 'Frans and I used to stop here on our bike rides before the War and watch the tankers and traders passing close to the beach. It was here that I discussed my ideas of being a priest with my younger brother. The troubles in Germany were gathering, and Adolf Hitler's career already had momentum. Because the world seemed to be turning away from God, I felt an inner urge to turn towards Him.' He looked up and down the boulevard. 'It was here that I stood by myself one day and, looking out into the North Sea, received the call to be a priest.' He paused. 'It is a funny thing. Many religious will tell you the same. At a certain moment, one feels a decisive urge, a call that cannot be resisted.'

'Did you know what you would do?' said Truus.

'No, I had no idea really what lay before me. I only felt the call to devote myself entirely to God's work, to conform my will to His.'

There was another period of silence.

'Do you remember,' he said, at length, 'that fifteen years ago you asked me whether it was difficult to give up having a wife and family?' Truus nodded. 'All these years later, the idea of clerical celibacy is becoming ever more incomprehensible to people moulded in our secular society. Indeed, for some people, the idea is repulsive to the point of psychological sickness or criminal disorder. So, to answer your question more fully, I should explain the basis of the Church's teaching on celibacy and consecrated virginity.

'The Church has always taught that celibacy chosen for the love of God is a higher state of life than marriage. I believe some of our Protestant brothers and sisters find that teaching somehow unbiblical. This is not true. For example, St Paul's clear meaning in chapter seven of his first letter to the Corinthians is that the celibate or virginal state chosen for the love of God is superior to the married state. Our Lord says in St Luke's Gospel that the person who leaves family and possessions for the sake of God will be rewarded many times over in this life and will enjoy life with God in the next. There is an unassailable joy in turning one's back on the world for love of God and Jesus Our Saviour, no matter what sorrows appear along the way. That's what I have experienced. This is important for you to meditate upon as you reflect on your undertaking.'

Truus looked towards the horizon over the limitless sea. Fr. van Engelen, aware of the momentous decisions that lay before her, waited. He, too, turned towards the horizon.

'You are reminded of that decision, aren't you?' said Truus.

'Is it obvious?'

'Very.'

'It was the decisive point in my life. I thought God had tapped me on the shoulder.'

'I know now what you felt.'

ON THE following Saturday afternoon, there was a knock on the front door of the Winterbine house. Aine went to answer it and returned to the lounge room where Fr. van Engelen sat with Charles, Estella, Geoff, and Miss Barker.

'There's a letter for you,' she said, handing it to the priest. 'It was a seminarian from the Melbourne house. He did not wish to stay.'

The envelope contained keys and a sheet of paper.

'Good heavens,' Fr. van Engelen exclaimed after he had perused it. 'Here, Charles, you read it. I am too surprised to talk. Read it out for us, please, so I know I am not imagining things.'

Charles took the letter.

Dear Fr van Engelen,

We have reviewed our recent decision. Although my priestly colleagues and I are still of the opinion that your views no longer correspond with those of our priestly fraternity, we have come to the conclusion that all that is required is that you separate yourself from us to carry on your duties as you see fit.

We are mindful that you minister to a group of faithful, no matter how misguided you and they are about the decrees of the Second Vatican Council. We are now of the opinion that it's not proper to put obstacles in the way of that ministry, thus causing a rupture between you and the Church. In a word, you are not required to vacate St Philomena's church and presbytery.

However, as you are no longer a member of our order, it is only right that you support yourself and maintain the property. We will look at this more closely in the coming weeks when we will have a formal agreement drawn up.

Yours in The Holy Spirit who guides His Church,

Fr H de Jonge, MWH

Keys enclosed

'Well, I never,' said the priest. 'Miss Barker, is this your doing?'

'Miss Barker ...?' said Aine.

'All right,' she said, with a smile, 'I will tell you. You will have to know about it eventually, anyhow. Just before I left for Holland, I rang my solicitors in Sydney and asked them to investigate the legality of the order's decision. That included the laws of the Church. I also suggested they raise a few points of interest to the provincial about bad publicity, persecution, and that sort of thing. You must excuse me, Father, for the application of a few secular tactics. Well, when I arrived back here, I asked my solicitors to make certain representations to the provincial, of a business nature. To be brief, with a few adjustments the provincial seemed susceptible to those representations. That is all.'

'That's all!' said Fr. van Engelen. 'Miss Barker, you have saved our congregation. For the moment, at least. You have been an instrument of God's Providence.'

'I thought he would say something like that,' Miss Barker whispered to Geoff. 'Next moment he is going to talk about conversion and so on.'

'Miss Barker, whether you like it or not, you are on the way.'

'Father, I did it for you and my family here. You can make of that what you will.'

'Then you did it for God.'

Chapter 37

A new start

ESTELLA AND Geoff sat on the verandah, enjoying the mild autumn weather. The clear blue sky and the freshness in the leafy air devoid of summer insects had a cleansing effect on their mind and spirit. During their quiet conversation, Estella glanced now and then up the road. 'She's coming!' she cried, jumping to her feet and running to the front gate.

Jenny Brougham, dressed modestly in slacks, blouse, and jumper, and with her long blond hair bound in a single plait, gave her a cautious wave.

'I'm so glad you are home, safe,' said Estella, grabbing her in a hug.

'I am, too,' said Jenny, unresponsive to her hug.

'Come on, come and meet Geoff, and then we can talk.'

'Let me first say hello to your parents.' She was back a minute later. 'I wanted to apologise. Your mum and dad have always been good to me. I'm ashamed of the way I behaved towards them.'

'They will like that,' said Estella. 'Now tell me what happened.'

Jenny looked at Geoff. Geoff understood. He left them, saying he would walk around the garden for a while.

'He seems a nice man,' said Jenny when he had gone. 'Not really handsome, but certainly not ugly. I suppose you'll tell me that what's on inside counts.' There was no irony or sneer in her words.

'Yes, you must know Geoff well to appreciate him. He's courageous and principled, someone you can trust.'

'I suppose when you finally decide to pick a boyfriend, you must be different from the rest of us.'

'I didn't decide anything, Jenny. It just happened. I wasn't looking. I told you—'

'Yes, you did. So you don't have to tell me again. Ten years older, too?'

'A little more. I didn't decide that either. Is that an objection?'

'I'm not looking anymore, but if I were, I would prefer someone closer to my age.'

'Why does age make a difference?'

'It just does. It's natural.' She had been looking vacantly across the road, but now turned to Estella. 'You're seventeen.'

'Nearly eighteen. I can't see why it matters if I love him. I told you, Cleopatra—'

'Yes, yes, I know. That's the way I feel. Twenty-eight is too old for me.' She shook her head slightly, and her pretty lips shaped in disgust.

'Would you ... would you be attracted to a man in his fifties?'

'It wouldn't enter my head,' said Jenny, focusing. 'My grandfather is not that much older.'

'Even if the man was handsome, elegant, with the best manners, full of respect for you—?'

'Estella, I can't believe what I am hearing. Is that what you got mixed up in?'

'Part of it.'

Jenny contemplated Estella. 'I suppose someone who looks like Estella Winterbine could not be satisfied with the snivelling juveniles that chase us in this town. It may well have to be someone older, rich, and handsome to deal with such awesome female beauty.'

'Jenny ... please!'

'Come to think of it, will Geoff be enough in the long run?' she continued, unmoved by Estella's cry. 'Beauty without comparison and talking about love in Dickens and Jane Austen, and Cleopatra and Julius Caesar, it could be no ordinary bloke to deal with that.'

'That's cruel.'

'I don't mean to sound cruel, Estella,' said Jenny, waving her hand. 'I only mean to say you deserve more than the Len Dawson types that seem to set the standards.'

The possible truth in Jenny's comment rather than the possible offence caused Estella's exclamation. It was a penetration of her character and behaviour that had not occurred to her. The implications were daunting if it were true. Could she have been so dramatically mistaken about her school friends since they had reached puberty? Had she merely postponed similar behaviour because of fussiness, a fussy pride, a judgment that others were not up to her standard? She could not face those questions. It was too difficult and too painful.

'Besides, you could change your mind. It's your first love.'

'Never.'

'You can't know.'

'Never.'

'Then I'm curious how you will deal with the other.'

'Tell me what happened,' Estella said, drawing Jenny to the swing seat to redirect the conversation.

'My shame seems endless, and my self-respect totally destroyed,' Jenny began, showing no further interest in the question of Estella's constancy and self-control. 'How I could have got into that situation, I don't know.' She sighed. 'And who would have thought that Paul Egan—?' The dispassionate manner dissolved, and a single tear rolled over a cheek. 'It's coming back to punish me. How could I have said those things about him?' She let Estella put her arm around her. She wiped her cheek. 'I'm really sorry for how I spoke to you that day. I was so upset. I thought something was going on between you and Len.'

'But there was nothing.'

'I know, I know. I could see his attention to you developing. There were little things, things that boys don't know girls notice. I thought you might have been encouraging him. So that night at Tricia's place, when you disappeared and then Len—when he came back to the party covered in dirt and his clothes out of place, I didn't know what to think. He told us you had given him the come-on. Then someone jumped him and roughed him up. He said it was a set-up. He called you a ... well, you know what ... and you were leading him on. I believed him. Everybody did. They all called you the same thing.'

'It was not like that at all. I was on my way—'

'You don't have to tell me the details. I know it was all lies. Anyhow, that's why I spoke the way I did. Jealousy. I'm such a fool. I'm so sorry. Then I heard about the fight between Len and Larry. Len said you and Larry had mocked him about being roughed up and that Larry had been the loser in the fight that followed. I was glad to hear it and said it was a pity you had not suffered the same.' She stopped and shook her head.

'I'm sorry,' she continued. 'I didn't know what was happening to me. Looking back, it was like an evil spirit had control of my mind. I can't understand why I swallowed Len's lies ... and it was not just the fact that his friends kept backing him up. I don't know ... it was like my mind was not my own. It hadn't been for months. Anyhow, the next day, some of the girls told me one of Len's friends had tried to set your hair on fire, and Larry had tried to intervene and had been beaten up by those crawlers that hang around Len. It was a shock. I didn't know what to think. I was so stupid.'

She stopped and shook her head again. She seemed on the point of getting up and leaving. Then she began a slow, broken account of how Len came to her after Anzac Day and said he was clearing out to Melbourne because Sergeant Willis was out to get him. He wanted to know whether she was coming with him. Of course, she said. She loved him. She was ready to go everywhere with him. But when they got to Melbourne, everything changed.

Almost at once, Len began to ignore her. He lolled about smoking marijuana with other idiot boys. Some girls arrived, and he went out with them and his friends. When she objected, he told her that if she wasn't happy, she could leave. It was then that it dawned on her how much he had used her. In her abandonment, Stephen Calder turned up and propositioned her. Next thing, to her amazement, Paul Egan appeared. He had a few private words with Calder, after which Calder left. He helped her pack up her things and took her to his house, where he spent time consoling her.

'What have I learned in my stupidity?' she said when she came to the end of her story. 'For one thing, I learned what a despicable rat Len Dawson is and what a good person Paul Egan is. All the way back to Binawarra, he talked reassuringly with me. He knew what I was feeling and wanted to encourage me to put it behind me.' She stood up and leaned on the verandah railing for a moment before turning to face Estella. 'But I can't forget it. It has affected me. I have a feeling it has only just begun. I don't know when I will get over it. If ever. I feel so defiled, so very defiled. And I don't want to face everybody at school, especially those snivelling morons who probably heard every detail of— Oh, I can't bear the thought of it. You're the only one I want to see here, if you'll still have me.'

'Of course, Jenny, it changes nothing.' Estella rose and put her arm around her shoulder. Jenny was unresponsive. 'I know now a little of the way you felt. I know now what it means to feel strongly about someone.'

'But never strongly enough to throw everything away as I did. I know you. You would never give in. You would suffer in silence and pray that everything would come good.' She absently slapped the railing. 'Anyhow, that's what happened. I thought you would want to know—and I still want your friendship.' She stopped and then released an ironic laugh. 'You know, after the way I behaved with Paul Egan and all the rotten things I said, I wish he were around now.'

'You have his affection,' said Estella. 'He told me to contact him if ever you were in trouble.'

'Oh no, did he? I thought it was you who asked him to find me.'

'He gave me his card that day Uncle Bill told us he was in town, you know, while we were in the park. He came to visit later in the day to warn me about Len Dawson and—'

'Oh no, don't tell me any more! I can't bear it.' She put her hands over her face but did not cry. 'It's all coming back to haunt me. It'll haunt me forever.'

'Jenny, we all make mistakes. God forgives us—'

'No, no religious talk. I couldn't bear it.'

Silence endured for some time.

'I'm always here for you,' said Estella.

'That's all I want.' She paused. 'I don't know what happened with Edith Bicknell, but there's one thing I can say about her. She always encouraged me to find my best inner self and let it bloom as it should. I will remember that. Now I must go. I told my parents I would be away for a short while.'

'Before you go, can I ask you how you feel about Mr Egan now?'

'I understand why he showed an interest in me. There are things I have learned. I'm not offended anymore. But I have the sort of affection for him I would have for a favourite uncle.' She looked at the bush in the vacant land opposite. 'Now I would be careful how I behaved, out of respect for him and his feelings.' She looked Estella full in the face. 'Estella, I am seeing a side of you I have not seen before.'

'What are you seeing?'

'I'm sorry, I must go now. We will talk again. I need time to sort myself out.'

They embraced, and Jenny hurried away. Estella stood against the railing, watching her walk up the street with her head bowed. There were no longer the skimpy, tight clothing and the flowing golden locks. It seemed symbolic that Jenny's hair was tied into a plait, so it poked straight and rigid down her back. She remained where she was, even when Jenny was out of sight. If Jenny did not want to answer her question, she could not ignore it. It was as if her embrace and the long, lingering kiss with Geoff had opened a door, and she had been pushed through it whether she liked it or not. The first assault of intense desire had changed her forever. There was no change to her vision of life with its religious consciousness and all its objective moral principles; the change was in how she now perceived her relationship with Geoff, her relationship with other men, and her friends' relationships.

She had been in denial over her response to Mr Al Refai's efforts to seduce her. She had been fooling herself about having a sisterly affection for Didi. That was no purely sisterly inclination to accept his kiss. How could it happen? Before her embrace with Geoff, she would have been indignant and disgusted with the suggestion that she could love Geoff as much as she did and still feel that sort of inclination. If her inclination to kiss Didi disgusted her, what would she have felt if it had been suggested that she would have a similar response to Mr Al Refai? She could not answer that question because she would not have been able to conceive of acting in such a way. But she did.

She could not understand what it was exactly that impelled her to admire him and find his attention pleasing. She shivered, and her face burned as she imagined how far it could have gone. Anneke's description of her dramatic lapse brought more vividness and reality to the picture in her mind. And now she was hearing repeated within her, 'There but for the grace of God go I,' despite Fr. van Engelen's assurance that she had enough moral strength and purpose ultimately to pull back.

When she thought of her friends' relationships, she was still disgusted at their lack of respect for themselves, but that disgust now had a different colour. It had been disgust, filled with incomprehension. The incomprehension had gone; she understood the temptation and the social pressures they had exposed themselves to. The misery that so often followed their succumbing—Jenny was an outstanding case—did not seem to make clear the lesson to most of them. She hoped she had learned as Jenny seemed to have learned, but she understood that despite the resolve at that moment, there was brittleness in her where she never thought it existed.

As these thoughts turned in her mind, she unconsciously fiddled (as she now often did) with the medal hanging on the silver chain around her neck, the chain that Fr. van Engelen had given her, and Geoff had fixed during her stay in Bendigo. Now she became conscious of the medal and the crippled priest's warning that she would be confronted with temptations she could not imagine. Miss Barker had also warned her. How right they were. As she left the verandah, she thought how strange it was that Fr. van Engelen was so accurate in his assessment of the feelings she would experience and the situations she could get herself into.

ESTELLA FOUND Geoff sitting under the rose-covered archway. She was sitting next to him before he was aware of her presence. 'You were so deep in thought,' she said, taking his hand and holding it tightly.

'I was thinking about that time you came and found me here.'

'I was so in love with you.'

'That's what I was wondering. I can hardly believe it.'

'You must believe it. You must not question it anymore. Daddy has set a test for me this year. But I will not change. I will love you more for the absence.'

'How could you love such a boring person like me?'

'Boring?' She could hear Jenny's voice. 'You mean not like Bruce Butcher or Len Dawson?'

'Whatever you can say about them, they were not ugly or boring.'

'You don't mean that.'

'I suppose not.'

'You did not love me at first sight, did you?'

'I first saw you in the park on the square,' said Geoff, after some thought. 'It wasn't that sort of situation. Besides, I never thought— You were so young, too.'

'I saw you looking at me in a way I had never seen before. You were looking at me as a person. I saw the reasons. I realised later that I fell in love with you at that instant. Age does not come into it. Afterwards, I only saw more clearly what I had seen in that first moment. That's the person I fell in love with, not the outward appearance.' She paused. 'I never saw whether Len Dawson was handsome or not. He was always ugly on the inside. I never really trusted the outward change.' That realisation, now enunciated so clearly, was encouraging after her raw conversation with Jenny.

'It did not take me long to see what you were like on the inside,' he said, 'especially after I had walked around this garden.'

'My appearance never really bothered you, did it?'

'Not in the important sense, I suppose.'

'You see.'

'I'm not blind, though. There's no point in denying it.'

ESTELLA AND Geoff had to be together longer than the two weeks. First, there were the police inquiries into Nasser Saladin's death. Then Uncle Bill's problems in the school came up for discussion. He spoke with Estella about her experiences with her fellow students and teachers. He kept coming back to her as if attempting to understand how he could have missed the signals Gerda van den Donker gave about her intentions. Similarly, he had ignored the political activity taking place, as Miss Barker put it, right under his nose. In the end, he admitted his culpability and apologised profusely for not being attentive to Estella's needs. During this time, he announced the resignations of Jane Cox, Faye Crofts, and Lesley Cognos and informed several others that they were on notice. Suzie McNamara resigned of her own accord.

Interviews with Government officials followed. Estella was shocked to learn of Bruce Butcher's role in the affair. She was never comfortable with him, but at the time did not understand why Ruby was so strict about him. She now understood. Ruby's worry was about his reputation as a sexual predator. There was never any danger there. His obsession with her was only ever a nuisance. No, the real danger was his connection with Gerda van den Donker and her use of his relations with international businessmen.

More disturbing was the role she seemed to have played in his violent death, the details of which nobody would tell her, leaving her prey to her imagination. Although she could never be held responsible for Bruce's death, she could not ignore that his obsession led to his death. That same obsession provided the critical clue to where she had gone, thus enabling Geoff to find and free her. She was indebted to him, to a person she would have shunned. He redeemed himself with a true act of selfless Christian charity. She could not help but admire him for that. He was indeed her Sydney Carton.

Geoff, who seemed to know more about the process than was obvious, guided her through the interviews and helped her reconcile her place in it all. They spoke for hours. Sometimes he did not leave until quite late for his drive back to the farm. Surprisingly, her parents left them alone. When she asked them later if it was all right that Geoff stayed so late, especially on a school night, her father said Geoff was there to help her get over her experiences, some of which were quite shocking for a young woman. There was nobody they could trust more to reassure her.

On top of bringing Geoff more out of himself, the investigation and debriefing, together with her parents' supervision, functioned as a buffer.

The raw feelings of her potential weakness and the possible moral traps she may blindly walk into receded with Geoff's comfort and companionship. With no loss of understanding of what it meant to have passed through that door in Bendigo, she became more confident about her inner strength, the strength to control her circumstances and resist what may confront her. She was by degrees recovering her former innocence.

But there was something else to confront her now. She had only had one passionate episode with Geoff, which was spontaneous. Now, with their open commitment and the disappearance of some of the previous limitations, she was not entirely sure how she should behave with him. Geoff's manhood was unknown territory. This period before formal separation helped her adjust and to understand what it meant to love a man. Geoff understood, too. He showed understanding from the first moments of their open declaration of love. He was anxious to let her take her time and lead the way. Sometimes when they sat silently on the verandah, she would turn her face towards him, and he would kiss her lingeringly. It was enough to make her face burn, and appearing to sense that, and ever mindful of his commitment, he drew back.

If Estella was cautious about dealing with his manhood, he was in the same measure in awe of her femaleness. Those essential aspects of being female, he saw almost perfected in Estella. She was beautiful to look at, but he had gradually seen past her appearance. Within was where the real person, the real beauty, subsisted. Her inner beauty permeated her physical appearance, endowing her with extraordinary qualities that reduced people to staring silence. Ruby had been right. It gave her that indefinable quality that people unwilling to reflect could not explain. It was what Geoff saw, and it was what filled him with an attitude akin to reverence. How could he not treat her as someone precious?

When at last the temporary separation came, they accepted it without complaint. Then, as they began their exchange of letters, they found that all they had experienced together on the way to knowing each other passed fluidly into their writing. Estella had no trouble filling sheets of paper with her thoughts and daily experiences, but Geoff surprised them by writing almost as much detail. Indeed, he said more in writing than he usually spoke, removing the last barriers of unfamiliarity between them.

When they had settled into their routines—Estella attending to her schoolwork and Geoff to his farm—there came an unexpected change. Charles told Geoff that, although they thought it wise for them to be apart until Estella finished school, he and Aine no longer saw the need for a complete break. They were satisfied that he and Estella had accepted the reasons for staying apart. There were also practical concerns, like meeting Geoff's family and family celebrations. Estella's eighteenth birthday was in September, and they planned a celebration of this milestone. He must be there.

Estella saw little of Miss Barker after she had returned to school. She said Estella needed to be left alone to reconcile her experiences and resume her studies in this most important of years. She and Geoff also needed time to find themselves. It was not until Estella's birthday gathering that she spoke with her for the first time since the final confrontation with Saladin on Death Rock. Estella noticed a change. Miss Barker was softer in her manner and speech. She even took to calling Geoff by his Christian name, something that brought a wry smile to Geoff's face.

'You have to pass a test, Geoff,' she said, for he was present during this conversation.

'I am honoured,' said Geoff.

In the following weeks, it seemed Geoff's connection with Miss Barker had not ended. She arrived unannounced one evening to tell Estella that Geoff would be away and out of reach for a few weeks, and she was not to worry. It had nothing to do with her recent experiences. Geoff was sorry he could not tell her in person and must send a message through her. Miss Barker urged her to trust Geoff and not ask questions that could not be answered, which seemed to suggest Miss Barker was involved in whatever

Geoff was doing. Her trust in Geoff and Miss Barker was unshakeable, and she accepted the separation. Geoff turned up after three weeks but said he could not speak. Estella knew enough now about Miss Barker's other life to conclude that Geoff was on some sort of secret mission. She did not press for an explanation. Intentionally or unintentionally, Geoff let slip a vague comment about events in Canberra that gave her an idea of what it was about. Without warning, he was away twice before the end of the year—at least twice she knew about.

Time did not weigh heavily. Her father arranged a meeting with the townspeople to correct the lies and misrepresentations peddled by the media about Bill and Fr. van Engelen. Alan Collins departed soon after, having sold his newspaper to a city tabloid. Unknown to the townspeople, Miss Barker engineered Stephen Calder's resignation from teaching. She also kept Estella up to date with the investigations into Gerda van den Donker. There was no trace of her to be found. Her London office said she had been on an extended field trip since January. Investigations could trace Gerda only as far as Holland in January. There the trail ended. The real Edith Bicknell, a teacher from Sale in Gippsland, was found travelling around England and Scotland. Her passport showed she had been there all along. Apart from the real Edith Bicknell being a teacher with part-time teaching experience in England, there was no discoverable connection between her and Gerda. Investigations were continuing.

When this subject arose, Estella's thoughts always went to Didi. She had to struggle with Didi's declaration of love, followed by his violent death and the guilt his death aroused in her. Surely, he did not deserve to die straight after an undertaking made with such unimpeachable intentions as if those pure intentions caused it. It seemed so unfair. Didi and his father belonged to that small compartment in her life that she could not fully open to Geoff. Fortunately, Fr. van Engelen was there to assuage her sorrow and self-blame. Didi's declaration of love and firm resolution to lead a good life, he said, were, in terms of Catholic teaching, a baptism of desire and a confession of sins.

'Nobody can say with certainty what God's final judgment is, but on the evidence, Didi is now enjoying heavenly bliss.'

That Didi should be enjoying heavenly bliss was an irony, given he had been motivated by her inner goodness, goodness that had shown regrettable brittleness. And the pleasure she was now experiencing in Geoff's love added to her guilt. For a moment, she thought Fr. van Engelen's comment could have a double meaning. But, no, he would never say things that flowed from her confession.

Shortly before her birthday, Estella received a note from Aisha and Tahini Al Refai. Conveying their heartiest birthday wishes, they wrote that they truly regretted any discomfort they had caused her. They hoped they could make up for it. Their father had one consolation: Didi was truly in love with a beautiful person and was full of resolution to lead a good life. He would be forever grateful for Estella's influence on his life. They were charged to convey their father's most respectful best wishes.

Estella was surprised to receive the letter and even more surprised that they should refer to her time with them. As Bruce Butcher had predicted, Mr Al Refai's Melbourne associates said she never turned up for the work experience weekend. All other documentation showed that the two sisters were the only females aboard Mr Al Refai's private jet when it departed Brisbane. Then again, they knew she would not betray them. She burnt the letter. In the meantime, she would pray fervently that Mr Al Refai would understand how wrong it was to place young women in the way of such strong temptation. Jenny could tell him about the worthlessness that gripped her after the surface glitter, and the promises of steadfast love had evaporated, and only the deception remained.

If Estella and Geoff acted as if nothing was more important than the pleasures of their companionship, others in Binawarra had much to attract their attention. Not long after Estella's birthday, Anneke van Engelen and

Truus van den Donker arrived in response to Charles and Aine's insistent invitation. The arrangement was excellent, Miss Barker commented. Charles and Aine could return the Van Engelen's hospitality and Anneke could be a guide while Truus tested her decision to leave Holland to assist Fr. van Engelen in his needs. As it turned out, Anneke did not need to be constantly translating. With Anneke's help and Truus's sustained study, Truus could follow much of the ordinary conversation around her. She was confident she would make progress.

Aine and Charles provided not only accommodation. They took Truus and Anneke on many outings, introducing them to the Dutch members of Fr. van Engelen's congregation. And when Ruby arrived after a special invitation to meet Anneke, nobody was surprised to see the two young women of similar age and temperament hit it off. Nor was it a surprise for Estella to see Anneke spend a week with Ruby in Bendigo and Ruby later accompany her on a trip to Sydney. It was just as well. She and Geoff could do with a break from Ruby.

Jenny was the only part of Estella's life now that caused sorrow and apprehension. She was no longer the cheerful, bubbly girl she had been. A depressive seriousness had overcome her. She devoted herself to her schoolwork, avoiding her former friends and giving up most of her earlier interests. She now spent the morning break with Estella or went to the library. At lunch, they walked home together, taking turns eating at each other's house. Larry was sometimes tolerated at their lunches, where the talk was almost exclusively about their schoolwork and the final exams.

Jenny remained reserved but friendly to Larry, even apologising for her manner in the past. The only friend she saw outside school was Estella. She did not want to know about anyone else. There was no time for it. She would not make a mess of her life anymore. She was determined to earn a pass in her final exams to pave the way to professional independence. She would be at nobody's mercy ever again. A career in law was what she sought. When Estella asked why, she took Estella's hand and put it on her tummy. She put her hand on Estella's tummy.

'The origin and cradle of humanity,' she said gravely. 'We must protect ourselves against the constant assault and desecration of this sacred place. We must preserve our natural authority.'

'What purpose does becoming a lawyer serve?' Estella asked, ignoring for the moment the extravagant terms. 'Surely this is a question of right moral behaviour and our own personal moral choices? Where is the place of law in this?'

Jenny hesitated. 'You say that because of the context of your beliefs. You must review the sense of that context.'

'That sounds like Gerda—Miss Bicknell,' said Estella.

'They are my thoughts.'

Estella was not inclined to debate the issue. She had had enough of Gerda van den Donker and would not let such talk disturb her pleasure with Geoff. She countered by asking if Jenny thought any more about Len Dawson.

'Only as a motivation for my goals,' she said stiffly. 'Nobody is happier than me that he has not returned to Binawarra. Good riddance. I couldn't care less where he is as long as he's not where I have to see him.'

Later in the year, she had nothing to say when they learned that Stephen Calder and Len were active members of the Building Employees Confederacy. There was one pleasing benefit, however, from Jenny's change in spirits and the accompanying resoluteness. She constantly sought Estella's advice on the subjects they were doing, which meant they were often studying together.

'I have three years of study to catch up on,' she stressed, 'and I want you to tell me everything you know, everything, no matter how small. I'm way behind.'

She would not let Estella be distracted during their study sessions, either. She banned the topic of Geoff, putting her hands over her ears when Estella mentioned his name by mistake. The happy result was that her resoluteness forced Estella to undertake a close revision of the material she had already covered and to focus more intensely than she otherwise would have. Only once did Jenny let her thoughts wander to Len and his friends.

'The thought really pleases me,' she murmured, leaning back during a break, 'that I will eventually be in a superior position to Dawson and his grovelling mates. I may even get them one day. How much that thought pleases me, you can't imagine.'

'I hope you're not blaming all boys for the way Len treated you,' said Estella.

Jenny gave her a superior glance as if she was tolerating her appalling naivety before returning to her books.

MID-AFTERNOON on Christmas Day, Estella went to her bedroom, leaving Geoff to keep Ruby and Larry company. She was taking the book Ruby had returned to her room. She placed the long-missing book on her bedside cabinet from where Ruby had picked it up. She took a hesitant hand away from it as the events of the intervening period rushed back to her. She understood Ruby's incomprehension. She had an impulse to take the thin book and push it between the books on the bottom shelf of her bookcase. But, no, she could not be so weak—or forgetful.

She looked at herself in the mirror just as she had looked at herself on the first day of the school year. She wore fashionable slacks and a short sleeve blouse. Her hair, a little shorter, hung loosely. On her feet were elegant leather sandals. But it was in her expression and demeanour that she saw the real change.

She turned to the shrine as she had done that same day, noticing the dead, withered flowers in the small vases. With a resolute movement, she took the vases and emptied them outside her bedroom window. She left the room and returned with freshly picked flowers from the back garden. With ceremony, she placed the vases on either side of the statue, bowed her head, and made the sign of the cross. She then rejoined Geoff on the verandah, who was parrying a tease from a voluble Ruby, while Larry looked on amused. With Geoff's help, Charles had erected a marquee on the lawn in the back garden. The marquee was positioned so the people approaching the lawn would walk through the rose-covered archway and emerge a few paces away from the marquee. Charles called the guests together at twilight.

'This is one of the great occasions of our family life. To see all our dear family and friends present on this occasion fills us with joy and gratitude to God for all the blessings we have received.'

'It is almost twenty years since, for some reason only known to himself, the usually relaxed and jovial Father Bertollo suddenly became agitated about what I was doing with myself.' He nodded at Father Bertollo, whose plump, florid face wore an affectionate smile. 'Before I knew it and could comprehend what I was doing, I was off on a walkabout to find myself, as he put it. My walkabout brought me to Binawarra, where a man with a big heart, for some reason only known to himself, invited me home for Sunday dinner, prepared by his devoted wife, Joanne. Then, in a series of events that revealed the supervising hand of Providence, I met Aine O'Riordan. Aine was God's gift to me, and I thank Him daily for her presence in my life. Then, if Providence had not been kind enough, Aine and I received the gift of our daughter. Let me not forget here the strength and support Miss Barker has given to us through the years.

'Now, to top everything off, a quiet, unassuming man walked almost unnoticed into our lives. We have Ruby Waiting to thank for that. Geoff Shawcross did not stay unnoticed for very long. Soon, we saw a young man of great inner strength, both of purpose and principle. You all know his courage, perseverance, and planning saved our daughter from great danger. Geoff, we are forever in your debt. I come now to the purpose of these few words.' He held out his hand to Aine, who came and stood with him. 'Geoff formally requested our permission to propose marriage to Estella. We feel our daughter is now mature enough to know what she is doing, and we willingly gave it. So now, as we celebrate the birth of Our Lord, we announce their betrothal. Estella and Geoff, please—'

Geoff and Estella walked hand in hand to the entrance of the rose-covered archway. Geoff placed a ring on Estella's finger, saying, 'Please accept this ring as a sign of my love and my commitment to you,' to which Estella replied, 'I accept the ring and will wear it as a sign of my love and commitment.' They embraced to the applause of all present. Aine came forward.

'As an end to all that has befallen Estella this year, and before we sit down to our celebratory meal, I would like to read verses from Psalm 101.'

Will not the heathen learn reverence, O Lord, for Thy glorious name, and all those monarchs of the earth?
When they hear that the Lord has built Sion anew, ready to be revealed there in glory.

'Enjoy yourselves. *Deo gratias.*'

Aine and Charles's aunts began serving dinner. The continual chatter and the hearty congratulations to the betrothed couple ensured the dinner proceeded with uninterrupted pleasure. When darkness fell in the balmy evening air, and the light from the many garden torches took over, bathing everything in a shimmering glow and glitter, many of the guests experienced for the first time the otherworldly atmosphere that prevailed in the Winterbine household.

AT FIFTEEN minutes before midnight, a long line of robed and veiled figures holding candles issued from the Castle of Heavenly Bliss. The leader, dressed in black, led the line of chanting women over the bailey bridge and along the white gravel path that wound its way to the edge of the forest below the dunes. Behind her was a tall, handsome woman dressed in flowing purple robes. There, waiting for them, under the shelter of the great oaks, were a small stone altar, a fire, and a large iron bowl positioned on a tripod over the fire. Near the stone altar was a small animal cage. The white-robed women drew together in a circle around the black robe, supported by acolytes on each side.

'On the day of the celebration of the impostor Prince of Peace,' Gerda Vrouwendijk intoned over the low chanting, while the handsome woman in the purple robes spiralled gracefully within the circle, 'we are present to celebrate the beginning of the end of his devastating reign.' She held up her arms, and the acolytes, Lesley Conos and Faye Crofts, moved forward to hold up the edge of her black veil. 'In reconsecrating this altar to the goddess Nehalennia, we are restoring the rightful religion to this region after two thousand years of desecration.' She waved her arms in a blessing. 'In the depths of the winter solstice, we are here to atone for the scarring of Mother Earth by the masculine spirit of the fraudulent Prince of Peace and to herald the dawn of the age of the Divine Feminine.'

On the porch of the castle stood a group dressed in long robes with their faces concealed behind masks of different sorts and different colours. They stood motionless, watching the proceedings under the dunes.

END

Dutch words or phrases

Goedemorgen – Good morning (formal)

Goeiemorgen – Good morning (everyday)

Goedemiddag – Good Afternoon (formal)

Goeiemiddag – Good afternoon (everyday)

Goedenavond – Good evening

Plein – square

Straat – street

Lieverd, schat – darling or dear

Goede hemel – good heavens (an exclamation)

Allemachtig – lit. almighty (an exclamation like 'my goodness' or 'good lord')

Kasteel Zaligheid – Castle Bliss or Castle of Heavenly Bliss

Meneer – Mr or sir

Mevrouw – Mrs or madam

Juffrouw – Miss

Stroopwafel – Sweet syrupy cookie or biscuit

Bolus – a syrupy pastry, speciality of Zeeland

Mof — a pejorative word for the Germans during World War 2

Papegaai — Parrot

Notes on spelling and pronunciation

Dutch spelling deviates in some respects from English. The 'ee' in the name 'Cees' is a pure vowel sound and approximates the 'a' in 'case', without the diphthong slide; 'c' is usually pronounced as 's', but in the case of the name 'Cees', it is pronounced as a 'k'. Cees is thus roughly pronounced as 'Kayse' without the diphthong slide; the 'ij' that appears in Marijke (and many other Dutch words) is equivalent to the diphthong 'ay' in English, thus with a diphthong slide; 'v' is usually pronounced as an 'f'; 'j' is pronounced as a 'y'; 'w' is pronounced like 'v'. Here are the main Dutch names in the story, spelt *roughly* the English way:

Cees van den Donker: Kayse fun den donker

Zeeland: Zayland

Jos van Engelen: Yos fun Engelen

Jannie de Kam: Yunnie de kum;

Anneke: Ann-e-ke

Marijke: Maray-ke ('ke' is short)

Select Bibliography

For background on the occult and goddess worship, the author relied primarily on these titles:

Goddess Unmasked: The Rise of Neopagan Feminist Spirituality, Philip G. Davis, Spence Publishing Company, 1998

Occult Feminism: The Secret Story of Women's Liberation, Rachel Wilson 2021

The Inner Goddess, Josephine Robinson, Gracewing, 1998

Women: Why Are You Weeping? Margaret E. Mills, News Weekly Books, 1997

Awakening Your Goddess, Liz Simpson, Barron's, 2001

Also By Gerard Charles Wilson

FICTION

Sixties Series

Times of Distress (Book 1)
In This Vale of Tears (Book 2)
Counterculture Dreams (Book 3) 2024
The Counterculture Goddess (Book 4) 2025
Love in the Counterculture (Book 5) due 2026
Dreams to Nightmare (Book 6) due 2026
The Castle of Heavenly Bliss (Book 7)
A Sense of Loss (Book 8) due 2027

Editing Constancy: A Jane Austen Story
Seeking the Divine Spark: A Satire in the Style of Evelyn Waugh

NON-FICTION

Social History Series

Prison Hulk to Redemption (Part 1)

War Depression War (Part 2)

Me 'n' Pete: Recalling a Fifties' Childhood (Part 3)

Communists, Billycarts and Two-Wheelers (Part 4) due 2027□

Politics and Media Series

Tony Abbott and the Times of Revolution

The Media of the Republic: Who Killed Diana?

The Telecard Affair: Diary of a Media Lynching 2nd Edition 2024